He'll stop at nothing to get what he wants...

With war looming on the horizon, Methusal and her kaavl teammates risk everything to infiltrate the enemy, undermine the insane Zindedi Presidente, and bring peace to their continent. But the challenge she faces from the enemy may pale in comparison to the challenge she faces from her own team.

Fireworks erupt when Methusal and Mentàll Solboshn must pose as newlyweds in Zindedi. Torn between her distrust and growing attraction for him, Methusal must set aside their differences to win the battle against the enemy. Even as she struggles to trust her kaavl leader, signs point to a spy within their midst.

In the end, her determination and creativity must win out, or their homeland will face an army far more imposing than any that have come before.

KAAVL CHRONICLES
(Book Three of Quadrilogy)

KAAVL CALAMITY

Jennette Green

DIAMOND PRESS

Kaavl Calamity

A Diamond Press book / published in arrangement with the author

ISBN: 978-1-62964-018-1

Library of Congress Control Number: 2016962601
Library of Congress Subject Headings:
Man-woman relationships—Fiction
Paranormal romance—Fiction
Saga—Fiction

Diamond Press
3400 Pegasus Drive
P.O. Box 80043
Bakersfield CA 93380-0043
www.diamondpresspublishing.com

Published in the United States of America.

I'd like to

express my deepest,

abiding appreciation for

my terrific beta readers,

Betty, Lori, Debbie, McKenna and Kristy.

I couldn't do it without you.

Thank you!

Also by Jennette Green

ROMANCE NOVELS

The Commander's Desire
Her Reluctant Bodyguard
Ice Baron
The Pirate's Desire
Kaavl Conspiracy
Kaavl Quest
Kaavl Calamity
(Kaavl Chronicles Quadrilogy)
Beyond the Rapture
(Christian Apocalyptic)

Castaways
(a novelette)

SHORTER WORKS

Toot of Fruit
(a children's story)

Murder by Nightmare
(a novelette)

KOBLAN

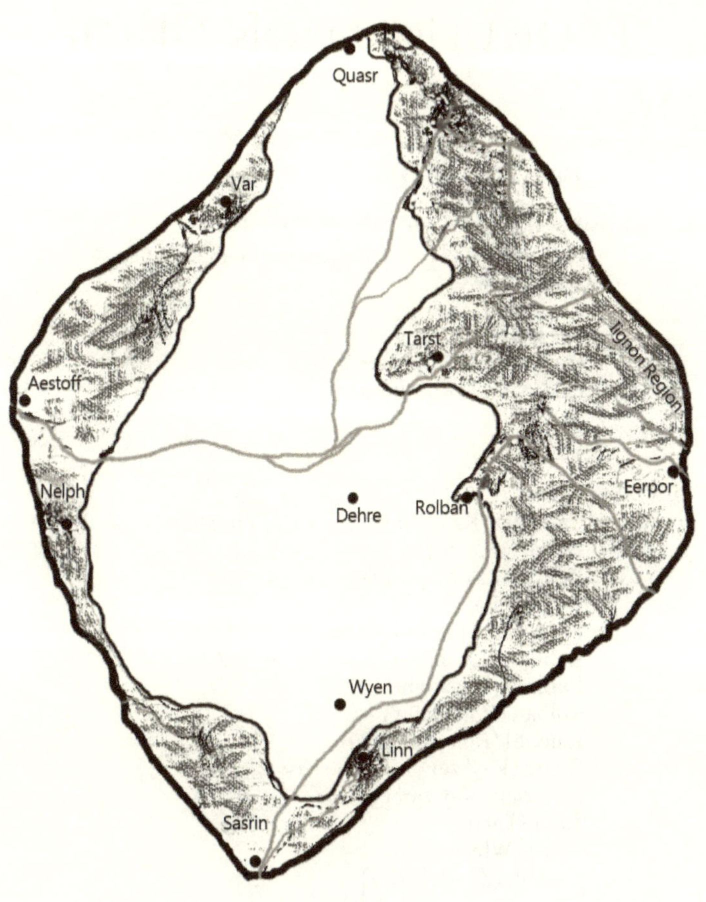

Quasr
Var
Tarst
Aestoff
Tignon Region
Nelph
Dehre
Rolban
Eerpor
Wyen
Linn
Sasrin

Pronunciation Guide

Kaavl (Kah' vl)

Kaavl levels (from highest to lowest):

Ultimate level (only Mahre ever achieved)
Primary level
Bi-level
Tri-level
Quatr-level (Kwah' tra level)
Quint-level (Kint level)

Places

Aestoff (Ay' stoff)
Carachki (Ka ra' chki) capitol of Zindedi
Dehre (Deh' ree)
Dehrien (Deh' ree un)
Eerpor (Ear poor')
Eerporian (Ear por' ee un)
Koblan (Koe' blun)
Koblani (Koe blane' ee)
Rolban (Role bane')
Rolbani (Role bane' ee)
Quasr (Kay' zer)
Quasrian (Kay zar' ee un)
Tarst (Tarst)
Wyen (Why en')
Zindedi (Zin deh' dee)

Characters

Rolban

Aalicaa (A lee shaw') (Aali (A' lee)) Deccia's sister/cousin, Methusal's cousin, Tri-level
Barak Mehl (Bare' uk Mel) Kitran's brother
Behran Amil (Bee' hrhun/Beh' rhun Uh meel') Tri-level
Ben Amil, Behran's father
Deccia (Day' shuh) Methusal's twin sister
Erl (Earl) Methusal's father
Goric (Gor' ik) Tri-level
Hanuh (Han' nah) Methusal's mother
Mahre (Mah' ree) The Old Kaavl Master
Methusal Maahr (Meth u' zul Mare) Tri-level
Petr (Pet' r) Deccia and Aali's father, Bi-Level
Poli Amil (Pol' ee Uh meel') Behran's mother
Sims Nalg (Sims Nalg) Supply room supervisor
Timaeus (Tim' ay us)

Dehre

Hendra (Hen' druh) Quatr-level
Mentàll Solboshn (Mn tall' Sole' bah shn) Chief of Dehre, Primary level
Tabor (Tay' bor), Bi-level, Mentàll's second-in-command

Tarst

Aenill (Uh neel') Pan's wife
Dastn (Das' tn), runner for Tarst
Doc, Tarst's doctor
Pan Patn (Pan Pat' tn) Tarst Chief, Primary level
Riln, Bi-level

Quasr

Calbn M'ntoyan (Kal'bn Mn toy'un)
Lylitha (Lil eeth' uh) Calbn's wife
Rartn (Rare' tun) Calbn's son
Trori (Tror' ee) Calbn's daughter
GG Calbn's grandmother

Chief Aarabst (Air' uh bast) of Aestoff
Sozla (Soz' luh) from Eerpor

Zindedi

Ceri (Sair' ee)
Euphira (U fire' uh) shopkeeper in Carachki
General Fitrn (Fie' turn)
Matron Machblin (Mrn. M) Mock' blin), landlady in Carachki
Nygev (Nie' gev) Vitnia's husband
Olita (Oh lee' tuh) friend of Vitnia
Ostl (Oss' tl) the Commander in the Carachki's military base
Presidente of Zindedi
Tisnia (Tiz' nee uh) friend of Vitnia
Vitnia (Vit' nee uh) rents cabins to team on Dakarra
Yalin (Yah leen') Presidente's secretary

PROLOGUE

CARACHKI
CAPITOL OF THE ZINDEDI CONTINENT

TINY PEBBLES CLATTERED, as sharp as Zindedi gun blasts, in Methusal Maahr's sensitive ears. Someone was climbing up the plateau ten lengths behind her. Kaavl training recognized the person's gait, and a quick visual carry verified her deduction. Relaxing out of kaavl, she turned with a smile.

"Another letter, Thusa." Timaeus Rolnnt, who was her brother-in-law and also a runner for Rolban, tapped the folded parchment into her hand.

"Thank you." Methusal did not particularly want the letter burning into her palm, but she wouldn't refuse it, either. The letter had come from Dehre this time. Once a month, over the last six months, a letter had come for her, sent from different places all over the Koblan continent. From Quasr to the north, and all the way from Aestoff, the sea port over the western mountains.

Timaeus hesitated for a moment, his curiosity evident. "It's the full moon tonight. I guess you expected it."

"Yes." She managed a weak smile. In an ideal world, she'd love to rip the parchment into tiny pieces. But its sender knew she never would. That was why his continual, successful attempts to get under her skin must satisfy him so deeply.

"Why don't you tell him to stop?"

Methusal bit her lip and broke open the seal. The page fluttered open and revealed the familiar, bold handwriting scrawling across the page. It was page eight of the long lost *Second Book of Kaavl.* Only ninety-two pages left to go.

"Because it's the only way Rolban will ever get a copy of the *Second Book of Kaavl,*" she said quietly. That was true, even though the ancient book belonged to her home community of Rolban, and even though her ancestor, Mahre, had written it. ...And even though Methusal had found it seven months ago.

Her enemy, Mentàll Solboshn, Chief of Dehre, had stolen the book from her at the end of the Quasr War. He now played a whip and apte game with her by sending one copied page at a time, month after month. At this rate, it would take eight years to read the entire book.

Timaeus nodded. "Deccia is waiting for me." He blushed a little. Methusal's twin sister and Timaeus had been married for almost six months, and were deeply in love. Timaeus had just returned from a two day trip to deliver messages to Dehre.

Methusal smiled, and after he left glanced at the parchment again. Reluctantly, her gaze fell to the bottom of the page, where her adversary always left a cryptic message for her.

Prepare for another adventure.
See you soon.
Mentàll

Unease immediately gripped her. What did he mean? And why was he coming to visit Rolban?

Once again, she wondered why he continued to send her one copied page of the book, month after month. With Mentàll, the reasons went far beyond a simple desire to get under her skin. He was plotting something; she felt it, deep in her bones. Truthfully, when wasn't he?

She considered all the places from which he'd sent the letters; Quasr, Aestoff, Wyen... From communities all over Koblan. They were clues. He wanted her to know that he'd been traveling the continent. Was he pursuing that secret alliance he'd initiated before the Quasr War began? The alliance she had unfortunately discovered precious little about six months ago.

The Dehrien Chief loved power, and he relished needling under her skin. What scheme would deliver to him the fruit of both objectives?

She supposed she was about to find out.

But whatever the Dehrien was planning, she would stop it. His games, manipulations, and his greedy lust for power would find no foothold in Rolban, ever again. She'd make certain of that once and for all.

Δ Δ Δ Δ Δ

CARACHKI, ZINDEDI

"We are nearly prepared for the invasion of Rolban." The clipped words were uttered through thin lips, edged by a razor perfect moustache.

The new General sat across from the Presidente of Zindedi. As was true every time he saw him, something about the man bothered the Presidente.

He was too neat. That was it. General Fitrn's clothes were ruthlessly pressed to perfection. Not a wrinkle could be seen. Every hair was in place, and his nails were as smooth as a woman's. Discontent rose in the Presidente. Is this what life had brought him? Association with pompous, preening fools?

And yet the General had proven himself.

Before pulling out of Koblan's southern port seven months ago, this man had personally killed every Koblani prisoner. He had shown no mercy. Yes. A vicious soul lurked beneath the pampered exterior. It was the only virtue the Presidente could understand and appreciate. And the only proof of the man's pure-blood lineage.

The Zindedi leader cleared his throat. "What remains to be done?"

"We need more men."

More men. A repeated demand, and one the Presidente had chosen to ignore; whether it was to prove his power over the young General, or to make him feel impotent, he wasn't sure. Likely both.

Golden brown eyes, sharp with dislike, stared at the Presidente. Was that resentment he saw? Yes.

A smile worked at one corner of the Presidente's jowly mouth. He relished keeping his highest officers firmly under his boot. It was the boon of power he loved most—making it clear to his subordinates that he held the power to crush out their lives, if he so chose.

"More men." He settled comfortably back into his chair, but said no more. Pleasurable anticipation arose. Now he would watch the General squirm and then demand—no, beg—for the troops needed to complete his mission.

General Fitrn stared back, his eyes expressionless. His square face was cut in perfectly symmetrical planes. A lock of dark blond hair, trimmed to razor precision, edged his high, smooth forehead beneath his black military beret. He said nothing.

A power play.

Fury surged at the insolence, but the Presidente masked it. The young man would not guess that his actions bore any impact upon him.

Fitrn's golden eyes now looked black. His intense stare felt like a sword thrust.

Was it becoming warm in the office?

The Presidente allowed his lids to fall half shut, as if growing bored with the interchange.

Although the General sat ramrod straight, the Presidente sensed no nerves or fear in him. Only focused, calculated aggression.

The Presidente's thick fingers tugged at his neck cloth. The soft fabric suddenly felt suffocating. A warning pain shot from his chest to his belly. *Be calm,* he told himself. *Do not show weakness to this young pup.* The General had been bred for power, but the Presidente would make certain he received it only at the time *he* appointed.

General Fitrn's eyes flickered as he watched the Presidente fumble with his neck cloth. A small, vicious smile curved his thin lips. He crossed his legs and visibly relaxed. "We require men to sail the ships. We also need men to move the weapons and powder to the docks."

The young pup thought he had won! The Presidente's fingers convulsed. Should he crush him now? Grind him as a rocher beneath his heel?

Another sharp pain shot down his arm.

No. The General must remain ready. He must stay in power.

The Presidente inclined his head. "Initiate the draft. Volunteers only." He knew, as did the General, that few men would sign up. It was another way to keep the General dancing at the end of his string, but granted a small bone to help with his task.

Displeasure pressed the General's thin lips into oblivion.

The Presidente smiled, feeling well satisfied. Even better, the last pain in his chest subsided. "Send in my secretary when you leave."

General Fitrn stood, snapped a salute, and marched out the door.

The Presidente chuckled softly. Yes, victory tasted sweet, even if it was only a small bite.

His secretary, a skinny young man with a pasty complexion, hurried in. "Yes, sir?" He clutched parchment and ink at the ready.

The Presidente folded his thick arms across his barrel chest. Relish for the task ahead rushed through his veins. At long last, it was time. If victory tasted sweet, vengeance satisfied like only a thick, bloody steak. Time to strike flame to powder.

Soon his enemies would join his brother in hell.

"Send a letter to Kilum, and also to my deepest spy in Koblan. Write, 'Kill the man who murdered my brother. Kill Mentàll Solboshn and Methusal Maahr. Destiny awaits.'" He chopped his hand through the air, and the secretary scuttled from the office.

A smile curled the Presidente's lips, and his mind turned to his deepest spy. The General had proven himself. Now would his other branch?

CHAPTER ONE

DAY 1
ROLBAN, KOBLAN

"Mentàll Solboshn is arriving this afternoon," Erl Maahr announced at the lunch table.

Methusal put down her fork and stared at her father. So soon? She had received his letter only yesterday. "What does he want, Papa?"

The others at the table—Hanuh, Old Sims, Ben and Poli Amil, and their son Behran—stopped eating to listen.

"He's requested a private meeting with Petr and me."

Petr Storst was Methusal's uncle, and also the former Chief of Rolban. Erl Maahr was the current Chief.

"Why?" Behran rested his forearms on the table and leaned forward so he could see down the table better. Methusal again reflected upon how handsome her fiancé was. He was tall and lean, but the sculpted muscles in his forearms gave testimony to how strong he really was. His leather tunic emphasized his broad shoulders.

"He wants to discuss the Zindedi threat. That's all I know."

"Be careful," Methusal said. "You know we can't trust him."

"I will be cautious. But he proved himself during the Quasr War. I will not turn him away."

Methusal wished her father would speak to the Dehrien outside the gates. Her entire body felt tense with the urgency to keep the Dehrien Chief out of Rolban—and far from her, as well.

"Even a Dehrien can learn a thing or two," Old Sims said. At an indeterminate age over eighty, Sims had spent most of his life traveling Koblan. He had friends everywhere, and one of his friends included the famous Prophet, whom Methusal had last spoken to during the Quasr War. The elderly Prophet had given her difficult instructions to live by, and they had changed her forever. While the Prophet was a wanderer, Sims had settled in Rolban over thirty years ago, but he lived a solitary life. He had no family, and so Methusal had invited him to join her family three years ago as her adopted grandfather.

"You mean he can learn another *trick* or two," she muttered.

Across the table, Behran caught her eye and offered a smile. His deep blue gaze steadied her, and his warm, secure hand closed over hers. He, too, remembered how the Dehrien had left Rolban last time: by forcing a searing kiss on Methusal.

It wasn't the only time Mentàll had kissed her. Behran didn't know that. He didn't need to know, she told herself again. It would only upset him. Besides, the Dehrien had only done it to torment her. In truth, the kiss was a petty trifle, compared to the dangerous games the calculating Dehrien loved to play. Power was his obsession—as proven when he'd tried to take Rolban by force three years ago—and revenge, his lust.

On the surface, Mentàll had played all the right notes during the Quasr War. He had helped to defeat the Zindedi invaders. Koblan could not have won without him. Methusal knew this. But she also knew that underneath it all, he was plotting to advance his own selfish interests. Stealing the *Second Book of Kaavl* right out of her hands was one example, as were the cryptic, suspicious letters to the other Chiefs that she had found in his pack. She'd bet anything that he wanted to achieve more power in the Koblan continent.

Unfortunately, second only to Mentàll's lust for power was his ruthless desire to see her suffer for the humiliating defeat she had served him in Rolban three years ago. Hence his disturbing kisses six months ago, and especially the one right under Behran's nose.

Behran said in a low voice, "The past is finished. He can't hurt you again."

She squeezed his hand. "I hope you're right. But I don't trust him. Look." She pulled the folded parchment from her pocket. "He's planning something. I know it."

As Behran studied the document, a lock of dark blond hair fell across his tanned forehead. His sharp features grew grim. "I guess we're about to hear his plan."

She glanced at her father. Maybe she couldn't stop the Dehrien from coming to Rolban. But she could provide a surprise he wouldn't expect.

"Papa, I'd like to be at that meeting."

△ △ △ △ △

Methusal's stomach twisted in sick knots as she waited in her father's office for the Dehrien Chief to arrive. She hadn't seen him in six months. Unfortunately, every time she did see him felt like a shock to her system. She struggled not to think about how he had left her that last time. Nor his veiled promise—or threat—to finish what he had begun.

Petr Storst settled his large, paunchy frame into a wooden chair. It creaked alarmingly.

Her father, the only other occupant in the room, sat at his desk, scratching words onto a parchment. He glanced at Methusal. "Remember what I said. 'Seen, but not heard.'"

"I'll do my best, Papa."

Erl smiled. "I showed him to the guest quarters. He should be here any moment."

As if summoned by the words, a sharp knock came at the wooden door. Erl rose and welcomed in the giant, blond-haired Dehrien Chief.

Methusal's heart lurched at the sight of her long-time enemy. He was a handsome man, if one liked angles and planes, and a harsh line of a mouth. His straight nose had a hump in it near the bridge, as if broken and never properly reset, and his cheekbones were wide. A glance told her nothing about him had changed in the last six months. Nothing from the short, white-blond hair that kicked up a bit at his temple, to the broad shoulders and powerful, sleek frame outlined by his bleached leather tunic and breeches. He must be just over thirty now.

He strode with soundless, predatory grace, and although she made no sound to announce her presence, the shock of his ice blue eyes immediately focused upon her. She'd once likened their color to a glacier. Now they seared into her like blue fire. His gaze held hers for several beats too long, and her skin unaccountably warmed.

A small smile tugged at his lips. "Methusal." She'd forgotten the harsh timbre of his voice. "I did not expect to be honored by your presence."

As courtesy demanded, she rose and gave a curt nod. "I'm here as an observer."

"Of course."

Her presence pleased him.

This realization disturbed her even further. The men shook hands and everyone settled into their respective chairs.

"Mentàll, we're pleased to have you here," Erl said. "But your message sounded urgent. Do you have news?"

"A brief report. Several of our spies were killed while trying to infiltrate Zindedi. One fact is clear. The Zindedis are building up arms."

Petr cursed. "The filthy whips."

Erl winced, but said calmly, "They're planning another invasion. That's not a surprise."

"No," agreed Mentàll. "I have spent the last six months traveling Koblan. I have discussed the threat of the invaders with the other Chiefs."

Methusal doubted that was all he had been doing, but remained silent.

Erl sat forward in his chair. "When do the invaders plan to attack?"

"I do not know. It could happen at any time, and we would be forced into another defensive position. I do not like that idea. I want to strike Zindedi first."

"Attack the invader land?" Derision laced Petr's deep rumble. His hatred for the Dehrien Chief had not diminished over the last three years. His humiliation at being duped by the Dehrien still rankled deep.

"No." That pale gaze hardened into ice. "I have devised a plan to ensure lasting peace with the invaders."

"You have a plan." Petr Storst sounded disbelieving. A sound like *hrrmmph!* came from behind his white beard. His stocky body shifted on his chair, and a sharp, cracking sound rent the air. Amazingly, the chair held firm while Petr shot a frown at her father. "He's untrustworthy, Erl. You know that."

It was the one point on which Methusal and Petr agreed perfectly, and she was glad he had brought it up. At least someone remembered that only eight short months ago Mentàll had been considered Rolban's number one enemy. That was because three years ago he had manipulated a fake Alliance with Rolban, fooled Petr into championing a secret second agreement, and started a war to take over their mountain community. Actually, an invader, Maxmil Verdnt, had started the war, but that was a technicality. Mentàll had decided to finish it—and he had lost. He had been warned over pain of death never to darken Rolban's gates again.

But eight months ago, Zindedis from across the sea had attacked the coastal villages of Koblan. As a result, Rolban, Tarst, and Dehre had allied together to fight the enemy in Quasr. The Dehrien Chief, as the leader of the kaavl team, had proven to be a vital ally in defeating the invaders. Consequently, Rolban and Tarst had resumed cordial relations with Dehre—provided, of course, Mentàll continued to behave himself. An unlikely possibility, in Methusal's opinion.

Mentàll leaned forward in his chair. "You are wrong, Petr. I have proven my loyalty. However, it is time to say I regret attacking Rolban." He looked at Methusal. "I was wrong to try to do so."

With disbelief, she stared back. What game was he playing now? Self-interest no doubt inspired his humble, conciliatory words.

"I hope you will forgive me." Mentàll glanced at Erl and Petr, and then again at Methusal. She gazed back, her eyes slightly narrowed. He had the gall to offer her a small, unreadable smile.

Erl spoke. "Thank you, Mentàll, for your words. They are received and accepted. Petr, Mentàll has earned the right to speak in this assembly. What is your plan, Chief?"

After that dubious apology, and the letter she had just received, taunting his soon arrival, she didn't trust him. Not one finger width.

"The invader land is a danger to us. I have spoken to leaders all over Koblan. Everyone agrees. We must take steps to neutralize that threat."

"How?" Erl wanted to know.

"Our spies failed because they lacked kaavl skills. I will take a kaavl team to the invader land. After assessing their strengths and weaknesses, I will present a peace agreement to their Presidente."

Petr guffawed, and his pot belly shook. "Good one, Solboshn! And when they catch you, you're dead."

Erl waved his hand. "Go on," he said patiently.

"We have several of their ships," the Dehrien Chief said. "We also have charts, books, and clothing that belong to their native land. Skilled kaavl players would easily blend into their community. We would scout the main city and the surrounding areas to understand their culture and attitude toward Koblan. We could find out how strong their army is. We would discover their weaknesses, and use those as bargaining tools for a lasting peace."

Petr remained silent, but he looked skeptical; much how Methusal felt. She spoke for the first time.

"They want our ore. How does one bargain away greed?" Greed was the Dehrien's middle name. He had wanted to seize power in Rolban three years ago. And during the Quasr War he had stolen the coveted *Second Book of Kaavl* right out of her hands. In fact, it resided in Dehre right now.

His gaze seared into her. "Sharing can satisfy both parties."

He referred to the copied pages of the *Second Book of Kaavl* that he sent her each month.

She said, "They want all of our ore. I don't think they'll be satisfied with scraps."

The Dehrien Chief's teeth flashed. "When they understand that is all they will possess, they will be content."

"To one consumed with greed, that will never be enough. You, of all people, should understand that."

"Methusal," Erl said.

Apparently tiring of the game, the Dehrien returned his attention to Erl. "We annihilated the invaders when they attacked us here. Only a few escaped home to tell the tale. We won without guns. We only used swords and kaavl. We have also learned that the Zindedis are a superstitious people. The job of the peace delegation will be to build up the mystique of our kaavl abilities. Then they will fear us. They will not attempt another invasion."

"Do you really think that will work?" Petr objected.

"Would you rather wait to be invaded again?" Mentàll asked. "I choose offensive action."

"Of course you would," she murmured.

"Yes, Methusal?" Mentàll impaled her with an icy look. "Speak if you have something to say."

"Who would be on your kaavl team? All Dehriens, no doubt."

"On the contrary." Methusal did not like his smile. "I want only the best kaavl players. That means the top ones from each community would come. As well as Doc, from Tarst, in case of injury, and men to sail the ship."

Erl asked, "Which Rolbani kaavl players would you take on this mission?"

"Methusal and Behran. Goric, as well." His blue eyes rested on Methusal again, and she instinctively stiffened, sure she would not like his next words. "Behran will team with my cousin Hendra, Goric, and a few others to scout the countryside. Methusal," and he smiled when he said her name, "will team with me. We will infiltrate the main invader city, Carachki. Eventually, we will obtain an audience with the Presidente and present to him the peace plan."

Methusal had been required to submit to Mentàll's kaavl leadership during the Quasr War. During that time, he had made it his mission to get under her skin as much as possible, and it seemed very likely that he wanted to continue this fun activity during the dangerous trip to the invader land.

"Are you insane?" she demanded. Was this the adventure he had referred to in his last letter? "I'm not going anywhere teamed with you!"

"Afraid, Methusal?"

"I'm not afraid of you," she snapped. "And how could we trust you on a peace mission? What do you hope to gain from it?"

"Methusal," her father said. "I agreed that you could sit in on this meeting if you remain silent."

"Methusal cannot stay silent when confronted with a challenge. Nor will she run from one."

He was baiting her, of course. Provoking her to take the challenge.

Methusal leaned back in the chair and folded her arms. "Your whole plan sounds crazy. The invaders have far more warriors and guns than we do. We don't have any leverage to coerce a peace agreement from them. And don't tell me again about the supposed 'kaavl mystique.' They believe in guns.

They lost the last war, so they'll come back with more fire power."

"So you agree with me. They will return."

Methusal hissed out a frustrated breath. How could he twist her words so easily to his advantage?

The Dehrien addressed Erl and Petr now. "The documents we found on a ship at Aestoff indicate the invader land is smaller than Koblan, but it has more people. The ships hold carved images of many creatures believed by them to be The Ones. As I mentioned before, they are superstitious and fearful, according to the books taken from their ships."

Erl nodded. "Interesting information. It's a bold plan, and it has risks. But I like it, and I like the idea of being proactive. What do you think, Petr?"

"We can't trust him," Petr blustered. "Look what he did three years ago!"

"He fooled you," Erl's shrewd gaze rested upon the Dehrien Chief. "If anyone could carry out this plan, it's you, Mentàll. You're a master at battle plans. You proved that during the Quasr War."

"And a master manipulator," Methusal said. "Don't you see, Papa? He's plotting more than just a peace alliance here."

The Dehrien Chief's gaze returned to her. "And what additional, diabolical goal would I be plotting, fair Methusal?"

She glared at his soft, amused tone. "You tell me."

Petr spoke up. "For once, Methusal is right. You are a master manipulator, Dehrien. Maybe that would qualify you to carry out this crazy plan."

The Dehrien Chief looked pleased. "Then I have your approval? You will sign the preliminary peace agreement, Erl?"

"Yes, after I read it over. What about Tarst and the other communities?"

"All agree. Several are sending people to help with the mission. Aestoff is providing the sailors, since the ship we'll take is anchored there now."

"How long will it take to reach the invader land?"

"Ten days."

Although Methusal had been listening quietly, her mouth gaped open in disbelief. Finally, she shut it and spluttered, "Papa, how can you agree with his plan? We can't trust him. You know that!"

"He proved himself to be a strong ally during the Quasr War. Now he's willing to risk his life to bring peace to Koblan. It's a worthy goal, and a brave thing to do."

"But who's going to watch *him?* Who will make sure he doesn't ally with the invaders and come back and take over all of Koblan?"

Maybe that last bit was unlikely. However...

Mentàll gave a harsh laugh. "You see, Methusal, you must come. The safety of the entire Koblan continent depends upon you."

He was twisting her words yet again to achieve his goals. She eyed him. "Why are you so desperate for me to come with you?"

"Desperate is a stretch, Methusal. However, during the war you proved to be my most valuable kaavl player. I need the best with me."

She wasn't about to fall prey to his flattery. "Tell me the rest of it."

He said nothing for a moment, as if reluctant to disclose his full strategy.

Erl spoke. "Mentàll? We need to know it all."

A cool mask wiped the expression from the Dehrien's face. "In order to infiltrate the invader city without suspicion, I need a foolproof cover. Methusal will provide it."

She knew, in her gut, that she would not like what he'd say next.

"A strange man, alone in a new city, would be noticed. However, a man from the country, honeymooning in the city with his new bride, would create little suspicion."

Methusal's mouth went suddenly dry. "Are you *insane?*" She leaped to her feet. "I am not going to pretend to be your wife!" The very idea made her heart pound, and she felt dizzy. It was crazy. Ludicrous. "You've leaped off the bluff of reason, Mentàll. I would never do anything that stupid!"

Erl frowned. "Sit down." She complied, but with arms defensively crossed. "Mentàll, don't you have a Dehrien woman who could play the role? I agree it would be a clever cover."

"None with Methusal's qualifications." The Dehrien's eyes gleamed at her, and she choked back more words. So this was his plan. To draw her into a tight situation. Then she'd never be able to escape from him. It was exactly what he'd always wanted. Finally, he could exact the revenge he'd threatened so long ago, and never fully implemented.

She would never go on the mission as his fake wife. *Never.*

"I'll call a Council meeting," Erl said. "If everyone agrees, we'll meet again tomorrow morning, and I'll sign the document. I'll ask Behran and Goric to join us. Methusal, it's up to you if you'd like to attend, as well."

"Oh, I'll attend."

"Very well. This meeting is ended."

Methusal bolted from the room, unable to escape Mentàll's icy, amused scrutiny fast enough. She needed to talk to her sister. Deccia would help her make sense of the situation. Then she would decide what to do next.

△ △ △ △ △

Deccia did not show up for dinner. Evidently she and Timaeus had decided to dine in their compartment tonight, which was not surprising for the newlyweds. Methusal would have to speak to her tomorrow.

When dinner was over, Methusal hesitated in the doorway of the dining room. With unease, she observed Mentàll talking to her father. The Dehrien could be charismatic when he chose to be, and was a proven genius at manipulating to get his own way. Not for the first time, she wondered what exactly the "preliminary" peace agreement said. She was sure her father would read it carefully before he signed it, since Mentàll's first Alliance had caused Rolban untold grief three years ago.

"Methusal." Behran came up behind her, and put his arms around her waist, drawing her close to his hard chest. He was almost a handbreadth taller than she was—no mean feat, since she was tall for a woman. She smiled, and affectionately covered his hands with hers. His lips grazed her cheek. "I hear a plan's afoot. And I heard that you shouted at our Dehrien friend." Humor warmed his voice.

"He's up to no good." She frowned across the room. The Dehrien Chief seemed to sense it, for he looked up. He sent her a narrowed, calculating look before he returned his attention to Erl.

"Come on. Tell me all about it," Behran urged. He put his arm around her shoulders, and she put one around his waist, hugging him close. They descended the Grand Staircase to the entry hall below, which was shielded from the night and the wild beasts by the closed, massive gates made of wrought ore. Lounge chairs lined the walls, and they chose to sit on one together.

"Tell me," he insisted again.

She told him about Mentàll's plan to make peace with the invaders. And how he wanted Behran to go as part of the kaavl team, too.

"It sounds dangerous, but the stakes are worth it," Behran said after a small silence. "And we could work together again, like during the war."

"No. I haven't told you the best part. Mentàll wants to pair you up with Hendra."

Behran stiffened. In a heartbeat, all of her old insecurities rushed back. She knew they were only friends, but the two had become very close during the war. She wondered again what he felt for the Dehrien girl.

"And?" he prompted, relaxing a bit.

"And he wants you to infiltrate the countryside. He wants me to team up with him in the city as—get this—his newly wedded wife!" Hysteria edged her laugh.

Now Behran grew even quieter. He removed his arm from her shoulders.

She felt suddenly cold. "I won't do it."

Behran stood up and paced. "Why does he want you to be with him?"

She explained the Dehrien's twisted logic and the plan which would help him to escape invader suspicion. "And he claims I'm the best kaavl player for the job. He seems to think the job in the city will be the hardest."

"I'm sure he's right. And you are the best, Thusa." He abruptly stopped pacing. "I don't like it."

"I won't do it, Behran. That man hates me, and I know he wants to needle under my skin every chance he can get. Even if I do want peace with the invaders for Koblan's sake, I don't want to subject myself to that kind of misery again."

"You mean like during the war."

"Yes. Exactly."

"You never did tell me what happened...what he did to you."

"Nothing." She forced a bright smile to her lips. "It's over and done."

Behran's midnight blue eyes held hers. "Is it?"

Her stomach clenched, and she didn't know what to say. "Yes," she insisted softly.

"Okay." He said nothing for another moment. "I don't like the specifics of the plan, but I think we should both go."

She stared at him in surprise. "But it's crazy, Behran!"

"We need a peace agreement with the invaders."

"Yes, if that's possible!"

"Even if it isn't, we could assess their threat to us firsthand. It's vital information that we'd need to help us defend Koblan."

"You mean we'd be spies."

"Exactly. We're good at it. You know it."

"Yes."

"If Zindedi does plan to attack Koblan, we'd know how many ships and men they plan to send. How many guns, too. When they'd sail, where they'd land. We have to do this, even if a peace agreement is impossible."

He was right, she realized. She hadn't thought it through so clearly, because apprehension had distorted her perspective. Mentàll was going to get his way.

"I'm scared, Behran," she said in a low voice.

"Thusa." He pulled her into his arms again, and she held him tightly. "I'll protect you from Mentàll."

She wished that was possible. She pressed her cheek into his comforting shoulder, and took several calming breaths. Finally, she pulled back a little. "I won't team up with him. I'll go with you, and Hendra can go with him. Or some other woman kaavl player."

"Hendra is only at the Tri-level. You're at the Bi-level. Almost Primary. And you're the only woman in all of Koblan who is."

"So?" Unfortunately, she didn't want to be logical. The idea of being teamed with Mentàll made her feel like an apte about to be stalked by a wild beast. She had stood up to him during the Quasr War, and she could do that again, but at what cost?

Just thinking about how the Quasr War had ended, and how she had felt when Mentàll had kissed her at base camp again coursed guilt and confusion—and anger—through her. The Dehrien knew how to twist her mind so she didn't know if up was down. She hated him and distrusted him, but he also confused her. His occasional flashes of vulnerability tugged at her heart. He'd tormented her, and yet saved her life four times. He baited her, and he hated her.

Or did he? Just the question made her close her eyes, overcome with a feeling akin to panic.

The truth was, he was a man with a lot of experience with women, and the thought of being forced into close proximity with him scared her to death.

How long could she maintain her defenses against him? How long before he burrowed under her skin so deep that she wouldn't know herself anymore—and until she forgot who he truly was? She had nearly done that at the end of the Quasr War. It could not happen again.

She could not team up with him in the city. She said, "Mentàll's brilliant, isn't he? Let him figure out that small problem."

Behran's arms tightened around her, but she couldn't relax. "I don't like Mentàll's plan, either. But we can try to change the parts we don't like."

Methusal nodded, but she didn't believe for one moment that it would be easy. Not when the Dehrien Chief had obviously been planning this mission for months. He'd probably worked out every tiny, logical detail, as well as every argument necessary to succeed in getting his own way.

△ △ △ △ △

"Behran said you were looking for me." Later that evening, Deccia slipped into the supply room where Methusal was working to sort out supplies for breakfast. The afternoon meeting had cut into her work schedule, so now she needed to finish her neglected tasks.

"I was wondering if you'd ever come out," Methusal teased.

Her identical twin flushed and giggled. She was tall and slim, with long dark hair, a lightly tanned complexion, and green eyes. The only differences in appearance between the two were that Methusal's skin was a faintly darker hue, and she wore fewer decorative bits of feathers and beads on her tunic. Deccia's personality was softer than Methusal's, too, and she was empathic, just like their mother, Hanuh. Methusal wished she possessed even a pinch of her sister's gentleness and tact, but thankfully she had grown a little in that direction over the last three years.

"Wait until you and Behran get married," Deccia said.

"Mhmm." She quickly finished sorting, and waved for her sister to sit on a sack of grain.

Deccia sent her a shrewd look. "Why haven't you set a date yet?"

"We've only been engaged for six months."

"And you've been dating for three years. Isn't Behran getting impatient? Aren't you? You're over twenty-one—we'll be twenty-two in a few months. Certainly old enough for your parents' approval."

"I don't know, Decc. We don't seem to talk about it much." Correction—she sensed Behran wanted to talk about it, but she didn't. "I don't feel like the time is right. Not yet."

"If you say so." Deccia did not look satisfied with the answer, but changed the subject. "Timaeus heard about the trip. He says they'll need a runner to keep communication going between all the teams in the invader land. He wants to go, too."

"Papa's having a meeting tomorrow morning. He should come to it."

"I'm coming, too."

"You are?" After all that Deccia had suffered at the hands of the invader General, the last place she imagined her sister ever wanting to go would be the land that had spawned that devil. Thankfully, he was dead.

"I want to go." A core of cooled ore hardened her soft voice. "I want to be with Timaeus, but I think I'd be an asset to the team, too. I feel like I *have* to go. I wasn't able to do anything to defeat the invaders the last time. I want to do something now. I have to." Tears filled her eyes.

"Oh, Deccia." Methusal hugged her. Deccia had suffered violation after horrifying violation from the insane General. In her place, wouldn't she want revenge? Or at least want to prevent Koblan from becoming a victim to invader hands again? "I'd love it if you came. Selfishly, it would make everything so much better."

"Why?" Deccia pulled away, wiping her eyes.

"I want to go, too, but..." Methusal explained about the Dehrien's disturbing plans. "I won't team with him. I *won't*."

"What if he won't let you go on the mission otherwise?"

"He'll let me come. He said himself I'm the best qualified woman."

"Are you afraid, Thusa?" Deccia asked softly.

"No. Well, yes," she admitted. "I can't work with him. I'd have to find another assignment. Behran and I should work together."

"Instead of Behran and Hendra."

"Exactly." Troubled, Methusal looked at her sister.

"Behran loves you."

"I know. But I'm not sure what he feels for her. Tonight when I mentioned her name, he stiffened and went all weird on me."

"Everything will work out the way it's supposed to. Look at Timaeus and me. I thought the General had corrupted me, and I was afraid Timaeus would never want me as his wife. But he did. He loves me. That's how true love is. It never gives up."

Methusal felt better. "I know you're right."

"And however much Mentàll plots and plans, he'll never change that, unless..."

"Unless what?"

Deccia went still. Methusal recognized that far off look. Her sister had retreated into an empathetic trance, seeing something no one else could. "Unless *you* want it changed."

"I don't!" Methusal said, more sharply than she had intended.

Deccia blinked, and glanced at her through narrowed eyes. "Of course you don't."

Δ Δ Δ Δ Δ

Deccia slipped into the pallet she shared with Timaeus. The rocky compartment felt empty without him tonight. Cold, too, although a warm torch flickered on the wall. She shivered and tucked the covers more tightly around herself. He'd be back soon. The whaal card game was almost over. Unless, of course, his friends convinced him to play another hand.

Deccia shivered again and closed her eyes to shut out the black shadows. She'd pretended to feel calm to Methusal, but fear licked through her when she thought about traveling to the invader land.

And yet she had to do it. The General had stripped away more of her self-worth than she'd let anyone know. He'd stolen her dignity and a piece of her soul.

Going to Zindedi seemed like the only way she could fight back, and also maybe reclaim a little of what she'd lost. At the very least, she would make sure that a Zindedi never hurt another Koblani again. *Ever.*

The torch sputtered and dimmed. Shadows crept closer, and Deccia squeezed her eyes shut. She would not be afraid. Timaeus would be home soon. He would protect her. *Always.* She clung to this truth as she slipped into the lonely blackness of sleep.

The General stalked her. His black military uniform was perfectly in place, with the red sash across his chest, and so was his black cap, perched on his black hair, which was sprinkled with gray. Amber eyes glowed at her, looking as hot as hell's fires. He reached for her, and the red from his mutilated thumb made her choke back a cry.

She backed away, but the door stopped her. Fear sickened her. "No! You can't have me. It's too late."

He laughed. It was an awful, insane sound. His touch scored her flesh like acid. "I can touch you whenever I want. You are mine, now. Forever."

"No," Deccia screamed. "No!"

He gripped her arm.

"No." She shrank back. "No! Don't touch me."

"Deccia." The grip on her arm tightened.

"Don't touch me," she sobbed out, twisting and writhing to free herself. "Don't touch me!"

"Deccia! *Deccia.*" A deeper voice than the General's filled her ears.

"No," she whimpered. "Don't touch me."

"Deccia, I love you." Pain roughened the male voice.

Her eyes blinked open to dim light, and Timaeus' worried face above her.

"Timaeus!" She burst into tears.

"Can I hold you?" He sounded anxious.

"Yes," she whispered.

He pulled her into his arms. She crumpled against him and wept until she felt dried up inside.

He kissed her temple. "Are you all right?" Worry still roughened his voice.

"Yes, now that you're holding me."

"You had another nightmare." It wasn't a question. "It's the first one in weeks."

Deccia sniffed and wiped her eyes. "I've been thinking about the invader land."

"You don't have to go."

"I do. Six months ago I couldn't do anything. Now I can."

"You're shaking."

She was. "I'll be fine."

He frowned. "Are you sure?"

"Yes." She whispered, "But I worry about you. What if the Presidente finds out you're the one who killed his brother, General Greisn?"

"How? We killed every Zindedi in that room. Only Koblanis were left."

Deccia didn't answer. But this dark worry had surfaced the instant she'd found out Timaeus wanted to go to Zindedi. The trouble was, she couldn't tell if her anxiety was a premonition or an irrational fear. She'd already lost half of her soul to one Zindedi. She wouldn't lose the other half of her heart—Timaeus—to the Presidente.

Chapter Two

When Methusal entered her father's office the next morning, everyone else had arrived. Erl and Petr sat near the desk, since they were the Rolbani elders in charge of the assembly. Currently, Mentàll stood speaking to Erl. Parchment pages lay on the desk. Methusal guessed it was the preliminary peace agreement, and wondered if her father had signed it yet.

To Petr's right sat Deccia, Timaeus, and Goric, and to Erl's left was Behran. Two empty chairs sat next to Behran. Methusal slipped into the chair nearest him. Which left one for Mentàll. Next to her. Surreptitiously, she pushed it, so the armrest did not touch her own. The more space, the better.

Unfortunately, before she had shoved it far, the Dehrien grabbed it with one large hand and scooted it back as he sat down. Temper warmed her cheeks, but she ignored him. This was another small way he could needle under her skin. His close proximity disturbed her, and he clearly knew it.

With a faint frown, she leaned on her left elbow, toward Behran, and away from the Dehrien's large frame. His long legs stretched out before him, ankles crossed. He looked like the picture of relaxation. On the other hand, her skin prickled, urging her to jump up and flee to the other side of the room.

She was being ridiculous. What could the Dehrien do to her in a roomful of people, for goodness sake?

Erl opened the meeting. "I spoke with the Council last night, and all agree that your plan, Mentàll, has merit. I signed the preliminary peace statement, and saw that all of the other Chiefs of Koblan have signed, as well. It will take courage to lead this mission, and to be the spokesman for Koblan. I commend you, and thank you for your initiative."

Mentàll nodded, but he looked away for a moment, as if he felt uncomfortable. Maybe he was not used to receiving such high praise. Or perhaps he thought he didn't deserve it.

Methusal still believed this peace agreement was not all Mentàll had been plotting for the past six months. In fact, she knew it, because a half a year ago, she'd uncovered letters in his pack that had proven he was trying to make alliances all over Koblan—*before* the Quasr War had even started. Before they'd realized Zindedi was a huge threat.

Erl continued, "We will fully support you by providing the people and supplies you need. Timaeus would like to join the team, too. Go ahead and speak your piece, Timaeus."

The tall, dark-haired young man edged forward in his seat. "It sounds to me like this mission could use a runner. I don't know all the facts, but I'm guessing you'll have at least two different teams, plus the men on the ship. You'll need to keep in contact with everyone as often as possible. I'm the man for the job."

"Timaeus is the best runner I have," Erl offered. Erl was not only Chief of Rolban, but had also been chief of the messenger team in Rolban for many years.

Mentàll's low, harsh voice said, "And what about Deccia?"

Deccia bit her lip. She looked a little nervous, but determined. "I would be a valuable asset to the team, too. I may not know kaavl, but I am good at reading people. I can tell when they tell the truth, or when they tell lies. And I can tell if someone can be trusted—not only now, but how that person will affect a certain plan of action well into the future. I will be able to tell which people in Zindedi will be the most dangerous to us."

The Dehrien leaned forward. "Empathic." He sounded faintly surprised. "My mother was an empath."

Methusal shot a glance at the Dehrien Chief. He never spoke about his long dead mother.

He leaned back in his chair again, his light eyes narrowed. "I have never met another one."

"My mother is an empath, as well," Deccia said.

Mentàll cast Methusal a quick glance, and then returned his attention to her sister. "An empath would be helpful on our journey. Reading the motives of the Zindedis you'll meet in Dakarra will help protect the team from unexpected threats."

"Then I can go? I want to be with Timaeus," Deccia clarified.

"Yes."

Deccia jumped a little in her chair and hugged Timaeus.

"Good. That's settled." Erl looked pleased.

But if his heavy scowl was any indication, Petr did not like the idea of his adopted daughter traveling to the dangerous invader land. He growled, "What plan do you have to keep these kids safe?"

"I make no guarantees," Mentàll said. "The mission is dangerous. Timaeus and Deccia know that."

Erl said, "Behran? Methusal? Do you want to go? Goric has already said he does."

The thin young man with the murky gray eyes and dirty blond hair said nothing. Rather, he watched everyone else like a whip eyeing an apte. During the Quasr War, he had teamed up with Jascr, Mentàll's horrible cousin, to make Methusal's life miserable. However, during the last battle with the Zindedis, Goric had warned Methusal about Jascr's attack, and had helped to save her life. She still wasn't sure what to think about him.

"I'll go," Behran said. "And I think Methusal would like to, as well." He looked at her, and she nodded. "But we'd like to change assignments. I'd like for Methusal to be on my team."

As much as Mentàll had been surprisingly willing to change his plans to allow Timaeus and Deccia to join the team, a cold, implacable mask fell over his features at Behran's suggestion.

"No. That is not possible."

"I would be just as useful scouting information with Behran in the country," Methusal said in her most reasonable tone.

"Doubtless you would be useful in the country." Those light, icy eyes were even more disturbing at close range, but she lifted her chin and met the Dehrien's gaze head on. "But your skills are most needed with me. In the city."

"Why?"

"Because the city has more targets. High level targets. The Presidente lives there. A warrior base is located on the outskirts. Top commanders work there, plan there, and meet there. We need to know those plans. Our job in the city will be the most dangerous, and the most profitable. Much as you might want to choose an easier assignment, I am the commander, and if you come, you will go where I assign you."

She drew a sharp breath. "Easier?" she sputtered. "I'm not asking for an easier assignment!"

"No? You want to be in the country with your fiancé. Perhaps a pre-honeymoon? I see you still are not wearing his marriage necklace."

"It's not about that," she hissed.

"No. It is not, is it?" His eyes glinted. "You fear me. That is why you will not take the critical assignment."

"I hate you, I don't fear you," she retorted, anxious to make that point clear.

"You fear me."

"I do not!"

His lips curled up, and he said softly, "Then take my marriage necklace. Join me in the city."

Methusal's cheeks flushed hot. Unknown layers of meaning lived in those soft words, and the anxiety again gripped her. He'd blocked her into an impossible corner. Why was she surprised? She's already guessed that he'd planned out every detail so he would get his own way. She blurted, "You just want to torture me. Like you did during the war."

"Torture you?" Erl interjected. "Mentàll, did you hurt my daughter during the war?"

"Did I, Methusal? Tell him how."

She bit her lip, but said nothing. She couldn't. She had never even told Behran.

"Methusal?" Erl said with a frown.

"He never harmed me. Not physically, Papa."

Erl looked from one to the other with a frown. "You will agree to treat my daughter like a gentleman on this trip, Mentàll. And you will not touch her at all."

"A small amount of physical contact will be necessary in public. But I promise I will not lay a hand on her in private. We will be sharing close quarters, but I will give her all of the privacy she needs, and more."

Methusal hadn't even thought about staying in close quarters with Mentàll. In the same *room?* The memory of that night six months ago, alone with him on the rocky hillside of base camp, hit her again with the force of a punch. He had been released from all promises then. She'd be a fool to willingly walk into a tight situation with him again, promises or not. A situation where they would spend unknown amounts of time together, alone in a small room!

All the air left her lungs, and she gulped for air. *Impossible.*

"This job takes courage, Methusal," the Dehrien Chief said, as if reading her mind. "If you cannot conquer your fear of me, then you have no place on the mission."

She cast Behran a tormented look.

"We need you, Thusa." His low voice gave her courage. "I believe in you. You can do whatever it takes. And if that Dehrien lays a hand on you, I will personally make him pay." Methusal had never heard that hard note in his voice before. His hand closed over hers, and it steadied her.

"I'll do it." She didn't know where the words came from, or how they could sound so firm and cool, but she looked at the Dehrien Chief as she said them.

Triumph flared in his eyes. He looked at Erl. "All is settled, then. I have a copy of the supply list. These five will meet me in Dehre in two days' time."

Methusal felt shaken. How had she been trapped into this mess—exactly where Mentàll had schemed for her to be all along? He was a master manipulator, and he had already won his first battle. Next time, she'd need to be better prepared.

△ △ △ △ △

"Come to my compartment for tea," Deccia urged after the meeting ended.

Methusal looked down at her list of supplies. "But I need to put together food rations."

"It'll wait." Her sister grabbed her arm. "Come on."

When she was sipping tea a few minutes later, Methusal realized she was glad she could relax for a few minutes in a protected environment—a place where she didn't have to worry about running into that confounded Dehrien.

Deccia gave Methusal a shrewd look. "Very impressive, the Dehrien Chief. And ruthless and intimidating. I'd never seen him in action before."

"Now do you see what I mean?" She still felt shaken by the meeting.

"I see how much he wants you on his team. He fired every piece of ammunition he had to make things go his way."

"Should I feel flattered?" she said sarcastically.

"No. You should be careful. But you know that." Deccia hesitated. "He won't...you know...?"

"No. Mentàll takes his word seriously." This, she knew.

"So you'll be safe with him, alone in a room."

Apprehension again gripped her. "He may not lay a hand on me, but I won't be safe. His games never end."

"Are you talking about when he kissed you?" Deccia eyed her with discernment. She was the only one Methusal had told what had happened in those rocky foothills.

Her face heated, and she hated the reaction. "Not just that. He likes to get under my skin and...upset me, I guess is the best description. It's his way to take revenge on me for three years ago."

"Ignore him."

"I would if I could!"

"His words mean so much to you?"

"No! Of course not. But he drives me crazy."

"And you don't provoke him, ever?"

A rueful smile crossed her lips. "Maybe I did. A few times during the war."

"I remember." Her sister's gaze shadowed. "Please be careful, Thusa."

"Do you sense something about the future?"

"Nothing specific. But I do sense danger ahead for you."

"That's not surprising. Deccia, he's plotting something else, I know it."

"Concerning you?"

That idea surprised her. "I don't know. I mean I think he has a secret plan regarding the mission—or after the mission."

"Then it's good you'll be able to keep a close eye on him."

"True." Methusal relaxed a little. She'd not only spy on the invaders, but she'd spy on a spy.

Mentàll would never be able to carry out any plan to hurt Koblan as long as she was privy to every move he made.

For the first time, she felt better about the situation. She would figure out what his ultimate goal was, one way or another, and if necessary, put a stop to it.

△ △ △ △ △

In the dining hall that evening, Mentàll approached Methusal. She fought her immediate urge to flee.

A faint smile curved those hard lips, and his gaze seemed to gauge her every flicker of emotion. "I am pleased that you agreed to pair with me on the mission. I anticipate complete victory."

A double meaning, as always, seemed to color his words. "What victory do you mean?"

He smiled. "Peace with my enemies. What other victory would I desire?"

Bumps prickled up on her arms. She still could not tell what he was really saying, but she suspected she wouldn't like it if she did.

"Methusal." Her mother's voice startled her. She turned to see Hanuh watching the Dehrien Chief. Her shrewd gaze looked troubled. "Treat my daughter with courtesy, young man."

Mentàll inclined his head. "Yes, Matron Maahr." He spoke with surprising respect.

Hanuh nodded once. "See that you do. Methusal?" She turned to her daughter. "Come dine with your father and me tonight. Behran will enjoy your company for the next few weeks. But we will miss you."

"Thank you. I'd love to." She left the Dehrien Chief standing alone.

△ △ △ △ △

Aalicaa watched Methusal and Mentàll part ways. She sat alone at the Storst dining table, chewing on her lip. Another exciting mission was about to take place, but no one had asked her to join it.

Not that she was surprised. She'd earned a reputation for being rash. While yes, it was true she had mistakenly blown up a valley full of ammunition, hadn't she also destroyed the invaders' munitions building? She had played an important role in helping to defeat the Zindedis.

Now Koblan needed her ability to think outside the box again. They needed her to help think of ways to defeat that tricky Presidente and his minions.

Pain stung her raw lip. A dose of truth did, too. She didn't want to sit here in Rolban, bored to death, while the others had all the fun. She wanted to go on the trip, too.

CHAPTER THREE

"ANOTHER LETTER, HENDRA." With a grin, Dastn, the Tarst runner, extended a folded parchment to her.

A flush scored Hendra's cheeks. She couldn't help it, because she knew whom it was from. "Thank you, Dastn," she said softly.

"You're welcome." He headed for Mentàll's tent. Hendra's cousin had just returned from Rolban. Soon she'd ask him if Behran and Methusal had agreed to go on the mission.

But first, she wanted to read the letter from Doc.

The first letter from the Tarst doctor had arrived three weeks after the Quasr War had ended. Hendra still remembered that clear, sparkling day, which had chased away two days of rain. For the first time in months, plenty of water filled the well.

"Hendra!" On that day, Dastn had walked toward her, letter extended. "Something for you."

"For *me?*" Hendra wondered who would send her a letter. She had never received one before in her life.

She turned the folded paper over. A bold, masculine scrawl spelled out her name. A familiar scrawl. Her heart jumped a little. *Could it be?* He was Dastn's cousin. She looked up to ask, but Dastn had already strolled away.

With suddenly trembling fingers, she quickly unfolded the parchment. Her eyes jumped to the bottom of the page. *Doc.*

He had sent her a letter! Her heart pounded harder, and she retreated to her tent to read it in privacy. Not that she expected him to say anything personal to her, of course. She'd assumed the end of the war meant the end of their relationship. It had been a working relationship only, she reminded herself.

Hendra sat on her cot and smoothed the precious paper flat on her lap.

Hendra, I miss your nursing skills. Are you sure I can't bribe you to move to Tarst? No. I didn't think so.

You mentioned that you work with the orphaned children in Dehre. I know a few remedies for childhood sicknesses. Maybe you or the doctor in Dehre already know these things. In case you don't, here are a few tips.

He'd listed a page of childhood ailments and treatments, and signed it simply, *Doc.* While the letter was purely professional, the fact that he'd thought to write the note made Hendra feel happy.

Hesitantly, because she'd never corresponded with a man before—in fact, she'd rarely spoken to any men except for her relatives before the Quasr War—Hendra wrote back and thanked him. She also asked him how to treat a young boy's lingering cough. She gave the letter to Dastn.

Dastn always brought Doc's letters, and Hendra always gave him her replies. As far as she knew, no one else knew that she was writing to the Tarst doctor. She wanted it to stay that way.

And so the intermittent correspondence had continued over the last seven months. After the first letter, Doc had included snippets about his own life. And he casually scrawled a question or two for her, too. She kept all of his letters—as a future reference for medical cases, she told herself.

And now she'd received another one!

She quickly opened it, and eagerly drank in each word.

Hendra, Mentàll asked me to go to the invader land. That means I will be in Dehre on Fourthday. I'll see you soon. Doc

Doc was coming to *Dehre?* And he was going to the invader land? Her heart leaped with excitement. Anxiety chased it.

Hendra spotted her tall cousin striding across the dirt compound, and sprinted to join him. "Mentàll!"

One of his rare, small smiles flashed. "Hendra." He glanced at the letter in her hand. "You have news?"

"Doc is *coming?* You asked him on the mission?" Hendra didn't care that she'd just revealed Doc had been writing to her.

He stopped and his smile widened. "You are pleased, little cousin?"

He *knew.* How had he known? But how did Mentàll know anything? He seemed to have a seventh sense about him. It was probably one reason why he had achieved the highest possible level of kaavl, and the highest political office in Dehre. He'd held that office for the last seven years.

Mentàll was a powerful man, and had earned the deep respect—and perhaps fear—of all Dehriens. Still, being Chief of Dehre was not enough for him. Hendra sensed this. Others, such as her friend Methusal, thought he was a power hungry wild beast. Maybe that was true. Or perhaps quests for power were how he tried to fill an empty void inside of him.

Her cousin started walking again. "Do you still want to come?"

"Of course." Last week Mentàll had asked her to join the mission. She had felt honored, because he'd asked no other Dehrien to come, except for Tabor, his first-in-command.

"Good. Methusal, Behran, and Goric will arrive tomorrow."

Her surprise mounted. "Methusal agreed to your plan?" Why was she so amazed? Mentàll always got what he wanted, one way or another.

Satisfaction glimmered. "Of course."

"You are happy," she said softly.

"I will be happy when all works out according to my plan." With those cryptic words, he left her. Hendra felt a bit unsettled as she watched him go. She still did not know her cousin's entire plan, and that disturbed her. But she was also certain that he'd told no one else, either. He let no one into his heart or his confidence.

A lonely place to live. While she didn't understand her cousin completely, she did know he loved her, in his own way. He had always protected her. Once, he had almost killed a man for her.

Too bad the damage had already been done.

Hendra closed her eyes against the painful memories. Jascr was dead. And yet the fear he'd left in her heart toward men—*all* men—would not subside. Fighting in the war had helped. But she wasn't healed. Not even close. She glanced at the letter in her hand. *Doc was coming.*

Did he still have feelings for her?

She would *see* him soon!

What would he expect from her?

Excitement and apprehension battled. The touch of a man still scared her to death. But did she want to live in fear for the rest of her life?

Biting her suddenly trembling lip, Hendra carefully folded the letter again. *No.* No, she did not.

△ △ △ △ △

"Are you sure, Methusal?" Hanuh's gaze looked troubled.

"I am." Apprehension stirred in her, however. Right now her empathic mother seemed to be sensing something ominous about the future. "It's my duty. I've been given the gift of Mahre's kaavl skills. I have to use them to protect Koblan." This was the first time she had admitted that truth to anyone. Although Mentàll had guessed.

After a short silence, Hanuh said, "It will be dangerous. Not only because of the Zindedis, but to your heart. Are you prepared for it to be broken over the man you want, but will not have?"

"What do you mean? Will Behran and I break up?" Dismay and fear clashed within her. A horrible suspicion dawned. "Is it because he loves Hendra?"

"I don't know. That's for you to find out. But here's my best advice: Don't just listen to your head. Listen to your heart to find the answers."

"And what about the peace mission?"

"Your bravery will make a difference. Remember that. And remember that I love you, no matter what. And I'm proud of you. So is your father."

"What about Deccia? She won't be hurt by another invader, will she?"

"Your sister knows what she must do. Both of you will struggle. I'm praying that you'll both follow the higher path. Don't forget, Methusal, that not everything in life is about kaavl."

"Are you saying kaavl isn't important on this mission?"

"No." She fell abruptly silent. Worry clouded her eyes.

"Mama?"

"Make sure you learn every scrap of kaavl you can. Your safety will depend upon it."

∆ ∆ ∆ ∆ ∆

At the dining table that evening, Aali glared at Methusal and Deccia. "I want to come!"

"You're only fifteen," Deccia pointed out.

"Almost sixteen, and I know kaavl. And I'm at the Quatr-level! I could help beat those nasty invaders. I can use a kaavl stick just as well as Methusal can."

"Kaavl sticks probably won't play a big part in the mission," Methusal said. "We'll be spying. And if we're in danger, we'll have to use knives." She still had nightmares about killing the two invaders when she'd run for her life through the Quasr Mountains. She had never forgotten the looks on their faces when they died at her hands, nor their blood, spurting onto her arms.

Methusal swallowed back a feeling of nausea. She put a gentle hand on Aali's arm. "You don't want to go, Aali. You don't."

"Are you afraid you'll die?"

"I hope I won't. But it'll be dangerous." An idea struck her. "But you can help out here."

"How?" Suspicion wrinkled her brow.

"Mentàll's been traveling all over Koblan. He wants us to believe it was to build support for the peace mission. But in my gut, I'm certain he's plotting something else—maybe a power grab."

"I could talk to our runners." At last, Aali's gaze lit up. "My friend Dastn would tell me stuff."

"I'm sure he would." Methusal hid a smile. Although Aali was only fifteen, she'd had her eye on the handsome Tarst runner ever since the Quasr War. Of course he was five years older than she was, so she might be in the throes of a first infatuation, but all the same, her cousin wasn't one to let grass grow under her feet. She'd pursue his friendship with all of her considerable powers of charm, persuasion, and spunk.

Aali's eyes narrowed. "I know a lot more runners, too. I'll ask the best ones, like Dastn, to spy out answers when they go to Quasr and Aestoff. And then I'll write down all the information in a report. I'll give it to you when you get home!" She seemed to become more excited with the idea by the moment.

"Good idea." Deccia glanced at Methusal. "You really think he's planning a power grab, Thusa?"

"I'm pretty certain. During the Quasr War, I found correspondence with other Chiefs in his pack. And I also overheard a few conversations that seemed to indicate he wants to form a large alliance of some kind. When we get home, we'll need Aali's information. Then we can stay one step ahead of him, and we can stop him before it's too late."

"What if you're wrong? What if he has a good plan?"

"Then no harm done. But over and over again, he's proven he's power hungry and dangerous, and he can't be trusted."

Deccia's eyes narrowed, but she did not disagree.

"If Mentàll's up to something nasty again, I'll find out," Aali vowed, rubbing her hands together with clear relish. "I'll get started right now!" She leaped up and darted for the messenger cave.

Deccia said dryly, "At least now we won't have to worry about her following us to Aestoff and stowing aboard the ship."

Methusal giggled, but her smile soon faded. Tomorrow their adventure would begin. And tomorrow she would see Mentàll. Just thinking about spending time in close contact with him for days on end in Zindedi made her feel anxious.

Behran would not be with her in Carachki. Much as he wanted to protect her, he could not be her buffer.

Her mother was right. She did need to learn more ways to protect herself.

△ △ △ △ △

Methusal again flipped through the papers on the battered desk in Kitran Mehl's old office. Nothing. She had already searched twice through all of her kaavl instructor's books.

Kitran had died while mutinying against the Dehrien Chief's leadership during the Quasr War. No one had taken his place as kaavl instructor, because no one in Rolban had achieved the Primary level yet. She, Behran, and Petr were the only Rolbanis currently at the Bi-level. And Petr knew next to nothing about the Primary level. He'd plateaued at the Bi-level, and had taken little time to learn more.

Everything she had learned over the past six months had come from three sources: the *First Book of Kaavl*, which contained a few cryptic paragraphs about the Primary level; Kitran's papers; and the few pages of the *Second Book of Kaavl* that Mentàll had sent.

Nothing. Frustrated, Methusal shoved the papers aside. Kitran had written *nothing* about achieving the Primary level. He'd only listed the required skills necessary to reach that level, but no instructions about how to achieve those goals.

The *Second Book of Kaavl* explained how to reach the Primary level. When it had vanished two hundred years ago, that knowledge had passed down through oral tradition from one Primary level kaavl player to another. But now Kitran was dead, and she had no one to ask.

The prospect of sailing to Zindedi and infiltrating the invader land scared her—especially after her mother's warning. She needed to learn Primary level skills, and now.

Her mind returned to the *Second Book of Kaavl,* which Mentàll had stolen. If only she could read it. Familiar resentment simmered. If the book was in Rolban, as it rightfully should be, she'd surely know how to advance to the Primary by now, and possibly the Ultimate level, too. But Mentàll kept the stolen book in Dehre. And he certainly wouldn't bring the old book on the trip. It was far too fragile.

So, how could she achieve the Primary level?

A sudden, brilliant plan occurred to her.

Reckless anticipation stirred. The plan was dangerous and possibly foolish. Maybe even a stunt Aali would have considered in the past. But the fruit of this first, preliminary spy mission would be worth it.

A small smile tugged at her lips. Spying on a spy would begin tomorrow, in Dehre.

CHAPTER FOUR

Day 4

EXCITEMENT JUMPED IN HENDRA when five travelers appeared on the horizon.

Fifteen minutes later, they were close enough to greet. Hendra ran and hugged Methusal and Deccia. She offered a grin to Behran, Timaeus, and Goric, and then they walked together in the warm sunshine to Dehre. It had been seven long months since she'd seen them. She'd missed them.

Mentàll emerged from his tent and greeted the men.

"No Aali?" Hendra asked. "For sure?"

Methusal laughed. "I gave her an assignment. Hopefully it'll keep her busy until we get back." She cast a faint frown in Mentàll's direction.

Hendra tactfully didn't ask what Aali's mission might be.

"Look!" Behran said. "It's Doc and Riln."

Hendra quickly turned. The tall, muscle-bound Riln strode ahead of Doc. His large body partially obscured the Tarst doctor and someone who walked beside him. During the Quasr War, Riln and two Tarst men had mutinied with Kitran against Mentàll's leadership.

"Who's with them?" Deccia wanted to know.

A petite, dark-haired woman was laughing up at Doc. Hendra's heart gave a sickening lurch. Who was she? Surely he wasn't married...

The Tarst doctor hadn't changed. His dark red hair was still short, and his beard neatly trimmed against his jaw. He was medium height, which meant he was two finger widths taller than she was, because she was tall for a woman. His tunic had short sleeves—a testament to the heat—and lean, hard muscles rippled.

Hendra knew when Doc spotted their small group, and when he saw her. His intent gaze didn't leave her after that. Hendra's heart beat faster as the three Tarst pilgrims joined their little group. She quickly dropped her gaze from Doc's and sized up the newcomer. The woman's short, straight dark hair swung about her chin, and her dark eyes sparkled with fun. She wore no marriage necklace, Hendra was relieved to see.

"I'm Methusal." The Rolbani girl introduced the others. "And who are you?"

"I am Sozla." The petite woman spoke with an accent. "I am from Eerpor...to the east."

The Eerporians had lived in virtual seclusion for many centuries. Only the Quasr War had lured them out to fight for their continent.

Hendra realized it was time for her to speak. "Welcome to Dehre, Sozla. Will you be joining us on our trip?"

"Yes. When Mentàll visited our village, he said you had need of one who understands how things work. Irrigation...such things."

"Engineering," Behran spoke up. "I'm an engineer, too."

Sozla's smile blossomed. "Then we have much to discuss, you and I."

A faint red stained Behran's cheekbones. "Yes. I'm sure we do."

Hendra cast a quick glance at each of the men in the group. Yes, to a one, all appeared fascinated by the tiny Sozla. She offered a smile to the other young woman. "Please. Let me show you to your cabin. I hope you don't mind sharing with Methusal."

"Of course not. I am pleased to be here."

"And Mentàll. I'm sure he will want to talk to you," Hendra said.

"Yes. I see Mentàll is busy. I will speak with him later."

Hendra escorted the others to their cabins. "Dinner will be ready in an hour. Mentàll has asked us to dine in his tent tonight."

"Oh, goodie." Methusal murmured.

Hendra smiled. "I see your feelings for my cousin haven't changed."

"They will never change." Her friend headed inside the cabin.

Hendra realized that only Doc remained standing beside her. She glanced at him. "Isn't your pack getting heavy?"

A faint smile lurked in his smoky blue eyes. "Hendra. You are looking well."

Feeling a bit self-conscious, she said, "Thank you. So are you."

He extended his hand. "It's nice to see you again."

She stared at his extended hand. The ridiculous, illogical fear gripped her. And she hated it.

She took a breath and forced her hand out. He made no move to touch her. Doc understood why she feared physical contact with men. She glanced at him. His gaze steadily held hers. She swallowed and curled her hand around his. It felt calloused, solid, and warm. She whispered, "Nice to see you too, Doc."

He smiled, gave her hand a gentle squeeze, and then let it go. "Are you ready for the mission?"

"I hope so. I'll be a spy this time around."

"That will be dangerous."

"Isn't that why you're coming? To pick up the pieces?"

"And who will put together my pieces?"

Flustered, Hendra said, "I'll help you, if you need a nurse."

"Thank you. I appreciate every step you're willing to take. I'll see you at dinner," he said quietly.

Hendra watched him go. How could one man make her feel so flummoxed inside? Excited, fearful... And joyful to finally see him again. He scared her, because she sensed he wanted them to take a trip of their own. A journey she might be a fool to start, because she may not be able to finish it.

△ △ △ △ △

Dinner would soon begin in one of Mentàll's large tents. But not in his living structure, Methusal noted. She and Behran were currently strolling around the Dehrien Chief's compound, which was composed of seven tents, including Hendra's.

Good. All the better to set her plan in motion later.

She calculated the distance between the Dehrien's main tent and the dining tent. At least twenty lengths. Soon it would be twilight. When it was dark, she would make her move.

"What are you staring at?" Behran's gaze looked darker than normal, and troubled.

"Just thinking."

"About the mission?"

"A bit." She didn't want to involve Behran in her underhanded scheme.

He nodded, but remained silent.

She touched his arm. "What's wrong?"

"I don't know." After a moment, he admitted, "I have a bad feeling about this."

"The trip? The mission?"

"Mentàll."

She glanced over her shoulder at the Dehrien's tent. As if summoned by their conversation, the blond-haired Chief emerged.

"Who *doesn't* have a bad feeling about him?"

"It's not that," he said fiercely. "It's you...and him."

"Me? And *him?*" She felt sting of surprise. "You have nothing to worry about, Behran. I hate him. You know that."

"Yes, but I'm not so sure..." He nodded. "Mentàll."

Methusal spun. The Dehrien Chief had obviously come over to them for a reason, for he held a small leather pouch in his hand.

"Behran. Methusal." The low voice prickled down her nerves.

Methusal gave a nod for the sake of politeness, and waited for him to speak.

"I have a present for you, Methusal."

"A present?" Her voice lilted with surprise. She glanced quickly at Behran. "I don't want a present." Then she added, "Thank you all the same," for the sake of being polite.

Mentàll tipped the bag over, and shimmering strands of precious metal and gems pooled into his hand. "Take my marriage necklace, Methusal. You will need it for the trip."

Words escaped her as she stared at the necklace. It was intricately woven of silver and gold threads, and linked by pale blue gems which were flanked by tiny, dark green gem leaves. The blue stones exactly matched its owner's eyes. A genuine marriage necklace. And worth a fortune, no doubt.

With trepidation, she raised her hand to receive it. The chain fell in a stream from Mentàll's fingers into her palm.

The weight felt warm and silky in her hand. "It's beautiful," she couldn't help but say softly. "Is it a family heirloom?"

Of course it couldn't be an heirloom. He had no father, so he had no heirloom. His line would begin with him.

"No. I had it especially made for you—for our mission."

Methusal's gaze shot to his. She could not decipher his inscrutable look, but she felt like he had just put a claim on her.

Behran stiffened. "You are rude to both of us, Mentàll."

"I apologize." Now Mentàll sounded coolly contrite. "So, when is your happy day?"

Methusal and Behran glanced at each other. It was the one decision they couldn't quite make.

"You are a patient man, Behran. I would not be so passive." Mentàll looked at Methusal. "If I desired a woman enough to marry her, I would do everything in my power to make her mine."

Her stomach muscles clenched for a reason she could not fathom. "Hopefully she'd have the sense to run in the opposite direction."

The Dehrien Chief's gaze held hers. "Would she? Or would she relish the danger, and choose to face her destiny? Perhaps she would find the answers to the questions she seeks."

"She would find no answers with you, Mentàll."

He smiled faintly. "So sure of yourself."

"Back off." She had never heard Behran use that low, threatening tone before.

"Do you fear me—or Methusal?" A veiled challenge lurked in edged the Dehrien Chief's words.

What were they talking about, Methusal wondered, confused by the sudden fury in Behran's eyes.

"She wouldn't be with you if I could help it," Behran gritted.

"Then perhaps you should marry her before we sail, to ensure her devotion to you. We have a preacher. I could set it up." The Dehrien was all helpful solicitation, but his eyes looked hard.

"We will get married after the mission," Methusal hugged an arm tightly around Behran's waist. She looked up at her fiancé. "Isn't that right, Behran?"

The anger in his eyes softened when he looked at her. "After the mission?"

"Yes."

He smiled. "After the mission."

"Congratulations," the Dehrien Chief interjected. His voice sounded harsher than normal. Methusal got the impression the conversation hadn't gone in the direction he had expected, and she smiled.

Of course the Dehrien had to have the last word. "I ask that you invite me to the happy event. I could not miss Methusal's wedding."

"If this peace mission is a success, you are welcome to come," Behran said. His smile looked relaxed now, and they continued on their walk, leaving the Dehrien Chief alone.

∆ ∆ ∆ ∆ ∆

Laughter echoed up and down the long table in the Dehrien Chief's dining tent. It felt good to be with old friends like Hendra and Doc, Methusal reflected. Even Sozla, their new friend, interjected bright bits of wry observations that made everyone laugh. Mentàll laughed a few times, too. In Methusal's opinion, his chuckles appeared too hearty to be real. No doubt this was his charming, public façade. And likely the one he adopted whenever he wanted to beguile the Chiefs of Koblan to consider his nefarious schemes.

Methusal turned and flipped her legs over the bench. She whispered to Deccia and Behran, "I'll be back in a minute."

They'd both think she needed a trip to the relief hut. So would Mentàll. Methusal smiled to herself and exited from the dining tent.

No one was outside. Likely it was dinner time for all of the Dehriens. Methusal headed for the relief hut first, in case someone was watching her. After she emerged again, she took a circuitous route back to the dining hall. She sharpened her senses into kaavl, and listened.

Her sensitive ears picked up on people talking in their huts. Even further away, guards' footsteps patrolled Dehre's eastern outskirts, vigilantly keeping the nocturnal wild beasts out. The other three sides of Dehre were walled with timber hauled from the Tarst Mountains. The final, eastern side was only partially completed.

No one patrolled inside Mentàll's small compound, however. Was he so trusting? Or utterly confident in his ability to detect and thwart any attacks against him? Or maybe the Dehriens held him in such fearful reverence that they didn't dare cross him.

What did it matter?

Here it was. His living tent. She sharpened her hearing, but heard no sounds within. She slipped inside.

She'd been in his tent once, three years ago. It was still neat and orderly. To the left were a table and chairs, to the right, a long couch with a table, and beyond that, a desk. A curtain partitioned off a room directly across from her. Probably his sleeping compartment. She wouldn't go in there unless she had to.

Knowing the Dehrien, he'd put the book in a prominent location. That way he could see it every day and gloat over possessing it.

Methusal circled the room, checking the far table and in the desk drawers.

Nowhere to be found. Hands on her hips, she contemplated searching the main area again. But time was speeding by. She didn't want anyone to get suspicious. And she'd already checked this room thoroughly.

She took a deep breath. Brushing aside the heavy, soft leather curtain, she entered Mentàll's bed chamber. A small taper burned on a stand near the door, pushing the darkness back into soft, shadowed corners. Rich browns gave the chamber a warm feeling. The lingering sense of the Dehrien Chief's presence momentarily overpowered her. As did the scent of clean leather and that raw, indefinable male essence that was purely Mentàll.

She took an unsteady breath and surveyed the room. It was neat, just like the others were. A high bed pallet took up most of the space to her left, and was covered in a patchwork of dyed, multi-hued brown pieces sewn into a decorative quilt. The supple leather looked soft and inviting.

Feeling a bit uncomfortable, Methusal turned her attention to a high table flanking the right wall. Candle holders stood at each end, and parchments, a writing stick, and ink lay on top. A drawer was built into the table. Swiftly, she pulled it open.

The *Second Book of Kaavl* lay nestled in the dark interior. Reverently, she touched the book's cracked leather cover and then carefully gathered it up in her arms and slipped outside.

In her cabin, she hid the book under her coverlet, and felt a vague sense of guilt as she did so—as if she had just done something wrong. But hadn't he stolen the book from her? And he'd stolen her tablet necklace too, three years ago, and had never given it back. It was the least he deserved. Besides, she'd return the book later.

No one remarked upon her absence when she returned to the dining table. Mentàll appeared to be deep in conversation with Doc and Tabor, his first-in-command; a man with mud colored eyes and hair.

Good. She finished her meal.

Afterward, she told the others she was tired and wanted to rest for the trek tomorrow. Behran walked her to her cabin, and after a warm kiss, left her for the night.

Eagerly, Methusal retrieved the precious book and sat cross-legged on her cot. Then she drank in every word of the pilfered *Second Book of Kaavl* as fast as she could.

A knock at the door startled her.

It couldn't be Sozla, because she'd come right in. Maybe Behran had come back?

Or maybe...

Unease surged. Surely Mentàll was still in the dining tent with the others. Even if he'd gone to his tent for a moment, he couldn't have noticed anything amiss so quickly.

Someone knocked again, harder this time. Whoever it was meant business. It definitely wasn't Behran. He'd never knock like that.

Anxiety tightened in her chest. Mentàll was excruciatingly observant. During the war, she'd once rifled through his pack and afterward had knotted it up exactly the way he'd left it. But he'd known someone had touched it before untying the first knot.

Methusal bit her lip. She wanted to ignore the intruder, because she was afraid of who it might be. Right now she needed every minute to peruse the important book.

Already little nuggets of information swirled in her brain. Such as letting down her guard to let sensory input rush into her ears, eyes, and brain. That instruction seemed counter-intuitive, especially since kaavl had always been used for war during Mahre's time. Was she really supposed to relax her defenses in order to outmaneuver her enemy?

She would need to think about that idea for a while. Still, she'd found nothing that directly addressed reaching the Primary level, even though she'd quickly flipped through the entire book.

She returned to page nine and quickly read each line, drinking in the precious information as fast as she could.

A flicker of movement teased her peripheral vision, but hearing nothing, she dismissed it and concentrated harder. Her lips moved, softly repeating the confusing words she'd just read, "Victory can be achieved; not by force, but through discernment. Be aware..."

"Enjoying your studies, Methusal?" Mentàll said softly, and jerked the book from her fingers. He flipped it shut.

Fright exploded, followed by outrage. She leaped to her feet. "Get out!"

"Social courtesies do not appear to matter to you." A hard edge bit through the words.

"How did you know I had the book?"

"You do not want to cross me, Methusal. Didn't you learn that during the Quasr War?" His icy eyes watched her. "If you wanted to visit my bed chamber, you need only ask."

Methusal gasped, and warmth flushed her skin. "Give me the book!"

"If you ask nicely, I will consider lending it to you."

Her gaze dropped to the book he held in his large hand. There had to be a catch. And yet she wanted it. Desperately. She couldn't help it.

Although it galled her to ask, she said, "Please, may I read it?"

A small smile appeared. It looked calculating. "You may. Come to my tent, and you can read it there." Those light eyes watched her. A challenge...and a suggestion?

Her face burned. "I will not *go to your tent!*"

"Have I propositioned you?"

"Tell me what you mean, or get out."

"Do not play games with me, Methusal."

"*You* are the one..."

"You know that Dehre has strict laws about respecting personal property. You entered my bed chamber. What am I to think about that?"

Heat seared her cheeks. "You stole the book from me. It only seems only fair that I could borrow it for a few hours."

"I would have leant it to you, if you had asked."

"No, you wouldn't."

He stepped closer. "Ask me anything, and I will give it to you, Methusal."

She stared up at him. Her heart beat very fast. If she'd felt threatened before, she felt doubly so now.

"I love Behran," she told him. "Remember your promise to my father."

He smiled, but it didn't reach his eyes. "I am not asking you to love me, Methusal. I am making it clear I will do whatever it takes to make our marriage partnership work. You can trust me now. Can I trust you?"

Methusal didn't know which outlandish statement to address first. "First of all, we will not be *married*. Second of all, I will never trust you."

"Sneaking into my tent and stealing the book behind my back is dishonorable." Harshly, he said, "Can I trust you?"

She looked away, ignoring an unwelcome stab of guilt. "You're a fine one to talk about stealing."

"Can I trust you?"

She frowned, but did not reply.

"If you want something from me, ask. If possible, I will give it to you."

"Fine. I'm sorry. But the book belongs to me. I found it."

"I am the one who found the cave. Not you."

"Still, you ripped the book out of my hands, just like you did right now!" Methusal's pulse jumped alarmingly, and suddenly all of her frustrated, pent up emotions, built up since he'd kissed her in Rolban, exploded. "The *only* reason I'll work with you is for Koblan's sake. I *hate* you. I want you out of my life forever!"

"You do not hate me, Methusal."

"I *do*."

He took a step toward her.

She backed up. "Leave me alone." Her low voice trembled.

Mentàll stopped moving and looked at the book in his hand. Then he dropped it onto her cot and turned for the door. Harshly, he said, "Return it to me in the morning."

The door closed with a hard snap.

Methusal stared at the door. She couldn't believe that he'd left the book behind, or that he'd left the room so abruptly, either. But he hadn't liked her fear. She had seen that surprising truth in his eyes.

CHAPTER FIVE

DAY 5

THE NEXT MORNING, Methusal's brain ached when she awoke, and she didn't feel like she could process another drop of information.

She wanted to return the book. Hopefully before he woke up, because she'd prefer not to talk to him again.

Dawn barely peeped over the horizon when she stepped into the chilly spring morning and headed for the Dehrien Chief's large tent.

Reaching the tent, Methusal knocked once, softly, for courtesy, on the wooden knocker beside the tent flap. She was about to shove the book under the door when the flap twitched open. Mentàll stood there, fully dressed. In fact, she got the impression he'd been up for quite some time.

She thrust the book at him. "Thank you for letting me read it."

When he took the book, he pressed something cold, hard, and rectangular into her palm. Methusal drew a quick breath of surprise.

Her tablet necklace. It was an heirloom that had been passed down through the oldest Maahr child for generations. A raised "M" was embossed on the front, and scratches on the back had led Mentàll to find the cave where the *Second Book of Kaavl* was hidden. He had taken the precious necklace from her three years ago, when he'd tried to take over Rolban.

With disbelief, she looked up. "Why?"

"I was wrong to take it from you."

She couldn't speak for a moment. What was his motive? Was he trying to make peace with her?

Her fingers closed around the familiar, heavy object. "Thank you," she said stiffly, and left.

Δ Δ Δ Δ Δ

The peace party departed from Dehre after breakfast. So far the sky was clear, and a light breeze accented the cool morning. Hendra hoped the good weather would last for the two day hike to Aestoff. At this time of year, the plains weather could change in a matter of hours.

Mentàll and Tabor led the way. Riln, the tall, dark-haired Tarst man, followed a little behind them, and he was talking to Goric. Hendra walked in the middle of the pack, talking to the friendly Sozla. Her gaze kept straying to Doc, however, who strode ahead of her. He carried his heavy pack and bow and arrows with ease, and right now he was talking to Timaeus and Deccia.

"What is Eerpor like?" Hendra asked Sozla.

"It is a quiet village. We have much rain, and many crops."

"Must be nice. Dehre is dry. Three years ago, our water almost ran out and our crops died."

"That is terrible," Sozla said. "Perhaps now, since we are friends, that need not happen. We can trade for goods."

"That would be wonderful." After a moment, Hendra said, "Did you travel through Tarst on your way here?"

"Yes. It is not the shortest way, but my father was visiting Tarst. And Mentàll said Doc and Riln would be coming this way, too. So we could travel together. He is a nice man, the good doctor." Sozla gave Hendra an inquisitive look. "You and he are..." she held two fingers close together.

Hendra flushed. "Oh. No! Of course not."

Sozla smiled. "Why not? He spoke of you during the trip."

"Really? Well, he was probably telling you about each of us. We're just friends. I helped him take care of patients during the war. I haven't even seen him in seven months." Of course she did not mention the letters they had exchanged.

"I see. Tell me more about the others, then."

Hendra briefly explained the relationships that had grown between them all over the last three years.

Doc's steps slowed down, so they'd catch up with him. "Hendra. Sozla." He smiled.

"Morning," Hendra murmured. It was the first time she'd spoken with him today.

"Doc," Sozla said. With a small smile for Hendra, she said, "I see Behran is free. I will speak to him about the mission now."

Sozla moved ahead, and Hendra cast a quick glance at Doc. Nerves danced in her stomach. Softly, she said, "Thank you for the letters. They were helpful for the children."

His smile intensified the color of his eyes to a deep, smoky blue. "I'm glad you corresponded with me. I enjoyed reading your letters."

Hendra blushed, and didn't know what to say. So she changed the subject. "I think Mentàll has put together a good team. I'm surprised he asked Riln to come, though, since he mutinied against Mentàll during the war."

"He was a good friend of Kitran's," Doc said. "And you know Kitran hated Mentàll."

"So he mutinied for Kitran. Not because he hates Mentàll?"

Doc glanced at his Tarst compatriot, who was walking by himself a short distance away. After the barest hesitation, he said, "I believe so. He's the best kaavl player we have in Tarst, besides Pan."

So Mentàll needed him. And she knew Riln hated the Zindedis. In the General's compound during the war, she had witnessed the brutal way he'd killed every invader in his path. Almost as if he had enjoyed it.

As if sensing they spoke about him, Riln headed their way. "Doc! I spotted our dinner."

He shouldered close to Hendra, which meant she was sandwiched between the two men. It appeared that he didn't even notice her. His leather sleeve brushed against her arm and she instinctively sidestepped, which meant she bumped into Doc. Alarmed, she jerked away from him and almost tripped over her own feet.

Doc caught her shoulder. "Careful."

She flushed. Unfortunately, when she'd sidestepped into Doc, Riln had moved even closer to her. Hendra felt trapped, overwhelmed by the two men flanking her. Touching her. Panic clawed at her and she slowed down so she could escape from the situation. She moved to Doc's free side.

"Want to give it a shot?" Riln asked, still apparently oblivious to her existence. "Or will you let me?"

Doc pulled the bow and quiver of arrows off his shoulder. "You go ahead. I'm talking to Hendra."

"Great." Riln plucked the weapons from Doc's hand and headed with purposeful aggression across the plains floor. Hendra pitied the poor apte he was stalking. Clearly, he already relished the thought of killing it.

"Are you all right?"

"Yes." Although she still felt flustered, Hendra didn't let it show. "I felt squashed."

"Riln can be overbearing." A few silent moments passed. "This isn't going to be easy, is it?"

She quickly glanced over and found him watching her with sober acceptance. "We can be friends," she said softly.

"I hope we are friends, Hendra."

"Yes. But it's been a long time since we've seen each other."

"You're right." He smiled. "Want to play a game?"

"Okay," she said softly.

"Tell me your three most favorite things in the world."

She grinned. "Anything?"

"Anything at all. As long as you absolutely love them."

"Well, I love days like today. It's so clear and fresh and bright. Anything seems possible."

His smile deepened. "Go on."

"I love the children in the orphanage."

"I knew you would say that."

"And I love..." What could she say that she loved more than those things, or more than walking in the glorious sunshine with him? She swallowed back the sudden lump in her throat. "I love my cousin and my friends." Of whom Doc featured prominently. "Now it's your turn," she said quickly. "What are your three favorite things?"

"Healing patients," he said at once.

"I knew you'd say that," she teased.

"And my family. And walking with you."

With a flush, she looked down.

"Hendra." She felt his fleeting, warm touch on her wrist. "I don't want to make you feel uncomfortable, but I do need to be honest."

"What do you mean?"

"I sent you those letters for a reason. I couldn't stand the thought of losing contact with you. I hoped we would meet again."

She smiled a little. "I'm glad you wrote. Your friendship means a lot to me."

"It does?" His gaze held hers.

Fear quivered in Hendra's stomach, but she said, "Yes, it does."

His smile edged higher. Softly, he said, "Thank you."

She'd given him hope, and she had done so deliberately. She hoped she hadn't made a mistake.

Shyly, she smiled back and changed the subject.

△ △ △ △ △

"Are you all right, Methusal?" Behran asked.

It was evening now. Soon they would set up camp. Methusal was glad, because her pack felt heavier with every step.

"Hmm?" Behran's words pulled her from her thoughts. She'd been trying to formulate strategies for how to deal with Mentàll in the invader land. When she gazed into Behran's deep blue eyes, she felt chagrined.

How could she possibly waste time thinking about the Dehrien when she was walking with Behran right now?

She reached for his hand and smiled. "I'm fine. I'm trying to deal with problems before they happen."

"Mentàll," he said quietly.

"Of course. Who else?"

"You haven't told me everything that happened during the Quasr War. Why not?"

Methusal glanced at him in surprise. The old guilt stung, as neatly as Behran's gaze pinned her.

"It's in the past."

"No, it's not. I see the way he looks at you. Why does he do that?"

The low intensity in Behran's voice made it clear that the matter had been troubling him for quite a while. But she didn't want to discuss it. She pulled her hand from his.

He recaptured it, and laced their fingers together. "Tell me, Methusal. I need to know."

"It's nothing." She looked away. "I don't want to upset you."

"Instead, you've dealt with it all by yourself. *Tell me.*" Behran had never used that tone with her before.

"Fine." She tugged her hand free. He waited, his eyes very dark.

"He likes to get under my skin. You know that. That's all it's ever been about, and that's the truth. You say he looks at me a certain way? Well, it's like a whip playing with an apte. That man hates me."

"I'm not so..."

"Listen, Behran," she interrupted. "I'm not sure how he did it, but he tried to twist and confuse my mind during the war. He wanted to hurt me in the deepest way possible, and somehow, he figured out he could do that by interfering in *our* relationship."

"How?"

Methusal fumbled for the right words. She couldn't make sense of it, even now. "I'm not sure," she admitted. "But he...kissed me. A few times."

Behran's gaze intensified. No shock registered, however.

"I think he did it in the hope that I'd feel guilty. That if I kissed him, I'd feel like I was being unfaithful to you."

"*You* kissed him?"

Methusal gasped. "*I* didn't kiss him, Behran! He kissed *me.*" Although she had certainly allowed him to continue the kiss, there in the rocky hills of base camp. A temporary lapse of sanity. And guilt still plagued her for it. But why? Hadn't he forced the kiss upon her? Why would she feel guilty when his obvious experience had muddled her head for one minute?

"Oh, Behran, it's a mess! That's why I didn't tell you. It didn't mean *anything!*"

"I know."

Relief rushed through her. "Then you're not mad at me?"

"Is that why you didn't tell me?"

"I didn't want you to think... I didn't want *him* between us. I wanted to forget all about it. Do you understand?"

"Yes," he said slowly. His eyes still looked dark. "But I wish you'd trusted me enough to tell me sooner."

"I'm sorry."

Roughly, his palm stroked her forearm. "I don't want you to feel bad, Thusa. I want to be there for you. Always. And I don't want you to go through this trip feeling alone."

"But I will be alone with him most of the time." She reached for his hand. "What am I going to do?"

He pulled her close. "We'll get through this together."

She closed her eyes, and wanted to believe him. She whispered, "Everything will be all right."

His arms tightened around her. "Of course it will."

CHAPTER SIX

"C'MON, DASTN," Aali pleaded up at the Tarst runner. She was getting tall for a girl. Last winter, during the Quasr War, she'd been just shy of his shoulder, but now she reached his chin.

Dastn had broad shoulders and was solid and strong...and brave. During the Quasr War, he'd saved her from Pogul's vicious attack. Aali thought he was cute, too, but would never tell him that. She liked his brown hair and dark brown eyes, and the way he smiled at her, with that little curl at the side of his mouth. As if he found her amusing. That was okay. She didn't mind being amusing, as long as that meant he liked her and would talk to her.

He shook his head. "I'm not going to spy for you, Aali."

"Just ask a few questions when you're in Quasr. It's top secret important. For Koblan's security."

"Says you?"

"Says Thusa." Aali knew it was time to throw in the big guns. Mentioning Methusal, the Chief's daughter, might make Dastn listen to reason. Though she definitely felt piqued that he wouldn't listen to her.

"Methusal, huh? What does she want?"

"She wants to know what Mentàll's been up to, traveling all over Koblan. I mean," she added in a whisper, "what he's *really* been up to."

"What do you mean?"

Was Dastn really so thick-headed? "How am I supposed to know? That's where you come in!"

He looked amused. "So let me get this straight. You want me to ask questions all over Quasr. You want me to try to find out Mentàll's secret, evil plan."

"Not *all* over Quasr! Are you dense, Dastn? I never thought so, but now I wonder." She put her hands on her hips and shook her head, putting on her most disappointed face. "Maybe I'd better speak to someone else. Someone a little...sharper."

He laughed out loud. Aali admired his flashing white teeth, and how his short, spiky hair tipped just so to the left, which made him look dangerous and exciting. His tanned face settled into more serious lines, but his mouth still curled up at one corner. "Okay. I'll ask around the Chief's compound. I have a few friends there. If I hear anything, I'll let you know. I'll be back in a few weeks."

"Thank you." She threw a dramatic hand to her forehead. "I thought I was going to have to wash my hands of you."

"Never that, Aali. Never that." With a grin, he left her.

Aali hugged her arms across her chest. Her finally developing chest. She felt self-conscious about that. Sometimes she still felt like a kid, and other times she felt ready to take a step beyond. She didn't want to grow up. Not really. Not yet. Boring, that would be, with all kinds of dull responsibilities.

Her mind returned to her exciting new project. Now that she'd lined up her first recruit, she had four more to go. She had narrowed her spies down to five total, because those were the runners she trusted the most. And definitely this mission had to stay top secret. Methusal said so. If the whole security of Koblan depended on Aalicaa Storst, then so be it. She hurried off to find her next victim.

△ △ △ △ △

Dark clouds billowed on the horizon when Methusal strapped on her pack that morning. The gray morning felt gloomy. Behran was unusually quiet, too. She was still worried about what she'd told him last night. Was he upset? He'd said everything was okay between them, but was it really? She should have told him everything long ago.

Riln, Goric, and Tabor were already underway when Methusal fell into step beside Behran, who was chewing on a meat strip. She offered him a smile. "I have some dried tagma berries. Want some? I know you love sweets."

A small smile lifted the corners of his mouth, and he unexpectedly cupped the back of her head and kissed her. "You're sweet enough for me."

Methusal flushed, surprised, but pleased. Behran was usually not so demonstrative. Especially not in front of other people.

"Good morning, Methusal. Behran." Mentàll's harsh voice interrupted her thoughts. He was striding beside her. Where had he come from?

"Mentàll." Behran's voice sounded hard.

The Dehrien flicked Behran an expressionless glance. "Enjoy your sunshine. It will end soon." He increased his pace to take the lead.

Behran's brows drew together.

"Ignore him. He's a whip."

Behran took her hand. "I trust *you*, Thusa," he said in a low voice. "That's all that matters."

Methusal's fingers closed around his, and she held them tightly as they walked.

The clouds rolled closer. At midmorning, sheets of rain darkened the landscape ahead. Methusal pulled her cloak over her pack and hair, and so did the others. Cold, damp wind brushed her cheeks. Unfortunately, they would have to go straight through the storm.

An odd ray of sunshine lit the plain just before the advancing wall of water. It seemed to shine down from heaven like a golden pillar of light. Iridescent rain drops shimmered behind it.

The bright spot grew wider as they drew closer. The streaming wall of rain seemed to have stopped its eastward progression in that location.

"Look at that," Deccia whispered.

But Methusal had spotted something else. "*Who* is that?" A man knelt in the middle of the circle of sunshine, his face bent to the ground. Her heart leaped when she saw a ragged tuft of white hair. *Could it be?*

They drew still closer. The rain splashed like a waterfall west of the circle of light. Except for the rush of the rain, all was silent as the little group gathered at the edge of the circle.

Only Mentàll dared to step inside. "Prophet."

The old, dark skinned man with white tufts hair lifted his head. Tattered animal skins covered his body. Serenity and joy radiated from his smile.

"You have come." His voice boomed and resonated. It was deeper than Methusal remembered.

"We have come," the Dehrien agreed. "We are on our way to Aestoff."

The old man's smile broadened. "You think I do not know this?" He raised his hands. "Come into the light. Sit."

Deccia and Sozla stared at each other, clearly excited, and obeyed. Neither had seen the Prophet before. In fact, Methusal realized that only a few people in the group had. She was one, as were Mentàll and Hendra.

After a hesitation, even Mentàll went down on his haunches before the Prophet.

"Good." The Prophet raised a hand toward heaven. "I have a word for you, Mentàll. The One says, 'If you repent, I will restore you, so that you may serve me.'"

Methusal's brow lifted in surprise at the blatant rebuke to the Dehrien.

"Methusal." The Prophet's dark brown eyes found her. "Forgive, because you have been forgiven."

Taken aback, she remained silent. Who was she supposed to forgive?

"You know, Methusal. Deccia, do not take revenge. 'It is mine to avenge; I will repay,' says the Lord."

Deccia looked just as confused as Methusal felt.

"'A new command I give you,'" the Prophet's voice rose, and he climbed to his feet. Hands stretched toward the heavens, he cried, "Love one another!" He flung his head back and gazed heavenward, as if seeing the face of The One. "'I have seen a wicked and ruthless man flourishing like a green tree in its native soil, but he soon passed away and was no more; though I looked for him, he could not be found!'"

Who did he mean? Mentàll? A Zindedi?

The Prophet's eyes closed. Serenity smoothed the lines of his face. "Blessed are the peacemakers, for they will be called children of The One.'"

The Prophet fell silent, but remained still, eyes closed. Was he praying?

Methusal felt awed, and a little uncomfortable. Clearly, The One was speaking through this man. She needed to listen to whatever he said to her—whether she liked it or not.

In the past the Prophet had given her two directives. Three years ago he'd told her to pray for her enemies. She had not—at least, not really. During the Quasr War, he had told her to love her enemies, and to treat them with kindness. She had tried. And she'd even succeeded a little with Mentàll, although not so much with Jascr and Goric. Now he had just told her she must forgive. Who? Mentàll? The Zindedis? And how?

The Prophet opened his eyes. "Forgiveness does not mean that you are saying the other person's actions were right. And it does not mean that you should trust them again. But you must let go of the bitterness. It only hurts you. And you must give up your desire for vengeance. It belongs to The One."

Had he just read her mind?

The Prophet crossed his arms. "Blessings on your peace mission."

After a moment, everyone awkwardly climbed to their feet. No one seemed to know what to do next. Goric and Riln abruptly bolted for the curtain of rain and disappeared into the downpour. Tabor followed.

Methusal approached the Prophet.

His old brown eyes sparkled. "I see you want answers, Methusal. I will give you more words, but first, remember what I told you in the past: Pray for those who mistreat you, and love your enemies. You have begun to walk on the higher path. Now, it is time to grow still more. Pursue peace. Love one another. Again, this means your enemies."

Pray. Love. Forgive. Be a peacemaker. Odd commands for a troop about to infiltrate the enemy land.

"Sounds very familiar." She had been hoping for a new message. Frankly, once again his esoteric commands seemed impossible.

A kind smile softened the Prophet's face. "Loving The One and loving others is what it is about, Methusal. It is what life is always about."

"How? Tell me *how*." She needed some practical advice here. Last time, just tending Mentàll's wounds kindly had stretched her beyond the limits. In fact, it had added to her confusion about the Dehrien. What did the Prophet expect from her now?

The Prophet's deep voice rumbled like thunder, "You must forge peace with each other before you can achieve peace in the invader land."

"How?" she insisted again.

"Nothing is impossible with The One. Ask for help."

Frustration grew within her. She wanted to do the right thing, but it seemed completely impossible.

Quietly, Deccia said, "I think what Methusal means is *why?* If we understand why, maybe the how will become easier."

"Yes." The Prophet's eyes gleamed with approval. Gently, he said, "The One wants us to be whole. We can never be whole when we are filled with hatred. The One is about restoring broken relationships. We are separated from The One when we do wrong. We must repent and ask his forgiveness. He wants a whole relationship with each of us, and he wants us to have whole, healthy relationships with each other." He glanced at her, and then at Mentàll. "You must forgive."

The Dehrien Chief watched Methusal. With a frustrated frown, she said, "I can leave his fate in The One's hands. But I don't trust him." Her gaze returned to her longtime enemy. "I will *never* trust him."

The Prophet inclined his head. "Again, I remind you; you possess more than one enemy. I will see you again, Methusal."

"So I will come back alive?"

Shadows dimmed the Prophet's eyes. "Not everyone will return. Seek peace while you may still find it." He looked at Deccia. "You too, Deccia." He turned and suddenly the wall of rain descended on them, battering into Methusal's skull. She gasped in shock. When she came up for air, the Prophet was gone, and the others were only dark shadows, running west through the rain.

"Come, Methusal." The Dehrien Chief stood at her elbow. "The rain is clearing to the south."

Even though a glance confirmed what he said was true, Methusal stifled the overwhelming urge to flee from him.

Behran. Where was Behran? She looked around, baffled. Why would he leave her?

"Follow me, Methusal," the Dehrien urged, and started walking south.

Now she saw Behran a few lengths ahead. He'd turned back, and was looking for her.

She ran through the beating rain to him, and then grabbed his arm and pointed to the south. They followed the Dehrien Chief's large, dripping form. He strode on alone, and didn't look back.

Methusal tried to dismiss that short encounter with her enemy. She had actually wanted to *run from* him. It chagrined her. She couldn't even bear to walk with him for a few moments to escape from the rain. How was she supposed to live at peace with that man in the invader land?

She faced a deeper truth. Every time she was near him, she wanted to push him away. She didn't want him close. And she knew why. When she'd opened up a little during the war and had treated him with kindness, like the Prophet had directed, that's when he'd started to confuse her. That's when he'd shown a little of his vulnerable side and burrowed under her skin, and even, a little, into her heart.

She could not let that happen again. She would not open up her heart to him, because she could not trust him. He was a dangerous, power hungry man. She knew this. If she forgot it for one moment, he could unsheathe his sharpest weapon and destroy her. He hated her, after all. Wasn't destroying her one of his primary goals?

Why was the Prophet asking the impossible of her?

She knew now that this mission would be far more dangerous to her peace of mind than both the Rolban invasion and the Quasr War put together. If only she could stay in this downpour, slogging by Behran's side forever. Better that, than the future she must face in Zindedi.

CHAPTER SEVEN

METHUSAL AND THE OTHERS HIKED over the low, forested mountains, paralleling the swollen, southern side of the rushing Tarst River. At twilight, they descended into Aestoff's grassy valley. Lights twinkled near the sea, across the river, but any hopes that they'd have comfortable cots to sleep on tonight died a swift death. There were no bridges across the swiftly moving Tarst River. Aestoff was on the north side. She wondered how they would cross it in the morning.

They set up camp on saturated grass mixed with red clay.

It made for a cold, miserable night.

Methusal awoke to a pink dawn and a blue and white streaked sky. Lengths away, the Tarst River still rushed toward the sea. She joined Deccia and Sozla at the edge of the brown, churning river.

"What will we do?" Deccia wondered. "We couldn't cross in the mountains, but it looks even worse here."

"Perhaps there are boats," Sozla said. "The fishermen, they are experienced sailors."

Methusal glanced toward the sea. In the distance, waves thundered on the shore. "You mean we could sail around the mouth of the river and land in Aestoff?"

"Exactly." Sozla smiled.

A great shout went up, and Methusal whirled.

A score of burly men, brandishing guns, advanced upon camp. Fear shot through her when Mentàll strode out to meet them. What was he *doing*? Anxiety ratcheted higher when Behran, Timaeus, Tabor, and Riln joined him. A meager line of defense against the dangerous, armed men.

Mentàll lifted a hand in a gesture of peace. After a long moment, a stocky, dark-haired man stepped forward and offered his hand to the Dehrien Chief. A clear gesture of friendship.

Relief made her relax. She sharpened her hearing to listen, and moved closer.

"I am the Chief of Dehre," Mentàll said. "Chief Aarabst is expecting us. We require safe passage to Aestoff."

"You are Mentàll Solboshn." The swarthy man's moustache lifted in a smile. "I have heard much about you. I am Captain Swartzi." He waved a hand over his shoulder. A clear order for the rest of his men to stand down. "You have picked a rough day to cross the river."

"I understand that your men are resourceful."

White teeth flashed in his dark face. "It is why we have been honored with the task of defending Aestoff's coast."

After the Zindedi invasion, coastal patrols had been formed to protect and warn Koblanis about any imminent attacks. All of Koblan was protected by these sparse groups of men—all except for the rocky Iignon coast, to the northeast. No one could patrol that dangerous coastline. Most of it consisted of sheer cliffs.

"I understand that you coordinate all of the patrols on Koblan's west coast."

The man nodded, and gave a pleased smile. "You hear correctly. And I do have resources to transport your team to Aestoff. Chief Aarabst told me to expect you. When you have struck camp, follow me."

"We have hot tea," Deccia said. "Would your men like a cup while we pack?"

Captain Swartzi grinned. "Of course. We always have time for a hot drink."

Methusal, Hendra, and Sozla helped serve Captain Swartzi's men, and then swiftly packed up. Methusal's coverlet was covered in sticky red clay and wet grass, so she carefully folded it in on itself and hoped for an opportunity to wash it in Aestoff. Her moccasins were disgusting and dirty, too, as were her clothes. She decided to wait until Aestoff to change.

After breaking up camp, Captain Swartzi and his men led the team to the shoreline, where an almost chest high surf thundered on the beach. Two long boats were pulled up on the beach, just beyond the frothing, darting tongues of the waves.

"I hope you can swim," Captain Swartzi said with a grin.

Deccia had never learned how to swim. She gripped Timaeus' elbow so tightly that her knuckles showed white.

The Captain and his men muscled the smallest boat into the water. "Women first," he shouted. "One of your men can go in this boat, too."

One of the larger Aestoff men lifted tiny Sozla up on his shoulder and battled through the surf to the waiting, bobbing boat beyond. Methusal envied Sozla, because besides wet legs, she still looked mostly dry when she climbed into the boat. The man returned, but Methusal knew she was too big to carry. She'd have to get to the boat on her own power, but she didn't relish the idea of wading through that surf. She hadn't touched the water yet, but she was pretty sure it was ice cold.

Fear whitened Deccia's face, and her hold on Timaeus' arm looked like a death grip. Methusal decided to go next, just to prove it was safe, and to bolster her sister's confidence.

Gulping in a deep breath, she walked forward. The seawater felt like melted ice as it swirled inside her moccasins and rose to her ankles. Everything in her pack was going to get wet. Maybe she should hold it overhead. But what if the surf knocked her down? What if she lost the pack in the pounding waves?

Behind her, Mentàll muttered, "Behran?"

"I'll go with you." Behran moved beside her.

She sent him a look of gratitude. "I'll be fine. Your boat isn't out yet. No sense in you going through that horrible surf more than once. You'll freeze to death."

Nearby, the Dehrien Chief watched Behran like a wild beast with an apte, but he remained silent. Behran didn't appear to notice. "I don't know, Thusa. Are you sure?"

"You can rescue me if something happens." She smiled, and injected a note of confidence into her voice. "I'll be fine."

The water sucked at her feet and swirled out to sea. She stepped forward. But instead of touching wet sand, her feet walked on empty air, and her stomach dropped in a dizzying spin as she flew skyward and landed on a broad, bleach clad shoulder. Hard hands bit into her hips.

"Hold on, Methusal." One hand released her, and the other moved to her thigh to steady her.

With a gasp, she instinctively grabbed Mentàll's wide wrist and his head for balance. The white-blond hair, which she'd always assumed to be as hard and prickly as the man, felt surprisingly soft. One shock among too many to comprehend.

"What are you doing?" she gasped. "I didn't ask... Put me down!"

But he was already walking toward the surf. Frosty white water churned around his knees.

Methusal cast a helpless glance backward at Behran. His eyes looked dark and unhappy.

The surf hit Mentàll's chest. His whole body shuddered from the impact, and fear quivered through her. Her grip tightened.

"I cannot see." Hard fingers pried her arm from his head, and she gripped his hand as another, higher wave swept toward them. His wide palm felt comfortingly strong. The wave broke at his shoulders and swirled cold water through her breeches. She gasped from the shock of it, but still the Dehrien moved forward.

Now they were beyond the breaking waves. Another step, and they reached the boat, which the Aestoff men held in place with long poles. It was an easy matter to tumble into the boat. She was half dry, thanks to Mentàll, and her pack was completely dry.

She looked at her enemy, who now stood below her eye level. He looked surprisingly vulnerable, with only his shoulders and head above the water; as if a strong ocean wave could sweep him under forever. He was mortal, like any other man. Surprisingly, the thought scared her a little.

He'd risked something to carry her out here.

The Dehrien Chief watched her, as if waiting for some response. Not receiving it, he turned for shore.

"Mentàll. Thank you." She was grateful. Very much so.

He glanced back. "You are welcome, Methusal." That penetrating, ice blue gaze held hers. Unfortunately, instinctual hairs prickled up on her arms. Why did she suddenly have the feeling that he was trying to make a point to her, or put some sort of a claim on her?

Her gratitude faded rather abruptly. Had he carried her out to prove his superiority over Behran? Behran wasn't tall enough to make it through the waves with her on his shoulder. If he could have done it, he would have, she knew.

Just as Timaeus would have helped Deccia, too. Mentàll carried Deccia and Hendra to the boat, too. To his credit, those were kind acts, but as far as why he'd carried her... With a faint frown, she averted her eyes when he climbed into the boat after he'd helped Deccia aboard. He took the place across from Methusal. She watched Behran and the other men climb into the other boat.

"What have I done to displease you now, Methusal?"

She sent him a narrowed glance, and didn't answer.

"Do you think you understand me, Methusal?"

"I know I do."

"You know nothing. But you will." He smiled faintly. "I promise by the end of our mission you will know me quite well."

Her face warmed, and unfortunately, so did her temper. "You will keep your word to my father."

"I always keep my word. I finish what I have begun. Remember the promise I made to you."

He had said those exact words in Rolban, at the end of the war. He'd also said he made no promises he would not keep.

"If you're plotting evil, I'll stop you. Count on it."

He gave a harsh, rusty laugh. "I am not the devil, Methusal. You will learn to trust me."

"I won't. *Ever.*" Her rising voice must have captured Hendra and Deccia's attention, because both looked over with questions in their eyes.

She lowered her voice. "Leave me alone, Mentàll. I want nothing to do with you. In fact, until we reach the invader land, leave both Behran and me alone. Your games annoy me."

"You did not want me to rescue you from the cold surf?"

"If I had a choice between being indebted to you, or freezing to death, which do you think I would choose?"

Softly, he said, "You would choose to be rescued. Your thank you was heartfelt. I will not forget your words."

It was amazing how quickly he could provoke her. "I didn't realize then..."

"Realize what?" How could he sound so reasonable? Was she misinterpreting his actions, after all? But she *knew* him. She suspected very strongly that he'd played the hero—at least in part—in order to create problems between Behran and herself.

"Never mind," she told him. She looked at the swirling sea. To the east, the Tarst River churned into the ocean. Beyond it, and to the north, lay a hook of green land. Aestoff.

"If you want our mission to succeed, Methusal, you must learn to trust me."

"When aptes fly." From then on, she ignored him. She glanced back at Behran's boat and waved. Her heart fluttered with happiness when he waved back. Behran loved her, and she loved him. That Dehrien's schemes would never change that. Never.

△ △ △ △ △

Captain Swartzi's men rowed for one of the two long docks nestled within the arm of the bay protecting Aestoff. Small fishing boats were tied to one, and the other was flanked by two large, dark-hulled wooden ships with three masts each. Zindedi ships.

Shivering from her wet clothes, she scanned the shoreline, trying to get a feel for this strange new place. She hoped, at the very least, for a warm bath sometime soon.

Trees and pink, clay-colored buildings lined the streets behind the dock, and also edged the entire bay. Most of the town appeared to lie on the other side of the bay. It looked like a large community. Methusal guessed a thousand people lived there. About twice the size of Rolban.

Her legs felt like ice, and her teeth chattered, even though the rising sun warmed her back. The Dehrien Chief was soaking wet. He must be freezing. Behran must be, too.

The two boats bumped up against the fishing dock at the same time, and Methusal was the first one out. Goric was the first from the other boat, and they both moved to the side of the dock to allow room for the others to disembark.

Goric's dirty blond hair was plastered to his head. Since he was about the same height as Methusal, he must have had to swim to his boat. Water dripped from his pack, but he didn't seem to notice. He stared west, his face blank, at the main part of Aestoff.

"You're from Aestoff, right?"

Murky gray eyes looked at her. "Yes." Wet hair spiked down his forehead, accentuating his thin face.

"When were you here last?"

"Six years ago." His gaze swung back to the town.

Goric was hard to read. During the war, she'd thought he was a whip. And then he had helped to save her life.

She looked back at Aestoff. The morning sun toasted the buildings a warm, dull red. Lush trees and a road followed the curve of the bay. High on a hill outside of town, white walls glistened. The Chief's compound?

She sensed a brooding quality in Goric's stare. Unable to help her curiosity, she said, "Do your mother and father live here?"

He frowned. "I only have a father and an older brother." His eyes flashed, looking dark and hard, and he muttered under his breath, "He's my father's prize."

Not a close family, she guessed. "Why did you move to Rolban?"

"Why do you care?" he snapped back.

Stung, she tugged her pack higher up on her shoulder. "We're on the same team. I thought we could try to get along this time."

His gray eyes looked murkier than ever before. "We are not on the same team."

Oddly enough, his words hurt. "Right. You'll be in the country. But we're still on the same team."

"Sorry."

Surprised, she glanced back.

"My family..." He paused, as if finding it difficult to choose the right words. "We're not close, like yours is."

"Is that why you came to Rolban? To escape?"

"My father wanted me to prove myself. So he sent me out into the world." Goric's lips pressed into a thin, grim line.

"Are you going to visit him, now that we're here?"

His gaze shifted, and he shrugged. "My father sets the rules. If he wants to see me, he'll ask for me."

Goric had never fit into Rolban, and Methusal suddenly wondered if he'd ever fit into Aestoff, either. It certainly didn't sound like it. How hard that must be. No wonder he seemed so angry all the time. What kind of a family would treat their son like that?

"Thusa." Behran appeared beside her. His face looked white from the cold, and his saturated leather clothes looked almost black.

"Behran!" She clasped his cold hand. "You're shaking."

"Come!" Captain Swartzi called. "The Chief awaits."

Methusal hoped warm baths awaited them, too. Behran and all of the men would get sick if they stayed in their wet clothes for much longer.

△ △ △ △ △

Thankfully, warm baths did await them in Chief Aarabst's comfortable complex. Servants took their dirty clothes and coverlets and washed them. Later, the team joined Chief Aarabst for a meal of freshly baked bread, fruit, and smoked meat.

While eating the delicious food, Methusal finally relaxed. What a wonderful place this was. After the hard hike, the peace of Chief Aarabst's compound seemed unbelievable. Almost like paradise.

Afterward, while the Chiefs of Dehre and Aestoff sat in comfortable chairs and talked, Methusal, Behran, Deccia, and Timaeus explored the compound. Outdoors, the warm breeze smelled of salt and they wandered around the stone-flagged courtyard, enjoying the lush foliage, enormous yellow and orange flowers, and tall trees. From one tree hung a round, red fruit Methusal had never seen before. She wondered if it was ripe. It looked juicy.

The paths in the courtyard twisted and turned, and were bordered by flowers and trimmed bushes, and shaded by a variety of trees. Benches were nestled into tiny alcoves, and after a while Deccia and Timaeus stopped to sit on one. Methusal and Behran wandered until they found a bench placed beside a clear green pool of water. Little yellow and blue fish darted in it.

"It's so relaxing here." She sighed when Behran put his arm around her shoulders.

"Totally different from that cold surf."

She rested her head on his shoulder. "That was awful. And scary."

"I'm glad Mentàll carried you." Although his words were quiet, Methusal sensed the tension behind them. Behran wished he could have carried her.

She did not want to think about Mentàll. "When do you think we'll sail for Zindedi?"

"Day after tomorrow."

And then it would be a ten day trip to Zindedi. At least for now they could enjoy a few days of peace in Chief Aarabst's home. Even better, the compound was big enough that she and Behran could find plenty of places to spend time alone. And hopefully it was large enough that she could avoid the Dehrien entirely.

An hour or more peacefully drifted by, and then the low, mournful sound of a slug monster shell sounded. Investigation proved that another feast lay spread out on the dining room tables, including pieces of the red fruit Methusal had seen earlier. It was juicy and delicious. At the end of the meal Mentàll stood and claimed everyone's attention.

"We will need new clothes for our stay in Zindedi. Our leather ones will immediately mark us as outsiders. Chief Aarabst's seamstresses have taken the Zindedi's clothing from their ships. This afternoon they will modify them to fit us."

As if waiting for this introduction, a small army of women entered through a large doorway on the east side of the dining room. Their leather dresses were made of multicolored patches, and very beautiful.

"These clothes, we will have enough for our stay in Zindedi?" Sozla asked.

"We will buy more. The invaders left all their money on the ships." A hint of ghoulish humor tinged Mentàll's words.

"Enough to pay for room and board, too?" Timaeus asked. As a runner, he knew—more than anyone—the importance of finding a safe, comfortable place to lay his head at night.

"Yes. If you are finished with your meal, go with the women."

The men and women split up, and soon Methusal found herself trying on black breeches made of a soft, supple material. The fabric appeared to be finely woven of strong, slender fibers. It wasn't as warm as leather, but definitely more loose fitting and comfortable.

She noticed an open book on a nearby bench. Drawings of men and women were depicted. Their clothing looked foreign, much like the pants she wore now. The women wore dresses.

Methusal looked at her black pants, which a seamstress even now tucked up with pins, slimming down the lines to fit her. "Do the women in Zindedi wear breeches?" she asked.

By way of an answer, the seamstress flipped the page. More women were drawn there. Some wore mid-calf length pants, and some knee length skirts. The shirts the women wore had artistic-looking large collars, whereas the men's were more utilitarian. Men wore the top buttons of their shirts undone, but the women's were buttoned to their necks.

A pin poked into Methusal's calf, and she bit back a small sound of discomfort. After the breeches were pinned up, she tried on the white shirt. Clearly the garment had already been altered with scraps of cloth, because the soldier's utilitarian collar had been replaced by an ornate, drooping, scalloped one. It fit perfectly.

"Good," the seamstress mumbled with satisfaction, pins in her mouth. She whisked the shirt off Methusal and indicated she should go to another woman, who was fitting black jackets.

The afternoon sped by, and when Methusal and the others left the sewing room, they were told the new clothes would be finished tomorrow.

"I love that cloth, don't you?" Deccia's voice was full of wonder. "I've never felt anything so soft and smooth in my life."

"In Eerpor, we have a few fine garments made of such cloth," Sozla said. "But in Zindedi, it must be common." With a faint frown, she fell silent. Methusal remembered that Sozla was good at engineering, just like Behran. Maybe she was trying to figure out how the Zindedis made such rich cloth in mass quantities.

One thing had already become clear while examining the book and the cloth—not to mention remembering the deadly Zindedi guns. The invaders were far more advanced than the Koblanis. How, then, could Koblan ever hope to win against such a well-developed country? Koblan possessed only kaavl, knives, and bows and arrows as defensive weapons. And a few invader guns. Who knew what other wonders the Zindedis could manufacture? Or what additional weapons they might be able to deploy against Koblan.

The peace plan had to work, Methusal realized. It just had to.

Chapter Eight

DAY 8

THE NEXT DAY PASSED QUICKLY. Methusal tried to enjoy every minute of it, and spent the day walking through the town with Deccia, Hendra, and Sozla, trading for small items she'd need on the trip. After dinner, under a star-speckled black sky, she meandered around the courtyard with Behran. The lingering, unsettled feeling from the trip had finally dissipated into nothing, and she felt closer to him than she had since Mentàll had arrived in Rolban.

To her delight, she had seen little of the Dehrien Chief that day, because he had spent most of his time down at the docks, making sure the ship was well-supplied and ready for the voyage. She'd seen little of Goric, either, and she wondered if he'd gone to visit his father.

The idyllic day finally ended. Methusal suspected it would be the last day of peace she'd experience for weeks—maybe months.

She felt reluctant to go to bed, and when she did, anxiety tightened like a band around her chest when she thought about the trip ahead. She awoke repeatedly throughout the night.

At last she gave up trying to sleep, and lay awake on her soft cot, staring out the window at the black sky.

Her mother had warned her of danger. The Prophet had warned that not everyone would return to Koblan alive. And Methusal herself had the awful feeling that this trip would change her life forever.

She felt restless and on edge, and couldn't lie still for another minute. In the pre-dawn darkness, she quietly arose and dressed. Maybe spending a few quiet moments in the courtyard would help.

Methusal slipped into the hall and softly drew the door shut. Her moccasins whispered over the stone floor. Although torches burned in the hall, everything was silent. She unconsciously slipped into kaavl, because it seemed as natural as breathing in this quiet, shadowed place.

To her surprise, voices immediately seeped into her ears. They came from Chief Aarabst's office, down the hall and to the left.

A familiar, harsh tone slid like a shiver down her spine. "We are agreed, then."

Mentàll! Methusal bypassed the door to the courtyard and slipped toward the Chief's office.

"You have my word," Aarabst said. "Aestoff will abide by the agreement."

Light filtered under the door. She placed her center of kaavl vision on that slim crack and mentally carried from that position. It was as if she was actually peering under the door and into the brightly lit room.

Mentàll and Chief Aarabst sat across from each other at a round conference table. Mentàll's pack lay at his feet, and right now he stuffed a sheaf of papers inside. Obviously, those papers must have something to do with the agreement the two men had just been discussing. Papers lay before Chief Aarabst, too. If only she could see them...

Methusal concentrated hard and focused on the candelabra suspended over the table. If she could carry from there, she would see the papers clearly... But Mentàll's white-blond head swiveled toward the door, distracting her. She could almost feel him looking right at her, even though the thick wooden door was closed.

She froze.

Harshly, the Dehrien Chief said, "Not a word about it, until the time is right."

"What's wrong?"

"It is nothing." But Mentàll's lips pulled back a little into a frightening, feral snarl. His body uncoiled like a predatory animal.

Methusal turned and ran. Mentàll had sensed—or heard—her presence. Hopefully he would assume a servant had passed by in the hall.

Heart thumping, she slipped back into her room and curled up in a tight ball on her cot and pulled the blanket over her shoulders. Mentàll was up to something. Which meant she'd been right all along—he was still the same secretive, power-hungry man he'd always been. She felt vaguely sick, but wasn't sure why.

She listened intently for sounds in the hall that might indicate he had followed her.

Nothing.

Methusal closed her eyes and faced the newest unpleasant facts. Secret meetings and secret pacts clearly implied that Mentàll wanted to hide his true plans. But from whom? And how would the Alliance benefit both Mentàll and Chief Aarabst?

Furthermore, if Mentàll had made an agreement with Aestoff, it wasn't a far stretch to assume he might have made similar agreements with other communities on Koblan. If she was correct, this was the plan he'd begun to implement before the Quasr War began.

Most alarming, she was certain he had made no similar, additional agreement with Rolban. Her father would have mentioned it, or Petr would have. Neither man fully trusted Mentàll, and they would have discussed the matter with the Council. Methusal would have heard rumors, if that had been the case.

Logical deduction seemed to indicate that Rolban was excluded from the additional Alliance Mentàll was setting in motion.

Methusal's stomach ached, and she realized she been curled up in a tight, tense position for a long time. Outside, dawn pinkened the sky.

She'd need to find out exactly what he was up to. And if she found proof of treacherous plans, she'd bring the facts to her father in Rolban.

Finding proof meant going through Mentàll's pack at her first opportunity.

She closed her eyes. Mentàll was still the same man he'd always been: charismatic, manipulative, and a master at tricking people to get what he wanted. Once and for all, she would expose his underhanded plans, and depose him as a threat to Koblan forever.

It wouldn't be easy. Nothing with Mentàll was ever easy—and rarely black and white, either. Going to the invader land and being paired with her enemy would probably prove to be the most difficult assignment she would ever face in her life.

The One, please help me.

Chapter Nine

"ARE YOU READY?" Doc walked with Hendra down the wooden pier, heading for the Zindedi sailing ship.

Heart fluttering a little, she said, "I hope so."

The ship was about fourteen lengths long, and it was probably four wide. The black ship reared high above them now, and she smelled an acrid, sharp smell—perhaps the oil for the decks. The salty scent of the sea teased her nostrils, too.

Red letters spelled *Sea Mistress* across the stern of the boat. In that moment, the enormity of what they were about to do truly hit her. They were going to sail in a foreign ship and spy in a dangerous land.

Ahead of her, Mentàll climbed a ladder onto the ship.

Knotted ropes and wire rigging connected the outer edges of the ship to the masts. It looked like a jungle, and she was amazed that anyone could make sense of it all. Aestoff sailors had grown up sailing on the ocean, so a ship—any ship—probably seemed as familiar to them as Dehre's plains did to her. But to her, everything looked strange and unfamiliar.

It was her turn to climb the rope ladder. It swayed as the ship moved, restlessly tugging at the creaking lines that bound it to the dock. She tightly clutched the rough rope fibers, afraid of falling into the dark, water swirling below.

"Are you all right?" Doc looked up at her with concern. "You're not moving."

She expelled a short laugh. "Just trying to get my balance." A few steps later, Mentàll's steadying hand helped her onto the deck. To her surprise, her cousin gave her one of his rare smiles. It lifted her spirits, and made her feel safe, too. That one smile imparted comfort to her—he'd wanted to convey to her that he believed everything would go fine on the ship, and on this mission. And so she found herself believing it, too.

On board, she surveyed the ship. For some reason, she'd thought a ship's deck would be empty, except for the masts, of course. Flat walkways did encircle the ship, and there was a wide, cleared path across the middle section. But low, boxy structures rose from the bow and stern decks of the boat. A mast was embedded in each of these, and more ropes lay looped on the deck, mixed with tied down barrels and an upside down skiff boat. Large, square hatches appeared to provide access to the interior of the ship. Hendra couldn't wait to explore.

Doc joined her, and then Methusal climbed up. She ignored Mentàll's helping hand and staggered onto the ship under her own power. Though Hendra's cousin said nothing, a faint smile of a very different kind curved his lips. His gaze briefly followed Methusal as she joined Hendra and Doc. Unease slipped through her when she noticed it, and she wondered what he was thinking.

During the Quasr War, he'd determinedly set out to make the Rolbani girl pay for his humiliation during the two hour Rolbani skirmish. But by the end of the Quasr War his attitude toward her had changed. Hendra wasn't sure what that meant for Methusal now.

Goric was the last person to board the ship. As he did so, a stocky man strode down the deck. He wore a dark blue leather uniform studded with shiny metal buttons. Short white hair bristled from his head, and a thick beard hid his mouth.

"Welcome aboard!" His deep voice seemed to rumble from the depths of his belly.

Mentàll greeted the Captain with a firm handshake.

The Captain surveyed the team with his legs braced apart, as if was still riding the high seas. "I am Captain Hilrae. Call me Hil for short."

He ticked up one finger. "Rules. No one goes on deck in a storm. Period. Except for my crew. If you feel sick, don't vomit on my deck. At sundown the crew passes the brew. You're welcome to join us. If you have questions, speak to my first mate, Skyl." A skinny young man in a dark blue shirt and tan breeches stepped forward, and quickly ducked his head. He immediately stepped back again.

"Good." The Captain turned and bellowed, "Cast the lines! Ready the sails!"

A flurry of men sprang across the deck. Two scurried up the masts and others pulled lines from the docks. Sails unfurled, and the *Sea Mistress* drifted away from the dock. The wind caught in the sails, and the boat heeled a bit to the right as they sailed close into the wind, heading for the southwestern harbor entrance. The wind blew from the southeast, which should help speed them on their way north to Zindedi.

The smooth glide of the boat felt foreign to Hendra. It seemed strange to float across the water—to move without walking. She slipped over to the railing and looked down at the water far below. Swirling eddies followed the ship as it nosed toward open water.

"Do you like it?" Doc spoke beside her.

She drew a startled breath. "It seems...magical."

Doc grinned. He rested his forearms on the polished wooden railing. "Our adventure is about to begin."

Nerves fluttered in her stomach.

He sent her a quick glance. "Are you all right?"

She tried to relax. "I was thinking about the trip. All of a sudden I'm not sure I'm ready."

He frowned. "For the mission?"

"Yes, of course. For the mission." She looked away.

A pause elapsed. Carefully, he said, "Friends are good to have around. Especially when the mission seems scary."

She met his steady gaze. "Friends. Yes. That's exactly what I need."

Quietly, he said, "Well, you have one here."

"Thank you."

He smiled, and looked out at the bay. The strengthening breeze ruffled his short, dark red hair and her gaze fell to his trimmed beard. It still edged his jaw, just like during the war. Hendra remembered the feel of it, when he had kissed her that once. For one insane moment, she wanted to touch it again.

Quickly, she looked away, aghast at her thoughts. What was wrong with her? How could she want to run from him one minute and want to touch him the next? Poor Doc. He didn't deserve a person as broken and mixed up as she was.

She drew a deep breath. "Maybe I should go down to the cabin and drop off my backpack."

"Will you stay for a few more minutes?" She saw in his expression how much he wanted that.

She could. And more than that, she wanted to stand beside him for a few minutes, too. With a smile, she said, "I'm interested to see how choppy the ocean will be. The water in this bay is so smooth."

"It will be rough," he predicted. "We're partly protected by the bay, but the breeze is stiff. It'll be stronger out on the ocean. But our goal is Zindedi. No prize worth winning ever comes easily." He glanced at her, and she saw in his serious gaze that he knew their relationship would not be easy. But he was determined to pursue it anyway.

Hendra hoped she wasn't giving him false hope. When she was near him, her emotions wavered from one extreme to another. *The One, please help me.*

△ △ △ △ △

Methusal stepped through a square hatch near the back of the boat and climbed down a narrow ladder into the dim interior of the ship. The warm air smelled stale, and of old meals. She spotted a stove, counters, and two built-in tables with wide benches. Nearby, Skyl appeared to be giving a running commentary to Mentàll, Deccia, and Timaeus about the different sections of the ship's interior.

So far, Methusal had managed to avoid Mentàll all morning. She had decided to treat him exactly like normal. If he suspected she had overheard his secret conversation with Chief Aarabst, he'd watch her and might even hide the papers he'd tucked into his pack.

"The kitchen is called the galley, and the tables lower down to make extra beds. We'll need them for the crew. We have one aft cabin," Skyl pointed to the back of the ship. "That's the Captain's quarters. Forward," and now he pointed to the bow of the boat, "is the relief chamber and more bunks, and four private cabins. Come with me."

The plank floorboards felt smooth beneath her moccasins. She scanned the interior of the ship as she followed the others. The inside was entirely paneled in dark, polished wood, and small, round windows let in light from outside. As they moved forward, the ceiling lowered in height, but she could still stand up straight. Mentàll had to stoop.

An open space to the left revealed two sets of triple bunks. On the other side of the hall, to Methusal's right, were two closed doors. The blond sailor pointed to the first. "That one is used for storage, and the next one is the relief room."

A few steps further down the narrow passage revealed doors to the left and right. "The men will sleep here, and the women in there. The two small forward cabins are for you, Chief Solboshn, and the married couple."

Deccia and Timaeus looked at each other and smiled. Skyl said, "If you have questions, I'll be on deck."

"Thank you, Skyl."

Sozla entered the girls' room to the right, which had two sets of built-in bunk beds. Curiosity made her follow Deccia, though.

A ladder attached to a narrow wall separated Mentàll and Deccia's cabins, and it led up to a closed, square hatch. A quick peek proved that Deccia and Timaeus' quarters was shaped like a long, narrow triangle. The bed was on the right side, and it tapered, narrowing in width to the end— obviously to accommodate the bow of the boat. The narrow walkway beside the medium-sized bed allowed for enough room to accommodate one skinny chair.

"It's so cute." Deccia touched the blue fabric on the bed. "Smooth invader cloth."

"And look, we have windows." Timaeus pointed to two small, round portholes.

Methusal remembered her quick peek into her own cabin. It had looked bright, too. And the ceiling was higher here. This must be the raised portion that she'd seen out on deck. And the hatch... To get a better look, she backed out of the room, which meant she accidentally stepped through Mentàll's open doorway.

"Do you wish to enter, Methusal?" His harsh voice made her spin. He was untying his pack, which lay on his bed.

He'd clearly said it to annoy her.

"Thank you for the kind invitation." She smiled, "But I couldn't want anything less."

A smile curved his lips. "When you want to practice for our marital duties, you need only to say so. I will be ready and willing."

With an eye roll, Methusal left without answering.

In her own cabin, she unpacked her belongings into a small drawer beneath her bunk. As she did so, the boat moved underfoot.

"We are under way." Sozla leaped to her feet. "I am going on deck. Do you want to come, too?"

"Soon," Methusal agreed. After unpacking, she poked her head in the open door of the men's cabin, where Behran was stuffing his deflated pack in a drawer. A lone bag rested in the middle of the floor. "Whose is that?" She realized the five remaining men on the mission outnumbered the four bunks in the small cabin.

"Riln's. He said he doesn't mind bunking with the crew in the hall."

Fitting. Riln never appeared to be intimidated by anyone or any new situation.

"We have an extra bunk, but..."

Behran grinned. "Don't worry about it. Skyl said there are plenty of beds."

"It's hard to imagine nineteen people living in this small space for ten days." Methusal moved into the main cabin and tried out one of the wide, cushioned benches. "Comfortable." The fabric felt smooth to the touch. More of the wondrous invader fabric.

Behran sat across from her in the quiet cabin. Feet scuffled overhead. He said, "Are you ready for the trip?"

"For the mission, you mean?"

Deep blue eyes held hers. "For the whole adventure."

She felt uncomfortable. "Are you talking about Mentàll again? Because there is *nothing* to worry about. I told you that."

"I love you, Thusa, but I'll admit I'm scared. I feel like we're about to be tested."

Her mother had said the same thing. She captured his hand and held it tight. "I love you, Behran. Everything will be fine. Don't worry."

His eyes looked darker than she'd ever seen them. And steadier. "I trust you. I know you mean that. But I have a feeling..."

"We'll only be in the invader land for two or three weeks. What could change in three weeks? Unless one of us gets hurt. I'll pray against that."

"Me, too." The tension in his frame relaxed a little. "I think I'll go on deck. Want to come?"

"In a minute. I need to stop by the relief chamber first."

By the time Methusal exited from the relief chamber, the deck rolled beneath her feet. They must have reached the open sea. Mentàll's cabin door was shut, so she wasn't sure if he was inside or not. She'd better make sure before she tried to search his belongings.

The boat shuddered and jerked, and she grabbed an overhead handrail to keep from falling. Slats held books into shelves, and raised ledges kept cabin cushions in place. Nothing in the large cabin moved, although the ship rose and dipped like a live beast. A lot of preparation must go into making a boat seaworthy.

The cabin felt warm, and the aroma of stale, greasy food touched her nostrils. She held onto the handrail, trying to get a feel for the rolling movement of the boat. It wasn't easy. She felt vaguely sick.

Doc climbed down the ladder. His discerning gaze narrowed. "You look a little green."

The nausea intensified. "I guess I'm not used to the floor moving." She managed to smile.

"Go up on deck. The sea air should help you feel better."

Glad to know something could help her feel better, Methusal carefully climbed up on deck and found a warm spot on the raised, forward cabin. The sun toasted her skin as she leaned back against a barrel. The boat dipped and swayed beneath her, and the ocean breeze caressed her cheek. The cool breeze did help her feel a little better. The refreshing scent was a vast improvement over the stale air in the cabin. Just thinking about that made her throat convulse.

She gazed out at the sparkling sea. After long while her stomach settled a little. Good.

Sailors shouted from the back—stern, she remembered—of the boat, and she turned to look. High overhead, a sailor clung to the top of the mast. The pole traced invisible, jerky lines against the sky as the ship moved. A dizzying wave of nausea attacked her. Prickles of a peculiar sensation pooled behind her jaw, just below her ear.

She gulped and closed her eyes. Maybe she shouldn't have moved so suddenly. Maybe if she sat very still…

She did feel a bit better, sitting absolutely still. But unfortunately, that did not last for long.

Long minutes later, she slitted her eyes open and peered at the horizon. She swallowed. No denying it. She felt awful. And it was getting worse.

No one else seemed to be affected. Sailors shouted cheerfully to each other and Deccia and Timaeus strolled by, deep in conversation.

Tears filled her eyes. How long would this last?

Doc sat beside her. He pressed a grain disc into her hand. "Sometimes dry bread helps."

"What's wrong with me?"

"You're seasick. It's a common malady."

It felt too awful to be a common malady. "When will it go away?"

In her peripheral vision, his shoulder shrugged. She still didn't dare move her head. "A day or two."

"A day or *two?*" How could *talking* make her feel queasy, too? She swallowed, feeling utterly miserable.

"I'm sorry, Methusal. I wish I could help you more. Stay out on deck as much as possible."

Through her teeth, she said, "I will, believe me."

"Take a bite," he urged. "I'll check back on you later."

She took a small nibble, but it didn't help her feel better at all.

Behran appeared. "Thusa. I've been looking for you."

She allowed only her eyes to follow him.

He frowned and sat beside her. "What's wrong?"

"I'm seasick, apparently. It could last a few days." She slid her hand across the cabin top, seeking his, and Behran immediately took it.

"Can I do something to help?"

"I wish you could." Nausea gripped her again, and she closed her eyes. She also pulled her hand away from Behran's because she suddenly felt close to vomiting. "I think I want to be alone for a while. If that's okay."

"Are you sure?" He sounded worried.

She managed a faint smile. "For now."

After another long hesitation, he pressed a kiss into her hair and left.

Methusal quickly realized she didn't feel any better. Now she was alone and miserable. But at least Behran could enjoy himself, talk to the others, and explore. She wished she could do the same.

Tears burned in her eyes when another surge of nausea hit her. She grimaced, trying to hold it back.

Slowly, the urge abated a little.

If only she could be perfectly still, she would be fine. If only the boat would stop rising and plunging. The waves didn't look large or rough, and the ship appeared to be running with the wind. The sails billowed out, and the ship heeled down to the left, to the port side, so her body weight rested against the barrel. A perfectly sunny, comfortable spot. If only...

The ship surged forward with the waves and rose, and then dropped and rushed forward again. Sea water hissed and slapped against the hull. The bow rose again, higher this time. Nausea gathered in the back of her throat. The ship dove down and raced forward, and all of a sudden Methusal knew she was going to lose it.

"Don't vomit on my deck!" The Captain's words swam through her thick, befuddled mind. She bolted to her feet. Moving on blind instinct, she moved left, for the edge of the ship skimming closest to the sea. She didn't realize the deck was tilted so dramatically to port until she involuntarily ran forward two steps. The boat unexpectedly lurched. She stumbled sideways and quickly ducked to avoid hitting her head on the sail boom. Another surge of the waves, and she found herself running for the edge. For one wild moment, Methusal thought she'd flip over the rail and fall into the sea. She threw out her arms to protect herself and instinctively twisted sideways.

She collided with a solid body. A swift, hard arm across her chest stopped her from smashing into the railing. Nausea roiled so high now that she could barely think, except for the need to get to the edge of the ship. She fought. "Let me go!"

"Methusal." That hated harsh voice.

"Let me *go!*"

Whether he let her go or she fought free, she wasn't sure, but the next moment the railing pressed into her stomach and she helplessly retched into the sea.

She heaved a breath, feeling dizzy. An odd sound buzzed in her ears. The boat jerked down and she gripped the rail, fighting for balance. Hard fingers bit into her shoulders, steadying her. Another violent surge of nausea overtook her, and she vomited again into the frothy white sea.

Methusal threw up twice more, and then a shot of icy spray blasted her face. Another shock to her system. Her stomach twisted, and she stood very still, trembling. Was that it?

She felt shaky and as weak as a baby apte. She didn't let go of the railing because she was afraid of falling on the unsteady deck.

"Are you done?" She became aware that strong hands gripped her shoulders and Mentàll's large body protected her from the wind.

Mutely, she nodded and allowed him to lead her to the cabin top where she could sit again. She rubbed her face with her sleeve to wipe off the dripping water. She shook now from cold. Her hands trembled as she gripped the deck, trying to hold herself steady on the rising and dipping ship. Instinctively, she also struggled to find the protective wall she needed with her enemy.

"Thank you." Her voice quavered. "I'm okay now."

"You are not all right, Methusal. What do you need? I will bring it."

A glance took in his faint frown, although his eyes were the usual ice blue. But she did sense that he'd shelved the games he liked to play. "Even you are powerless against sea sickness, Mentàll."

"You want me to leave you alone."

"Isn't that what I always want?"

"So you say." The familiar, arrogant twist in his voice was back.

"Wild beast."

Mentàll unexpectedly smiled, and for a second those light eyes were disconcertingly close. As was his large, hard body. "Color has returned to your face. Perhaps I am good for that much."

His gaze dropped to run over her lips and more warmth flared in her cheeks. "Leave me alone," she snapped. "Thank you for your help. But I'm fine now."

"What's going on?" Behran appeared. "Hendra said..." His gaze went from the Dehrien Chief to Methusal. "Are you all right, Thusa?"

"I will be." She glared at Mentàll.

The Dehrien stood. "You would like me to leave. So I will." When he glanced at Behran, his expression was difficult to interpret. A turn to his shoulders and he headed down the deck toward the cockpit, where the Captain was steering the ship.

Behran sat beside her. "What happened?"

"I almost toppled over the railing in my hurry to throw up."

He digested that. "You look better."

"A little. I don't feel very well, Behran."

He slid an arm around her shoulders and urged her to lean back with him against the barrels tied to the mast. "I'm not going to leave you this time."

Methusal rested her head against his shoulder. "Thank you." Nausea crept back up into her throat again. From the bottom of her heart, she hoped she would feel better soon.

Chapter Ten

"Are you sure I can't get you anything?" With worried eyes, Hendra observed Methusal, who hadn't risen from her bunk all morning. In fact, it was almost noon. Her friend's face looked faintly green. A bucket was tied to the bunk leg, and Deccia had already emptied it twice this morning. "Doc says you need to drink more liquids."

Methusal closed her eyes. "Maybe later. You'll come back...and tell me about the meeting, won't you?"

"Of course."

She nodded and averted her face, clearly wanting to be left in peace.

Against her better judgment, Hendra left her. Doc had already urged Methusal to go up on deck, but she had said she felt too awful to get out of bed, and claimed she hadn't felt much better on deck anyway. Hendra hoped she'd feel better soon. It scared her to see her spunky friend looking so pale and listless.

Softly, she closed the door behind her.

"How is she?" Mentàll appeared by her side.

To her surprised satisfaction, she saw genuine concern in her cousin's eyes. "Bad. She won't eat or drink, and just lies there, looking like...death."

Mentàll's hand twitched, perhaps involuntarily, for the door knob. He seemed to think better of it. A wise idea, given Methusal's feelings for her cousin.

"Can anything be done?"

"No. Doc says she should start feeling better tomorrow."

Mentàll hesitated for a fraction longer, and then strode for the main compartment. "The meeting begins now."

The other team members already sat at the table, which was piled high with books. One small spot was left for her, across from Doc. Mentàll remained standing. After a few introductory remarks, he said, "This first strategy meeting belongs to you. I will give you an overview of the information available, and then leave you to discuss it."

Hendra felt a little surprised by her cousin's strategy, until a flash of intuition helped her to understand. Everyone at the table would work together in the country portion of Zindedi. He wanted them to own their mission—not just take orders from him.

"You will stay in the village of Dakarra, located in the northwestern part of the country. It is a seaside community and new people visit often. You should easily blend in. Dakarra is also located near Zindedi's second largest military base. The largest base is in Carachki, the capitol city."

"Where are Zindedi's other bases?" Timaeus wanted to know.

"One was in the northeast, but it was destroyed a few years ago during their bloody civil war. That is when the Presidente and his brother, General Greisn Rohasch, unified the country."

Deccia glanced down, and her fingers convulsed on the table. Timaeus took her hand. Hendra felt compassion for her. She knew, better than anyone, how Deccia felt. Both had suffered at the hands of cruel men. For Hendra, it had happened when she was a young teen, and the torture had lasted for years. Her emotional scars still had not healed. On the other hand, Deccia had suffered a shorter, but more horrifying experience. Hendra was still amazed that Deccia had recovered so swiftly from the traumatic ordeal. ...Or maybe she hadn't. The other girl's eyes looked shadowed.

Mentàll said, "The books on the table will provide you with vital information that you will need to know in order to complete your mission successfully. I would like you to start working together as a team now. Read the books and start planning your strategy. We will meet again and fine tune the details. Any questions?"

"Not yet," Timaeus said. "But I'm sure we'll have plenty later."

Mentàll nodded and headed for the ladder.

Timaeus discovered a map of Zindedi, and since Doc was interested in that, Hendra changed places with Timaeus and sat at the opposite end of the table, flanked on her right side by the cabinets built into the hull, which abutted the table and bench seat. She perused a book, as did the others, except for Riln, who sat on her left. His big body fidgeted in the confined space. He glanced at a book, and then shoved it aside. His aggressive restlessness made her feel uneasy. She edged closer to the cabinet and tried to focus on her book, which appeared to be about social customs.

Riln's finger jabbed at the map. "How far is it from Carachki to Dakarra?"

Timaeus said, "The markings seemed to indicate a finger span is an hour's journey. Looks like six hours between the two. And here are the bases." Hendra looked, but couldn't see around Riln's burly shoulder, which was leaning forward.

"Looks like the Dakarran base is east of town, about a half hour's walk," Doc commented. "And the Carachki base is just north of Carachki. Looks huge. At least a good twenty minute walk across that."

Deccia looked up from her book. "It says here the Dakarran base assembles weapons. Two powder mines are located nearby, but it doesn't say where. It also says the Carachki base is primarily a training facility."

"There aren't many towns on the continent," Timaeus observed. "Carachki and a city in the northeast are the largest ones. All the others look like villages."

Hendra finally found something interesting in her book. "Dakarra is a popular vacation spot. I guess that's why Mentàll said new people visit all the time. It says people rent cabins to newcomers."

"Perfect," Deccia said. "Our first job will be to find a house to rent."

"Will we all stay together?" Hendra wanted to know.

"That might look suspicious," Doc said. "It might be better to arrive in two groups."

"Deccia and I could rent our own hut," Timaeus suggested. "Everyone else could rent another cabin."

"I think it would be a good idea if Hendra and I scout before anyone goes in," Behran said. "We'll get the lay of the land. Then Deccia will get a read on the people renting the huts, and tell us what she senses about them and the other people we'll see in the town."

"I like this plan," Sozla interjected. "But when will we inspect the military facilities, Behran? We must not forget—that is our true mission."

"Finally!" Riln's fist hit the table. Hendra jumped. "Someone's making sense. I'm scouting the base first. Are you with me, Tabor?"

Hendra took a small, shallow breath. Her heart pounded, but she tried to ignore a swell of fear.

Tabor nodded, but his mud brown eyes revealed nothing.

"Scouting the perimeter is a good idea," Behran agreed.

"I'm going into the base, if I get the chance," Riln stated, with a belligerent jaw thrust.

"No," Behran said. "We need to plan our missions first. One mistake could cost us everything."

"I'll kill every Zindedi who sees me. One less Zindedi to deal with later."

Aghast, Hendra at last spoke up. "We can't kill Zindedis. We're supposed to make peace with them."

Riln shot her a black, violent look. The shock of it felt like a slap to her face. His expression mirrored the hatred she'd seen in Jascr's eyes every time he'd tormented her and used his physical strength to subdue her. To terrify her. Hendra mouth went dry. Unable to help herself, she shrank back against the cabinet.

Thankfully, Riln swiftly returned his attention to the others. "All I'm saying..."

"No," Behran said. "No killing. The Zindedis will come looking for us. Then the peace plan will be dead, and so will we."

Riln crossed his arms. His elbow brushed Hendra's arm. With a soft gasp, she pressed harder against the cabinet.

Sozla said, "I do not know the kaavl, but I would like to go on the base, too. I would like to see their weapon making facilities. Perhaps then I will understand how they make such weapons. Koblan could benefit from such knowledge."

"I agree," Behran said with a smile. "But first, the kaavl team will scout it out. We'll take you in later, Sozla. Hopefully knowing the base layout and their guard schedule will help to keep you safe."

"I wish to be safe," she agreed with a smile.

Behran nodded. "And you will be. I'll make sure of it."

Sozla blushed. "Thank you, Behran. But let's speak about the cabins again. We will rent two?" When Behran nodded, she said, "Deccia and Timaeus will stay in one, and the seven of us will stay in the other?"

Riln's arm was still only a breath away from Hendra's. Her flesh crept, and she wanted to be freed of him. She wanted to escape from this tiny space and this tiny room. Her lungs felt uncomfortably tight. That frightened her, because during the war she had suffered several panic attacks. She'd barely been able to breathe. She was afraid that could happen again.

"I think Deccia and Timaeus' marriage will provide a good cover for the team," Behran said. "Tabor could stay with them and pretend he's Timaeus' brother. It might be a good idea if another 'married' couple rents the other cabin. It would look better that way than if unmarried women are staying with unmarried men."

Hendra drew a small breath through her teeth, and then another, fighting for calm.

Timaeus spoke. "Since you and Hendra will scout the town first, I think you two should pretend to be married when you rent the second cabin."

Behran shot Hendra a quick glance. "Is that all right with you, Hendra?"

She struggled to concentrate on the conversation. Had Behran just said he wanted to pretend to be married to her?

Doc glanced at her, and his eyes were the color of intense, blue-gray smoke.

Hendra's chest tightened even more. Long ago, she had accepted that she'd never get married. And now, she was supposed to agree so quickly and casually to pretend to be married to Behran? Of course it wasn't real, but...

"I...I guess," she said faintly. The urge to climb over everyone and flee was suddenly overwhelming. A thought flashed. This plan meant she'd live in a small cabin with *four* men, including Riln and Doc. A soft, gasping breath whistled through her teeth. Her heart pounded harder. "Maybe...maybe we should rent an extra cabin. Riln, Doc and Goric could have their own..."

"Why?" Riln demanded. "It'll cost us more."

"It might be best to stick together," Doc said. "I'll need to stay close in case anyone is injured."

"Okay," Behran agreed. "We'll pretend to be friends from school who are taking a vacation together."

"It's set, then," Tabor said.

Hendra wanted to cry out that it wasn't okay. At all.

Riln stretched. His elbow poked into Hendra's side. She recoiled, and anger suddenly exploded. "It'll be crowded. I don't think it's a good idea."

Doc's gaze met hers. "Why not?"

Because he already flummoxed her every time she saw him. And Riln...she shuddered. "It'll be crowded," she repeated. "Besides, what if the Zindedis begin to suspect one of us? They'll suspect everyone in the same cabin. We could all be captured at once."

"That is possible," Doc agreed. "But I doubt we'll all be in the hut at the same time. I think we'll be scouting day and night. It might be best if we stay together in one place. That way we'll know where everyone is. Everyone can be accounted for at all times."

Behran spoke up. "Checking in and out. Good idea, Doc. We'll need someone to coordinate where we are at all times."

"I'll do that," the doctor said. "Since I won't be doing much unless someone is injured."

"Perhaps you and I can speak to the local people," Sozla said. "They will give us tips about the area, and the people. We are tourists, correct? We will want to know these things. Then, perhaps they will tell us more."

Doc smiled. "Good idea, Sozla."

"So, most of us will stay together in one cabin," Behran summed up. "But your concern is legitimate, Hendra. A potential risk we'll need to cover."

So the decision was made. She would need to live in a deeply uncomfortable situation for several weeks. Suddenly, she desperately needed to be alone so she could get her head around all of it.

"Great. We have a plan," Behran said. "Let's break for now."

The others slowly filed out of the cabin. Doc remained in his seat. Hendra felt his glance when she quickly slid out and rose to follow the others. A pluck on her sleeve made her halt.

"Talk to me for a minute," he said quietly.

She did not want to talk to him. It felt as if he had sided against her in the discussion. But wasn't she being childish to think that?

With reluctance, she sat down across from him.

"What is wrong?"

"I felt claustrophobic with Riln so close. It made me realize how crowded the cabin will be."

"Does it bother you that I'll be in the cabin, too?"

She didn't answer.

"Hendra, what's wrong?"

"Nothing!" she blurted. If she'd ever cherished any hope that she might someday get over her fear of men and possibly develop a deeper relationship with Doc, she'd just had a bucket of cold reason poured over her head. She'd almost had a panic attack sitting next to Riln, for heaven's sake.

"Hendra, look at me." Reluctantly, she did so. "Are you afraid of me?"

"No." Tears filled her eyes. "I'm *broken*," she whispered. "I can't be fixed. Don't you understand?"

"I believe you can heal, Hendra. With time." *And with patience*, his compassionate gaze said.

"Thank you. I'm glad we can be friends."

"I agree." After a pause, he said, "I enjoyed your letters. I felt like I came to know you a little better through them."

She had opened up a bit in her letters, especially when she'd written about her dreams regarding improving the care of the orphans. And she'd written about a few other small things, too.

"I enjoyed yours, too." She offered a hesitant smile. "But it's easier to write, than to talk."

"I know." He was silent for a long time. Finally, he said, "I know you're not ready yet. But I'd like our friendship to grow." She heard the carefully muted intensity in his low voice. "I'd like to know the real you, Hendra."

He wanted more than friendship. That was clear. And it felt wonderful and terrifying, all at the same time. A part of her wanted the same thing. And she wanted it more than anything she'd ever wanted anything in her entire life. But deep down, she was afraid that her fear of men would never leave her soul. If that was true, how could she ever be enough of a woman for a wonderful man like Doc?

"I'm sorry. We can be friends. That's all. Please...please don't hate me." She lunged to her feet.

"Hendra, I would never..." His dismayed words followed her flight up the ladder to the deck.

She hated herself. She was a coward. And so very lonely. She found a quiet spot and wept. It hurt terribly to turn away the one man with the power to touch her heart. Unfortunately, he was also the man she was destined to disappoint. So she'd save them both the pain, and end any hope of a deeper relationship now, before it ever began.

Chapter Eleven

METHUSAL EXITED FROM THE CABIN. She still felt weak, but had managed to keep down broth and a grain disk this morning. A bit of queasiness remained, but she felt much better. Now she just wanted to leave the stifling, miserable cabin, and go up on deck and breathe the fresh, clean air.

"Methusal." She turned at the harsh voice, and her defenses automatically rose. While she'd been sick, she had had plenty of time to think about Mentàll's secret agreement with Aestoff's Chief, and where he might have hidden the documents. She meant to find out everything she could—today, if possible.

Her eyes narrowed when Mentàll paused beside her, but she was unable to read anything in his pale gaze.

"You are well?"

"I'm better." Then she said, with a bit of humor, "Even talking to you is better than feeling sick in my cabin."

A smile glimmered. "Careful. Your compliments may turn my head."

"Heaven forbid. Your ego is enormous enough already."

"Confidence does not equal arrogance."

"Maybe not *usually*," she sallied back. With an arched brow, she left him.

"Thusa!" On deck, Behran caught her close in a warm hug. "You're feeling better?"

"Much." She inhaled a lungful of the crisp salt air. Sun glinted off of the gently rolling blue sea. Not a cloud was overhead, although dark ones bunched on the horizon. "What a beautiful day."

"Want to sit with me?"

"Actually, I'd like to walk."

He offered his arm. Methusal found her sea legs as they slowly approached the bow, and then doubled back. Along the way, Behran recounted yesterday's meeting and the general plan for the country team. He finished up, "After we get the lay of the land, Mentàll wants Sozla and me to work on detonators and explosive devices."

"Explosive devices! What for?"

"In case something goes wrong, we'll need to destroy their weapons."

That made sense. It also sounded dangerous. "Do you know how to make a detonator?"

"Not yet. But I've studied the guns, and I have ideas. I'll get more ideas after we spy on their weapons making facility."

"Sounds dangerous."

"Your mission will be, too. Mentàll said the top military men work at the base you'll scout. You'll be in the most danger of all." A pause elapsed as they bypassed the cockpit, where Skyl was steering the boat, and then they rounded the corner to head for the bow again.

Behran said slowly, "I need to tell you something else. Hendra and I will go into Dakarra first. We'll pretend to be married when we rent our cabin. I'm hoping we'll find one a long distance away from the village. I don't think we'll need to do much acting afterward." He glanced at her.

The old insecurities threatened to arise, but Methusal swallowed them back. "Sounds logical."

His shoulders relaxed. "Just wanted you to know." They passed by Hendra, who sat alone on deck with her knees drawn to her chin, staring out to sea. She didn't look particularly happy.

Behran said in a low voice, "She's been upset for the past few days."

"Why?"

"I don't know. Would you talk to her? She thinks of you as a friend."

Methusal was glad Hendra considered her as a friend. However, she wasn't sure if the other girl wanted anyone to intrude right now. But Behran looked worried.

"I'll try," she agreed softly.

"Thanks, Thusa." He strolled on while she doubled back and perched on the cabin next to the Dehrien girl.

"You're feeling better." A genuine smile lit Hendra's dark brown eyes. "I'm so glad. We've been worried about you."

"Yes. But I'm not looking forward to sailing back home." She offered a rueful smile. "Deccia found out it'll take fourteen days, and it will be against the wind. That means it'll be rougher."

Hendra gave a sympathetic nod, but her thoughts appeared to be far away.

"Is everything all right? You seem sad."

"Oh." Her laugh sounded self-conscious. "I'm okay. Just thinking about the mission."

Methusal waited for more.

"It'll be fine, of course. We'll rent two cabins."

"Behran told me."

"Mine will be crowded."

"With whom?"

"Well, Sozla, of course. And Behran. And Goric, Riln, and Doc."

"Does that bother you?"

Hendra rubbed her palms over her pant legs. "It's been a long time since I lived in a cabin with men. And those were my brothers." She gave a short laugh. "I just think... I don't know. It makes me feel nervous."

Methusal had guessed, through conversations with her sister, that Hendra had suffered some terrible things at the hands of a man, just like Deccia had. Deccia had certainly revealed no confidences, but all the clues added up to one picture. Gently, she said, "I feel for you. I don't know if I could stand being cooped up with all of those guys, either. Especially Riln. That man belongs outside."

Hendra gasped out a tiny laugh.

Methusal said, "Behran and Doc would never let anyone behave inappropriately. You know they'll keep Riln under control."

"I'm sure you're right."

Methusal decided to turn the subject a bit. "I'm not looking forward to staying with your cousin, either. I know you think highly of him, but..."

"He won't hurt you." Her doubts must have shown, because Hendra insisted, "He won't."

"One thing is for sure. We're both nervous about staying in Zindedi."

"The Prophet said to follow the higher way. To love people and live at peace with one another. Do you think it will help if we do that?"

"Probably. But it will be hard to follow that path."

"If I pray, maybe I won't feel so afraid."

Methusal nodded. "I need to pray, too." Because she had no idea how in creation she'd ever cohabitate peacefully with her enemy. But on the other hand, if they battled for weeks on end, she was afraid that she would end up being the one destroyed.

Δ Δ Δ Δ Δ

It was almost lunch time, and the dark clouds that had smoldered on the horizon this morning were almost overhead now. A stiff wind blew, and the boat hissed through the waves, heeled sharply to port. Spray periodically hit the deck, and the sailors had closed all hatches except for the main one. Methusal remained on deck, as did Behran and a few others who were playing a ten questions guessing game for points.

She slid a glance toward the cockpit. Mentàll appeared well ensconced and relaxed in the cockpit, talking to Skyl and eating a bowl of soup. He had just started his lunch. Now was the perfect time to search his room.

Methusal turned to Behran. "Want some soup? I'll bring you a bowl."

He frowned. "You've been sick. Let me get one for you."

She touched his sleeve. "I need to go below anyway. I'll be back in a minute."

"Are you sure?"

"Of course. Be right back."

Down below in the main cabin, she swiftly slipped down the hall, and after making sure no one was watching her, entered Mentàll's cabin.

Mentàll's room was as neat as a pin, as usual. In addition, his pack was nowhere to be seen. She knelt and opened the two cupboards beneath his bunk. Those were the only storage spaces in the cabin, which made her job a lot easier.

The left cupboard contained the pack, which was neatly flattened, and obviously empty. Folded tunics and breeches lay on top of it. Methusal slid her fingers between the garments, searching for hidden papers. Nothing. Her attention turned to the other cupboard, which held shaving and other personal items, a thick pouch of foreign money, and a book on Zindedi. The man certainly traveled light.

She pulled out the book and flipped through it. Neatly folded papers slipped from the back. The secret Alliance! Pulse accelerating, Methusal unfolded the parchments.

Peace Agreement

We, the Chiefs of Koblan, do propose...

Disappointment crushed her soaring hopes. It was the preliminary peace agreement her father had signed. Just to make sure, she turned to the last page. Sure enough, there was her father's distinctive signature, right along with those of the other chiefs of Koblan.

She sat back on her heels. Where was the secret document that Mentàll had discussed with Chief Aarabst?

Maybe she had missed it. Methodically, she checked through the book and cupboards again, but found nothing. A quick flip up of his mattress proved no papers were hidden under there, either.

But she had seen Mentàll tuck the agreement into his pack in Aestoff. Where was it, then? Uneasily aware that Mentàll could enter at any moment, she quickly straightened everything so it looked just as it had when she had first arrived. She could not get out of his room fast enough.

She joined the growing line of people waiting for soup. Deccia and Timaeus were ahead of her. Someone had closed the hatch overhead. The boat's hull hummed as it rose and dipped on the waves, and occasionally the floor jerked when a rogue wave hit. Methusal glanced out a porthole streaked with seawater and dotted with clumped salt crystals. After lunch they'd probably need to retreat below, especially if a storm was brewing.

Methusal moved forward in line, and wondered again where Mentàll had put the papers. She had *seen* him put them inside his pack. But maybe he had left them in Aestoff, or maybe a Dehrien runner had returned them to Dehre for safekeeping.

This last idea made the most sense. The documents were obviously important to Mentàll. He'd want to protect them at all costs. What was more, the agreement with Aestoff's Chief probably had to do with Koblan—not Zindedi. So it made sense that Mentàll would not bring those papers to the invader land.

The realization disappointed her.

Maybe Aali would find solid evidence against him back home. If she knew her tenacious cousin at all, Aali would not disappoint her. Still, to wait weeks until she knew what was really going on frustrated and worried her. Unless she missed her guess, all of his plots would come to fruition as soon as everyone returned home from Zindedi. Somehow, she had to find out what was going on before then.

"Bowl of soup?" The cook's deep rumble interrupted her thoughts.

"Two, please."

The deep bowls of vegetable stew smelled heavenly. The burly cook added chunks of bread to the tray. Her stomach rumbled as she headed for the ladder. It felt good to be hungry again, and to look forward to a meal.

The boat jogged beneath her feet. Thankfully a high, protective lip encircled the outer edge of the tray, and the bowls were deep, so the stew didn't slosh out.

She balanced the tray against her hip and reached for the ladder just as the hatch overhead lifted. A bleach clad leg appeared. She moved aside at once.

Once inside, Mentàll lowered the hatch against a shower of spray. When he saw her standing there, he paused on the ladder, his hand still on the hatch.

"You are going out?"

"Yes."

He moved back up the ladder and held the hatch up with one arm so ship's movements would not make it slam shut on her. It also meant she would have to climb by him up the narrow ladder. His actions appeared to be merely chivalrous.

As she climbed up, her wrist brushed against his leather tunic. An unwelcome memory flashed—of wearing his warm tunic after her bath during the Quasr War. Hairs prickled up on the back of her neck, and the point of contact felt suddenly warm. Disturbed by her inappropriate response, she frowned at him. They were now at eye level. "Thank you. But I can manage by myself."

A wave hit the side of the boat, jerking the vessel sideways. Methusal wobbled, but he gripped her arm to steady her.

Her heart beat faster. "Thank you. But please don't." She twisted free.

"Don't what? Help you?"

"Yes. Stop pretending. I know you hate me."

"Do I hate you, Methusal?" he asked softly. A curious light gleamed in his eyes. He was enjoying this.

"Stop with the games, Mentàll." She swept the tray upward. Unfortunately, the corner caught on a ladder rung and for one horrifying moment, the bowls tilted.

His quick reflexes saved the tray. The hatch slammed shut overhead.

Her heart pounded. The bowls had sloshed out a bit of broth, but that was all. "Thank you," she managed to say. "I'm fine now. Give it back, please."

"Climb out, and I will hand it to you."

She didn't want to stand face to face with him on the ladder for one more moment. Swiftly, she climbed out, and then reached back inside for the tray. As the transfer took place, his fingers brushed hers. It might have been an accident, but then again, maybe not, because the glint in his eyes had returned.

"You are welcome, Methusal."

She spun and left him. Clearly, he still relished antagonizing her. *The One, please help me.*

△ △ △ △ △

At dusk that evening, Hendra stood at the rail. The cool breeze ruffled her long, white-blond hair as she thought about Methusal's words.

The Rolbani girl was right. Neither Doc nor Behran would allow inappropriate behavior in the cabin.

Thinking logically about it now, it seemed clear that fear had distorted her perspective at the meeting. And then Riln's aggression had pushed her over the edge.

She closed her eyes. *The One, please deliver me from my fears. I want to live again. I want to live so badly!* She opened her eyes, and watched the frothy wake behind the boat. Clouds hid the setting sun, and gray shadows shrouded the seascape. Just like fear enshrouded her heart.

"Hendra."

With a soft gasp of surprise, she spun.

Doc held up a hand. "I didn't mean to frighten you." He moved to the railing.

"You didn't." she felt foolish. "I'm sorry."

"You have nothing to apologize for." He rested his forearms on the rail and gazed out to sea.

"I've sent you mixed messages. I'm sorry about that."

He shook his head. "You haven't." He remained silent after that, and his calm presence slowly relaxed her.

"Is everything all right, then?" she asked cautiously. "We're still friends?"

"Of course we are. In fact, I'm afraid you have a friend for life."

Another knot of apprehension loosened. Even though she was afraid to take their relationship deeper, he still wanted to remain her friend. "Thank you."

He stood in companionable silence beside her for a while, watching the waves slide by. "It's so peaceful here. It reminds me of Tarst."

She thought back to the letters she had received from him. She'd learned a few things about him, but wanted to learn much more. "What was it like to grow up there?"

"It was a good childhood." He smiled. "I had lots of cousins around. We had a great time making forts and playing in the forest."

"I know Dastn is your cousin. But he's a bit younger?"

"Eight years. Yes. But we've always been close. He's been like a little brother to me."

"That must be nice," Hendra said wistfully.

"Dastn is the one who inspired me to become a doctor."

"Really? Why?"

"When he was two he got a terrible fever and rash. The doctor had never seen anything like it before. It was bad. He nearly died, and I was scared. My father's mother knew a lot about herbs, and she thought she could help, but my mother's sister wouldn't listen until it was almost too late. When Dastn stopped eating, she changed her mind. My grandmother used special plants from the forest and made poultices and weak tea, and he slowly improved. I watched and learned from her. She taught me everything she knew."

"So you learned to become a healer."

"But it wasn't enough. I wanted to learn how to set broken bones. I wanted to learn every medicine and technique possible to help my friends and relatives get well when they were sick. So I went to school to become a doctor."

"That explains why you're such an excellent doctor," she said softly. "And you care about people. Tarst couldn't have a better doctor."

He grinned. "High praise, Hendra. I'm not perfect. I want to research and learn so much more. I'd like to learn if it's possible to prevent childhood diseases. Children's health is very important to me."

She smiled. "It is to me, too." They talked more about the children they cared for, and finally headed back inside for dinner.

On the way inside, she reflected that she had enjoyed their talk. And she was glad Doc wanted to be friends. However, that didn't explain why friendship didn't feel like enough to her.

She felt confused, because he had given her what she wanted.

Chapter Twelve

The morning's daily strategy meeting bothered Methusal, so afterward she headed for Behran, who was out on deck. She wanted to get his take on it.

She skirted around Timaeus and a few others, who had set up a fishing line, and sat beside Behran. "Sounds like our trip will be a spy mission, not a peace mission," she told him.

"You're right. Mentàll hasn't said much about peace."

"He hasn't said *anything* about peace." She eyed the Dehrien Chief, who was currently speaking to the captain in the rear of the boat. His tall frame easily dwarfed the short, stocky Hil. "Don't you find it interesting that he only talks about positive outcomes, and no one seems to notice? He focuses on the mission and the benefits we'll enjoy when we succeed. He's so..."

"Charismatic?"

"Yes. No one questions him about anything."

He nodded. "If you want to talk to him, here's your chance." The Dehrien Chief headed in their direction.

Methusal felt reluctant to confront him, but not because she was confused by his smooth talk and questionable charm. It was because she'd prefer not to speak to him at all. However, when he was almost upon them, she stood and blocked his path. "Mentàll. I'd like a word."

The Dehrien Chief smiled faintly. He glanced at Behran. "Here? Or in private?"

Methusal counted to ten. "I want to learn about the peace part of the mission. You've said little about it. Do you have a plan?"

Amusement glinted. "Of course. In fact, you and I will partner closely to achieve it."

"I'd love to hear the specifics."

"Of course." He glanced at Behran. "I assume you would like to hear as well, Behran."

"Behran!" Timaeus called out. "We've hooked a fish. A big one! Come see."

A silent beat elapsed. Behran opened his mouth, but before he could speak, the Dehrien said, "Go. Methusal may question me for as long as she desires. She can report to you all of my answers."

She did not want to be left alone with Mentàll. At the same time, she had seen the sharp flash of interest in Behran's eyes when Timaeus had called. He wanted to witness the catching of the fish.

She touched his arm. "Go ahead. This conversation won't last long."

Behran hesitated for another fraction of a second. He glanced from Methusal to the Dehrien. "Sure, Thusa. See you in a minute." He moved away.

"He is well trained. Is that the type of man you desire?"

She counted to ten again. "He's caring and sensitive. Qualities foreign to you."

"You know little about the qualities that mean the most to me, Methusal. But you will."

Her annoyance grew. "Stop playing games with me."

"We could sit and be more comfortable. Perhaps over there..."

"Tell me! *Please*. Everything about the peace mission."

The amused façade vanished. After a moment, he said harshly, "We will infiltrate Carachki. I will send a letter to the Presidente, offering peace. He will either reject it or accept it. Regardless, we will gather all the intelligence we need, should he prove to be treacherous."

"And what if he rejects peace?"

Mentàll smiled, and it wasn't a nice one. "Then I will convince him to reconsider."

"How?"

"I will tell you when the time is right."

"I will not follow you blindly. I need to know all of your plans. I expect to be treated as an equal partner."

A small smile curved his lips. "You want to be equal partners with me?"

Again, she did not like his subtle insinuations.

Fiercely, she said, "Stop it."

"Stop what?" But that sharp, calculating look said he knew exactly what she was talking about.

"You *know* what. I won't be able to do a good job if you keep provoking me."

"You prefer quiet, sweet conversations, like you enjoy with Behran?"

She drew a quick breath of irritation.

He continued with a thin smile, "You do not have to respond to me. And yet you do."

"You are *insinuating* a relationship between us."

"We have a relationship. You want to forget the war, and what happened between us, but I cannot."

The guilt, confusion, and anger she'd felt at the end of the Quasr War washed through her again.

"That was a mistake! A *mistake,* Mentàll. It will never happen again. So stop baiting me. Stop..." She floundered. "Stop pretending! Stop taunting Behran."

"Behran can stand up for himself.

"*Listen* to me," she said fiercely. "I'm only teaming up with you for the good of Koblan. But if you keep poking in, trying to upset my relationship with Behran, or trying to upset *me,* I will refuse to work with you. You'll have to find another partner for Carachki."

Swift, unknown emotions flickered across his features. A moment passed. Stiffly, he said, "I apologize."

Methusal tried to read his closed expression, but couldn't. "I hope you mean that. Because if you don't, the mission is off." She turned and left him.

CHAPTER THIRTEEN

DAY 14

DECCIA COULD NOT BELIEVE that they'd already been on the ship for six days. Only four more remained until they reached Zindedi.

She had been enjoying the lazy, idyllic time on the *Sea Mistress*—but much more so after Methusal had started to feel better. Deccia liked the soft, swishing sounds of the sea and the powerful, controlled lunges of the vessel through the waves. In fact, she'd be happy to enjoy another six days at sea, instead of only four.

The sun toasted her closed lids. A heavy Zindedi history book, bound by leather laces, lay open on her lap. Each member of the team had agreed to read two Zindedi books before landing. The more they knew, the better prepared they would be to fit in.

"Must be an interesting book," Timaeus teased, sitting beside her.

She opened her eyes to bright sunshine and the smile of the man she loved. Impulsively, she kissed him. His smile widened, and he kissed her back with passion. He murmured, "If you're tired, we could take a nap."

She blushed. "Timaeus! It's the middle of the day."

"So?"

"Everyone will *know*," she hissed.

"Doesn't bother me." After a second glance at her face, he said, "All right, Decc. I can see it bothers you. Maybe I'll take a nap right here, beside you."

"Want me to read to you? This book will put anyone to sleep."

"I'm all ears."

Deccia flipped the book over and turned the page. Thank goodness only one more chapter remained. These last pages were a bright white color, and looked newer, and she soon saw why.

"The Unification War," she read. "East and West Zindedi were unified after three years of bloody battles. Eastern Zindedi suffered thousands of casualties before surrendering to unification. All Eastern officers were executed in order to purge the seeds of rebellion." She stopped. "They were *executed?* After they surrendered? What kind of a ruler..."

"A dirt eating whip."

Worse than a whip, in Deccia's opinion. She read on, "In year eleven of the Presidente Supreme, honorable and without peer..." She snorted. "Do they actually talk like that?"

"They probably want to stay on the Presidente Supreme's good side," he muttered. "Is he the current Presidente?"

"I think so. These pages look new." She flipped another page, looking for confirmation, and gasped when a familiar face stared back at her.

"Decc?" After one look at her expression, he reached for the book and scanned the sketch. "Is that the Presidente?"

Fear curled through her, feeling like a vicious whip about to strike. "It's *him.*"

General Greisn Rohasch. During her studies, she had finally learned the name of the man who had raped her.

Her husband scanned the drawing again. "It's not General Greisn, Deccia. Look, it says 'Presidente Supreme.'"

Her pounding heart slowed down a little, and she looked at the picture again more closely. "He does look a little different because he's not wearing a uniform, but...but...they could be *twins.*"

With a frown, Timaeus scanned the picture again. "I only saw him once, at the end of the war. But you would know, Decc."

It *was* him. For a moment, logic flew from her head. And in a flash, the old memories clawed through her: the feel of the General's hands upon her, the helplessness she'd felt, and the humiliating sounds of her own pleas in her ears— until she had learned that begging only made things worse.

Hot tears burned her eyes.

"Deccia." Timaeus' arm went around her shoulders, urging her to sink into him, to share her pain with him.

"Timaeus." She wept quietly into his chest, struggling to keep quiet; not wanting the others to hear. Each ragged breath sliced through her throat like fire. The pain wouldn't leave. It would *never* go away. Rage trembled through her at that helpless realization. The wounds still felt raw and deep and fresh. From the grave, the General was still able to claw through her soul.

And another man, just like him, was still living. An evil one. A man who lusted after power, instead of women. One who had murdered untold numbers of people, just to gain what he wanted.

She gritted her teeth, trying to stifle the searing gasps. It wasn't fair. It wasn't *fair*.

She realized that she'd pressed her balled fists hard into Timaeus' chest. "I'm sorry," she choked out.

"It's all right."

"It's not. It's *not,* Timaeus. It's not right that evil people hurt thousands of people."

"Of course not. But that's our mission. To stop him from hurting Koblan again."

"Yes." Deccia bit her lip. "I'm glad I can help this time. I would do *anything* to stop him."

"He'll never hurt you. I'll make sure of it."

"I'm not afraid of him." Surprisingly, she wasn't. The fact disturbed her a little, but she refused to think about why.

In fact, the Presidente would learn that *she* was the one to be feared. Soon, he'd learn to fear all Koblanis. On that day, she would finally feel victorious over all of her enemies.

"I can't wait to start on our mission," she whispered. "We'll win. I can feel it."

A shadow crept over her spirit, and she sucked in a breath at the feeling of panic that gripped her. Her premonitions—a vision coupled with overwhelming feelings—always came unexpectedly.

Blackness separated her from those she loved most. She couldn't see through the writhing cloud. And someone was lost. "Timaeus?"

"Timaeus." She clutched his tunic and pressed her cheek against his chest. *The One, no,* she pled through the swirling terror. *Protect us all. Please.*

Chapter Fourteen

Only a gentle breeze stirred the gently rolling sea this evening. Captain Hil confirmed that they'd arrive in Zindedi in two days. Methusal wanted to enjoy this last bit of peace.

"Behran. Methusal." The Dehrien Chief briefly nodded to them, and strode down the deck.

"He's been civil lately," Behran commented.

The Dehrien Chief had been behaving in an exemplary fashion for the last three days. Clearly, he had taken her threat to heart. His good behavior now proved how much he wanted her to be on the Carachki mission. It also proved that he would go to any extreme to secure that goal. That realization made her feel uneasy.

Deccia approached with a steaming plate. "Dinner's ready. Timaeus and I are going to eat in the cockpit. Want to join us?"

"Sure. What did Coyl make today?" Methusal sniffed. "Smells good." Coyl was an excellent cook. It always surprised her that such a burly, gruff man could make such light, delectable dishes.

"Seared fish and tubers. And whipped fruit pudding."

"Pudding! Yum." Methusal jumped up.

"Better hurry before it's all gone. You know how much Goric loves it."

Goric had kept to himself during the trip. The only time he'd caused a drama was when he'd gone back for second and third helpings of pudding. Riln had teased him unmercifully about it.

As it happened, Goric was just ahead of her in line, and already half of his plate was heaped with pudding.

"Please leave some for us," she murmured. He cast her a look of dislike. "Sorry. But there are still a lot of people in line."

"Half the pot is still there." He jammed the ladle back into the pan and headed out the hatch.

Outside, Riln guffawed. "Pudding boy! Didn't your mama make you enough soft food?"

"*Shut it.*"

"Apte baby."

Hendra, who was behind Methusal, said, "Riln is so rude."

"Dakarra should be interesting with Goric and Riln living in the same cabin."

"I try not to think about it."

Footsteps *thunked* down the ladder. "Anyone up for whaal later?" Doc said.

"Oh." Hendra drew a quick breath. "I'd like to play."

They had been playing card games every night. Methusal would miss those quiet, peaceful moments when they reached Zindedi.

Outside, she noticed that Goric was sitting by himself near the bow of the boat. Did he *want* to distance himself from everyone? He never joined in their games.

Maybe because no one had asked him.

Love your enemies.

Strange, how the Prophet's words came to mind at the oddest times. Wasn't it time to listen again, and try to do the right thing?

"I'll be back," she told the others, and headed forward. Her steps lagged when she neared him, though, because she felt apprehensive about her reception. "Goric. We're playing whaal later. Want to join us?"

"*No.*" Narrowed gray eyes flashed up at her. "Your charity mission is done. Go on back."

She held her ground. "I'm trying to be nice…"

"Don't try. It doesn't suit you."

Stung, she bit back sharp words. "I thought we were past this."

"Some things never change. And pity can never be mistaken for friendship."

"I don't pity...." Methusal drew a breath. "We'd love it if you joined us. It's up to you." She left him.

Maybe the past would always rise up to bite her. For years, Goric had treated her like a whip, and she had retaliated by doing the same to him. This was the result, and she didn't like it.

Please help me, The One.

△ △ △ △ △

"Good game," Behran said with a yawn.

Doc gathered up the cards from the lamp lit table.

Hendra stifled a yawn, too. It *had* been fun.

"Another round?"

Everyone demurred, and Hendra waited for Sozla, Methusal, and Deccia to slide down the bench and exit from the table. Confined in the corner again, she had little choice but to wait.

"I like this game. Whaal." Sozla sparkled a smile down at Doc, who was wrapping a band around the gold mottled cards. "I will have to teach my friends and family when I return home."

With a grin, he said, "Then we'll need to play it often in Dakarra. That way you'll learn all the strategies."

Sozla laughed merrily. "And I will win. Yes, I like your plan, Doc."

Did his smile looked brighter, and his eyes more alive as he talked to Sozla?

And why not, Hendra thought with a sudden lump in her throat. Sozla was a fun, bubbly person. Everyone liked her. And she didn't walk around with a black cloud following her.

She blinked quickly. Hadn't she just told Doc that she was only interested in friendship?

He appeared to have taken her at her word. Ever since their conversation four days ago, his demeanor toward her had remained warm and friendly, but she'd detected no hint of anything else. Much as she knew this was for the best, her heart broke a little each time she saw him. Of course, she had no right to feel that way, but her heart did not appear to be very logical.

Sozla followed the others into the hall.

Finally, Hendra rose from the table. "Good night, Doc."

"Hendra." A deep, unknown emotion flickered. "Did you enjoy the game?"

"Of course."

"Then why do you look so sad?"

She offered a small smile. "I'm tired."

"You need to take better care of yourself."

"What do you mean?"

"I mean, stop judging yourself. In my opinion, you're wonderful just the way you are."

Unexpected tears flooded her eyes, but she blinked them back. Her throat ached. "Thank you."

His warm gaze held hers. "See that you don't forget that." A moment elapsed as he seemed to consider saying more. But he simply said, "Good night."

"'Night."

As Hendra headed for her cabin, she felt better. Doc cared for her very much. That was obvious. Couldn't she feel grateful to have such a good friend?

She was grateful. Very grateful.

She *was*. But she tossed and turned all night long, trying to find peace for her torn soul.

CHAPTER FIFTEEN

TOMORROW EVENING they would reach Zindedi. Nerves and excitement tangled in Methusal as she stood at the bow of the boat, watching the sun set in a blaze of orange and pink. Captain Hil had said they'd slow down tomorrow afternoon. He didn't want to sight land until dusk. Although they'd anchor along an uninhabited, forested stretch of shoreline, he wanted to take no chances of being spotted by Zindedis on the way in.

A cool breeze caressed her skin. It was nice to be all alone at the bow of the ship. She wasn't used to living in such close proximity to so many people. Up here she could breathe, and her mind felt free. She felt a connection to the boat and the sea. Almost if she was one with the elements.

The temperature had steadily dropped as they had sailed north. Zindedi must be a cool land. Certainly, it had a cold, merciless leader.

Half of the sun hovered above the horizon, looking like a blazing fireball, and then slipped utterly under the sea. Dusk fell swiftly, enshrouding the ship in shadows.

"Methusal."

The Dehrien's harsh voice startled her. He had approached silently, but that was no excuse. She needed to practice kaavl.

"Mentàll."

"It is time to discuss our plan for Carachki."

"Now?"

"Now, or later. Does it matter?"

Reluctantly, she faced him. "All right. Tell me your plan. I still would like to know all of it."

He didn't like her words. She saw it in the faint hardening of his jaw. "Respect, Methusal. I am your commanding officer."

"That sounds familiar."

"You learned to treat me with respect during the Quasr War. You will do the same now." In a low voice, he added, "And do not threaten me again, or you will not like the consequence."

"I meant what I said before. I won't team up with you if you act like a wild beast to me."

"I understand that, Methusal. And I will not." The cold ore in his voice proved that he spoke a simple fact. "But if you will not team with me, then you will stay on this ship."

Her jaw dropped. "You'd jeopardize the mission..."

"No. *You* are the one who would jeopardize the mission. I will not allow an insubordinate soldier on Zindedi soil. Are you with me, or not?"

She briefly closed her eyes, and then stared out at the black, rolling sea. "I'll go with you. You know that."

Tension relaxed out of his large frame. He hadn't been sure she'd agree. She said, "You will treat *me* with respect, too. At all times."

"I will. And you may trust me when we are alone in our room."

She drew an unsteady breath. Finally, he'd come to the crux of what was bothering her the most. Being alone with him at night, and working closely with him during the day. So many opportunities for him to burrow under her skin, as he'd done during the Quasr War.

As far as his promise not to take advantage of her in their close quarters—she would have to trust him. After all, his word meant everything to him.

"Okay. I'll trust you. What is your plan?"

"When we reach Carachki, we will look for a Matron Machblin. She lives in the heart of town, and not far from the Presidente's palace. Personal papers from a Zindedi soldier state she has a room for rent."

"What if it's filled?"

"I have a list of other names and addresses. But she would be the best one. She is a military widow, and she may have contacts in the Presidente's palace."

"How do you know she's a widow?"

"Her husband was the Commander in Quasr. Those were his papers."

She remembered the dead Commander. He had wanted to take General Greisn's position. Instinct had told her he was dangerous, violent, and unpredictable. What sort of a person would his widow be? "And then what?"

"We will scout Carachki's military base on the first day, and spy on the Presidente's compound the next day. Afterward, I will send a note to the Presidente and offer peace. His response will determine our next course of action."

She nodded. "Okay."

"No arguments, Methusal? I feel...disappointed."

"Feel anything you like. As long as you treat me with respect and leave me in peace, we'll get along just fine." She made to brush past him, but he caught her arm and held it.

"Will you not forgive me, Methusal?"

"Forgive you for what?"

"You are still angry with me."

She expelled an exasperated breath. "Why wouldn't I feel upset? You taunt Behran. You needle under my skin every chance you get. What am I supposed to feel for you?"

"I apologize, Methusal. Will you accept that?"

"If I thought you meant it, I would."

He said nothing for a moment. Then, "It is time for you to accept my word as the truth."

"I accept nothing from you as the simple truth. You always have another plot you're working on. What is it this time?"

He pulled her closer. "You searched my room." It wasn't a question.

Methusal went very still. So he knew. And he probably knew she had been the one spying on him in the hall in Aestoff, as well. She shouldn't be surprised. However, she wouldn't admit to it, either. "Do you have something to hide?"

His icy gaze bit like frostbite into her soul. She managed not to shiver. When he didn't answer, she decided her best defense would be a good offense. "Tell me why you've been traveling all over Koblan."

His expression closed. "You do not need to know. Not yet."

"Not *yet?* This is why I don't trust you." She twisted her arm free. "I will *never* trust you. It's time for you to accept that word as the truth."

She left him alone. And tried not to think about the days ahead when she would not be able to leave him at all. Her stomach tightened into knots, thinking about the weeks ahead. *Oh The One, please help me.*

△ △ △ △ △

The cell door squeaked open. The guard cackled. "It is time. Come now."

"No. You're dead. This is a dream."

"It is not a dream. The General awaits you in hell."

Fear slashed through her. "I'm not going to hell."

"You're one flight up. Come into the hall. I'll give you your freedom."

Deccia huddled harder into her dark corner.

The guard hissed, "You are trapped. It is time to escape and make your choice."

"What choice?" Fear overwhelmed her.

The guard swung the door open wide. Light from the passageway spilled into her dark cell. "Come out."

The light beckoned. She did want to escape. So badly. But why would the General free her? This must be a trap.

The guard laughed again. The evil of it slicked fear through her veins. "You cannot resist. Just as you will not resist your fate. The General awaits you."

She did not move. But the warmth beckoned. So did freedom

"That's right," the man hissed. "You know how you can be free forever, don't you?"

"No."

"Of course you do. The General must die."

"He's already dead."

"You must kill him. It is the only way to free yourself." His manic cackle echoed in the dank cell.

An unseen force sucked her toward the hall. She stumbled forward.

"No!" She clutched at the door, trying to stop herself.

"You must face the General. You must choose your fate. It is time."

"*No!*" Deccia sat straight up in bed, heart pounding. She shook uncontrollably.

Beside her, Timaeus slept soundly.

It was her fourth nightmare in as many days. She wouldn't wake Timaeus. He'd held her and suffered with her after every one of the others. Tonight she would leave him in peace.

The guard's words still shivered through her soul. Only a cold dose of reality would banish the ghosts from her mind.

She slipped out of bed, pulled on her cloak and moccasins, and quietly let herself out of the room. Snores rattled from Behran's cabin. A few crew members snorted in their open air cabin. A lone lantern lit the common area, but the hatch was open, and a chilly breeze swirled down inside.

When Deccia climbed out, the stiff, freezing wind hit her full in the face. The boat raced through the waves, booms creaking, sails humming. Moonlight glistened on the water.

"Nice night for a sail." Skyl's voice startled her. He stood at the wheel.

"Yes." Deccia wrapped her cloak more tightly around herself, and headed toward the bow.

"Be careful," Skyl called after her. "It's a might rough, and a bit wet in patches."

"I will. Thank you."

Deccia stopped at the forward cabin and sat facing the bow. The ship surfed the waves and dove into the troughs. Spray flew back, stinging her cheeks. The cabin top felt slick, and slightly greasy and gritty from salt spray. She didn't care, because right now she felt awake and alive.

With the good came the bad. The darkness enshrouding the ship reminded her of the cell. The fear wouldn't release her spirit.

She wept quietly at first, but the crash and hiss of the boat's movements drowned it. The pain inside of her billowed up, so black and endless that she wanted to scream. She was so tired of bottling it up. So tired of pretending she was all right to everyone. She wasn't. *She wasn't.*

Her keening wails matched the high pitched hum of the wind through the rigging, and the crashing plunges through the sea mirrored her desire to throttle the General. To *kill* him.

The One help her, she did want to kill him! Deccia felt horrified. More sobs gasped out.

He was *dead*. His fate was sealed. But she was still left feeling powerless and empty. Defeated. *The One, please make the pain go away. I can't take it anymore.*

Something hard crushed onto her foot and a hard, compact body hit her knees as someone tripped and fell.

A male voice swore. Moonlight glinted off dirty blond hair.

Goric glared up at her, and scrambled to his feet. "*You!*"

Deccia felt slapped. "What is your problem?"

He peered at her. Uncertainty flickered. "Deccia?"

"Yes."

He stuck his hands in his pockets. "Sorry," he said gruffly. "Thought you were Methusal."

"I'm sorry you tripped."

"I didn't expect anyone to be out here." He glanced at her again, obviously noticing her distress. "What's wrong?"

"Nothing." She looked away. "Just nightmares."

Long moments elapsed. He shuffled his feet. "Oh." Goric had probably put together the *why* of the nightmares and felt uncomfortable with the subject matter.

"I'm fine." Yet another lie, and she told it while looking at the sea.

"He was awful."

Deccia glanced back. A note in Goric's voice sounded odd–almost as if he knew what she was talking about. "Did you meet him?"

"I've heard things. He reminds me of someone I know."

Deccia didn't say anything for a long time. "He's dead. Why doesn't that make me feel better?"

"Memories stay with you. You can't outrun them. Believe me, I've tried."

"Do you mean your father?" Although Deccia knew the question was nosy, she wanted to turn the conversation away from herself. "Methusal said he lives in Aestoff."

Goric glanced away. "I want to be different than him, but I don't know if I can."

"Why not?"

"I'm a whip. A cheat. All things sluggish. Hasn't Methusal told you?"

"It's never too late to change."

"Choices. But what if some choices are built into our blood?"

"I don't believe that," she said fiercely. "We can always choose good over evil."

"When the moment of truth comes, we'll see." With those cryptic words, Goric left her.

Deccia uneasily wondered if his words had been directed to himself, or to her.

Chapter Sixteen

Not even Ryon lit the black night. They had lowered the sails earlier, in the mid-afternoon, when they were still far enough away from shore that Zindedi lookouts would not be able to see their mast. At twilight the sailors raised the sails again, and now gusting wind pushed them toward Zindedi. A squall was brewing, but Skyl had said they should reach the anchorage before it hit.

Methusal stood at the railing beside Behran and Deccia, and struggled to see the wild coastland ahead. But she only saw the black, choppy sea, faintly lit by the stars.

"How does he know where he's going?" Deccia whispered.

"He navigates by the stars," Behran replied.

A little earlier Captain Hil had announced that they'd head for a small, isolated cove shown on the Zindedi maps. It was located a day's journey from both Dakarra and Carachki.

The icy wind bit through Methusal's new invader clothing. Hopefully the storm would come and go before they left the ship the next morning.

Doc rested his forearms on the rail beside Behran. "Anyone see Zindedi yet?"

Hendra, on the other side of Deccia, gasped a little. Softly, she said, "It's *coming*."

"You had a flash?" Doc asked.

Methusal remembered that Hendra was able to see into the future when she focused on one object or location.

"Yes. We're too far east. We'll run aground..."

"I'll go with you," Doc offered.

"Thanks." Gratitude colored Hendra's voice, and she and Doc headed for the cockpit.

Her words must have held sway, for soon sailors ran forward and trimmed the sails to the wind. The ship nudged west.

Methusal shivered and wished for her leather tunic. She'd decided to wear the invader clothing today to try to get used to it. While it was soft and comfortable, it wasn't very warm.

Behran's warm arm came around her shoulders. "Are you ready?" he said in her ear.

She leaned into him and wrapped both arms around his waist. A hollow sort of fear had plagued her all day long. No matter how tightly she held onto him now, tomorrow they would be separated. "I'll miss you."

"I'll miss you, too." He hugged her tighter and kissed her hair.

"It's only for a few weeks."

"And we'll meet up a couple times. It'll be fine, Thusa."

"I know."

"Look!" Deccia said. "I think I see trees."

Black, jagged shapes loomed against the dark, star speckled sky. "We're so close!" she gasped. "Does the Captain see?"

Captain Hil shouted, "Port!" The boat slid further west, as smooth as water on silver.

"Looks like Hendra's warning saved us," Timaeus said. "If we'd been further east, we'd have run aground."

More sailors ran forward again to man the sails and ready the anchor.

Silent as the night, the *Sea Mistress* slipped north, around a corner, and into a sheltered cove. The breeze slackened to nothing in the protected inlet. Sails dropped and chain rattled as the anchor dropped into the calm water. A hard tug as the anchor caught in the mud and stopped the ship's forward movement.

"We're here."

Black forest loomed all around them, encircling the small cove. It was quiet. Eerily so. It was as silent as death.

CHAPTER SEVENTEEN

AALI WAS PLEASED WITH the accomplices she'd managed to cobble together. Three runners from Rolban, one from Tarst, and one from Aestoff. Unfortunately, four had already returned and reported little information of importance. They'd promised to try to find more information on their next trip, and she hoped for the best, but...

Much as Methusal had tried to convince Aali that this job—discovering Mentàll's unknown plot—was exciting and vital, so far it had proven to be deadly dull. Waiting for people to show up and report news was not exciting. She wanted to be out in the field, investigating for herself.

And maybe she could.

Over the last few days an idea had taken shape in her mind. A runner had told her that Mentàll had spent lots of time in Quasr over the last few months. Quasr must be important to the Dehrien Chief's plan. Maybe his biggest ally lived there. If so, it must be Quasr's new Chief.

Aali smiled. She was waiting for one last report—Dastn's. Hopefully, he would arrive soon. If he didn't bring any information either, she'd have no choice but to take matters into her own hands.

Δ Δ Δ Δ Δ

Today was the day.

Methusal hadn't slept well last night. The boat had barely moved, even though the storm had hit at midnight. It felt strange to lie on a level, quiet bed after ten days at sea.

She had lain awake in the dark for hours, listening to the howling wind, and wondering what the next day would bring. What would Carachki be like? Would the Commander's wife—the one who might rent them a room—be as coarse and unpleasant as her husband?

And Mentàll. She refused to think about him.

The wind died down at dawn.

Methusal dressed in the fine cloth of the Zindedis. Her outfit consisted of a white tunic with a soft, folded neckline, and trim black breeches. Her black jacket and a pack filled with supplies lay on her bunk.

It was time.

She untied her pack. With reluctant fingers, she pulled out Mentàll's marriage necklace. The silver and gold chain felt warm and silky in her hand. The necklace was beautiful. Light blue flowers were linked with green petals all the way around. Beautiful...and dangerous. She slipped it over her head.

Time for the deception to begin.

"Ready, Thusa?" Deccia appeared in the doorway. Her gaze fell to the necklace. "Oh! Where did you get that?"

"Mentàll. It's my fake marriage necklace."

Books on board confirmed that the Zindedis wore marriage necklaces, too. It was a custom both continents shared. Mentàll must have learned that, of course. In fact, she realized he must have ordered the necklace made months ago. It must have taken a long time for an artisan to fashion the intricate necklace.

Deccia stepped closer. "It's beautiful. Is it an heirloom?"

"That's what I asked. No. He made it specially for..." Methusal stopped. "For this trip," she ended lamely.

Deccia gave her an odd look. "For you, you mean."

She felt uncomfortable. "Yes, that's what he said."

"I can tell." Her sister touched the necklace. "The blue stones are the exact color of his eyes. And the green are yours."

Dismay made her automatically say, "No." But she lifted the silky chain to examine it more closely. The blue, of course, she had noticed, but the green... She looked at the clear dark green, and then into her twin's eyes—which were the same exact color as her own. A clear, dark green. An absolutely perfect match. "It must be a coincidence."

"Do you really think so?"

Her heart thumped with apprehension. The necklace must have cost a fortune. And Mentàll had apparently ordered it made especially for her. Months ago.

"Be careful, Thusa."

△ △ △ △ △

With the unfamiliar Zindedi socks and shoes in hand, Deccia stepped out of the small boat into freezing, knee deep water. Early morning sunlight peeped over the thick forest. The water was dark green. Small swells urged her forward. She stepped over smooth stones and jagged, biting pebbles toward the rocky beach. Wild grasses bordered the coastline, and beyond them loomed tall, dark trees.

Cold water clung to her feet as she stepped onto the beach. A sharp rock dug into one heel, and tiny stones prickled painfully into her toes.

A violent, soul deep shudder rippled through her.

Zindedi. The home of the General.

Timaeus' warm arm hugged her cold shoulders. "Are you all right?"

The forest seemed unnaturally still.

Deccia shivered again, unable to help herself. Foreboding seeped like the dark Zindedi water into the deepest recesses of her spirit.

"It's a seven hour hike to Dakarra, which is on the northwest shore," Timaeus said. "That should warm us up."

Had she made a mistake in coming? What further horrors would this land, the General's birthplace, inflict upon her? Upon them all?

Deccia shivered again. "Hold me, Timaeus," she whispered.

Δ Δ Δ Δ Δ

Methusal waited for the last boatload to arrive from the ship. In the distance, Goric and Riln climbed into the tiny, rocking craft with packs on their shoulders.

Sozla said, "It is so quiet. It reminds me of the forests of Eerpor."

"Where are the flying beasts?" Deccia's voice sounded strained.

"Perhaps they are searching for their morning food."

The last boat rowed closer to shore, gently bobbing on the small swells. When it came as close to shore as it could, Behran and Mentàll held it steady, their forearm muscles rippling, as the final kaavl spies climbed out. Behran wore a dark blue shirt, rolled to the elbows, and tan pants, rolled above the knee. Methusal had already noticed how the shirt intensified the deep blue of his eyes.

Mentàll wore the complete opposite; a white shirt and black breeches. It seemed strange to see him in anything but bleached leather. The Zindedi shirt emphasized his broad shoulders and the pants delineated lean hips and long legs. Methusal turned her gaze back to Behran.

"Your men are so strong and good looking," Sozla said. "Is this the way of all men in your communities?"

Seeing Behran—and even Mentàll—in the new clothes helped Methusal to see the two from Sozla's fresh perspective. "We have the best ones here, I think."

"I believe this."

"Aren't there attractive men in Eerpor?"

Sozla gave a tiny, one shouldered shrug. "None have captured me. Though there is one..." She fell silent for a moment, but a frown tugged at her brow. "Perhaps it is because I've known them since childhood."

"Maybe," Methusal agreed. "Or maybe not. Deccia has known Timaeus her whole life. Although she didn't know him very well until a few years ago. And I've known Behran since I was thirteen."

"But Hendra and her Doc. They met last year, true?"

Hendra's Doc? Methusal smiled at that surprising thought, and glanced at the two who were sitting on a fallen log. Currently, the Dehrien girl was not looking at Doc— although, if the questioning lift of his brow was any indication, he had just asked her a question. Hendra shook her head. Abruptly, she jumped up and left him. With a gaze of compassionate, but frustrated determination, Doc stared after her.

Hendra and *Doc?*

Surely she would have noticed something before now. But Sozla struck her as a perceptive person. And Doc's expression just now made her wonder.

Methusal turned her attention back to the dark-haired girl. "When we go home, maybe you would like to visit Rolban for a few weeks. You would be very welcome. My father is Chief."

Sozla smiled. "I would like that, Methusal. Thank you. My father is Chief, as well. Did you know?"

"No, I didn't."

"Yes. Mentàll has come on two occasions to speak to my father."

"Why?" Suspicion flared. Was Eerpor one of the communities with whom he had made a secret agreement?

Sozla's clear laugh tinkled. "They spoke of Chief matters. My father does not confide in me. He thinks women are...decorative."

It was Methusal's turn to laugh. "He does? I mean, Mentàll did ask you to come on the mission."

"I am honored that Mentàll asked me. He is a rare man, to think so highly of women."

Methusal hadn't thought about that idea before, but Sozla was right. Mentàll clearly valued her kaavl skills, and that of his cousin, and Deccia, as well. "You're right. That is true."

Sozla sent Methusal a sharp, smiling glance. "He is a handsome man, too, is he not? And powerful."

Methusal felt surprised, and also a bit taken aback. "You're interested in Mentàll?"

"I see he is otherwise engaged. You wear his marriage necklace, after all."

"We're not married," she quickly reminded her. "It's just a cover."

"Still, I will leave him to you."

"I don't want him. Behran is the man I will marry."

Sozla's smile faded. "True enough. You are a lucky woman to have two fine men."

"After the mission, it will only be one."

"Yes. But which one?" With this strange comment, she left to speak to Deccia.

△ △ △ △ △

"Time to go." Sadness shadowed Behran's gaze as he looked down at Methusal. Over his shoulder, Deccia and Timaeus strapped on their packs, and the Dehrien Chief shouldered on his own.

"I wish we didn't have to split up." Behran had no idea how fervently she wished this.

"It'll be okay." He leaned forward to kiss her. At that moment Mentàll glanced their way. It felt strange to kiss Behran in front of him, so she turned a little, so she didn't have to see him, and kissed Behran. Her lips lingered on his warm ones. "I'll miss you."

"I'll miss you, too," he said huskily, and kissed her again. "'Bye, Thusa."

Within moments, Behran and the others headed for the thick trees. Methusal watched until his dark shirt disappeared into the black forest. Sadness ached in her heart. She felt bereft.

And uncomfortably alone with the Dehrien Chief.

She picked up her pack, slung it on her back, and headed east. The maps she'd studied had indicated that Carachki would be easy to find. The great port city had been built around a deep bay. She couldn't miss it if she followed the shoreline.

After she left the beach, the forest grew down to the rocky edges of the water. So she hiked through the trees. Faint sounds told her that Mentàll was following her. She sharpened her senses into kaavl and walked faster, but did not look back. She did not want to speak to him right now. Yes, that was terribly rude. Unfortunately, she was afraid she would lose her current peaceful frame of mind if she talked to him. Once they reached Carachki, her peace would end for good.

Long minutes...perhaps an hour passed. She pushed herself hard, and tried to ignore the discomfort she felt about her behavior. Ignoring him wasn't nice or kind.

She plunged on, moving at a fast clip, and slapped aside low branches.

Methusal felt his presence close behind her now. In fact, that was one of the things that always disturbed her the most about him. She could never ignore him. It was as if a part of her actually wanted to be aware of him. The implications of that realization disturbed her even more.

She walked even faster, wanting to escape from him, and the confusion and torment she was certain he intended to engineer for her in the coming weeks. Fueled by frustration, she shoved a branch aside harder than intended. It accidentally snapped back behind her. The *thwack* of a branch hitting flesh broke the silence, and his steps lagged. Horrified, she said over her shoulder, "I'm sorry."

He said nothing, but she sensed that he was hard on her heels again. She walked even more swiftly. She didn't want him to catch her. She wanted him to leave her *alone*.

Love your enemies.

During the war, it had been so hard to be nice to the Dehrien Chief. And when she had, he had grown much too close.

Another branch accidentally snapped back. Tears of regret filled her eyes.

A hard hand unexpectedly gripped her wrist and made her halt. His face looked like a bleak, harsh mask. "You are acting like a child."

Methusal didn't like it. Not at all. She blinked back the confounded tears. "I'm sorry."

"You cannot run from me any longer," he gritted. "You must face me at last."

"Stop it." She freed her wrist. "I don't want to be near you!"

"You have made that very clear." If possible, his voice sounded even harsher. "But now it is time for you to follow me."

He wanted her to submit to his leadership—not only on this trail, but for the entire mission.

"Do you understand?"

Rebellion surged in her, fed by her overwrought emotions. She did not want a repeat of the Quasr War!

Those discerning eyes watched her. "You do not want us to grow close again. But we will, Methusal. We will."

"*Never,*" she said through her teeth.

"Follow me."

She said nothing.

"Do you want to go back to the ship? I can still arrange..."

"No." She finally looked away. Running from him wouldn't solve her problems. And she would *not* fear him. "I don't want to go back to the ship."

"Then you will follow me."

"Yes," she said evenly. "I will follow you."

"Good." Abruptly, he turned and stalked ahead. He was not happy. Perhaps that was a good thing. Maybe that would keep a safe amount of distance between them.

∆ ∆ ∆ ∆ ∆

More hours passed, and finally they stopped to rest. Mentàll sat on a log and gulped from his water skin.

Methusal sat across the clearing on her own log. She eyed him as she recorked her water. She had done quite a bit of thinking over the last few hours. The Prophet had said to pursue peace with her enemy. Well, it was time to try to take more steps in that direction. They did need to live at peace in order to succeed in this mission.

"I'm sorry for earlier."

He continued to drink. When he finally lowered the skin, he said, "I understand why you behaved as you did, Methusal."

"What do you mean?"

He stood and placed the water skin inside his pack. "We will finish this conversation on another day."

His answer frustrated her, but if he didn't want to have a conversation, that was fine with her.

Methusal followed his long, silent strides through the forest. He held back branches so they did not slap her in the face.

When they stopped for a late lunch, Methusal ate quietly. She felt the Dehrien's gaze upon her a few times, but he said nothing until they had both finished. Then he said, "Are you ready? We are almost there."

She wasn't. "As ready as I'll ever be."

"Good." He stood. "From now on, I am Lozar Solar, and you are Midi. My wife."

She took a deep breath, and suppressed a flutter of panic. Mentàll—Lozar—was to be her fake husband. She nodded.

In silence, she followed him through the forest. It cleared ahead and a wide, gravel road bisected their path. It stretched east and west. Carts rattled to the right, heading for Carachki. Large urchets pulled them.

Hoof clops and men's shouts filled the air. One cart was almost upon them.

All of a sudden the mission seemed very real. A new kind of apprehension gripped her. But this time it wasn't the fear of being teamed with Mentàll. He was the only person she knew in this land. In fact, she realized that he would be her only ally in Carachki. She would have to rely upon him, and trust him with her life. More so than than she had in the Quasr War.

Taking a deep, steadying breath, she fell into step beside her familiar enemy and headed for the unknown in Carachki.

"Heyyup!" A cart slowed down alongside Mentàll. A rough looking man with a cap pulled low over his black, shadowed eyes stared down at them. "Country folk, are you?" He spat a nasty globule onto the ground. "Maybe you don't know the way of things around here. If you want safe passage into the city, I'll give it to you. For a price." He smiled, revealing crooked, missing teeth. "Your choice, of course. But you know the Presidente's directive. Law breakers pay with their lives."

△ △ △ △ △

Hendra and the others had been traveling all day over dirt roads. Chilly dusk now settled around them as they trudged still further north, toward Dakarra. They'd left most of the forest behind.

Tabor, Riln, and Goric had separated from the group at lunch time. The three men had elected to cut across farmland and wild grasses and head straight for the Dakarran military base. Hendra wondered if they'd reached it yet.

Her heels and little toes felt sore from walking in the stiff, unfamiliar Zindedi boots. She touched the pretend marriage necklace at her neck. Sozla wore one, too—fictionally from Doc. Hendra swallowed back an irrational tug of jealousy. Both necklaces had been fashioned on the ship from leather thongs and a few beads. Crude, but serviceable.

She wondered what Dakarra would be like.

The steady clop of urchet hooves and clattering wheels drew up close behind them. Hendra swerved to the road's edge and fell in behind Deccia. Fear sickened her, as it had every time a Zindedi had passed them today. She was afraid someone might order them to stop, or demand to know who they were.

Even more frightening were the military soldiers in the familiar black uniforms with the red, sideways sash across their chests. If those Zindedis had known they were Koblanis, they would all be dead right now.

"It's getting dark," Timaeus muttered to Behran. "If we don't reach Dakarra soon, we'll have to hide."

The cart rumbled closer and Behran unexpectedly turned and raised his arm.

Horror made her gasp. What was he *doing?*

To her relief, the cart didn't slow down.

But then the driver shouted, "Hiy!" And the large wooden vehicle slowed to a stop up ahead. "Yeh?" said the driver. Grizzled white hair curled from beneath his cap. He wore rough brown breeches and a dirty white tunic.

"We're traveling to Dakarra. How much further?"

"Visitors, are yeh?"

"We've come to vacation."

The Zindedi scratched beneath his cap. "'Nother twenty minutes. Maybe more, on foot. Have a place to stay?"

"Not yet."

"Best hurry." He glanced down the road. "Those soldiers a comin' are ready for sport."

"What do you mean?" Deccia said.

"Ah, missy." A faint frown touched his features. "You oughtn't be out. Visitors often mistake the country for being lax."

The fear growing in Hendra impelled her to speak. "What are you talking about?"

"The military don't shoot to kill. But they take their entertainment in other ways, if yeh know what I mean."

Fear knifed through Hendra, and a matching, fine tremor shook Deccia's body.

The man chuckled. "Better than death. Or maybe not."

△ △ △ △ △

What law could they possibly be breaking? Methusal glanced from the disreputable looking man to Mentàll, and hated the fear she felt.

"Relax," Mentàll murmured to her. "All is well." To the driver, he said, "We will reach Carachki by curfew. Your concern is appreciated."

"Iy, it's your head." With a disappointed lip curl, the man snapped the reins and the urchets bolted forward.

"Carachki has a curfew?" She walked a little faster.

"All of Zindedi has a curfew. It has been law ever since their civil war."

"Do the others know?"

"Yes. We spoke of it while you were ill."

In silence, they walked closer to Carachki. The road sloped uphill. Small shacks, painted in faded sea blue, pink, and yellow lined the roads. Weeds clustered around their foundations, and broken carts littered a few front yards.

The road grew firmer and darker the closer they got to Carachki, and as the sun set they entered the city. Trees lined the street, and two story buildings loomed above them. The structures were painted every color of the rainbow, but most were muted colors. Every building looked well kept, and glass shone in the windows, providing tantalizing glimpses of the interiors. Signs advertised a mercantile, a grocer, a baker, and a leather worker.

Tall, black, twisted ore lamps stood on each street corner. The lantern globes were so high that Methusal wondered how people lit them.

Multitudes of carts and urchets crowded the streets, and people...there were so many! All wore beautiful cloth garments. Many of the women wore dresses in soft, multicolored hues. The men's clothing was more utilitarian, with fitted breeches and shirts in single colors.

No one paid the least bit of attention to either Methusal or Mentàll. In their Zindedi clothing, they easily blended in—although she noticed that very few women wore dark pants. She would need to find different clothes if she wanted to blend in better.

A cool ocean breeze drifted up from the harbor, which was three blocks downhill, to the right. The dark blue bay looked enormous. Ships—perhaps twenty or more—were anchored there. More were tied up at the docks.

"Look." Mentàll nudged her arm. "Ahead."

About seven blocks straight ahead a massive structure rose four stories high, and towered above the other buildings in the city. It was painted a dusky tan, and a spire rose from an oddly shaped structure which sat on top of the massive building. Strips of twisted metal barred the high windows, and dark figures with guns paced on the roof. She glimpsed the high wall that surrounded the building.

"Six soldiers," Mentàll murmured.

"Is that the Presidente's palace?"

"Yes," he said shortly. "Here is Feldon Street. We turn left and go north three blocks."

They hiked up the lush, tree-lined lane. The buildings here were smaller than on the main street, and appeared to be individual homes. Flowering bushes bordered the street, and formed a protective barrier between the small, grassy yards and the well-kept cottages.

Mentàll at last stopped in front of a house with a green hedge with thriving, massive yellow blooms bordering the lane. An arched green trellis and gate marked the entry, and beyond it, pink, red, and purple flowers lined the walk to the shadowed front porch.

It looked like a quiet, pleasant place. Nothing at all like the crude Zindedi Commander she had met in Quasr. But this had been his home.

Mentàll unlatched the gate and ducked under the trellis to enter the yard. Methusal followed. The mission was about to begin, and all of a sudden she felt sick with nerves.

"Take my hand," Mentàll told her.

She hesitated, reluctant to begin the lie of their marriage.

"Remember," he said in a low voice, "we are on our honeymoon. We must look happy."

"How can you *do* this?" she whispered. "I thought you hate telling lies."

"For Koblan's sake, I will do anything. For our safety, we must prove this lie to be the truth."

For Koblan. After the barest hesitation, her fingers slid into his large, calloused palm.

His hand curled around hers. "No arguments?"

"I'm ready to work as a team, as long as you keep your word."

"As long as I do not cross the line?"

"You will *not* cross the line."

Amusement glinted, and Methusal actually felt a small bit of relief to see it.

"I would never cross the line with you, Methusal."

She looked away, fighting a small, inexplicable smile. Maybe it was foolish, but she liked this relaxed footing with him better than the cold estrangement that had been simmering for so long. "See that you don't."

Hands interlinked, they climbed the two steps to the porch and Mentàll rapped on the wooden door.

△ △ △ △ △

Tiny, black uniformed soldiers grew larger on the horizon as they marched toward Hendra and the others. The future flashed before her eyes.

The rough band of soldiers surrounded them. "Sun's about to go down," one taunted. Thick brows bristled across his narrow face.

"Move aside," Doc said. His arm settled around Hendra's shoulders. The close contact didn't frighten her. The soldiers, however, with their wide grins and cruel eyes, terrified her.

"No need to tire yourself out," the soldier said. "We've got a cart a comin'. We'll give you a nice ride back to town."

Another soldier choked on laughter.

Horror spiraled in Hendra. How could they escape? There were so many of them...

She swayed, and the world went black.

"Hendra. *Hendra!*"

She opened her eyes and saw Doc's worried face. Deccia and Sozla hovered overhead, too. Her shoulder hurt. She was lying on the ground.

The soldiers hadn't arrived yet. This fact penetrated her foggy brain. And the old man's cart was still here.

In the background, Behran spoke. "We'd be obliged for a ride."

"Ye'would, would yeh?" Interest brightened the man's mumble. "I might help yeh. For a price," he added craftily.

"How much?"

"Fifty dascals."

"Too much."

The old man shrugged, and slapped the reins. The urchets surged forward.

"Behran, pay it!" Hendra cried out.

The man pulled on the reins and glanced back expectantly.

Behran frowned. "Are you sure? It's not far..."

"Pay it, Behran," Doc said quietly.

Behran dug into his pack and paid the man.

Hendra felt foolish to have fainted from a panic attack. She accepted Doc's helping hand up and brushed off her clothes. Her cheeks felt warm, and she averted her gaze from the others.

A few moments later, all six Rolbanis climbed into the cart and the man slapped the reins. The cart jolted down the lane.

Hendra sat wedged between Doc and Deccia. Behran perched next to the driver, making small talk.

"You had a flash?" Doc spoke in a low voice.

"Yes. The soldiers..." She shivered, and couldn't go on.

"Ten are coming," Deccia murmured.

The orange, burning crescent of the sun hovered low on the pastoral horizon now.

As the soldiers drew closer, Hendra finally spotted the low buildings of Dakarra in the distance.

The soldiers glanced at them as they passed. The leader had a narrow face and black, bristling eyebrows. The man from her flash.

With a shudder, she closed her eyes. Doc's warm arm against her own felt solid and secure. After a moment, she realized she'd leaned into him for comfort. Carefully, she pulled away. He didn't appear to have noticed, thank goodness. She didn't want to send him mixed signals. She was mixed up enough for the both of them.

"My wife rents cabins," the old man told Behran. "They belonged to her father."

"Really? We need to rent two."

"In town? Outside town?"

"Somewhere quiet."

"Eh. I know the place." He jerked his chin over his shoulder. "Those two want a cabin of their own?" His chuckle sounded rusty. "Newlyweds, right?"

With a frown, Behran glanced back at Hendra and the others. "You mean Deccia and..."

"I mean the pretty blond and the red-headed fella. Been a while since I treated m'wife with such tender care."

Heat, and then ice washed over Hendra's skin. The man was mistaken. "I'm sorr..."

"You have a discerning eye," Doc interrupted calmly.

The man guffawed again and slapped the reins harder.

Hendra wasn't sure how to wrap her head around this new development. She'd barely adjusted to the idea of a fake marriage to Behran, and now suddenly she and Doc were supposed to be married? Her gaze met Doc's, so close to her own.

His blue eyes looked calm. Quietly, he said, "It will be no different."

Than if he were Behran. And yet it *was* different.

She nodded. Even though it was a lie, she felt strangely connected to him now. As if she belonged to him. In the eyes of the Zindedi, she would.

Panic skittered through her insides.

It's only make believe. Calm down.

△ △ △ △ △

Methusal waited with baited breath for someone to open the door. What would the Commander's widow be like? A razor toothed wild beast? Smelly and unwashed, like her dead husband? And yet the yard looked so clean and well kept.

No one answered the door.

"Maybe she's not home."

Mentàll knocked harder.

Tiny clicks sounded, and she sharpened her hearing into kaavl. "She's coming. Five lengths away." She glanced up and discovered that Mentàll had affixed a pleasant smile upon his face. It looked so out of character that she almost laughed. But when the doorknob turned, she quickly applied a matching one.

The door swung open to reveal a short, round woman with curly gray hair. She wore a pale green dress which was covered by a flowered apron. She wiped floured hands on her apron. "Yes?" Black, alert eyes peered out of a round face with a small nose, and her mouth was bracketed by deep lines.

"I am Lozar. This is my wife, Midi. We're from Dakarra, and newly married. An acquaintance said you have a room to rent for a week or two?"

"Dakarra." The woman wiped her fingers again on the apron. "Haven't been there in a time. Who is your acquaintance?"

"Danyl Kir," Mentàll said smoothly. Obviously, it was a name he had gleaned after poring over the ships' records. "He died in the war, alongside your husband. We would like to express condolences for your loss, Matron Machblin."

"Danyl." A smile sparkled in the woman's black eyes. "A fine young man. I'm sorry to hear of his death. And thank you for your condolences." Her small mouth pursed. "How long did you know Danyl?"

"Not for long. We trained together in Dakarra, but I fought in the south of Koblan during the war, and returned safely. Danyl did not, I was sorry to learn."

"Yes." The woman gave Mentàll a long, searching look, and then glanced at Methusal. Her face softened. "And you a new bride. I see the nerves in your eyes. My man was always uprooting me and dragging me thither and yon."

"We would like to make a good beginning for our marriage," Mentàll said. "We only want a quiet spot where we can spend time together."

"And I've always wanted to visit the city," Methusal interjected. "Lozar has promised to show me the sights." It would probably be a good idea to let Matron Machblin know that they'd be out often.

"Of course." A small smile lit those dark eyes. She moved aside. "Well, come on in. The room is available. It's five hundred dascals per week."

Mentàll pulled off his pack and counted out the bills into the woman's palm. Her smile seemed to relax when her fingers curled around the money. "You may call me Mrn. M."

"Thank you for letting us stay here," Methusal said softly. She still didn't have a good read on the woman, and sensed that taking things slowly and talking softly might be the best bet. "I was worried your room might be filled. I wasn't sure where we'd go."

"Well, of course." Mrn. Machblin's eyes softened still more. "I have a daughter about your age. She moved north a while back. It will be nice to have you here."

Methusal smiled. "Thank you."

"Well, come." Mrn. Machblin bustled across the small living room, which was floored in flat, rectangular stones. A door to the immediate left led to the kitchen, and beyond this was a small, open dining area. After this a hall led left, to the back of the house. Mrn. Machblin, however, moved straight ahead and opened a door leading directly off of the living room.

Bright sunshine spilled into a large room through a wide window curtained by soft white drapes. This floor was made of flat, smooth stones too, and a wide bed dominated the right side of the room. It was covered in a quilt made of soft blue and yellow colors. Another quilt lay folded at the foot of the massive bed. To the left, a door led into a small, boxy chamber. Mrn. Machblin hurried toward this.

"This is the bath," she said, with obvious pride. The spotless room contained a small relief bench, and a high wash basin with spigots. But its main feature was a large, white tub. Spigots arched over this, too.

Mrn. Machblin smiled. "We have running water. Every morning Gorj heats a big caldron, and we have enough for baths. Use the left tap for hot, and the right for cold. When it drains, it flushes away the relief chamber deposits."

Methusal didn't have to fake her amazement. "I've never seen such luxury! I mean, I've seen cold running water, but never hot."

"Yes." Pleasure pinkened Mrn. Machblin's face. "My husband was high in the Presidente's command. These small luxuries were a benefit of his position."

Methusal began to relax. What a nice place this was. Much better than she had expected.

Mrn. Machblin bustled back out. "Your room includes meals, of course. Breakfast and dinner. But seeing I didn't expect you..."

"We'll buy something for dinner," Methusal said quickly. "Don't worry."

"I have pie, if you'd like to come back for dessert."

"That would be wonderful."

"Well." Mrn. Machblin smiled. "Towels and linens are in the hall closet. Gorj washes clothes twice a week. Just put them in that basket in the corner."

"Thank you." Mentàll spoke. His voice sounded harsh in the small room. "We appreciate your kind hospitality."

"Of course." Mrn. Machblin glanced from him to Methusal. "I wish you both the best." With that odd comment, she left them and clicked the door closed.

"She seems nice," Methusal ventured. "Nothing like her husband."

"She is a Zindedi. We cannot trust her. Ever."

"Of course not. But we can be friendly."

"I will be charm itself to Mrn. Machblin."

Methusal smiled at that unlikely picture.

Mentàll carried his pack to the other side of the room, near the window.

Methusal eyed the wide bed with trepidation. Her fake husband now sat on the far side and tucked a wad of money into a secure pocket in the inner leg of his breeches. Although the room and bed were large and spacious, both appeared dwarfed by the Dehrien Chief's large frame.

"I assume we'll take turns sleeping on the bed," she said into the silence.

He looked over his shoulder and his lips twitched. "No."

Her mouth opened immediately in shock. "You promised to give me privacy. You said you wouldn't lay a hand on me."

"I will not. You will be safe. This bed is huge, Methusal. It is more than big enough for both of us."

"You have *got* to be joking."

"No." His voice sounded cool.

"I will not sleep on that bed with you."

"Why? You think you would be unfaithful to Behran if you lie here with me? Beside me," he corrected. Methusal did not imagine the evil smile he quickly straightened out of his lips.

So, already the torment would begin. "Fine. You take the bed, you selfish beast. I'll sleep on the floor."

The humor left his eyes. "It is just a place to sleep. I promise I will not touch you."

"No thank you. The floor will be fine. It will just be like during the war."

After a moment, he stood to face her. "I promise I will not lay a hand on you. You can either trust me, or choose not to. But I will not sleep on the floor just because of your misplaced fear in me."

"Misplaced fear? You've been my enemy for three years! And now I'm suddenly supposed to trust you?"

"I thought our relationship had grown during the war."

"I grew to know you better," she agreed. "But not to trust you."

He turned abruptly. "So be it."

△ △ △ △ △

On the far edge of Dakarra, Hendra and the others filed into a small, brown building. Their footsteps echoed on the wooden floor. The damp, acrid scent of boiled vegetables lingered in the air.

Only a desk, lit by a lamp, occupied the narrow, shallow room. It appeared that most of the building lay beyond a closed door in the back.

A woman sat at the desk. Black and gray streaked her hair, which was pulled into a bun, and her dark blue dress accentuated her sharp, bony shoulders. The cart driver had said her name was Vitnia. Glasses made her eyes look small, and her mouth looked pinched. "Nygev, what have you brought me?"

"Yeh'll thank me, woman. Customers."

"Customers, hmm." Her eyes sharpened. "See to the urchet. I'll take care of them."

Nygev didn't seem to mind being dismissed so rudely. With a cheerful whistle, he shut the door behind him.

Behran spoke. "We'd like to rent two cabins."

"How much money do you want to spend?"

"We'd like to stay somewhere quiet."

"Near the beach? That's more."

"No."

The woman's mouth pinched even tighter. "I have a property at the edge of the forest. It's a good twenty minute walk from town."

"How much?"

Vitnia eyed him for a moment. "Five hundred dascals."

Hendra drew a breath of relief. Between the six of them, they had two thousand dascals stashed. Tabor and the others had a little more.

The woman's sharp voice cut into her thoughts. "That's each cabin. Per week."

Hendra glanced quickly at Behran. It was too much. Especially if they ended up staying two or more weeks.

Sozla unexpectedly stepped forward. "The amenities. What do you offer for such a steep price? You have food stocked in the cabins?"

"Of course not. Linens and cooking utensils are provided."

Behran pulled a slip of paper from his pack. "Where can we find Sindhl?"

The woman frowned harder. "You don't want to see that no good laze about."

"I've been told he rents cabins for two hundred dascals apiece."

Vitnia snorted. "If you want to live with insects."

"A little cleaning does not frighten us," Sozla said. "We cannot pay five hundred dascals per cabin."

The Zindedi woman said nothing for a moment.

"Perhaps we should go?"

Vitnia cast Sozla a grudging look of respect, and then turned her attention to Behran. "Your wife drives a hard bargain. Three hundred dascals per week. But you must pay for two weeks, and you must pay all of the money now." She let that sink in. "Twelve hundred dascals total." A small smile curved her thin lips.

Behran pulled off his pack and counted out all the money he had. Doc offered some, and so did Timaeus. To an outside observer, it might appear that Vitnia had bled them dry.

Vitnia licked her fingers and counted the bills. Twice. Then she neatly stacked them. "Turn right on the street when you exit. Take your third left. Walk until you see a hill with a forest behind it. The cabins are at the top."

"But what about the soldiers?" Deccia said. "It's almost dark."

The woman's small smile looked unpleasant. "Where are you from, again?"

"Carachki."

"My brother owns a boardinghouse. Stay with him if you want to feel safe."

"Thank you," Behran said into the awkward silence. Vitnia's suggestion had sounded more contemptuous than solicitous.

The woman said nothing, so Doc led the Koblani team outside. "I think we should go to the cabins now."

Fear crawled into Hendra's throat, threatening to suffocate her. "But the soldiers..."

Doc's steady gaze found hers. "Vitnia clearly doesn't think they're a threat."

"I disagree. Those soldiers were dangerous. I felt it."

"We have ten minutes until dark," Timaeus spoke up. "Besides, we'll probably be walking on a country road. The soldiers will probably stay on the main road."

"Let's do it," Behran agreed.

Hendra wanted to argue, but the men headed down the street, per Vitnia's instructions.

It *was* a rough country road, she soon discovered. Little more than two rutted paths with crushed weeds between them. Darkness descended swiftly, and only a sliver of Ryon's green light lit their path. Every rustle in the high weeds sent a shiver of fear down her spine.

It sounded like someone was following them. Hendra stopped twice, and strained her ears to listen. If only Methusal was here, she'd be able to tell not only what it was, but how far away it was.

Deccia stopped with her the second time. "What is it?" she whispered.

"I hear something."

They both stood still and listened. Grasses rustled. It was impossible to tell if it was caused by the rippling breeze, or by soldiers creeping up on them.

Deccia hurried forward and touched Timaeus' arm. "Let's hurry."

They jogged for the last five minutes, which was just fine with Hendra. Unfortunately, her feet burned more with each step. She couldn't wait to take off the infernal Zindedi boots.

"I see a hill," Doc called out.

A moment later she also saw the two dark, squat structures on top of the hill.

Doc and Behran cut uphill and mashed a path through the high grass for the others to follow. The first cabin was the smallest, and was about two lengths by three. The front door faced the forest, which bristled high on the next hill, to the south. A creek ran through the little valley below, glinting silvery green in the moonlight.

Doc rattled the door handle. "Locked."

Locked! Why hadn't Vitnia given them the key? After the long, wearing day, frustration made Hendra's temper spark. "Knock it down."

Doc shot her a surprised glance. A smile tugged at his lips. "Didn't know a wild beast lived inside you, Hendra."

"Maybe we can pick the lock," Deccia suggested.

"I've tried that back home," Behran said. "It's tough to impossible."

"Anyone have a wire?" Doc asked.

Timaeus produced a short length from his pack. "Runners are always prepared."

Doc went down on one knee and threaded the wire into the dark, shadowed keyhole. Head cocked, as if he was listening for something, his sensitive physician fingers delicately probed the lock. "Got it," he said softly. The door swung open to reveal a pitch black room.

"I see a lamp."

A moment later, a firestick flared in the dark, illuminating a lantern hanging from an overhead beam. Doc lit it. The sharp scent of smoke drifted to her nostrils.

The warm glow lit the small room. A crude counter with a stove and sink occupied the left side of the room, and a table with a couch and three chairs were arranged to the right. An open door straight ahead led to another room. Probably a bedroom. The brown curtains at the windows looked insect bitten, and a fine layer of dust covered everything.

"Let's check out the other cabin." Doc led the way, wire in hand. But that door was unlocked.

The second cabin was much larger than the first, although it was just as dirty. Couches and chairs upholstered in a nubby brown fabric furnished the main, large room. A door to the left led to a large kitchen furnished with a table and chairs. From the kitchen a door opened outside, leading to a small porch littered with rickety chairs. Back in the main, large sitting room, two doors led to bedrooms. One was larger than the other. Cots furnished both rooms, and each was topped with blankets. Hendra uneasily wondered how clean they were.

Right now, however, her body demanded a different kind of relief.

"I saw a small building down the hill," Sozla said. "Perhaps it is the relief chamber."

"How about all of us girls take a trip down there," Deccia proposed.

The relief hut smelled awful. Hendra took care of business, and then waited for the others outside in the darkness.

Deep in the forest a flying beast screeched, and she shivered. And then...was that that *rustling* sound again?

A twig broke a length away.

The large, dark shape of a man loomed out of the darkness.

She screamed.

△ △ △ △ △

Methusal's stomach rumbled as they entered a small shop which advertised fresh food. Just like in Mrn. Machblin's house, smooth stones paved the floor. The walls were painted a burnt yellow, and twelve tables, flanked by chairs, filled the room. Most were occupied. The sign near the door said to seat themselves. The aroma of freshly baked bread, savory stew, and grilled meat filled her nostrils.

The Dehrien Chief pulled out a chair out for her, and he waited for her to sit before sitting opposite her.

A man shortly appeared with a cold pitcher of water and he filled their mugs. Ice tinkled against the pottery as he poured.

Methusal guessed the man was their server. This was a new experience. She'd never been in a shop before that served food. She'd always eaten in the dining hall in Rolban, or around a campfire during the war.

The server put a crisp parchment in her hand. "The menu." He bowed and left them.

The ornate writing on the parchment described all sorts of mouthwatering dishes: tubers and baked slug monster, filet of urchet, and fish and salad. She had no idea how much money Mentàll had. It cost twelve dascals for a meal. Four more for a drink. Methusal decided to try the fish, and when the waiter returned, she said water would be fine for her. Mentàll chose the filet and water, also.

It all seemed so civilized. She glanced around the room after the waiter left, and noted the pairings of men and women at the tables. All were dressed nicely, and many shared intimate smiles. As if being in this shop was a special treat for them.

All of them were *couples*. Methusal felt even more uncomfortable. She glanced at Mentàll. His white shirt still looked crisp and fresh against his tanned skin. Reluctantly, she acknowledged that other women might think her long-time enemy was a handsome man. Certainly the Zindedis would believe they were a married couple. Her discomfort increased. She was grateful when the waiter placed a dish of colorful vegetables before her, because it distracted her from her present train of thought.

"Looks delicious," she murmured.

Mentàll thanked the waiter and picked up his fork. When the man left, he said, "You are disturbed. Why?"

Methusal had no intention of telling him her true thoughts. She forked up a tender red vegetable. It tasted sweet. "Mrn. Machblin seemed suspicious of you."

"She would not have rented the room to me if I had been alone. The plan is working."

She nodded.

"You will need to make friends with her."

"What about you?"

"I will make an attempt to charm her."

She smiled, because she couldn't help herself. "Oh, that's your strength."

"Do not underestimate me."

"Never. I *never* underestimate you."

Those ice blue eyes held hers, and a tiny smile curled his mouth, too. "I am pleased to hear it."

"You enjoy pushing me to walk the fine edge of the cliff, don't you?"

"Yes."

So he admitted that he liked to needle under her skin. "Do you *like* being a problem to me?"

"You need to stay alert. I am happy to walk that fine edge with you."

She couldn't tell exactly what he meant by that comment. So she changed the subject. "What's the next step?"

"Tomorrow we will tour our main objective."

Of course, he couldn't speak plainly in public.

The waiter arrived and placed large meat platters before them. Delicious smelling steam wafted to Methusal's nostrils, making her mouth water.

"Will we make an early start?"

His smile widened. "I think honeymooners sleep in."

Her face warmed. Keeping her tone even, she said, "I told Mrn. Machblin that I want to tour Carachki. I'll make it clear that's my main objective."

"And I have made it clear that I want to spend time with my beautiful wife."

Heat washed over her skin. "*Stop it.*" She glanced over her shoulder. "You don't have to pretend. No one is listening."

"You do not like it when I say you are beautiful?"

"Of course not. It's totally unnecessary."

"But you are beautiful. Most men in this shop have glanced at you several times."

She sipped water to cover her confusion. "They have not."

"Do I ever lie, Methusal?"

"This whole *cover* is a lie," she hissed.

"Perhaps." His gaze gleamed with amusement, and slowly drifted down her face. "But I am telling you the truth, Methusal. You are beautiful. Accept it or not."

She flushed. What was wrong with her? She was *providing* him with opportunities to needle under her skin. Silently, she ate. Near the end of the meal she made the mistake of glancing up, and found him watching her with a pleased glint in his eyes.

She cut her gaze away when the waiter placed the bill on the table. Mentàll paid, and in silence they left the small shop and entered the dark street. Only streetlamps lit the block. It was quiet outside. The breeze from the harbor felt cold, and she shivered, wishing she had brought her coat. At least Mrn. Machblin's house was only a few blocks away. She wondered about the curfew. Did it apply only outside the city, or in Carachki, as well? The other diners hadn't seemed in any hurry to leave.

In silence, they walked back up the hill.

When they were on their new landlady's porch, the Dehrien Chief's large, warm hand took hers. "Appearances," he muttered, and opened the door.

A fire burned in the grate, casting a warm glow over the yellow couch and blue chair where Mrn. Machblin sat working on a tapestry. Two cups and saucers sat on the small table before her. It appeared that she'd had a visitor while they were away.

"Oh!" That lady jabbed the needle into the fabric. "You're back. I promised dessert. Would you like a piece of pie?"

It sounded like a wonderful idea to Methusal for a number of reasons. One was that she did not want to enter the bedchamber with the Dehrien Chief. Not yet. She wasn't ready yet—as if she ever would be. "Sounds wonderful.'"

"I have berry pie." Mrn. Machblin hurried toward the kitchen. "Take a seat at the table."

Methusal followed her. "Can I help?"

A small smile flashed. "Aren't you a sweet one. You can help carry the plates."

An easy enough task. Methusal carried the two dishes, each heaped with a large slice of pie. One for her, and one for her fake husband. Their hostess had insisted that she'd already eaten, but she joined them at the table.

"What sights do you want to see?"

Methusal quickly jumped on this topic. "The whole city. I can't wait. I'd like to get an early start tomorrow morning."

"One day you'll have to visit the Presidente's gardens. They're lovely this time of year."

"The Presidente's gardens? You mean anyone can visit?"

"Of course." Mrn. Machblin smiled. "He donated the land to the city. They're kept in pristine condition. He loves flowers. Fruit trees, too."

Interesting. A bloodthirsty dictator loved green, living things.

Methusal asked a few questions about Mrn. Machblin's garden. The Zindedi woman seemed to love flowers, too. A bouquet of fresh orange blossoms rested in the center of the table. She couldn't remember if they had been there earlier.

With a yawn, their hostess finally left them. Since Methusal had insisted that she would clean up, she took the empty dishes to the kitchen and washed them.

A lamp cast a warm glow in the small kitchen. A large window faced the front walk, and painted pottery canisters lined the counters, making the room feel homey. So did the flower print curtains, and the small table and chairs in the corner.

She wondered about Mrn. Machblin and her husband. Much as the Commander had seemed horrific to Methusal, surely he'd had a good side, if Mrn. Machblin loved him so much. And she must have, because during the conversation she'd said they'd been married for twenty-five years, and she'd smiled whenever she'd spoken of him. She seemed lonely.

Methusal again wondered if someone had visited earlier. Then she wondered why she was so curious. Back home, she wouldn't think twice about extra cups out. Friends came to call all the time.

The silence in the kitchen comforted her unsettled spirit. The new country, the new living situation—not to mention being in close company with her enemy all day.

It was time.

Methusal folded the dish towel, blew out the lamp, and with reluctant steps left her quiet sanctuary. Darkness shrouded the living room now, except for the orange embers in the grate. A sliver of warm light spilled from their partially open bedroom door.

The Dehrien Chief sat on the bed, writing notes on a small scrap of paper. He glanced up. "You did well. She likes you."

"Thank you." She slowly untied her pack. Her long, warm nightgown, which was long-sleeved and high-necked, would be perfectly decent. While that was true, she still felt uncomfortable about wearing the thin garment all night alone with the Dehrien Chief. The idea made her feel vulnerable.

Mentàll rustled in his pack on the other side of the bed.

Time to stop stalling. She clutched her nightgown to her chest and straightened at the same time he did. In one swift motion, Mentàll stripped off his shirt. His powerful shoulders gleamed golden in the lamplight.

She froze. When he turned toward her, the warm glow revealed sleekly sculpted chest muscles. Of course she had seen him shirtless many times during the war, when she had cared for his injury. But that had been months ago.

She could not seem to look away. "Don't take off your clothes in front of me." To her chagrin, her voice was a horrified squeak.

"It bothers you?"

She did not like his smile. "Of course it bothers me." She averted her eyes. "You're half naked."

"I like to sleep naked."

Heat swamped her face. Fiercely, she said, "Well, you won't here!"

After a slow, maddening moment, he lifted a thinner tunic from the bed and pulled it on. "I will not, since it bothers you so much."

So, he'd never planned to sleep naked in the first place.

Methusal escaped into the bathroom, trembling a little with exasperation. That *man*. He got under her skin much too easily. And he clearly relished every moment of it.

Quickly, she changed, but she ignored him when she left the bath chamber. After putting her clothes away, she pulled the extra quilt from the end of the bed and folded it on the floor on her side of the bed. A pillow, and she was ready for the night. She stretched out on the hard floor. Even with the quilt doubled, the stones bit uncomfortably into her hip and shoulder. It was definitely a much harder and unforgiving surface than the earth she had slept on during the Quasr War. She pulled a small edge of the blanket over herself and closed her eyes.

Her enemy said nothing. After a moment, the light went out.

It was cold. She pulled more of the quilt over her. As a consequence, the stones bit more sharply into her flesh.

After a while, she heard his quiet, deep breaths. He was asleep.

One day was finished.

She lay there, stones digging into her flesh, until exhaustion overtook her.

∆ ∆ ∆ ∆ ∆

The huge, black shape of the man loomed out of the darkness. Hendra let out another blood curdling scream.

The relief hut door slammed. "What is wrong?" Sozla exclaimed.

A deep, dark laugh rolled from the horrifying figure. To Hendra's terrified mind, it sounded evil, as if from the very devil himself.

"I've caught me a little apte." Riln's familiar voice registered. He laughed loudly again.

"Hendra!" Doc shouted. Dark shapes ran down the hill.

Hendra still felt petrified. And then she felt foolish.

Finally, she felt furious. "How *dare* you frighten me like that?" she shouted, surprising even herself. Her whole body trembled. "I thought you were a soldier!"

Riln laughed again. "It's a joke. Can't you take a joke?"

Shaking, Hendra shoved by him and marched up the hill. Inside the brightly lit cabin, she stood still, arms crossed, hugging herself tightly. Tears hovered. Riln had made a fool of her.

Footsteps sounded on the front steps and she slipped into the kitchen.

"That was cruel, Riln." Timaeus' voice sounded hard.

"It was just a joke. She's an apte girl. She needs to toughen up."

Hendra felt the violent urge to grab a pan and pop Riln over the head with it.

Deccia slipped into the kitchen. "Hendra? Are you all right?"

"I feel embarrassed." Hands trembling, she pumped water into a mug. "Otherwise, I'm fine."

"He's a whip. Forget him."

"I know." How could her voice sound so steady? Inside, pieces of her felt shattered. The familiar, dark fear urged her to run and hide in one of the dark bedrooms and lick her wounds until she felt better. But she knew that she had to pretend to feel completely the opposite. If for nothing else than to prove Riln wrong. She knew men like him. Bullies. Her brother Jascr had been one. He'd taught her a very important lesson—never let an enemy know her fear. Because then he'd use that fear to manipulate her, and to wield power over her whenever the fancy took him.

No. She couldn't run. Instead, she had to put on the performance of a lifetime.

Carefully, she placed the mug on the counter. Her fingers still trembled a little, but that couldn't be helped. She glanced at Deccia, who was frowning. "I'm fine," she said quietly. She forced her legs to move for the door to the living room. A dead calm enveloped her, and a bit of the old ice that used to protect her heart cooled her nerves.

She stepped into the sitting room, where Riln was still laughing, but a bit of red tinged his features. Doc was speaking to him in a low voice, with a clenched jaw.

Riln laughed again and shrugged, as if to dismiss Doc's comments. He spotted her. His dark eyes looked black, and they glittered. "Well, here she is. The apte herself."

"Hendra," Doc said, but she ignored him. Instead, she moved as close to Riln as her trembling legs would allow, and locked her gaze with his.

"Do not *ever* treat me with such contempt again." She allowed a small pause to elapse. "Only a small man frightens other people."

"Well." He still smiled, but it was smaller. "The apte has spunk."

"My name is *Hendra*. Use it." After holding his gaze for another long moment, she looked for a comfortable chair to sit on. Relaxing into it, she surveyed the tableau of people calmly, as if she did not feel foolish, embarrassed, and, most importantly, afraid. Of anyone.

Riln continued to watch her, as if trying to gauge the sincerity of her performance. She gazed right back, allowing only cool disinterest to color her expression. Finally, he looked away. He told the others, "I need a hot drink. We've got a load of information about the military base."

For the first time, Hendra noticed that Goric and Tabor had arrived, as well. Most people followed Riln into the kitchen.

Doc he knelt beside her chair. "Great job, Hendra." Pride gleamed in his gaze. "He won't bother you again."

"I hope not." For the first time since leaving the kitchen, her voice trembled.

His hand covered hers and gripped it gently. "You're a strong woman. I know it, and now Riln knows it." His sudden smile warmed her shivering heart. "Come with me into the kitchen."

Hendra suddenly didn't feel so alone anymore. Instead, she felt grateful. She smiled. "Thank you."

CHAPTER EIGHTEEN

WHEN METHUSAL WOKE UP, her hip and shoulder hurt. She was also freezing. Sometime during the night she had wrapped the entire quilt around her body, which left little padding against the stone floor. Her bones had pressed so hard against the floor all night long that it felt like she had bruises from the inside out. She winced as she sat up, and pulled the quilt more tightly around herself to try to keep out the morning chill.

Soft, muffled movements came from behind her. Mentàll.

Was he getting dressed? Her cheeks instantly warmed in embarrassment. That would be just like him. He seemed to get some sort of perverse sort of satisfaction in getting under her skin.

Well, she wouldn't sit here, hiding, until he showed himself fully clothed. If he wanted to strip to the altogether, he'd have to endure her gaze. Not that she *wanted* to look at him, of course. Her skin flushed even warmer. But she would not be intimidated by him. Maybe he'd even feel embarrassed.

Pain flashed in her joints as she arose. She glanced over at the Dehrien Chief and drew a quick breath of relief. He wore a beige shirt and tan breeches, and stood rifling through his pack on the bed. He glanced up. "You are awake."

"Yes." She wondered how long he'd been up. His wet blond hair stood up in spikes, and the fresh scent of soap drifted to her. A bath. It sounded heavenly. Taking a full bath had been impossible on the ship. Methusal folded the quilt back onto the bed, so Mrn. M wouldn't know she'd slept on the floor.

"We will leave soon."

"Will we scout the military base today? And tomorrow the Presidente's compound?"

"Yes. Wear tan garments. It will help us blend into the landscape today."

"Okay." After gathering up her clothes, she retreated into the relief room. She turned the bone colored handles and water gushed into the tub, linking together the drops left behind from Mentàll's bath.

She struggled not to think of his powerful frame submerged in the water just moments before. She dropped in a few bath crystals and watched them fizz into clouds of soapy bubbles. Happy anticipation grew with them. She couldn't wait to get clean. Hastily, she pulled off her nightgown.

A sharp rap came at the door. Methusal froze with her nightgown pooled at her feet. She crossed her arms.

"Mrn. M says breakfast is ready," he said harshly.

"I'll be quick." She slipped into the tub and took a regrettably short, but thorough bath. A few minutes later she joined the Dehrien and Mrn. Machblin in the dining room. That lady had cooked a feast of eggs, fried meat, and warm toast with preserves.

"Thank you! It looks delicious," Methusal exclaimed.

"My wife has a healthy appetite," Mentàll said. He sent her an intense, searing look. "Don't you, sweet lips?"

Methusal sputtered, and juice dribbled down her chin. Quickly, she mopped up the liquid.

Amusement glittered. The wild beast. He turned to Mrn. Machblin with a smile. "Midi is embarrassed when I speak of my love for her in public."

Her face felt red hot. "Mrn. Machblin doesn't want to hear..."

"Nonsense." Mrn. Machblin waved a hand. A little pink touched her cheeks. "It's healthy for a couple to speak their love to one another. I'm not embarrassed at all. Sometimes my Charlie would do the very same thing. At first I felt self-conscious and wanted to smack him, but it made me love him all the more."

Methusal felt it was high time to change the subject. "Your husband sounds like a wonderful man. What was he like?"

"Oh my, aren't you sweet to ask." She smiled. "He was rough on the outside—some even believed he was hard and cruel. It was all an act, though. It was the only way he could climb the military ladder. He had high aspirations, did my Charlie."

Methusal remembered she'd heard the Commander say in Quasr that he wanted to take over General Greisn's position. A feat only possible by the General's death. How far would he have taken the *act,* as Mrn. M claimed? Or had his home life been the true deception? Much like Mentàll's fiction was right now.

"Inside, he was as soft and cuddly as a pillow," Mrn. M went on. "Of a night, we'd sit by the fire and he'd hold me until it burned low." She brushed a tear from the corner of her eye.

"I'm sorry," Methusal said softly. Although she had no idea what the Commander had truly been like, Mrn. M had obviously loved him with her whole heart.

"Ach. Well." She stood. "It's time to clean up. Will you be back for supper tonight?"

Methusal glanced at the Dehrien Chief.

"Yes," he said. "Thank you for breakfast."

A dimple flashed. "You are more than welcome."

Moments later, Methusal and Mentàll left the cottage. Neither carried a pack. Once out of sight of the house, Mentàll retrieved two items from a concealed pocket in the thigh of his breeches and handed them to her. "Hide these. You may need them."

A folded wad of dascal notes and a small, sharp looking knife. She eyed the latter with revulsion. During the Quasr War she had killed two men. She never wanted to kill anyone else again.

"You did not bring your knife, did you?"

He knew her too well. "I won't kill again."

"You will kill, if necessary. Take it, for your own protection."

She stared at it. The knife looked small in his large palm, but she knew the damage it could inflict. It could slice into someone's throat, just like...

With a shudder, she said, "No. I'll take the money, but you keep the knife."

"Methusal."

"I said *no.*" She walked faster in the direction of the military base, which was located in the northwest.

His fingers caught hers, which shocked her into stopping in her tracks. The Dehrien Chief's stronger ones flattened out her palm.

Ire rose. "I *said...*"

He pushed the dascal notes into her palm. Her fingers curled around the money. He held her gaze for another long moment, and then he released her. "Tomorrow you will carry the knife."

Although her temper simmered, she said nothing. If she'd learned one thing during the Quasr War, it was to choose her battles with care with the Dehrien. Although she may not want to carry the knife, it was a small issue. She'd carry it, and save her energy for the matters that were truly important.

She put the money in a hidden pocket and followed the Dehrien's long strides toward Carachki's military base. Her nerves thrummed with tension the closer they came, and she wondered if she would need the knife after all.

△ △ △ △ △

Hendra slept fairly well, although her skin itched wherever the blanket had touched her. Today she'd beat it outside. Wash it, too, if possible.

Pale morning sunlight streamed through the dirty window panes, which were framed by bedraggled curtains. One corner was frayed, as if gnawed off by a hungry rodent. She hadn't seen any so far, but in this filthy cabin, who knew.

Sozla had already left the room, so Hendra hurried to get dressed.

A sweet smell welcomed her nose when she opened the door. Another delicious scent, of something being cooked, mingled with it, too. Although the living room was empty, she heard voices in the kitchen.

What could those delicious aromas be? They'd eaten the last of their rations last night, and would need to buy food today.

"Morning, Hendra," Deccia said. Tired lines scored her mouth, and purple circles shadowed her eyes. She must not have slept well. The Rolbani girl set plates and forks on the table, where Goric sat alone. Sozla stood at the stove, stirring something in a large, flat pan, and Timaeus and Doc waited in line behind Behran at the counter. He poured steaming water into a mug.

Tagma juice! That was the sweet smell. Powdered tagma berries steamed in hot water. Hendra grabbed a mug and stepped in behind Timaeus. "What's Sozla making?"

Riln strode into the kitchen, exuding aggression and vitality.

She stiffened her spine, determined not to shrink away from him.

"Tabor and Riln found eggs this morning."

"Where? In the fields?"

Riln laughed loudly. "No. We relieved a farmer of his choicest eggs."

Hendra felt aghast, but Deccia spoke before she could. "You *stole* those eggs?"

Riln shrugged. "He won't know how many are missing."

"Let's buy our food from now on," Behran said. "We don't want the locals to get upset with us. Remember, we need to keep a low profile."

Derision curled Riln's lips. "The Zindedis must learn to fear us."

"We are on a peace mission, Riln." Warning sounded in Behran's tone.

"Are we?" He bared his teeth in a smile. "We're here to discover how to crush them."

"Peace is our first goal."

He shrugged. "Fool yourself, Behran. But I see clearly. I know my true mission."

Timaeus spoke. "If you do something stupid, you'll sabotage our mission."

Riln rolled his eyes.

Behran said, "We will live at peace with the Zindedis while we're here, Riln."

"I'll keep quiet until the time is right. For now I can pretend to be an apte just as well as you can."

Red flushed Behran's face. His fingers clenched white around his mug, but he kept his temper. "See that you do."

An uncomfortable silence followed. Doc headed for the table with his steaming drink. Hendra glimpsed the creamy scrambled eggs Sozla stirred in the pan. Her stomach rumbled.

"Hungry?" Riln's elbow jabbed into her side.

Shock slackened her jaw. Then fierce terror billowed. All reason left her mind, except for the need to flee.

Riln's dark side glance slowly pierced the fog. He was watching her, testing her reaction.

He'd lost the power struggle with Behran. This logical thought trickled in, but her lungs felt tight, and she struggled to breathe normally. Riln wanted to gain power over her, instead. She sucked in a shallow breath. Her face felt frozen, but survival, learned hard and well over the years from Jascr, made her jaw tighten. "Show some manners. Step off."

He laughed and cut ahead of her in line, taking the spot Timaeus had just vacated.

Although that was rude too, Hendra ignored it. Another lesson learned from her awful brother—unless directly attacked, ignore your enemy. When Riln learned he couldn't get a rise out of her, he'd leave her alone. She hoped.

She also hoped Riln's mission took him far away today.

△ △ △ △ △

"You had another nightmare, didn't you?" Timaeus' hand on Deccia's shoulder stopped her from leaving their bedroom. Breakfast was done, and she, Timaeus, Doc, and Sozla were about to travel to town for supplies. The other members of the team had just left to scout the military base.

"Yes." No sense denying it. Timaeus read her too easily. Last night's had been a particularly bad one, and had probably been inspired by seeing the soldiers on the road last night. Their uniforms, their sneer—all of it had reminded her of General Greisn.

"Why didn't you wake me?"

Love filled her heart for this man who stared at her with such concern in his brown eyes. How lucky she was that such a wonderful man had fallen in love with her, and still want to marry her after all the General had taken from them both.

She curled her hands around his muscular biceps and kissed him. "I love you, Timaeus. But you need to sleep. I don't want my nightmares to torture us both."

"I don't care about sleep," he said roughly. "I love *you*. Promise you'll wake me next time. You said it helps make you feel better."

It was true. Whenever Timaeus held her, a balm seemed to heal her soul.

"Promise me," he said again.

"All right." Maybe next time. But not...

"*Every* time," he stated.

"Timaeus."

"Every time."

His hands felt strong on her shoulders. Softness tempered the intensity of his dark gaze.

"All right."

"Good." He gently kissed her. "Ready to get supplies?"

She laughed a little. "How much can you carry?"

On the walk to town, Timaeus fell behind to talk to Doc, and Deccia seized the opportunity to talk to Sozla. She still didn't know the Eerporian girl very well, but liked the little she did know.

Sozla cast her a quick smile. "You are lucky."

"What do you mean?"

"Timaeus. It is clear how much he loves you. You are lucky."

"I know," she said softly. "What about you? Do you have a special man back home?"

Sozla shrugged a shoulder. "Perhaps. A man wishes to marry me when I return home."

Deccia's eyebrows winged up. "Really?" It was the first time she'd heard about it, but then again, she didn't know Sozla very well. "What is he like?"

"He is nice." Sozla faintly shrugged again. It seemed like a strange reaction.

"Have you known him for long?"

"All of my life. His parents and mine are good friends. It would please my father if I married him."

Now it began to make sense. "Do you love him?"

Sozla's dark eyes looked troubled. "What is love? I feel affection for him."

"Affection is important, but love is more than that. At least, it is for Timaeus and me."

"What is it like, then? How will I know if I'm in love?" Sozla genuinely seemed to want to know.

"For me... Well, my insides get twisted up every time I see Timaeus. I can't *wait* to see him every morning and talk to him. Every time he looks at me, I feel it in my heart. And besides all that...well, he's the most wonderful man I've ever met."

Sozla shook her head. "I do not feel those things." She sounded wistful.

"Then why consider marrying him?"

"It is my parents' wishes. My father wants me to live a secure life." She explained, "My suitor's father owns much land. It would be a good match. Besides, my parents' marriage was arranged. They are fond of one another."

"Maybe it's good that you have this time away to think."

"Yes."

For the remainder of the way into town they discussed less life altering decisions, such as how much grain and meat to buy. But Deccia felt concerned for Sozla. Clearly, she did not love the young man she was being pressured to marry. She said a quick prayer that Sozla would meet the right man before it was too late.

And she wondered what Dakarra would be like. She hoped there would be no soldiers in town.

△ △ △ △ △

Methusal and Mentàll crossed the sprawling Zindedi city, and at the northernmost edge, the buildings petered out and Carachki's high hill sloped downward. They stopped beside an old abandoned shack and surveyed the situation. The tan earth closely matched the earth-toned clothes they wore. Mentàll pulled on a cap of the same color to hide his gleaming white-blond hair.

Below, the flat plains afforded a good view of rolling hills to the east, and mountains to the west. And directly to the north, just beyond a huge, weed infested tract of land, lay Carachki's huge military compound. A fence of crisscrossed wires enclosed it, affording a clear view of the inner structures of the base.

Large buildings, painted a dull gray, dotted the compound. Wide, dark paths connected them, and the black clad men striding over them looked as small as rochers from this distance.

"We need to discover the purpose of each building," the Dehrien said.

"How?" Methusal asked simply. "If we get much closer, they'll see us. There's nowhere to hide."

He scanned the base, then grunted with satisfaction. "They are foolish. They have no watch towers. We can approach unseen."

"How?"

"We will crawl through the weeds."

Methusal tried to imagine the proud Dehrien Chief crawling through the weeds. "Isn't that beneath you?"

That pale gaze focused upon her. He appeared amused, which confused her. "How little you know me, Methusal. You must know I will do anything to achieve my goals."

"Then in this situation I'm glad you're ruthless. Since it serves Koblan's interests so well."

He gave a rusty chuckle, and glanced at the military base again. The familiar, determined mask hardened his features again. "It is time."

He headed directly east, hugging the edge of town, and keeping close to the buildings. A few people and children in raggedly clothing roamed about, but few paid attention to them.

After several minutes, Methusal understood why they had headed this way. A shallow ravine cut south from the eastern side of the base and meandered toward the eastern corner of Carachki. The old stream appeared to be dry, although bushy green plants grew in it. They were the only spots of green in the desert landscape.

Finally, Mentàll paused. This northeastern section of town was quiet. Only flying beast wings rippled overhead. "Do you hear anyone?"

Although Methusal had been focused into kaavl for the entire trek, she intensified still more, fanning out her hearing, and then her vision, looking down side streets, and into windows. "It's safe."

Mentàll headed down the steep slope and slipped into the ravine. Bushes closed behind him, concealing him from sight. Methusal followed. The plant leaves felt cool against her cheeks, and she realized she'd grown warm from the sun. Although cold at night, it was warm in Carachki during the day.

A trickle of water wet the center of the tiny ravine. The gully was a half-length deep. To approach the base unseen, they'd have to hike there bent over double. Better than crawling through the dry, scratchy weeds. She followed Mentàll's silent footsteps, and wondered what they'd do when they reached the military base.

△ △ △ △ △

An open air market flanked each side of Dakarra's main road. Black uniformed soldiers thronged with the villagers, sampling wares from each stall. A group of eight or more swerved close to the Kolbanis as they entered the street.

In a flash, Deccia's dream scorched through her mind. The fear she'd felt—and yes, the hatred for the General—billowed through her again. She trembled with it. She forced herself to look at the soldiers. To remind herself they weren't General Greisn, even though they wore the same black uniform, with the same red slash from hell. Blood red, like the General's mutilated thumb. She shuddered.

"Decc." Timaeus' arm closed around her shoulders. In a low voice, he said, "Are you all right?"

"Of course." She tried to smile, but failed. "My nightmare flashed back."

"You're safe." His arm felt strong and steady, and when the group of soldiers moved away, Deccia relaxed. Gratefully, she squeezed Timaeus' hand and took in the bright, lively scene before her.

Tubers, fruit, grain, fresh baked bread... An abundance of every kind overflowed from the stalls. Bright red, yellow, and blue skirts and dresses caught her eye, and she wondered if she could take time to look at the pretty clothes.

Vitnia suddenly appeared, her sharp face just as unpleasant in the daylight. Today she wore a drab brown dress. She said, "I see you made it to the cabins unmolested."

No one replied, although Deccia felt, as clear as a fist punch, the malice festering in the other woman. The Dakarran enjoyed causing trouble. It gave her a perverse sort of pleasure.

"You've come on a good day," Vitnia continued. "The farmers visit town once a week. Best to stock up." She peered at them. "Where are the others?"

Sozla said, "Our cabins require much cleaning. But you knew that, did you not? We have decided to split the labor."

"Of course." A fake smile revealed Vitnia's cramped set of teeth. "How long will you stay in Dakarra, did you say?"

"At least two weeks. We have paid for as much, have we not?"

"Will more people visit you? Is that why you required two cabins?"

Goodness, the woman was nosy! Deccia felt an unexpected rush of resentment. What right did the Zindedi woman have to pry into their lives?

Coolly, she interposed, "We have shopping to do. Good day." Guilt nipped her as she walked to another stall, leaving Vitnia behind. It wasn't like her to be so rude. But she couldn't stand the idea of talking to the woman for another moment.

As they shopped, Deccia noticed other townspeople, especially women, watching the Koblani group. They talked behind their hands to fellow Dakarrans. She sensed their curiosity, laced with disapproval, while she haggled prices with a vendor.

Sozla proved to be an expert negotiator, and within an hour they'd gathered all the supplies they needed. Timaeus and Doc shoved the heavier items into their packs and led the way home.

Deccia wasn't sorry to leave. She would have liked to have had a chance to finger the soft, colorful Zindedi dresses on display. But in Dakarra she'd felt like an insect inspected by a wild beast and found wanting. The Zindedis weren't friendly, and certainly Vitnia had appeared suspicious of them.

All of the Dakarrans had seemed very interested in them. But it hadn't felt like a simple fascination with strangers. Instead, it had felt like a malevolent curiosity. Did they treat all newcomers this way? Or did the Koblani team members appear or act differently than other Zindedis?

If so, they might need to try harder to fit in. Maybe she should have been friendlier this morning.

She'd report her impressions to Behran and Timaeus, too, so he could report them to Mentàll. One thing was for certain—they'd need to be careful. Dakarra was not safe. They could not let their guards down for one moment.

△ △ △ △ △

Hendra wriggled uphill through the dry, knee high weeds on her stomach, elbows digging into the sandy earth to pull herself forward. Her elbows felt raw, and sand sifted down her sleeves with every wriggle forward. She wondered how much further it was to the top of the hill. At least her feet felt comfortable today, because she wore moccasins. Her feet couldn't take another day in those Zindedi shoes.

After breakfast, while Deccia and the others went to town, the kaavl team had hiked north, following the thickly forested tree line past Dakarra. When the road to the beach was clear in both directions, they'd melted into another copse of trees and trekked east twenty minutes until they reached the far edge of the military base. A small hill rose there, obstructing their view. Riln claimed it was the perfect observation post. All they had to do was reach the top unnoticed. That was what Hendra was trying to do right now.

She lifted her head. Ahead of her, Behran appeared to have reached the top, because he'd stopped moving. Goric followed behind her. Thankfully, Riln and Tabor had decided to find a new observation point for themselves today.

Waves thundered on the beach a short distance away, masking any sounds they made. Not that many people were about. They'd only seen one cart on the beach road. Yesterday Tabor had reported that they'd spotted three military carts on the road where it split east and west at the beach. The carts were covered with tarps, and appeared to be heavy, for the urchets were straining to pull them. Discovering what they were carrying was one of the many answers they needed to discover today, if possible.

Hendra finally pulled up even with Behran. Putting a finger to his lips, he pointed. She parted the weed stalks so she could see better. Three lengths away, inside a wire mesh fence, five Zindedi soldiers argued. Sunshine glinted off the clusters of medals on their uniforms.

Officers. She couldn't help but wonder why they had congregated to talk at this back corner of the base.

Frustratingly, the thunder of the surf drowned out most of their words.

"...coming!"

A hum of low, vehement voices.

"...Presidente...."

"Top General!"

"...be ready..."

An older officer, who had a pot belly and balding head, grew red in the face. "My base! Won't..."

Clearly, they were having an argument about something important, and possibly top secret. Why else congregate at this back fence? They didn't want to be overheard.

Hendra crept forward a bit. If only she could hear better.

Behran gripped her shoulder. "Careful."

But the men still couldn't see her. The grass was too thick. A little further wouldn't hurt. Maybe another arm length would make all the difference. Hendra scooted forward another handbreadth, feeling proud of her bravery. Then another little scoot...

A loud squawk pierced her ears, and wildly fluttering black wings beat her nose. She cried out in shock. A flying beast shot skyward.

Behind her, Goric cursed. The men on the base turned around, and seemed to look right at her.

△ △ △ △ △

The stealthy hike to the base seemed to last forever. Methusal's back ached by the time the Dehrien knelt and put a finger to his lips. Methusal did a quick visual carry over the edge of the gulch and spotted the wire fence two lengths away. A soldier carrying a gun on his shoulder patrolled the area.

"One soldier, four lengths," she whispered.

"Tell me when he's gone."

"Why?"

"We need to get inside the compound."

Her jaw dropped. "Are you serious?"

"We need to scout the base. We will not discover information about our enemies if we hide in a creek bed."

"Wouldn't *nighttime* be better? If they see us..."

"They will not."

"Are you really that sure of yourself? Or maybe you've lost your mind."

The pale eyes glittered. "You can do it, Methusal. I believe in you."

"You do?" His confidence took her aback. It also unexpectedly bolstered her courage.

"It is why I chose you for my team, Methusal. We are well matched." More softly, he added, "If we work together, there is no end to what we can accomplish."

She was not sure what to make of that enigmatic comment. "What is your plan, once we're inside?"

"We will scout the eastern and northern perimeters."

"So, not the heart of the compound?" In order to take the bite out of her next words, she offered a half smile. "You won't stroll into their offices and demand a map of the place?"

"Not today." Humor glinted, and vanished.

She performed another visual carry over the edge of the gulch. "The soldier disappeared around a building. Now is our chance." However, she had no idea how Mentàll planned to get through the thick, crossed metal wires.

Light and quick as a whip, the Dehrien Chief sprang up from the gully. His broad hands gripped the wires, and with apparent ease he pulled them up at the weed choked base. Wide enough for a man to slither through on his belly. In a moment, he was through. Methusal quickly followed. Dry, stick-like weeds scratched her cheek and hands.

After waiting to see her safely on the other side, the Dehrien pushed the wires back in place and slipped north, moving fast. Methusal followed him around the nearest building. Nerves made her heart pound like a herd of wild beasts.

All remained silent. This portion of the base appeared deserted. She wondered what was stored in the rows of identical buildings.

The Dehrien Chief tried a door handle, but it was locked. Methusal slipped over to a small window. No curtains obstructed the view, but it looked black inside.

"What do you see?"

She cupped her hands around her eyes to keep out the light. "Barrels," she reported. "Floor to ceiling, it's filled with barrels."

"Powder." He sounded grim.

"Probably."

"Come." He headed for the next building.

"Shouldn't we listen?" she hissed. "Soldiers could be around any corner."

"You listen, if you do not feel comfortable. I know it is safe."

During the Quasr War, the Dehrien had negotiated dangerous streets without error. He'd never really needed her sharp kaavl hearing to tell them the safest route to take. He just seemed to know. A seventh sense of some kind? Or an advanced kaavl ability she'd never heard about before?

Three years ago, he had boasted of nearing the Ultimate level. She wondered if he had finally achieved it. With his pilfered *Second Book of Kaavl*, who knew? And she was still struggling to discover how to reach the Primary level, even though she was Mahre's multiple great-great... granddaughter. She had to admit it bothered her.

They checked several more buildings. All contained either barrels, bags, or guns. The Zindedis were armed to the teeth for war with Koblan.

Low voices touched her ears. She whispered, "Soldiers."

Mentàll tried another door, and it unexpectedly opened.

Silent as the night, they slipped into the dark building. Methusal's eyes slowly adjusted to the dark. Except for barrels along the far wall and the left wall, this building was empty, except for a lone table pushed under the window. A sheaf of papers rested upon it. Methusal itched to peek through them. In fact, she'd taken a step forward when a shaky voice outside said, "I just finished the report...."

"Show me." The words sounded sharp and clipped.

"Of course. Right away, sir!"

Keys rattled in the lock. Methusal fled after Mentàll to the far side of the room. Stacked barrels made of dark wood could hide them from view, but they were stacked flush against the wall.

"Come." The Dehrien gripped her sleeve and slipped between the two rows of barrels in the corner. A small space lived behind them, enough for Mentàll to stand with his back to the wall, with Methusal in front of him. She hoped the shadows would hide them, because in this spot there was gap of space between the topmost stacks of barrels, and her face was in plain sight if someone looked straight at them.

More rattling came from the door. The first try hadn't opened it. Likely because it had been unlocked to begin with.

"Sorry!" The soldier sounded agitated.

A second later the door swung open, revealing a short, stocky young man. Behind him, a slim man with sun streaked brown hair walked with clipped precision into the room. His features were sharp, and his thin mouth pressed into a line beneath a razor thin moustache. His black and red uniform boasted rows of glittering medals. A high ranking officer.

"Here." The portly man shoved the papers into the officer's hands. A few slipped free and fluttered to the floor.

"Idiot!" The officer whipped out a black baton and smacked the soldier's head.

The other man's face flushed bright red. "I'm so sorry, General Fitrn!" With shaking fingers, he gathered up the loose papers. His beefy hands crumpled them in his haste.

"You are incompetent, Hostn." The General spat the words. Ignoring the pages in the soldier's shaking hands, he dropped the remainder of the report to the floor. Papers flew everywhere.

He strolled across the room, out of Methusal's sight. "What other incompetencies will I uncover if I look hard enough?"

"None, sir. None! I...I have been very thorough. If only you will look at this report..."

"Put it in order, and be quick about it." General Fitrn's footsteps strolled closer to the hidden Koblanis. A quick carry told Methusal that he was only two lengths away, and getting closer. He snapped, "How many powder barrels are in here?"

"Th...thirty, sir!" Hostn dumped the papers on the desk and frantically struggled to put them in order. In his haste, he shuffled and reshuffled the same papers. His mouth worked silently, as if in a panic.

"How many in *all* of this compound?"

"Four hundred! General, sir. And more is expected from Dakarra within the week."

The General whirled, boots scratching on the wood floor. "*Within* the week? The shipment was due *last* week."

"I...I know, sir. But I..."

"It is good I'm going to Dakarra soon." General Fitrn walked closer to Methusal and Mentàll. "Meanwhile, I will count these barrels. If your numbers are not precisely correct, you will exchange this comfortable office for the rings."

Tears spilled down Hostn's face. His chubby hands moved even faster.

"And your report had better be ready, and in pristine condition by the time I finish counting. Eleven...twelve..."

The General's footsteps clicked closer and closer. Methusal felt frozen with fear. In a moment, the General would see them. What could they do?

△ △ △ △ △

"Down!" Behran hissed, and shoved Hendra's shoulder toward the earth.

"There!" a man shouted.

Hendra's heart raced.

More arguing erupted.

"Come on." Behran slid backwards, down the hill.

Had they really been seen?

"Hendra!" Behran hissed. "Come on."

She peeked through the grass again. The red-faced man glared in her direction, gesticulating wildly. Another, calmer looking officer, shook his head.

"Infernal kids!" bellowed the first man. "Send soldiers! Find out what they heard."

Another argument ensued, but Hendra quickly crawled backwards, so she didn't hear anything else. Behran was right. They weren't safe any longer. Weeds poked into her belly. Within moments, she joined Behran and Goric in the woods.

"I'm sorry." She felt awful. "Maybe we could find somewhere else to scout."

"No. We need to play it safe, and keep the area clear."

"What about Tabor and Riln?"

"They can take care of themselves."

Disappointment lodged deeper in her heart with every step they took away from the military base. They had failed. She had failed. Today they had discovered no information, and it was all her fault.

"Sorry," she whispered again.

Goric sent her a frown. The return trip to the cabins was silent.

Doc and the others had returned by the time they got back. Heaps of supplies filled the kitchen table. They'd had a fruitful mission, at least.

Deccia and Sozla were the first to notice them. Surprise registered. "You're back already? What happened?"

Hendra's face warmed. "It's my..."

"A flying beast gave away our position," Behran interrupted. "I decided it would be safest to come home. We'll try again tomorrow. Riln and Tabor are still out there."

"Too bad," Deccia sympathized. "But you can help us shelve this stuff. And we have lots of cleaning to do. Maybe this is for the best."

Hendra was grateful to Behran for covering for her, but she still felt bad. She threw herself into the work, cleaning and scrubbing and hanging up more laundry than anyone else. It helped her feel better—but only a little bit.

△ △ △ △ △

"General! Here. It is finished." Hostn shoved the report into a folder and extended it to the General.

Methusal's heart leaped in relief when the General retreated across the room. Using just his fingertips, he plucked the report from Hostn's hand. "Only accuracy will keep you from the rings, Hostn. I have lost patience with you."

The stocky man ducked his head, hands visibly trembling.

"Come." General Fitrn put a hand on Hostn's shoulder, as if in friendship. But his knuckles showed white. Pain spasmed across Hostn's face. "We will count barrels together. That will be a fun exercise, will it not?"

"Yes, sir," he said faintly.

Methusal's heart slammed harder. That horrible General was fixated upon counting barrels! How could they escape detection now?

Mentàll's hands curled around her shoulders and she stiffened still more. In a whisper that only the sharpest kaavl hearing could detect, he said, "Relax, Methusal. Remember Mahre's words that you read in Dehre. What did you learn?"

"Not enough," she breathed back. "I didn't have months to study it, like you did."

"Listen. I will teach you an elementary principle of the Ultimate level. Relax your defenses. Let the sensory input flow in."

How could she possibly relax? That psychotic General and Hostn had started counting barrels on the opposite end of the room.

"Relax."

She remembered reading the same words in the *Second Book of Kaavl.* They'd made no sense then, and made no more sense now, either. But if Mahre had said it, and the Dehrien had found it to be true, too...

She took a calming breath and exhaled slowly, struggling to relax and become in tune with her environment. After another, deeper breath, she relaxed utterly into kaavl. Perhaps more deeply than ever before.

Sensory input rushed in. The woodsy, timber smell of the wooden barrels. She could almost taste the texture. The cool breeze swirling through the open door. The click clack of the General's polished boots on the floor. Hostn's small, panting breaths. A faint, sickly sweet scent. Perhaps the General's cologne. Two lengths still separated their hiding place from the Zindedis.

Other sounds drifted in, too. An insect, buzzing... The heat of the man behind her. It sizzled, like a brand down her skin. She stiffened again, and her breathing accelerated.

He was close. Much too close. She felt the insane urge to run, regardless of the fatal consequences.

"Relax, Methusal." His warm breath teased the outer curve of her ear.

It tingled alarmingly. "*Stop it.*" Trembling a little, she forced another fingerbreadth of space between them. "I can't relax here...with you. Surrounded by my enemies. It's impossible."

"You are talented, Methusal. Do you not want to advance in kaavl?"

"Teach me another time," she whispered. "We need to escape."

She tilted her head away from his warm breaths, but his strong hands gripped her upper arms. "Face me. They will not see us."

How could facing him...? Then she realized that her dark hair would blend together with barrels and look like a shadow to the General.

But turning to face her oldest enemy felt dangerous, too. With her back to him, she felt a safe measure of distance. But facing him would bring him too close. And she didn't want to turn her back on her new enemies, either. It would make her vulnerable to attack. It also meant she would need to completely trust Mentàll to defend her, if necessary.

The General's precise, clicking steps were a half-length away now. She could not be an apte. She must face her fear of this man and trust him, at least for these short moments.

Silently, she turned, and Mentàll pulled her with him further back into the shadows. He felt hard and warm and very powerful against her. The last time they had been this close, with their bodies touching, had been when he had kissed her at base camp. Her mind shut out that disturbing, vivid memory, but another drifted in to replace it.

In Quasr they'd had to fool the Zindedi soldiers into thinking they were lovers. They had succeeded. He had hated her then.

She didn't know what he felt now.

The clean scent of soap and that raw, indefinable male essence that was purely Mentàll filled her senses. For one wild moment she felt like she was drowning in him. She drew an unsteady breath.

Mentàll's tense alertness was her only clue that the General was close. She'd lost all sense of time and place for a moment. The disorientation alarmed her.

Breaths whispered behind her. One sounded like a faint whistle through a nose, and the other like a wheeze.

Methusal froze.

"Twenty-nine. Thirty." Disappointment registered in the clipped voice. "You've escaped the rings today, Hostn."

A waft of displaced air tickled Methusal's ears. Maybe they had turned. She held her breath.

Footsteps clicked away.

"Finish your shift at the offices. The Commander needs filing done."

"Yes, sir!" Hostn sounded pathetically eager to please.

The door shut. All was silent, except for the two fading sets of footsteps.

Above her, the Dehrien's breath tickled her hair. "Follow him."

"What?"

"With kaavl hearing. Follow the General."

She backed away from the Dehrien. Finally, she could breathe a whole lot easier.

Without conscious thought, she crossed the room, mimicking the direction the General was heading now—west, toward the center of the compound.

The wall stopped her. She splayed her fingers over its rough surface and listened intently. Except for the footsteps, no sounds tickled her ears for a good while, and then...

"Commander." General Fitrn's clipped voice. "All is in order. I leave for Dakarra the day after tomorrow."

An older, rough sounding voice spoke. "Good. Beat that powder out of them, if you have to. All we'll lack then is soldiers. When will you see the Presidente next?"

A thin, mirthless laugh. "If he has his way, not until the ball."

"We cannot invade without more troops."

"I know, Ostl. What about the ball? Have you received your invitation?"

"Last night. The missus is pleased. More than I can say for myself."

"At least your woman has not fled to the far side of the country."

"Will you retrieve her?"

A soft, mirthless chuckle. "I am pressing her mother for information. It is only a matter of time."

"Tread carefully. The Presidente holds her mother in the highest regard."

"I know this!" Temper flashed. "The Presidente will not hold me back forever. It is only a matter of time."

A pause elapsed. The Commander said, "Time until what?"

A slap. Perhaps a clap on the shoulder. "Good friend, our conversation will end now. I will return at the end of the week."

"Success go with you."

General Fitrn laughed. "Success follows wherever I tread."

Footsteps faded away. Quickly, Methusal relayed the information to Mentàll.

He nodded. "Our work here is done. We will go back to town and watch the road."

"Why?" Although she certainly would be glad to leave the base.

"We will follow the General home. The Commander too, if we can."

"Why does it matter where they live?"

"Every piece of information about our enemies is important." The cold words sounded merciless.

"What do you plan to do?"

"When you need to know, I will tell you."

Annoyed, she reminded him, "We're in this together. Please," she added that word in a thin effort to be tactful, "tell me what you're planning."

He headed out the door. "The less you know, the better."

"What do you mean by that?" Her annoyance grew.

He turned back suddenly, making her stop in her tracks. "What it means, Methusal, is that if you are captured, you will have no secrets to hide."

"You don't trust me. That's what you're saying."

His lips twisted. "I do not want you to be tortured for my secrets. Your innocence will shine through. They will understand you know nothing and stop."

Methusal could not imagine General Fitrn taking note of anyone's innocence. "Really? I'll bet that General tortures people just for the fun of it."

The Dehrien did not reply, but headed for the fence, moving with sure, silent steps. Abruptly, he stopped and pressed his back to the closest building. Footsteps headed toward them, and then pivoted and paced away.

When it was clear, they both slipped through the wires again and into the gulch. Methusal longed to say more about the subject, but it was difficult, bent double, hurrying through the gulch. The words simmered on her tongue, however, as they slipped back into Carachki. There, he took her hand and strolled for the base road.

She discreetly struggled to free herself. "Let go. I'm not finished talking to you yet."

"That conversation is over. We have a new topic to discuss."

"What?" she said shortly.

"Our camouflage as lovers needs work."

She willed herself not to flush. He could needle under her skin until Ryon turned purple, but she would not respond. "You mean honeymooners."

His lips twitched. "It is the same thing."

Her hand felt uncomfortably warm, enfolded in his strong grip. "You love this, don't you?" she hissed.

He didn't deny it, and in fact, appeared even more pleased. "You must think of a name of affection for me."

"What?" Her jaw dropped.

"Did you like sweet lips? I can think of other names for you, if you wish."

She yanked at her hand. "I *don't* like sweet lips. And you can take your names and..."

An old lady frowned as she passed by. They had now entered the market area. Stalls filled with vegetables and fruits lined the sides of the street.

"You are jeopardizing our cover, Methusal."

She stopped struggling, but her pulse still hammered alarmingly. "Honeymooners argue."

"A name of affection, Methusal."

With a sudden smile, she cooed, "How about low-bellied whip beast? Or slug? Or maybe razor-toothed wild beast is more to your liking."

Amusement continued to glint in his eyes. "Your voice could lull a wild beast to sleep. But your words cut straight to the heart."

"You like plain speaking, don't you?"

"Admirable." He stopped suddenly, and backed her against a wall.

"What are you *do...*"

"Look over my left shoulder."

She looked. Mrn. Machblin! And she was talking to a slim man in a military uniform. She gasped when the Zindedi turned his head, confirming her suspicion. General Fitrn. "Why is she talking to *him?*"

"No doubt they are acquaintances," Mentàll murmured. "Her husband was a high ranking officer. It is likely he associated closely with both the Presidente and General Fitrn."

"We can't let him see us."

"Agreed. Follow me." He reversed direction and headed east again, and then cut south. Then they prowled the street, waiting for the General to reappear. He finally did, and they followed him west to a massive, two-story house, high in the hills. It boasted a semi-circular drive, ornate grillwork on the front of the mansion, and fancy curtains in the windows. It dwarfed the neighboring houses. A servant opened the door and bowed, ushering General Fitrn inside.

After watching for a while and discovering nothing further, they returned to the market area to eat lunch. One corner street provided a particularly good view of the road to the base. As the day wore on, they observed only a few soldiers, some with urchets and carts, traveling the dusty road.

Finally, as dusk descended, a burly man in a cart appeared, heading toward Carachki. He had thinning gray hair, a hooked nose, and a number of medals gleamed on his chest. His voice confirmed that he was the Commander. They followed him to his home, too.

He lived in a two story house only a few blocks from the General, but his home and neighborhood were not nearly as grand as General Fitrn's. A young blond woman met him at the door, and they disappeared inside.

"A fruitful day's work," Mentàll said, as they headed back to Mrn. M's house. Feldon Street wasn't far. "Tomorrow we will scout the Presidente's palace."

"You mean break in."

"Of course."

Anxiety slid into her heart. The compound looked impregnable. How could they break in, let alone scout that highly secured area?

As they turned into Mrn. M's gate, Mentàll said, "You are not afraid, are you?"

"No. Well, a little. I'll be fine." She didn't want to be afraid. Surely that counted for something.

They climbed the steps together. He stopped unexpectedly near the front door.

She looked up. "What?"

"We have had a good day. Smile at me."

She wondered if that was truly necessary. However, the request was harmless enough, so she reluctantly affixed a smile upon her lips.

He murmured, "Mrn. M is watching us through the kitchen window."

A prickle ran down her spine, and she wondered where he intended to go with this line of conversation. "And?"

"It is time to give my wife some affection."

Panic gripped her. It was clear what he meant. She felt caught, like an apte in a trap. She licked her lips. "Don't."

"It is so repulsive to you?"

"Yes."

His gaze held hers. "Then what do you suggest?"

"Anything else." She wasn't ready. Not yet.

He leaned toward her, and for one horrifying second she thought he'd kiss her anyway. Instead, his bristled cheek gently scraped her own. In a low voice, he said, "Put your arms around me." His arms enfolded her, holding her securely against him.

What choice did she have? Her arms trembled as they slipped around him. She buried her head into his shoulder.

"Is this so bad?" he murmured.

She didn't answer. He smelled nice, and his arms felt strong and secure, and for one crazy moment she felt no fear... Of anything at all.

He released her sooner than expected. "Good job, sweet lips."

Flushing, she retorted, "Thanks, love beast." Then she blushed furiously, because Mrn. M had just opened the door.

"Well." That lady smiled. "I see you two have had a good day. Come in to dinner."

△ △ △ △ △

It didn't help Hendra's low spirits that Riln and Tabor came back that night full of important news about Dakarra's military base. She quietly ate her soup and listened.

"I got close enough to see a pit," Riln boasted. "It's ten lengths deep, but stripped down to dirt. It might have been an ore deposits mine."

And maybe it was why Zindedi wanted Koblan's ore deposits, Hendra thought.

Tabor's deep, quiet voice spoke. "I think a weapons making facility is next to the pit. The windows are too high to see inside the building. But I spotted unusual structures inside when a man came out a door. One structure was a big tube on wheels. It reminded me of their guns, only bigger."

"We've circled that base three times." Riln belched, and leaned back in his chair. "Now it's time to get inside."

"How?" Hendra dared to speak. "It's surrounded by a mesh fence."

Riln shot her a contemptuous glance. "Courage and a little fire power is all we need."

"Riln, you're right," Behran said. "We do need to get inside. But we'll do it at night, and we'll do it undetected."

Riln rolled his eyes to the ceiling. "Apte," he muttered.

Behran ignored this. "Tomorrow we'll record the guard rotations. Then tomorrow night we'll break into the base."

"We'll need wire cutters," Tabor said.

"Yes. If we can find a pair."

Sozla spoke up from the couch, where she sat next to Doc. "If we cannot find cutters?"

"Send Doc," Timaeus said. "He has the magic touch. He could unlock one of the gates."

Everyone looked at Doc. Hendra had been trying to avoid that as much as possible this evening. Today, the Tarst doctor and Sozla had teamed up, washing and wringing out blankets together. Sozla had done a lot of laughing, and Doc seemed to have had a good time, too. Now they sat together. Hendra tried to ignore the jealousy she felt. Doc deserved to be happy. Maybe Sozla was the right woman for him. She looked away again, trying to dismiss the pain cutting through her heart.

"Well?" Behran asked.

"I'm for it," Doc said. "I'd be glad to help out the mission."

"Great."

"I think powder is in those carts." Tabor unexpectedly said. "We need to find out where it's coming from."

Behran nodded. "Any suggestions?"

"Riln and I will follow the carts. It may take a day or two, since we don't know how far they're traveling."

"Good plan. You'll start tomorrow?"

Tabor gave a silent nod. Riln frowned. Hendra guessed he didn't want to miss breaking into the base. But when Tabor sent him a level, speaking look, he nodded abruptly.

"So we have a plan." Behran sounded pleased.

"What about the detonators, Behran?" Sozla said. "Is it not our mission to begin making those?"

"I'm hoping we'll find information on the base that will show us how to make one. At the very least, we'll steal powder to use."

"Perhaps this weapons making facility has diagrams, or useful information," Sozla said. "I would like to see these things. It may help me figure out how to make a detonator."

"Come with us."

She smiled. "I hoped you would say that. But I know not the kaavl."

"That's okay," Behran said. "Stick close to us. We'll get you in and out safely."

"Indeed, yes. I will stick...as close as possible." She gave him a bright smile.

Behran shifted his shoulders a tiny bit, as if uncomfortable with the interchange. Hendra glanced from

Sozla, to Behran, to Doc. Who was the Eerporian girl interested in? One, both? Or neither?

What a suspicious mind she had! And it was none of her business, anyway. Selfishly, though, she wished Sozla would be interested in Behran instead of Doc, because she knew Behran was completely devoted to Methusal. Her friend had nothing whatsoever to fear.

Hendra glanced at Doc again. Unexpectedly, she discovered he was watching her, his smoky gaze assessing. Flustered, she looked away. Did he sense her jealousy? Was it written in bold letters across her face, *Please don't be interested in Sozla*? What a pathetic creature she was.

"I think I'll turn in." Behran stretched. "It's been a long day, and tomorrow will be even longer."

Hendra also said a general goodnight to everyone, and headed for her room. Doc hadn't heard her. He was too busy talking to Sozla.

Hendra crawled into bed and wept into her clean pillow. *Please The One, let tomorrow be better.*

CHAPTER NINETEEN

DAY 3

METHUSAL DIDN'T SLEEP very well. She woke up multiple times in the night. Her hip and shoulder hurt. Even sleeping on her back on the stone floor didn't help. And it was so cold.

She woke up grumpy, tired, and shivering the next morning, only to find Mentàll standing over her, fully dressed and his hair damp. He looked completely refreshed. And why wouldn't he feel refreshed? He had slept on a soft bed all night long.

She frowned up at him. "What?"

"It is time to get up. We have a full day ahead of us."

"Forgive me for being tired."

"If you are not well rested, perhaps you should go to bed earlier." He referred to the fact that she had stayed up late in the living room last night, reading a newspaper. Spending all day with him had been difficult. She had needed time to herself.

"Why didn't I think of that?" If it killed her, she wouldn't let him know how miserably she'd slept on the floor.

"Are you cold?"

Those sharp eyes must have spotted her quivering shoulders. "I'm fine."

He stared down at her. "Do not lie to me, Methusal."

"Okay, I'm cold." She raised her eyebrows. "Does that satisfy you?" She glared. "Does it make you *happy?*"

"It does not make me happy."

"Why not?" She tried to spring to her feet, but pain pierced into her hip. She twisted away to hide the agony distorting her features. More anger surged. The whip beast, making her sleep on the floor! Her hip hurt, her back hurt, her head hurt, and she was exhausted.

Turning back again, she snapped, "I know making me suffer is one of your main goals."

He opened his mouth.

"Don't deny it! You needled under my skin all through the Quasr War. It started again when you came to Rolban. When you *forced* me to team with you. But I'm happy to do it. Because at least here I can keep an eye on you."

"Are you finished?" His low voice sent a shiver of warning down her spine.

She ignored it. "I'll be finished when this mission is done, and I've defeated every underhanded plot you're cooking up for Koblan."

Faster than thought, he moved forward and his fingers sliced through her hair. He cupped the back of her head. She didn't dare move. What did he intend by this?

"Don't *touch* me." Her voice lowered to a shiver.

"Why not?" His gaze slowly scanned her face. "You are flushed. You are clearly upset with me. Do you want me to act like the wild beast you say I am?"

"Let me go." Her voice trembled, and her heart pounded.

He released her. "Watch yourself. The walls are thin. Mrn. Machblin can hear you."

"Don't touch me again."

"I will touch you whenever it is necessary." His gaze hardened.

"Don't threaten me."

"Unlike you, I do not threaten. I promise. And you know I will not break my word."

"Wild beast."

"Convincing yourself of that makes you feel safe, doesn't it?"

"I don't need convincing. Your behavior just now proves it."

He stepped back. It was hard to read his expression.

Without a word, she snatched up her clothes and shut herself in the relief room.

In there, she sank down on the cold floor and put her head in her hands. *This is an impossible situation. Oh The One, help me.*

△ △ △ △ △

At breakfast, Mrn. M's quick glances at them looked concerned. It was clear she had overheard their fight, and Methusal didn't even try to smile, because she knew it would look fake. When Mrn. M glanced at Mentàll, he looked down at his plate, and then over at Methusal. His expression was impossible to read.

The incident wasn't over. This became clear the moment they left the house.

"We need to work on our relationship." Mentàll's voice sounded stiff. "Mrn. M is suspicious."

"Our relationship will improve," she said through her teeth, "when you stop *touching* me."

"I will touch you again. Accept it. It is part of our cover."

"Not alone in our room. Not like that. Not ever again."

A pause elapsed. "You are right. I am sorry."

She blinked in surprise. "Oh." After a pause, she said, "I'm sorry for starting the fight."

"We cannot jeopardize our cover again. We have to make this work."

"I don't know how."

"We cannot live at war with each other."

She gasped on a laugh. "I don't know how to live at peace with you." But he was right. Mrn. M would become very suspicious if they kept fighting with each other. "I don't trust you."

"I will not touch you again in our room. I was wrong to do it. Will you accept that?"

What choice did she have? For Koblan, she was here. For Koblan she had to make this work. "Fine. But remember that Behran is the man I love. I cannot stand it when another man touches me."

He said nothing.

"Do you understand?" she repeated.

Coolly, he said, "I understand you perfectly, Methusal."

"As long as you keep your word to me, I will live at peace with you." She would, as much as humanly possible. She would obey the Prophet's words to her—The One's words to her. She would do anything for her homeland. Even if that meant spending every waking minute of the next few weeks chained to Mentàll's side, and sleeping on that horrible floor.

"Good," he said harshly. "It is time to focus on the mission." He strode toward the Presidente's massive palace. Methusal was not looking forward to breaking into that compound.

△ △ △ △ △

The Zindedi morning dawned bright and clear. Hendra had slept like the dead last night, and had woken up before everyone else. At the moment, she measured berry powder into water for juice. Today would be different than yesterday. A fresh start.

Behind her, heavy footsteps entered the kitchen. "Ah. The little apte." Riln's rough voice mocked her.

Fear sizzled down her nerves. They were alone in the kitchen. No one else was up. "Good morning." Ice cloaked her tone, and she stiffened her spine and turned back to her task.

"Good morning to you, too." Thick, hard hands closed over the tops of her shoulders and squeezed.

Terror soared. With a gasp, she twisted away. "Don't *touch* me." Her voice shivered hatred.

She heard footsteps behind her, but didn't dare take her eyes off of her adversary to see who it was.

Something flickered in Riln's gaze. He raised his hands above his head. "Hey, I didn't mean anything by it."

"Didn't mean what?" Behran's sharp gaze flicked from Hendra's tense expression to Riln's small, cocky smile.

"Nothing. Isn't that right, ap...Hendra?"

Rage scalded her cheeks. Did Riln think she'd feel ashamed? That she'd keep it a secret? She'd lived with enough shame and secrets to last her a lifetime. And no man would ever terrorize her like Jascr had again. She wouldn't allow it.

"Riln touched me."

A short laugh gusted from Riln's barrel chest. "I squeezed her shoulders and said 'good morning.' No need to jump off a cliff."

He was ridiculing her! To her chagrin, shame did creep into her heart. Shame for her fear, and shame that she overreacted every time a man touched her. But Riln had done it purposefully–he had wanted to scare her.

Now he was silently laughing at her. He seemed so big and indomitable. How could she ever win against a man like him?

Fear clogged her throat, but she forced herself to speak. "I don't like you. I don't trust you. Don't *ever* touch me again."

Hands lifted high again, he said, "Don't worry. I won't. Scared aptes aren't my *thing*, if you know what I mean." Turning his back, he poured juice into a cup.

Behran's concerned gaze rested on Hendra. He knew a little of her past. Enough to understand her fear of men. "Are you all right?"

"I'm fine." She injected strength and conviction into the words. She would not play the victim. Riln needed to believe that he held no power over her.

Behran glanced at Riln, and then back to her. "Good. After breakfast, we're going to observe guard rotations. I'd like you on my team."

In a low voice, she said, "Even after yesterday?"

He smiled gently. "Forget yesterday. I'd like you to practice seeing the future today. I need to figure out how to mesh that skill with our break-in tonight."

Hendra felt a little better. Behran valued her. "Thank you. That sounds like a good idea."

Grimly, he said, "Tonight will be dangerous."

△ △ △ △ △

In the cold, bright morning sunlight, Methusal and Mentàll strolled around the Presidente's compound. She wished her jacket was warmer. It was quiet and cold in the shade. Trees lined the street around the compound, and flying beasts chirped overhead. A dark pink stone wall, two lengths high, surrounded the Presidente's palace, and lush vines spilled over the top.

It was peaceful, walking in the quiet morning beside the Dehrien Chief. Perhaps it also felt peaceful because they weren't speaking to each other.

After one trip around the compound, Mentàll cut over to a park across the street. He sat on a bench and she slid in beside him.

"Impressions?" he said.

"Two entrances. One is a large, arched wooden door, guarded by six men. The other is a main entrance gate, made of wrought ore. Fifteen guards patrol the entrance gate." Which was closed. And the guards had eyed them with suspicion when they'd strolled by. "I saw soldiers walking the perimeter inside." In fact, from her limited glimpse inside the gate, it appeared that dozens of soldiers guarded the Presidente's grounds. "I don't see how we can get inside."

"At night, we could scale the wall. It is only two lengths high. Or disguise ourselves as soldiers."

"You're too tall to blend in. Maybe I could try to dress like a soldier."

"No," he said shortly. "We will stay together." He was silent for a minute. "We need to see over that wall. We need to count exactly how many soldiers are guarding the compound."

"Good idea. But how?"

They both scanned the northern and southern streets flanking the compound. Three buildings—one on the south side and two on the north side—were two stories tall. If they could somehow get to the upper floor, they could see over the wall and into the interior of the Presidente's compound.

"One is a dress shop." With effort, she offered a faint smile. "I could buy new clothes so I'll blend in better."

He looked at her for a moment, as if surprised by her tiny smile. "You want to shop."

She stood. "And who better to take me shopping than my wonderful husband?"

"Now I am your wonderful husband?"

"I'm trying, Mentàll." She bit her lip. But trying seemed so wrong. Illogically, it felt like a step toward the edge of a cliff. If she let him in—if she let him get closer to her emotionally—what would happen then? The situation between them could escalate far beyond what had happened in Quasr. That thought scared her to death. For self-protection, she needed to keep her distance from him. But for the mission, she needed to pursue peace.

He reached for her hand, and after a hesitation, she slipped hers into it. He said nothing, but the stiffness lingering from their fight finally relaxed out of his shoulders. Methusal finally relaxed a little, too.

Together, they walked across the street to the first shop. Beautiful dresses in soft pastel colors of yellow, pink, orange, green, and blue hung on racks inside. Many had designs printed on them. They were so pretty. Her fingers lingered on a pale green gown with tiny stars sprinkled across the hem. She'd never seen anything so beautiful in her life. And it was so soft! However, it was completely impractical for the mission.

Reluctantly, she turned away. "I need pants and tunics," she told Mentàll in a low voice. "I don't think this shop has any."

The shopkeeper, a woman in a flowing purple dress and glasses on her nose, hovered nearby. "I have more clothes upstairs. Would you like to take a look?"

Methusal smiled. "I'd love to, thanks."

Upstairs, while she perused the racks of clothes, Mentàll paced before the windows, looking bored. But Methusal knew those sharp eyes spotted and catalogued every movement across the street in the Presidente's compound.

More dresses filled the small upstairs room, as well as a few sleeveless tunics. They didn't seem practical, either. But in the corner she spotted a soft, brown leather jacket, tapered at the waist with a fashionable belt. She missed leather. And she knew it would be warmer than the jacket she wore now. She was tired of feeling cold.

Mentàll appeared near her elbow. "You like that?"

"It would be warm."

Mentàll looked over her head at the shopkeeper. "We will be back. Thank you."

His words had seemed brusque. She followed him outside. "Why did we run out like that?"

"Our mission, Methusal. Activity is going on in the north side of the compound. We will go to those shops now."

One of the two story buildings on the street north of the compound had a "Closed" sign posted on the door. The other was a clothing shop, and it advertised that both men's and women's garments were inside. Methusal perked up. Maybe she'd find something here. And maybe they'd see into the Presidente's compound, too.

"May I help you?" A short, thin man with receding black hair approached them. He wore a rumpled, gray striped shirt.

A quick glance proved the downstairs level showcased women's clothing.

"Do you carry men's clothes?" Mentàll asked.

"Of course. Upstairs."

"I will be back," he told Methusal.

When Mentàll disappeared up the stairs, the shopkeeper crept closer to Methusal. "Are you looking for something in particular?"

"Shirts."

He eyed her, and his glance lingered a little too long on her bosom. "You look like a healthy medium. Follow me."

Methusal's flesh crept in revulsion. She followed him, but at a good distance.

With flourish, he indicated a rack filled with flowery tunics. The necklines plunged to an indecent level. But several other tunics nearby weren't nearly so gaudy, and were nice soft brown and mauve colors.

"Thank you," she told him. "I'll look around here."

Still, he lingered. "If you need help, just ask. We have a dressing room in the back." He indicated a curtained doorway.

Methusal only relaxed when he moved away, and then lost herself in looking at the lovely tunics. How many should she buy? One? Maybe two? She didn't want to spend too much of their money.

And she wasn't sure what size to get, either. She found two she particularly liked. One was brown, and the other was a soft color she'd only seen in a sunset. Both the small and the medium sizes looked like they might fit her.

She called to the shopkeeper. "You said you have a dressing room?"

He smiled. "Yes, of course. In the back."

She slipped through the curtain and found another curtained room to the right. It had a bench in one corner, and a swollen door that didn't quite close, as well. She pulled open the door and peeked inside. Dark. She shut it again, as best she could. Maybe a storage room. She pulled the privacy curtain shut and took off her own shirt, leaving her bra, and tried on the pale, sunset colored tunics. The small one fit, but tightly hugged all of her curves. She'd never worn anything that revealed her shape so clearly before, and embarrassment warmed her cheeks. No. She could never wear that one.

With a quick flip, she lifted the edge of the shirt, but a tiny movement caught her eye. The door. The one that didn't quite close. Did it *move*?

Frozen, Methusal intensified into kaavl. Quiet breaths panted behind the door. And a tiny sniff. Revulsion, like tiny rocher feet, crept over her skin. And horror, too. She saw an eye peering through the cracked door.

With a soft, choking gasp, she grabbed her own tunic and fled from the room.

Of course the storekeeper was nowhere in sight. But Mentàll was pacing near the front windows. When he turned, his gaze went straight to the tight tunic she wore. For the barest second his eyes widened, and his gaze shot to her face. "Methusal." His brows came together. "What is it?"

She drew a gulping, shaky breath. Tears burned her eyes. She just wanted to get out of this shop, and get out now. "I want to *go*." She tried to push past him, but he stopped her.

"*Please*." She felt violated and horribly embarrassed. "Let's just go."

"What happened?" he said harshly.

"Nothing."

"You're wearing the shop's shirt. Do you want to buy it?"

No, she didn't want it! She wanted to rip it off and put on her own, safe tunic. But she wouldn't go back to that awful room, with that horrible *man*.

Mentàll pushed Methusal behind him. "What happened here?" He addressed the shopkeeper now.

"Does the lady wish to buy the shirt?" The man's voice sounded oily. "Only twenty dascals."

Methusal averted her eyes, unwilling to look at the man. The Dehrien Chief's gaze flickered from her to the shopkeeper. Much too softly, he said, "Tell me what happened, Methusal."

With a shudder, she cast a quick glance at the man. She choked out, "He spied on me. While I was getting dressed."

Instant tension stiffened the Dehrien's body. He addressed the shopkeeper. "Is this true?"

The man emitted a high little laugh. "Your wife is an imaginative woman..." The words choked off in a gasp, because as swift as a wild beast, Mentàll grabbed the man by the throat and slammed him against the wall. The man's eyes bugged out.

"You looked at my *wife?*" he hissed.

He gurgled, "I didn't..."

"Tell the truth. Or do you prefer to die?"

The man's eyes bugged wider, and his face turned purple. His toes scrabbled for the ground. "I never meant...harm..."

"You hurt my wife. Therefore, you have hurt me." The Dehrien's lips curled back in a feral snarl. "I am not a man you want to cross."

Tears rolled down the man's face. He gurgled, "I see...that."

"Do you want the shirt, Methusal?"

"*No.*"

"Change. The shopkeeper and I will have a conversation while you are gone."

The man's eyes fluttered wildly as Methusal walked quickly past them into the dressing room. With haste, she stripped off the pretty tunic and put on her own. When she returned to the main part of the store, the shopkeeper lay doubled up on the floor, holding his stomach and gasping for air.

Mentàll held the door open, and they walked into the sunshine.

She still trembled from the encounter. The Dehrien walked silently, and tension simmered from him like a palpable force.

The wild beast in him had leaped from its lair once again; it was the first time she'd seen it since the Quasr War. A few minutes ago, he had looked like he could have happily killed the shopkeeper. But why? Male possessiveness? After all, during this trip, she belonged to him—in the eyes of the Zindedis, at least. Maybe Mentàll was not a man to allow another to infringe upon his territory.

"I'm sorry," she offered. "I didn't mean..."

"*You* are sorry?" He suddenly faced her. "You have nothing to feel sorry for."

"What if the Presidente hears about it? What if the shopkeeper tells the military? What if they start looking for you?"

He resumed walking. "He will not. I made sure of it."

Methusal didn't want to ask how he'd elicited such a promise. And she wondered if anything could be certain in this foreign country.

"When you were upstairs, did you see into the compound?"

"Yes. I saw a garden. Tables were set up, as if for a party. Soldiers cover the compound."

"So we can't get in."

"No. Not unless we can discover a secret entrance."

"What will we do, then?"

"I will write a letter to the Presidente tonight, offering peace. His response will determine our next course of action."

Methusal still felt unsettled. That awful shopkeeper could report the incident to the authorities. Their cover could be compromised. But she did feel grateful that Mentàll had defended her honor. Rightly or wrongly, it seemed like he cared, and that meant something to her.

"Thank you."

With surprise, he glanced at her. His unexpected smile took her breath away, because it completely transformed his face. "You are welcome, Methusal. I would do nothing else."

She smiled, too.

They spent the rest of the day spying on the Presidente's palace, and watching guard rotations. In the late afternoon they watched the comings and goings on the base, too. In the evening, when it grew cool again, they headed back in the direction of the Presidente's palace.

"Maybe we should be careful," she said. "They might get suspicious if they see us too often."

But he only smiled a bit and opened the door to the first dress shop they had visited that morning. The lady in purple immediately hurried over.

Mentàll said, "My wife would like to buy the jacket."

"The one upstairs?"

He nodded. Methusal stared at him in surprise. Within moments, the woman returned with the coat folded over her arm.

"It is the best quality," she gushed. "Would you like it wrapped?"

The Dehrien Chief said, "No. I believe she would like to wear it."

Lost in wonder, Methusal slipped her arms into the soft jacket. It fit perfectly, as if it had been made for her. She'd never owned anything so fine in her entire life.

Dascal notes changed hands. They left the shop and headed back to Feldon Street.

"Thank you, Mentàll."

"You are welcome."

"It didn't cost too much?"

"No." He didn't appear to want to talk about it. He opened Mrn. Machblin's door and ushered her inside.

Their landlady came out of the kitchen. Her gaze assessed each of their faces. Methusal had already forgotten about the fight that morning. But that was the last time Mrn. M had seen them. "You had a good day?"

Methusal smiled. "Yes, thank you. Did you?"

Mrn. M raised a quick shoulder. "It was busy." She glanced at Mentàll again, as if trying to measure the level of true healing in their relationship. "What did you do?"

His arm went around her shoulders. "Midi needed a new coat."

Methusal flashed him a quick smile. She didn't even have to fake it.

In a low voice, he said, "Now you will be warm at night." He kissed the top of her head. The gesture confused her, because for a second it actually felt real.

"Well." Approval sparkled. "I hope you're hungry. I've cooked a cobbler for desert. I know what a sweet tooth you have, Lozar."

Mentàll grinned widely. Glimpsing it, Methusal stared in utter shock. His smile earlier today had been unusual, but she'd certainly never seen him *grin* before. He almost looked boyish.

"Thank you, Mrn. M."

"You're welcome." She wiped her hands on a dishtowel. "Gorj washed clothes today, so they're on your bed. He noticed the quilt has been used. Do you need another? The house gets cold at night."

"Yes, thank you," Methusal said quickly. "I've been a little chilly."

"Help yourself. Look in the hall closet."

Methusal would have liked to get two or three quilts. One to sleep on, folded up, and two more to keep her warm. But that would make Mrn. M suspicious. So she chose a beautifully quilted one in creams, oranges and browns. The invisible Gorj, whom she had yet to see, kept the house well swept. At least the quilt wouldn't get dirty on the floor.

Mrn. M served a delicious dinner of roast meat and tubers, with a salad and the promised berry cobbler. The Dehrien Chief ate two helpings of everything.

Mrn. M watched him with a twinkle in her eyes. "I remember when my man used to eat up everything I cooked. It is good to feed a healthy appetite again."

He sat back in his chair. The perpetual lines of tension on his face had relaxed. He actually looked peaceful.

Methusal said, "Were you able to do something fun today, Mrn. M?"

A faint frown touched her brows, and she cast a quick glance at the front door. "Well... I had lunch with an old friend."

"Did you enjoy it?"

Mrn. M laughed shortly. "Of course. The flowers on the living room table are from him."

Him. Methusal glanced into the living room, and for the first time noticed the lush bouquet of yellow flowers. They dripped over the edges of the vase. Mrn. M's obvious discomfort continued to feed her curiosity. "He's a good friend, then?"

Tears suddenly wet Mrn. M's eyes. "No one will ever take my Charlie's place."

"Of course not." With compassion, Methusal touched her hand.

"But, well...I've known him for years. He was a good friend of Charlie's."

"If you're not ready, maybe you should take the relationship slowly. Not that it's any of my business," she added hastily. "I'm certainly no expert. I've dated the same man for three years, and..." She stopped abruptly and glanced at Mentàll. His eyes had narrowed.

"Really, now?" Interest sharpened Mrn. M's voice. "You two have seen each other for three years?" She glanced at the two of them. "I would never have guessed."

Methusal fumbled to find the right words. "I *did* date a man for three years. But then...well, uh..."

"She fell in love with me," Mentàll inserted smoothly.

She frowned. "It wasn't nearly so simple." Then she caught herself. What was she saying? *Just agree with him!*

Confusion registered in the Zindedi woman's expression.

"Yes," Methusal said stiffly. "I fell in love with Lozar. It caught me by surprise. It caught *everyone* by surprise."

"Except for me," her fake husband asserted.

She frowned at him again. "Life isn't nearly as simple as I thought it would be."

Mrn. M's eyes softened. "And your other young man. Was he heartbroken?"

"Um...yes. I felt awful about it."

Mentàll said, "We needed a new start. That is why we came here for our honeymoon. I thought Carachki would be the perfect place. No distractions can come between us. We can become very close."

Mrn. M said, "Yes. A good way to start your marriage. Well, I'm off to wash dishes."

"I'll help," Methusal offered instantly.

"No. Spend time with your new husband." She smiled. "That's why you're here."

Methusal and the Dehrien Chief helped carry dishes into the kitchen, and then they retreated to their room.

"That's quite the fiction you cooked up," she told him, arranging her quilts on the cold stone floor.

"Choosing the truth seemed like the best idea."

"Truth?" She gasped in exasperation. "Yes, I've dated Behran for three years, but that's the only truth in the story."

"Tell me, Methusal. Why haven't you married him yet?"

"What business is that of yours?"

"Behran is a more patient man than I would ever be."

"*Behran* is a gentleman. A quality you'll never understand."

"I understand passion. If I wanted a woman, I would not wait three years to have her."

"Of course not. All you care about is your base lusts. The love Behran and I share has evolved beyond that."

"At last you admit the truth," he said softly.

"What truth?"

"No passion lives between you."

Anger swamped her. With vengeance, she pitched a pillow at him. "I love him!"

He caught it easily. In an infuriatingly calm voice, he said, "Do you?"

Methusal heaved a breath to try to calm temper. How could the peace that had built between them earlier in the day disintegrate so quickly? "You know *nothing* about love. Nothing! How could you?"

"What does that mean?"

She bit her lip. "Never mind. I hate this. I don't want to fight."

"Tell me what you were going to say."

She stared at him for a moment, and then said softly. "I don't think you've been loved by very many people, Mentàll. How could you possibly know what love is?"

He went very still. A faint flush touched his cheekbones. "My mother loved me."

"I'm sure she did. But…"

"I understand what love is not, Methusal. It is not stringing a man along for three years, while you *try* to decide when you can stomach marrying him."

"How dare you? I want to marry Behran. I agreed to marry him…"

"You didn't set the date until I pushed you, in Dehre. Isn't that right? If it wasn't for me, Behran would still be dangling at the end of your string."

She trembled with anger, but fought to keep her voice low so Mrn. M wouldn't hear. "What does it matter to you what I feel for Behran? You just like making me miserable! And I understand why."

His eyes narrowed. "Why?"

"I'm sorry that you lived an awful childhood. And I'm very sorry that you were beaten so horribly. But now hurting people is the only way you know how to live. And you're good at it. You're *excellent* at it."

His fists briefly clenched at his sides. "This argument is accomplishing nothing."

"You're right. But it's also true that you're the one who doesn't want to hear the truth. You hurt people, Mentàll."

"You know *nothing* about pain. Or what hurts."

"I do."

His hands fisted. With a quick twist of his shoulders, he stalked away. "You would never understand."

"Why not?"

"Because you haven't *lived* it," he snarled. Unexpectedly, he stripped his shirt over his head and advanced toward her. "Do you know what it's like to be beaten every day of your life, just for *breathing*? To be told you're a worthless, dirt eating rocher since the day you turned five?" She backed away. "To be told no one will ever love you because you're a bastard and the son of a bastard. Do you know what it's like to feel alone? To cry yourself to sleep every night until you can't cry anymore? Until you can't *feel* anymore?"

He turned, so that only his scarred back faced her. Hundreds of lines had sliced through his flesh as a child, leaving long white scars. In a low hiss, he said, "Those lashes were the only thing I felt. Only the pain told me I was still alive."

He yanked his shirt back on and stalked away. "Do not talk to me about pain, or hurt, Methusal. You will *never* understand it."

Methusal stood silently, trembling a little. "I'm sorry."

He said nothing, just sat on his side of the bed, back to her.

She said, "I'm sorry those terrible things happened to you." Tears slipped down her face. She wiped them away, and retreated into the relief room to change.

Methusal slowly dressed. It had hurt him when she'd said he knew little about love. It was clear that he knew a lot about pain.

She should have stopped the argument before hurting him still more. Yes, he sliced under her skin like a flaying knife. But he'd done that during the war, too. And she'd learned to treat his wounds with kindness.

Because she'd asked The One for help. For the first time in months, she remembered that.

Raw pain festered inside Mentàll, and she'd had no idea. She'd wrongly believed that he felt nothing because icy control permeated every word he spoke, and every decision he made. Except she'd seen his fury with the shopkeeper today. And once, during the Quasr War, his hatred for his father, the man who had abandoned both him and his mother, had blazed as white hot as the sun.

Maybe that was why the Prophet had admonished her to live at peace with her enemies. To *love* them, and treat them kindly. To forgive them. It was easy to judge. But she was beginning to see she knew little about the Dehrien Chief. In fact, right now she suspected she'd only seen a glimpse of the true man, encased under all that ice.

Deep, raw pain lived inside the Dehrien. She'd felt it several months ago, and just now she'd felt it again. She also felt terrible that she'd opened his old wounds again. Even more perplexing, the healer in her wanted to soothe the hurt, just like she'd cared for his physical wounds during the war.

If these wounds could ever be healed.

The One, I'm sorry. Please help me. Because no matter how good my intentions are right now, I know I'll slip again. Help me to do the right thing all *the time, no matter how hard it is.*

And then she knew one small thing she could do to make things better now.

Gathering up her clothes, she opened the door. Tension still simmered in the room.

Mentàll appeared to be writing on a parchment. Not a movement or eye flicker indicated that he'd noticed her leave the relief room.

Methusal gathered her courage and walked over to him. Finally, he looked up. That pale gaze looked as remote as a glacier.

"I'm sorry," she said again. "And I was wrong earlier, too. I know you love Hendra. I know you've done everything in your power to protect her for her whole life." Mentàll had saved his cousin from many of those same beatings, and had instead taken them upon himself. What stronger proof of love could there be? "And I know that she loves you, too."

"Your apology is accepted." He returned to his task.

She retreated to her own side of the bed, arranged the quilts and pillow to her liking, and lay down. Even with a little padding, the stone floor bit like the sharpest teeth into her hip. She flipped onto her back and looked at the ceiling. The lamp on Mentàll's side cast the black shadow of his head, larger than life, on the ceiling. The flame flickered, and so did the shadow. Ephemeral. Fleeting. ...How fragile their lives were.

A flickering shadow one moment. Gone the next. Melancholy gripped her. Surely life had to be about more than pain and war and hard circumstances.

She missed Behran suddenly, and fiercely. She missed his warmth and comfort, and his smile that always made her feel better. And the security she felt in his arms. She wanted this mission done. She wanted to go home.

△ △ △ △ △

Black night cloaked Hendra, Behran, Sozla, Doc, and Goric as they crouched on a hilltop overlooking the military encampment. The sun had set four hours ago, and a cold breeze rippled through the tall, dry grass surrounding them. Adrenaline and fear made Hendra feel jittery.

Riln and Tabor had left that morning to follow the Zindedi military carts, and they hadn't returned yet. Hendra was glad. Knowing Riln's impulsive, violent nature, she was happy he wouldn't join them on the mission tonight.

Tomorrow Timaeus would run to Carachki and report the information they discovered to Mentàll.

Hendra had a clear view of the small, western side entrance of the base. One guard strolled by with a gun on his shoulder. A few lamps hung on poles inside the compound. Most of the buildings lay dark and quiet on the western and northern sides of the base. Behran thought they were storehouses. The eastern side housed the soldiers' quarters and kitchen. Lights still blazed from those windows.

When more lights went out, they would make their move.

"Remember," Behran whispered. "No more than an hour on the base. If someone gets in trouble chirp three times, loudly, like a flying beast."

Behran and Goric would infiltrate the storehouses, and Hendra would take Sozla to the weapons making building. It might be locked, so Doc would go with them. Neither Doc nor Sozla knew kaavl. It was up to Hendra to protect their lives.

Everyone wore dark clothes like the Zindedi soldiers. Hendra had piled her hair under a dark cap.

The cold breeze made her shiver, and by the time most of lights had gone out on the base, her hands felt like ice and she shivered uncontrollably.

"Hendra," Behran whispered. "Can you see when the guard will leave the gate?"

She concentrated on the wire mesh gate. The soldier strolled by again...and then she felt the subtle shift into the future. The soldier strolled left, and leaned on a building. A match flickered. The smokestick tip flared red in the dark. He sighed with contentment. More minutes ticked by, but he remained where he stood.

With a small gasp, Hendra returned to the present. After reporting what she'd seen, she said, "He's staying within sight of the gate. How will we get past him?"

"A diversion. I'll go north and make noise. Doc, you and Hendra go to the gate. When it's clear, get inside. Someone may need to take out the guard if he heads back before I can get inside."

"I'll do it." Perspiration slicked Hendra's palms. "I have kaavl strips."

The soldier wandered north and leaned against the building.

"Now," Behran hissed. Bending low, he ran down the dark hillside. It was a good thing Ryon hadn't risen yet, or he'd be clearly seen.

Far down the fence line now, Behran threw rocks and a stick against the fence. The soldier abruptly straightened and strolled toward the sound.

Without speaking, Hendra and Doc sprinted for the gate. Doc knelt before the gate and inserted the wire pin while Behran flung more sticks. He'd taken refuge behind a small bush. It was large enough to hide his body in the dark, moonless night.

Doc's fingers delicately worked the wire. Long seconds ticked by, and then a minute.

It was taking too long.

Heart pounding, Hendra stared at the building the soldier would have to round when he returned. She concentrated, shifting into the future. Nothing... Oh no.

"He's coming!" she gasped. "Oh Doc, hurry."

"How long?" He sounded calm.

"Two minutes. Maybe."

"I'll get it." Doc put his ear to the lock. The wire clicked on. Endlessly.

Any second now...

"Got it."

The next moment, the two of them slipped inside, and so did Sozla and Goric. And then Behran appeared like a tall, dark ghost, and slipped inside, too. He pulled the gate to, and the five sprinted for the quiet, northern part of the base.

They stopped in the black shadow of a huge building.

"That was exciting," Sozla murmured.

"We'll meet here in an hour," Behran whispered.

The small party split up. Hendra, Doc and Sozla headed for the northeastern corner of the base, where, according to Tabor, the weapons making facility was located.

Hendra advanced slowly, shifting into the future from time to time. But this part of the base currently appeared to be deserted. Finally, they reached the huge, silent warehouse. A locked door met them.

"Let's circle the building," she whispered to the others.

This silent trek took a few minutes as they picked through the weeds growing against the large building. They didn't dare walk on the black paths, which were lit by lanterns on poles.

The weapons facility was at least twenty lengths long, and ten wide.

On the southern side of the building they discovered two massive double doors, locked with chains. The warehouse hugged the eastern fence, and when they rounded the northern end, a small road separated the building from a deep chasm. A fence enclosed it. This must be the pit Riln had seen.

The lamps cast only a little light into the monstrous pit, but from the little Hendra could see, it looked very deep. Perhaps ten lengths or more, as Riln had reported.

Sozla peered in. "I would hate to fall in there."

Huge double doors led into the weapons facility on the northern side, too. They were locked with chains and two locks.

"Let's try the first door we saw," Doc said.

Stealthily, they slipped back. "I have seen no windows," Sozla hissed.

"Look up," Doc whispered.

Far overhead, black glass glinted in the starlight. Hendra wondered why there weren't windows on the lower level. Perhaps what went on in the weapons making facility was top secret.

Still, they saw no one. In the distance, though, she heard doors slam, and a loud laugh.

Only starlight illumined the western door. Doc struggled with the lock for a long time before it popped it open.

The door swung open, revealing pitch black.

"Perhaps a lantern is near the door," Sozla whispered.

One benefit of the windows being so high was that no one would see a bright light moving around inside.

After closing the door behind them, Hendra searched the wall. Her fingers touched a smooth, polished surface. "I found one." She sneezed.

Doc lit a match. Orange light flared across his features. Quickly, he turned the wick down low so no light would glow through the upper windows and spill out into the night.

They surveyed their surroundings.

The warehouse consisted of one enormous room. The ceiling towered at least four lengths overhead. Tools lined the walls, and pieces of ore lay in piles along the edges. In the middle of the room were platforms with monstrous tubes mounted on wheels. Tabor was right. They looked like giant guns.

"They're *huge*," Hendra whispered. She sneezed again, and realized a thick layer of dust covered everything. "I don't think they've manufactured weapons for a while."

"Tabor said the mine looked picked clean. Probably ran out of ore a while back."

They circled the room, carrying the lantern, and in one corner discovered deep vats and giant molds. Probably to make the huge guns.

Hendra found round ore balls, as big as a man's hand, stacked in open wooden crates. "Look," she said softly. "Do you think these are the bullets for the big tubes?"

Doc squatted beside her. "Those could cause a lot of damage."

"Why make such large guns? Their smaller ones can already kill men."

"These are meant to destroy larger things. Like ships, or buildings. Maybe the Presidente used them during their civil war."

"Doc, may I have the lantern, please?" Sozla said.

"Sure."

Sozla climbed onto one of the platforms and inspected the closed end of the gun-like tube.

Just thinking about men inflicting such damage on other Zindedis, and on their homes and places of business made Hendra feel sick. An awful thought crossed her mind.

"What if they put these guns on ships? They could stay safely at sea while they attack Koblan's coastal towns!"

"That's why we're here," Doc said grimly. "To stop them."

"Doc, please would you hold the lantern?" Sozla said. "I need to remove the back panel of the gun."

Hendra spotted a desk and slipped over to investigate.

Although the surface was bare, a lone drawer contained two sheaves of papers. An inventory list and diagrams. She drew a quick breath of excitement. These were diagrams of the giant guns! If she could just find one with a close-up of the firing mechanism. Rapidly, she flipped pages. Notes indicated the giant guns were called cannons. This diagram looked promising...

A door slam interrupted her concentration.

Instantly, the lantern went black, and smoke drifted to her nostrils.

Her heart pounded and she grabbed the diagram, swiftly folded it, and tucked it into her waistband. Silently, she moved toward the platform where Doc and Sozla were. Or had been.

Boot steps sounded on the wooden floor. And the click of a gun.

Zindedi soldiers.

∆ ∆ ∆ ∆ ∆

Methusal woke with a gasp. It seemed like she'd only been asleep for moments. Silent footsteps alerted her to why she'd awoken.

Mentàll headed for the door, fully dressed in dark clothes.

She sat up. "Where are you going?"

"I am delivering the letter to the Presidente." His voice sounded harsh in the silent room.

"Do you want me to come with you? I could be your lookout."

"No. Go back to sleep, Methusal."

Quietly, he pulled the door closed behind him. After a moment, she lay back down, pulling the warm quilts over her body. But now she was wide awake. Why hadn't he told her that he'd planned to deliver the letter to the Presidente tonight?

Minutes crept by, and then perhaps an hour. She felt unsettled, and then realized she was listening intently, waiting for him to return. She wasn't sure why. Mentàll could certainly take care of himself.

More long minutes passed. Exhaustion pulled at her mind, and she was drifting on the edge of sleep when he finally returned.

Silently, he crossed to his side of the room. Soft, muffled movements told her he had stripped off his clothes, readying for bed. She closed her eyes, even though the room was pitch dark and the bulk of the bed hid him from sight. A faint squeak and sigh told her he lay on the bed.

She didn't have to ask if the mission had been a success. Of course it had.

Would the Presidente accept peace? She also wondered if he'd think the letter had been delivered by ship, or if he'd guess they were in Zindedi. The game had begun.

△ △ △ △ △

Hendra's heart raced. The soldiers had seen the light. Of course they'd head straight for it.

She heard nothing. No breaths. Just eerie silence.

She had no idea where Doc and Sozla might be, but guessed they would head for the door, if they could.

Pitch black enfolded her like a living, suffocating thing. She needed to escape. But how could she find the door without accidentally running into a Zindedi soldier?

She tried to shift into the future, but fear gripped her, holding her back.

She saw nothing but pitch black.

Hendra followed the edge of the platform with her fingertips until it ended in empty air. How far away was the next canon platform? *Where* was the next one?

More cautious steps forward, and her knee connected with a corner. She swallowed back a soft gasp of pain.

Although she couldn't hear them, the Zindedis felt close. Shivers crept down her spine.

She moved faster, following the platform, and then blindly walked to the next one. She was heading for the southern wall. After reaching it, she could follow it west to find the exit.

Silent breaths seemed to reach out and envelop her. Warmth touched her skin, as if someone was close enough to touch her. In a blinding moment of panic she realized that she'd slipped into the future. It hadn't happened yet.

Hendra hurried faster. Her nose began to itch. She pinched it, and slammed into yet another platform

Searing, blinding pain ripped down her knee.

Now she felt the warmth for real, touching her skin, soft as a caress.

"*No!*" Too late, she realized she panted it.

Fingers bit into her shoulder. A scream gathered in her throat. "Hendra," Doc whispered.

Doc. Her racing, panicked heart rate slowed down. "Where's Sozla?"

"We split up." His hand found hers. Warm and secure, he clasped it tightly, as if he didn't want to let her go. "She has great night vision, so she's heading directly for the door. She has a piece of the mechanism."

"Why didn't you go with her?"

"She thought she'd be safer alone. I wanted to find you."

"I'm supposed to be protecting *you*. I'm the one who knows kaavl."

"Help, by all means." She heard the smile in his voice. "We're not out of here yet."

Five lengths away, a slice of gray flashed. A dark figure slipped out the door.

A light flashed and a gun exploded. Hendra gasped. Sozla!

"Doc."

"Shh." He pulled her against the southern wall.

Footsteps *clunked*, and someone threw the door open wide. Pale starlight filtered in, revealing that a heap of ore lay between them and the door. She and Doc swiftly crawled over and hid beside it. Another soldier joined the one in the doorway.

"Get him?"

"No."

"Who was it? What was he doing in here?"

A lantern flared to life. Warm orange light licked over Hendra's curled legs. She shrank back, against Doc. His chest felt warm and solid, and beneath her, his thighs, taut with muscle. Embarrassment flared. She was practically sitting in his lap! She tried to move away, but his hands curled around her shoulders, stopping her. He said nothing, but she sensed his calm.

The soldiers walked closer.

"Do you think it was an eastern Zindedi spy?"

"We crushed them. They wouldn't dare."

They were less than a length away. Hendra closed her mind to the panic and concentrated hard to shift into the future.

Two Zindedi soldiers stared down at her, jaws slack with surprise. Then the larger one bellowed, "Seize them!"

With a gasp, she slipped back into the present.

She looked around for something to throw so she could divert their attention, but saw nothing but giant ore rods. "The wire," she whispered to Doc.

His thighs shifted. His hand slid by her leg, and she realized he was searching in his pocket. A hot blush seared her skin. If it wasn't for this life and death situation, she'd bolt to the other side of the room.

Cold wire slipped into her palm. Hendra crept forward. The wire had to hit metal. From her limited angle right now, she saw only one cannon, and that was too far away. But she'd glimpsed another, closer one, before ducking behind the ore heap. It was located just beyond the soldiers. She moved forward, ignoring her fear. Right now she had to act, or die.

Black Zindedi legs. She didn't dare look up, for fear she'd freeze in panic. Swiftly, she threw the wire at the nearest cannon.

Ping.

At first she thought they hadn't heard it.

Then one man clicked his gun. "What was that?"

"A rodent." But they moved to investigate. Their backs were to Hendra and Doc.

"*Now,*" she whispered. Bent double, she shot for the door.

A gun blasted. Pain seared her arm. Still, she kept running through the door, and into the cold, dark night. Another gun blast. Doc! A quick glance proved he was right behind her.

"Stop!"

Hendra darted around the nearest building. Her arm throbbed, but she ignored it, and shifted into the future before turning each corner.

Shouts erupted from all over the compound. Hendra saw soldiers coming and slipped north, and then west. She suddenly realized that she saw only the future, although she ran in the present. Surreal.

Soldiers rounded a corner. They needed to move faster! She grabbed Doc's hand and shot for the next building. Safety. Now the western fence loomed.

The guard. And where were Behran and the others?

Seconds later, they neared the last building before the gate. She peeked around the corner. Behran and Sozla looked down at the unconscious guard. But that was the *future.*

Confused, Hendra closed her eyes, trying to catch her breath.

A gurgle caught her attention. She peeked around the corner again. Behran had just attacked the guard with a kaavl stick. As soon as the man fell, Sozla darted up and pulled the keys from his pocket.

Meanwhile, Goric struggled with the gate. He hissed, "It's locked!"

"Here." Sozla ran and fit a key in the lock. It clicked open. Everyone slipped outside.

"Give those to me," Behran whispered. "We'll need to trick them into thinking we're still on the base."

Sozla handed over the keys, and Behran swiftly locked the gate and then tossed the keys inside, so they landed in the guard's lax hand. "Let's go!"

Silently, they ran for the forest. On the hilltop, they paused and looked out over the military compound. Lights blazed, and men shouted. Zindedi soldiers swarmed the base.

A pack of men discovered their fallen comrade at the western gate. One rattled the gate's lock and shouted, "They're still inside!"

"Come on," Behran said tersely. "If we're lucky, they'll think they have eastern Zindedi spies on the base."

It was a smart idea. Hendra had wondered why Behran hadn't kept the keys, but now she understood that the suspicious activity on the base, combined with their recent arrival in Dakarra, could send up warning flags to the military. Hopefully, Behran's trick would protect them from suspicion. For now, at least.

Hendra sprinted after the others. Doc followed. Her arm burned more with each step. By the time she reached the cabin, it felt like it was on fire.

Deccia and Timaeus waited for them in the largest cabin. The anxiety on Deccia's face relaxed when she saw them all enter. She jumped up. "What happened?"

"Soldiers discovered us in the weapons facility," Sozla said. Carefully, she lay a black metal part on the table.

Doc said, "I've been wondering how. The windows were three lengths up. How did they see our light?"

Hendra didn't want to draw attention to her arm, although it burned like crazy. Blood soaked through her shirt, and she pressed the bloody patch hard with her hand to stop the flow. "It was pitch dark out. Maybe the faint light caught their attention," she said.

"I broke into one storehouse," Behran reported. "It's full of powder barrels."

Goric said, "I saw carts in another warehouse filled with barrels."

"We saw no powder in the weapons facility," Sozla said. She examined the black part on the table.

Behran moved closer to look at it. "What is it?"

Sozla told him, and the two leaned over it, heads close together, examining it. Doc told the rest of the story, and Behran interjected a few bits here and there. It turned out they'd heard the shots and figured it was time to leave. Sozla had caught up with them at the gate.

"At least no one got hurt," Deccia said with clear relief.

Timaeus stood up. "I need get an early start for my trip to Carachki tomorrow. 'Night."

After goodnights were said, Goric retreated outside, probably to the relief chamber, and Sozla and Behran remained engrossed in the piece of machinery that she'd pilfered. That reminded Hendra of something. Biting her lip against the pain, she shifted her arm and pulled out the diagram. "I found this. Will it help?"

Doc moved closer to take a look. Too late, she saw her bloody fingerprints stamped across it. His brows wrenched together. "*Hendra.*"

"I'm fine." Even though she felt a bit light-headed. "Maybe I should sit down for a minute."

"You need to sit down for more than a minute." Doc said vehemently, and directed her to the couch. "Why didn't you tell me?" He crouched beside her and gently peeled her blood soaked sleeve away from her skin.

It hurt. Tears sprang to her eyes, but she didn't want to cry.

Sozla and Behran clustered behind Doc. "Are you all right?" Sozla sounded worried. "Do you need bandages, Doc?"

"I have those in my bag. I need hot water."

Sozla hurried to the kitchen.

"I'll get your bag." Behran retreated into the men's room.

Doc flipped out a pocket knife and carefully cut away her sleeve.

"I don't want to make a fuss. I'm all right." Then why did ice pins prickle across her scalp? Why did she feel so woozy?

"You're as white as death." Concern roughened Doc's voice. "Lie down."

She obeyed, and closed her eyes while Doc dealt with her wound. "A bullet creased your arm. It's not too deep. That's the good news. But we need to prevent infection."

He urged her to drink a bitter pain powder. Although she knew he was being as gentle as possible, it hurt when he cleaned the wound. Tears slipped down her face.

"I'm sorry, Hendra."

The pain powder kicked in by the time he started the stitches. She only felt vague pinches on her arm.

When he was done, Hendra opened her eyes to find him looking down at her. Although she logically knew he was close, he seemed very far away...untouchable. Her limbs felt weightless, as if she was floating on air. "I'm done?" she murmured sleepily.

"I'll carry you to bed."

"Okay." Belated concern made her say, "Aren't I too heavy?"

He chuckled. "I'm stronger than I look." With ease, he gathered her in his arms and carried her to bed. There, he pulled the blanket over her.

She lifted her hand in the air...to him. It wavered there for a moment before he took it. "Come here," she murmured.

He went down on one knee beside her cot.

With a slow, beatific smile, she said, "Thank you." She tugged him still closer, so his face hovered inches from hers. "You're my hero."

His gaze flickered to her lips. His breaths sounded suddenly harsh. "Hendra."

Hendra felt no fear. She slid her fingers into his gleaming, dark red hair. He went very still.

"Hendra." The word sounded scratchy.

She stroked his hair and he continued to watch her, his eyes bemused and dark...and a little glazed. Lifting her head, she pressed her lips to his. "You mean so much to me," she whispered, "Don't you know that?" She tried to kiss him again, but he pulled back, pressing against her hand that was still woven through his hair.

"Hendra. You're not..."

She reached up and kissed him again. A jagged breath escaped from his throat, and then he suddenly kissed her back, hungrily accepting what she offered. Then, with a soft word, he gently freed himself. "The pain powder is affecting your thinking."

"No." She yawned in protest.

Regret flickered. "Good night, Hendra." He closed his eyes and kissed her forehead.

"Doc." But it only came out a drowsy mumble. Why did her eyelids have to feel so heavy? She wanted...no, she *needed* to talk to him.

From far away, he said, "I'll see you in the morning."

But she needed to speak to him *now*. Morning may be too late. When again would she ever feel so free to speak what she really felt for him?

CHAPTER TWENTY

Day 4

"Two letters, Presidente." With a bow, the skinny secretary deposited them on his desk and quickly retreated from the room.

The Presidente scowled after the retreating pup. *Backbone.* Too many of the next generation possessed backbones of invertebrates.

His thick fingers plucked up his small, jeweled dagger and slit open the first envelope. "What is this?" To his annoyance, his voice sounded slightly slurred and thick. As if his voice was growing fat, too. He didn't like to look at himself in the mirrors anymore, or to see the swelling flesh distorting his jowls and neck. And the launderer kept shrinking his clothes... And his tailor. The last time he'd visited, the man had scuttled away, begging entreaties for forgiveness. The fool couldn't get his measurements right.

The Presidente plucked the parchment from the envelope. The crude scrawl identified the sender. His spy in Wyen. Swiftly, he scanned the short document.

Koblanis sailed for Zindedi a few days ago. Mission unknown. Number of people on ship: crew plus eleven kaavl players. Mentàll Solboshn and Methusal Maahr are on board.

Unease rose in the Presidente. Mentàll and Methusal. The Kaavl Master and his enemy. An odd combination. Yet both were leaders of the resistance against the Zindedi invasion.

"Well." He sat back abruptly. His first stab of alarm faded quickly, replaced by contempt. A short breath escaped from his lungs. So, the Koblani rodents meant to invade his land. He laughed, and the effort sounded breathy and wheezing.

"Fools!" He crumpled the paper and hurled it to the floor. The Dehrien scum and Maahr harlot dared come to his land? They'd played perfectly into his hand. He would find them. He would crush them like insects!

His breaths came in short pants as he fantasized about meting justice to his worthless enemies. His fists clenched hard, nails digging into his palms. Perhaps one of them had murdered his brother. A pain stabbed in the area of his heart.

He struggled to quiet his pulse. He would mete out justice to every living Koblani. And when he found the one who had killed his brother, he would order him tortured until he screamed for mercy.

Cheeks folding into a smile, he licked his lips. What a sweet day of justice that would be. He would turn Koblan upside down until he found that guilty man...or woman.

The Presidente's gaze fell to the other envelope. Impatiently, he ripped it open with his bare hands.

Bold black letters, written in all capitals, scored the page. There was no humble salutation. The Presidente frowned. What *impertinent...*

Presidente. We are willing to set aside our right for vengeance. Koblan offers peace to Zindedi. We hope you will accept our generous offer. If you agree, I am authorized to offer a peace agreement for your signature.

Speak the truth in your response to this offer, because we will discover if you are lying. Violated promises will result in brutal punishment for you, and for all of Zindedi.

We await your response. Affix your return letter beneath the southern bench on the main ship dock.

Mentàll Solboshn, Chief of Dehre, Elected Spokesman for all Koblan.

"Ha!" Immediate pain skewered his chest. The Presidente drew short, impatient breaths until it subsided.

So. The Dehrien scum offered peace, and threatened war. He chuckled at the utter absurdity of it. Eleven Koblanis against all of Zindedi? What did they think they could do?

"*Ha.*" He wiped streaming eyes. It was outrageous.

Eventually mirth vanished, replaced by a steadily rising, righteous rage. "Yalin!"

"Yes, sir!" The skinny lad trembled in the doorway.

"Take down my order. The draft is initiated. Now! All un-enlisted men must join. Order the General in here."

"He...he is in Dakarra, sir. He left this morning."

The Presidente cut a fist through the air. "Then send him a missive. Tell him we will sail for Koblan in two weeks. All must be ready!"

"Yes, sir." The lad swayed in the doorway. "Anything more?"

"Yes. Tell Fitrn to get over that woman. He may not have her. That is the end of it! The *end!*" His fist slammed on the desk. "He will focus his full attention on my mission. Is that clear?"

"Yes. Yes, perfectly." Yalin fled.

The Presidente folded his hands across his soft midriff. A cruel smile curled his lips as he imagined the horrible tortures the Koblanis would suffer under General Fitrn's boot. The boy may be prissy, but he possessed a vicious streak as deep as his own...perhaps even deeper. Even better, he accomplished every task assigned to him. Worthy qualities.

His mind switched to his spy in Koblan. Would he prove himself, as well? He hadn't heard from that pup in weeks. Was he in Koblan, still?

His eyes narrowed. Or had he come to Zindedi, still cloaked as his deepest spy?

Time would tell. In the meantime, he would order the Commander of the military to start looking for Methusal Maahr and Mentàll Solboshn. They had to be in Carachki. Too bad he knew little of their physical descriptions. He knew the Dehrien was a blond giant, but the girl...she had dark hair, according to his dead brother. That was all he knew.

△ △ △ △ △

Hendra awoke slowly the next morning. Her head ached a little, and dull pain throbbed in her right arm. Last night flashed back. Escaping from the base, running home, and almost fainting. Doc bending over her, his fingers deft, but gentle on her wound. The bitter pain potion, and then...things went a little fuzzy. She couldn't remember how she'd gotten into bed.

A memory oozed in, like a slow trickle of glue. Doc had carried her. He'd laid her down on the bed, and...

Alarm stabbed her, twisting her stomach into a sick knot. No. Surely not.

Had she kissed him? Her heart pumped uncomfortably fast, and she tried harder to penetrate the syrupy, viscous memories.

Drop by drop, more memories trickled in. Doc had knelt by her bed and she'd slipped her fingers through his hair, and then...

She drew a horrified breath. She *had* kissed him! Brazenly, too. When he'd tried to pull away, she had kissed him again.

Mortification burned her cheeks. *He had kissed her back.* She remembered that, too. More heat flushed through her. It had felt nice, and she hadn't been afraid.

Hendra put her hands over her face, wanting to die from embarrassment. What must he think of her now?

She didn't want to get up or dressed. She didn't want to face him again. An unrealistic wish, living in this small cabin.

The ache in her temple sharpened when she sat up, and then slowly subsided.

Hendra dressed slowly. Her arm hurt every time she moved it. After brushing her long, white-blond hair much longer than was necessary, she drew a fortifying breath and opened the door.

Everyone appeared to be up. A babble of voices, punctuated by laughter, came from the kitchen. Forcing herself to move, she entered the warm room. Bread sizzled in a pan that Sozla tended. Most people sat the table, laughing. Including Doc. He went very still when he saw her.

Wonderful. Turning her back, Hendra poured juice into a cup. Her face felt hot, and she wondered if it was bright red. Hands trembling a bit, she lifted the cup to her lips. She wouldn't turn to face him again until her color settled down.

"Good morning, Hendra." Doc stood right beside her. She gasped, and trembled from suddenly jumping nerves.

With slow, casual movements, he poured juice into a mug. "How's your arm this morning?"

Her mouth felt as dry as the sun baked desert of Dehre. "Fine. Thank you."

"Did you sleep well?"

"Yes." She swallowed. "I'm sorry about last night."

Calmly, he said, "I'm not."

Heat washed her cheeks. "But I threw myself at you," she whispered. "I'm so embarrassed."

"Hendra." He grinned. "You can throw yourself at me any time you want."

More heat washed her face. "But...that wasn't *me*. I wasn't myself. "

His thumb rubbed the edge of his mug. "Are you sure?"

She wasn't sure. She was very confused, in fact. "I don't want to lead you on."

"You're not."

Her gaze flew to his. "I'm not?"

That blue-gray gaze held hers. "I understand who you are. Nothing has changed."

Relief flooded her. "Are you sure?"

"We're still friends."

"I'm glad." Feeling free from fear last night had felt so good. She wished she could feel that way all the time. Unfortunately, it was the drug which had helped her to relax—certainly not a solution to her problems.

She whispered, "You mean a lot to me. I don't want to lose..."

"You won't."

Mutely, she nodded.

"I'd like to take a look at your wound after breakfast. I'm not sure if you're well enough to scout with Behran and Goric today."

She felt relieved that their conversation had returned to a normal subject. "It's only a scrape. I'll be fine."

"I'll be the judge of that."

But Hendra wanted to scout. No. She *needed* to scout. In so many areas of her life, she felt like half of a person. She wanted to be worthwhile. She wanted her life to count for something. Spying on Zindedi achieved that goal. She would convince Doc that she was fine.

Δ Δ Δ Δ Δ

Deccia finished drying the last of the breakfast dishes. Timaeus had gone to their cabin to get his pack. Then he'd leave for Carachki.

Although she knew the trip was necessary, she didn't like it. Timaeus would be alone today in this awful, foreign land. The home of General Greisn–the man Timaeus had killed. What if the Presidente discovered that he had killed his brother? What if he found out Timaeus was in Zindedi?

He wouldn't. How could he learn either of those things?

Logic did not calm her fears. She didn't want Timaeus to go, and she wasn't particularly looking forward to going into Dakarra today, either. But they needed supplies.

Voices at the table interrupted her thoughts.

"Are you sure?" The Tarst doctor had just examined Hendra's bullet wound. The Dehrien girl looked a little pale, and no wonder. Her bullet wound looked raw and red, and it was at least three finger widths long, and one wide.

"It's just a little headache."

"It would be best if you stayed here. Behran and Goric can scout without you."

"I want to go." Hendra's belligerent tone surprised her. It seemed out of character for the normally soft-spoken girl.

The doctor shifted back in his chair, eyes narrowing. "Why?"

"I'm fine. Really. I'm here to help. That's what I want to do."

"I can't stop you. You know that. But..."

"Good." Hendra stood. "I appreciate your concern. I do. But I'm going." She headed out the door.

With a frown, Doc watched her go. Deccia saw the pain in his eyes, and the worry–and the mute, frustrated heat of affection.

He loved her. The realization surprised her.

For being empathic, she felt chagrined that she hadn't noticed before. She wondered if Hendra felt the same way about him.

Hendra had once told Deccia about the sexual abuse she'd suffered from her step-brother. Deccia knew how much that changed a person. That lingering horror twisted normal feelings until every healthy attraction to a man was mangled by fear. Hendra was still suffering, almost ten years after the abuse had ended.

And if Doc was in love with Hendra... Deccia eyed him with compassion. *Please help them both, The One. Even if the road ahead is rough, I pray it won't be impossible.*

She'd do whatever she could to help, too.

"Decc." Timaeus' warm hand cupped the back of her head and she drew a quick, startled breath.

"Timaeus." A smile softened her lips, and she relaxed.

His fingers stroked her hair. He seemed very large and capable, standing so close to her, but she still didn't like thinking about his trip today. She touched his chest, reassuring herself of how very strong and solid he was. "Be safe," she whispered. "I'll miss you."

His dark brown eyes smiled. "I'll be back tomorrow afternoon."

A whole day and a half. Deccia realized that she was tightly clutching his tunic. "Timaeus..." Her voice broke, and she hated it, because she wanted to be strong for him.

"It's all right." He kissed her, and pulled her close. "I'll be back before you know it."

"I know." Struggling to stiffen her backbone, Deccia pulled back and offered a small, wobbly smile. "I'll see you tomorrow."

He offered her a lingering kiss, and then Deccia walked him to the front door. She watched him until he reached the main road, and then slipped back inside. Arms crossed, she leaned against the wall, fighting tears. *Oh The One, please go with Timaeus. Keep him safe. Please! I love him so much.*

△ △ △ △ △

Sharp pains stabbed into Methusal's back when she sat up that morning—her reward for sleeping on her back all night long. Her joints felt stiff, and she was exhausted, because she'd only slept in fits and starts after Mentàll had returned. Although sleeping on her back had been uncomfortable, sleeping on her side was even worse. Every time she'd tried to do it, the bruises on her hips had ached with deep, bone drilling pain.

At least the extra blanket had kept her warm last night.

Her mind returned to the Dehrien Chief's midnight mission, and she wondered if the Presidente had read Mentàll's letter yet.

Water splashed in the relief room. Wincing with pain, she climbed to her feet and folded the quilts onto the end of the bed. A plop of the pillow beside Mentàll's crushed one, a rumpling of the covers on her side, and it appeared that she'd slept all night next to her fake husband. She surveyed her handiwork. Gorj and Mrn. M would be completely fooled.

The chill morning air bit through her nightgown, and she shivered as she gathered up her clothes. When Mentàll left the relief room, she took his place and quickly pulled on her clean tan shirt and dark pants. The beautiful pastel tunic from yesterday flitted to mind, and so did the awful man in the shop. She'd love to own more colorful tunics made from the wondrous Zindedi fabric, but not at that cost.

After pulling a brush through her long hair, she exited from the room. Mentàll sat on the bed, obviously waiting for her. He wore a dark blue shirt that intensified the glacier blue of his eyes, and light tan breeches. He appeared larger than ever.

A new day. Time for a new start.

She said, "That shirt is a good color for you."

"We have peace today, Methusal?"

"Yes. I hope you want it, too."

Those light eyes searched hers, but she could read none of his emotions. Iced away, as usual. "Yes."

"What is our plan for today?" She pulled on her wonderful, warm leather jacket.

"The Presidente will deliver his response today."

"Where?"

"Under a bench near the docks."

"They'll watch to see who picks it up."

"Of course. I hired a fisherman to pick it up this afternoon. He will deliver it to a bake shop and hide it in the napkins. We will see if he is followed. If he is, I will hire someone else to deliver the letter to me."

"What if the military questions the fisherman? Won't he be able to describe you?"

Faint amusement glimmered, and she felt an unexpected rush of relief. Everything truly was okay again.

"Are you are worried about me now, Methusal?"

"I'm worried about the *mission*," she told him. "We can't let the Presidente find us."

"He will not." Again, that supreme, arrogant confidence.

She managed not to roll her eyes, and moved toward the door. "Whatever you say. So we'll watch the bake shop all day?"

"We will watch the docks, and then the bake shop."

At the door, she turned suddenly, and the movement seemed to surprise him, because his eyelids flickered. He stopped only a few short handbreadths away from her.

Although it unnerved her that he didn't retreat a step, she tried to ignore it. "Do you mean we'll watch together? Isn't that a waste of time? One person could watch the docks and the other could spy on the Presidente's compound."

"We will stay together."

"Like last night?" The words slipped out before she could stop them.

"I accomplished that task best on my own." Gaze suddenly cool and remote, he watched her.

Suspicion flared. "What else did you do? You were gone for a long time."

A smile kicked up the corners of his lips. "You waited for me to return?"

"I couldn't sleep."

"I see." He watched her intently, as if cataloguing every emotion touching her face. "I spied on the General's house."

"What did you find out?"

"He keeps late nights, entertaining friends."

"What kind of friends?"

His gaze flickered. "You do not want to know."

"Tell me. I'm not a child."

"You are an innocent, Methusal."

A laugh caught in her throat. "You didn't think that last year. You judged me—and Rolban—guilty for all of the awful things done to you."

"I was wrong about Rolban. My father was not from your community. And I was wrong about you."

"You admit that you were wrong?"

"I always tell the truth. Have you not realized that yet?"

"I know you tell truths that benefit you."

He gave a harsh laugh and reached behind her to open the door. Cool air from the living room wafted in, scented with the aroma of warm, sweet bread and scrambled eggs.

With a faint smile, she said, "Are you trying to escape now? You've come to the end of the truths you want to tell?" She stepped out into the living room.

As he followed her out, he murmured close to her ear, "If you want to speak the complete truth to me, I would be happy to finish this conversation."

She felt as if he'd subtly turned the conversation on her. She also saw Mrn. M working on an embroidered tapestry across the room.

She whispered, "Tell me one more truth. If you find me so innocent, why do you enjoy getting under my skin every minute of the day? You take pleasure in it. Admit it. You still want to punish me for defeating you three years ago. For crushing your enormous pride."

He smiled. "You are so transparent."

"What?"

Softly, he said, "You are the one who always runs from the truth."

He was too close. She backed up a tiny step. "I don't."

"You want to flee right now."

"You're full of yourself."

"When will you admit it?"

"I want no part of *your* truth."

"Don't you?" Still, those blue eyes watched her. He moved forward, closing the space between them. Her heart jumped with sudden alarm. "Why do you want to run right now?"

Stubbornly, she held her ground. "I'm not afraid of you."

"No. You are afraid of yourself."

"I am *not*."

He moved even closer. Alarm sizzled. Mrn. M was watching them. How could she escape from this situation?

Their breaths intermingled, and her pulse seared faster.

"Stop it." Rearing back, she licked dry lips.

"Why? You are not innocent to my kisses."

"That's the problem. I can't take any more of those than I can handle." She realized that didn't make any sense at all.

He turned his head the barest fraction and slid in closer. In her ear, he said softly, "Is this better?" His warm breath caressed that delicate instrument. She shuddered in response, unable to help herself. He pressed a kiss to her jaw point, and muttered, "I am famished."

When he pulled back, amusement warmed his ice blue gaze. "Mrn. M has cooked us a feast."

Without reply, Methusal retreated to the table. Her hands trembled as she poured juice into her cup.

It was all just an act so Mrn. M will believe our marriage, she told herself. But if it was only fiction, why did she feel so shaken?

△ △ △ △ △

Under a gloomy sky, Deccia, Sozla, and Doc turned onto the main, dirt packed street of Dakarra. Deccia worried about the reaction of the soldiers and townspeople to the break-in at the military base last night. She wondered if the Dakarrans would suspect them, since they were new to the area. Or would they believe the attack had come from eastern Zindedi spies, as Behran had tried to make it appear?

She'd try to get a read on the Dakarrans today.

The heavy gray clouds threatened rain. Today only a few people wandered between the weathered buildings of Dakarra, which were separated by vacant strips of land bristling with weeds. She hoped they'd find the milk and bread they needed in one of the shops.

A cold breeze cut through Deccia's black jacket, and in the vacant lots the wind bowed the tall grasses, crowned with tiny purple flowers. How similar the Zindedi clothing was to those flowers, she thought. Beautiful, and yet unable to stand against the wind.

Few people paid them any attention this morning, for which she was grateful. She also sensed no more unfriendliness than normal from the Dakarrans. She relaxed a little more with each step. They passed Vitnia's shop. Hopefully they wouldn't see that unpleasant woman today. In fact, Deccia would prefer to purchase supplies and hurry home without talking to anyone at all.

But one of the reasons for coming into town was to see if something new might be brewing, particularly concerning the military. The people in town surely had a finger on the pulse at the base. It seemed likely that some of their men worked there.

Doc hadn't needed to come along this morning, but he'd insisted. Probably for protection, although he didn't say so. Deccia knew Sozla itched to hurry back and examine her piece of machinery.

"Where is the food shop?" Sozla said. She held her pack in her hand, carrying it like a bag. It was a good idea, because Deccia saw that the Dakarran women clutched their large bags in a similar fashion. Deccia dropped her pack down to her fingers, too.

"Over there," Doc said. He indicated a large, dark brown building across the street. "Market" was painted in green letters above the entrance. A long set of windows flanking the door displayed canned goods, cloth, and tools.

"I need a length of wire," Sozla said. "And perhaps string."

Doc held the door open for them. Inside, it took Deccia's eyes a moment to get used to the dim lighting. Gray light filtered through the windows, brightening the front half of the store, and a lamp flickered on the counter across the room. There, two women waited to buy goods.

Sozla went to investigate a display of twine and pots of nails. Doc fingered plain beige cloth. Perhaps to make more bandages.

Deccia spied the bread and plucked up several loaves. Dried fruit caught her eye, too. And a fresh piece of meat would be welcome for stew. Why had she thought they'd only need bread and milk? Tubers...

A loaf of bread toppled out of her overflowing arms.

A light laugh tinkled, and a girl with a gamin face and short, wispy blonde hair, grinned at her. She handed back the loaf. "You need a basket." She wore a green apron.

"I suppose you're right," Deccia smiled back. Finally, a friendly Dakarran. "I hadn't planned to buy so much."

The girl, who looked to be about her own age, fetched a basket and helped Deccia unload her items.

A friendly Dakarran could be a help to the team's mission, Deccia realized. "We're new here," she offered. "We're vacationing."

"I'm new, too." The girl grinned. "It's nice, if you ignore the sour busybodies."

Deccia couldn't help but smile. "I'm afraid we've met a few of those."

The door opened, letting in a waft of cold air. The shop girl made a quick face. "Here they come. Nice to meet you." She vanished toward a door in the back.

Vitnia led two other gray and black clad women inside the market. The two women flanking Vitnia's skinny form were stout, and one moved with a limping waddle. That one headed for the counter. "Hasr!" Her strident tone cut like a knife. "I need urchet meat. Do you have any fresh?"

Deccia turned away, but wasn't quick enough.

"Well." Vitnia appeared in her side vision. "You've come to town again. I hope you're finding your cabin comfortable."

Deccia reluctantly faced the repellent woman. "Yes. We've cleaned it, and it's very nice now, thank you."

Vitnia's lips curled back in the semblance of a smile. "You're new to town. You'll want to make acquaintances. Come meet my friends."

Reluctantly, Deccia followed the woman.

"Tisnia, this is..." Vitnia turned to Deccia. "What was your name again, dear?"

The fake endearment set her teeth on edge. "Deccia."

Vitnia turned back to her friend. "Deccia. Our other friend, Olita, is at the counter."

"Pleased to meet you."

"Tell us," Tisnia spoke in a high, breathy voice. "Why are you here in town?"

"We're on vacation. My husband loves the beach." True enough. Timaeus did like to visit Aestoff, on Koblan's coast.

Tisnia stared at her, as if waiting for more information. When Deccia didn't supply it, she prodded, "Where are you from?"

"Carachki." Deccia noticed that both Sozla and Doc were finished gathering necessities, so she edged toward the counter.

"Carachki!" Her dark eyes glittered. "What part? I grew up there."

Deccia's mind went blank. In a panic, she struggled to recall the books she'd studied on the ship.

"What street do you live on?" pressed the woman.

Deccia felt Vitnia staring at her. Her black eyes felt beady and intense, like a whip beast.

The street Methusal and Mentàll lived on popped to mind. "Feldon."

The woman's eyes narrowed. A little of the plump seemed to leave her feathers. "A nice area."

Vitnia interjected, "Your family must be rich, then."

Deccia could not believe the woman's nerve. Desperately, she glanced at Sozla and Doc, silently pleading for support. Within moments, the two closed ranks beside her. "Not rich," she said. "But comfortable."

Olita approached, huffing and puffing from her short trek from the counter. "Who are these people?"

Introductions were made, and all the while Deccia itched to be gone. She touched Doc's arm, silently urging him to start moving toward the counter so they could pay for their goods.

"Vacationers! Are you going fishing?" Olita's strident voice stopped them in their tracks. "My man has a boat he'll rent. He'll pilot. You don't have to do work. Just relax." Her murky green eyes narrowed, and glanced from Deccia to Sozla. "You do have husbands, don't you? I see one, but where's the other?"

Deccia wanted to say that it was none of her business.

"Fishing sounds wonderful," Sozla interjected in a cool tone. "We will tell our husbands when we return home."

"Good." A smile eased the suspicion from Olita's face. "My man's shop is across the street. Two hundred dascals for a trip. That includes transport to the beach. A good deal."

"We'll keep it in mind," Doc said. "But we need to go now. Nice to meet you." His smile looked genuine, and Olita emitted a giggle. Tisnia fanned herself and dimpled.

"You do that," Olita said.

After they paid for their goods, Deccia couldn't leave the store fast enough. Once out of earshot of the Dakarrans on the street, she said, "I've never met such nosy people."

Sozla shuddered. "To me...they are creepy. Like rochers crawling down my back."

Deccia completely agreed. If it wasn't for the nice shop girl, she might start to think all Zindedis were as unpleasant and awful as the dead General.

An involuntary shudder went through her, and she hurried faster for the cabins. Worry lodged like a nut caught in her throat. She prayed for Timaeus' protection. And she wished they could go home soon. She didn't like it here at all.

Δ Δ Δ Δ Δ

Hendra hoped it wouldn't rain. Her headache was worse, but she ignored it. She lay full length on the sandy hilltop, peering through the tall grasses down at the base. Men bustled about in a flurry of activity. They reminded her of panicked insects after an apte stirred their nest. She wondered why they were so agitated.

Suddenly, all of the men ran and lined up in straight rows, right arms bent, stiff fingers touching the opposite shoulder. The main gate slowly opened.

Hendra went up on her elbows in order to see better. A large black cart approached, pulled by two urchets. Black blankets, slashed with a stripe of red, covered the creatures' backs. Two men sat in the cart. One was the driver, and the other was a slim, light-haired man, whose back looked as straight as a tent pole. Every line of his uniform looked as crisp as an arrow. His black beret was perched at a slight angle on his head. A few of the lined up soldiers hastily fiddled with their berets, clearly trying to make them match the military man's.

He was obviously an officer of high rank.

He did not descend from the cart until two men arrived with a small staircase and positioned it perfectly so he could easily step down. One of the men carrying the steps was the potbellied, apoplectic officer she'd seen at the back fence two days ago. He'd protested this top officer coming, she realized. Was the newcomer the new top ranking General? From the reactions of everyone at the base, it seemed likely.

Perhaps he was the man who had replaced the insane General Greisn, whom Timaeus had killed in Quasr.

The breeze picked up, pitching the grasses into swaying, bobbing dances about her.

The General approached the men. Instantly, all of them stiffened their spines and took a collective breath. They stood rigidly motionless. The military officer slowly moved down the line, inspecting each person. He spoke to the thick-waisted, bald man again.

Hendra wished she was closer, so she could hear what they were saying. The portly man nodded, and the General continued. He stopped before a blond soldier. From this distance, Hendra could not see what had caught the General's interest, or what made that man different from the others. A black stick appeared in the General's hand, and he struck the soldier's face.

Crack!

Hendra gasped. The young man's head whipped right. Red suffused it.

The other troops stiffened their stance.

Feeling sick to her stomach, she watched the military officer pace down the line. Two more men did not meet his satisfaction. Hendra cringed with each cruel snap. And still more soldiers remained to inspect.

The man savored terror.

The evil of him collected in Hendra's gut, frightening her. Urging her to run. Escape. Because she understood men like him. The dead General had been one. And her dead step-brother, Jascr, had been another.

She pressed her cheek into the cold, prickly grass and closed her eyes. The pain intensified in her head, and she felt nauseous. *The One, please help the soldiers.* She couldn't stand it. She couldn't bear to watch that monster hurt one more soldier.

A cold drop of rain splashed onto her cheek. Then another. It felt refreshing. Cleansing. More rain pattered down. Drops trickled into her scalp, reminding her that she couldn't hide. She needed to watch. It was her job.

The pain behind her temple sharply intensified when she raised her head. She waited for it to subside, as it had done all day, but it did not. She peered through the grass again.

All but five soldiers had disappeared. All five bore identical red welts across their cheeks. The disfiguring slashes reminded her of the welts her father had lashed into her skin as a child. And into Mentàll's.

Horror welled in her, gathering into a sick lump inside of her.

Rain steadily dripped down. All five soldiers remained frozen in a salute, looking like statues.

She spotted the last of the other men disappearing inside the dining hall. So the unworthy soldiers had to stay out in the rain. A sick feeling told her she didn't want to know how long they would have to stay there.

With most of the soldiers inside, spying seemed a bit pointless. She could see and hear nothing. If only Methusal was here, she could carry with hearing and discover what the General was saying in the dining hall.

Going up on her hands and knees, Hendra scooted back into the protection of the forest. She wasn't sure if she should stay until the rain stopped, or head back to the cabin.

Wet splotches soaked her tunic. The fabric clung to her arm. A quick touch told her the bandage over her wound was damp, too. Doc wouldn't be thrilled.

But Hendra remained where she was, shivering and watching the military compound, until Behran and Goric suddenly appeared. Her head hurt more with every passing minute.

Behran frowned when he saw her shaking shoulders. "Come on. We're done for today."

She fell into step with them. "Who was that man? Is he the top General?"

"Yes," Goric said shortly. "General Fitrn."

"He's awful." She shuddered with cold. "Just like the old General. Does the Presidente only hire insane people?"

No one answered. Silently, they tramped through the undergrowth in the fragrant forest.

"We need to get closer to the base, so we can hear what's going on," Goric said abruptly. Those murky gray eyes looked hard. "I'll go tonight. Alone."

Behran said, "Let's wait until Riln and Tabor get back."

"We'll spy at night, too?" Hendra asked.

"Goric is right. We need do to get closer, so we can hear what they're saying. Watching from a distance has benefits, but I think we need to split up into teams. One to scout during the day, and one at night."

"I'll scout at night." Hendra liked the idea of gathering useful information.

"We'll see what Doc has to say about that."

She frowned. "Why?" Her headache sharpened again. She closed her eyes, struggling not to wince.

"You're injured. He decides what is best for you." Thankfully, ahead of her, Behran did not notice her pain-contorted face.

Back at the cabin again, she longed for dry clothes and to lie down, but Behran and Goric pulled up chairs and related their discoveries to the others. She thought she should participate in the meeting, too.

However, she could barely think now through the blinding, pulsing pain in her head. Spots danced before her eyes, and she drew a slow, shaky breath. *I am all right.*

Behran's voice droned on and on. Would he ever stop? She shivered from cold, and she felt nauseous. Peculiar prickling sensations crept over her skin. The room dimmed, and she drew a quick breath of panic. She was going to be sick. She lurched to her feet and bolted for the door.

She felt cold, and then hot, and then sweaty cold again as she stumbled down the porch steps.

She spied a bush and lurched for it. But retching convulsions seized her before she reached it. Strong hands gripped her shoulders. "Hendra." Doc's calm, soothing voice murmured things that barely registered.

She threw up until all that remained were dry heaves. And still she felt no better.

"Hendra?"

"My head's spinning," she whimpered.

Without a word, Doc picked her up and carried her inside to her room. "She's freezing." He spoke to someone. "Help her change into dry clothes. I'll be back when you're done."

Deccia's kind, concerned face swam above her, and Hendra struggled to help wriggle out of the wet clothes. Dry clothes went on easier. "There." Deccia touched her forehead with the back of a warm hand. "You feel cold. Here's Doc."

"How are you feeling?"

She shivered. "Cold. Strange." Her head still didn't feel quite right, and she closed her eyes as he pulled a blanket over her.

"I'm going to check your wound."

She felt his gentle hands on her arm, but the bandage stuck to her scab when he pulled it off. Tears ran out the corners of her closed eyes. His hand touched her temple in quiet apology. The wound burned as he cleaned it and wrapped it back up again.

She opened her eyes again. The gray sunlight blinded her, intensifying the pain in her head. With a moan, she squeezed them shut.

"Headache?" he said sympathetically. "I'll give you something for it. Your arm is fine. No sign of infection."

She mumbled, "So what's wrong with me?"

"You did too much too soon."

He'd warned her, and she hadn't listened.

"You'll be fine. Sip this." Doc put a cup to her lips and cradled her head up so she could drink.

Afterward, he crossed the room and closed the curtains. The dark shadows soothed her eyes. She sensed when he came back, and dared to open her eyes again. He stood over her.

"Sleep," he advised. "Stay in bed for the rest of the day."

She felt awful enough that she didn't argue.

He smiled, and unexpectedly kissed her forehead. His lips lingered for a moment, and a sweet curl of pleasure drifted through her.

"Sleep, sweet Hendra. You'll feel better later. I promise."

"I hope so," she whispered. She had to feel better. Because right now, she couldn't possibly feel any worse.

△ △ △ △ △

They spied in downtown Carachki, near the docks, waiting for the letter from the Presidente to arrive. Mentàll wore a dark cap, as did many of the Zindedi men. It covered his distinctive white blond hair.

So far, the morning had crept by with slow boredom. At least Mentàll had let her wander off a few times, in pretext of watching the bench from different angles. It hadn't added much excitement to the task, but she'd liked being on her own for a little while.

Just after noon, a black clad soldier strode onto the dock and adhered the letter beneath the bench. Four other men in civilian clothes lingered on the street nearby. When their companion returned, they all split up. Two stationed themselves at the end of the dock, and the other three took up residence on nearby street corners.

A quick scouting trip confirmed Methusal's suspicion. She looked for Mentàll and found him sitting on a bench on a narrow side street with a clear view of the dock. He sat hunched over, reading a newspaper. If not for his long legs, she wouldn't recognize him, hidden behind the paper as he was.

"I only saw the five soldiers," she reported.

"We will still take every precaution. Are you hungry?"

Her stomach growled, answering for her. "What do you have?"

The newspaper lowered a fraction. Amusement glimmered. "You are hungry. Does it matter what I have?"

"I'm choosy."

"Yes, you are." His gaze held hers. "A good quality."

Why did everything he say end up sounding suggestive, and fraught with double meanings? Or was she imagining things? "What did you buy?"

He poked into a white paper bag beside him and pulled out two paper wrapped items. "A meat sandwich. Or a fluffy egg sandwich." His amusement still lingered, perplexing her.

"I like meat."

He handed her the sandwich. His calloused fingers brushed hers. "I knew you would. You require substance to satisfy you."

Her cheeks flushed. She snatched the sandwich and scooted none too discretely down the bench, far away from him.

A quiet chuckle rumbled in his throat.

She tore off a hungry bite. Through a full mouth, she said, "You can't help but be a wild beast, can you?"

"Not when it is so easy to provoke you." He took a big bite of the egg sandwich. "It is gratifying."

She rolled her eyes. So, the maddening man admitted he liked playing with her because it amused him. In silence, she finished her lunch. She crumpled up the paper and looked around for a trash bin.

"Give it to me." Mentàll extended a wide-palmed hand.

She eyed it with suspicion. "What game are you planning now?"

A short, rusty chuckle erupted. "I am sorry, Methusal. But you tempt me. I cannot help myself."

With a faint "Hmph," she ignored his hand and tossed the wadded paper into the lunch bag.

His smile lingered. "Your skills continue to surprise me."

"Enough," she told him.

He stiffened. "Look."

She glanced over at the docks. A blue capped, burly fisherman fumbled under the bench. A white envelope appeared in his hand. He straightened and turned it over, and then over again in his hands, examining it. Finally, with a shrug, he stuffed it in his pocket and ambled down the dock.

The soldiers at the end of the pier melted away, trying to look inconspicuous. However, as the fisherman shuffled down the street, all five followed him. The Zindedi fisherman didn't seem to notice.

Methusal followed behind the soldiers, while Mentàll, with a murmured word that he would be back, disappeared around the corner of a building.

She followed the procession at a discrete distance, and paused from time to time to peer in store windows. She didn't have to pretend interest. The Zindedis made so many beautiful things. Red glass vases, ore twisted into table stands and lamps...the variety seemed endless. Each thing looked more exotic than the last.

The fisherman entered a shop that had a carved ship plaque above the door. Minutes later, when he left, two Zindedi soldiers entered the store. Methusal moved closer, pretending to be absorbed in the cookware displayed in the window of the shop next door. She projected her hearing into the ship store. Raised voices blasted her eardrums.

"What did he want? What did he do?"

"I don't know." The man, probably the shopkeeper, had a thick accent. Methusal glanced at the shop's doorway and carried with vision so she could see through the glass.

A dark-haired, bespectacled man cowered inside, hands raised above his head. "I swear it. He left nothing. He bought nothing. You may look through my shop."

"We will." One soldier swept a violent arm down the counter, scattering trinkets all over the floor. An ore bell let out a harsh clang and lay still. The other soldier kicked a glass display of a model ship. Glass shattered. Another kick, and the ship splintered to pieces. Methusal gasped, appalled.

The shopkeeper cowered even lower, hands laced over his head. "Stop, *stop*," he begged. "This is my livelihood."

The first soldier ducked behind the counter and cleaned out the money till. He stuffed the dascal notes in his pocket. After a few more destructive kicks, and shoving tablefuls of breakable merchandise onto the floor, they left. Outside, they laughed and split up the money. Inside, the man knelt on the floor and wept.

Methusal trembled with fury. The wild beasts!

"Methusal." Mentàll appeared at her side. "Come with me."

"But those soldiers! They..."

"I have the note."

That caught her attention. "How?"

"I paid a thief to steal it from his pocket."

So simple. Ahead, the fisherman entered the bake shop. Three soldiers closed in behind him. A shout erupted, and they dragged him out. The fisherman cursed at them, struggling hard.

"Come, Methusal."

"Wait! People are suffering because of us. We have..."

"They are suffering because of the Presidente. He hires the wild beasts. He encourages them to terrorize the people."

"It's *our* fault. We have to do something!"

His hard fingers gripped her arm. "We are doing something. We are seeking peace for Koblan."

"Don't you care?"

"Come, *now*. And stop arguing," he said harshly. "Our lives are in danger. That man will survive." Even now, the soldiers kicked the fisherman and left him. His clothes were torn, pockets ripped out, and blood dripped from his nose. He sat up, looking groggy and dazed.

Two soldiers headed toward Methusal and Mentàll. Without a word, she allowed the Dehrien to pull her down a side street, and then around quick corners until the quiet streets told them they were safe.

Methusal still trembled from the things she had witnessed. What if men had died today because of them? Could she have left them? Did Mentàll feel no responsibility or guilt? She twisted her arm free and stopped in her tracks.

Mentàll stopped, too. That hard gaze latched on her face. "You are a soldier, Maahr. Act like one."

"You have no heart!" She itched to do something—anything—and go back and help the poor people who had just suffered because of them, and their mission.

"Better them, than you or me."

"Why? Are they worthless because they're Zindedis? Because of where they're born? But that's what you used to think about Rolban, isn't it? Everyone from Rolban had to be evil, because you thought your father was from Rolban."

"I told you I was wrong about Rolban." His voice sounded tight. "Do you want me to apologize yet again?"

"No. I want you to care about innocent people's lives."

"What did you want me to do to the soldiers?" He sounded exasperated. "Attack them? Kill them? Punish them for their crimes?"

"Of course not. But maybe we could have bribed the thief to steal the store owner's money back. Then we could have given it to the shopkeeper."

"I will not use that thief again. He will recognize me."

"We could have done *something*."

"What?"

"I don't know! Anything."

"Nothing. We could do nothing. I do not like it either, Methusal. But we have a mission to accomplish. That is more important than any Zindedis who might get hurt. Or have you forgotten that they are the enemy?"

"The *Presidente* is our enemy. The soldiers are our enemies. Not the common people."

Silently, he walked beside her. They turned in Mrn. M's gate and climbed the steps. She said, "Finally, I've won the argument?"

"You have won nothing, Methusal." He stopped abruptly in front of her, forcing her to face him. His gaze burned with blue heat, and maroon edged his cheekbones.

She stubbornly stared back. "Everything is not as black and white as you want it to be, Mentàll."

"No. It is not, is it?" The red slash on his cheekbones began to fade. "But you know that, don't you Methusal? One truth appears black. The other white. But sometimes..." his hands closed around her arms, and he tugged her closer, "the two meet and make gray."

Her breaths came faster. "What are you doing?"

"Mrn. M is watching through the window. It is time to make sure no doubt lives in her mind that we are very happily married."

She drew a quick, jerky breath. "N..." But his mouth touched hers. It lingered, without moving for a moment, and then seared across her lips. Violent heat scorched her. Methusal closed her eyes, and a low tremble seized her. She seemed unable to move, to fight. Her hands fisted into his hard shoulders, and she quivered, absorbing every single sensation.

Why was it always like this with him?

Time stood still, until her head felt befuddled and her skin felt warm and too tight. When at last it ended, she found him watching her. The light eyes searched her own, as if trying read her thoughts.

In a low, harsh voice he said, "That was worth the wait."

Horrified, she bolted into the house. She'd *let* him kiss her. With barely a "hello" to Mrn. M, she escaped into their room. She heard his silent footsteps following her, and whirled when he shut the door. "I have had *enough* of your kisses."

"I have only kissed you once." His eyes gleamed.

She clenched her fists. He liked to get under her skin, that's what he really meant. But knowing how deeply he'd done so would only please him all the more. Somehow, she had to regain control of this situation. She must prevent further "affectionate" embraces at all costs.

Coldly, she said, "We need to look more realistic."

"More realistic. What better way to prove I love my wife than to kiss her?"

Her face warmed, and that bothered her, too. "That's not the only way a husband and wife can show affection."

"It is an important one."

"Be creative, Mentàll. Married people don't grope each other all the time."

"Then what do you suggest?"

Although she didn't want to endure another kiss, she hadn't thought of any other solutions, either. "You know," she fumbled. "Like... Well, like my parents. They do kind, thoughtful things for one another."

Curiosity registered. "Like what?"

Could he possibly have no idea? But then again, he hadn't grown up in a loving family. Instead, an abusive one.

She groped for an analogy that would resonate with him. "Try to remember how your mother treated you. Little things she did that made you feel special. Love is about putting someone else's needs before your own. It's selfless, not self*ish*."

Quietly, he said, "If you want that, Methusal, I am willing to do it."

She shot him an uncertain glance. But he looked perfectly serious.

"Fine. Good." She felt uncomfortable. "Then that's the plan. And no more love names, either. They sound completely fake."

"Agreed."

She turned her back and pulled a parchment from her pack. Using the bedside table as a hard surface, she began to write.

"What are you doing?"

"Writing to Behran." She concentrated fully upon her task, and refused to look at him. She hated that she felt so guilty right now.

"You need to reaffirm your love for him?"

She bit back an irritated reply. Never mind that he was right. Why had her whole body responded when he had kissed her? She loved *Behran.* How could that man's kisses always disturb her so deeply?

It must be because he had years of experience wooing women. It was the only explanation she could accept.

She wrote a few newsy bits, reassurances that she was fine, and then a full paragraph about how much she loved and missed him. There. She folded it into a small square and wrote his name on it.

A knock came at the door. "Timaeus is here," Mrn. M said.

Methusal shot Mentàll a surprised glance. Perfect timing.

Timaeus stood in the living room, looking uncomfortable.

Methusal made the introductions. "Timaeus is my sister's husband, Mrn. M." When Methusal hugged him, she slipped the note into his hand. She pulled back. "How is she?"

Timaeus smiled. "She has a letter for you."

She accepted the parchment he extended. "Are you here for long?"

"No. I came to visit my father. I'll head back soon."

Mrn. M spoke said, "Would you like some cake, or something to drink?"

"Thank you, but no. I need to go."

"I'll walk you out," Mentàll said smoothly.

"Tell Deccia we'll be back soon."

"I will." The two men disappeared outside.

Mrn. M frowned. "That was a short visit."

Methusal swiftly improvised, "He has to hurry back to his job."

"I see." She retreated into the kitchen.

Did their landlady suspect something wasn't quite right? Methusal thought about going in and offering to help with dinner. Then she realized that if she'd really received a letter from her sister, she'd behave differently. She went to the doorway. "After I read my letter, I'll help with dinner, if you'd like."

"Oh." Mrn. M flashed her a quick smile. "Only if you'd like to, dear."

Methusal did want to. She needed to make certain Mrn. M suspected nothing out of the ordinary regarding her or Mentàll. Better to cultivate a Zindedi friend than to neglect a suspicious enemy.

Timaeus' note contained brief, cryptic notes on the Dakarran mission.

It wasn't until much later, when Mentàll asked for the letter from Timaeus, that Methusal remembered the letter from the Presidente. She asked, "What does it say?"

He made no effort to show it to her. "He proclaims peace."

She snorted. "That's why the soldiers beat up that fisherman. Yes, peace does seem to be his primary goal."

"I do not trust him, either." He tucked both letters into his pack. "Tomorrow we will go on base and discover the truth."

CHAPTER TWENTY-ONE

DAY 5

FINALLY, DASTN ARRIVED IN ROLBAN. It had been at least three weeks since Aali had seen him last.

He called greetings to guys he knew. A faint swagger marked his steps. Runners were well respected, and many people envied them their exciting jobs. Aali did, that was for sure. Maybe she should become a runner. She was old enough to practice now. And she knew the way to Tarst, Dehre, and Quasr, and how to camp and cook. What more did she need to know?

Aali watched Dastn enter Erl's office, messenger pack in hand. She leaned nonchalantly in the hall, picking her fingernails as he delivered his messages.

Kaavl helped her sense the door knob turning before the door actually opened. Before he could see that she'd been waiting for him, she strolled toward the dining room. Dastn's footsteps followed her. She smiled to herself. Easy.

She slipped into the dining hall and rooted around in the dried meat bin, searching for the tastiest bit she could find. Dastn stopped beside her. Perfect. She'd known hungry runners always stopped by for a snack.

She selected a meat strip and turned. "Oh! Dastn, hi." Her hand fluttered to chest—no, her throat—self-consciously, she redirected it away from her now obvious feminine attributes. "What a surprise!"

"Is it?" He gave her a knowing smile. She watched his mouth curl up to his right, just the way she liked.

"Why, yes," she agreed. "I believe you have a report for me?"

"A report...for a little girl like you?"

Anger flamed her cheeks hot. "Don't tell me you forgot. Not an old man like you."

With a laugh, he leaned against the stone counter. "Tell me. Am I spying for you out of the kindness of my heart? Or do you have payment in mind?"

"You mercenary!" she said indignantly. "Your pay is the satisfaction of protecting Koblan from an evil plot."

"I see." He continued to grin, and while he seemed relaxed, his brown eyes looked very intent. "Are you ready, then?"

"Of course. I have a paper right here." Aali slipped it out of the waist band of her tunic. "Prepared for all occasions," she informed him.

He crossed his arms as she licked the end of the charcoal writing stick. She raised her eyebrows. "Go ahead, then."

"Let's see, I talked to at least five people."

"Good! Good."

"Shall I give you their names? Ages too, might help," he suggested.

"Names..." She looked up suspiciously, and saw him trying to swallow a laugh.

He was making fun of her! The whip beast! He did think she was a little girl. Clearly, he was just humoring her, and laughing at her the whole time!

Hurt sickened her stomach, but she schooled her face into frozen lines. Kaavl concentration helped her do it. She had a job to do, and my goodness, she would get it done, whip beast or not standing before her.

"Please go on. Names and ages are unnecessary, don't you think?" She smiled sweetly.

His eyes narrowed. "I found out that Mentàll has spent a lot of time in Quasr lately. He and the Chief are friends, and one guy said he saw them working on documents together."

"Documents. Mmmhmm. What sort of documents?"

Dastn threw his hands up. "How am I supposed to know? I spied like you asked. I gave you the information. Isn't that enough?"

"Enough would be answers, Dastn." Aali drew herself up to her full height. She wished she could glare down her nose at him. Up her nose would have to do. The thought struck her funny bone, but she scowled harder, trying to suppress the inappropriate giggle.

Her accomplice wasn't treating her with proper respect. In fact, he wasn't treating this entire mission with proper respect. She said, "Perhaps you feel this mission is stupid? Something a *little girl* made up—just a game. Is that what you think, Dastn?"

He smiled again, and his lips curled up in that certain, very cute way. Darn him. *Stop looking at it,* she told herself.

"Pretty fierce, Aali. Should I be scared?"

"You would be, if you were smart," she informed him. "But if you're not willing to help me any further, I'll scratch you off my list of informants." A glacial smile stretched her lips. "You may go."

He straightened. "If you say so. See you around."

"Not if I see you first," she countered sweetly, and stalked out of the dining hall. Time for stage two of her plan. Dastn might sneer at the idea of helping her, but he'd help her still more. He just didn't know it yet.

△ △ △ △ △

Once again, Methusal slept terribly. She was tired to the bone when she woke up to the faint sound of splashes in the relief room. Her limbs felt like dead weights. She was exhausted. And her back and hips both ached with pain. She was sick of it. She frowned at the ceiling. That selfish man, lying in comfort every night...

Yesterday's kiss re-entered her mind, and she closed her eyes, feeling a flutter of panic. If she was going to survive this mission in Carachki, she must keep him emotionally and physically at arm's length. No more repeats of that kiss.

As she lay on the hard stones, she realized it was time to start finding answers to her questions about the Dehrien Chief. Hopefully Aali was making headway with her investigation in Koblan. And Methusal would search for clues here. For one, she wanted to read the letter the Presidente had sent Mentàll yesterday. It seemed a bit odd that he hadn't offered to let her look at it.

Water gurgled in the relief room. The tub was draining. She didn't have much time. She slipped over to the Dehrien's pack. Parchment crinkled in one of the pockets, and she swiftly pulled out the Presidente's letter.

Honorable Mentàll Solboshn, Chief of Dehre, Elected Spokesman for all of Koblan,

We welcome the spirit of friendship that you and Koblan offer Zindedi. Peace will be profitable for both of our lands. Come to the royal palace tomorrow at noon, and we will discuss these matters further.

The Presidente Supreme of Zindedi, most Honorable and without Peer

Methusal rolled her eyes at the grandiose name posturing. Clearly, the Presidente was besotted with himself. As for Mentàll's name... She frowned.

"Have you read your fill?" Softly, Mentàll spoke behind her.

She jumped. But with cool composure, she replied, "You've been invited to the Presidente's palace. What a surprise. Were you going to tell me?"

He pulled the letter from her fingers. "Are you finished rifling through my pack?"

"Answer my question."

"What would be the point? I do not intend to visit the palace." He tucked the letter away again.

"Why not? Surely the Honorable Mentàll Solboshn, Chief of Dehre, *Elected* Spokesman for *all* of Koblan, would want to meet with the Presidente."

"Speak your true question, Methusal." An edge bit through his tone. "I do not have a death wish. I will not visit the palace under the Presidente's terms."

"All right. Your title bothers me. Who elected you to be spokesman for all of Koblan?"

"You know the Chiefs agreed that I would be the spokesman for Koblan."

"But the title the Presidente gives you suggests so much more. In fact, it sounds like you're one step away from becoming the *Presidente* elect of all Koblan."

He smiled. "If the Presidente believes that, then my letter has achieved its purpose."

"What?"

"Methusal. The Presidente despises Koblan. He thinks we are weak because we are not unified. He knows who I am.

He fears my name. If he thinks I am about to become Presidente of Koblan, he will respect our peace agreement much more."

That made sense. "Are you saying he won't attack us if he thinks Koblan is unified?"

"That is my hope."

"The letter says he wants peace. I don't believe him."

"We will discover the truth today."

"At the base."

"Yes. Wear your black pants, and bring a white military shirt. Today we will dress as soldiers and infiltrate the compound." With a grim curl to his lips, he added, "We will see if they have stopped preparing for war."

∆ ∆ ∆ ∆ ∆

Hendra slept all afternoon, evening, and through the night. When she awoke, weak sunlight filtered in through the curtains. She gingerly tested her head by tilting it left, and then right. No pain, thank goodness. Sitting up didn't bother it either, but her stomach gurgled.

After quickly dressing, she joined the others in the kitchen. Deccia sat on a stool, chatting to Sozla. Both held steaming, fragrant mugs of tea.

"Where is everyone?" Hendra asked. Now that she noticed, the kitchen looked clean, as if breakfast had long since been eaten.

"Behran and Goric are spying. Timaeus, Tabor, and Riln aren't back yet," Deccia glanced out the window at the gray, misty day. A frown knit her brows together.

"When did they leave?"

"Before sun-up. Behran thought the fog would let them get close enough to hear conversations."

"It is nearly lunch time," Sozla said, sipping from her mug.

"It *is*?" She'd slept for almost twenty-four hours.

"Doc said to let you sleep," Deccia said with a smile.

"Where is he?" Hendra wasn't sure what the Tarst doctor might think of her now. One day she attacked him with a kiss, and the next she almost fainted in his arms. It would be no wonder if he saw her as a problem, with a capital "P".

Boots *thunked* on the stairs outside.

"That's probably him," Deccia said. "He was getting the meat from the stream."

The freezing cold stream kept their perishables cool enough to keep overnight.

But the dark hair and tall, broad shoulders of the man in the doorway did not belong to Doc. Rain glistened in his hair and darkened his jacket.

"Timaeus!" Deccia nearly knocked over her stool in her haste to reach him. She flung herself into his arms and hugged him tightly, burying her face in his shoulder. "I was so worried," she said, voice muffled. "I'm so glad you're back." She pulled back to take a good look at him. "You're all right? You had a safe trip?"

Timaeus grinned and kissed her. Deccia flushed pink, and released her hold on him, clearly remembering the other people in the room.

Doc appeared, and everyone gathered around the table while Timaeus told them about his trip. "Three days from now, I'll meet Mentàll again. We'll meet early in the morning at a bake shop. He thinks it'll be safer than going to their house. He also told me it's important that we look like tourists, so the Dakarrans don't get suspicious."

"Olita said her husband gives boat tours," Deccia said. "But it's expensive."

"The beach is close enough to walk to, and visiting it is free," Doc said.

Timaeus nodded. "Sounds good to me."

"Now? You're not too tired?" Deccia said, clearly concerned.

"No. But I could use some lunch."

"Perhaps all four of you could get lunch in Dakarra," Sozla suggested. "Then they will see you walking around, looking like tourists."

"Won't you come with us, Sozla?"

"No. It is bothering me, that I still do not understand how the mechanism works. I would like to stay and work on it, and take another look at the paper you found, Hendra. Also, Behran is not here. They might think it strange if I go to the beach without him."

So it would be a couples outing, Hendra realized. Deccia and Timaeus, and Doc and herself. The thought made her nerves jump uncomfortably.

Cool mist kissed her face as soon as she stepped outside. To the west, a patch of pale blue peeked through a break in the low clouds. She hoped the clouds would break up even more, and soon. With a shiver, she tucked her jacket more tightly around herself against the damp, and followed the others down the cabin's stairs to the crushed grass at the base.

Doc waited for her. Already the light, misting rain collected in tiny silver balls on his brows and hair. He stuffed his hands deep in his coat pockets. "You're feeling better today?"

"Yes. My arm doesn't hurt as much."

"Good. I'll check it when we get back."

Hendra followed the others down the narrow path that threaded through the tall grasses. Below, on the road, Deccia tucked her arm through Timaeus' and shivered. "Hope that blue sky gets here soon."

Doc walked with an easy stride beside her. He appeared to feel relaxed. After a while, his undemanding presence relaxed Hendra, too.

"You don't mind the cold?" she ventured after a while.

He smiled. "Tarst is often like this in the winter. Sometimes the mist doesn't clear off until noon."

"I remember."

He sent her a quick look. "You've been to Tarst?"

"Once, for the Kaavl Games three years ago."

He nodded. "I was gone then, getting additional medical training in Wyen."

"Wyen?" Now he'd surprised her.

"A few of the best doctors in Koblan have started a small new school there. I learned all I could," he said simply. "And I taught several classes about the use of different herbs, and how they can aid in healing."

Hendra had never known he taught classes, as well. "That's wonderful. I wish our doctor in Dehre was interested in learning new techniques. He disapproved of some of the healing methods you suggested for the orphans. I did them anyway, and they got well quickly. He seemed to ignore the results."

"That's unfortunate." They walked on in silence. "Are you happy in Dehre?"

"I've often wished I could move. Maybe to escape all the painful memories. But of course I love the children, and

Mentàll lives there. He's my only family." The only family that mattered. All of the others had rejected her.

Dark shapes loomed out of the mist. Dakarra. The four turned down the main road. Warm lights spilled from windows. Hendra shivered from cold now, and hoped they'd find a food shop soon.

"Let's ask in here." Deccia opened the door to the market.

Hendra almost swooned as delicious heat enveloped her.

A slight, blond girl wearing a green apron flitted over to Deccia with a grin. "You're back! No sour busybodies today. It's safe."

"Good." Deccia laughed. "By the way, I'm Deccia, and this is my husband, Timaeus."

Timaeus' big hand enveloped the girl's, and with a smile, he shook it gently. The girl pinkened a little. Deccia turned. "And this is Hendra and Doc."

"Pleased to meet you. I'm Ceri." She pronounced it Sair' ee. "Why are you out in this weather?"

"We hoped it would clear up," Deccia said ruefully. "Right now, we're looking for a place to buy lunch."

"We make sandwiches here. We even have a table in the back." She waved to the far corner. "How about it? May I fix you lunch?"

"Yes, please," Timaeus said with feeling, and Hendra was glad he'd said it, because she was starving, too. She hadn't eaten in over twenty-four hours.

Within moments, they'd ordered cheese and meat sandwiches, and draped their wet coats on chairs which flanked a small wooden table.

Ceri whipped up the sandwiches amazingly fast, and soon carried the plates, garnished with greens, to the table, along with cups of water. She lingered, as if waiting for something else. Besides the man behind the counter, the shop was empty.

"Join us," Hendra invited with a smile.

With a quick glance at the counter, she said, "Well, maybe for a minute," and pulled up a chair.

After eating a mouthful, Deccia asked, "Where are you from, Ceri? You mentioned you were new here, too."

Ceri glanced again at the counter. The bald man appeared to be paying no attention. "Carachki," she said quietly.

Hendra wondered why that might be a secret. "Why did you move here?"

She gave a light, quick shrug. "To get away from home."

Hendra wondered what stories lurked behind the girl's sharp, pale green eyes. But she did understand why someone might want to escape from her family. If Ceri's reasons were anything like her own, she wouldn't welcome questions.

△ △ △ △ △

Methusal stood in plain sight, leaning against the wall of the Commander's office building on the military base. Being out in the open, in full view of the Zindedi military officers, made her feel nervous. At least the uneasiness pushed back the weariness that four nights of poor sleep had bought her. She wore a black beret and the military shirt Mentàll had carried in his pack.

With her hair up, she probably looked just like a soldier. Much like Mentàll did. She glanced over at him, two buildings away. The crisp, black uniform made him look larger than normal, and added an austerity to his features that was not unattractive. He looked every bit the Commander that his medals proclaimed him to be. No. In truth, he possessed the bearing of a General.

Inside the building, the Commander spoke. "The General will be back soon. He will take charge of the influx of men..."

"I told you, six carts are coming from Dakarra today."

Inside the building, two different conversations competed for her attention. The base Commander currently spoke to a Sergeant, and the Commander's secretary lectured a Private.

Soldiers approached, and Methusal quickly strode for the back of the building, trying to look purposeful, as if she knew where she was going. To her chagrin, the conversations inside faded, swallowed up by the crunch of the approaching feet. Fear raised the hairs on her arms. It was difficult to stay focused with so many enemy soldiers nearby.

But Mahre had said that to achieve the highest level of kaavl, one must relax and let all sensory input flow in.

She struggled to do so yet again. But just like every time she'd tried to relax today, a multitude of input rushed in. A score of conversations tangled in her ears, confusing her. She had to focus, which meant excluding most of the input.

How had Mahre compartmentalized it all? Had he been capable of tracking dozens of systems of input all at the same time? Methusal still struggled just to follow two or three, and it frustrated her.

A broken down cart behind the building caught her attention. A dusty tarp lay on its floor. What if she climbed inside and lay down? No one would see her if she pulled the tarp over her. It would provide a safe, concealed place to stay while she focused into kaavl.

A quick glance proved that no one was looking. She swiftly slid into her hiding place and pulled the dry, dusty tarp over her. A sneeze caught her by surprise. Quickly, she pinched her nose. An insect droned above the cart. She sharpened into kaavl and listened for the conversations once more.

A door slammed.

The sun beat down on the tarp. She lifted an edge to let the cool air in.

"The Presidente wants that ore. We ship out in two weeks."

"The new men won't be ready."

"They'll train on the ships. Until then, I expect you to beat them into shape. They should start arriving today."

A silence elapsed.

"You have your orders, soldier! Prepare the barracks."

"Yes, sir. But, well... A few of the men are wondering..."

"What?" The Commander sounded impatient.

"What about Koblan's kaavl, sir? How will we fight that?"

"With firepower."

"But..."

"Dismissed!"

Boot clumps, and then another door slam. Silence.

It seemed clear from that conversation that the Zindedis still planned to attack Koblan, but which ports and when remained to be seen. So much for the Presidente's proclamations of peace. Not a big surprise.

Methusal continued to listen. Maybe the Commander would relay more information to his secretary. But only papers rustled now.

It was warm under the tarp. Methusal closed her eyes, relaxing completely into kaavl. Conversations murmured far away. That persistent insect buzzed just above the tarp. Carts rolled onto the base, punctuated by the soft clop clop of urchet hooves.

All of the sounds merged into an undulating, undistinguishable murmur as Methusal slipped into a peaceful dream.

△ △ △ △ △

Doc asked Ceri, "How do you like Dakarra, compared to Carachki?"

"Definitely more peaceful. I like it. It feels safe here."

"Especially with all the military nearby," Deccia added dryly.

Ceri froze for a second, and then gave a thin laugh. "Yes. Exactly. Especially if we stay inside at night."

Timaeus changed the subject. "You probably know the best places to visit around here. What do you recommend?"

"If you haven't gone yet, the beach. It's divine. Other than that..." she shrugged. "It's wild, which I love. I like to go on long walks by myself."

"Olita mentioned a boat tour," Deccia said. "Is it worth the money?"

"Only if it's calm. The boat is small and beaten up. But I wouldn't waste my time on it. I'd rather walk on the beach."

"Ceri!" The man at the counter scowled. "You've sweeping to do."

"Sorry," she told the foursome in a low voice, and darted off to resume her duties.

Hendra felt much better after eating. They waved goodbye to Ceri, who was still sweeping, and entered the gloom and drizzling rain of the street again. Across the street and down one building, bright windows cut a swath of warmth through the gray light. Earth colored wares perched on shelves inside. So did cookware, dried herbs, and even books.

"Let's go in," Hendra suggested. After all, wasn't that what a tourist would do? And maybe they'd learn something new from the patrons inside—provided any Dakarrans were out in this cold damp.

A bell tinkled when Timaeus opened the door, and the sweet scent of dried herbs and incense filled Hendra's nostrils. Deccia cut immediately left to investigate the scented candles, dragging a good humored Timaeus in tow.

A stout woman with brown, curly hair waddled from the recesses of the store. Her black eyes flickered from Deccia to Doc, and then lingered on Doc. A smile curved her small lips. "Well," she said in a high, breathy voice. "I'm pleased to see you again."

Hendra didn't like the way she looked at Doc. As if she'd like to eat him up. Instinctively, she moved closer to him.

"Is this your wife?" said the woman. She smiled at Hendra, although the smile did not reach her eyes. "I'm Tisnia."

Doc's arm went around Hendra's shoulders. It felt solid and secure, and very safe. She allowed him to pull her even closer, so their torsos touched. The embrace did not frighten her.

Hendra smiled and introduced herself.

Tisnia's small eyes narrowed. "Do you need help finding something?"

"We're just looking," Doc said pleasantly.

Tisnia left them. Like a large, plump flying beast, she swooped across the store to roost beside Deccia and Timaeus.

"I'm not sure if I like her."

"She's one of Vitnia's friends."

Hendra realized he still held her close to his side, and she felt a small flush of embarrassment. Discreetly, she tugged free, pretending interest in a woven basket made of colorful, dried grasses.

"She's coming back," Doc muttered. "We should hold hands." Before she could process what he meant, Doc's warm hand curled around hers, securing them intimately together, palm to palm. Her heart beat faster.

They stood side by side, arms brushing, and she blindly examined the soft, wonderful blankets on a nearby table. The man at her side stole all of her attention.

He murmured, "Are you cold at night?"

"A little," she admitted, fingering one made of a particularly beautiful, smoky blue. The color of Doc's eyes.

"You like that one?"

She nodded.

"I'll buy it for you."

"Are you sure?" she shot him a quick glance. "It's twenty dascals."

He smiled. The dark warmth of his gaze captured her full attention. She couldn't look away. Pleasure filled her heart, drinking in the unspoken promise of his steadfast, unending patience. She offered a small smile. "Thank you."

"Any time," he said quietly.

Hendra's heart thrummed as he paid for the blanket, and she felt so good that she totally ignored Tisnia's baleful looks. Still keeping a firm clasp on her hand, Doc walked with her to the door, where Deccia and Timaeus waited, clearly ready to go.

The sky outside looked lighter.

"It stopped raining!" Deccia did a little dance and twirl of joy. Timaeus looked on with an indulgent grin. With a mock frown, she grabbed his hand. "Are you making fun of me, Timaeus Rolnnt?"

"I'm enjoying you." He drew her in for a lingering kiss.

Flushed, and with a breathless laugh, Deccia pulled away. "You've redeemed yourself. Shall we go to the beach?" Her look included Hendra and Doc.

"I'd love to," Hendra agreed.

So they headed down the wet, muddy street for the road to the beach. Doc released Hendra's hand once they left sight of Dakarra, but continued to walk beside her, and engaged her in light conversation. And he insisted on carrying the bag with the blanket. After a while, the foursome walked together and the men joked with each other.

At last the beach stretched before them. It was a long, silver crescent of sand flanked by foaming gray breakers. Overhead, clouds leant a silvery white light to the scene. The wet sand squished beneath their footsteps.

Deccia and Timaeus fell behind, holding hands and talking quietly. Hendra and Doc walked together, skirting the skimming, lapping water's edge. The sharp, briny scent of seaweed swirled on the breeze. White-headed flying beasts strutted across the sand, and shot skyward with noisy, admonishing squawks when they got too close. Clumps of driftwood glistened, shining silver in the muted half-light. Everything was silent, except for the thunder of the breakers and the flying beast cries.

"I hope Behran and Goric learn something today," she commented. "It feels like we haven't learned much so far." The cold, damp wind tugged at her hair, and flipped it to the side. She hoped it hadn't stung Doc's cheek.

He didn't seem disturbed, and walked with hands stuffed in his pockets again. It felt colder on the beach than it had inland. "Riln and Tabor should be back this evening, too."

Riln. Hendra had temporarily forgotten about him, and her happy spirits dimmed. "I'd like to scout tonight."

Doc said nothing, so she looked at him.

He raised an eyebrow. "You know I can't stop you."

"But?"

"I'd feel better if you wait another day. Give your body a chance to recover."

Hendra said nothing. She felt fine.

"I can read your mind," he said quietly.

"Really? What am I thinking?"

"When you get obstinate, your bottom lip turns white, like you're mashing it."

An unexpected giggle escaped. "It does not."

"Sure it does. Look at me." He stopped.

Deccia and Timaeus had also paused far down the beach. They seemed to be deep in conversation. She glanced at Doc, and then back at them.

Doc watched her. Amusement deepened the lines at the corners of his eyes. "Give me your full attention, please."

She frowned. "You have it."

"Your lip is all white again."

"No, it's not!"

"It looks painful." He laughed openly at her now.

"You slug." She fingered her lip. It did feel thin and hard. "See?"

Not to be outdone, she said, "You're a good one to talk. You bottle up your emotions, too."

His smile faded. His eyes reflected the crashing breakers. A quiet color, and yet full of power and deep emotion. "Is that right?" he said softly.

"Yes. I know you pretty well."

He glanced down and gently took her hand. That blue-gray gaze met hers. "You're not afraid when I hold your hand."

"No," she whispered. Her heart beat as fast as flying beast wings. Panic battered against the pleasure.

Doc watched her, but seemed to understand the conflict within her, because he released her hand.

Relief mixed with disappointment.

Doc asked questions about her childhood—the good parts, when her mother was alive. And when she'd learned kaavl.

In time, the sky darkened again, and they headed home. They made a dash up the last hill just as thunder rolled and the sky unzipped.

Inside the cabin, damp and gasping for air, the four looked at each other and laughed.

Goric strolled out of the kitchen, his wet blond hair plastered in spikes against his forehead. Moisture darkened his clothes. "You're back. Riln and Tabor are in the kitchen. We have news."

△ △ △ △ △

Cold air hit Methusal's face. Before she could open her eyes, pain exploded across her temple.

"Get up, you lazy Pit!" A rough hand grabbed her arm. Methusal barely had the presence of mind to clutch her beret over her hidden hair before she was dragged bodily out of the cart. She landed on her hip on the hard earth. Bone jarring pain stole her breath away.

"On your feet!" Another cruel yank on her arm.

Methusal awkwardly scrambled to her feet.

A man—a Sergeant, according to the medals on his jacket—thrust his face close to hers. "*Straighten up, Pit!*" he screamed.

With a gasp, she jerked back. Cruelty curved his lips. "A new one, are you? Good. You'll be an example to the others." He shoved at her shoulder. "Get moving."

Prodded by the gun poking into the base of her skull, Methusal trotted across the compound. Mentàll was nowhere to be seen. Panic fluttered. A quick glance at the sun said it was almost evening. That meant she'd slept for over three hours. Aghast, she struggled to outpace the soldier and ease the painful pressure against her neck.

They wove between clumps and streams of Zindedi soldiers, heading toward the barracks. Her heart pounded. If only she could make a break for it.

They neared the first large dormitory. She carried with vision, looking around the far corner. Dozens more men.

The scent of roasted meat wafted from the kitchen, located to the east. Most of the men were heading there now.

The Sergeant grabbed her shoulder, forcing her to turn right, into a darkened doorway. A wooden slat held the door propped open. When she entered, she understood why. The close, warm air, loaded with the acrid smell of sweat and unwashed clothes enveloped her. It took a moment for her eyes to adjust to the dim lighting. By then, the Sergeant had maneuvered her over to a cot. A large trunk rested beside it. The officer opened this and extracted something long and snake-like.

He shoved her toward the door again. An unpleasant suspicion uncurled in her mind. She struggled to make her voice deep, but fear lent it a breathless edge. "What are you doing?" She slowed down, fighting against the painful pressure against her neck.

A crack across the back of her head brought tears to her eyes. She stumbled forward again.

"Get going, you lazy Pit," he snarled.

Against her will, she stumbled into the sunlight again. A post embedded with rings lay before them. Ropes dangled from them.

"No!" she gasped, and tried to break sideways.

Grabbing her tightly by the shirt neck, choking her, the Sergeant forced Methusal to the small, circular pit ringing the pole. Boot prints trampled the dark earth. Instead of light brown, the soil here looked red.

"Strip off your shirt."

"No!"

"Strip it off, or I'll cut it off." A curved knife with jagged teeth appeared in her side vision.

Why couldn't she think? Her mind was frozen with terror.

Kaavl. Relax into kaavl.

"Fine," she said. "Let go."

He shoved her, so she almost fell to her knees. A quick step saved her. Now she saw the deep gouges in the post. Were they bitten there by hundreds of scrabbling fingernails? How many splinters had sliced beneath the nails of the men tortured at this pole? Had it felt like nothing, compared to the lashes of the whip?

Methusal lifted her fingers to her shirt and slowly undid the first button. Although terror fogged her mind, kaavl input finally began to trickle in. The harsh, panting breaths of the man behind her...

Another man shouted, telling others of the beating about to take place.

Murmuring voices drew nearer.

"Faster, soldier!" Pain exploded across her back. The whip licked around her, biting into her arms and stomach. She let out a sharp, involuntary sob.

The Sergeant released the whip. "Fifty lashes now," he said with satisfaction. "If your shirt is not off by the time I count to ten, it'll be a hundred. One...two..."

Panic clouded her mind. If she made a break for it, someone would catch her. If she unbuttoned her shirt, they'd see she was a woman. Maybe that would be the best course of action. Then the Sergeant may not beat her. Maybe he'd drag her to the Commander. And then what? Death? Rape? By now, three buttons were undone. One more would reveal her unmistakably as a woman. She slowly worked the button.

The whip hissed.

"Stop!" That familiar, harsh voice brooked no disobedience.

The whip snapped into the ground. Men murmured with discontent. Tears of gratitude swam to her eyes.

"Commander." The Sergeant sounded surly. "You're new. Where are you from?"

"The Private is with me. I will see to his punishment."

A small silence elapsed. "You're visitors?" His reluctance to believe it was clear.

"We're from Oesten. I am leaving now to prepare our base for new recruits."

The Sergeant spit onto the ground. "Take him, then. Scourge him. I found him asleep under a tarp."

"The Private will receive everything he deserves." Mentàll's hard hand gripped Methusal's shoulder and hustled her toward the entrance gate.

Kaavl told her that the Sergeant followed them for a few paces, and then stopped; probably to watch them go. Like magic, the gate to the base opened, letting them escape. Mentàll kept up the brutal pace toward town, his grip as hard as when they'd left the compound. Methusal began to feel uncomfortable when it continued, even far away from the base. Was he truly upset with her? Finally, he released her.

Once they reached the outskirts of Carachki, he marched down a narrow, deserted street, and then into the abandoned, two room shack where they'd changed shirts this morning. His pack was still where he'd left it.

Inside, she swiftly faced him.

His cold gaze seared into her like frostbite. It dropped to the open "v" of her shirt. The fourth button had popped open. Embarrassment scalded her, and she clutched the material together, trying to hide the curve of her breasts.

Much too quietly, he said, "You planned to strip for him?"

More heat scalded her face. "I didn't *plan...*"

"No. You did not plan at all, did you? You fell asleep on the job."

"I didn't mean to. I've been so t..." She broke off, because she didn't want to let him know how sleeping—rather, *not* sleeping—on that stone floor had stolen hours of her sleep. She was exhausted. Well, after that nap, she felt better. But now the anger seen in his curled lips made her want to shrivel up inside.

"You could have cost us our cover. You could have been *killed.*"

He was furious. This was clear.

"I wasn't killed." She lifted her chin. "Thank you for rescuing me."

His gaze dropped again to her still gaping shirt, and darkness flushed his cheekbones. He seemed to be at a loss for words, which was very unlike him.

Methusal took advantage of his uncharacteristic silence. Softly, she said, "I'm sorry for failing my duty. But I learned that they're still planning war."

Jaw visibly tense, he listened as she recounted what she'd overheard. Then his eyes flickered to her tunic again. Abruptly, he ordered, "Change your shirt."

Without a word, Methusal retreated into the next room and did as he asked. Anything to escape from that thick tension. Maybe he needed a minute to cool down. The ice and the angry heat warring in him confused her. She was used to the ice. His deep, hot emotions unnerved her.

After several minutes passed—enough time for him to calm down, she hoped—she exited the room with the white Zindedi shirt folded neatly in her arms.

The Dehrien watched her. Now she read nothing in his expression. Strangely, that didn't make her feel any better.

The issue needed to be resolved. "Are you still angry with me?"

One large hand clenched his pack, and his knuckles showed briefly white. "Yes. I am angry with you. I am disappointed in you."

With a quick breath, she looked away, surprised that his displeasure could affect her so deeply. She met his gaze. "It won't happen again."

"No, it will not," he agreed harshly. "Or I will send you to the ship."

"Okay," she said quietly.

"No arguments? That is not like you."

"I was scared, Mentàll." Unwanted tears filled her eyes, and she blinked them back. "I was really scared. He was going to beat me. Or I could unbutton my shirt and…"

"Stop!" he said harshly.

Of course he didn't understand. More tears scalded her eyes. "I'm sorry." Her voice wavered.

"Stop," he told her again. A flush scored his cheekbones.

She turned her back on him, fighting the hated tears. "It won't happen again. I promise."

"No, it will *not*. Or I will kill the *scienth* and ruin our cover forever!" Violence shivered through the low words.

Shocked, she glanced back. Dark red slashes made his high cheekbones stand out. Yes, he was angry. But not at *her*. At least, not primarily. He was angry with the man who had hurt her. "Please, can we put it behind us?"

"Yes." He moved his shoulders, as if ordering himself to relax. "Come." He strode out of the shack.

Methusal was hard-pressed to keep up with him. Silence stretched on for so long that it began to feel uncomfortable. Finally, she said, "What did you learn?"

"They fear kaavl," he said shortly. "As I knew. They want to kill every kaavl player they meet. Or capture them, and try to learn kaavl secrets."

That was a new twist. "Anything else?"

"They still want Rolban's ore. They are sending double the ships and men to Koblan. They set sail in two weeks."

"Two weeks! That doesn't give us much time. How will we stop them?"

They now neared Mrn. M's house. "Before the ships set sail, I will force the Presidente's hand. He will choose peace."

"How can you force him to choose peace?"

He did not answer, but held Mrn. M's gate open for her.

"How?" she repeated. "And even if he agreed to peace, how could we trust him?"

"Leave those questions to me, Methusal."

"Tell me." She stopped on the path in front of him, forcing him to halt, too. "I'm an equal partner with you. I need to know everything."

"It is safer if you know nothing." His face looked like a cold, withdrawn mask. "Trust me."

She would not address the trust issue right now. "Do you plan to meet him, after all? Promise you won't go alone."

He remained silent, looking at her, almost with distaste—as if wishing he was far away from her. "I will meet him. I will deliver my terms and the peace agreement signed by Koblan's Chiefs."

"When?"

Finally, that cold, remote gaze looked away, releasing her. "I do not know."

"I do," she said suddenly.

When he looked back, the disturbing coldness had softened a bit. "When?" He sounded patient.

"The ships leave in two weeks, right? Well, the ball the General spoke about is in two weeks, too. It must be an important event for the Presidente. I doubt he'll cancel it. In fact, he'll probably turn it into a sendoff party for the ships."

Swift, calculating thoughts flickered. "You may be right."

"So, let's get invitations to the ball. We'll surprise him. He won't expect us there. It would be the perfect time to give him the peace agreement."

He nodded. "Yes. If the ships set sail after the ball, that could work."

Methusal still sensed the tension in him, like a shield behind which he'd withdrawn. It puzzled her. The mission had not been compromised. They had gained vital information. But he was still visibly upset. Clearly, however, he did not want to be, if that icy shell was any indication.

She said, "So, what should we do in the meantime? Besides trying to get invitations."

"We'll find out the exact date the ships leave. And the exact date of the ball."

"Mrn. M might know, since her husband was a Commander."

Mentàll nodded. "We need to learn all the information we can about the powder and weapons shipments on base. I know they are expecting more men and powder from Dakarra soon. I want to understand the purpose for every building on that military base. And I need to understand how and when they plan to transport the weapons to the ships, and where they plan to land on Koblan."

More trips to the military compound. More danger. An involuntary shiver slid through her, and pain pinched her back. The whip lash.

"Are you ready for what is to come?" Mentàll's gaze held hers.

"Yes. But I'm glad we're done for today."

"Tomorrow we will take a break," he said unexpectedly.

"No scouting?"

"Not during the day. It is time we behaved like tourists. Then, when Mrn. M asks questions, we will have typical honeymooner answers."

Methusal wanted to laugh at that thought. "We're anything but typical."

"You are correct about that, Methusal." He brushed by her to enter Mrn. M's house.

△ △ △ △ △

"The General ordered the Commander to start moving inventory in a few days," Behran reported that evening.

"What inventory?"

"I don't know. But carts will head for Carachki soon. Maybe to another port, too."

"Why?" Timaeus wondered grimly.

"If they're transporting weapons or powder, it can only mean one thing. They're planning another attack on Koblan."

That made sense to Hendra. And it proved that Mentàll's suspicions were correct. The Zindedis still wanted Koblan's ore. "They'll probably send more ships to Koblan this time."

"Right. More of everything," Behran agreed.

"We followed the carts down the beach road," Tabor said in his quiet, deep voice. "They traveled east and stopped at a powder mine. It appeared to be a small one. They accessed it through a passage into a hill. About five men work it. It produces one barrel of powder a day."

"I thought you said 'carts.'" Deccia said. "Why would they need so many carts for one barrel of powder?"

"That's what we wondered, once we realized how small the mine was. Riln followed more carts down the road while I kept an eye on the first one. Tell them what happened, Riln."

Hendra glanced at Riln for the first time. It had been so peaceful and pleasant with him gone that she'd wanted to pretend he wasn't there at all. She blinked in shock at his face. His nose was bent sideways, and his lips cracked and swollen.

Riln laughed loudly. At least his spirits appeared to be uninjured. "I followed them for an hour. Then a Zin spotted me. I didn't run. Thought that would look suspicious, so I stood my ground. He popped me in the face with the butt of his gun." His lips curled with satisfaction. "Then I beat him to a bloody pulp."

When Tabor raised his eyebrows, Riln shrugged. "Maybe not a bloody pulp. But I walloped him good before the Zins rushed me. Then I ran. I didn't see where the carts went after that."

He'd assaulted a Zindedi soldier. Aghast, Hendra said, "They'll be looking for you."

"Yeah." He shrugged. "So?"

"You could have compromised our cover! If they see you with us..."

"Don't get your pants in a bunch, apte girl." He rolled his eyes to the ceiling. "War's messy. Skirmishes happen."

Hendra could not believe it. Was he truly so thick-headed? "If they spot us together, we'll all be in danger."

"They won't *spot,*" his fingers waggled derisive quotes in the air, "me. We're pretty much living in the wilderness. Two steps from the forest. No one's going to come here."

"We don't know that," Behran said. "Hendra has a good point. You'll need to stay out of sight. Anyone who teams up with you now is in danger."

"I'll go by myself. *Sheesh.*" He appealed to the others. "What do we have here? A bunch of old ladies?"

"Your behavior is reckless," Doc said. "It needs to stop."

Riln's mouth gaped open, and he appealed to Tabor. "Can you believe this? Our team is made up of women and aptes." His narrowed gaze took in Behran and Doc. "I can't tell which is which."

Behran's fists clenched, but then relaxed. "Let's take a vote. Should we give Riln one more chance, or should we send him back to the ship?"

Riln's face turned crimson. "You can't do that! You're not the team leader."

"That's why we're voting," he said calmly. "Who's for sending Riln to the ship?"

Hendra glanced at the others. She was all for that course of action. However, she didn't want to be the only one raising her hand. Then again, wasn't she sick of playing the scared apte to bullies like Riln? Staring him right in the eye, she raised her hand. His swollen lips curled, and his eyes flickered away.

Deccia raised her hand, too, and so did Doc. Riln rolled his eyes and glanced at the door, his discomfort obvious.

A long silence elapsed. No one else raised their hand.

"See?" Riln's triumph sounded like pure bluster.

"I see we've elected to give you one more chance," Behran said. "Next time you fight a Zindedi or endanger this mission, you're gone."

"Mentàll's in charge of this mission. He'll give me my marching orders."

"I'll make sure Timaeus relays that message to him," Behran returned evenly.

"That reminds me." Timaeus pulled a note from his pocket. "This note is from Methusal."

A smile eased Behran's tense expression. He slipped the note into his pocket. "Do you agree, Riln? You're not to be seen or heard by the Zindedis again."

Riln's face was dark red. "Fine. I'll be an apte. But I'm not whipped, like you." He surged to his feet. "When this mission needs a real man, you know where to find one." He strode out. The front door slammed.

Doc spoke into the uncomfortable silence. "What's next?"

Tabor shoved a small pouch into the center of the table. "I stole powder. I figured it could help make the detonators."

Sozla spoke for the first time. "I still cannot figure out how the mechanism works. Even Hendra's paper does not help. It only shows part of the firing mechanism. It also shows that we are missing several pieces."

"I think we should keep studying, but I think the cannons are triggered by a match and a fuse. I'd like to invent something that can fire on its own, without us lighting a wick. And I want to work on a timer." Behran said. "I'll scout at night, so we can work on the detonator during the day."

"What wonderful ideas, Behran! But you will become exhausted," Sozla said with a frown.

"Lights are out on base at ten o'clock. After that, it's pretty quiet. I won't be out too late."

Tabor spoke up. "I think we need to watch the base all the time. Anything could happen, at any time."

A small silence elapsed. "You're probably right," Behran agreed.

"I'll take the night shift," Tabor offered.

"I'll help you," Goric said quickly. "We'll need someone at each end of the base."

Tabor shook his head. "Riln should go with me. That way he'll stay out of sight."

Goric's lips briefly thinned, and he looked away. But he said nothing more.

It was decided that everyone else would rotate through the day shifts, based on the needs of the day.

"Let's find out when they're moving those carts from the base to Carachki," Behran said. "And let's find out for sure what's in them. We're pretty sure it's powder, but it might be weapons, too. Mentàll will want to know every detail when Timaeus goes back to Carachki.

"And the next time the base sends empty carts toward the beach, we'll need to follow them. They're probably using those carts to steadily build up their powder supply, but that's just a guess. If I'm right, those carts will lead us to Dakarra's biggest powder mine."

Chapter Twenty-Two

Day 6

THE NEXT MORNING, Methusal asked Mrn. M about the ball. Mentàll slathered jam on his toast, appearing to pay no attention to their conversation.

His attitude toward her had thawed a little. She couldn't decide whether she was glad or not. Last night he'd kept his distance. His manner had been remote, but polite. He'd certainly made no attempt to touch or kiss her. A benefit, to be sure, but the lingering tension had felt uncomfortable. Today he seemed a little more like himself. Which meant she wasn't sure what to expect from him.

"The Presidente holds the ball once a year," Mrn. M said. "It's in honor of his late wife's birthday. And it coincides with the full blooming of the flowers in his garden. Both mean the world to him."

"What is a ball like?" Methusal asked. "I've never been to one."

"Well." Mrn. M smiled. Her eyes softened and took on a dreamy, far off look. "My Charlie and I used to go every year, of course, being he was high in the ranks. Most people don't know this, but the Presidente and Charlie were first cousins, and they shared the same tutor when they were young, at the Presidente's palace. The Presidente was good to Charlie. He never forgot him."

From Mrn. M's rapturous descriptions, one would think the Presidente was a saint—still in love with his dead wife, never forgetting an old friend and cousin, and cherishing tender flower blooms. Methusal managed to keep from rolling her eyes. Never mind the thousands of eastern Zindedis he'd ordered murdered, or his brutal, greedy attempt to conquer Koblan.

Mrn. M sighed. "The balls were splendid. I always bought a gorgeous new gown. Charlie insisted I have the best one in Carachki. And Charlie," she smiled softly, "always wore a black dress jacket and pants. So handsome, was my Charlie. And then, at the ball...my goodness, the splendid finery the women wore. Sparkling jewels at their throats, long, shimmering dresses... And of course, all the men wore black. And the food was divine. And we danced until midnight." Still smiling, she fell silent.

"It sounds wonderful. I imagine you need to be invited to be able to go."

"Oh my, yes. The invitations are engraved, you know. And your name has to be on the list to get inside the palace. Security is very strict, as you'd probably guess."

"Mmhm," Methusal agreed. Important to keep out those pesky assassins.

Mrn. M drew a quick breath, her dark eyes still sparkling. "Well. What do you two plan to do today?"

Methusal glanced at Mentàll. "We were hoping you might have some suggestions. We've walked all over town, and shopped, too. I'd like to do something different today. Something special."

"Have you visited the Presidente's gardens yet?"

"No. Are they near the palace?"

"Only a few blocks east. They're along the waterfront."

They hadn't explored the waterfront, except for the one dock and the carefully watched bench.

"Sounds nice. What do you think, M...Lozar?"

His sharp eyes glanced at her, obviously noticing her near fumble. "The gardens sound wonderful," he said placidly. Methusal shot him a suspicious look.

Mrn. M bustled into the kitchen and returned with a paper in hand. Huffing the tiniest bit, she sat down at the table. "I thought I had a map, and here it is! Now look here. Here are the ortangias..." She launched into describing which flowers would be the most beautiful at this time of the year.

Methusal wasn't sure she if could remember them all.

"You'll so enjoy yourself!" Mrn. M enthused, folding the map back up. "I haven't been in ages, but I imagine the trees have grown. And the Presidente mentioned that he'd ordered more yellow nasrias planted this year."

Mentàll said, "Why don't you come with us?"

Both Methusal and their landlady stared at him in surprise. Mrn. M recovered first. "But I couldn't intrude! This is your special time..."

"It would be an honor," Mentàll insisted. "I know nothing about flowers, and I feel certain my wife doesn't, either. We would enjoy it if you would come and tell us more." His smile flashed, loaded with pure charm.

Mrn. M blinked a little, and so did Methusal. She'd forgotten how charming he could be when he so chose. Unfortunately, he was also a master manipulator. Uneasily, she wondered why he wanted Mrn. M to come with them today.

Mrn. M appealed to Methusal. "Are you sure?"

How could she say "no"? Not that she wanted to object, of course. She smiled. "Yes! It would be fun." And it should be—it was only Mentàll's ulterior motive that made her feel apprehensive.

"Well, if you're sure." Mrn. M looked from one to the other. Seeing only welcoming smiles, she laughed and jumped to her feet. "I'll freshen up. Would you like to go soon?"

"Take your time," Mentàll said. "We are in no rush."

As soon as Mrn. M left, Methusal hissed, "What is this all about?"

He smiled. "You will not have to be alone with me. Does that not please you?"

It wasn't an answer, and her frown made that clear. "*Lozar*. Nothing is ever so simple with you."

His smile vanished. "Perhaps today it is."

On a sudden hunch, she said, "Or is it *you* who doesn't want to be alone with me?"

Hot, unreadable emotion flashed in his gaze, which jarred her. "You do not want to know what I wish."

She had thought... But no. "You're still upset with me. Aren't you?"

Mentàll rose and strode into their room. After an indecisive moment, she followed.

Carefully, she shut the door behind her. "Why?"

Back to her, he pulled several items from his pack and stuffed them in the pockets of his breeches. He did not answer.

"Are you ignoring me?"

Finally, he faced her, his cool expression under complete control once more. "It is time to go, Methusal." He headed for the door.

Methusal moved in front of it, blocking it with her body. "Not until you tell me what's wrong."

The Dehrien stopped two paces from her. That's when she knew something was really troubling him. On a normal day, he would invade her personal space and attempt to force her hand, or intimidate her into doing his will. Now he couldn't seem to keep enough distance between them.

A blessing, to be sure. So why, again, was she pushing the issue?

She said, "For the mission's sake, tell me what's wrong. Please. And besides that, Mrn. M will pick up on it."

He did not reply. In frustration, she exclaimed, "You are the most stubborn, contrary... *infuriating* man I know."

"Are you finished?"

"I'll be finished when you quit hiding like an apte and tell me what's wrong."

His features hardened until they looked bleak and harsh. "You do not want to know the truth."

"Yes. I do."

His fists clenched. "You won't like it. It will prove I am the wild beast you've always accused me of being."

"What do you mean?"

"Here is the truth, Methusal," intensity shivered in his low voice. "I wanted to gut the man who whipped you. I wanted to kill the *scienth*! You put yourself in danger. If not for me, you would be dead right now."

Although yesterday he'd clearly felt angry and upset, learning the true depth of his feelings now surprised and confused her. "Three years ago you're the one who held a blade to my throat. Why would it matter if someone else wanted to kill me now?"

"You need to ask?"

"Yes! Why do you care? Or are *you* the only who can pass sentence on me? You'll give that pleasure to no one else— isn't that what you said during the Quasr War?"

He glanced at the ceiling, as if pushed beyond endurance. "Methusal, I said I was wrong for how I treated you. That is *over*. It is done!"

Shakily, she said, "Is it? Really?"

His fingers raked through his hair, leaving it standing on end. A guttural sound escaped. "Sometimes, Methusal, you drive me to the edge of the bluff of reason. I don't know what to do with you."

"It upsets you that I don't stay in the box you put me in? It drives you crazy that I have a mind of mind own? That I dare to argue with you and make you see reason? That I might actually be *right* sometimes."

"No."

"Yes."

A grim smile twisted his lips. "You have no idea what I think of you, Methusal."

"I think my death yesterday would have upset all of your plans. Isn't that right?"

"You still understand so little about me."

"How can I, if you won't tell me why you're so upset?"

A long pause elapsed. "I did not want you to get hurt." The admission seemed difficult for him to make. "He hurt you, and I wanted to kill him."

She stared at him in complete silence. He was upset because *she had been hurt*.

It appeared that much more meaning lived behind those stark words than he'd articulated, however. Perhaps he didn't want to care at all. Likely. Maybe he was also upset with her for failing her duty and putting herself at risk. But at last she'd discovered the basic truth. He did not want to see her hurt. Perhaps that explained—at least partly—why he had saved her life so many times over the last seven months.

"Really?" she said softly.

"Yes." He drew a harsh breath. "I am no longer upset with you, Methusal."

Bewildered, she said, "Why not?"

"Our fights accomplish one benefit."

"They release your frustrations?"

A smile that wasn't a smile curled his lips. "The world is as it should be once again."

What did he mean by *that*?

She didn't know what to feel. Even more bewildering, his remoteness still lingered. Something was still bothering him, although he clearly did not intend to share that with her, either. He appeared quite ready to leave her presence.

A thought struck her. "Are you still disapp..."

"Enough, Methusal." He gripped her upper arms and firmly removed her from blocking the door. "It is time to go."

She did not like him looking at her like that; as if he could not wait to get away from her. But why? Why did she care?

She pulled free from his grasp. "Don't touch me."

He paused and took in her expression. A real smile flickered. "All is well now, Methusal. Come."

Frowning, she followed him. All was not well. And she wasn't sure why it mattered.

△ △ △ △ △

Timaeus walked with Deccia toward Dakarra. Goric walked a few lengths ahead by himself. The team needed bread again, and meat. Deccia dreaded entering the town, even though yesterday had been pleasant enough.

Timaeus had just told her more about his harrowing trip home from Carachki. After leaving the capitol city, he'd immediately started back. Unfortunately, it had turned dark before he found a town in which to spend the night. He'd had to dive into a bush at the side of the road when soldiers straggled into view, dragging an ill-kempt, wild-eyed man with them.

"They poked him with guns. They kicked him and spit on him." Timaeus' voice deepened with disgust. "They enjoyed it."

Deccia felt sick, listening to this. What if Timaeus had been caught, too? "Promise you won't be out again at dark."

"I can take care of myself, Decc."

"Not against ten men! Promise me."

"I won't walk on the road at night. But if it's dark and I need to get somewhere fast, I won't curl up and hide, either."

"Timaeus." Deccia touched his arm. It felt hard and corded with muscle.

"I won't." His tone gentled. "I love you, Deccia. But at some point, my messages might mean life or death. The Zindedis won't stop me."

Maybe he was right, but she didn't like it. "Do you think soldiers patrol the whole road from Carachki to Dakarra?"

"They must. I saw a few barracks along the way. Must be where they live."

Deccia felt a fresh stab of homesickness. She missed Rolban. And while she always worried when Timaeus ran messages between villages on Koblan, she never worried about him being attacked by packs of evil soldiers. Only wild beasts. But maybe they weren't so different.

They approached the main street of Dakarra now. Goric had already turned the corner and disappeared from view.

Deccia said, "Let's just get our supplies and go."

"What's your feel for this place?"

"Bad," she said shortly. "I mean, Ceri's nice, but most of the other people..." Timaeus gripped her arm, abruptly pulling her into the shelter of a tree.

Soldiers thronged the streets. A few nailed up flyers. Two men gripped a young man by the elbows. "*No!*" a woman screamed, arms outstretched. "My *son.*" It was Olita, Deccia realized with shock. Vitnia and another woman held her back. Her son didn't struggle when the soldiers shoved him toward a cart where other young men sat, looking scared. Olita collapsed to the ground, wailing.

"What on *earth...*" she whispered.

Timaeus slipped sideways and yanked a flyer off a lamp post. He returned, frowning. Deccia read over his arm, "Draft in force. All men years eighteen to twenty-two must join the military now. Report to your home district for duty."

"*All* men?" Fresh fear hit Deccia. "What if they think you... What if they try to drag *you* off?"

"Looks like they're dragging off Dakarrans. It says men are to report to their home district."

"But..." Panic overwhelmed her. "You have to hide, Timaeus!"

"I won't hide."

She'd never known her husband could be so stubborn. "But it's foolish..."

"I'll have to face them sooner or later."

"They're grabbing everyone they see. Look!" Soldiers seized a man who looked to be thirty years old. "They're drunk with power. You need to leave now, Timaeus. What would we do if they grabbed you? You can't prove who you are, or where you live!"

Indecision hovered on his face for the first time. The soldiers swarmed closer.

"Go!" She shoved him. "I'll grab the food and meet you back at the cabin."

"I won't leave you alone."

"Yes, you will! Go," she begged. "They won't bother me. I'm a woman."

"Where's Goric?"

"If he's smart, he's heading back, too. Don't worry. He's good at kaavl."

Another excruciating moment passed. He didn't want to leave her, that was clear. Finally, he turned silently and disappeared around the corner. Deccia drew a breath of relief. Straightening her shoulders, she darted across the street and headed for the market.

She passed Vitnia and Olita. The large woman wept, her face red and blotchy. Deccia couldn't help but feel sorry for her. How would she feel if her son was ripped from her arms and forced to join the horrible Zindedi army? She touched her stomach protectively, even though no life stirred there yet.

Other Dakarrans crowded the walkways, gawking at the scene in the street. Young mothers wept for their husbands, and older women wept for their sons. Their heartache touched Deccia, but she hurried on, trying to close her mind to it. Zindedis were savaging their own. It was unconscionable, wild beast behavior.

She ducked into the market, glad for the sudden, dim quiet.

Ceri crept forward, her face as pale as a ghost. "Did you see him?"

"See who?" Behind Deccia, the door opened.

A visible tremor seized the other girl. She backed up, her round green eyes focused on the person behind Deccia. She backed up again, and stumbled over a box of fruit.

Deccia whirled. A thin man stood there. He was about her height, with a black beret perched jauntily on his dark blond head. Something about him seemed vaguely familiar. The high, broad forehead, or the sharp, aquiline nose? Or was it his square face? His military uniform was unnaturally neat. Medals, lined in crisp rows, adorned his uniform. Deccia recognized the patterning of the medals. That particular clustering of colors and metal shapes had been burned into her brain nine months ago...on the uniform of the General who had raped her.

Her chest tightened, and she couldn't breathe. She tried to reach for something to steady herself, but touched only empty air.

The General's eyes were not fixed upon her, though, but on Ceri. A smile tugged at his thin lips. He stepped forward. Polished boots clicked across the wooden floor. "So," he said. "This is where you've been hiding yourself."

If anything, Ceri looked even paler, but bright spots of color burned on her cheeks. "Leave me alone, Fitrn."

So, this was General Fitrn, whom Hendra and the others had seen at the military base.

"Come with me, and all will be well."

"*You* are not well," she spat.

"You are mine. Your father promised you to me. The Presidente's son."

Deccia swallowed a silent gasp at this revelation.

"No. He didn't promise me to *you*. In any case, my father is dead. Leave me alone." She backed up again.

The cruel lips curled. Now General Fitrn was almost level with Deccia. His eyes were a flat, goldish brown color. A shiver began, deep inside her. The heart of a beast lived in him, just like it had in the dead General Greisn. His uncle.

No wonder he seemed so familiar. They had the same square face and dark eyebrows, and cruel set to his thin lips. Deccia broke out in a sweat of pure terror. She glanced at Ceri. Her friend needed help. Much as she wanted to run out the door, she couldn't. If she could do anything to help free Ceri from this man, she would do it.

Deccia slowly backed up. Her shaking fingers closed around a metal can. She watched the General, waiting to see what he'd do next.

He said, "Come with me now. Make it simple on yourself. I will lavish you with every expensive jewel and gown you could desire."

"I won't sell my soul to the devil." Ceri spat on the floor. "I would sooner die than go with you."

Red flooded General Fitrn's face. "You may have your wish!" A thin whip appeared in his hand.

Deccia gasped, and her heart pounded. Time seemed to stand still as she watched the whip flick back and forth. It was black, with a flat, black, triangular head. He flipped it again. Ceri did not back away.

He walked closer to the slight girl. Now his back was to Deccia. She gripped the heavy can tighter, fingers slippery with perspiration.

The General's red flush had faded, leaving his face a pale, unnatural white. "When you are mine, you will not talk back to me."

"I am not yours. I will never be yours!"

The whip flicked, faster than thought. A snap ricocheted, and then a long, red welt appeared on Ceri's face.

Deccia gasped. "Stop!" she cried out. "Stop it!"

The General whirled.

Ceri shouted, "Look at *me!* I'm the one you want."

The General glanced back. Deccia took that opportunity to hurl the can at his face. It hit his temple with a satisfying *thunk*. Surprise flared in those dead eyes, and he slowly spun on his heel and crumpled to the floor. Ceri stared in surprise at him, and then at Deccia.

"Run!" she cried out. "And don't come back until he's gone!" She whirled and darted out the back door.

Already, the General was stirring on the floor.

Deccia dashed out the door and down the street as if the hound of hell was on her heels. She didn't slow down, even when she reached their quiet country road.

"Deccia!" Timaeus appeared, and ran beside her. "What happened?"

She explained, gasping with fear.

"He saw you?"

"Yes, but only for a second."

Grimly, he said, "We'll keep watch. If he comes, you'll have to hide in the forest."

"I'm sorry, Timaeus. I didn't know what else to do. What he did to Ceri..."

"You did the right thing," he assured her in a gruff voice.

Panting, they burst into the large cabin. Sozla and Behran looked up in surprise.

Deccia explained what had happened again. Then everyone sat silently, digesting her revelation that General Fitrn was the Presidente's son.

"You did the right thing," Sozla agreed. "Behran, should we watch now for the soldiers?"

"I'll do it," Timaeus said. "You two keep working on the detonator. Deccia, you stay here." The door slammed behind him.

Deccia couldn't keep still. She couldn't sit down. Too much adrenaline pumped through her. Still trembling, she exited from the kitchen and slipped into the side yard.

Laundry was piled high in a tub, near the well. Physical exercise. That's what she needed. She lowered the large bucket into the well and then pulled the full, heavy load back up again. She dashed the water into the laundry tub, imagining the General's face crumpling with the dirty linen.

She flung the bucket down again and savagely jerked it back up. "That horrible man. The *horrible man!*" Tears stung her eyes and slid down her cheeks. She threw the bucket down the well again. She trembled uncontrollably. "I hate these Zindedis! I *hate* them!"

"Trying to kill the bucket?" Goric appeared in her side vision. His straight, dirty blond hair poked down his forehead. Murky eyes watched her with a faint hint of curiosity.

Deccia pulled up the bucket. Hands trembling, she dumped it in the tub a little more gently. She would not let Goric witness her tantrum, nor see her fear or her rage. Despite this lofty resolve, she flung the bucket to the ground with unnecessary force.

"Man, you *are* mad." Goric fetched the bucket before it rolled into a mud puddle. He stepped back and watched her as if she were some sort of unpredictable animal. "You hate all Zindedis, then?"

"Not all of them." Deccia pressed her trembling hands together. "But the ones who are in charge, yes. The evil ones. The soldiers."

He said nothing, and Deccia wondered in a sudden rage why he was staring at her like that. Didn't he know it made her feel uncomfortable? And yet politeness had been ingrained into her very core, so she tightly pressed her lips together.

Goric said, "You hate them all. Isn't that what you just said, before you saw me?"

Deccia glared, despite herself. "What's it to you? Are you my conscience?"

"Want me to disappear? Or maybe you want to ignore me, just like everyone else?"

His words caught her by surprise. But they were true. No one asked Goric's opinion about anything. He was shuffled onto assignments, and his wishes weren't given any thought.

Like when he'd wanted to scout at night, and Behran and Tabor had dismissed the idea immediately.

All the same, she didn't understand why he still stood here, talking to her. What was his purpose? And then she recalled their brief talk on the ship. Maybe he saw her as a bit of a friend. Maybe he was actually trying to be one for her.

She wiped her cheeks. "I'm sorry, Goric. I didn't mean to snap at you. I'm really upset." She grabbed the bucket again and lowered it down the well for more water.

A moment elapsed. "What happened?"

"General Fitrn attacked the girl who works at the market. He said she belongs to him. When she refused to go with him, he hit Ceri's face with a whip."

Goric flinched.

With satisfaction, she added, "I threw a heavy can at his head and knocked him out."

She dumped the cold water onto the clothes. Now perspiration dampened her skin. The sun felt hot, and filling the tub was hard work. And yet she relished it. The physical labor and the ability to lash her emotions onto the hapless clothes, rather than on the people around her, helped.

Goric digested this information. Then he said, "I saw General Fitrn when I was out scouting the other day. He's a piece of work."

"He's insane," she panted, struggling with another bucket. The rope dug into her hands. She was getting tired. Pleasantly so. "Just like his uncle."

"His uncle?"

"The horrible General who came to Quasr. General Greisn. I wonder if everyone in that family is insane."

Goric fell silent.

She said, "What do you think of the Zindedis?"

He shrugged a shoulder. "I don't know. They're people, like any other."

Deccia shook her head. "They're not like Koblanis."

"What do you mean?"

"I think they're bred to hate. Almost every single one I've met so far has been vile and awful."

"You'd judge a whole continent based on two Generals?"

"And the soldiers," she agreed. "Terrorizing citizens just for the joy of it is barbaric. They're sick, like wild beasts. Who would raise their children to behave like that?"

"Maybe you're right. Maybe they are all worthless." His voice sounded hard.

Now she was passing her prejudice on to someone else. "No," she said. "Don't think that. I'm biased. I'm afraid I can't see the Zindedis clearly. Especially not the soldiers or the General."

"Because of General Greisn. In Quasr."

Hot tears flooded her eyes. "Yes. Because of him."

"I understand." He made a small movement, as if to convey sympathy but instead he remained very still. "I understand what it means to hate. Don't be too hard on yourself." He moved by and headed for the kitchen.

Deccia dumped the last bucket of water into the tub and watched Goric enter the house. He really had been trying to be her friend. A surprising overture. She'd never seen him offer friendship to anyone else.

△ △ △ △ △

The botanical gardens were gorgeous. Methusal, Mentàll and Mrn. M had already been walking for an hour, and they still hadn't reached the end of the grounds. Tall trees shaded the stone walkways, and flying beasts chattered overhead. Lush bushes laden with flowers grew tall in a few places, serving to hide other, crisscrossing pathways. In other areas clipped grass formed a verdant background for individual plants covered in gigantic, breathtaking blooms.

"Nasrias," Mrn. M said happily, sniffing a large yellow flower. Black spots speckled the center. Taking her turn, Methusal inhaled the sweet, heavy fragrance. A petal touched her chin. It felt as soft as a baby's skin.

Mentàll did not stoop to smell the flowers. Instead, he studied the map. He extended the paper to Mrn. M. "What is this structure?"

"A maze." Mrn. M chuckled. "The Presidente loves a good puzzle."

"What is a maze?" Methusal wanted to know.

"We're not far. I'll show you."

After wandering down a few more paths, they approached a towering, dark green hedge. Its perimeter stretched west and disappeared north into the looming trees. It was hard to see how big the maze was, but it appeared to be enormous.

A narrow stone path led inside. To the right of the entrance rested a stone tablet on a raised platform. Mrn. M went to this. "See? It's a map of the maze. If you look hard enough you'll find the way through."

"Are other markers placed inside the maze?" A glimpse inside the maze left an impression of unfriendly darkness.

"No. That's the fun of it. It's a memory test. But I'll leave that adventure to the young ones. Would you two like to go in?"

"No," Methusal said quickly. She felt the Dehrien Chief's gaze upon her. "I mean, it looks spooky. Has anyone gotten lost in there?"

"Gardeners go through twice a day to rescue lost guests," Mrn. M said comfortably.

Still. The foliage of the maze was an unnatural, inky green. Menacing. She shivered. "I'll stick to the sunshine, thank you."

To her shock, Mentàll's large, warm hand closed around hers. "Are you cold?" he murmured.

She couldn't tug free. Not with Mrn. M watching with bright, interested eyes. So she smiled. "Yes, thank you. It looks frightening in there."

Mentàll drew her closer, so their forearms touched from wrist to elbow. "I will protect you. You need not fear." A little amusement flickered across his features. So, he was enjoying this. Perhaps she should feel grateful that he appeared to be fully himself again, and relishing every opportunity to needle under her skin. Well, two could play at that game.

"Oh, Lozar." She fluttered her eyelashes. Breathlessly, she simpered, "I feel so safe with you. Not even the wildest beast would dare attack me with you at my side."

A small smile appeared and vanished. They continued down the path, hand in hand.

Mrn. M rushed toward a bush bearing enormous purple flowers. "A flasrian!" she cried. "I've never seen one so large."

She flitted next to a plant dripping huge clusters of delicate orange petals. "Ortangias." She breathed in the scent and closed her eyes with an expression of rapture. "Come, Midi. Smell them. You too, Lozar," she encouraged.

Methusal sniffed, and almost swooned with delight. A sweet, delicate aroma, like the sweetest, purest tagma juice, or sweet cakes filled her senses. Mentàll dutifully bent to sniff. Surprise registered, and he inhaled again.

Mrn. M smiled. "Carachki is the only place ortangias grow on Zindedi. A bottle of ortangia perfume costs a month's wages. It is the rarest, most exquisite perfume available."

"Like my wife," Mentàll said. Startled, Methusal looked up at him. Those glacier blue eyes penetrated deep into her own, as if searching for her soul. "She is a bloom of perfection. Found nowhere else in the world."

Her jaw dropped, and her face warmed. He seemed sincere. But of course it was only an act. With difficulty, she closed the ridiculous, naïve place in her heart that had actually believed it for a moment, and reminded herself of the truth. Mentàll, once again, was behaving true to form. And why would anything he say affect her, anyway? She loved *Behran*. Unfortunately, in Carachki, Behran seemed very far away. Only Mentàll, and her tumultuous relationship with him, seemed real. The realization disturbed her.

Mrn. M sidled away with a smile tugging at her lips. She'd bought the deception, just as the Dehrien had intended.

Methusal discreetly tugged at her hand. "Let me go."

He did not. Instead, he raised it. His lips warmed the back. "I speak only the truth. But you know that, don't you?"

Flummoxed again, her face warmed. "You love this, don't you?"

His eyes glinted. "What?"

"Playing games with me!" She tugged at her hand again, but he didn't let go.

"Lovers walk hand in hand," he murmured. "We cannot keep Mrn. M waiting."

She growled beneath her breath. Up ahead, their landlady stopped beside another stone plaque. This one marked the exterior of a waist high hedge, on which flourished hundreds of tiny, multi-colored flowers.

Mrn. M turned to them with a smile. "Another maze. Would you like to try it?"

It was much smaller than the other one. And if worse came to worst, they could climb over the short bushes and escape to freedom.

"Sounds fun," she agreed. And hopefully Mentàll would release his grip on her once they'd entered the narrow walkway.

Her fake husband studied the map for a moment before declaring himself ready to go.

For a while Mrn. M led the way, and she bobbed left and right, following dead end paths. Last in the group, Mentàll walked more slowly, and Methusal did, too, although thankfully now her appendage was her own once again. At one point, when Mrn. M flitted left, Mentàll touched Methusal's shoulder, urging her to go right. Mrn. M joined them a moment later. At another fork, Mentàll's touched her left arm. Mrn. M brushed by and headed right. She seemed to have an unerring knack to go the wrong way.

Methusal glanced back at him. "You know where you're going, don't you? Why don't you lead the way?"

"You trust me so completely, then? You will follow wherever I lead?"

She ignored this. "Did you memorize the map?"

"Yes."

He had done little more than glance at it. "So do we turn left or right here to get out?"

"We are heading for the center of the maze. Not the exit."

"Why?"

"Because therein lies the prize."

"What?"

It was amazing how his smile could look both patient and arrogant at the same time. "Those who enter a maze think the purpose is to escape."

"It's not?"

"No."

"How do you know? Have you ever been in a maze before?"

"No. But the Presidente designed this. The plaque said so."

Methusal began to see. "You understand how complex, twisted minds work."

His teeth bared white in the sun. "Yes."

"Then lead the way."

"I'm out!" Mrn. M's cry reached their ears. She waved madly to them. Methusal waved back, but followed the Dehrien Chief deeper into the maze. She was curious, too, what they might find. And if there was a prize in the center of this small maze, what could lie in the center of the larger, darker, more frightening one?

Nine increasingly intricate turns later, Mentàll paused, his broad back blocking her view. She touched his shirt, meaning to urge him on, but the warm muscles beneath the thin cloth felt like hard stone. Memories from the war flashed; of smoothing coltac juice into his wounds, and kneading the hard muscles when they'd begun to pull apart the healing flesh. And later, when the wound had healed, she'd seen those broad shoulders flash bronze in the setting sun. She'd wanted to touch him then. She wanted...

She snatched her hand free. The pads of her fingers felt warm and tingly and she rubbed them on her pant leg, trying to erase the sensation.

Mentàll finally moved to the side, and she gasped at the beauty of the small, secret garden. Slowly, she walked inside. Beds of flowers bordered the square space. Blood red blooms tumbled from a bush living in the center of a two tier fountain. The water flowed over the top edge of the fountain in a sheer curtain, and then sluiced soundlessly down a sloped edge to the trough beneath. The near silence of that center alcove proved that the Presidente had planned it to remain a secret. No sound of falling water would entice curious visitors to come here. Only the curious—or those with suspicious, twisted minds like Mentàll—would ever find it.

She moved closer. A bronze colored plaque, nearly hidden in the grass underfoot, caught her attention. "The Blood Fountain," she read. "What do you suppose that means?"

"The blood of innocents stains his hands. Perhaps he wants to imagine he can wash himself clean."

Insightful. But perhaps more so into the Dehrien's soul than the Presidente's. "Do you ever wish that a fountain could wash away all of your sins?"

The Dehrien Chief remained silent for a long time. "If I did, it would mean I would want to return to The One who abandoned me."

He'd said something similar during the Quasr War. "You believe The One left you when your mother died?"

He looked away. His fists briefly clenched. "Yes. It is the only explanation."

"The scriptures teach that The One will never leave us nor forsake us. Not after we've asked him to be Lord of our life. Then we need to trust him and obey him."

"I do not trust him," he said shortly. The Dehrien turned his back on her and inspected the fountain. He was clearly finished with the conversation.

If she was smart, she would let the conversation die. But something inside of her would not allow it.

And she was curious. "Why don't you trust The One?"

"Methusal." That low grate warned her.

"Because your mother died a horrible death? Because you were abused as a child?"

"If The One was good, he would not allow those things to happen to her. Or to me. Or to Hendra." His voice was harsher than she'd ever heard it before.

"People do evil things. Not The One."

"It should never have happened. *None* of it!" Pain lashed. "Drop it, Methusal. It's a beautiful day. I do not want to feel angry."

But now she finally understood several new, deep truths about her enemy. "You're angry at your father for abandoning your mother. And you're angry at everyone who's ever hurt you. To top it off, you've wrapped up that whole ugly package and put it on The One's shoulders. Has it helped you, being angry at the entire world?"

His gaze flashed freezing ice. "Methusal. As usual, you do not know when to stop speaking."

"You mean I'm the only one who dares to stand up to you. To tell you the truth." She moved closer. Now she was the one invading his personal space. "Isn't that right?"

His hands whipped out, gripping her arms. "You cannot have the secrets to my soul."

"I want to know the truth. You always speak the truth, right?"

"Drop it." he gritted.

"Then be honest with yourself. You've done evil. To me. Do I blame The One for that? No. I blame you. And only you. Your uncle was evil. He hurt you horribly. Put the blame where it belongs."

"And then what?" His eyes seared like blue fire.

"Forgive," she whispered. "The One has asked me to forgive you."

That pale gaze flickered. A moment passed. "And will you?"

"I'm trying to forgive you, and let it all go. I try every day." She should try harder. She understood this now.

His hard grip eased, and his hands gently ran down her arms before releasing her. "I am sorry."

"For what?"

"You know I am sorry for how I treated you in the past."

She searched his eyes. Part of her did believe him. Another part was afraid to fully trust him. She was afraid that at his core he ultimately cared about no one but himself. That even if he did regret his past actions, he wouldn't hesitate to use her to get what he wanted. ...Whatever *it* was that he wanted.

"I forgive you," she said. Saying that felt like stepping off of a cliff. "But that doesn't mean I trust you."

"Just as I do not trust The One."

"Don't you think you should judge yourself, first? You're far from perfect."

"I expect a higher standard from The One."

"Did you ever think that he expects a higher standard from you? That the reason you're rejecting him is because if you turn back to him, you'd have to face the bad things in your own heart? I know you were hurt. But I think you use that as an excuse to avoid the truth. You're the one who's lost. And maybe The One is the only one who can rescue you."

"You are arrogant, Methusal. You do not know everything."

"I know. But you are willfully blind."

She headed back the way they had come. In her heart she felt sad, but she wasn't sure why. Maybe because it seemed like he'd condemned himself to live in that blood red, dark heart of the maze forever.

△ △ △ △ △

Hendra spied on the Dakarran military compound all day. She lay in the tall grasses on the northern slope, not far from the beach. It was deserted back here. The ore quarry inside the base lay silent and empty. So did the cannon making facility.

It was unbelievably boring.

She itched to gather useful information to help the team. They needed to discover what was in the carts before the military sent them to Carachki. Mentàll needed to know every detail. The team especially needed to find out where the huge powder deposit was located.

A few carts rolled south through the compound, and she hoped Doc was having better luck on the southern hill. Since kaavl wasn't needed for daytime spying—they didn't get close enough to risk capture—Doc had insisted that he wanted to help. He felt worthless, he said, otherwise.

He certainly wasn't worthless. Hendra's arm still ached when she moved it, but it was healing nicely. Thanks to Doc.

A cool breeze caressed her cheek, and she stared down into the compound through the waving grasses. A dreamy smile curved her lips. Doc had been so tender, and yes, even sweet with her yesterday when they'd walked along the beach.

She remembered holding his hand, and how happy she had felt with him. For once, her fears hadn't overwhelmed her. And yet the thought of stepping further down the path of intimacy with him still absolutely petrified her. Small steps, she told herself. Small steps.

Screeching flying beasts circled overhead. Grasses sang, whispering in the breeze. So peaceful. So quiet. And she was so alone.

A twig snapped, and Hendra quickly glanced over her shoulder. She slithered backward, heading for a protective bush. A hand touched her foot and she stifled a scream.

Goric's blond head appeared, blending in with the dried, waving grasses. He actually grinned. She scooted still further back to be level with him. "What are you doing here?"

"I'm your relief," he whispered. "Behran sent me. I'll take over for you and Doc until Tabor and Riln get here later."

Disappointment stabbed her. Spying all day had netted her zero information. A complete waste of time.

"Nothing is happening here," she whispered back. "You might find out more from Doc's position."

"I'll check it out." Those murky gray eyes revealed nothing. Clearly, Goric would spy as he saw fit. He'd be alone for a few hours, so he certainly could go wherever he liked.

"Good luck." She wriggled back into the cover of the woods. Her muscles felt stiff when she sat up. Dried grass poked into her tunic, scratching her skin. When she stood up, her legs felt a bit numb and wobbly, but after a few steps normal feeling returned. She headed toward the main road.

A twig snapped a four lengths north, in the direction of the beach. Heart pounding, Hendra paused. The forest lay silent around her.

Feeling a bit spooked, she hurried faster for the road, and nearly cried out when Doc stepped from behind a tree.

"Doc!" she gasped, throwing out her hands to stop herself, but still she careened into his hard chest. "What are you doing here?" With a blush, she quickly disengaged herself."

"Dakarra is dangerous right now. I came to bring you home the long way."

"What's going on?"

"Let's cross, first." They checked the road both ways and dashed across to the thick forest beyond. Then he told her about the forced draft and the cartloads of men rolling into the base. "The soldiers seem drunk with power right now. After they delivered the men, a group returned to town and tried to force their way on women, too."

Horror seized her. "No." With a choked gasp, she stopped in her tracks. "What if they go to our cabin?"

"Timaeus is watching the road. And we'll stick to the woods. We'll see them long before they see us."

"Are you sure?" Uncontrollable tremors raced through her. Hendra hated displaying such weakness, but she couldn't seem to stop her reaction.

"I'm sure."

She believed the quiet certainty in his voice. And the compassion in his eyes prevented her from feeling ashamed for her clear overreaction.

"All right." She stepped forward, although fear still threatened to swallow her whole. "We'll be fine."

"We'll be fine," he agreed.

She kept her breathing even and steady. She wouldn't succumb to a panic attack. Not with Doc walking beside her. She didn't want to become that weak, pitiable apte that Riln accused her of being.

"Can I hold your hand?" Doc offered his hand to her.

"Okay." Her trembling hand clutched his. His palm felt warm. Quiet strength flowed from his firm grip into the sinews of her own body. Bit by bit, as they walked, the fear ebbed from her heart. Doc would not let anything bad happen to her. He would not.

And of course he was right. They reached the cabins unmolested. Deccia greeted them with clear relief. "Have you seen Timaeus?"

"An hour ago," Doc reported. "He said he'd come back when everything has calmed down in Dakarra."

Deccia glanced at the road, worry clearly etched between her brows.

Inside, Sozla and Behran sat close together. Sozla touched a ball of wax, and said something in a low voice.

"Yes," Behran agreed. "But we'll need to test this bit first." His finger touched the attached wick, pointing to what he meant.

Sozla blushed and removed her hand. "Yes. Yes, I see." When she saw Hendra and Doc, she quickly jumped up. "You are back! I just pumped cool water. Perhaps you are thirsty?"

"Thank you." With a smile, she accepted the mug Sozla offered, and followed Doc toward the living room, but halted in the doorway when saw saw Riln pacing in that room. Curses muttered from his lips. Clearly, he wished he was outside and a part of the action.

She retreated to the kitchen and started dinner. It was a sparse one of fried bread and cheese, since Deccia explained what had happened at the market today.

A horrible day, all in all, Hendra thought. Nothing learned. A Zindedi draft enforced. Soldiers carrying off people at will.

Zindedi had just become a whole lot more dangerous. And the General was the Presidente's son. Mentàll would be interested to learn that bit of information.

A yawning Tabor soon entered the kitchen, and she reported her findings at the northern fence to him and Behran. Both men agreed that the northern fence would be given a lower priority in the future.

Deccia visibly relaxed when Timaeus finally returned at dusk. He reported that the General had apparently ordered the carousing soldiers to return to base.

He grinned. "He has a knot the size of an egg on his head."

"You got that close?" Deccia scolded.

"He's as mad as a blinded wild beast." Timaeus' tone sobered. "He ordered men to look for Ceri. Maybe that was their excuse for carting off women. In any case, it's stopped. I don't know if he's given up the hunt, though."

With a pale face, Deccia clasped Timaeus' hand so tightly her fingers showed white. "Was he looking for me, too?"

"No. I don't know why. I know he saw you for that split second."

Doc said, "Sometimes a blow to the head can affect memory. The amnesia may be temporary."

Deccia looked a little sick. "Do you think he'll stay at the base much longer?"

"I don't know." Timaeus hugged her. "But we'll keep a close watch on the road to the cabin. Don't worry, Deccia."

After dinner, Tabor and Riln slipped off into the night. Hendra finished cleaning up the meal with Sozla.

"What happened to you?" Deccia's exclamation brought Hendra into the living room, wiping her hands on a towel.

Goric had returned, and everyone stared at his face. A bright red mark scored one cheek.

He turned away. "It's nothing." His voice sounded faintly sullen. "I couldn't see where I was going, and ran into a tree."

With a frown, Deccia stepped closer. "Does it hurt? Maybe some cold water would help."

"No." Surliness edged the words.

Deccia stepped back and crossed her arms.

"Sorry," he muttered. "Guess I'm fried I walked into a tree. And I didn't find any new information, either."

"No one has today," Hendra commiserated.

Hopefully, Tabor and Riln would discover vital information tonight.

△ △ △ △ △

Methusal took a nap that afternoon on the soft bed in their room. Mentàll had already told Mrn. M that they'd be out late that night. Of course Mrn. M thought Mentàll planned to take Methusal out to dinner, and maybe to a play in a theatre downtown.

"It's safe enough in the center of town," Mrn. M cautioned. "But soldiers patrol the borders of the city. You could be arrested," a frown worried her forehead, "or worse."

"We'll be careful," Mentàll had assured her.

Now Methusal sleepily pried her eyelids open. The soft, downy comfort of the bed urged her to drift back into slumber. The dim light outside didn't help matters. It was almost time for bed. Maybe she could sleep for just a little while longer...

"Methusal." The Dehrien Chief's harsh voice jarred her. Strong fingers gripped shoulder. "It is time to leave."

Reluctantly, she turned over and gazed up at him. He brought cool air with him, as if he had been outside. It felt crisp and refreshing on her sleep flushed cheeks.

An odd expression crossed his features as he looked down at her. "Get up, Methusal," he said, a bit more gently. "It is time to go."

With a sigh, she sat up. Her head swam for a moment. Sleep still clung to her mind, and lethargy dragged at her limbs. "Give me a minute," she yawned. "I'll be ready soon."

Her feet touched the cold floor and she swayed a bit when she stood up. He steadied her shoulder. "You are all right? You are not sick?"

"I'm fine. Thank you." She headed for the relief room, and after changing into dark colored clothes and refreshing herself, she entered the living room.

Mentàll sat on the back of the couch, his long legs stretched out before him, talking to Mrn. M. He stood when he saw her. He wore a partially unbuttoned black jacket. It emphasized the breadth of his shoulders, and made his features appear even more austere...and even handsome. Her heart skipped a beat, and she quickly looked down and buttoned her jacket.

"You are ready?"

Methusal glanced back into those steady, disturbing pale eyes. "Yes."

"Have fun," Mrn. M fussed. "I'll leave the key under the door mat."

"Goodnight," Methusal called, and preceded Mentàll out into the dark, cold night. She curled her fingers into the warm pockets of her jacket.

On the street, she addressed him. "Are we going to eat first?"

"We will get a sandwich."

His tall body flanked her as they walked down the lamp lit street. Water glistened in patches on the dark, paved stones. It didn't smell like rain. Perhaps people had watered their gardens.

All was silent except for their footsteps. It felt strangely intimate, walking beside him in the dark like this. As if they truly were a couple, and going out for a night on the town.

She looked away from him, trying to ignore the mood that seemed to envelop them both.

"Here." Mentàll opened the door to a bright lit shop, and allowed her to enter first.

The warm smell of spiced meat and freshly baked bread filled her nostrils. Her mouth watered as she followed the Dehrien to the counter.

"What can I get for you two?" A man with a smudged apron covering his paunchy belly greeted them.

"Urchet meat with white cheese on a roll." Mentàll's black clad elbow brushed her arm as he pulled bills from his pocket.

Again, he seemed very large, and very near. It felt disturbingly more like a date with every passing moment.

"The same." Her tongue felt a little dry.

"Two cups of water, please."

Mentàll paid. While they waited, Methusal wandered around the shop, taking an interest in the dessert confections displayed in the glass case. In truth, she needed to put space between herself and the Dehrien Chief.

"Here you go." The shopkeeper put a white bag on the counter. "Have a good evening."

"You, too."

Mentàll headed for the door. Relieved, Methusal followed. At least they wouldn't have to sit facing each other over a table while they ate. In her bizarre frame of mind, that would have been too much.

"Here." Mentàll handed her a sandwich, and his calloused fingers briefly brushed hers.

"Thanks." Her skin tingled where he had touched her.

She needed to snap *out* of it. Her heart hammered uncomfortably fast. What was wrong with her? She stuffed a big corner of the sandwich in her mouth and concentrated on chewing.

Why were his fingers so calloused?

She blinked and looked away from the Dehrien, and into the dark night. Did she care? No. In silence, she finished her sandwich and drink. A toss in the trash and Mentàll pulled on his dark cap, tugging it down over his white-blond head. They headed for the northern side of town.

Now he strode at a fast clip. It diminished the odd sense of intimacy she'd felt between them. Good. Time to focus on the mission.

They climbed down the short bluff and followed the familiar gully to the eastern edge of the base. A pull of the wires and they were inside. Only one soldier patrolled this back fence, and he was easy to avoid. Soundlessly, they made their way toward the center of the base.

Methusal remembered the last time she'd been there, and the Sergeant and his whip. Her skin crept as they approached the barracks which hugged the northern fence.

"What is our plan?" she whispered.

"We will break into the Commander's office."

Into the Commander's office? The base was quiet, although laughter rumbled from the barracks, and shouts came from a large, rectangular building. A peek inside proved it was some sort of huge, open room. Men threw balls at one another, and ran with no apparent purpose back and forth across the floor.

Mentàll headed on, looking like a large, silent shadow. After cutting south across the base's main road, they reached the Commander's building. It looked dark inside. All the same, Methusal listened while the Dehrien Chief went down on one knee and picked the door lock with a wire.

"You have unknown talents," she whispered.

He glanced up. In the gloom, his teeth flashed a feral white. "You know about very few of my talents, Methusal."

Heat, mixed with that uncomfortable awareness, flashed back in full force.

Within moments, they were inside. Mentàll struck a firestick and lit two candles that he'd brought. He handed one to her. "Look for maps."

Wooden chairs flanked a desk in the outer office, and a tall cabinet stood in one corner. Mentàll disappeared through a door in the back. She guessed it led to the Commander's office.

No curtains covered the windows, so Methusal cupped the candle flame with her hand. Hopefully no one would notice the lights flickering inside. She opened the tall cabinet. At first glance, it appeared to be a treasure trove of books and boxes of papers. However, she soon realized that the papers were inventories for the base; food stuffs brought in, logs of who came and went on the base... Data of no use to her. She saw no mention of powder or guns.

Four drawers located in the bottom of the cabinet were loaded with files. Names were written on the top of each. Soldiers' names, by the look of it, and divided up alphabetically. She found a section labeled "Zindedi Officers." Smaller tabs broke them down by rank. She wondered if there was a file on the evil General Fitrn, or on the whip happy Sergeant who had threatened to beat her. But that information wasn't important right now. She sifted through more papers, looking for any reference to powder or weapons.

A sound tickled her ears. Stealthy footsteps crunched outside the building.

Instantly, she snuffed out her candle and slipped into the Commander's office. The room was pitch black. "Mentàll?"

"Here." The whisper came from behind the door.

"They must know we're here."

He pulled her back with him, into the shadows.

Outside, a key scraped in the lock.

"The man is foolish," he said quietly, behind her. "He is alone."

Methusal listened intently. He was right. She only heard one man's breaths. The lock clicked, and the door swung open. Carrying with vision, Methusal peered around the corner. A match flickered, illuminating the soldier's face. Not the Commander, as she'd guessed, but the Sergeant who had tried to beat her. She involuntarily pressed back harder against Mentàll. When she realized what she had done, she jerked forward again, as if scalded. Even so, every hard line and plane of him was imprinted in her memory.

"The Sergeant," he guessed softly. "Get behind me."

"No. He'd hear." Still carrying with vision, she watched the enemy soldier. He held a candle, also. Glancing furtively at the black windows, he pulled a large envelope from a box on the desk labeled "Out." He broke the seal. After extracting a slim folder, he set this on the desk and read it. Swiftly, he grabbed a writing stick and scrawled something on the paper. Then he shoved it back in the folder and into the envelope, and headed for the Commander's office.

"He's coming." Methusal stiffened again, and struggled to suppress her desire to shrink back against Mentàll. Apparently, she'd been wrong—the man didn't know they were there. He'd come to the office for some unsavory purpose of his own.

The light flickered, revealing a large wooden desk. The Sergeant circled the desk, still carrying the envelope. Although most of the open door still protected their hiding place, he could see their arms if he looked. Thankfully, he seemed intent on rummaging through a drawer. "Ah," he muttered. He extracted a blob of red wax and a metal stamp.

He scratched off the old seal on the envelope. The light flickered on his face, revealing dark circles under his eyes and a determined set to his lips. He was young. Younger than Methusal had thought when he'd marched her across camp yesterday. He had short brown hair, and a hint of puffiness in his jaw line predicted jowls to come. His black Zindedi uniform fell in crisp lines from his shoulders, and the handle of his knife glinted silver in the candlelight.

He looked so *ordinary*. And yet he was obviously doctoring records for his own purposes. He did not look nervous. And as far as looking ordinary—she already knew a love for cruelty lived beneath that boyish exterior.

The Sergeant affixed the new seal, using heat from his candle, and pressed the stamp into it. Then he commenced a thorough, drawer by drawer search of the Commander's desk. With a grunt of satisfaction, he flipped two files onto the desk and quickly paged through them.

She needed to see what he was looking at.

"Carry. See what he's seeing." Mentàll's breath curled into her ear. She jumped a little, once again brought to full awareness of the man behind her. She wanted to retort that she'd been about to do exactly that, but said nothing.

Using the tip of the Sergeant's nose as a reference point, she carried. The man's quiet breaths seemed louder now, and she had a perfect view of the papers before him.

They listed shipments leaving Zindedi towns. Dates were noted, and so were the contents. Powder. Weapons. Uniforms, ship supplies. To her frustration, the Sergeant speedily flipped through the other papers in the file, and then folded three of them together and stuffed them into his shirt pocket.

The next file listed ships and locations. Methusal scanned these as fast as she could. Thirty or more were listed in Carachki alone. A smattering of others appeared to be located in the southern port of Oesten, and still fewer in the eastern Zindedi town of Paraski.

The Sergeant stared at this for a while, and then abruptly returned the folders to their original locations. Methusal's kaavl concentration broke when he stood.

He looked up, and for a second, she could have sworn his dark eyes bored right into her. She froze, not daring to breathe.

Slowly, he picked up the envelope and sauntered toward the door. He unexpectedly blew out the candle just before reaching it. Swifter than thought, Mentàll shoved her behind him, inserting his body between her and the Zindedi officer. Now she saw nothing but his broad back.

A faint whistle indicated that the Sergeant had returned to the outer office. A door click indicated that he'd gone.

"He saw us," Mentàll said, releasing her from her prison. "But he said nothing."

"We need to get out of here. He'll send soldiers for us."

"Perhaps." He headed for the door.

Methusal didn't feel at ease until they'd reached the relative safety of the back fence. There, she reported the contents of the papers.

He listened, but his gaze continued to stray in the direction of the Commander's office. "No shouts," he murmured. "No soldiers."

"Are you sure he saw us?"

"Yes. He is a spy."

Her jaw dropped open. "For whom? Not Koblan?"

"Most likely for eastern Zindedi."

"But weren't they conquered a few years ago?"

"Perhaps not as thoroughly as the Presidente wants to believe."

This was a new twist. "So he didn't report us because he thinks we're spies, too?"

"He knows we are spies. Why else would we break into the Commander's office?"

"Do you think we could make an alliance with him? Maybe pool our resources?" Methusal couldn't believe she was suggesting an alliance with the man who had nearly whipped her to death.

"No. We can trust no one but ourselves. However, the sergeant may prove useful in the future."

Methusal digested this. "So now what? Do we head back?"

"Now we discover the purpose for every building on this base. We will start at the front gate and work our way back."

There must be over fifty buildings on the base. Methusal's jaw dropped for a second time. "That'll take all night! We'll need to split up."

"Can you pick locks?"

"No."

"Are you at the primary level?"

Her hackles rose. "No."

"Then you will stay with me."

"If I'm so useless, maybe you should search by yourself," she snapped.

"Petulance does not suit you, Methusal."

"Then teach me to reach the Primary level."

Surprise flashed. "You want me to teach you?"

"Who else is there? Kitran is dead. Pan's not here. That leaves you."

A moment elapsed. In a quiet voice, he said, "I would be honored to teach you, Methusal."

"Yes. Well." She felt a little uncomfortable. She hadn't expected him to accept the responsibility so soberly; as if it was an appreciated honor. "When do we start?"

"Now. Tell me where the nearest soldier is."

Methusal intensified into kaavl, and carried with hearing, too. Finally, she heard what she was searching for. Footsteps. A visual carry confirmed it. "A soldier is twelve lengths south, and he's heading north."

"No."

"What?"

"Relax completely into kaavl, like Mahre taught."

Her old frustration arose. "I can't."

His eyebrows raised the barest bit. "You cannot?"

"I *can*. But too much input rushes in. I can't make sense of it all."

The soldier's footsteps grew louder, and Methusal and the Dehrien Chief slipped into the shadow of the next building. Ryon glowed overhead, almost as bright as daylight. Methusal carried with vision, and continued to watch the soldier.

"Relax." Mentàll's arm bumped into hers. He stood so close that the heat from his body warmed her. "Close your eyes. Let the input rush in."

"Do you have to stand so close?" she said irritably, and then wished she'd bitten her tongue.

"We are standing in the same place." Amusement glimmered. "We are receiving the same input. Relax."

Methusal struggled to block out the Dehrien. Finally, she relaxed totally into kaavl.

"Tell me what you sense," he murmured.

His words broke her block against him, and the sensation of his close physical presence nearly overwhelmed her. She struggled to regain her equilibrium and block him again. "I hear men talking about training tomorrow. Urchets chomping grass. Two soldiers walking across the front gate..."

"What about vision?" he murmured.

As effortless as a flying beast coasting on a breeze, her vision flew around building corners, into open doorways, into... She gasped, and her concentration broke again.

"What did you see?" he prompted.

Her face felt warm. "A man, in a relief hut. He'd left the door open."

"Surely that is not the first naked man you have ever seen."

Her cheeks flushed even hotter. "I didn't see *all* of him. But yes, it is."

A small silence elapsed. "You truly are an innocent, then."

She felt vulnerable now, having exposed her unworldliness to the Dehrien. "Don't look down on me. Purity is nothing to be ashamed of."

"I do not look down on you, Methusal." His whisper softened. "It is a gift. The man who takes you will cherish you."

Her clothes felt hot now, and she felt the insane urge to peel off her jacket, even though it was so cold that her breaths made frosty white puffs in the air. "No man will *take* me," she retorted. Why was she having this outrageous conversation with him? "I will *choose* the man. And I've chosen Behran."

A breath of a laugh touched her ears. She frowned. "What?"

"Behran will not be the man who awakens you."

She gasped. The audacity of the man. "Let's get back on subject, please. Teach me how to make sense of all of this kaavl input."

"You are beginning with the right idea. Concentrate on one sense at a time. Afterward, flip from one sense to another as fast as you can."

"It sounds impossible."

"It takes practice."

"Is that what you do?"

"It is some of what I do."

Methusal tried again. Struggled, would have been a better word, over the next ten minutes. The constant discipline and razor sharp concentration needed seemed impossible to achieve. Not to mention mentally exhausting. She felt truly overwhelmed, and wondered how much his kaavl surpassed her own.

Battling the constant sensory stimuli made her head ache. She closed her mind to kaavl for a moment, in order to relax. "What's the difference between the Primary and Ultimate levels?"

"Kaavl becomes completely effortless, at all times. I am still learning the rest."

"You haven't achieved the Ultimate level yet?"

"Who will judge if I have?"

Good question. No one had achieved it for centuries. "Doesn't Mahre lay out specific guidelines in the *Second Book of Kaavl*?"

"A few. But I believe it was a journey he traveled until his death."

"So you could reach the Ultimate level at any time." She thought about how very dangerous he could be then. Who knew what abilities or powers he might possess.

Softly, he said, "It will be a few years, I am sure. Would you like for me to tell you when I reach the Ultimate level?"

Methusal eyed the man looming over her—her enemy and persistent thorn in her side for more than three years. She wanted to say 'no,' but wouldn't it be smarter to stay apprised of the advantages her enemy gained? "Yes."

"So you expect our relationship to continue for many years?" His eyes gleamed down at her.

She felt uncomfortable. "No." Unfortunately, at this moment, she couldn't imagine her life without him in it.

"Believe what you will, Methusal."

"You believe *me*. When this mission is over, I will see you as little as possible."

His teeth flashed, but he did not answer.

She swallowed a grumble of frustration. The insufferable man. "Let's scout. I'd prefer not to be here all night."

"We will scout until two, and then we will return tomorrow."

"Thank goodness for small favors."

"Relax into kaavl."

She wanted to retort that she was still in kaavl, but that would be a lie. And he'd know it. "Fine. I'm ready." With a hint of sarcasm, she added, "Any last words of instruction, Kaavl Master?"

"I have many things to teach you," he murmured. Her spine prickled. "But you are not ready to hear them."

Why, yet again, did his words feel fraught with double meanings? Or was she only imagining things? "I'm ready to learn everything about the Primary level."

"And afterward?" Still, he pushed. "You do not want to know how to achieve the Ultimate level?"

"I'll learn from the book. Aren't you sending me one page a month?"

"My personal lessons would make you grow faster."

No doubt. But she couldn't imagine intentionally placing herself in his hands after this mission ended. "Thank you. But I don't think so."

Footsteps sounded. Mentàll pulled her further back into the shadows, to where a shed met the building, creating a deeper corner of shadows in which they could hide. Thankfully, he was behind her, because she wanted a clear view. At the same time, she sensed him, close behind her, and as much as she tried to ignore it, it disturbed her greatly.

She tried to think about Behran, and what he might be doing right now, but that enterprise quickly ended when two soldiers appeared and leaned against the building opposite them. Minutes dragged by as they shared a smoke and inconsequential gossip.

She and the Dehrien were stuck. If they tried to escape, the soldiers would see them.

Mentàll hissed, "We must move on. Cut left when I tell you to." A second later, "*Now*."

She didn't move. The soldiers hadn't looked away. It wasn't safe. And honestly, she was tired of his insufferable high-handedness.

But even as she felt a small flare of satisfaction, a noise to the south caught the Zindedis' attention. A small rodent scuttled across the dirt. Both men glanced men that way, and then back in the space of a second.

Opportunity lost. Chagrined, she closed her eyes. How had he known?

Hard fingers bit into her shoulder. "Go when I tell you to, Maahr."

She twitched her shoulder. "You're hurting me."

His grip loosened at once. "Your arrogance cost us ten minutes."

She didn't ask how he knew. "Let go."

"You must trust me," he said near her ear. She shivered, despite herself. The heat of him imprinted into every nerve ending of her body. "Do you understand?" His scorching breath feathered down her neck.

"Yes," she whispered faintly.

He released her, and she found she was trembling. Her skin still burned from where his breath had touched it. She told herself that she hated him. She crossed her arms.

"Move. Now," he told her in a harsh whisper.

Without thinking, she cut left, out of the shadows, and then slipped into the concealing shadows at the back of the building. He was close behind her.

They'd made it. "Where now?" She wouldn't look at him.

"The barracks."

Moving fast, she followed his every order for the next few hours. Exhaustion pulled at her mind before he called it quits. But she did not complain. In fact, she did not speak to him again.

They'd discovered the purpose for half of the buildings on the base—the occupied portion. Most were office buildings and barracks. But a few housed carts and guns. Tomorrow they would survey the other half. Of course, they'd already scouted some of the back buildings when they had first arrived. So tomorrow should take less time than tonight had.

In silence, they made their way back into the heart of town, easily avoiding the soldiers stationed at the perimeter of the city. On Feldon Street, the Dehrien Chief stopped. Warily, she did, too.

He said, "You are angry."

She said nothing.

"I cannot allow insubordination to risk our lives." His voice cut as sharp as the cold wind swirling down the street.

"You've made your point." Irritation finally prompted her to speak. "Clearly you want a mindless slave who will obey your every order."

"No. I want you to trust me. And I need your loyalty."

"I haven't been disloyal to Koblan."

"Only one person can be the leader. If you disobey orders, one of us could die."

She finally met his gaze. "I heard you the first time. You don't need to harangue me about it again."

"Good." The Dehrien Chief started walking again. Annoyed, she followed a step behind his tall, black form. Weariness tussled with a bit of depression. Sarcastically, she muttered, "Your wish is my command, Kaavl Master."

When he glanced back. Of course, he'd heard. One corner of his mouth curled up. "Give no promises you cannot keep, Methusal. Because I would be happy to hold you to that one."

"Whip."

He slowed down to walk beside her.

She frowned and crossed her arms.

"Tell me the real reason why you are angry." His voice sounded deeper, harsher.

Could she hide nothing from him? "I'm tired. And I thought..."

The Dehrien stopped, and she unwittingly stopped, too. "You thought what?"

She waved a sharp, angry hand. "I don't know. That we were a team. But it's clear all you care about is power and control."

"We are a team. But I am the leader."

"You've made that abundantly clear!" She looked away.

"Tell me what is wrong."

"What is *wrong* is you don't care about anyone but yourself."

A pause elapsed. Roughly, he said, "Do you want me to care about you?"

"No!"

"I like your fire, Methusal. I enjoy our battles. I do not want to quench your spirit."

"But…"

"I am the leader," he said softly. "No more insubordination, Methusal."

"I understand." Surprisingly, she felt a little better. He had listened to her feelings just now, and he had tried to take a step of peace.

He opened the door for her to Mrn. M's house. After quick ablutions, she collapsed onto the stone floor. The pain in her hips and back did not stop her from falling into instant slumber, because she couldn't think anymore. She couldn't feel anymore. She felt utterly exhausted, both physically and emotionally.

CHAPTER TWENTY-THREE

"THAT TWISTED ZIN IS GONE." Riln belched.

Hendra sat at the opposite end of the table, sipping hot juice. The warm mug felt good in her hands on this cold morning.

Riln and Tabor had returned from scouting a little while ago. Goric had left at dawn—he'd volunteered to scout until she and Doc could get there.

"Thank goodness," Deccia said with clear relief. "When?"

"He shipped out for Carachki this morning. Two carts went with him."

"Did you see what was in the carts?" Behran asked.

"Nope. But next time I won't tiptoe around those filthy Zins like a woman-skirted apte. I'll get as close as I need to get." Riln's hard jaw radiated belligerence.

"We may need to take more risks," Behran agreed calmly. "We've found out almost nothing so far."

"Who'll stop the soldiers from attacking innocents now?" Timaeus wondered grimly.

Hendra said, "Hopefully the new recruits will keep the soldiers busy."

"Maybe," Timaeus allowed. "But I don't think anyone should go to Dakarra alone again. And Deccia, I don't want you to go at all."

Deccia's hand curled over his black clad forearm. Today he wore a black Zindedi uniform, because he'd leave soon to bring a message to Mentàll. Dressing as a soldier seemed wise, now that the draft was in place. "The General is gone," she said quietly. "I'll be fine. Maybe he didn't see me after all, back at the store. Or maybe he has amnesia, like Doc said."

"Or maybe he ordered soldiers to seize you. No."

"I won't stay here." Ore cooled her voice. "I feel useless enough as it is."

"Decc." Tenderness softened his dark eyes. "I don't want you to get hurt."

"And I don't want *you* to get hurt. But you have your mission, and I have mine."

With a frown, Timaeus fell silent, but his tanned fingers curled over his wife's and remained there.

Riln shoved back his chair, muttering something that sounded suspiciously like, "Bunch of women-skirted aptes." Louder, he said, "We've got important decisions to make."

Behran looked up from the cannon part he was rolling between his fingers. "What are you talking about?"

"The carts. Two went with the General. A score more are waiting to ship out. We need to find out what's in them. If it's powder or weapons, we've got to stop them from rolling to Carachki."

Much as Hendra didn't want to agree with Riln, he had a point. Powder and arms that reached Carachki would head next for Zindedi warships. And then on to attack Koblan.

"I'm scheduled to talk to Mentàll tomorrow morning," Timaeus said. "I'll ask what he wants us to do."

"I say we blow up the carts now. Before more leave Dakarra." Riln looked around. "Anyone with me?"

No one answered. With a disgusted snort, he folded his arms. "I didn't think so."

"I think you're right, Riln," Doc said unexpectedly. "We can't let many carts reach Carachki. Destroying them on or near the base makes the most sense. Fewer innocents would be killed."

"Zin innocents?" Riln rolled his eyes. "The more we kill, the better. Kill every last one, is my philosophy."

Evenly, Doc said, "I disagree with that, Riln. And while I do think we need to destroy the carts, we can't do it yet."

Riln rolled his eyes again. "Bunch of mother..."

"Riln!" Deccia said sharply.

"I can't believe it!" Riln surged to his feet. "What are we, a bunch of sniveling brats, hiding behind women's skirts?" His fist slammed the table, making both Hendra and her mug jump. "We need to act now! Destroy every Zin we see and take out their weapons. We're here to save Koblan! I won't slink around anymore, hiding my tail between my legs. I'm going to *kill* some Zins!"

Doc crossed his arms and leaned back in his chair. Calm emanated from his still frame. "And after you kill the Zindedis, then what? The military will come looking for you."

"They'll suspect eastern Zins. Remember, they thought you were eastern spies when you broke into the compound."

True. However, Hendra didn't realize anyone had told Riln that.

Doc said slowly, "Regardless, they'll come looking for someone suspicious. We're new to the area, so that would be us."

Riln turned away, his disgust clear. "We'll never win this war by sitting on our hands and *spying* for days on end."

Behran spoke up. "Remember, we're hoping for peace."

"Peace!" Riln snorted.

"It may not be possible," Behran agreed. "So we're gathering information. When it comes time to act, we'll know every point to attack. And when Sozla and I figure out how to make these detonators, we'll be able to time explosions down to the minute."

"Riln, that means we can blow up every cart, every powder mine, and all at the same moment," Sozla said. "After we make the detonator, Behran and I will figure out how to set fuses that will burn for six or more hours."

A little of the stiffness left Riln's stocky shoulders. "Explosions? All at the same time?"

"That would be a sight to see," Doc murmured.

Riln spun a chair around and sat on it backwards. "I'm all for blowing the Zins to Ryon."

"Until we get the order from Mentàll, we'll watch those carts. And we absolutely need to find that biggest powder deposit."

"Kaboom." An evil grin split Riln's face. "Sounds excellent. As long as we take action soon. Sitting here all day is going to drive me crazy."

And living in the same cabin with Riln was about to drive Hendra crazy. The man was a powder keg, ready to blow up at the slightest spark. He'd said he would wait until the right time to act, but who knew?

△ △ △ △ △

Methusal slept until midmorning. She was alone in the room, and breakfast aromas drifted under the door. Hunger, as well as body aches from lying on the stone floor, urged her to get up, and she slowly did so.

If she was honest, she was sick of spying, and sick of lying on the stone floor. Truly, she'd had enough. But for Koblan she could do anything.

She took a quick bath, and afterward combed her damp hair while eyeing herself in the mirror. It still seemed strange to clearly see what she looked like. Rolban's dull metal mirrors portrayed a fuzzier, softer image. This one clearly revealed her green eyes, which were underscored by violet shadows. And her dark hair fell past her pale shoulders. Well, they were pale except for several round discolorations. The imprints left from Mentàll's brief grip on her shoulder last night.

They would bruise, although they didn't hurt. She bruised easily.

She touched her shoulder and cautiously poked at last night's memories—specifically, her reaction to his searing breath on her skin. Why had she felt that way? Why did she always respond to him in such a visceral way? It disturbed her. Deeply.

Reluctantly, she finally left the room and joined Mentàll at the dining table.

"Juice?" Mrn. M bustled in, holding a silver pitcher. Condensation beaded on it, testifying to the cold, delicious juice inside.

"Yes, please."

Mrn. M cast her a stern look. "You look like you've been up half the night. You need more rest. Not that it's any of my business, of course."

"I'll try to get to bed earlier tonight." Not that she'd get much rest on that cold floor. And weren't they supposed to scout again tonight? She swallowed a soft sigh.

"I was just telling Lozar that the Presidente has ordered up the draft."

Methusal glanced from Mrn. M to Mentàll, wondering what that meant. Clearly, it was something she should understand.

Calmly, Mentàll said, "Only men under twenty-two are required to report. I told Mrn. M that we would visit Dakarra in two days to make certain my leave remains intact."

Mrn. M asked, "How much more time do you have?"

"Almost two weeks. I intend to take it all, if I can."

"A wise move. Once you set sail, you'll have no time to yourself." Mrn. M glanced at Methusal. A smile softened her face. "You must take full advantage of your time together."

The Zindedi woman passed around a plate of hot, buttered cakes. "So," their landlady said brightly, clearly deciding to change the subject, "what fun thing will you do today?"

Methusal thought about last night, and didn't think she could handle much more *fun*.

Mentàll's hand closed over hers, making her jump. With a voice warm with charm, he said, "I would like to take Midi on a picnic."

"A picnic!" Delighted approval bloomed on Mrn. M's face. She clasped her hands. "I'd be happy to pack you a basket. Would you like that?"

He smiled. "We would be in your debt."

"I'll get started right now." Pushing back from the table, Mrn. M hurried into the kitchen. Happy humming reached Methusal's ears. At least someone was excited about the idea of a picnic. Of course, there would be no picnic.

After breakfast, arms shaking a little, Mrn. M transferred a large, obviously heavy basket into Mentàll's steady hand.

"Now, you have a wonderful time," she said. "Will you be back for dinner?"

"Yes," Mentàll said.

"Good. See you later." Her waves followed them out the door.

Methusal followed him in silence to the street. "So what's the real plan?" she said abruptly.

"You do not seem excited by the idea of our picnic."

"I'm tired. When are we spying? Now, or tonight?"

"Now."

"Then let's go."

In silence, she walked with him south, toward the harbor, and then followed the walkway east, past the Presidente's gardens. She didn't ask why they'd gone this way, although clearly the military compound lay to the north.

The Presidente's gardens ended where a small stream cut into the ocean. A bridge crossed it, and then the walkway headed north for a good while, and then petered out into short, stubby grass on either side of the shallow stream. Clear water rushed over the brown and green pebbles in the bottom, and here and there dry boulders reared up. They did not cross the bridge, but instead headed north, through the grass. To their left was a thick forest. No doubt the far edge of the Presidente's garden. Beyond the grassy strip on the other side of the stream sprang another, although thinner, forest.

The Dehrien secreted their picnic basket in shrubbery up on the hill. Now she knew where they were. To the north lay the dry gully they used to reach the military base.

They walked on. Only the twitters of flying beasts broke the quiet. Mentàll didn't seem to mind the silence, although when she cast him a side glance, a faint frown tugged at his brows.

Long minutes later, on the military compound, Methusal executed kaavl with complete, clinical concentration. She reported every finding to Mentàll, who wrote details on a map he'd drawn of the base. They finished cataloguing every building. It was mid-afternoon when they headed back the way they had come.

Mentàll seemed satisfied with the information they had obtained. Privately, Methusal wondered why it mattered, knowing where the powder was located, or how many buildings housed guns and other weapons. The Zindedis were massively armed and completely formidable, and she had no idea how they could ever stop them.

Out of the gully at last, they walked in the weeds bordering the forest toward the place where he'd stashed the picnic basket. Methusal's stomach rumbled.

The silence between them, broken only by necessary exchanges on the base, had grown a bit uncomfortable. Logic didn't explain the unhappiness that twisted through her spirit, depressing her. She wasn't happy talking to Mentàll, and she wasn't happy with the silence between them, either. Could she never win? The man was a gigantic thorn in her side.

The Dehrien Chief stopped. A few paces later, she slowed down and reluctantly looked back to see what was keeping him. The grim expression on his face said he was ready for a confrontation.

"What?"

He closed the distance between. "Finally, you have decided to speak to me."

"I spoke to you on the base."

"Facts only. You know what I mean."

"I thought nothing bothered you."

"What do you want, Methusal?" A thin edge of patience marked the words.

Although she wouldn't share her true thoughts, she might as well get answers to a few of her questions. "Why do we need to know where all their weapons are located? They'll transport them to the ships soon."

"And we will watch the ships while they do so."

"Why? Does it matter how many arms they have? It's clear they have enough to decimate Koblan."

"I care only where they place the powder."

"Why?"

"Because then we can blow it up."

Methusal gasped. "What?"

"I await only detonators and timers from Behran and Sozla."

She blinked, trying to wrap her mind around this new development. "But I thought we were going to push for peace. Aren't we going to get invitations to the ball, and...and convince the Presidente..." Her voice faltered.

"Yes. We will do that, also. But words will not convince the President to embrace peace. His rejection of my first peace proposal is proof of that. The explosions will be a warning. He will know that more destruction will come if he does not comply with the peace agreement we present to him at the ball."

"Don't you think that will infuriate him? Then he'll be more determined than ever to destroy us."

"Then he will suffer complete destruction."

Methusal stared at the Dehrien. She could not believe he meant to employ such a ruthless plan. The Presidente would be enraged beyond reason. He'd probably torture and kill every Koblani he discovered on Zindedi, and order the same for those captured on Koblan during the next war.

"I don't like it. It's too risky."

"You have no say, Methusal. Do your part. It is the only way we will ensure victory." Those pale eyes looked as hard as ice. He had made up his mind. And on some level, she was thankful to be on his side, rather than against it.

"What exactly is your plan?"

"When we go to Dakarra I will explain everything."

△ △ △ △ △

"I wish you didn't have to go." Deccia hated herself for clinging so tightly to Timaeus. Where was her strength? This was a military mission, wasn't it? She wished she could be as strong as Methusal. Her sister had let Behran go with no tears or clinging farewells.

"I'll be okay, Decc." Timaeus' hungry kiss lingered. "I'll be back before you know it. Tomorrow afternoon at the latest. Promise."

"All right." Deccia stepped back and made herself smile. "I'll pray for your safe trip."

Timaeus touched her upper arm. "Try to get some rest. Go to bed earlier, if you need to."

She had tried not to wake Timaeus, but she had been up and down all night. Every time she'd closed her eyes, nightmares exploded in her mind. The dead General morphed into his nephew, but both wanted to kill her—or Ceri, who lingered on the periphery of her dreams. The good news was she woke up, gasping, before anyone managed to hurt her. The night had seemed endless. Finally, in the black dawn, she'd crept out of bed, weariness pulling like a dead weight on her mind, and started breakfast for the others.

"I'll try," she promised. Another kiss, and he was gone, cutting southeast through the grassy fields, heading for the edge of the forest. Deccia wished he could avoid roads all the way to Carachki.

When she turned back to go inside, black figures caught her eye. Two people were on the road, heading for the cabins. Her heart jerked hard in alarm, and then settled down when she recognized the women. One was thin, and the other was large and limped. Vitnia and Olita.

Deccia doubted they'd come to pay a neighborly visit. Fear gripped her again. Goric, Riln, and Tabor were in the cabin. Vitnia had never met any of them. Their presence would invite questions and suspicion.

"Hello!" Vitnia raised a long, skinny arm.

Deccia wanted to bolt into the cabin and warn the others, but the two women had already reached the bottom of the hill. Skirts in hand, they laboriously climbed up.

"Vitnia!" Deccia cried. "And Olita! How nice that you could stop by."

Vitnia's eyes narrowed above her sharp nose. "We're not deaf."

Olita paused for a moment, puffing mightily. Perspiration beaded on her forehead.

Deccia used her body as a barrier between the women and the cabins. As pleasantly as possible, she said, "What brings you here?"

"A social call." Vitnia brushed by her and headed for the first cabin. "And I need to check on my property."

Still wheezing, Olita rolled forward, intent on following her friend. Deccia side-stepped before she was mowed over.

Vitnia poked her head inside Deccia and Timaeus' cabin. Thankfully, it was empty. Everyone was in the other cabin.

Deccia hurried to reach the larger cabin's porch before the Dakarran women arrived.

Vitnia put her narrow, black clad foot on the bottom step. "The first one's not bad, but it could be cleaner. Let's have a look at this one."

Deccia offered a gracious smile. "Of course." She opened the door and called inside, "Sozla, Behran...you have company!"

"Come in."

Sozla met them in the living room. The door to the men's room was shut, and so was the one to the kitchen.

The Eerporian girl stepped forward. "How wonderful that you could stop by." Her sparkling smile seemed a bit forced. "Perhaps we could offer you some refreshment?"

"No time for that." Vitnia headed for the kitchen door. Without invitation, she pushed it open.

Sozla frowned. "May we be of assistance?"

Vitnia ignored her. With apprehension, Deccia followed her inside. But only Behran sat at the table. The springs and flints and other odd bits had disappeared, replaced by a book. Vitnia twisted her neck to look at Sozla. "This is your husband?"

Sozla flushed. "Well...yes."

A thin smile stretched Vitnia's lips. "Newlyweds?"

"Yes. Newly. That is an accurate description." Sozla recovered her poise with admirable swiftness.

Vitnia's black eyes zeroed in on Deccia. "And what about your husband and your friends? Where are they?"

"Out."

"Please. You have not told us the purpose for your visit," Sozla said.

Vitnia smiled. It looked patently fake. "Olita and I would like to invite you to tea this afternoon."

"Tea?"

"Yes, tea." Olita's strident voice took up the tale. Her huffs and puffs had quieted to gentle pants. "Aren't you acquainted with the custom?"

Neither girl answered.

"It follows the midday meal. It's a restful custom." Olita turned to Vitnia. "I didn't realize it was only a Dakarran practice."

"Nor I." Suspicion sharpened Vitnia's gimlet gaze.

Sozla's laugh tinkled. "I did not realize Dakarrans view tea as its own event. In Carachki, it is all part of the noonday meal."

Stiffly, Vitnia said, "Dakarran customs are different than Carachki's."

"We would be delighted to have tea," Sozla said. "Shall we arrive immediately following lunch?"

"Yes," Olita boomed. "Come to my shop. We'll have tea in the back. And," she added craftily, "my husband will be on hand, if you have questions about the boat tour."

"Sounds good." Behran spoke for the first time. "I'd like to catch some fresh fish."

Olita beamed. "Excellent! Come, Vitnia, let's prepare." Clutching her friend's arm, she waddled out the door.

Deccia only relaxed when the two Dakarran women headed down the hill.

Olita waved. "See you later!"

Behran muttered, "Timaeus isn't going to like this."

Sozla sent him a puzzled look. "Why, Behran?"

"It could be a trap."

△ △ △ △ △

Mrn. M had packed a large bed sheet, as well as the scrumptious food, into the basket. Uncomfortably, Methusal wondered what their landlady expected them to do on the sheet. Other than eat food, of course.

Sitting cross-legged and barefoot, since it was warm in the sun, Methusal unpacked roast meat sandwiches, fruit, and a bottle of an unknown beverage. And of course plates, napkins, and a mound of fluffy fruit tarts. Mentàll had already helped himself to two of those. Right now, he worked at the cork in the tall, slender bottle. When it popped free, he sniffed the open neck.

"What is it?" she asked.

He smiled. "Spirits."

Methusal had never drunk spirits before in her life. She watched the Dehrien pour amber liquid into one of the small cups that Mrn. M had thoughtfully provided. When he tilted the bottle over the other cup, she covered it with her hand.

He looked up, and amusement glinted for the first time in a long time. A bit of her tension relaxed. He said softly, "Be bold, Methusal. Try a sip."

"Do you want to get me drunk?"

"I believe Mrn. M intends for us to enjoy ourselves."

Methusal glanced at the sheet and warmth crept across her cheeks. "Mrn. M doesn't know what's really going on."

"Try a sip of mine." He extended his cup.

She would not drink out of the Dehrien's cup! It seemed entirely too intimate, and that disturbed her. "I'll try a little in mine."

Golden liquid splashed in, filling it halfway. It smelled vaguely fruity. Methusal raised the cup and allowed a drop to cool her tongue. It tasted tangy, with a faintly fiery aftertaste. "Interesting," she allowed, setting the cup back down.

Mentàll swallowed more of his. "I would think you'd like it, Methusal. You like fire. The sweetness should only add to the allure." His eyes gleamed before he tossed back the rest of his drink.

"*You* are going to get drunk," she disapproved.

"I never lose control. Have you not learned that yet?" He did not pour more spirits into his cup. Instead, he downed another sandwich and three tarts.

The sandwich was delicious, but the bread was dry. Methusal took a few more discreet sips of the spirits to wash it down. It left a pleasant, warm feeling in her throat. Then she tried a tart. Delicious. One more sip, just to wash it down... To her surprise, she'd emptied the cup.

"More?" he suggested with a wicked grin.

Methusal frowned. He never grinned—except when he was about to sample a sweet treat. Ignoring him, she packed up the remainder of the lunch. Her head felt a little funny when she moved too fast, but other than that, the spirits didn't seem to be affecting her. Good.

"I'll take the last tart," he said, before she wrapped it away.

He downed it in two bites and licked the jelly from his fingers. Methusal watched, mesmerized. She'd stowed away the food, and now her eyes seemed to have nowhere else to go.

He grinned again, taking note of her interest. "You know, Methusal," he said, "we will need to make it look as if we've enjoyed ourselves."

Her gaze slid to his, not sure what he meant. Then comprehension dawned.

She leaped to her feet. "I don't *think* so." Her head swam for a moment. Strangely, this impairment to her faculties didn't bother her. Not at all. In the recesses of her mind, something told her the dizziness should be a warning sign, but she chose to ignore it.

He leisurely unfolded his long body and stood up. He gazed down at her. "I am not suggesting anything inappropriate."

"Then what *are* you suggesting?" More words flipped off her tongue. "I don't think I can trust you, Chief Solboshn."

"No?" He laughed softly. "Muss your hair. Rub in a little grass."

Outrage swamped her. "To make it look like I've rolled around in the grass? With you?"

"We want Mrn. M to think we have had a good time."

He was utterly outrageous. Recklessly, she jutted her face closer to his. "The day I have fun with you is the day I leap off the bluff of reason."

"You are certain about that?"

Regaining a scrap of her better sense, she retreated and tugged up the sheet to fold it.

He turned away, as if abandoning the conversation. But then he unexpectedly bent and plucked up handfuls of grass. Methusal watched him suspiciously.

A swift turn to his shoulders made his intent clear. With a faint smile, he advanced on her.

Her heart jerked with a spike of delight and horror. Methusal squealed, and ran like the wind.

The cool, soft grass felt good, sliding through her toes. He was close. Her mind clarified into kaavl, but she felt no fear, no anxiety. Instead, she felt the insane urge to giggle.

His hand grazed her arm, and she shrieked and ran faster. *Cross the stream!* That would slow him down. She splashed through the ice cold water and up the bank on the other side. Then she headed back north, and glanced over her shoulder. He hadn't gained on her. Her feet flew over the ground. She exulted in the exercise, and in a wild sense of freedom. Still, he didn't gain on her. Or lose ground, either.

She ran until her chest heaved and a stitch pulled at her side. Finally, she jogged to a stop. When Mentàll reached her, he wasn't even breathing hard.

Panting, she accused, "You let me run until I collapsed from exhaustion."

"No. Until you let me catch you."

Her mind felt clear again, and free from the effects of the spirits. But the lighthearted adrenaline remained. "So you've caught me. Now what?"

He raised his fist over her head. Grass softly sprinkled down, kissing her skin, her lips, her hair. Another handful sifted over her clothes.

"Mentàll!" She swiped at her garments. The grass stuck, clinging to the fabric. And her hair...it felt like millions of grassy bits slid through the slippery strands. The more she brushed at it, the more the grass teased and tickled into her scalp. She frowned. "I can't get it all out."

"Let me." His big hands moved over her hair, plucking out grass. She stood very still, aware of how close he was, and the heat of his hands when he cupped her cheeks and tilted her head gently from one side to the other, looking for bits of grass. Her heart softly thundered in her chest.

Finally, he released her. She felt illogically bereft. "Is it all gone?"

"Most of it." Humor tinged his tone.

"You slug." She felt completely befuddled by his behavior, and worse, by her reaction to it. To cover, she swiftly plucked up fistfuls of grass and dunked them on his head. She pushed the strands into his soft hair. Grass fluttered over his broad shoulders.

His hair actually looked cute all mussed. Boyish, even. Her insides flip-flopped in even more alarming confusion. "Don't smile at me like that."

His smile turned wicked. "Will you return the favor? Help me brush it off?"

She backed up, her pulse still beating too fast. This time, she listened to the warning signals in her head. "That's your job, I'm afraid."

Mentàll swiped his hair and suddenly he looked like himself again—dangerous, and a bit intimidating. Softly, he said, "Apte."

Maybe so, but she knew when to retreat from a predatory wild beast.

△ △ △ △ △

Behran and Goric left Deccia and Sozla at the edge of Dakarra.

"Be careful," Behran said, for at least the third time. His frown made it clear that he didn't like the idea of the girls taking tea with the Dakarran women.

"We'll be fine," Deccia said. "Remember, this is my job. I'm supposed to get a read on their attitudes toward us. Right now it's unfriendly, but if it changes into something worse, I need to get a hint of it before they attack."

She hoped they weren't walking into a trap. So far, the town seemed to be empty of soldiers. Maybe they were all at the base, training new recruits. On the other hand, it was possible General Fitrn had ordered several to stay in town and grab her.

"We will be fine, Behran," Sozla said with a small smile. "But I am sure Timaeus appreciates that you are watching out for his wife."

Behran's frown deepened when he looked at Sozla. "Deccia isn't the only one I'm worried about."

Delicate color kissed Sozla's cheeks. "Thank you, Behran. But I am well used to handling difficult older women. My father has no patience with them, so settling their disputes has fallen to me. In fact, now my father believes it to be my primary purpose in life. Besides marrying, of course, and providing him with grandchildren." More color pinkened her face. Quickly, she looked at Deccia. "I am ready. Are you?"

"Goric and I will scout. I'll meet you at the market when you're done." Goric would not. So far, the Dakarrans had not noticed that he was connected with them, and it seemed prudent to keep it that way.

Olita's shop was located directly across from the market. Inside, the familiar scent of leather clashed with odd, metallic scents. Deccia soon saw why. Half of the shop was dedicated to fishing and boat supplies, and the other to footwear.

Sozla paused near the door and lifted a pair of soft leather boots. "Deccia, look. They are marvelous." Her dark eyes sparkled. "So much more comfortable than our boots, don't you think?"

Deccia touched the soft, supple leather. It did feel heavenly. Her blisters from the work boots had slowly turned to calluses. The price tag dangled from one shoe. She gasped. "One hundred dascals!"

Olita shuffled up, beaming. "For the best, it is well worth it. Would you like to try them on?"

"No. Thank you." Sozla replaced the boot.

They followed Olita's limping form to the back of the store. Deccia kept a sharp eye out for soldiers, but the shop appeared to be empty. Olita led them through a door and into a cozy back room furnished with a table and chairs. Bright orange curtains covered the window above the sink.

Vitnia perched on one chair, sipping steaming tea. She grimaced when they entered. "At last," she said, setting down her mug. "The guests of honor have arrived. Sit."

Deccia and Sozla did so while Olita lumbered around the small kitchen, setting down a platter of sweet cakes and a steaming pot of hot water on the table. Everyone served themselves.

An uneasy silence ensued. Deccia stirred her tea, searching for a promising line of conversation. "I'm sorry about your son. I saw what happened yesterday."

"He's a good boy." A sheen of moisture gleamed in Olita's eyes.

"Why aren't your men at the base?" Vitnia asked sharply. "Orders say all men are to report for duty."

"Our husbands are over twenty-two," Deccia said. She wasn't accustomed to lying, but to protect Timaeus, she would do anything necessary. "And they are already enlisted and trained. When their leave is up, we'll return home to Carachki. "

"Mmhm." Vitnia watched them with a sharp, disbelieving eye. "Where are their papers?"

Deccia glanced at Sozla in an attempt to hide her confusion.

"All papers are in order," Sozla said smoothly. "Don't worry, Vitnia. Our husbands will not be dragged from our arms like unwilling children. They are loyal and ready to fight for Zindedi."

Vitnia snorted softly. "Both my man and Olita's man were called in this morning."

An unfriendly gleam hardened Olita's eyes. "They are patriots! As is my son."

"Of course they are." Deccia frowned. "Why would they call your men? I thought the draft..."

"Our men don't need to be drafted," Vitnia said with scorn. "They have fought for Zindedi for years."

Olita unexpectedly blew her nose into her napkin. "I thought my husband was safe this time." Her jowls quivered. "Just this morning, he was safe abed, and then..." Tears spurted.

"There, there." Vitnia patted her hand. "They'll be home at night... Much good that does us."

"I'm sorry," Deccia offered.

"You are only a child. You don't understand pain." Vitnia's claw-like hands curled around her cup again. "You still have your man. Enjoy it. It won't be long until they call him, too." Black eyes stared at her. "And if he tries to hide, they'll hunt him down and drag him away."

The malignant hostility lurking in the other woman made Deccia feel sick. Angry, too. How dare this horrible woman presume that she knew anything about Deccia's pain, or her life? She clenched her fists under the table and remained silent.

Sozla sipped tea. "I hear we will soon go to war against the far continent."

"In two weeks," Vitnia said.

"That seems like a short time to train new recruits."

Vitnia cackled. "They will learn all they need to know on the ships."

Olita mopped her face again. "My boy." Her lower lip trembled.

"Now, now." Vitnia patted her hand again. "Your man will watch out for him. You've nothing to worry about."

"Your husbands are retired military men?" Sozla asked.

"Olita's husband earned higher honors than my lazy Nygev."

"He's a Commander," Olita said with pride. "He'll help train the new recruits."

"Good thing your men are trained and ready to go," Vitnia told Deccia and Sozla. "All the same, you'd better keep those papers handy."

"Thank you for your concern. But as Sozla said, we're prepared. Until that time, we'll enjoy our vacation."

"Do that. It could be your last vacation together." Vitnia's flat black eyes gleamed.

Deccia struggled to keep her face expressionless, but she finished the last of her tea in one big swallow. It burned her tongue.

That vile, mean-spirited woman. It was clear now why they had been invited to tea—to be interrogated and intimidated by bored, spiteful women.

It was time to leave. She didn't want to stay here one more moment. She glanced at Sozla, who apparently read her expression with no difficulty. Quickly, she finished her drink, too.

Deccia said, "Thank you for your hospitality. But we must be going."

"We must do this again," Vitnia dared to say.

When hell freezes over. The base, vulgar thought shocked Deccia. She never swore. She always followed the right and proper path. And yet these women...these *Zindedis* pulled darkness up from the depths of her soul. She didn't like it. Not one little bit.

She couldn't draw an easy breath until they had left the oppressive tea party. Then she shuddered, wanting to shake off the ugly feelings crawling through her.

"That was unpleasant, I agree," Sozla said with sympathy. "Those women are bored. It is why they play mean little games."

"Maybe. Or maybe they're just *evil*." There, she'd said it. "Am I wrong? It seems like every Zindedi I've met has been mean, and...and cruel on purpose."

"Many have," Sozla agreed. "But we have yet to meet every Zindedi, correct?"

"You're right." Deccia felt bad. Feeling prejudice against all Zindedis, just because of a few repellent ones she'd met, was wrong. Vitnia and her friends were awful. But the cruel Zindedi soldiers—and especially the insane Presidente and all of his twisted relatives—were the evil ones. She pulled open the market door. "At least Ceri is nice."

Inside, the store, Deccia looked for her friend, but only the balding shopkeeper occupied the store.

Surely the General hadn't caught her. Troubled, Deccia helped gather up the supplies they'd need.

Behran arrived as they paid for their supplies. As Deccia put the change back in her pocket, she asked the shopkeeper. "Where's Ceri?"

The man shrugged. "She took off. Probably'll be back in a few days."

Took off? Or had the General taken her?

Worry for both Timaeus and Ceri knotted within her.

More worries crowded her mind. Vitnia had warned that without the proper papers, soldiers could drag the men to the base at any time.

Back at the cabin, Deccia addressed her concerns to the group. "I think we need to get a copy of those papers," she finished.

"I'll do it," Goric volunteered. Clouds lurked in his gray eyes. "I don't have anything else to do."

So it was agreed that Goric would steal a set of papers. Afterward, Deccia would forge copies for the men.

Everything would be fine, she tried to assure herself. Goric would try to steal papers tonight. Timaeus would be back soon, and hopefully Ceri would be all right, too. And once the men had papers to keep them safe, all would be well.

△ △ △ △ △

Mrn. M seemed convinced that Methusal and Mentàll had thoroughly enjoyed themselves at their picnic. At dinner that night, her eyes lingered on the bits of grass in Mentàll's hair and on Methusal's clothes, and she smiled to herself.

During the meal, the Dehrien Chief outdid himself in the charm department. Mrn. M ate up every word he said, and from time to time her dark eyes twinkled at Methusal.

Clearly, she felt that Methusal had secured herself a fine specimen of a husband.

Methusal still felt disturbed by the playful interchange between herself and Mentàll at the picnic. She didn't know what to make of it, and wanted to forget it had happened. Mentàll's continued, charming attentiveness to her at Mrn. M's house did not help matters.

She should have known the Dehrien's performance would not end at the dinner table.

After talking for a while after the meal, He took Methusal's hand and urged her up from the table. "We are tired," he informed Mrn. M.

Methusal's face burned at the veiled insinuation.

Mrn. M smiled and gathered up dinner dishes. "Of course. See you in the morning." She bustled into the kitchen, leaving them alone.

Methusal wanted to glare at the Dehrien, but didn't get the opportunity, because he pulled her toward their bedroom door. Outside it, he paused. Her eyes narrowed.

Softly, he said, "You still have grass in your hair."

"Let's go in the room." Impatience to be freed from his disturbing presence overwhelmed her.

"Play your part, Methusal. Secure our cover." His warm fingers brushed her throat, and then slid into the hair at her nape. Her breath caught. "I thought I saw a piece of grass back here," he murmured. Dry grass tickled her neck a moment later. "See?"

In the background, she was aware of Mrn. M clinking dishes together at the table. She hurried back into the kitchen.

"Let me go," she hissed.

"Not yet." He smiled a little, clearly enjoying himself. "I see another piece." This time, he urged her chin left. His warm fingertips slid over her skull, and then plunged deep into her thick hair. She clenched her fists, fighting both the desire to bolt, and the insane temptation to surrender to his questionable charm.

"There." His breath flared suddenly hot on her temple.

She sucked in an involuntary breath.

He remained still, his warm breath caressing her skin. His hand slowly withdrew. "Last piece."

Her senses felt overloaded. "Thank you," she forced out, for Mrn. M's benefit.

"You are welcome, *ce'cemone.*" He smiled down at her, his blue eyes much darker than normal. One large hand cupped her jaw and he murmured, coming nearer, "I enjoyed today with you...my wife." She couldn't escape from his kiss. Helplessly, she watched his mouth come nearer, and her nerves knotted, anticipating the contact.

But when his lips touched hers, as soft and gentle as baby down, her mind closed to all thought, save that unexpectedly sweet, soft caress. Her heart thundered hard, flushing her skin hot. In that endless, gentle moment something melted inside of her.

When he withdrew, she stared up at him, unblinking. It had felt real. Everything just now. His words, his caresses...

A feeling akin to panic gripped her. No. This could not be happening. Not like Quasr. Not again.

She stumbled backwards. It wasn't possible.

But in the next instant she realized that his words...his kiss...had all been pitched perfectly to coincide with Mrn. M scurrying in and out to clear the dining room.

Feeling sick to her stomach for her naivety, she stepped backward again, but managed not to stumble this time. Without a word, she retreated inside their room. She took plenty of time in the relief chamber, getting ready for the night.

She was shaken and appalled by her own reactions. The Dehrien was a master actor. How could she, of all people, have been fooled for an instant?

Why had she wanted to believe him?

This question disturbed her the most. She tried to tell herself that it didn't matter. *He* didn't matter. Didn't he have years of experience, turning women's heads? She'd foolishly succumbed to his charm, that was all. It meant nothing. *Less* than nothing, she lectured herself.

When this mission was over, she'd go home with Behran. In fact, she'd see Behran in two days, in Dakarra. Methusal grabbed onto this thought with intense relief. Seeing Behran would put everything right. Nothing the Dehrien did mattered. He'd fooled her for an inconsequential moment, but never again.

At last, feeling more composed, she exited from the relief chamber. The Dehrien Chief sat on the bed, studying his map.

"Good job," she said, spreading her quilts on the hard floor. "Mrn. M is convinced you're my loving husband. Just as well she doesn't know the truth."

He barely glanced up. "What truth is that?"

"That you're a great actor, of course. I can't wait to see Behran."

"Your true love." The words sounded mocking.

"Of course he's my true love." She scowled.

The light flickered out, plunging the room into darkness. "Goodnight, Methusal." The bed springs squeaked as he lay back in comfort.

Frustration simmered. The slug, letting her continue to suffer on the floor. Behran would never let her suffer. Not for one moment.

Methusal dragged the cool quilts around her chilly shoulders and curled up into a tight ball. Behran. Everything would be all right when she saw him again.

Chapter Twenty-Four

"A letter, Presidente." His secretary beat a hasty retreat, and closed the heavy wooden door behind him.

The Presidente exhaled a pleasant lungful of smoke. He contemplated the familiar writing on the dirty envelope, and drew in a long, satisfying pull of smoke. His lungs expanded, filling with that pungent, warm cloud.

A smile twisted his lips. So. The boy had emerged at last. It didn't trouble the Presidente that he'd received no direct communication from him in three years. Reports from Quasr indicated that his spy had done his job. That was fitting, and the least to be expected.

Zindedi intelligence, fed to General Greisn, had resulted in Koblani deaths. Even better, Koblanis trusted his spy implicitly. As ordered, his deepest spy had stayed undercover even after the General's failed attempt on Koblan.

And now the boy dared to approach him directly. It must be important.

Carefully, he cradled his cigar—the best smoke available in Zindedi, and made of opulent, cured ortangia leaves—in a beautifully crafted, golden tray. His thick fingers plucked up his bejeweled dagger, and with one violent wrist flick, he sliced the letter open.

I am in Dakarra. Methusal and Mentàll live together in Carachki, as married. Koblanis seek peace, but prepare for war. Notes will reach me through Oortn in Sisln, to

*the west of Dakarra. I continue to do your work, as is
my duty.*

No signature. Yet none was needed.

The Presidente's pleasure at reading the missive cooled after the second sentence. Mentàll and Methusal, *married?* But they hated each other.

And yet, what if it was true?

Two formidable enemies, united as one. Unease surged, as unwelcome as a sour stomach. He'd known the Dehrien was in Carachki, of course. But the Dehrien and his *wife?* He must find and kill them. He'd set General Fitrn on it immediately. They must *die!*

Violence stabbed through him, as swift as a knife. He slammed his fist on the desk. Everything on it jumped. A quiver ran up his arm and shivered through his jowls. They should be dead *now*. Incompetent fools. Why must everyone about him be inferior? And his spy. Another disappointment!

How long had he been in Zindedi? The Dehrien's impertinent demand for peace had arrived four days ago. Surely his spy had arrived on the same ship. Why had he taken so long to make himself known? And why hadn't he provided more information about the Koblanis?

Pain stabbed like a dagger through his chest, and the muscles seized. For endless moments he gasped for breath, mouth gaping uselessly, like a beached fish. His vision blurred. Panic made him claw at his collar, but nothing helped. For a moment, he wondered if he would die.

Intolerable! He must live. It was not his time.

As if obeying the brute force of his will, the seizure eased its fierce grip, leaving aching pain behind. Harsh gasps soothed the starved suffocation of his lungs. Gradually, his breaths quieted, and the fear subsided.

His heart pounded in uneven bursts. Its clear weakness made him angry. So much so that determination boiled up, as hot as a youth's. He *must* see this mission through to the bitter end. And he would. None other could handle it as well as he could.

The spy must prove himself, and quickly.

The Presidente patted the perspiration from his forehead. Only when his breaths were completely normal did he shout, "Yalin!"

The skinny young man sped into the room, carrying parchment and ink. "Yes, sir?"

"Take down a letter!" The Presidente slapped the desk with his open palm. The secretary jumped, and scurried closer. He perched on the edge of a chair and waited, writing stick hovering at the ready.

"Write this: Tell me who killed my brother. Sabotage the Koblanis' plans."

Yalin scribbled speedily, and then waited.

"That is all, fool. Send it at once to Oortn in Sisln."

"Yes, sir!" With alacrity, he vanished from the room.

Disgusted, the Presidente took another comforting drag of his perfect cigar. No spine lived in his secretary. Intimidating him was an easy, ungratifying sport, to be sure. And yet Yalin was valuable—the only reason the Presidente kept him. And fear spurred his efficiency—an edge the Presidente was happy to sharpen from time to time.

His mind returned to his deepest spy. A heavy frown scored his forehead.

Would the boy prove himself worthy? Or would he prove to be the failure and disappointment the Presidente had always suspected him to be?

Time would tell. If it came down to it, he'd have no trouble delivering swift, vicious punishment. Only death would purge the stink of failure from his line.

∆ ∆ ∆ ∆ ∆

As usual, Methusal awoke exhausted. Of course, her huge purple and yellow bruises on her hips hurt, but she couldn't put all the blame for poor sleep on them. Instead, she placed it on herself.

Last night, that Dehrien's kiss had crept into her mind over and over again, much as she'd tried to explain it away with every argument under the sun. She couldn't seem to stop remembering the sweetness of it.

How could that hard, cold man kiss like that?

It wasn't the first time she'd asked that question. The last time had been at the end of The Quasr War, when his kiss had seared through her soul like fire. Last night, just like back then, she had responded to him.

Yes. For one brief moment, she had. Methusal couldn't deny it, and it confused and scared her.

She hated him. *Hated* him, she told herself. She was worse than a fool to let that man turn her head, even for a moment. Behran was the man whose kisses she longed for.

She loved *Behran*.

Methusal stood up and thumped her pillow hard onto the bed. It looked too...fluffy. Too *happy*. She thumped it again with the flat of her hand. A shallow scoop now made it look deflated. Good.

A waft of cool air indicated an open door. Methusal spun around as her fake husband entered the chamber. Today he wore a black tunic and tan pants—apparently they wouldn't spy on the base. She tried to ignore the way the black shirt emphasized his broad shoulders and contrasted sharply with his white-blond hair and shrewd, pale eyes.

With a faint frown, she folded her arms. "What's the mission for today?"

He crossed to his own side of the bed and tucked a note into his pack.

"Well?" she demanded, feeling further annoyed by his silence.

After a lengthy moment, in which he finished his small task, he finally faced her. That calm, calculating gaze regarded her. "Why are you in a bad temper?"

Methusal frowned harder. "I have no idea what we're doing today. I'm sick of being left in the dark."

"Then ask."

"What do you think I'm doing right now?"

"Did you not sleep well?"

Her mouth gaped open. "This has nothing to do with *sleep*. But no, I didn't. Do you care?"

"You could sleep with me on the bed," he said softly.

Heat flamed her cheeks. "After the way you've been kissing me? I don't think so."

"I said I would not touch on this bed." Harshly, he finished, "I will not."

"*No*."

A long silence stretched. "It is your choice, Methusal."

She clenched her fists and left the room. As if she would ever lie there, next to him. Never. And she didn't want to speak to him right now, either.

△ △ △ △ △

Goric returned from scouting the base just before Hendra and Doc left. Deccia set her breakfast bowl in the sink and wondered what he'd found out. Last night, he'd searched Dakarra for military papers, too. Little wonder dark smudges shadowed his eyes, making his thin face look sallow.

No one paid any attention to Goric as he stood in the kitchen doorway, and his lips tightened. Being continually ignored by the team must hurt. Deccia didn't need her empathic abilities to understand that. Riln was a wild beast to him, but Deccia knew the others weren't deliberately rude to him—they just didn't notice him. His withdrawn, silent nature kept him at the edges of the group.

She touched his arm. "Come sit down. You look exhausted. Would you like some hot cakes? Juice?"

A small smile momentarily lit his gray face. "Yes. Thank you."

Deccia's comments drew the attention of the others to Goric.

"Skipping your job?" Riln gibed unpleasantly.

"Stop." This was Hendra. "He must have news. What is it, Goric?"

"A cart is heading for the powder deposits."

"Which one?"

"The big one, I think. I heard a soldier talking about getting a lot of powder."

"We need to follow it," Doc said. "I volunteer."

Deccia set a steaming plate of cakes before Goric. "Hendra should go with you. If you go together, the soldiers will think you're on a romantic stroll."

Hendra nodded. "But who'll watch the base?"

"I will," Behran volunteered immediately.

Sozla opened her mouth, and then shut it. So far, they'd made little progress in figuring out a firing mechanism that would trigger by itself. However, they had experimented with the bits of powder encased in balls of candle wax. Behran had also done extensive testing to see how long it would take for a fuse to burn thru the wax and ignite the powder. Those tests had been done in the woods, but since the powder amounts had been so small, it had made little smoke or noise.

"I'll scout, too," Goric said, his mouth full.

He wouldn't appreciate being told that he needed to rest. He wasn't a child. Instead, Deccia said, "What happened last night? Were you able to find any military papers?"

He lowered his eyes and hunched over the table, forking up rapid bites. "No."

"Useless apte," Riln said derisively.

Again, Deccia bit her tongue. Goric did not need her defense. This was proven a moment later, when hatred blazed from his suddenly black eyes. "I will find what I need, Riln. Be sure of it."

Hendra joined her at the counter a few moments later and dumped her dishes in the sink. "What is it, Deccia? You look worried."

She'd been trying her best to ignore her endlessly circling worries this morning. "It's Timaeus. I just have this feeling... I can't ignore it. I'm afraid one of these times he won't make it back."

Hendra's brown eyes looked compassionate. "Timaeus is careful. He can take care of himself."

"I know. But what if... I know it's illogical, but I'm afraid the Presidente will find out who he is. That he's the one who killed General Greisn."

"How?" Hendra said simply. "Only those of us in this room know. No Zindedi witnessed it. How could he possibly find out?"

"I don't *know*. But sometimes this awful dread overwhelms me. And I've had a vision... It's not specific, but I'm so afraid, Hendra. I'm afraid something bad is going to happen to Timaeus."

Her friend gave her a reassuring hug. "Have your fears gotten worse since we've been in Zindedi?"

"Yes. And the nightmares about the General come every night now."

"Because we're in the General's homeland, and his brother just happens to be the Presidente. It's natural that all of those horrible feelings would come up here."

"Intensify, you mean." Deccia looked away. She didn't want to admit that her hatred for the General and Presidente had spilled over to include the Dakarran Zindedis, too. "It doesn't help that Vitnia is so hateful. I think she wants to make trouble for us."

Riln boomed behind Hendra, "She's a hag!"

Hendra jumped, paling with shock. She staggered away from him, her eyes large.

Riln laughed loudly, watching her reaction. "Apte girl."

At the table, Doc half rose, fists clenched. But when Hendra faced Riln, the doctor sank back down.

Lips white, Hendra said, "Vitnia isn't the only one who likes to make trouble."

Riln snorted. "I'm not a *Zin*."

"Interesting. Because your behavior fits right in."

Deccia's jaw dropped a little. Good for Hendra.

Ruddy color flooded Riln's face. "So, the apte has the tongue of a whip."

"At least I don't have the heart of a wild beast." Hendra turned her back on him and returned to the table.

Riln's ears were blood red now, and his mouth worked, trying to form a pride saving reply. Before he could speak, however, Behran said, "Good job on the information, Goric. Maybe Doc and Hendra will find the big powder deposit today."

"Yeah." Goric shrugged a narrow shoulder.

And hopefully Vitnia wouldn't set the military on the Koblani men out of pure spite. Deccia glanced outside. Much too soon for Timaeus to arrive. *The One, please bring him home safely.*

△ △ △ △ △

Hendra walked rapidly beside Doc. They headed for the beach. Overhead, the gray sky was lightening in patches as the sun tried to break through. Flying beasts fluttered over the white-capped breakers, riding the cold gusts of wind over the ocean.

Hendra's black Zindedi jacket barely protected her from the freezing breeze. Walking, however, had finally warmed her up. So far they hadn't spotted the cart that Goric had reported.

Doc walked with his hands in his pockets. The wind had roughened his cheeks to a dull red. His nose, too. Hendra's nose dripped, and she clutched a handkerchief in her hand. It seemed a waste of time to put it away, since she needed it every few minutes.

"Crossroads," Doc said. They'd reached the beach. Good news—no sign of Zindedi soldiers. Bad news—still no sign of the cart. A few scrubby trees and bushes lined the road. "Tabor said to turn right."

Hendra followed without speaking. They hadn't said much since leaving the cabin. Doc seemed lost in thoughts of his own. After a try or two at conversation, she'd fallen silent, too.

A particularly bitter gust blasted his hair upright. He hunched his shoulders and Hendra swerved closer, selfishly hoping his body would break the wind for her. Her ears ached with cold, and she raised hands from her warm pockets and covered them.

With a quick flip, Doc unwound the scarf he'd wisely wrapped around his neck. "Take this."

His ears were bright red, too. "You need it," she protested.

He stopped. Wondering why, she did so, too. His back blocked the wind. "Put it on," he said gently.

His smoky blue eyes were a warmer shade than the gray clouds behind him. With a smile, she accepted it. "Thank you." She made an awkward attempt to wind it round and round her head. He smiled, clearly finding the results interesting. After she knotted it under her chin, his skillful surgeon fingers adjusted her headdress so it didn't dip over her eye.

"There." His warm knuckles grazed her cold cheek.

Feeling a bit flustered, she offered a small smile and began walking again.

He matched her stride. Moments of companionable silence elapsed. At last, he said, "Can I talk to you about something, Hendra?"

Quickly, she glanced over. He sounded serious. "Of course."

"It's about Riln. You know I'm proud of the way you stood up to him today."

"But?"

He shoved his hands deeper into his pockets. "He's mad. His pride is hurt."

"He doesn't like an apte girl getting the best of him."

"Exactly."

Hendra waited for the fear to hit, but instead she felt anger. "Too bad for him."

A small smile curled up the corner of his mouth. "That's my girl."

"Then why did you bring it up?"

"Just be careful. Be aware that Riln might try to lash back at you."

Now the fear came. "Do you think he'd try to attack me? Alone?"

"Probably not. Riln's impulsive. He acts on his emotions when he feels them. So stay with the group. But he seems to enjoy scaring you. If his pride's hurt enough, he might think up a plan for revenge."

"I won't let him scare me."

"Good. I just want you to be aware. And I'm always available if you need me."

She smiled, but his serious gaze made her feel sober again. Although he spoke lightly, but Doc was more troubled than he wanted to let on.

"I'll be careful." She shivered, and it wasn't from the cold.

"Look." He pulled her suddenly behind a tall, bushy green tree.

Hendra peered through the fluttering leaves. Far ahead, black clad Zindedi soldiers, looking as small as rochers, strutted across the road. She saw a cart, and a hill rose to the right. Men exited, rolling barrels toward the cart.

"The powder deposits!" she whispered.

"We haven't come far enough."

"Do you think it's the small one?"

"Yes."

"Should we keep going? But isn't that the cart that left the base?"

"It must be."

"Goric thought it was going to the big deposits. He must have been wrong." Hendra shuddered when the wind gusted. "What should we do?"

"Keep walking. Mentàll's coming tomorrow. I'd like to be able to tell him where the bigger deposit is."

Hendra nodded. "It'll be tricky, getting around those soldiers. I don't see any trees we can hide behind. Only a few bushes."

Doc smiled. "But I'm with the girl who can see the future."

His steady confidence in her felt good.

Hendra took the lead, and they rushed from bush to bush toward the Zindedi soldiers. As they drew nearer, Hendra counted the men. Seven.

One gray-haired man sat in the cart, holding the reins to a docile urchet. Two men chatted, and two stood guard at the entrance. Two others emerged from a dark hole in the hill, rolling barrels with their feet. These wooden canisters were heaved into the cart, and a black tarp pulled over the entire thing.

Safely hidden across the road from the mine, Hendra concentrated on the cart before her. Time shifted, and the scene changed before her eyes.

The grizzled driver—probably a man pulled from retirement, like Vitnia's husband—paid no attention to anything. The two men re-entered the mine. Her heart pounded as a plan formed in her mind. The guards wouldn't see her. Neither would the conversing soldiers.

Another focus into the future proved that they didn't plan to move anytime soon.

She whispered, "Stay here. I'm going to count barrels in the cart."

"*Hendra.*"

Ignoring him, she darted across the open road.

Safely on the other side, she huddled against the wooden cart. The urchet snorted and pawed the ground.

"Easy," growled the driver.

The animal continued to snort and shake his head. Hendra hadn't foreseen that. She'd better quickly look in the cart. After rising to a half crouch, she plucked up the tarp. It took a moment for her eyes to adjust to the darkness under the rough black cloth. Six barrels. Certainly more than the one or two that Riln had reported coming from the mine last time.

"Urchet, calm!" The querulous voice rose. Movement made the cart shake.

Hendra froze in fear. The driver was climbing off of the cart. If he glanced back, he'd see her. Sweat wet her palms. Only one thing to do. Hoisting herself up, she slithered over the cart's rail and under the tarp. She fell inside, and her shoulder hit hard against a barrel. With a loud thump, it toppled over. Jarred, Hendra lay still, heart racing.

An unearthly screech rent the air, and teeth snapped. The driver cursed.

"Having trouble, old man?" asked a young male voice.

"Git in the cart. We're goin,'" replied the disgruntled driver.

"After we tie down the tarp."

Hendra pressed back against the barrels in the center of the cart. She wished she could hide between them, but moving them would make noise.

"Grab that end, Mikl." The tarp billowed up, letting in an alarming streak of daylight, and then fluttered back down. Ropes scraped. The tarp stretched as tight as a board above her. The cart shook as they yanked on something. Maybe testing the knots.

She was trapped. She had no knife to cut the ropes, so she was stuck in here until they untied them again. And discovered her.

She took a deep, steadying breath. Panicking wouldn't solve her problem. Doc was out there. Maybe he could help her.

But what if that got him captured, too?

What had she been thinking? Why had she run over here to count barrels in the first place? It wasn't absolutely vital to discover that knowledge.

An uncomfortable truth became clear. She'd done it to show off. Doc's confidence in her had felt so wonderful that she'd wanted to gain more of his admiration. In many ways, she felt like a failure in life. At least her kaavl skills made her useful for something. And now look what had happened.

Boots clumped onto the cart.

Hendra pushed up the front edge of the tarp. It wouldn't give much. Poking up at different intervals revealed that three men were sitting in the cart. She wondered where they planned to drive next. Maybe to the bigger powder deposit? Hope stirred.

But the cart turned in a tight semi-circle and headed back for Dakarra.

△ △ △ △ △

Still with no idea what their mission might be for today, Methusal accompanied the Dehrien Chief to the affluent, residential section in the hills of Carachki. Her silence did not appear to bother him in the least. In fact, she got the distinct impression that he liked it, because it gave him the full ability to focus on their surroundings.

They ducked into a narrow, tree-lined alley bordering the back of Commander Ostl's house. Only twittering flying beasts overhead broke the silence of the morning. They hid in the shadow of an enormous bush with spiky, prickly leaves. These jabbed uncomfortably into Methusal's exposed skin.

The silence had stretched on long enough for Methusal to begin to feel uncomfortable with it. However, she had no desire to break it, either.

The Dehrien, evidently satisfied with his visual inspection of the house, finally looked at her. Still annoyed beyond measure by the manipulative games he'd played with her over the past several days—as well as her own, foolish responses to them—she gave him a hard stare back, eyebrows raised in irritated question.

"You are angry with me."

"Good guess."

"Is it because I kissed you last night?"

She didn't answer.

"Are you angry because you hated it, or because you liked it?"

She gasped. "I love *Behran*. I hate *you*."

A faint smile curled his lips. "Do you feel better now? You have vowed your hatred for me. You have affirmed your love for Behran. All is well in your world." Mockery edged the conciliatory words.

"Don't kiss me again."

"It is necessary to secure our cover, Methusal. Mrn. M often hears our fights. We must keep her convinced that underneath it all, we are deeply in love, and happily married."

She didn't answer. Maybe it was necessary. Or maybe he took great delight in kissing her because he knew it got under her skin.

He turned toward the house. "I spoke to Timaeus this morning."

"What did he say?"

"The General left Dakarra. He's probably back here now."

Methusal digested this with little joy. "He's a horrible man."

"Evidently you sister feels the same. He made an advance on a Dakarran friend, so Deccia threw a heavy can at his head. If he sees her again, she is in danger."

"Hopefully he won't go back to Dakarra."

Mentàll glanced at her. "Hopefully he won't see *you*."

Of course. If the General saw her here in Carachki, he'd assume she was Deccia. And knowing his sick, twisted mind, she didn't want to imagine what tortures he'd like to inflict upon her. She shivered.

"Timaeus told me that General Fitrn is the Presidente's son."

She drew a quick breath of surprise. "I guess that makes sense. He's insane. General Greisn was insane. I'm willing to bet the Presidente is insane, too. What a horrible family. I'm starting to think peace isn't possible with them."

"Anything is possible, if the right pressure is applied."

Methusal marveled again at his supreme confidence—arrogance, she corrected herself.

"So what are we doing here?" She eyed the white, two-story house.

"We will look for the master list to the ball."

"You don't think it would be in the Presidente's palace?"

"It may be. We will also search for invitations to the ball here. If we find one, we will steal it and copy it."

"What good would that do? Our names have to be on the Presidente's list."

"We will fill in the names on the invitations later."

Methusal wondered what he was plotting. Whose names did he plan to use? Their own, or...? Suspicion dawned. "If we find that list, do you plan to hunt down two official guests and kill them, so we can take their place?"

He gave a harsh chuckle. "You have a suspicious mind, Methusal. But that is a good plan, if it comes to it."

"You'd kill them in cold blood?" she said, appalled.

"No. But I would ensure that they were detained."

"I see. I'm glad cold-blooded murder isn't at the top of your list."

"I do not like to kill, Methusal. Have you not learned that yet?"

"You had no trouble killing during the Quasr War. And when you invaded Rolban, you held me at knife point."

"But I didn't kill you. Did you never wonder why?"

"Because you didn't have the chance? Remember, I escaped."

Softly, he said, "I hate spilling the life blood of a man. I may not be on right terms with The One, but I do believe the life he created is sacred. That is why I dislike killing."

She said nothing, but she felt relieved by his answer, although for the life of her, she couldn't explain why.

"Come, Methusal." He headed for the house, his body a tall, dark shadow as he skirted around several large bushes.

The house was dimly lit, and they only saw one portly housekeeper on the ground floor. It was easy to break in, because the back door was unlocked. Searching the large living chamber proved simple, and mostly unfruitful. A paper in the Commander's desk provided the launch date for the mission—thirteen days from now—but the invitations were nowhere to be found.

However, Methusal remembered hearing the Commander tell the General that he had received the invitations.

"Maybe his wife has them," she whispered to Mentàll. They were skulking around on the second floor now.

A door slammed downstairs.

Footsteps clattered.

"You're home! Would you like tea?"

"Yes," drawled a lazy female voice. "My shoes are killing me."

"I'll have it ready when you return, madam." Bustling noises came from the kitchen, and shoes clicked on the wooden stairs.

Alarmed, Methusal glanced up and down the hall, but saw nowhere to hide.

"Here," the Dehrien Chief hissed, and slipped into an enormous room. Obviously the master bedroom. A closet adorned each end of the room. They slipped into the one holding the Commander's clothes, and watched through the cracked open closet door. Mentàll was behind Methusal; close, but not touching. He watched through the crack above her head.

A slim, blond woman swept into the room and threw several packages on the flower patterned bed covering. She wore a fawn colored, skin-tight jacket and a mid-length skirt with black stockings. She kicked off her offending shoes, and then peeled off her jacket, revealing a silky blouse. She threw open her closet and pulled out a new outfit, all in green, and began to unbutton her top.

The Dehrien drew in a quick breath—whether in surprise or appreciation, she wasn't certain. Appalled, Methusal shoved him further back in the closet. Clearly surprised, he stumbled a bit. "Don't stare at her!" she hissed beneath her breath. "Are you so depraved?"

"Are you jealous?" His almost silent whisper tickled into her kaavl tuned ears.

She gasped. Of all the egotistical...

His hand unerringly caught hers in the dark. It closed like a vice around her wrist. He pulled her further back into the dark recesses of the closet. Crisp military jackets brushed against her skin.

"What are you *doing?*" she hissed, being careful to pitch her voice low enough so the Commander's wife wouldn't hear. This couldn't be good. Not at all. To be trapped alone in the close warmth of the closet with him, and remembering his kiss last night. "Remember your promise to my father."

"I forget nothing, Methusal." He'd stopped. A touch proved the wall was at his back. He released her, and softly said, "Will you keep me from temptation, Methusal?"

"I'll keep you here," she told him with a grim smile. A knee to a well-chosen spot would cool him down.

He chuckled. She remained where she was, blocking his path to the open closet door. Preventing him from seeing the other, possibly undressed, woman.

When he shifted, she moved with him, blocking him. And then she realized that he'd only straightened. She felt foolish.

He murmured, "You are as protective of me as a wolmite with her cub, Methusal. Or a wild beast with her mate."

"*No.* I'm trying to protect basic decency. That poor woman doesn't deserve to have you leering at her."

"I was not leering at her."

"No? You were just enjoying the view, then."

"If it was lighter in here, I would enjoy this view much more."

Heat burned her ears. "Stop."

"You cannot take a compliment? Or perhaps it is the truth you cannot handle. The truth, Methusal, is a man cannot help but notice a beautiful woman. But to secure his whole interest and his entire passion...that is another matter completely."

She trembled a little. What was he saying to her? "Don't play games with me, Mentàll."

"Why not? Those are the games I enjoy the most."

So, he'd just admitted this was a game. Hadn't he?

"Enough," she hissed. "She left the room. We can go."

"Check her bedside table first."

As she searched her small dresser, Mentàll swiftly searched the Commander's dresser. Methusal kept her hearing sharp and tuned to the slightest sound in the house. Her fingers touched thick, rich parchment.

She pulled out an envelope. Flowing script addressed it to Commander Ostl. A broken red seal marked the back. Mentàll crossed to stand at her side as she pulled out the two invitations. Each card was one hand length long, and one half in width.

Raised black lettering stated the date—eleven days from now—and the place—the Presidente's palace, at six o'clock. Dinner would begin at seven, with dancing encouraged throughout the evening. The Commander's name was inscribed on the bottom, and below that the Presidente had signed in red ink. The wife's name was inscribed into her invitation.

It appeared simple enough. Find several good pieces of parchment and copy the invitation. Only two problems— getting their names on the Presidente's list, and copying the raised lettering. The other option was to steal invitations from lower ranking officers whom the Presidente may not know very well or recognize, and then try to impersonate them at the ball.

She whispered, "We could take an invitation to Dakarra. Deccia's good at copying."

Mentàll raked a thumb over the raised black letters. Unreadable thoughts flickered. Now that they'd emerged from the closet, he was all business. "We'll take the wife's, and leave the other." He stuffed it into his back waistband, under his tunic. Methusal quickly replaced everything else the way she'd found it, and followed Mentàll from the room.

Getting out proved to be a waiting game, because their exit was in full view of the Commander's wife, who lounged on a chair in the living room, idly swinging her crossed leg. Her skirt revealed her knees, and Methusal felt scandalized. She didn't look at Mentàll, who surely enjoyed the view.

Abruptly, the woman jumped up and stalked toward the kitchen. "I thought the tea would be ready by now..."

They darted out the door and into the alley, as silent as ghosts.

Methusal walked fast, intent on putting as much distance as possible between themselves and Ostl's house.

"Is fire burning your feet, Methusal?"

She came to a full stop and crossed her arms. "Where do you want to go, Commander?"

Quizzical amusement lightened those eyes to silver-blue. "Why are you upset now?"

"I am not upset." She did, however, feel frustrated by her own reactions to the Dehrien's flirting in the closet. What was wrong with her? It had meant nothing. Purposefully, she relaxed her defensive posture. "Our mission was a success. Now what would you like to do?"

"Spy on the docks. We will split up. If possible, I want to learn what arms they've already put on board the military ships."

An afternoon on her own. She smiled. "Wonderful idea."

"At six o'clock we will meet at the bench where we had lunch, and exchange information."

"Sounds fantastic."

He glanced at her a few times on the walk to the docks, as if trying to figure out what she was thinking. She didn't enlighten him. Even if the afternoon proved deadly boring, it would be better than staying in close proximity to him all day. She still felt off balance from last night and the close quarters with him in the closet, and needed to get her head squarely in place again. This time apart from him would help accomplish that goal.

At the docks he left her, his black cap pulled down low over his eyes. She wandered the part of the dock that appeared to be open to the public. She tried her best to blend in with the other women pushing babies in little carts.

The military end of the dock was barred by metal gates, but that didn't matter. It was easy to count the ships on both docks. Today there were eight on each, and eleven at anchor in the harbor. The only way to find out what was on board each one was to carry with hearing and listen.

As she leaned against the rail, inhaling lungfuls of the crisp, clean ocean breeze, Methusal listened to dozens of conversations on the ships. Most were of no consequence, but a few were very interesting indeed.

△ △ △ △ △

Hendra wouldn't think about the horrible things the soldiers might do to her if she was captured. She scooted to the back of the cart and ran her fingers along the top ledge of the railing, under the tarp, toward the corner. It was cinched down so tight that her fingers couldn't wiggle closer than within two handbreadths of the knot.

Time to try something else. She slid her hand along the top ledge of the rail again, pushing up until she found a place where she could slide her whole arm out. Then she scooted closer to the corner again. The tarp edge cut into her upper arm as she stretched forward, trying to find the knotted rope.

Finally, she touched it. Smooth and straight, it threaded downward. No knots. She followed it down as far as she could reach, until all the circulation threatened to leave her arm. Her fingers brushed a knot and a circular metal ring. Straining harder against the unyielding tarp proved fruitless. She withdrew her aching arm and contemplated her options. The tarp was tied to metal rings far below the railing. She couldn't reach the knots. So then how could she escape?

A search proved that the closest thing to a weapon in the dirty cart was a pebble. She was trapped. Trussed as neatly as an apte for the roasting.

Please help me, The One. Her foolishness was about to cost her her life.

The cart jounced down the road. Fighting despair, Hendra didn't notice or hear the men talking until long minutes later. She crept back to the front of the cart and listened.

"Too many men," grumbled the older man. "Too crowded."

A young soldier laughed. "You're too used to comfort, old man. Get tough, if you want to hang with us."

"Smart is what I am. You young ones waste energy running about, shooting off your mouths. A few smart moves is all is needed. I can outshoot you any day."

A chuckle. "You've got a bet, old man. Back at the base. After supper."

"I'll wup your baby-skin hiney," he muttered.

"When's the General coming back?" The tone of the young man changed.

A deeper voice answered. "When we've mined a lot more powder. In two weeks, when we're ready to move. The Presidente wants everything supervised."

A snort. "Like we can't do our job."

"It's delicate work. Don't forget the eastern Zins who broke in the other night. We're on high alert for a reason. Anything so much as moves outside the gates and we shoot."

A husky laugh. "Jaml shot three aptes last night. I love those critters fried. Hope the cook does'em up right." He sighed. "I know what else I'd like to do right. This girl..."

Hendra closed her ears and crept to the back of the cart again.

Apparently, the powder and arms wouldn't leave Dakarra until General Fitrn returned. And the base was on high alert.

The cart rolled on and on, and she wondered where Doc might be. More despair caught at her heart. She didn't want him to get killed or captured trying to rescue her. In addition, right now they should have been searching for the bigger powder deposit. Her cousin had made it clear to Timaeus that it was vital they discover its location.

Another failed mission, thanks to her.

The cart turned south, heading for Dakarra, and then slowed.

"What's this?" growled the driver. "How'd that driftwood get in the middle of the road?"

"Careful," said the deeper voice. "Could be a trap."

"Naw," scorned the youngest voice. "Nothing's out here but those screeching birds."

"I got my gun." The driver snapped the weapon into readiness.

Two men climbed down. Moments later, Hendra heard a hollow, clattering sound as they tossed the old driftwood to the side of the road.

The cart moved a bit, and Hendra thought the men had climbed back aboard. They hadn't—proven a moment later when boots clumped up onto the wooden cart. The vehicle swayed as they sat down.

"Drive on, old man. Told you there was nothing to worry about."

The vehicle lurched forward.

Hendra crawled around the barrels again, searching for a nail, a piece of wood—anything she could use to saw through the rope and try to escape.

She became aware of a tiny scraping sound in the far back corner. Finishing her fruitless search, she crept closer.

The next instant, daylight streamed inside. Doc's face appeared, and she nearly cried out with relief. "Come on." Grim lines etched the sides of his mouth.

A glance proved the laughing soldiers were looking straight ahead at the road before them. She swiftly climbed over the railing and joined Doc in a crouch on the back ledge. He must have climbed on board while the soldiers moved the driftwood.

"The tree line is ten lengths ahead," he whispered.

Hendra's heart thumped as they waited for the thick, protective cover to draw nearer. At any moment, she expected the soldiers to look back and notice the tarp sagging—or to see the tops of their heads.

"Now."

They jumped to the ground, causing a rattling spatter of pebbles, and darted for the woods.

"What was *that?*"

A gun snapped.

Hendra ran. A shot pinged off a tree near her head. Soldiers crashed into the woods, hot on their heels. Kaavl training kicked in, and she darted deeper into the forest, leaving a false trail, and then cut in a completely new direction. She ran over top of logs and rocks whenever she could, and Doc followed close on her heels.

Her breaths came in sharp gasps by the time they finally lost the Zindedi soldiers. Now they were deep in the forest, west of Dakarra.

Doc panted, "Good job."

"Right. I caused this mess. Now we're lost."

"It's not as bad as you think."

"How can you say that?"

"Look." He pointed. Overhead, the white-bellied ocean flying beasts dipped and flew, riding the coastal breeze. "We're not far from the beach. Let's follow them."

Hendra's legs felt tired and shaky, but she followed Doc. He was right. Five minutes later, they reached the beach. Now they just had to follow the coastline to the path that led home. They'd done it once before, and it was easy to find again.

Thankfully, it wasn't as cold in the woods, because the trees filtered the wind. They walked in silence until Hendra said, "I'm sorry."

His sharp glance snared hers. "How many barrels were in the cart?"

"Six." Then she told him what she'd overheard while she'd been trapped.

He nodded. "Important information."

She sensed that he was holding back his true thoughts, however. "It was a foolish move," she admitted into the silence.

"And dangerous." Emotion roughened his voice. A quick glance proved that stark lines scored his mouth.

A little fear went through her and she stopped. He did, too.

She wet her lips. "Are you mad at me?"

He closed the distance between them, so only handbreadths separated them. His black jacket seemed close, and while he wasn't much taller than she was, he seemed very big right now. Apprehensively, she stared at him.

"No, Hendra," His voice sounded harsh. "I was scared for you. When I saw you get in that cart..." His low words stopped. "And I saw them drive off with you trapped inside..." He halted again, as if trying to wrestle his emotions under control. "Hendra, it felt like someone tore out my insides. All I could think about was what those soldiers would do when they found you."

"Me too."

He gripped her arms. "Please. Don't ever do that again."

"I won't."

"Hendra!" He rubbed her arms once.

"Please don't be angry with me."

In answer, he drew her close and his breath feathered on her hairline. He gently kissed her forehead. "*Hendra.*"

For a second, she swayed into him. His care for her and his tender kiss felt lovely.

His hand tightened on the curve of her hip, and she involuntarily stiffened.

Unwanted memories shattered the pleasure of the moment. Memories of hard hands holding her still, forcing her to submit...

"No," she gasped out, and jerked free. "No!"

His gaze darkened with incomprehension, and then alarm.

She stumbled backward.

"Hendra."

She raised shaking hands. "No," she breathed, trying to tamp down her panic. "Don't touch me. Please. Just stay back."

In answer, he stuffed his hands into his pockets and stood very still.

The panic slowly subsided. He must have seen it, because he took a tiny step closer.

"*No.*" She backed up again. "I don't want to feel like this. I don't. But I can't help it."

"Did Jascr hold you like that?"

"Yes." She took low, deep gulps of air. "He'd grab me and push me against the wall..." Her breaths now came in sharp gasps. Tears rushed down her cheeks. "I hate him. *I hate him!*" She broke into uncontrollable sobs.

She felt very alone, standing there, weeping. And contradictorily she wanted comfort, too. Feeling foolish, she whispered, "Please, will you hold me?"

He enfolded her in his arms around her, as if she were a fragile, spun piece of glass.

"I'm sorry," she wept, pressing her cheek hard into his shoulder.

"Shh. It's all right."

After long minutes, she finally gulped into silence. He offered a clean handkerchief. Wiping her eyes, she stepped back. "I'm a mess."

"I understand why, Hendra."

She gasped on a laugh. "And you still want to be friends?"

"I want to be more than friends." He made a short, restless movement, as if afraid he'd said too much.

She looked at him, eyes still watery, and felt an unbearable sadness. She wanted more, too. Much more. But her hysterical fit had proven yet again why that wasn't possible. He had to understand. She couldn't let him expect something that would never happen. "I do, too. I'm sorry. But I can't."

"I know." He squared his shoulders, as if against the cold. "I know," he repeated. For himself? Or for her?

"Can we be friends?"

"I will always be your friend, Hendra." He headed for home again, but she couldn't read his expression.

She felt estranged from him now. And upset with herself. And she prayed for the millionth time to be delivered from the hell in which Jascr's abuse had bound her.

△ △ △ △ △

By the time it was time to meet Mentàll again, Methusal had come to terms with what had happened between them last night, and this morning. He enjoyed getting under her skin—this had been true for over three years. It had all been just more of the same.

If she forgot his true motivation and let down her guard again like last night, though, he just might gain the power to really hurt her. That thought sobered her, and she approached Mentàll at the bench with a calm, level feeling she hadn't possessed in days. A welcome feeling.

She sat down, leaving a large space between herself and the Dehrien's large body. Crisply, she reported, "Most of the powder will be delivered to the ships two days before departure. On the day of the ball. They want it kept dry and safe until then."

His light gaze searched her own, as if sensing something different about her. "Arms will be delivered soon to the ships."

"Will we try to stop them?"

"The powder is the danger. Without it, the arms are useless."

That made sense. "What else did you find out?"

"I heard men grumbling. They are not happy to go to war again."

"I heard the same. I also learned the name of the liquor house they like to visit at night. It's called 'Merry Spirits.'"

"I will pay it a visit." He stood. "Mrn. M is expecting us."

Their strides matched on the walk back to Feldon. "No more spying on the base?" she ventured.

"Not until we return from Dakarra. We'll leave early in the morning."

Tomorrow she would see Behran. In Behran's presence, the Dehrien would have to leave her alone. Only one more evening to endure. Once they left Mrn. M's, there would be no reason for them to behave as if they were married.

Finally, she would gain the emotional breathing room that she needed.

"I think I'll turn in early tonight," she said brightly. "So I'll be fresh for tomorrow. I can't wait to see Behran."

He said nothing.

Dinner with Mrn. M passed pleasantly. Mentàll was quiet, but courteous to their hostess. Methusal kept up a light chatter, asking their landlady more about the plants in her garden and the tapestries she made by hand. Mrn. M's eyes lit up, and the evening sped by.

Afterward, she helped Mrn. M clean up the dishes, and then bade her goodnight.

"You'll be leaving early, then?" their landlady said. "I'll have breakfast ready just after dawn."

"You're so kind. Thank you."

"You'll be back the next day? A fast trip."

"Lozar wants to protect our vacation time."

The woman nodded comfortably. "Hopefully all will go well at the Dakarran base." She followed Methusal to the living room and picked up her tapestry. Mentàll rose from a chair as they entered, and his gaze fixed upon Methusal. She couldn't read his expression.

She took a deep breath. One more hurdle to pass until she could retreat safely inside their room. Affixing a pleasant expression upon her face, she went to him and put a hand on each of his powerful wrists. It looked like an affectionate gesture, but she gripped them tight. Now he couldn't grab her close for another unpalatable kiss—at least he couldn't without putting up a suspicious struggle.

She smiled sweetly up at him. A thrill of unease went through her when his eyes narrowed the tiniest bit. "Goodnight, Lozar." For extra flair, she breathed, "I'll be waiting for you."

A quick twist of his wrists, and suddenly he gripped hers, instead. The long-fingered grasp was gentle until she tried to twist free. She subtly struggled against the vice-like grip.

He smiled faintly, obviously well pleased with himself. Methusal's temper surged, but she struggled to ignore it. She would not erupt at him, because it only encouraged his unconscionable behavior.

In a low voice, he said, "I will be looking forward to it."

He tugged her a little closer. Methusal did not struggle. But her fake smile felt brittle at the edges. Determined to play the game to the bitter end, she said, "Don't keep me waiting."

He tugged her still closer, so now their torsos touched. Unwelcome heat and irritation scorched her cheeks. How dare he? He said, "I would never keep you waiting, Midi. You should know that by now."

Time to end the game. She fluttered her eyelashes. "See you inside, then." She tugged at her wrists.

Instead of releasing her, he raised one of her curled fists to his mouth. His lips grazed the first knuckle. A pleasant warmth sizzled down her skin. The heavy-lidded blue gaze locked with hers, watching her every reaction. "A bite to whet my appetite."

Her temper heated still further, and so did her skin, which suddenly felt too hot. He was deliberately pressing the boundaries.

Jaw clenched, she whispered, "Let me go. Right *now*."

To her surprise, he released one hand. To her even greater surprise, he allowed her to pull the other one free, too. She stood there, quivering with fury. Slowly and distinctly, and in a voice only he could hear, she said, "I'll see Behran tomorrow. I cannot *wait*."

The flame in the blue gaze flickered out, leaving them cold. Anger and something else flashed, too quick to be discerned. He directed a thin smile over her head to Mrn. M. "I think I will turn in now, too. Good night."

"Goodnight."

Prickles ran down her back as the Dehrien followed her into their room. The confrontation clearly wasn't over. As soon as the door closed, she quickly turned to face him.

He remained still, watching her with a dark, calculating gaze. Nerves fluttered in her stomach. What did he plan to do now?

She demanded, "Why can't you just say goodnight? Why do you have to turn everything into a...a *torture* session?"

"Did I injure you?"

"You left red marks on my wrists. See? Now they'll match the bruises you left on my shoulder!"

"I did not bruise your shoulder."

"No?" She jerked her tunic off of her shoulder. Four yellowish gray bruises marred her skin.

He stepped closer, his eyes riveted upon them. "I..." His voice grated, sounding raspy. He cleared his throat. "I did that?"

"Yes. The night on the base."

"I didn't know I'd gripped you so hard. I am sorry."

"It doesn't hurt. It's the principle of the thing. You feel like you can manhandle me whenever you want to. It has to stop."

"I didn't intend to hurt you. But your disobedience could cost us our lives one day."

"I don't *deserve* to be manhandled for any reason. Just because you're stronger than me doesn't mean you can treat me however you want."

Red edged his cheekbones. "I am sorry. I swear I do not like violence. Whenever possible, I prefer persuasion."

"Is that what your treatment of me has been? Persuasion? Persuasion to hate you, maybe. Well, you've achieved that goal. It's clear you love to torment me. I'm *sick* of it. Enough!"

A step closed the distance between them. "No."

Infuriated, she said, "No, it's not enough?" Tears welled in her eyes. "I can't *wait* to see Behran. I can't wait to be with someone who treats me with love and respect!"

"Methusal!" It was not an anguished groan. It wasn't.

"Enough revenge." To her chagrin, her voice wavered. "No more. Please."

He whispered, "Is that what you think this is about?"

"I *know* it's what it's about."

"No. It is not about revenge. I have told you that, over and over again."

"Then what *is* it?" Not that she believed him.

"Listen, Methusal. I will tell you." His low voice sounded harsher than ever before. "Listen to my heart."

How could she listen to his heart? Did he have one? And then, to her surprise, he came closer and his lips touched hers with a gentleness that blazed through her last defense. For the longest moment, she could not think at all.

Finally, she came to her senses. "No," she choked out.

With a harsh breath, he stepped back.

She stood there, trembling, feeling as if every defense had been stripped from her. She wanted to run.

Instead, she straightened her spine, gathered up her clothes, and closeted herself in the relief chamber.

Inside, she washed her face with shaking hands. How could his kisses, or anything he said mean anything to her at all? And yet he ripped under her skin so effectively that trying to claw him free caused her soul to bleed.

After changing, she entered the room and silently set up her pallet. Then she sat on the edge of the comfortable bed, putting items in her pack for tomorrow. There. That should be everything she'd need. Before she could slip down to her cold, hard pallet, Mentàll suddenly sat beside her. The bed sagged from his weight, alarmingly tilting her toward him. Feeling a bit panicked, she sprang away from him.

"Methusal," he said quietly.

She sent him a dark look.

His gaze held hers. "I am sorry."

"It ends now," she told him.

"What ends?"

"Your calculated advances toward me."

"Our marriage contract has not ended. Our cover will remain intact. But I will limit my advances to no more than one per day. Barring unforeseen circumstances."

Probably the best concession she'd ever get from him. She stated, "Your feet are on my pallet."

He removed them and she slipped under the cold quilts, lying on her hip, which screamed pain, just so she could turn her back on him.

"Good night," he said harshly.

She didn't answer.

She couldn't wait to see Behran tomorrow. As far as Mentàll was concerned... *The One, please help me.* Because as always with him, she felt like she was walking on the edge of a cliff. One false step, and she would lose her soul forever.

Chapter Twenty-Five

DAY 9

THE NEXT MORNING IN THE BRIGHT, warm kitchen, Methusal ate silently. Night still blackened the windows, making the outdoors look chilly and uninviting. Mrn. M bustled about, delivering hot eggs and fried meat, but she said little. Methusal was glad. She was in a poor mood, and she didn't want to poison their hostess' day with it.

Yet again, she had slept abominably. Exhaustion felt like a physical weight on her mind, and it pressed all of her thoughts into disjointed jumbles.

When the sun brightened the horizon, they left Mrn. M's cozy cottage carrying a large sack lunch pressed upon them by that lady, and headed for the road to Dakarra. Cool air nipped Methusal's cheeks, and she tucked her hands into her warm leather pockets.

She walked a good half-length to the left of the Dehrien. They hadn't spoken all morning.

Yesterday continued to swirl through her mind like a thick, uncomfortable fog. He'd flirted with her and kissed her. Unfortunately, she knew him well enough to realize that every move he made was calculated. So he'd done it on purpose, but why? To try to drive a wedge between her and Behran?

Even worse, she'd responded to him. She hated herself for it.

He'd said he was sorry.

Methusal frowned and walked steadily on. She wouldn't think about him anymore. Instead, she pulled up a picture of her fiancé in her mind. His dark, calm blue eyes. The gentle way he teased her. She couldn't wait to see him. She couldn't wait to launch herself into his arms and feel safe once again.

Mentàll glanced at her once or twice as the morning wore on, but said nothing.

Weariness ached in her bones, and the misery became more oppressive with every hour that ticked by. She found herself longing for their lunch stop, but a nap would be even better.

The sun rose higher, and Methusal estimated they'd been walking for three hours when the Dehrien Chief broke the silence.

"You are upset."

No sense denying it. "Yes."

"Because of yesterday?"

"Because of *every* day. Day upon day, too many to count, you get under my skin. You hurt me. And you *like* doing it."

"That is not true. I told you this is not about revenge, Methusal. But you will not listen."

"I don't believe one word you say. Why *should* I?"

He stared at her in silence for a moment. A trace of bleakness sharpened his features. "So I am a lost cause. There is no hope for me?" Quietly, he said, "You think I have already been assigned a place in hell?"

"I never said that."

"But in your mind, I'm little better than the devil."

She looked away for a second. "I never said that, either. The Prophet says it's never too late. Not until we die."

"So I still have time to redeem myself." A statement, not a question.

"Make amends with The One. He's the one who'll judge you."

Softly, he said, "And how do I make peace with you, Methusal?"

That intense blue gaze held hers. Her skin warmed, and he wasn't even touching her.

He pressed, "Is it possible?"

"You don't want peace," she said at last. "Not with me, not with anyone. All you ever want is your own way, and to accomplish your own goals. You'll go on pretending peace with the Presidente, but you don't mean it. You pretended peace with Rolban all those years ago, but you didn't mean it.

Don't pretend you want peace with me now, because I don't believe it."

"You still know so little about me."

"I know all I need to know." Turning sharply, she marched on.

"I *do* want peace, Methusal," he said harshly. "With *you*."

She glanced back, unnerved by the vehemence in his voice. His gaze arrested hers, dark with unknown emotion. He never lied. But if he meant it, then what—besides the reason for the mission—was the purpose behind all of his kisses?

"You want peace? Then give me space. For the next two days I don't want to speak to you. Except when absolutely necessary, of course, during the meetings."

His tense shoulders conveyed frustration.

"I need space," she repeated. "Leave me alone."

"No."

She clenched her fists. "You just said you want peace."

"I do. But peace cannot be forged between two people who are not speaking."

She started walking again. If he refused to give her space...well then, she'd take it.

Despite her weariness, she pushed herself to walk faster, feeling impatient to reach Dakarra. And eager to finally be free of the Dehrien Chief and the thorn he poked deeper and deeper under her skin.

When it came time for lunch, she insisted that she did not want to stop, even though exhaustion settled more deeply into her bones with every step. Instead, they ate while walking. Mentàll appeared just as determined as she was to arrive swiftly in Dakarra.

Timaeus had given Mentàll directions to the cabins, so when they at last passed through the small town of Dakarra, they knew to turn left onto a rough country lane.

Methusal couldn't prevent her steps from lagging now. After six hours of walking, her head ached, her legs ached and she felt unbearably weary. Her mind felt thicker and foggier by the minute, and she found it difficult to string two coherent thoughts together. All she wanted to do was lie down and sleep for a week. Preferably on a soft, comfortable bed.

Up ahead, two cabins perched on the top of a tall, grassy hill. Dark forest stretched beyond them. At last. Rest. Weary eyes fixed upon the goal, she stumbled over a rock in her path.

Mentàll caught her before she went sprawling. Her shoulder hit hard into his chest and he pulled her up against him so she wouldn't fall. He was slow to release her. Tired as she was, she pulled away without a word. Then, belatedly, she mumbled, "Thank you."

"You are tired."

Tears filled her eyes. "I'm exhausted." She was so spent that anything but the truth seemed like too much of an effort to say.

They reached the base of the steep hill to the cabins. A beaten path marked the way up through long, waving grasses. From the bottom, it looked like an eternity to the top. Mentàll started up first.

Methusal remained where she was, trying to gather the internal resources needed to travel this last distance. When the Dehrien Chief glanced back and saw that she hadn't moved, he retreated and held out his hand. Methusal looked at that strong, capable hand, and then up the hill, and then back to his offered hand. More tears filled her eyes. She was so tired. Wordlessly, she took it. Slowly, they climbed the hill together. He didn't rush her, and in fact waited patiently, because for every one of his steps, she had to take two.

Finally, at the top, he released her without being asked. "You are all right?"

She nodded, unable to speak. Slowly, she followed him to the biggest cabin. Smoke streamed from its chimney. She climbed up weathered porch stairs, and then stood beside him as he knocked on the door.

The door flew open and Deccia's cheerful face appeared. "Methusal!" She hugged her. "Mentàll. You're here! Come in."

The warm cabin smelled of rich, simmering stew and freshly baked bread.

Methusal stumbled after the Dehrien Chief. At last, her searching eyes found whom she'd been longing to see. With a quick step, he came to meet her.

"Behran!" Methusal launched herself into his arms. When they closed around her, warm and secure, she closed her eyes. With her cheek resting on his shoulder, she relaxed for the first time in over a week. She felt safe, at last.

"Thusa," he murmured, stroking her hair.

After a few long, restful moments, she pulled back. She felt giddy with exhaustion. She wobbled a bit, and he gripped her arms, steadying her. Concern darkened his eyes. "Are you all right?"

"No, she's not." Deccia appeared. "Mentàll told me she's exhausted." To Methusal, "You need a nap."

"But the meeting..."

"It can wait." Deccia pulled her toward the door. The Dehrien Chief glanced at Methusal for a moment, watching her progress, and then returned his attention to his conversation with Tabor.

Methusal stumbled a little as she followed Deccia down the stairs. "That bossy man," she mumbled. "Thinks he knows everything."

Deccia sent her a sharp glance, and let them into the smaller cabin. "He's looking out for your best interests. It's clear you're about to fall dead on your feet. Now come in here. You can take our bed. Timaeus and I will be in the other cabin for the rest of the afternoon, so it'll be quiet."

Methusal sank down on the deliciously soft bed and closed her eyes with a small moan of delight. Deccia pulled the covers over her. "There. And don't get up until you're rested."

Methusal needed no exhortations. She instantly fell into a deep, dreamless sleep.

△ △ △ △ △

Perfect! Aali inhaled the tangy Tarst air and hurried out of the Tarst Chief's house, leaving her friend, Vaantra Pan, behind. She must do this mission alone. So far, everything was going according to plan. She'd wangled an invitation from Vaantra to visit Tarst, and she had arrived this morning. Now for the next step—the one that would get her to Quasr.

Smiling to herself, Aali hurried down the path, following the brown-haired girl whom Vaantra had pointed out.

"Excuse me!" she called out, and the other girl stopped.

When Aali caught up, she discovered the other girl was dismayingly pretty, with warm brown eyes. Dastn knew this girl? She looked to be about eighteen years old. "Vaantra said you know where Dastn lives?"

The brown haired girl smiled. "I should."

"Are you his girlfriend?" Aali asked point-blank, and then felt embarrassed. What did it matter if she was or not?

The girl laughed out loud. "No! I'm Gloriana, his sister. Who are you?"

"Aali."

"Aali—from Rolban?" Gloriana smiled, her eyes friendly but curious. "He's talked about you. I thought you were younger."

Aali frowned. Just like him—he still thought of her as a kid. "I'll be sixteen in a few days." In fact, now, for the first time, she realized that she wouldn't be home for this most important birthday. Oh well, she'd celebrate a few days late, after she completed her top secret mission.

Gloriana smiled. "Why do you want to know where we live?"

"I need to ask you a question, actually. Will you help me? Without telling him I'm here," Aali added quickly.

"Sure. I guess."

Aali felt bad that she'd have to deceive Gloriana, but she couldn't let Dastn suspect her true plans. Then everything would be ruined. She said guilelessly, "We had a fight, and I wanted to apologize to him. Has he gone to Quasr yet?"

"He leaves tomorrow morning."

"Oh! Well. Okay."

"Do you want to come up to the house?"

"Well, uh..." Maybe she shouldn't have said that about apologizing. Especially since she would not! Or maybe when aptes learned to fly. "Maybe later. I have things to do right now. Thanks, though."

"We live up that hill." Gloriana pointed. "Come by any time."

"Great—but don't tell him you saw me, okay? I want it to be a surprise."

"I'm sure he'll be pleased to see you." Gloriana waved goodbye.

Aali stared up the hill with an evil curl to her lips. Dastn would be surprised, all right, but not pleased.

△ △ △ △ △

It was dark outside, and Hendra was about to help serve dinner when the front door opened. Methusal slipped inside, blinking against the bright lights. She must have been exhausted, because she'd slept for over four hours. While she'd slept, the Dakarran team had exchanged information with Mentàll—including the fact that Goric had finally pilfered military papers to copy. However, Mentàll had refused to start the formal meeting until Methusal was present.

During the afternoon, Hendra had spoken to her cousin for a few moments, but had been unable to get a read on him. As always, he wore his cool reserve like a shield. But she sensed tension simmering in him. At the moment, he headed for the kitchen.

"We're serving up stew," Hendra called to the Rolbani girl.

"Thank you," she said, smothering a yawn, and headed in that direction, too.

Mentàll adjusted his course and intercepted Methusal halfway there. His tall body loomed close. "You are well?" he said in a low voice.

She looked up at him for a long, silent moment. And then she nodded briefly and moved on.

Mentàll watched her go, his expression inscrutable.

Hendra's eyes narrowed. Interesting. Her cousin's stance bore a possessive stamp...mixed with something else, too.

As they all settled down to dinner around the large kitchen table, Hendra continued to observe her cousin between bites of the flavorful, thick stew. Mentàll sat across from her, and Behran and Methusal to her right. Doc was at the end of the table next to Sozla, who laughed with delight at something he said. He grinned and said something else, which made her eyes snap with appreciation.

With a small frown, Hendra returned her attention to Mentàll, who ate silently. While she pretended to be completely absorbed in her meal as well, she shot quick, discerning glances at him.

Unaware he was being watched, her cousin's gaze repeatedly returned to Methusal and Behran. The two talked quietly, and when the Rolbani girl laughed, Mentàll's features imperceptibly tightened. As the mealtime wore on, her cousin's glances became infrequent—as if he'd retreated within his icy shell.

Methusal laughed again. It sounded lighter, this time. Happier, and freer. "You wouldn't, Behran!"

"Wait till I get you alone."

Unholy blue fire flashed in the glance Mentàll shot Behran. The ferocity and the heat of it made Hendra flinch back. If looks could kill, Behran would be ash right now.

Her cousin deliberately returned his attention to his meal, but a faint flush colored his high cheekbones, and his broad shoulders looked stiff. He spooned up another bite of stew meat.

Interesting. For her cool, emotionless cousin to display any sort of feeling at all was unusual, but this much took her by surprise. A crack had finally breached Mentàll's thick wall of ice. She wondered if he realized it.

Mentàll harbored deep feelings for the Rolbani girl. But she wondered exactly what kind of feelings they were, and what he intended to do with them. Yes, she sensed his possessiveness toward her. He wanted her. But she knew, better than anyone, how little love he'd received in his life. Would he recognize his emotions for what they could be? Or would he only understand his need to possess her?

Behran laughed, breaking into Hendra's thoughts. *Behran.* He loved Methusal. She didn't want to see him get hurt.

Maybe she should talk to Mentàll and try to figure out what he intended, because she'd sensed from the start of this trip that he was plotting something concerning the Rolbani girl. If that blue fire in his eyes was any indication, his determination to follow through on his plan had only strengthened.

Hendra wanted him to be happy. But not at the cost of her friends' happiness.

After dinner, Mentàll joined her outside to help empty the pot into the scrap pile. The move surprised her.

Holding the lamp while he scraped, Hendra said, "You never helped with kitchen work at home."

"You wanted to speak to me. You repeatedly looked at me throughout dinner."

Hendra colored a little. She'd thought she had been discreet. "I have a question."

He finished scraping the pot and gave her his full attention.

"Do you plan to steal Methusal from Behran?"

His teeth gleamed white in the moonlight. "It is not stealing if she comes willingly."

Her jaw went slack with shock. "Do you really think that will ever happen?"

"Do not underestimate me." His smile made her shiver, and she suddenly felt sorry for Behran. When her cousin made up his mind, it was impossible to sway him from his course of action.

He led the way back inside. Already the others had begun to gather in a circle of chairs in the warm kitchen room. The sweet, fruity aroma of a baking pie wafted from the oven.

"Tell me why," she pressed, following him. Not that she expected him to bare his heart to her. But to get a clue about his true motivation—that she did hope for.

"Why what?"

"Why are you pursuing her?" she hissed. "You know she hates you."

"Methusal will not admit what she wants."

"And you think that's *you?*"

Mentàll said nothing.

"Why do you want Thusa? I thought you hated her." Again, she pressed for the truth.

"I do not hate her, little cousin."

With that small scrap of information she had to be content, because Methusal entered the room, and her cousin fell silent. It didn't escape Hendra's notice that her friend circled the room in order to avoid Mentàll. It also didn't escape her notice that her cousin claimed the chair next to Methusal's, the instant she sat down. Her friend threw Mentàll a frown, but did not vacate her chair. He leaned toward her and said something near her ear, and Methusal's cheeks flushed. She glared at him, and averted her face, clearly endeavoring to ignore him.

Hendra sighed to herself. If Mentàll cared for Methusal, he was going about wooing her in a thick-headed sort of a way. Of course, he had little experience expressing his feelings. He probably did not know how. Perhaps conquering Methusal with strategic battle plans was his chosen course of action. If so, he was not going to get far.

Mentàll called for everyone's attention. "Report your progress, Behran."

Behran reported their success in finding powder and weapons supplies on the military base.

"Good. I want every munitions building searched. I want to know which ones contain powder barrels. Also how easy they are to access."

"What is your plan?" Doc asked.

"Prepare timed detonators. One for each building and powder mine you find, and add twenty for the ships and buildings we've found."

Behran spoke. "You plan to blow them up?"

"When the time is right."

Hendra's heart lurched at her cousin's brutal statement. "Isn't this a peace mission? Why would we blow up their buildings and ships?"

Her cousin's cool, level gaze met hers. "Because they cannot be trusted. I sent the Presidente a letter, offering peace. He replied that he wants peace, too. But soon after that Methusal and I heard his officers plotting to invade Koblan. The Presidente cannot be trusted. He cares only for power."

Methusal looked at him. "A common seduction of men."

Mentàll sent her an undisturbed glance. "Liars cannot be trusted. We will strategize as if we can trust no one."

"What if our attacks make them angry?" Hendra said. "You said they want to invade Koblan again. Won't that make them more determined to do it?"

"Another reason to destroy their fire power," Mentàll said. "That reminds me. We still need to find the largest powder mine in Dakarra. Tabor told me you've only found one."

"Then we'll blow them up, too?" Behran asked.

"Yes."

Riln growled in approval, "Finally, we'll get some action."

Hendra felt uneasy with the plan, but Mentàll was the Commander. And it did make a brutal kind of sense. Clearly, the invaders couldn't be trusted. They'd invaded Koblan once, and planned to do so again. Her cousin was right. They had to do everything within their power to prevent that from happening.

"Do we still plan to offer them a formal peace agreement?" Deccia wanted to know.

"Yes."

"But why? How can we forge peace with someone we can't trust?"

"We will tempt them with ore, and we will scare them with destruction. They are a fearful people. They fear kaavl, and they fear the unknown. If they think we are more powerful than they are, they will submit to our demands."

"How will they trust us, then?"

"They do not need to trust us. They need to fear us. Only then can a peace agreement last."

"Doesn't sound like peace to me," Methusal muttered.

"I understand these people, Methusal. I know how they reason, and what motivates them."

"Because you're just like them?"

Mentàll only smiled, as if amused. "Is the plan clear?"

Behran nodded. "What about the invitations? Is Deccia going to copy the one you brought?"

Methusal spoke up. "Yes. But her invitations will be our backup, just in case we need them. She'll leave the names blank because each one will have to match the guest list, and we don't know the names on that list. Our best bet would be to steal original invitations. But the owners might report it to the Presidente. If we show up with the stolen invitations we might be arrested."

"Methusal and I intend to secure invitations for ourselves by one means or another," Mentàll interjected. "Perhaps that will mean stealing them the night of the ball, and restraining the true owners until morning. By the way, note the ball is in ten days. Day Nineteen here. We will call it Day Zero."

"Will you go on this mission alone?" Sozla wanted to know. "Or will a few of us come to Carachki to help you?"

"Doc and Behran will come, and they'll bring the detonators with them the morning of the ball. The rest of you will be responsible for setting the other bombs in place here. Methusal and I will set the detonators on Carachki's base and on the ships."

"How will we get into the Presidente's compound for the ball?" Behran asked.

"You will slip in as servants. You will be there to help us if we need it. Afterward, when it's dark, we'll escape to the ship, which will be waiting in a small cove a half hour's walk west of Carachki. Then we'll sail to Dakarra and pick up the rest of the team before dawn."

Behran said, "You'll present the peace agreement at the ball?"

"Yes. Hendra, you and the others will stay in Dakarra. Riln and Tabor will blow up the mines. You see now why it is so important to find the largest powder mine. We must completely incapacitate their military. Hendra will lead the mission onto Dakarra's base and set those timers."

It sounded dangerous. Especially since Sozla, Deccia, and Timaeus didn't know kaavl. It would be up to her, she realized. Everyone's safety would be her responsibility.

"Can you do it, Hendra?" Her cousin regarded her across the room. He knew he'd placed a huge burden upon her, and she wondered suddenly if he had done it on purpose. To test her? Or because he believed in her?

"Yes. Of course I can."

"Good." A small smile touched his lips. His attention turned to Methusal's twin. "Deccia, what is the feeling you are getting about the Dakarrans? Are they hostile? Suspicious?"

Deccia rubbed her palms on her pants. "I... Well, they're hostile, as far as I can tell. They're unfriendly. I don't think they like newcomers."

"Can you make friends with a few?"

Discomfort crossed Deccia's features. "I'm friends with a girl named Ceri, but she's disappeared."

"What about the others? Pretending friendship could ease their suspicion."

Sozla spoke up. "Mentàll, they are like whip beasts. Vitnia is a good example. She is cruel, and likes to stir up trouble. That's why we are glad Goric has found the military papers to copy. If our men do not have them, the military will force them to the base to begin training."

"Why?" Methusal asked. "You're visitors. Why wouldn't they leave you alone?"

"Because they're *Zins!*" Riln bellowed. Hendra gripped her chair. Her heart raced, but she drew a calming breath. That man. He'd been docile ever since Mentàll had arrived, but evidently that pleasure had ended.

Mentàll flicked Riln a cold glance. "I require facts, not emotional outbursts."

The Tarst man's face flushed. "That Vitnia hag will make sure we're hounded." He settled back in his chair. "I say we take her out. One less Zin to worry about."

Deccia said, "Vitnia's friend Olita has a husband who's a retired Commander. Riln's right. She could stir up trouble for us. I'll keep an eye on her." If Deccia's downturned mouth was any indication, however, she was not looking forward to the task.

"Good. And Sozla and Behran," Mentàll said. "How close are you to finishing a detonator?"

Sozla looked at Behran. Slowly, she said, "We are close to finishing the self-firing detonator. But we are having trouble figuring out the timing device. Lighting a slow burning candle is possible, but it's dangerous, too. And it would probably be noticed by soldiers. We hope to find another solution."

"Keep working. You have nine days before Behran and Doc come to Carachki. We will blow up all of Zindedi's powder at midnight on the night of the ball."

"What if the powder carts leave the base before then?" Doc asked.

"Then Riln and Tabor will follow them and blow them up halfway to Carachki. From what we've discovered, it seems like they want to move the powder at the last minute to the ships. If at all possible, wait until the night of the ball to blow them up."

"Who will blow up the mines, then?" Deccia wanted to know.

"Goric will be in charge. He can take whomever he wants."

A small smile curled Goric's lips. A small vindication for the man who was perpetually ignored and underestimated.

Mentàll said, "We need to find that big powder mine. Goric, I'd like for you and Doc to follow the beach road tomorrow until you find it."

△ △ △ △ △

Methusal listened to more strategic planning, and contributed a few of her own ideas from time to time. In all, the plan seemed like a good one.

At least now her mind was sharp and clear. She even felt relaxed, for the first time in nine days. It was amazing what sound sleep could do. That, and feeling safe with Behran and her friends close by.

Gradually, the meeting wound down. She said, reminding the Dehrien Chief, "Is this our only meeting?"

"Yes. Thank you, Methusal. Timaeus will report progress to me every two days. Oh, and Methusal will need a dress for the ball." Mentàll directed his attention to her sister. "Deccia, you will come to the city with Behran and Doc. You'll find Methusal the perfect dress, and then you will report to the ship and make sure it's ready to sail that evening."

Deccia nodded, and the meeting officially ended. The men gathered around the bubbling berry pie that Sozla had just taken from the oven.

With a faint frown, Methusal turned to Mentàll. "Why can't I find my own dress?"

"You could, of course. But you will be busy, with me. This will give your sister two necessary jobs, and also keep her out of harm's way. I trust that meets with your approval."

His mildly mocking tone annoyed her. "Of course. Thank you. You're so thoughtful." Abruptly, she stood and headed across the room to speak to Behran, determined not to let Mentàll get under her skin again.

A few minutes later, while she nibbled on pie at the table with Behran, Mentàll took Riln and Tabor aside and spoke to them in a low voice. By the time she thought to spy on their conversation, all she heard was, "...east Zindedi, too."

Riln's teeth shone white in his dark, aggressive face. It was a scary looking smile. Clearly, he was pleased with the plan, whatever it might be. What was Mentàll plotting now?

Behran nudged her arm. "Are you finished? Want to go for a walk?"

She smiled, but then a yawn caught her. She clapped a hand over her mouth. "How can I be tired? I just woke up!"

"You've had a long day." Behran took her hand. "Walk with me for a few minutes?" His smile tipped up with promise.

She hesitated. For a surreal moment it felt odd that Behran was the one flirting with her, and not Mentàll. She tried to ignore the confusion she felt. "All right."

They both stood.

"Behran," Mentàll said. "I need to speak with you."

Behran hesitated. "Now?"

"Yes, now. About the mission." His hard gaze slid to Methusal. "We are leaving early in the morning."

Behran glanced at Methusal. With obvious reluctance, he released her hand. "Maybe later," he murmured.

Methusal directed a glare at Mentàll. He'd interrupted them on purpose. And if she knew him at all, he'd keep Behran occupied with endless details about the mission for a long time. Temper trembled through her, and she rudely brushed by him on her way to the living room.

Deccia sat talking quietly to Timaeus on the couch. When she saw Methusal's thunderous expression, she immediately rose to her feet. "What's wrong?"

Methusal glanced at Timaeus. "Nothing."

Wordless communication passed between Deccia and Timaeus. She smiled at Methusal. "Want to have tea at our cabin?"

"I'd love it. Thank you." But she sent Timaeus an anxious look, wondering if it would bother him that she'd stolen Deccia from him. But he gave her a relaxed smile and waved her toward the door.

In Deccia and Timaeus' blessedly quiet cabin, Deccia quickly set water on to boil, and Methusal chose the tea she'd like from a small basket.

When the fragrant mugs of liquid steamed on the table before them, Deccia came to the crux of the matter, "What happened? Why aren't you with Behran?"

"Mentàll interfered. He said he needed to speak to Behran about the mission."

"And you don't think that's true?"

"*No*. Well, maybe it is, but he didn't need to speak to Behran that very instant."

Deccia sent her a long look. "Tell me what's been going on in Carachki. Between you and Mentàll, I mean."

Methusal fiddled with the handle of her mug. Confusion and frustration threatened to overwhelm her. She'd felt completely relaxed until the end of the meeting. And then, within minutes, Mentàll had her in knots again.

"He keeps...kissing me. It's for cover. But it seems like he *creates* opportunities to do it."

Deccia gave her a sharp glance. "And how do you feel about that?"

"I hate it."

"Do you?" Compassion warmed her eyes.

Methusal looked away. "What am I supposed to feel?" Her voice caught.

"I'm not the one to tell you. But be honest, Thusa. You owe yourself the truth."

"I want to hate him."

Deccia waited patiently.

"I have to hate him," she stated. "I can't trust him. I know he's trying to form some sort of Alliance with the Chiefs on Koblan. I'll bet anything this peace mission ties into it somehow. He's ruthless, Dec."

"He is determined to get what he wants. I know."

"He'll hurt anybody to get his own way."

Deccia said, "Thusa, listen to yourself. You're talking about alliances and the peace mission. But from what I can see, the situation between the two of you is personal."

"It all ties together."

"Does it?"

Methusal didn't answer, because truthfully, she didn't know. "It has to. Mentàll cares about power. He says he doesn't hate me anymore. But either that's a lie, or he's trying to get under my skin for another reason."

"What reason?"

"I don't know. Sometimes I could swear that he...he *cares* for me." Methusal knew how foolish this sounded, but Deccia made no comment. "You want to know my biggest fear? I'm afraid he's trying to twist my mind, and lull me into trusting him. I think he wants to forge some sort of alliance with *me*. I don't know why, and I know this sounds completely crazy, but maybe he thinks I could be useful to him somehow. I don't know."

"Maybe."

Methusal frowned. "Tell me what you really think."

"I can't get a read on him." When Methusal lifted her brows, she said, "I know. That's unusual. When he was about to take over Rolban, I did sense that he was dangerous. But ever since the Quasr War, I'm just not sure. He keeps a thick wall of ice around his emotions. I'm sure you know that."

"I know he's a cold man." But the memory of his hot kisses scorched her mind, and she blushed.

It was Deccia's turn to raise her eyebrows. Carefully, she said, "I don't know him well. But he's clearly a complex man. I think it's a mistake for you to lump all of his motivations under one category. Lust for power and alliances, I mean. I think much more is going on under the surface."

Methusal said nothing, because it was true. He constantly surprised her. Like when he gently kissed her when it was the last thing she expected from him. "He says he wants peace with me."

Deccia's eyebrows raised even further. "He does?"

"That's what he *says*."

"You don't believe him?"

"I don't know what to believe anymore."

"Remember what the Prophet said? Pursue peace with your enemies. Forgive them."

"I have forgiven him. But it's like I have to do it over and over again. He's always doing something new to upset me. If only he'd leave me alone! But living with him twenty-four hours a day..." Her voice dropped to a whisper, "Sometimes I don't think I'm going to make it."

"What do you mean?"

"I mean, I feel like he's trying to take pieces of me. He keeps on..." She searched for words. "It's like he's building a chain between us, hammering each link into place, one at a time. He won't stop. I'm afraid..."

When she fell silent, Deccia prompted, "Afraid of what?"

Methusal twisted her fingers together. In a low voice, she said, "I'm afraid he's going to succeed." There it was; the truth she'd been unable to admit to herself until now.

"Are you afraid a point will come when the bond between you can't be broken?"

"It's crazy, isn't it? I love *Behran*."

Deccia's frown looked troubled. "Maybe it *is* about power."

Methusal looked down. "I told you."

"Or maybe it's about something else entirely."

She looked up again. "What?"

"That's for you to find out. If you have the courage."

Methusal wanted to feel offended, but her sister wasn't trying to hurt her.

Deccia said, "Sometimes the feelings we have are so mixed up we can't understand them. Sometimes we don't want to understand them." Her expression turned dark.

Now it was Methusal's turn to feel concerned. She touched her sister's hand. "What do you mean, Decc? Is something wrong?"

A poor smile pulled at her lips. "I'm a good one to tell you about forgiveness. I keep feeling more and more hatred in my heart toward the Zindedis."

"Why?"

Deccia explained her encounters with Vitnia, a few other Dakarrans, and General Fitrn.

Methusal said, "They don't sound nice. And I know the General is horrible. I've seen him in action."

"Yes. But I feel like I have this ugly...*blackness* in my heart that keeps growing. Sometimes Riln literally spews out his hatred for them. He says he wants to kill all the Zins, and in my heart...I wish we could do that."

Methusal tried not to reveal her shock. Hatred was brewing in her gentle, peaceful sister? She took her twin's hand. "We both need to forgive our enemies. It's the higher way, right?"

"But I can't. I've tried. And every time Timaeus goes to Carachki, I'm paralyzed with fear. If the Zindedis hurt him, I don't know what I'll do."

"I think we both need help," Methusal said softly. "Can we pray together?"

Deccia nodded, and clasped Methusal's hands tightly.

Methusal closed her eyes. "The One, Deccia and I feel overwhelmed. We're living with our enemies, but we don't know how to live at peace with them. We don't know how to forgive them completely. Please help us to walk your right path. We know your ways are right, and if we follow you, you'll heal us inside and make us whole again. Amen."

"Amen." With a gentle squeeze, Deccia released her hands. "Thank you, Thusa. I'll keep praying for you."

"And I'll do the same for you." She smiled. Her heart did feel lighter and freer again; as if maybe things could work out after all. "I'm going to turn in. Even after that nap, I'm exhausted."

Deccia saw her to the door, and Methusal walked through the dark to the other cabin, which blazed with light. When she walked inside, Mentàll looked up, snaring her gaze for the space of a long heartbeat. He sat on the couch, speaking to Behran. Fine. No problem. She would talk to Behran tomorrow. She didn't want to feel angry at Mentàll anymore. She wanted to cling to this feeling of peace.

Methusal touched Behran's shoulder. "Goodnight," she said softly.

Behran's serious expression gentled into a smile. "'Night, Thusa. Meet me on the porch at dawn?"

She grinned. "I'll look forward to it."

As she turned away, her glance briefly skimmed over the Dehrien. He looked withdrawn and watchful. "We will leave right after breakfast," he said harshly.

She nodded and retreated into the girls' room.

△ △ △ △ △

Later that night, when Methusal lay on the floor in Hendra and Sozla's room—on a soft pile of blankets they had thoughtfully provided—she heard indistinct voices outside. A closer listen revealed that Doc and Mentàll were talking together alone on the kitchen porch. It seemed a bit odd that the two would speak together. They appeared to have little in common.

She decided this thin excuse justified sharpening into kaavl to listen.

"I wish I could *kill* her stepbrother for what he did to her." Rage shivered in Doc's low voice.

"You know? She told you?"

"Yes."

A silence elapsed while Mentàll digested this. "Then you know I stopped it."

"Yes. You ended it. But that wasn't the first time. You know that, right?" Anger hardened Doc's words. "Jascr abused her for two years before you stepped in."

A curse whispered. Then a vicious one rent the air. "*No.*"

"Yes."

A long silence ensued.

Methusal had pieced together a little of Hendra's past, so the news didn't shock her. Not like it evidently just had the Dehrien Chief. And if she knew him at all, right now he was blaming himself for not protecting her better.

"I should have visited her more," Mentàll's harsh voice sounded strangled. "I should have taken care of her."

"You rescued her."

"Too *late!*"

"You stopped it before Jascr crossed that last boundary." Doc cleared his throat, as if it was hard for him to speak. "She's scarred emotionally. But you did take her out of that pit. For that, I thank you. If you hadn't taken her into your tents and protected her, she wouldn't be half the woman she is today."

"I wish I could kill Jascr again. This time with my bare *hands*." That violent hiss made the hairs stand up on Methusal's arms. Here was the merciless, frightening man she'd met three years before—a man little more than a barbaric wild beast wrapped in the veneer of civility.

"I feel the same way," Doc gritted.

More grim silence elapsed.

Mentàll grated, "I cannot change the past. But Hendra is my responsibility now. Any man who wants her must pass through me, first."

"Good."

"You agree?"

"I know you'll protect her. That's all I want."

"You want nothing more."

After another silence, Doc said quietly, "Hendra won't have me. I will accept her word."

"Protect her for me while she's here."

"You trust me?"

"I trust few people. But if she changes her mind, you have my blessing."

Doc laughed softly. "I appreciate that. But I doubt you'll need to give it."

A door closed. Someone had gone inside. That same man went into the room next door and prepared for bed. The footsteps told her it was Doc.

So, Mentàll still stood outside, alone. Just like him. A solitary figure. Methusal suspected he'd initiated the meeting with Doc. He'd probably meant to flush out the doctor's intentions toward Hendra, but had received an earful instead.

Although Methusal didn't want to, she felt sorry for the Dehrien. He believed he should have been there for Hendra. The fact that he hadn't been would eat away at him forever. For if nothing else, she knew he loved his cousin.

CHAPTER TWENTY-SIX

DAY 10

AALI SAT HUDDLED in a thicket nestled under a towering, spiky green tree. She was well off the path Dastn would travel to head to Quasr this morning. She'd snuck out here before dawn. She was all ready to go. Her pack was stuffed with rations, firesticks, and water. Everything she needed.

Her story had been rehearsed with Vaantra, too. Her friend would tell her own parents that Aali went home this morning. Petr would think she was still in Tarst. No one would miss her for days. Perfect!

She grinned to herself and slapped at a bug biting her arm. *Hurry up, Dastn!*

Again, since she was bored, she rehearsed her plan. She'd silently follow him off this mountain. This short part was the only part of the trip she hadn't traveled before. After that, it didn't matter if he went too fast and left her behind. After she reached the plains, she knew the way to Quasr.

Sort of.

She shrugged off any doubts.

All of the kaavl and sneaking skills she'd cultivated over the years were about to bear fruit. She itched to get started.

Footsteps crunched through the forest, and she heard Dastn's cheerful whistling. She grinned. Good. He'd never hear her following with all the racket he was making. ...Not that he'd hear her stalking him anyway, since she was the most silent kaavl player ever. She smiled again to herself, and waited for him to pass.

There he went, his tall, sturdy frame striding down the mountain. A large pack was on his back. Aali darted silently after him.

Just because his job was called "runner," didn't mean he'd run the whole way to Tarst. In fact, she figured she could easily keep up with him. She prided herself on her good physical condition; she ran forty minutes every day. It would be no problem to keep up with Dastn.

△ △ △ △ △

Just after breakfast at dawn, Methusal and Behran sat on Deccia's front porch step, at last alone together. A chill white mist blanketed the landscape. Later, the sun would burn it off, but for now it was cold. Yet again, Methusal was glad to have her warm leather jacket.

Mentàll had said they'd leave soon. The rest of the team stood talking together on the crushed grass outside the main cabin.

At least over here they could have a few moments of uninterrupted privacy.

Methusal tightened her grip on Behran's hand. Their thighs touched, and his warmth felt good on this chilly, foggy morning. "I'm going to miss you. I wish we'd had more time together."

"This mission will end in nine days." His dark blue eyes held hers. "Will you be all right until then?"

"Do you mean will I be able to survive that long with Mentàll?"

Quietly, he said, "How has it gone so far?"

"Good. And bad. It's more complicated than I want it to be."

His grip tightened. He looked down for a moment, and then said carefully, "He wants you, you know."

Surprised, she said, "*No.* You mean he wants to play games with me. Or to torment me."

"No. I mean he wants you," he said flatly.

Methusal felt even more flabbergasted. "Why do you say that?"

"Because of the way he looks at you. Among other things."

Methusal slid a glance over at Mentàll, who was currently speaking to Tabor. He appeared to be paying no attention to them at all. "You're wrong, Behran."

"Has he kissed you?"

Methusal flushed. "A few times. For cover."

Behran shook his head. "I'm telling you, Thusa, he wants you, and he means to have you. I've known it since Dehre." His fingers rubbed hers lightly. "Can you handle him?"

"Of course I can handle him." But she thought about what he'd just said.

She remembered the kaavl pages Mentàll had sent to her over the last six months. One at a time, each complete with a cryptic message from him. What had that been about? And the way he'd made sure she would accompany him on this mission as his make-believe wife. And the marriage necklace she wore. And his sizzling kisses...

Yes, she believed that he'd chosen her because her kaavl far outdistanced any other woman on Koblan, but she also remembered his smile when he'd gotten his way; as if he had accomplished his goal, and was pleased with himself about it.

She glanced at Mentàll again. The Dehrien Chief was watching them now.

"Why would he want me?"

"What is the usual purpose when a man wants a woman?"

"Nothing is ever so simple with Mentàll."

For one, she couldn't imagine the Dehrien wanting her for herself, ever. He might desire a base union, but nothing more—after all, he had said he desired her three years ago, even as he threatened to kill her. No, he would not go to all of this trouble for something so simple. And unattainable. Surely dozens of Dehrien women would willingly perform that service for him, anyway.

The idea of him wanting her personally, because he liked her, was extremely difficult to believe. Impossible, actually. As she'd told Deccia, his advances must be for a logical purpose. They must be, if he'd planned all of this months ago.

Feeling more confused than ever, she shot another glance at the Dehrien Chief, but he'd turned his back on them. All the same, she impulsively closed her other hand around Behran's. "Let's set a date."

Pleasure lit his features. "Sounds good to me. When?"

Methusal thought quickly. "How about six weeks after we get home? That way we'll have time to make all of the preparations."

Behran leaned over and gave her a slow kiss. Deep security wrapped around her heart, and she held him tight. "Sounds great."

She felt relieved. "I can't wait."

Holding hands, they rose and approached the Koblani team. Deccia greeted her with a hug and a tearful goodbye. "Hang in there," she whispered. "We'll both get through this."

The Dehrien Chief shook hands with the men, and then he approached Hendra, who had just said goodbye to Methusal, too. He touched her shoulder gently, as if she were a fragile piece of glass. "Hendra."

When she turned to him, a smile bloomed on her features. After the barest hesitation, she ducked into his chest for a hug. Wonder warred with the dark, brittle pain on his face. He stroked her shimmering fall of white-blond hair, so much like his own that they could be brother and sister. Bleak lines scored his features. "Be careful."

She smiled up at him and pulled back. "You, too."

But Mentàll's sharp, searching gaze remained on her face, as if trying to see inside her soul. Trying to discover how broken she still might be?

He pressed a kiss into her hair. "You will do well, Hendra. I will see you at the ship."

Pleasure lit her eyes. Compliments from Mentàll were rare, and obviously his words meant a great deal to her.

Methusal hugged Behran tight. His arms felt strong around her, and yet she felt very alone right now. Desperately, she clung to him. Her moments of safety and reprieve were over. Nine more days until the mission ended.

△ △ △ △ △

By lunch time, Aali had unfortunately begun to question her impeccable physical condition. Her legs ached, and her lungs hurt. Dastn walked really fast. And he never stopped to rest.

What was worse, nothing looked familiar. That didn't make sense, because nine months ago she remembered skirting mountains to get to Quasr, just as she was doing now. It must be the same route, but she just didn't remember it as clearly as she should.

She decided she'd better stick close to Dastn. She didn't want to get lost.

Thankfully, he stopped soon near a stream and perched on a rock to eat lunch. Aali felt hot and sticky, and longingly eyed the cool stream from behind her tall, bristly tagma bush. She sat in the dirt and gnawed on a dried meat strip, and peeked out every so often to make sure he hadn't left. She wished she could take a nap.

Stop it! she told herself. *You're not a baby anymore.*

Her legs felt sore when she stood again to follow him. She only dared to pause for a moment at the stream to splash water on her face. She couldn't lose him now. By this rate, they'd reach Quasr by tomorrow night. That would be good. Perfect, she decided, trying to ignore her aching legs.

The afternoon crept on, and it grew hotter and hotter. Now her feet hurt. She hoped she wasn't getting blisters. She gulped water and ate more snacks to keep up her energy. Ahead of her, Dastn's steps didn't falter.

Gradually, the sun crept toward the horizon. Now, not only did her legs and feet hurt, but the skin on her nose sizzled. Probably a sunburn. She pulled out the extra tunic she'd brought and draped it over her head.

Would Dastn ever stop?

Twilight fell fast at this time of the year, and soon after that the wild beasts would emerge from their caves. Her skin crept at the thought. One beast could easily rip her to shreds in seconds.

She didn't particularly want to die. Not even for this important mission. Yet tonight she'd sleep out in the open. How would she stay safe?

Unfortunately, she hadn't thought that far ahead, so she had no idea. Maybe she could find a cave.

△ △ △ △ △

Morning passed quickly as Methusal and Mentàll walked in silence through the cold mist. The dark wooden buildings of Dakarra appeared to be sleeping. No one was about, although she heard the hollow sound of a bucket being tossed down a well on the south side of town.

As the sun rose higher, burning off the light fog, the sweet smell of grass mixed with the dusty scents of earth. Mentàll set an easy pace. He appeared to be in no rush to return to Carachki.

The Dehrien appeared to be lost in his own thoughts, which was perfectly fine with her. She used the peaceful quiet to relive her moments with Behran over and over again, wanting to cling to the warm security she'd felt in his arms.

The sun beat down, warming her skin. In an hour or more, they'd stop for lunch. She took off her jacket and stuffed it into her pack.

Open farmland surrounded them. Here and there urchets roamed, penned in by fences. A few carts rattled down the road, but no one spoke to them.

She glanced at Mentàll. So far, he'd given her plenty of space today. But she wasn't foolish enough to think it would last.

Behran believed that the Dehrien Chief desired her. The idea sent a prickle down her skin and her heart beat faster...with alarm, she told herself.

That formidable—even handsome man, by some people's standards—could have any woman he wanted. Of this, Methusal had no doubt. She'd seen women fawn over him, eager for a small scrap of his attention. But Behran believed the Dehrien Chief wanted *her*. She didn't agree—although she did believe Mentàll wanted something *from* her.

But what? For three years, their roles had remained the same—she the hunted, and he the predator, circling, licking his chops, waiting to take a bite of her. Whatever purpose he pursued, Methusal wished for the millionth time that she could figure it out. More than that, she wished she could figure out what drove him, overall. But since she couldn't, one thing remained clear—she must remain wary at all times.

"You are hungry?" The Dehrien asked a little while later. Funny, how he phrased questions like statements. As always, he appeared so very certain of himself.

"Yes."

Large blocks of baled grass dotted the side of the road, and Mentàll headed for one. Methusal perched on the other end of the same bale.

The Dehrien pulled the wrapped bundle of sandwiches and fruit from his pack. "Both meat," he murmured, handing her a sandwich. "That should please you." His teeth flashed white and sharp as he took a big bite.

It was on the tip of her tongue to ask him to explain himself. Then she realized that he was baiting her. He was reminding her of their lunch together when they'd spied on the docks in Carachki.

Silently, she polished off her sandwich and fruit, and gulped water from her water skin. The sun felt hot now. The sound of rushing water tickled her ears. A few easy carries pinpointed the source to a stream to the south. A line of tall trees confirmed her guess.

Mentàll followed her gaze. "You want to find a cool place to rest?"

"We need to get back to Carachki." She avoided eye contact and took another sip of water.

Softly, he said, "You will have to endure my presence either here or there. Do you want to rest in the shade?"

"You're not in a rush to get back?"

That light gaze locked with hers. "No."

It felt dangerous, the idea of going to a secluded spot and whiling away a quiet hour with him in the shade. But the thought of soaking her hot feet in cold, rippling water tempted unbearably.

"All right," she said, and rose. "For a little while."

They cut directly across the field and walked for a good fifteen minutes before reaching the tree line. Thick, stickery bushes clogged the earth between the trees. It was tough going. Mentàll went first, holding back branches for her. She emerged at the bank of the swiftly rushing stream relatively unscathed, although angry red scratches marked the Dehrien's forearms.

A short descent led to a boulder strewn creek. Clear water rushed over the stones. It was only one length across, although erosion higher up the banks indicated it often flooded to higher levels. Methusal found a sun-warmed boulder to sit on and discarded her boots. The icy water shocked her system. "Ah," she gasped.

Mentàll sat on his haunches at the edge of the stream and sluiced water over his cut forearms. "I thought you were tough, Methusal," he murmured.

She tore her gaze away from the angry welts on his arms. His left one looked the worst. "It's freezing."

The pale eyes flashed with amusement. "It is not that cold."

"Having ice in your veins must help you out."

A rusty laugh erupted. "Of course you are right, Methusal. I feel nothing, because my heart is made of ice."

"You said it." Methusal felt a little uncomfortable with their light bantering, and turned away, dangling her legs off the other side of the boulder. Now her back was to him. A much safer position.

A touch on her neck startled her. "Stop!" She slapped at his hand like a bug.

"We are not alone," he murmured. "Put your boots back on."

She stiffened, and listened. Leaves soughed in the light breeze. No footsteps, but...the back of her neck prickled. Was it because Mentàll stood behind her, or because someone was watching them?

Swiftly, she pulled on her boots and knotted the laces.

The Dehrien helped her down from the boulder and across a few partly submerged stones. "Walk with me. No. Don't pull your hand away."

They followed the stream east, and she relaxed utterly into kaavl and listened. He was right. Quiet breaths and stealthy footsteps followed them.

The hairs rose on the back of her neck. "They mean us harm," she whispered, her heart suddenly racing. Never had she felt anything so strongly in her life. The malevolence in the people behind them slid out, wrapping tentacles of black terror around her soul. "We need to run!"

"No." He tightened his grip, holding her in check. "Walk calmly. Never run from danger."

Trembling a little from the panic gripping her, Methusal pressed closer to him, so their forearms interlocked. His strong hand felt very secure.

"Do not be afraid," he said in a low voice. "Relax into kaavl. Let in every sensory input."

Taking a deep breath, Methusal focused more fully into kaavl. As he had taught, she concentrated on hearing first, moving from sound to sound, identifying every leaf flutter, every babble of the stream, and every footstep behind her. "Two men," she muttered. And lighter, skittering noises. "And a wolmite."

"Good. There is a clearing ahead. We will cut left and head for the road."

A good plan, if their stalkers allowed it. Methusal scanned the ground, looking for a stick to use as a weapon. Nothing but small, broken branches.

Mentàll cut abruptly left at the edge of the clearing. Instead of going straight, through an open meadow, he ducked down and plowed straight between two leafy, stickery bushes. Methusal closed her eyes, shielding her face with her arm, and followed. They erupted into a cool, shady space. Mentàll directed her toward another bristling bush. "Hide behind that," he ordered.

She realized that he intended to face their stalkers alone. "No."

He dragged her close, his lips curled back in a feral snarl. "Do not question my orders, Maahr." He put her from him, hard, so she staggered back.

That light gaze looked hard. Savage, even. "Get back, Maahr," he hissed.

The truth dawned—he was purposefully trying to frighten her. She glanced at the far bushes, where stealthy movements tiptoed closer.

"Do it!" The words lashed, making her jump. Dark emotion now intensified that hard gaze.

Without a word, she slipped behind the bush. Maybe she could help him better from here. Their attackers wouldn't see her immediately, although she would be able to see them.

She searched the ground for a stout stick—to find one a half-length long would be the best. She found one half that size. It would have to do. Then she pulled the knife Mentàll had given her in Carachki from her pack. With revulsion, she eyed the cruel blade. She had killed men during the Quasr War.

She slipped it into her boot for easy access.

Their stalkers had split up. The Dehrien had moved behind a tree.

Methusal gripped the thick stick tighter. Its rough bark felt gritty beneath her palms.

A blood curdling yell rent the air and a wolmite erupted from the brush, galloping toward Mentàll. Yellow fangs gleamed with saliva. One snap from those powerful jaws could kill a man.

Methusal never saw the knife in Mentàll's hand until it flashed silver in the sunlight. It plunged deep into the beast's throat. With a muffled, "Arf," the beast crumpled and lay twitching on the ground.

Guns clicked and Mentàll lunged for deeper cover in the trees. A bullet whined, spraying bark near his head. A man erupted into the clearing. The black uniform that the stumpy figure wore identified him as a soldier. A taller, skinnier man lurked in the shadows at the edge of the clearing.

Methusal didn't see Mentàll now, but the stocky man obviously saw something, for he sighted down his barrel. Quicker than thought, she flung her stick. It struck his head with a loud crack. The man in the bushes fired at her. Something hot grazed her skull. She rolled away, seeking cover behind another bush. The man's next shot went wild.

The forest lay quiet now. Faint clicks indicated that the soldiers were reloading their guns. Any attempt to cross the wide stretch of open ground for the road would mean certain death. Even if they made the road, the soldiers would still probably hunt them down and kill them.

The stocky one spit on the ground. "Track'em, Kirl."

Methusal gripped her knife handle harder, fingers slippery with sweat. A touch on her shoulder almost made her gasp. Mentàll.

Silent as ghosts, they backtracked west. Methusal kept her hearing fixed on the Zindedis. One crunched through leaves in the clearing they'd left, but the tall, skinny one... She didn't hear him. Chills ran down her spine and she followed fast on Mentàll's heels. Her head throbbed, but she ignored it.

Every kaavl sense was heightened. Every leaf flutter, every bird claw scratching wood, and every sound behind them she swiftly catalogued and identified. He wasn't there. On a hunch, she shifted slightly ahead of them, listening to the south and west. A suspicious pebble rolled.

A swift visual carry proved that the Zindedi was running at an angle, moving to intercept them ahead. How had he known? She wondered if he possessed a natural kaavl gift.

Why not? Verdnt, the Zindedi spy in Rolban, had possessed one. He'd quickly reached the Bi-level in kaavl. A horrifying thought struck her. What if other Zindedis learned kaavl? That, combined with their guns could decimate Koblan.

She touched Mentàll's back. When he looked over his shoulder, she silently pointed south. Without asking questions, he altered his path. They reached the rushing stream. The man still crept through the woods, but he was further west than their current position. Whether he saw them or not could not be helped. They darted across the stream, and then into the woods on the other side. A shot rang out, breaking the silence.

"Run," Mentàll commanded.

She had forgotten how fast he was. They plunged through the forest, stickers tearing at their clothes and skin, and erupted into a wide open field. The nearest shack was a five minute run away. They'd be easy targets.

Mentàll ducked back into the woods. He gripped her arm. "Stay here."

Again, he meant to face their attacker alone. Lips sealed, she stared back, promising nothing. "Obey me, Methusal. I do not need to be distracted by you."

"I'll stay out of sight." It was the most she would promise. She would not abandon him.

When he slipped back into the shadows, heading toward the soft movements of the Zindedi, she followed. When he stopped, she stopped too, close enough that her knife throw would do some good. She hid behind a tree.

Mentàll waited behind an overgrown bush. The Zindedi stealthily entered the tiny clearing, gun poking forward, at the ready.

The tableau remained frozen for an impossibly long moment. Then the Zindedi suddenly whirled and fired at Methusal. A *thwack* hit the tree. His shoulders twisted left and he aimed at Mentàll. Without thinking, Methusal fired her blade, straight and true at the Zindedi. Another flash of silver paralleled hers. With a gurgle, the Zindedi grabbed for his throat. He sank to his knees, and then toppled sideways onto the ground.

The Dehrien Chief swiftly retrieved both blades, and wiped them on leaves. She met him in the clearing.

She swallowed. "Is he dead?"

"Yes." He handed over her knife.

"Whose blade killed him?"

A muscle twitched in his jaw and he turned away to resheath his knife. "Mine," he said harshly.

He never lied. But just now, he had not told her the full truth.

Was that to spare her the guilt of taking another man's life? During the Quasr War, he'd seen her fall apart after she'd killed a Zindedi soldier. In his cold, dispassionate way, he had tried to comfort her then. It hadn't helped. What could ever make right the act of killing a man? Except for forgiveness from The One.

She briefly touched his arm. "Thank you," she whispered. "But I can take the truth."

He looked at her for a long moment. "My blade finished him. Know that is the truth."

She nodded without speaking. It was the only truth he would allow her to know.

"Come." He headed for the edge of the woods again.

"I hear the other soldier. He's crossing the stream."

"Unless we want to kill another man, we must run."

Methusal sprinted as fast as she could, trying vainly to keep up with the Dehrien's long, ground eating strides. They'd almost gained the dilapidated shack when another shot rang out.

After a glance to see that she was still following, Mentàll kept running. He ducked out of sight behind the tilted shack. Panting, she joined him a moment later.

"We must keep going." He set off again, heading diagonally for the next building.

They ran for a half an hour before the Dehrien's steps slowed down. They stopped beside a cavernous barn, half-filled with baled dried grass. The sweet scent of grass and dust tickled her nose, and she sneezed and coughed as she panted for breath. She heard no sounds of people or animals. A water pump, encircled by a moat of mud, stood in the nearby yard.

Both of them rested in the shade of the barn, gulping water from skins, and then retreated to the yard to refill them. That's when Methusal saw the bloodstain on Mentàll's left arm.

"What's that?" She felt ridiculously offended that he'd said nothing about it.

He glanced down. "It is nothing. Just a scrape."

"It's bleeding. It needs to be tended."

"No. We must keep moving."

"It'll only take a minute." Not waiting for further denials, she grabbed his arm and pulled him toward the dark, cool shelter of the barn. Although she sensed no one was nearby, this location protected them. No one would see them while she tended his arm.

He allowed her to pull him into the barn—of this fact, she had no doubt. A herd of wild beasts could not drag that big man anywhere he didn't want to go.

Like an obedient child, he pushed up his sleeve, revealing the scratches mixed through the blond hair on his forearm. Above his elbow, the bullet wound dripped. It wasn't long or deep, she saw with relief.

"I told you."

She ignored him and pulled coltac leaves and a kaavl strip from her pack. After washing the wound with water from her water skin, she gently smoothed the antiseptic coltac juice over it.

He said, "This reminds me of the war."

His voice made her jump a little. She'd been so engrossed in her task that she'd managed to block out everything but tending to his wound. Just like during the war. She took a breath to calm her pounding heart.

"Some things never change," she returned flippantly, tying a kaavl strip over the flattened coltac leaf. She tucked the edges under the band. His skin felt warm, and the muscle beneath, very hard.

She longed to apply coltac juice to the long scratches on his arms, too, but before she could decide whether to broach the subject or not, he stepped back and abruptly stripped his tunic over his head. Smooth skin flashed, revealing defined muscles and broad shoulders.

With a silent gasp, she spun away. "What are you *doing*?"

"Mrn. M cannot see my bloody shirt." Softly, he added, "I do not mind if you look at me."

Her ears warmed, but she sealed her lips together and crossed her arms for good measure. She only turned back after he told her that he'd pulled on a new tunic.

That molten blue gaze met hers. Silently, it mocked her fear. That doused her awkward flush as effectively as a dash of cold water. Tersely, she said, "We need to go."

But with her first step, pain—as sharp as a knife—stabbed into her head. Her hand flew up. Wet stickiness came away on her fingers. Blood. With disbelief, she stared at it. Then she remembered the hot sensation that had creased her skull when the tall Zindedi shot at her.

A small breath hissed through Mentàll's teeth. "You are injured." With one step, his fingers slid into her hair, lifting it from the wound.

"No." She wanted to pull away, but was afraid that if she did her hair would catch on his fingers. She felt as neatly caught as a caged apte. "It's nothing. I'll put coltac juice on it..." She gasped when bright pain flashed. He'd touched the edge of the wound.

"I am sorry." That harsh voice sounded thick, and she sensed the tension in his body. A flush colored his cheekbones. "He almost killed you." Those light eyes glittered, as hard and sharp as crystal. Still, his fingers remained gentle on her.

"It's nothing," she insisted.

"Stop!" He drew a shallow breath. "It is not nothing. It almost went to the bone. Do not move. I will tend it."

Methusal stood very still while he swabbed the wound with the damp edge of his old tunic. When it stung bitterly, she didn't flinch.

"Good," he murmured.

With a sure, light touch, he applied the soothing coltac juice, applied the leaf over it, and then carefully arranged her hair to cover it. When the Dehrien was finished, he remained very close to her, and for a moment, his fingers softly stroked the last of the blood from her hair with the tunic.

He felt unbearably near. His large, sheltering presence reminded her of how he'd been with Hendra earlier— protective and gentle. And yet this felt completely different. Tension simmered between them, and awareness warmed her skin.

"Thank you. I...I'm fine, now." She stepped back and swiftly shouldered her pack. After a hesitation, he did the same.

Outside, she said, "Are we lost?"

"I always know where I am, Methusal."

She rolled her eyes, but felt relieved for the break in the tension between them. As they headed east, she maintained a good distance from him. She didn't like how she had felt when he had been so close. It wasn't right. She must concentrate upon Behran.

His small smile disturbed her.

"What?" she said with a touch of irritation.

"Why do you always flee from me, Methusal?"

"I've learned to be wary of wild beasts."

"You want to see me as a wild beast, and Behran as your savior."

"Behran is nothing like you. You are polar opposites."

"Yes, we are."

She felt vaguely surprised that he had agreed.

Mentàll said, "I understand who you are. Behran does not."

She bit her tongue, determined to remain silent.

Softly, he pressed, "You are an apte. You are afraid to see me as I really am. Instead, you insist on seeing me as a wild beast. It is a shield, so you can hide behind your fear."

"That is ridiculous."

"It is the truth. Tell me this, Methusal. Why do you tremble every time I touch you?"

"I'm *not* afraid of you!"

"No. You are afraid of yourself."

"I am *not!*" Aghast, she spat, "You're an egotistical whip. I hate you!"

His head jerked back.

It had been a cruel thing to say, and she regretted it immediately.

"Apte," he said through his teeth.

Methusal wanted to apologize. And yet she wanted distance between them far more. So she said nothing, and instead clung to the coldness between them.

Hours went by in silence. The sun dipped closer to the horizon, but Carachki still was not in sight.

△ △ △ △ △

As the sun set, Aali silently followed Dastn as he approached a rushing river. He veered to the right and climbed the rocky foothills to a shallow cave. At least he didn't plan to cross the river tonight, thank goodness. Aali hid behind a rock. She realized with dismay that this place didn't look familiar, either. She'd need to continue to follow Dastn. Actually, she was glad. She didn't want to be camping here alone with the wild beasts.

Dastn built a fire in front of the cave's mouth. It was to scare off the wild beasts, of course. But where would she sleep? She didn't want to get eaten up tonight!

She ate dried rations and refilled her water skin upstream, and then waited, her eyelids growing heavier by the moment.

It was nearly dark now, and every twig snap made her jump.

Enough of this. When Dastn fell asleep, she'd creep near the fire and unroll her pallet right next to it. Wild beasts feared fire—both its light and its heat—so she would be safe there. It seemed to be her only option. She didn't see any other caves, and it was too late now to gather up a big pile of wood like Dastn had done.

Finally, Dastn threw a huge bundle of wood on the fire and lay down inside the cave. By then, Aali felt about ready to keel over from exhaustion. She'd nodded off several times already, waiting for him to go to bed. Only the fear of being eaten alive by the wild beasts kept waking her up.

Quickly, she crept close to the fire near the cave entrance, and unrolled her pallet. She instantly fell asleep.

She awoke when a wet snuffle sucked the hair away from the nape of her neck. Hairs stood up all over her body, and she froze.

What was that?

Warm breath nuzzled her skin, and sharp teeth nipped. She screamed. Instinctively, she clamped her elbows over her head and rolled for the smoldering fire.

△ △ △ △ △

Dusk gathered like a soft blanket around them when the lights of Carachki finally shone in the distance. It was getting colder by the minute, and Methusal put her jacket back on.

It had been a long, silent journey. For this last bit of the trip they'd skirted the road, avoiding soldier patrols. The silence between them continued to feel uncomfortable. Worse, guilt plagued her for what she'd said to him.

Finally, as they slipped into the city, she said stiffly, "I'm sorry."

"Tell me the truth. Do you hate me?"

She did not. "No." Even though it went against every self-protective fiber in her being, she repeated, "No, I don't."

More silence passed, and then he said quietly, "I accept your apology."

When they headed down Feldon Street, Mentàll spoke again. "You and Behran have reason to celebrate?" The casualness of the question alerted her. He'd been itching to ask it for some time.

Finally, a reason to smile. "Yes, as a matter of fact. We've set our wedding date. It'll be six weeks after we get home."

They reached Mrn. M's cottage.

He said in a silky tone, "You must miss him terribly when you are apart."

"Yes, actually, I do."

"Do you."

She frowned. "Are questioning my feelings for Behran?"

Mentàll opened the cottage door for her—only partway, so she had to brush by his arm to get inside.

As she passed by, he murmured, "Your feelings for Behran could not warm milk."   She gasped in outrage. Mentàll spoke above her, "Good evening, Mrn. Machblin."

Mrn. M looked up from the tapestry work she held in her lap. She sat next to the blazing fire. The tiny living room looked cozy, warm, and safe. "Good evening, you two. Did you have a nice trip?"

"Fabulous," Methusal gave Mentàll a thin-lipped smile. She cooed, "My husband is faultless in all his ways." Under her breath, she added, "Or so he thinks."

Mrn. Machblin sighed and smiled. "Aah, young love."

She muttered beneath her breath, "Yes, but thankfully I'm not blind. I know a wild beast when I see one."

Mentàll's wide hand curled around her shoulder and he leaned close, as if responding to her comment. He said, "No, Mrn. Machblin does not mind."

"Mind what?" Methusal and the older lady asked at the same moment.

"Midi thinks it embarrasses you when I kiss her."

Mrn. Machblin giggled. "Oh, my, no. Young love is beautiful to see."

Methusal frowned at him.

He said, "So you see, sweet? You do not need to be embarrassed."

She hissed, "*Back off.*"

"Provoke me to your own sorrow," he returned in a low voice, and pulled her closer.

The nerve of him! She wrenched free from his grasp and trotted over to Mrn. Machblin, whose eyebrows had climbed her forehead, watching this interchange.

"What wonderful work, Mrn. Machblin. It's so beautiful! I wish I could stitch like you." Unfortunately, she could no more wield a needle than fly to Ryon. She looked up with a fake smile. "Look, Lozar, at the detail. The beadwork is exquisite."

"Thank you, dear." Mrn. Machblin glanced at Mentàll, and then at Methusal. "Come sit down, and I'll show you a simple stitch."

"Okay." Methusal pulled a stool close. She wanted Mentàll to leave the room. She needed space from that man.

"Now you see, dear, you hold the needle thus..." Mrn. M deftly wove the needle through the fabric, and as if by magic a design appeared. "Now, you try."

"I hope I don't ruin your work." She felt apprehensive.

"Nonsense. Stitches can be pulled out. No harm done. Go ahead."

As Methusal awkwardly attempted the stitch, Mentàll disappeared into their rented room. She heaved a sigh of relief. Finally, a moment's peace. She listened carefully to Mrn. Machblin's instructions and tried again, with more success this time.

After a little more instruction and practice tries, Methusal sat quietly, watching the older lady's needle fly, creating a deft, beautiful mosaic of stitches. After a long while, Methusal said goodnight. Mentàll was probably in bed by now. Good. And she had the lovely stone floor to look forward to again. After one night of relative comfort in Dakarra, the thought was unbearable.

Methusal let herself into their room.

"You like to play with fire," Mentàll commented when she closed the door. He sat relaxed, leaning back against the headboard of the bed.

"Don't manhandle me again," she retorted. "Behran and I are going to be married, so back off."

He said nothing, so she believed she had made her point. She headed for the bathroom, but two steps from it, she gasped when he soundlessly turned in front of her, blocking her way. "Do not jeopardize our mission again."

"Jeopardize? You were about to force yourself on me, and I'm jeopardizing the mission?"

"Invaders will get suspicious if you run every time I touch you."

"I don't. And I don't appreciate you manipulating me into that situation, just because you didn't like my comments."

"You goad me on purpose. I cannot respond?"

"And you bait me! Respond like a gentleman. If you know how."

His cheekbones tinged red. "I decide the rules of our behavior in public. I am your commanding officer. You will obey me."

"Power hungry whip." Methusal glared. "I am not your puppet! I have a mind of my own, and I have a purpose here, too. Isn't that why you asked me on this mission?"

"Even so, you will follow my orders to the letter. ...Or do you not trust my judgment and leadership skills?

"I don't trust you at all. That's the problem. Yes, you led well during the war, and your plans seem good here so far..."

"Then play the part. Both of our lives depend on it."

"I don't *like it*."

"What? Me touching you? Kissing you?"

"Yes!" she blurted. "You make my skin crawl." It was a blatant lie, but she didn't know how to describe her true feelings. She didn't like it, that much was certain.

"You lie."

"No."

"I hate liars. Speak the truth to me!"

She felt a bit shaken. "Okay, then. I hate it when you kiss me. I hate it when you touch me. That's the truth!"

"The truth is you are scared. You are afraid you will betray your precious Behran."

"Stop it! I don't want to speak to you anymore. I'll play the part, fine. But I don't have to like it. Step off and leave me alone!" She slammed the relief room door in his face.

Shaking, Methusal changed into her long nightgown and washed her face.

And he was wrong about everything. If only she could be indifferent to him, everything would be so much easier.

Methusal stared at herself in the mirror. Her eyes looked large and shadowed underneath, and her face pale. She looked tired and miserable. It had been a long day. But that wasn't the real problem. The stress of the mission, combined with the tension of living with Mentàll were taking their toll on her.

She squeezed her eyes shut. *Oh The One, please help me. I don't know what to do. This situation is impossible.* She had hoped the trip to Dakarra would help, but it hadn't. For a while, he had seemed almost human today, but here she was, stuck back in the same intolerable predicament again.

Slowly, she gathered her clothes together and exited from the bathroom.

The Dehrien Chief sat on the bed again, reading a parchment. He looked up and said in a harsh voice, "Tomorrow we will fix the damage with Mrn. M."

Tears sprang to her eyes. "I'll let you figure that out, since you think you know everything."

She grabbed the pillow from her side of the bed and flung it on the floor, and then yanked the quilts off the bed, too. She sat on the hard stone floor and pulled the blankets over her, and then curled up on her side. Stone bit into her shoulder and hip, and she gasped softly with pain. Bruises upon nine nights of bruises. More would torture her tonight.

She missed Dakarra. She missed the people who loved her.

Suddenly, it was all too much, and she began to cry. She pressed her hand to her mouth to silence the sobs. She *hated* everything—the hard floor, the impossible situation of working and living twenty-four hours a day with a man who clearly relished getting under her skin. That man who even now rested in comfort in that soft bed.

She longed for Behran and his teasing wit and strong, gentle arms. She felt so alone. And chained to her mortal enemy.

Everything became crystal clear right then—he liked making her feel miserable. He did. He had hated her for three long years, and now he calculated ways to make her suffer every moment!

Her sobs came harder. She pressed her face into the pillow and covered her head with her arm in an effort to silence the sobs. She wouldn't let him know that he had succeeded in hurting her yet again.

Her pillow became soaked from temple to cheek from her tears. It was scary, because now she couldn't seem to stop. Mouth twisted into a soundless cry, her shoulders shook, and she gulped for air between sobs. She curled inward on herself, her chest tight and heaving. Her cheekbones hurt from holding in the silent wails. *Oh, The One, help me. Help me!*

She gulped and sniffed, trying to clear her running nose. It didn't help. The stifled snort made too much noise. She clutched the pillow tighter, and the pain in her shoulder intensified. She gasped on a sob, helpless in unrelenting misery.

"Methusal." Her name seemed to come from a great height. She curled up into a tighter ball.

"Methusal!" Now he knelt beside her.

She gasped, "I'm not making any noise. And I'm not breaking your blasted cover. Go away!" It made it feel even more miserable that he was seeing her cry.

"Methusal."

She did not respond, and only wished she could stop crying.

To her everlasting shock, his hands slid underneath her, and suddenly she was lifted in the air and deposited on the soft bed. He stripped the blankets from her clutching fingers, and then the warm weight of the bed's quilt covered her shoulders. Her pillow touched the top of her head. She unthinkingly lifted her head, and he tugged it down beneath her cheek. This side was dry.

In bewilderment, her sobs slowed and she peeked through the crook of her arm at her enemy. He looked down at her, quilts clenched in his fist. She couldn't read his expression. Consternation...annoyance...regret? She couldn't be sure.

He disappeared from her line of vision. She waited for him to sit on the bed, but he didn't. She heard a whisper of sound as his pillow slipped off the bed, and then silence. The lamp flickered out, and darkness enclosed the room.

Was he going to sleep on the floor? She could barely believe it. Her tears finally stopped, and she wiped her cheeks with her sleeve and sniffed. She needed a tissue. Her nose was running. Silently, she slipped out of bed and took care of it in the relief room.

Coming back, the soft green light of Ryon shone through the sheer curtains and illuminated Mentàll's hulk on the floor beside the bed. So, he had decided to give her the bed tonight.

Why?

Silently, she crept back onto the bed and pulled the quilt up to her chin. Oh, blessed softness and comfort! She fell asleep the instant her head hit the pillow.

△ △ △ △ △

Claws scrabbled and jaws snapped, and Aali cringed away from the attacking wild beast. She screamed again. In her side vision a burning stick flew through the air. The varmint squealed in pain and ran.

Rough hands dragged her bodily into the cave. Aali cringed against the wall, shaking, arms covering her head.

"Are you hurt?" She heard Dastn's voice, but couldn't seem to respond. "Are you okay?" he repeated sharply, and stripped her arms away from her face. Terrified, she stared up at him. His eyes looked impossibly dark.

"Aali! What are you doing here?" His mouth was not curled up in the way she liked. In fact, it curled down in deep displeasure.

Still trembling, she scooted into a sitting position, feeling intimidated by his anger, made worse by her near death experience. "I'm...going to Quasr?"

"Quasr! Are you insane?"

She lifted her chin, trying to calm her racing heart. It was hard to do, after almost being eaten alive. "I have a job to do. Since someone didn't complete it."

"Me, you mean."

"If the moccasin fits..."

"You've done some crazy stunts, but this tops them all. You are the most foolish girl I've ever met!"

"Foolish? Not even. Koblan's security is at stake. I won't shirk my duty, even if you will."

"Does your father know you're here?"

"No."

"Of course not. Since he's not here, you'll listen to me. I'm taking you back to Tarst tomorrow."

"No. I'm going to Quasr."

"No. You're not."

"Yes. I am. I'm not afraid," she said coolly. "And you don't intimidate me. You're not my father, and I don't have to listen to you. And thank goodness I don't have any brothers, if they'd turn out anything like you!"

"If I was your relative, I'd find a switch and use it."

Fury swamped her. She snorted, "I'd like to see you try!"

He stared at her for a full minute, and then his mouth curled up—in the right direction, she was glad to see. "Irrepressible Aali. No one can tame you, can they?"

"Nope. Don't even try."

"I wouldn't dream of it."

He tossed more logs on the fire, and when he looked back at her again, the humor was gone. "Fix up your pallet in the back of the cave. I'll guard the entrance."

Aali quickly dragged her pallet and the remains of her pack into the shallow, cramped cave. Dastn's pallet touched her own, since the space was so small.

She stared at her shredded pack in dismay. "That wild beast! He ate all my food! And clawed a hole in my water skin."

Now all she had left were her spare clothes—and all of them were trampled with dirt.

"We'll have to share." Dastn flopped back on his pallet. "Go to sleep, Aali."

She settled back, but now noticed how close he was. Not a respectable distance. Inappropriate, even. Her father would burst a blood vessel if he could see her now.

She scooted back a bit further, until her back touched the cave wall. Then she shut her eyes. Then she opened them again.

Dastn lay on his side, with his broad back to her. His tunic stretched tight over it, outlining his different muscles. Aali's mouth went dry and a new, exciting song sang through her blood. What would it be like, if she touched him? She wanted to know. She needed—no, okay—she wanted to know.

His breathing slowed and became deep and steady. He was asleep.

She would not.

Yes, she would.

She should not!

Despite her better sense, Aali slowly stretched out her fingers and touched the thick corded muscles of his shoulders. They felt firm and strong. Solid and warm.

He felt nice. And she felt safe with him.

"What are you doing?" Dastn growled.

Aali jumped, snatching her hand back. "Uh...nothing! You were too close. I was pushing you away."

"You're lying," he said in a low, soft voice. "You're lucky I'm a good guy."

"I don't know what you mean!" She went for indignant. Really, her heart thumped hard, and she was thankful he was a man of integrity.

"Be ready for a long hike tomorrow. You won't have the energy to play games with me then."

She bit her lip. "I'm not going back to Tarst," she said experimentally.

"You'll go where I take you." His soft voice didn't trick her, because she heard the hard undertone.

She fell silent. Maybe she'd pushed him far enough for today. But neither Dastn nor wild beasts would stop her from going to Quasr tomorrow.

CHAPTER TWENTY-SEVEN

THE ROOM WAS BRIGHT WITH SUNSHINE when Methusal finally awoke the next morning. It was late—at least halfway to lunch. All of those nights of misery and poor sleep on the floor—not to mention the trip home from Dakarra—had finally caught up to her. She yawned. At long last she felt rested.

She was alone in the room. The only sounds she heard were voices in the living area.

It was nice to be alone. She hadn't been by herself in almost a month, except for in the relief room. She wished she could pretend it was a vacation day, and she could sleep in and enjoy a long, lazy morning, but she knew that was not to be.

The doorknob turned and Mentàll came in, shutting the door behind him. He kept one hand behind him, on the doorknob. His pale eyes scanned her face, and he stepped closer. Defensively, she struggled into a sitting position. She knew she must look like a mess, but surely he didn't care about that.

His low, grating voice spoke. "Are you rested?"

"Yes. Thank you."

He inclined his head, and then moved his right hand, which was still behind his back, into her line of vision. A single, long-stemmed flower, blood red in color, rested between his finger and thumb. He extended it to her.

"For me?" Confused, she cast a quick glance upward. His cool gaze watched her. Cautiously, she reached out to take it. "Why?"

"Mrn. Machblin guessed we'd fought. She thought I should make peace."

"And the flower? Was that her idea, too?"

"Does it matter?"

Hurt lodged in her throat. "It does," she snapped.

"The idea was mine," he returned, voice expressionless. "And I am sorry for my behavior last night."

"Thank you." A long moment elapsed. "Is our cover destroyed, then?"

"Mrn. Machblin seems to think all lovers quarrel."

"So it's okay, then." She felt relieved about that.

"Our fights must stop, Methusal. We need to make a plan so this does not happen again."

"We?"

A muscle clenched in his jaw. "*We* need to agree on a plan of action. Next time we might not be so lucky."

"I agree." She couldn't believe that he was going to treat her like a full partner with equal say now, but she'd assert as much as she could while she could. "Rule number one: No more manipulating me into uncomfortable situations, just because you're mad at me."

"Agreed. Rule number two: Watch your tongue. A man can only take so much."

"I'll try. Rule number three: You need to warn me in advance every time you plan to touch me."

"Impossible. Each situation will require different actions."

"I need a warning."

"You will not get one. Be prepared at all times. And do not run away from me again."

Methusal looked down. A rebellious lump caught in her throat, but she swallowed it back. "I can't take it."

"My attentions?"

"Yes! I feel wrong about it. I'm engaged to Behran. I feel like I'm doing something wrong when I allow you to...touch me, or kiss me."

"It is a cover. Make-believe. Nothing more."

"It's a whole lot more, and you know it."

In silence, that blue gaze meshed with hers. He didn't deny it. "Agree to my terms or we will have to scrap this mission."

Her jaw dropped. "It's not that serious!"

"It is," he said harshly. "We need a bullet proof cover, so we can spy and succeed in our mission. Our cover is vital to this whole plan. Have you forgotten the danger we are in right now? The danger to all of Koblan? I chose you because I thought you had the skills and determination to get this job done. You cannot balk every time I hold your hand or touch you."

Put in that light, Methusal realized how petty her complaints were. Just because she couldn't handle his kisses didn't mean she should jeopardize the mission. She had to pull herself together.

"You're right. I'm sorry."

A little of the tension relaxed out of his shoulders. "And I am sorry, as well. Much of the blame rests upon me."

She was surprised that he had admitted it.

His gaze held hers for a long moment. His acknowledgement of his fault in the matter created a new, tenuous feeling of peace between them. But many issues still needed to be resolved.

He said, "We need to settle one last thing. I know it is difficult for you to live in close quarters with me. Sharing a room...and a bed."

"We are *not* sharing a bed."

"We will share a bed. The floor is a miserable place to sleep. I will not sleep there again."

"Then I will."

"You get little sleep on the floor. That affects your mood, your concentration, and your ability to perform your job. You will not sleep on the floor again."

"I'm fine on the floor."

"Speak the truth, Methusal."

"I don't like it, but I'll survive," she insisted.

"And that is why you were crying last night."

"I was crying because..." she stopped, unwilling to admit that he could hurt her.

"Because of the hard floor."

"Yes, the floor, but not just that. It was everything. You do it on purpose, don't you? Admit it, you like to make me miserable."

"That is not logical. Why would I deliberately jeopardize our mission?"

"I don't understand how your mind works. All I know is that you've hated me for the last three years. Don't deny it. I know it. That's why this situation is intolerable. I feel like you *enjoy* needling under my skin. That you want to upset me. You say it's not about revenge, but I don't believe you."

"You still believe that I want to hurt you?" Disbelief roughened his voice.

In mute affirmation, she stared back.

"*Methusal.*" That low grate sounded pained. He looked away for a moment, as if trying to collect his thoughts. Then he sat down on the edge of the bed, beside her. Alarmed, she curled her legs away from him.

"Give me your hand."

She looked at him with distrust.

"Give me your hand." The ice was back.

She complied, so her right hand, the one without the flower, lay on top of his open hand, palm to palm. Hers looked small and delicate against his large one with the square, calloused palm and long fingers. His strong fingers closed over hers. Her heart jumped at the contact, but she forced herself to remain still and endure his touch.

"Now, look at me," he commanded.

She met his cool gaze.

"Does this hurt?"

"No. Of course not."

"Could I hurt you?"

"If you tightened your fingers, I suppose you could." Apprehension kindled.

"Have I?"

The pressure of his hand around hers remained firm and steady.

"No."

"Will I?"

The icy eyes wouldn't let her go. Methusal bit her lip, unable to put a name to the fear besieging her.

"Will I?" he repeated more harshly.

"I...I hope not."

"I will not. Do I lie?"

"No. I know you hate liars."

"Have I kept my word to your father?"

"Yes."

"Will I keep my word to you?"

"Yes." She believed he would, to her surprise.

"I will not hurt you. And when I lie in this bed with you at night I promise I will not touch you."

She searched his eyes. He meant it. He was telling the truth. She licked her lips. "Okay."

"That issue is settled. I do not want to speak of it again."

Had she just agreed to lie in this bed with him at night? Methusal felt a small flare of panic. "I can't."

"You still do not trust me?"

It wasn't that. "I just..."

"I said I will not harm you." That blue gaze was so sharp and intense it burned. "I swear," he said, low and vehemently, "I will never hurt you again."

A different promise. A deeper one, and a promise for forever. She could barely believe he'd offered it. Was this a turning point in their relationship? Voice a little shaky, she said, "You swear?"

"I swear by my word, and on my life."

The deepest oath he could possibly make. His gaze did not waver from hers. He meant it. She drew a small breath. For the first time, she actually believed him.

"You don't want to hurt me."

"That is not my purpose."

"Then what is?"

He released her hand and stood. It appeared to be a subtle emotional withdrawal. "To win this war."

That wasn't his whole purpose. "Why do you want peace with *me*, specifically?"

Unknown thoughts flickered. "I will tell you one day, Methusal. When you are ready to hear it."

"Why not now?"

"Fear still lives in your eyes," he said, his voice harsh. "When it is gone, I will tell you."

"That implies trust."

"Yes. Trust between both of us."

So he didn't trust her completely, either. Coming from a man like him, who lived behind layers of self-protective ice, that shouldn't surprise her.

He said, "You will need to trust me for our missions, as well. Will you?"

Last night flashed back. While he may not want to hurt her, it seemed unlikely that their relationship would become all sweetness and sunshine now. His personality was too strong—and so was hers, she had to admit. They would continue to butt heads.

Any peace with him would have to be a delicate balancing act. She still didn't know why he wanted peace with her, or what his plans were for all of Koblan. So she would need to remain wary, until she knew every last detail of it. But she did want peace, and she would strive for peace, as the Prophet had advised.

She said, "I'll try. As long as you agree not to manipulate me."

"Then you will agree to watch your tongue."

"I'll do my best."

"Then get dressed. We have work to do today."

"Yes, sir."

He shot her an unreadable glance. "Do not test me, please. I will keep my word to your father, and to you, but all other areas remain gray. Do you understand?"

"Yes," After a second, she added, "And thank you for last night."

Mentàll's posture relaxed. "I am not as cold as you want to believe, Methusal."

He left her alone with the blood red flower still in her hand. It's heavy, sweet fragrance drifted to her nose and she dipped her head and inhaled deeply. A full, rich, intoxicating scent.

She found a glass, filled it with water from the relief room, and placed the flower on the stand next to the bed. Maybe Mentàll was a dangerous, inscrutable man, but he had chosen a beautiful flower. He had good taste.

△ △ △ △ △

Dawn spread a deep pink canopy over the top of the Tarst Range. Aali sewed up her pack as the light slowly brightened the chilly morning. The water skin could not be salvaged.

Dastn moved around camp, silently readying for the day's trip. He shared his grain discs and dried meat with her for breakfast, and she drank from the stream.

She rued last night's unfortunate events. That horrible wild beast. Why did he have to eat her food and ruin her water skin? What if Dastn insisted on returning to Tarst? Of course she wouldn't go with him, but could she make it to Quasr with no food or water?

Dastn headed down the rocky hill. He was very quiet today. Maybe he wasn't a morning person.

The silence felt unnatural. She wondered if he was still mad at her.

"Where are you going?" she asked.

He eyed her with a frown. "Quasr. You're foolish and stubborn enough to go there on your own. I don't want your death on my conscience."

"Thanks!" Aali glared. So she'd get her way. However, she suspected Dastn would extract a price for it. Her suspicions proved correct.

He set a hard pace. Harder than yesterday. After they crossed the river, she had to run to keep up. But she didn't complain. She wouldn't give him the satisfaction. And she didn't talk to him, either.

The slug monster. The whip beast. She was very disappointed in him for behaving in such a mean, unforgiving manner.

△ △ △ △ △

"One man is dead, Presidente. He was killed between Dakarra and Carachki." The young sergeant held his shoulders stiffly at attention. It wasn't often that a low ranking officer delivered a report to the Presidente of Zindedi.

The Presidente fingered his cigar, and then drew a steady puff. "And the two who killed him? The soldier is sure of the description. A blond-haired giant and a woman."

"Yes. The Commander questioned him at length. It is all in his report."

With slow, deliberate movements, the Presidente creased the white parchment into benign folds. He wanted to viciously crush it into a wad and fling it across the room. However, he would display no temper to this young pup. He wanted to appear strong, and to inspire terror in his subordinates. Having an apoplectic fit would not serve his purposes well. His secretary occasionally saw them. Yalin could not hide his flash of pity, mixed with terror, when he came in while the Presidente shoved books and precious valuables—everything onto the floor, just to release the fury that occasionally overcame him.

Incompetence. That was the problem. He had to deal with incompetent fools! Why hadn't his men found the foul Dehrien and his whore yet?

He did not believe the Koblanis were married. Fiercely bitter enemies could never make peace. As he should well know. That was why he'd ordered the execution of every eastern Zindedi who had opposed him. Instead, he believed the Dehrien was using the Rolbani woman for his own purposes. When the Presidente found the two of them, he would use that division between them. He would crack it wide in order to defeat them both. And then all of Koblan's lush ore mines would be his. After that, the world...

Visions of power, glory, and being lavished with the worship and adulation of thousands upon thousands of people swelled his heart with joy. One day, everyone would see how great he was. They would say he was brilliant beyond description. They would fawn over him. He would be the most important and powerful man in the world.

It was what he deserved.

The sergeant made a tiny, nervous sound in his throat. He eyed the Presidente with confusion.

The Zindedi Presidente scowled, and felt the violent urge to put his thick fingers around the soldier's thin neck and squeeze until his eyes bugged out and he fainted in terror. He would allow no young pups to look at him as though he was insane...or worse, beneath them, and an object of their pity.

"Straighten up, soldier." He used his gentlest, calmest voice, but allowed a gravelly rasp to add sinister depth. Fine acting was one of his best skills. With it, he pretended to feel affection, so those closest to him would run to do his bidding. Sometimes his control slipped, however.

This young pup would see none of that. Instead, he would run, shaking with terror, back to his Commander. Fear would impart urgency to his words. The Commander would understand that the Presidente's orders must be carried out and fulfilled immediately. Failure would mean immediate death.

The Presidente's lips curled up into a false smile. Inside, he focused his fury into a hot, consuming ball of menace and stared at the soldier through narrowed, burning eyes. The sergeant blinked rapidly. A faint flush crept up his neck.

Pleased, the Presidente leaned forward and laced his fingers together. "I have words for your Commander."

"Yes, sir?" The words wavered.

"Come to the desk, so you may hear me distinctly."

He hesitated, face going very white, but obeyed.

The Presidente chuckled, and as quick as a whip, grabbed the soldier's starched shirt front and yanked him down, bent double over the desk. Round pebbles of stark terror stared straight into the Presidente's eyes. Good. Further satisfaction oozed. His other hand went for the sergeant's throat. One thick finger pressed in, hard beneath the point of the jaw, and his thumb did the same on the other side. He pressed in harder and harder, and then squeezed with all of his considerable strength.

The sergeant gagged. Choked breaths gurgled in his throat. The sensations and sounds were so satisfying that the Presidente didn't want to stop. But when the soldier's eyes rolled back in terror, he realized he had become distracted. The fool must be able to keep two thoughts together while he listened to the Presidente's important message.

He loosened his fingers, just a bit, and was pleased to see pure terror stare right back at him.

Softly, he said, "Tell your Commander I want the Dehrien and his slut found before the week is out."

"Yeth, sir," the sergeant gulped.

The Presidente smiled. A beautiful, satisfying plan had just come to him. "Do not capture them," he directed. "Instead, report their movements, and where they're staying. The next move will be mine."

Almost as an afterthought, he shoved the soldier away. The sergeant's hands went straight for his red throat, which still showed white marks from the Presidente's fingers. Harsh gasps trembled through that strong young frame.

The Presidente smiled in satisfaction. The strong dominated the weak. He was still in his prime, and the soldier, a mere boy. To be pitied, really.

"Go!"

"Yes, sir!" Snapping a sloppy salute, the sergeant stumbled from the room.

Chuckling softly, the Presidente sat back in his comfortable chair and laced his hands over his thick middle. Ah, yes. Victory tasted sweet. And blood, even better. The Commander would find the Koblani scum; of this, he had no doubt. And then...then, he would devise the slow, pleasurable retributions he would extract from each of his enemies.

Another idea illumined his mind and he chuckled again. Yes. Let them believe they were still free. All the while, he'd bait the perfect trap with sweet enticements. Too stupid to resist, they would be simple prey, unable to resist all the tortures he would order. A small giggle burbled from his chest. It sounded maniacal, even to his own ears. Ah, well. At least no one else had heard him.

All of the details would come to him in time. They always did. Usually in his best dreams.

△ △ △ △ △

A little later, Methusal joined Mentàll in the dining room for the hot breakfast Mrn. M had just cooked. Their landlady bustled in and out of the kitchen, carrying fragrant, piping hot dishes to the table. She'd already refused Methusal's help. "You're on vacation," she fussed. "Just relax and enjoy each other."

Methusal glanced at Mentàll. *Enjoying* each other was a stretch. However, Mrn. M couldn't know that. At the same time, the Zindedi woman *did* know they'd had a fight. She couldn't hide the worried little frowns she cast them every time she hurried into the room.

Methusal wasn't sure how to feel at ease with Mentàll. Their new agreement felt uncomfortable. It signaled a new start to their relationship, but she still didn't know what he wanted, or how far to trust him.

Could he really just want her for herself? Methusal shook her head.

"You don't want fried meat?" Voice puzzled, Mrn. M put down the meat platter.

Methusal drew a quick breath. She'd lost track of what was happening around her.

Mentàll glanced over, his gaze sharp, but unreadable.

"Um. I think I will, after all."

"What will you do today?"

"Stroll the city. Perhaps have a late lunch somewhere." Mentàll directed a slow, lazy smile at Methusal. "We will go anywhere Midi wants to go."

Mrn. M raised her eyebrows. "A good deal if I've ever heard one. Take advantage of it, Midi."

"I'll see how many dascals Lozar has. Then I'll know how many I can spend," she said with an arch, sweet smile at her fake husband.

His eyes narrowed, but his smile lingered, approving of the banter. Mrn. M seemed to approve, too, because her expression softened, and her worried looks disappeared.

A little while later, they left the house.

"What will we really do today?"

"Spy on the base." He set off in that direction, strides long and quick.

She hurried to keep up. "All day?"

"No. I want to see if more carts or troops have arrived. Afterward, we'll spy on the docks."

"So we won't actually go on the base."

"No."

She felt relieved. "We have eight more days until the ball. What are our goals? We can only spy so much. We know where the weapons are, and when they plan to sail for Koblan. What more can we do?"

Grimly, he said, "We will continue to spy, and make sure the Presidente does not change his mind and order the mission moved up. I also want to keep watch on all powder that leaves the base. We'll need to follow it to their destinations."

"So we can blow it up?"

"If necessary."

"I'd think that getting the invitations to the ball would be our most important goal," Methusal said.

"Perhaps."

"If we want the Presidente to sign the peace agreement..."

"He will not sign the agreement."

"Then why are we going to the ball?" A horrible thought struck her. "Do you plan to kill him?"

"No. Another would take his place. I will present the peace agreement. He will have plenty of time to look it over while explosions shake Zindedi."

"Then what?"

His lips curled back into a hard, unpleasant smile. "Then he will come to Koblan and beg for peace."

"He'll come to *Koblan*?" Methusal wondered if Mentàll had lost his mind. "We don't want that madman on our soil!"

"The peace agreement states that if he wants peace, he must come to Koblan. He will come."

"So, it *is* about power." Surprise, surprise. "If he submits to your demands..."

"It will prove his humility. It will prove he fears Koblan and our power to hurt him."

"It will prove he fears *you*. But that thought pleases you, doesn't it?"

"It does."

"What if he tries to trick you?"

"Then he will die."

Methusal gasped. "You *are* a wild beast."

His gave her a thin smile. "I never said that I have changed, Methusal. Only that I will never harm you."

"But you just said if you killed him, another would take his place."

"True. But that man will understand the consequences of treachery."

"You'd start another war."

That hard gaze held hers. "We have war now. We risk nothing."

Put that way, it did make sense. Scary, that she'd come to agree with Mentàll on any point of brutality. What did that say about her?

△ △ △ △ △

Aali's legs burned and her feet blazed with blisters. At last, Dastn decided to stop for lunch. He perched on a boulder and pulled out his food. She waited, feeling like a begging pet apte, for her portion. Why wait, she wondered suddenly. His water skin was sitting right there.

She scooped it up and gulped thirstily.

Dastn pulled it none too gently from her hands. "That water has got to last us all the way to Quasr."

Tears stung her eyes. Suddenly, it was all too much. "You're such a slug! I hate you. *I hate you!*" Her chin wobbled and she turned her back on him. She crossed her arms.

"You know how to push a man to the brink, Aali."

"You know how to behave like a whip beast!"

"Take some food." His voice sounded gentler.

She grabbed a grain disc from his hand and sat on a boulder far away. The food was so dry that her mouth burned with thirst by the end.

Dastn appeared in her side vision. "Time to go."

"I need a drink," she said frostily.

"A sip," he agreed.

She took three and shoved it back. His eyes narrowed, but he said nothing. They set off again. Now the terrain was starting to look familiar. Aali recognized the twin peaks rising to the east. That meant Quasr lay to the northwest. As the hours wore on, she spied the distant outline of the coastal town.

She walked faster, anxious to leave Dastn behind. His cold, mean attitude hurt badly. She hated that he was mad at her.

Was it her fault that a wild beast had eaten all of her supplies? Was it her fault that he was forced to travel with her?

Well, maybe. But it hurt that he didn't want to travel with her. And it hurt that he'd barely spoken to her all day. Okay, she'd done the same to him. But it still hurt.

Tears blurred her eyes again. She hated him. Really, she did. She didn't know what she'd ever seen in him in the first place.

Just one more clump of boulders to climb over, and then they'd could cross the flatland to Quasr. Maybe forty more minutes. She climbed over the rough rocks and jumped down on the other side. She was going faster than Dastn, she thought with relish.

Perching for a second on a high boulder, she glanced back. He was three lengths behind her. What an oldie, climbing so carefully. He should know kaavl, like she did.

She slid down the boulder. Too late, she saw the long, narrow hunting pit in the earth below it. She tried to sprawl forward, to miss it, but her right foot fell in it, and her forward momentum wrenched at her leg. It all seemed to happen so slowly...her shin jammed...the awful snapping sound... Her scream of agony.

△ △ △ △ △

Spying had been boring, and largely a waste time, Methusal reflected as they headed back to Mrn. M's at dusk. Two new carts of powder had arrived on the base. From what she'd overheard, they'd come from a powder mine in eastern Zindedi. No powder had been loaded onto the ships yet.

Mentàll appeared satisfied with the day's work, but Methusal still felt that their main priority should be to steal official invitations, so they could go to the ball.

Although she wasn't entirely sure why Mentàll wanted to present the peace agreement in person to the Presidente, she had a guess. He wanted to confront his adversary face to face and, if possible, intimidate him. Part one of his ruthless plan to wrestle the entire Zindedi continent into submission to Koblan.

If it was anyone's plan but Mentàll's, she would laugh. But she knew, better than anyone else, not only the unbending determination that fueled the man, but the dark, cold-blooded side of him, too. No scruples—nothing would get in his way, once he'd set his mind on a goal. Nothing.

She sent him a wary glance. Nothing at all.

They approached Feldon Street.

He said, "Today I am giving you advance warning."

She shot him a look. "What do you mean?"

"Mrn. M is worried about us. If we do not soothe her concerns, they will build into suspicion."

Methusal swallowed. "Oh. So you plan to kiss me."

"Yes." Amusement flashed. "Are you pleased for the warning?"

She drew a fortifying breath. "Of course." She could do this. She *could*.

Mentàll suddenly grabbed her arm and drew her sideways, into the shelter of a clipped bush. Methusal did a quick visual carry around the corner, curious what he'd seen.

A gasp caught in her throat. General Fitrn was latching Mrn. M's gate shut! He headed their way.

"He's coming," she hissed.

Mentàll tugged his dark cap down harder over his white-blond hair and sagged backwards into the prickly bush. He was trying to appear shorter. "Come to me," he whispered. "Put your arms around my neck."

The General was almost upon them. Fear made it easy to press herself against Mentàll's hard chest and wrap her arms around his neck.

"Good," he murmured thickly. His arms came around her, holding her hard and secure against him. Her heart beat faster, and to her surprise, his heart thundered in slow, heavy beats, too. Ice blue eyes looked deep into hers. "Kiss me."

He dared her.

Her heart beat faster as she contemplated it. His straight lips were very near her own. What would it be like if she kissed him deliberately, of her own accord? Would the power switch to her, or would he pull her under, drowning her in a sea of feelings she didn't want?

General Fitrn's rapid steps passed behind them. The Dehrien Chief had managed to finagle their position so the Zindedi could only see the back of her head.

The Zindedi kept walking. He hadn't appeared to notice them at all. He wouldn't know if they had kissed or not.

It wasn't necessary. Relief flooded her.

Fitrn was gone now, around the corner, heading toward his house. Methusal pulled back from the Dehrien, but was unable to ignore how warm and disturbed she felt.

Mentàll drew a harsh breath and straightened. "You have won a reprieve, Methusal." He meant he still intended to kiss her.

Ignoring him, she headed fast for Mrn. M's house. Dusk pooled deep shadows beneath the trees lining the street.

"On her porch."

Her steps slowed.

Mentàll caught her hand and urged her through the gate, steps quick. He appeared eager to gain the porch. She'd felt the heat in him when he'd held her anchored tight against him. This kiss wouldn't be light and meaningless.

More unease flooded her as she followed him up the steps. She felt like a bride about to be ravaged by her eager husband. "Mentàll. Wait."

△ △ △ △ △

The pain in her leg was so intense that Aali couldn't think. She'd hurt it. She couldn't seem to think or feel anything beyond pain and shock.

"*Aali!* Oh, The One." The last sounded like an anguished prayer. Dastn knelt beside her, his face white beneath his tan. "Aali, are you all right?"

She stared at him, dazed. "My leg," she whispered.

"Don't move."

He nudged her calf, and a torrent of pain slammed through her again. She cried out. "Don't! Dastn, that hurts. Oww!" She wept uncontrollably.

"I'm sorry. Aali, honey, I need to move you a little."

More excruciating pain shot through her body, and then her foot was free. She lifted her head, and through her blurred vision saw that the bottom half of her right calf was bent at a strange angle.

"It's broken." Dastn sounded tense, but calm and soothing. "Don't move. I need to find some branches." He stood up.

"Don't leave me. Please!" she begged, hiccupping now.

"I have to, just for a minute. Be right back."

She had never known pain could be so intense. It went on and on, like a hot piece of ore drilling through her body.

"I'm back." Dastn knelt beside her and pulled a tunic from his pack. He sliced it into strips with his sharp knife. Then he gently felt her leg. She tried not to cry out. It was hard. She gulped back her sobs. She needed to be brave.

He looked at her, his eyes gentle. "You need to lie back and relax, hon. Here, I'll put my pack under your head."

"What are you going to do?" She was afraid.

"Doc showed me how to set broken bones during the war. I did it at least a half a dozen times. You've broken both bones in your calf. Both look like clean breaks. I can set them. Are you ready?" He sounded firm, matter-of-fact.

"Is it...is it going to hurt?" Her voice wobbled.

"Yes."

More tears spurted out, but she bit her lip, trying to stop them.

His large, warm palm brushed the hair out of her eyes. "I'm sorry," he whispered.

"Just do it," she choked out.

"Bite on this piece of leather."

Obediently, she let him slide the thick piece between her teeth. How bad could it be, she wondered, in a fog of pain. It was already broken.

Aali felt his hands on her calf, and then a quick movement. Blinding white pain flashed through her. She heard a scream, and then everything went blessedly black.

She awoke slowly. Her mind groped, searching for the pain. It was there, but not so bad now. She opened her eyes and stared up at Dastn. He sat close beside her. She felt his fingers stroking her hair.

"Welcome back." He smiled at her.

"Did you fix it...them?"

"Yes."

"Thank you." She lifted her head. Her leg was immobilized by several straight, thick branches secured by rows of tight leather strips.

"I'm sorry, Aali."

Surprised, she asked, "Why?"

"For being such a whip all day."

"Yeah. Why were you?" She grinned a little, to let him know she was joking.

He laughed, and his fingers stopped their delicious stroking sensation.

"You don't have to stop," she encouraged.

"Oh, you like that, do you? You must be feeling better." To her regret, his fingers fell away. He fell silent for a minute. "When I heard you scream, it scared me to death. I think that sound is going to haunt me forever."

"I've been a brat. I'm sorry. And I'm sorry I stalked you— I mean, followed you—to Quasr." She managed an impish grin.

"We're almost there." Dastn looked over his shoulder. "But you can't walk."

"Leave me here. Go get help." She didn't want to be left alone. But she had caused enough trouble already.

"I won't. Besides, it'll be dark soon."

He was right. The angle of the sun said twilight would arrive within the hour.

He gathered up both of their packs and strapped them on his back.

"What are you planning to do?" She sat up. Her leg burned with pain, but she tried to ignore it.

"Carry you." He easily scooped her up, with one arm beneath her knees and one at her back. "Put your arms around my neck."

She obeyed. The joy of being close to him far outweighed the discomfort in her leg. He felt solid, warm, and sturdy. "I'm too heavy," she protested.

"You're just a scrap, Aali."

Dastn walked slowly, picking his way over the remaining boulders. Soon they reached the desert floor, and he increased his pace.

Aali knew she must be getting heavy. "Put me down when you need a rest," she ordered.

He laughed softly into her hair. "Thanks for your concern. But I'm okay."

He carried her all the way to Quasr. She couldn't believe it. He must be exhausted, she thought, as he walked through the courtyard of the Quasr Chief's compound. It was a tropical paradise, with tall, lush trees, and flowering plants in pots. The warm, sweet scent of fresh flowers teased her nostrils.

Dastn set her down on a bench. "Stay here. I'll get the Chief."

Amazed, she looked around after he'd left. How could such a beautiful place exist in the middle of the desert?

"Hi." A dark-haired little girl appeared at her elbow.

"Hi," Aali grinned. The little girl looked like she was about six years old, and had the palest blue eyes she'd ever seen. They looked startling, paired with her dark hair. "Who are you?"

"I'm Trori. Who are you?"

"Aali. I'm from Rolban."

"I'm from here. My daddy is the Chief."

"Nice to meet you, Trori."

"What happened to your leg?"

Aali grinned. She loved kids. Probably because she still felt like one sometimes. "I was dumb and broke it."

"Did Dastn save you?"

"Yes."

"Dastn's my friend."

"Mine, too."

"I have a brother. He's two," Trori said. "Do you want to meet him? Oh, here comes my daddy."

A short, dark-haired man approached with Dastn. His eyes were a dark, cordial gray. "I'm Calbn, Chief of Quasr. I understand you're Erl's niece?"

"Yes."

"Looks like you'll be staying with us awhile. You'll be our guest. Dastn will show you to your room, and I'll send for the doctor."

She felt dismayed. "Thank you. But I can't stay here. I have to go home."

Dastn said, "That's impossible. You can't walk. The doctor will get you crutches, but you can't walk for three days to get home."

Aali felt even more dismayed. "But my father will wonder where I am!"

"I'll leave here tomorrow. I'll go to Rolban first and tell him."

She stared at the two men, still trying to wrap her head around this new development. "You mean I'll have to stay here until my leg heals? How long will that take?"

"At least eight weeks."

"Eight weeks!" she said, horrified. She'd come all this way, and now her leg was broken. Not only couldn't she sneak around and spy like she had planned, but she'd be housebound. And alone in a strange place, and living with strangers. Even worse, her sixteenth birthday was tomorrow. She hadn't planned out this mission very well at all. She loved her birthday. And no one here would know it. Dastn didn't know. No presents. No laughter, no teasing. No party. An empty pit opened up in her soul.

Sudden hope flashed. "What about an urchet?" She pleaded to the Quasrian Chief. "It could carry me home."

"I am sorry. We have none to spare."

"It's not the end of the world," Dastn said. "Chief Calbn and his family are very nice. You'll feel right at home in no time."

"Of course. I appreciate them letting me stay. It's just... I didn't expect this."

Chief Calbn inclined his head. "You're welcome to join my family for meals. I have business to attend. If you'll excuse me." He gave her a curt nod and strode away.

Trori touched Aali's arm. "We can be friends." Her hopeful grin looked like sunshine, and Aali smiled back.

"I'd like that," she said softly.

△ △ △ △ △

Hendra stared out the window at the deepening dusk and mist swirling across the panes and hugged her arms tighter against herself, trying to ignore the worry nagging at her.

Where could Doc be? Why hadn't he and Goric returned yet?

Behind her, Sozla giggled at something Behran had said. They believed they were finally close to discovering how to make the self-igniting detonator work. Dark head and light one were close together, murmuring words as they tinkered with the delicate mechanism they were trying to create.

Hendra and Deccia had gone to town earlier and bought supplies, including parchment, so Deccia could try to copy the military papers and invitations. Laundry had occupied the rest of the empty day.

Doc had been gone for two days now. He and Goric had left yesterday morning to search for the biggest powder deposit. Riln and Tabor had disappeared shortly afterward for parts unknown, apparently assigned a new, secret mission by Mentàll.

Only five people remained at the cabins. It was quiet. Too quiet. Not that Hendra missed Riln's outbursts, of course. But she did miss Doc. Worry for him felt like an ache in her heart. Now she understood what Deccia felt like when Timaeus traveled the long distance alone to Carachki.

Hendra had eaten an early dinner, because soon she and Behran would scout the base.

Darkness deepened over the landscape, and drops of mist clung to the fogged over windowpane. She shivered. She didn't look forward to going out into the freezing damp.

Behran appeared beside her, shrugging on his coat. "Ready?"

"I guess."

He fixed his collar with his thumb. "We won't stay out all night. Just until lights out."

"Okay."

After saying their goodbyes, they went. Cold, misty air slid inside the crevices of Hendra's jacket, and damp grasses slapped at her pant legs, soaking them. The chill damp clung to her skin, icing her legs from the ankles up. Ryon was at its quarter; a thin, pale stream of green light over the wild landscape.

Behran led the way. Hendra's cheeks and nose felt colder by the moment, and she kept her hands in her pockets. Doc and Goric must be out in this cold damp, too. Only they wouldn't sleep under a warm, dry roof tonight. They'd probably shiver in misery all night long. She wondered if they had found the other powder deposit yet.

By the time her ears went numb, they'd reached the forested hill near the military base.

Behran blew on his cupped hands. "Not many people are out."

A few soldiers patrolled the compound, and lights blazed from the dining hall. A cluster of soldiers smoked outside. Maybe they were saying something important.

A little excitement energized Hendra's spirits. "Let's spy near the dining hall."

"You do that. I'll circle around the base to see what else is going on."

Behran split left, and Hendra went right, carefully following the tree line downhill to the plain. Few bushes covered this sandy, grassy land. She didn't relish the idea of crawling on her belly the thirty lengths to the base. Crawling would have to do. At least her hair color blended in with the grain colored grass.

Within moments her knees and the lower half of her pants were soaked, and sand trickled into her boots. Gritty sand scratched her hands and had found its way up the cuffs of her jacket, too.

Ignoring the chilly discomfort, she crept closer to the dining hall, which was located in the southeastern corner of the base. Ten lengths away, she sank down to a belly crawl and wiggled closer.

Tall, damp grasses waved above her head. She was soaked from head to toe, and freezing. Shuddering, she lay still and listened. Foul smelling smoke teased her nostrils. It smelled like burnt, rotting weeds.

"Too many men," grumbled one soldier.

"I get to visit home soon," said another.

Slapping sounds. "I miss your sweet Aldina," smirked another. "She knows how to send a man off."

Coarse guffaws followed this crude remark.

Hendra rolled her eyes. She'd crawled through the mud to hear this?

"When are we leaving?"

"When the Commander says so."

"Isn't the General coming back first?"

"Maybe. He wants to catch his pretty firefly. He's iced about what happened."

"I heard he's coming back for sure," said another. "He's the escort for the powder to Carachki."

"When're we moving that?"

"Who knows?" And who cared, appeared to be the man's attitude.

While taking deep puffs of their smokesticks, the men mumbled about the tough discipline the Commander had enforced after General Fitrn's visit. The putrid clouds drifted Hendra's way. The smell was disgusting.

The conversation turned to card games and gambling their paychecks, and then they wandered inside.

Hendra continued to wait and listen, but heard nothing more of importance from the few men who wandered in and out of the dining hall.

Her teeth chattered from cold, and she wondered where Behran was.

It seemed like she'd been lying in the mud for hours. Maybe she should head for the hills. Though she'd be just as cold there.

"Hendra." The soft whisper came from behind her. Behran crawled through the grass ten lengths away. She turned and crawled out to meet him. It was a relief to go up on her hands and knees, and then crouch low and run up the hill to the protective tree line.

She shuddered uncontrollably now.

"Run," Behran advised. "It'll warm you up."

So they ran back to the cabin. In her room, Hendra stripped off her wet clothes, put on new pants and two dry tunics, wrapped a blanket around her, and hurried to the warm kitchen, teeth still chattering.

Deccia handed her a cup of tea, and then delivered one to Behran at the table. "Did you learn anything?"

Behran shook his head and wrapped both hands around his mug and lifted it to his face. It steamed gently.

"The General will return," Hendra reported. "The soldiers said he'll escort the powder to Carachki." She didn't care that the tea burned her tongue. The hotness felt good sliding down her cold throat.

"Wonder when that will be," Deccia mused. She moved to the table, where parchments lay in neat stacks.

"Have you finished the military papers?"

"One set. They're long—two pages each. And I copied the invitations, too. But I'm not sure if they're good enough."

"What do you mean?"

"I couldn't copy that raised ink."

Hendra compared the original documents with Deccia's copies. "I can't tell the difference," she said with admiration. "As long as they don't touch the paper, it'll be fine."

"Thank you." Deccia looked pleased. "Now just five sets of military papers to go."

Her words reminded Hendra of the four men still missing from the cabins.

"Are you all right?" Deccia asked.

"I hope Doc and the others get home soon. It's going to be a cold, miserable night."

"They'll make a fire to keep warm."

Hendra kept her worries to herself, and sipped more hot tea.

The tea kettle whistled. Deccia touched her shoulder as she got up. "I know how you feel," she said in a low voice. "It's a sick kind of worry. You're afraid a piece of you will never come home."

Surprised, Hendra glanced at her.

Compassion lurked in the other girl's green eyes. "It's hard, isn't it, when our hearts and our heads tell us two different things?"

She nodded.

"Pray. It's the only thing that helps."

Hendra did. When she went to bed, she prayed fervently for Doc and his safety, and for the broken pieces of her own heart. While her heart was damaged now, it would be shattered beyond repair if she never saw him again. This, she knew for a fact.

△ △ △ △ △

Mentàll tugged Methusal up onto the lighted porch. A glance through the kitchen window showed Mrn. M busily whipping batter in a bowl. "The perfect position," he murmured. "When she looks out, she will see us."

Heat lingered in his eyes, melting their color to a scorching silver blue. Methusal's heart beat faster. Behran was right. The Dehrien did appear to desire her. She needed to cool him down. Their last kiss, before leaving for Dakarra, had undone her. She needed to break the tension between them.

"Let's ask Mrn. M about the General."

"After I kiss you," he murmured.

"Maybe he discovered that we live here. Maybe he'll be back with an army of soldiers."

"After I kiss you, we will find out." He pulled her into his arms, tugging her close to his hard chest.

She glared. "You drive me absolutely crazy."

His eyes glittered. "I am sorry."

"No, you're not."

"I am," he said softly. His hands fanned up her back, and then down, in gentle, soothing caresses, as if he sensed how agitated she felt. An alarming warmth stole through her.

"I hate you." To her chagrin, the words lacked conviction. Even more alarming, a warm sensation pooled, deep within her, fueled by every stroke of his hands.

"I know you hate being in my arms. You hate it when I kiss you." His breath teased her lips.

She licked them. "Yes. Yes, that's right."

Still, his hands soothed her skin. With each stroke, a nameless longing quivered, deep within her.

He moved closer, as if to kiss her, but his mouth moved by without touching her. Methusal involuntarily arched toward him, until she realized what she was doing.

His heavy-lidded eyes gleamed. "Yes, I can see that is true."

"Stop it." She felt flushed.

"I can't. Mrn. M is watching." His mouth hovered a hair's breadth from hers.

A quick glance proved he was right. "Oh," she said breathlessly.

"You see?" he whispered. His lips touched hers and she helplessly closed her eyes at the delicious sensation of it.

His lips lingered on hers, moving by the barest degrees over the sensitive skin. Her fingers curled tight into his shoulders. Wanting more than he gave her, she imperceptibly leaned into his kiss. A guttural sound erupted from his throat and his arms tightened around her. Tension hardened his frame, but still his touch remained gentle.

Time seemed to stop while his lips feathered magic over her own. Heat suffused her every pore, and an unknowable, frustrated longing grew as his kiss lingered, brushing her mouth, teasing her again and again. How long could it go on, she wondered hazily. How long could she endure his velvet caresses before she lost her mind?

A little sob caught in her throat. "Mentàll."

"Hmm?" he murmured, leisurely exploring each corner of her mouth.

Methusal felt desperate. She didn't know how long she could take this without...without...

"Our cover," she said incoherently, and opened her eyes.

His slightly unfocussed gaze told her that he'd forgotten both Mrn. M and their cover. That blue gaze sharpened.

"Enough," she said, desperate to push free from him. Her whole body trembled. She needed to be free of him, and she needed to be free *now*.

He released her. But before she could take a step, his large, warm hand enveloped hers. Of course. Their cover. He opened the door for her. Warmth, and the aroma of baking muffins and simmering meat flooded out to meet them. Scents of home.

Methusal wanted to break free from his grasp, but that would be foolish. They had kissed for a reason.

Mrn. M exited from the kitchen, wiping floury fingers on a towel. With a tiny, approving smile, she eyed Methusal's flushed cheeks. "Did you have a good day?"

"Wonderful," Mentàll said, above her. Charm himself, as usual. "Dinner smells delicious."

Mrn. M dimpled. "I've put a pie in. It'll be warm for dinner."

"Thank you," he murmured.

"Go and relax." She waved a white dusted hand. "I'll call you when it's ready."

As soon as their landlady disappeared inside the kitchen, Methusal pulled her hand free. She couldn't look at him, or remember his kisses. She didn't want to think about her moral failure again to Behran. To herself. She walked quickly to a chair and snatched up a newspaper.

Something *had* to be wrong with her. It had to be. How else could she enjoy the kisses of a man who had been a thorn in her side for three years?

But for the first time, she realized that she was grasping for reasons to vilify him. He wasn't a saint, true. But the real problem was with *herself.* Why did she keep responding to him? Behran was the man she'd chosen; the man she loved.

His harsh voice spoke above her. "Methusal."

She found she couldn't speak to him.

A blur of movement alerted her that he'd crouched beside her. "Methusal."

"Please leave me alone."

He remained silent for a long moment, and then rose. "I will speak to Mrn. M about renting our room for another week."

"Okay."

She sat quietly after he left. At long last, she admitted the truth to herself. She did respond every time he kissed her. In fact, she always had—from the sleepwalking kiss when he'd hated her, until now.

She did not know why. She didn't understand herself, not one bit. That frightened her, but at the same time she was tired of feeling afraid of her emotions. Running from them hadn't solved anything. In fact, it was creating more problems.

Maybe it would help if she tried to think about this logically. She could compare the two men in her life.

Mentàll and Behran were as different as night and day, and so were her feelings for each of them. Behran was her anchor in the storm. Mentàll *was* the storm. He was elemental, and some primitive part of her did respond to him.

It disturbed her to admit it, but perhaps she was physically attracted to Mentàll. Without question, he was a handsome, powerful man. But physical attraction alone meant nothing. What counted were love and commitment. She had chosen Behran because he was the man she loved.

The simple, disturbing fact was, Mentàll would continue to kiss her here in Carachki, and she would continue to respond to him. She did not have to like it. But perhaps she could accept it and endure it. And then, when the time here was finished, she would put it behind her, forget it, and move on with her commitment and upcoming marriage to Behran.

This logical plan gave her a measure of peace, and soothed a bit of the guilt in her soul. She may not have to like that she responded to Mentàll, but she did not have to let it destroy her, either.

And Behran was right: The Dehrien Chief did desire her. It seemed foolish to deny it, when faced with the proof moments ago.

So, he desired a base union with her. In and of itself, that meant nothing. But the reason he *allowed* himself to desire her—that was what worried her.

From their long, uncomfortable relationship she'd learned one fact well—the Dehrien followed no course of action without cold, hard logic backing it. Yes, he wanted her, but probably for a reason beyond bodily gratification. He was a complex man, and she'd be a fool take his advances at face value—as if he desired her, the person, and not for how she might further his goals.

What could he want from her?

He wanted her to desire him, too.

This flash of intuition made her sink back in the chair and think harder. He desired her, and she responded to him. Her failings to both herself and Behran would continue unless she could somehow gain control of this situation.

Another, more dangerous thought surfaced. Could she possibly turn the knowledge of his desire—his possible weakness—to her own advantage?

She didn't like the idea. It reeked of dishonesty and manipulation. However, she did know that some women did use a man's desire as a means to wield power over him. Even as her heart skittered rapidly at the prospect, Methusal wondered if she could do it. Could she be that coldly manipulative? The idea of wielding any sort of power over him enticed unbearably. But could she separate her mind and emotions when he kissed her? If she could somehow gain some sort of advantage over him—any advantage— perhaps then he would let down his guard, and she could discover what he truly wanted from her, and from Koblan.

Her heart beat unsteadily as she contemplated the plan. She wanted to try. How else could she finally get the answers she needed? But she would need to wait for the perfect opportunity, when he was weak, or tired or discouraged. ...If that ever happened.

She tried to ignore an uncomfortable, niggling feeling of guilt. She must do it. For Koblan. Learning the truth of the Dehrien's plans would benefit her entire continent. And it would benefit her relationship with Behran, too. If she could succeed in this new plan, then the little game Mentàll had started would finally end.

△ △ △ △ △

The Quasr doctor complimented Dastn on how well he had set Aali's broken leg. "With this new clay cast, you'll be as good as new in no time," the white haired doctor promised Aali. "Stay off of it as much as possible. And take these herbs after dinner. They'll help with the pain, and will help you sleep, too."

Aali took the pouch, and Dastn helped her maneuver upright and grab the crutches. Slowly, she limped down the hall beside him.

The aroma of roasted meat and fresh baked bread welcomed them into the dining hall. Trori, Calbn, and a dark-haired little boy sat at the long table. A petite, hugely pregnant woman entered from a hallway on the other side of the dining room. Her dark hair wisped around her tired face, but she smiled when she saw them.

"Hello, Dastn. And you must be Aali. I'm Lylitha, Calbn's wife."

Aali smiled in return. "Hi! Nice to meet you."

"It's a shame about your leg. Here. You two sit here, between Calbn and Trori."

Dastn pulled out Aali's chair and deposited her crutches against the wall a few lengths away.

"Thank you for letting me stay." She included both Calbn and Lylitha in her smile. "But I don't want to be a burden. Please tell me what I can do to help while I'm here."

Lylitha glanced at her husband. He frowned, but said nothing. She turned to Aali. "Perhaps you would help me with Trori and Rartn? Trori is very taken with you. And I get very tired these days. I can't seem to keep up."

"I'd be happy to," Aali assured her. She grinned at Trori, and the little girl grinned back.

"Good." Lylitha looked relieved.

A woman in a servant's uniform hurried up and muttered to Lylitha, "*She* wants you. Now."

Lylitha's mouth drooped down at the corners, and she clumsily pushed back her chair and stood. "Please excuse me."

Aali watched her waddle down the same hall she had emerged from earlier. She wondered why someone would call for her in the middle of dinner.

The food was delicious. She gobbled up every morsel on her plate. Good thing she would be running—or hobbling—after the kids. Otherwise she'd get fat in no time on the Quasrian food.

"You're eating like a starved apte," Dastn said with a small smile.

Indignantly, she said, "I've trekked miles today, Dastn. Or have you forgotten already? I didn't know memory loss could start so young."

He chuckled. "Good to see your spirit isn't broken. You'll be okay here?"

"Yes, of course." She met his serious gaze. "Thank you for asking."

His reply was cut off by a loud crash of pottery. It came from the hallway down which Lylitha had disappeared. A servant woman scuttled out.

"And don't come back until it's *right,*" screamed a querulous voice. A door slammed.

The servant woman scurried into the nearby kitchen, clutching a tray of broken pottery. Then she hurried back out with a mop and towel.

What in the world...?

"It's Great-Grandmother," Trori said. She matter-of-factly poked another bite into her mouth. "She's having a fit."

"A fit? Is she dangerous?"

"Not usually. Just don't get too close," the little girl advised.

A great-grandmother who threw fits? What kind of a household was this? She glanced at Dastn, but he shook his head. "First time I've heard of it."

She quietly ate her food, straining to hear more of the drama down the hall. All she heard was an irritable voice raised in complaint. Gradually, the indignant screeches quieted. A fresh tray was delivered, and finally Lylitha returned to the table. Perspiration dampened her forehead, and her expression looked pinched. Aali decided it wouldn't be polite to mention the incident.

Dinner finished, she contemplated her bag of herbs. Her leg throbbed now. "How much should I take?" she wondered. The doctor had neglected to tell her.

"Just a bit," Lylitha said. "Let me show you." Aali handed her the pouch, and the Quasrian woman pinched just a tiny bit between her thumb and finger and dropped it into Aali's water cup. "This will help you sleep until morning."

But Dastn would leave in the morning. How long would the herbs make her sleep? She couldn't let him leave without saying goodbye!

Lylitha said, as if reading her mind, "If you take it now, you won't oversleep. Dawn should awaken you."

Aali smiled. "Thank you." After she drank the herbs, she bid everyone goodnight, and Dastn retrieved her crutches. He patiently walked beside her as she hobbled to her room.

"'Night, Dastn." She turned, halfway in her doorway. "Thank you for everything."

"My pleasure." His eyes glinted. "Anything for a certain red-nosed, blond..."

"Red nose!" Offended, she glared and touched her nose. It stung like fire. She must look ridiculous. "You're laughing at me!"

"I'm not," he said with a grin.

"I'm burned and broken! How dare you?"

"Aali," he said contritely. "I..."

When she raised a hand to halt his pathetic apology, one crutch crashed to the floor. She wobbled dangerously.

His strong hand caught her arm and steadied her. With a swift move, he retrieved the crutch and tucked it again under her armpit. "You really do need a hat," he said softly, looking down at her. He stood very close now, and her heart beat faster.

"Guess I didn't plan very well."

"Guess not." That brown gaze held hers for another moment, and then his warm hand released her arm. "Goodnight."

"'Night."

With a small smile, he left her. Aali watched him go, her heart thumping. She definitely needed to wake up in time to see him off tomorrow. After all, he was probably the last friend she'd see for weeks.

The herbs were already making her feel sleepy. She shut the door and readied for bed. On the soft cot, she closed her eyes with a sigh. Dastn was so strong. Maybe he could carry her all the way back to Rolban. She giggled at the thought, and drifted into a world where even the unlikely was possible.

∆ ∆ ∆ ∆ ∆

At dinner, Mentàll casually brought up the matter of General Fitrn's visit. "How was your day, Mrn. M?"

"I've had better." Her tone belied her casual shrug.

"The flowers on the table are beautiful. Did they come from your garden?" Methusal was willing to bet they hadn't. The large, purple blooms looked bruised around the edges. They were light purple on the inside, and darkened to almost black on the edges. Their hostess seemed to prefer pink and orange flowers. Bright, cheerful hues.

Mrn. M's lips thinned. "The Presidente's son came by."

"General Fitrn?"

"Yes."

"What did he want?"

Mrn. M frowned. "Nothing much. Just nosing about, asking questions."

Mentàll spoke. "What kind of questions? Was he bothering you?" He sounded concerned, and this earned him a faint smile.

"He doesn't listen very well. He thinks I have information I don't have." Her scowl deepened. "And it's his fault I don't."

"What do you mean?"

Mrn. M blinked rapidly. "My daughter ran away because of him. I don't know where she is. She's safer that way."

"Oh." So the General was a predator. Not a surprise.

"He thinks I'm lying, of course."

The man was cruel. Troubled, Methusal said, "Has he threatened you? Do you think he'd hurt you?"

Mrn. M laughed, but it didn't sound happy. "He doesn't dare hurt me. His father would punish him severely. But make my life miserable? Yes. That he enjoys doing."

Casually, Mentàll said, "Does he come by often?"

"No. But I was foolish. I let him in because I thought he was delivering my invitation to the ball."

Methusal shot a quick glance at the Dehrien Chief. "Isn't the ball coming up soon? I thought you had already received your invitation."

"No." Mrn. M fiddled with her spoon. "Usually the Presidente delivers ours right away. But now that Charlie's dead... I guess I'm not so important to him anymore."

"I'm sorry."

"Oh, it's all right. We'll see what happens. The Presidente often likes to draw the suspense out to the last minute. Keeps people on the edge, wondering if they'll be invited. Or, if not, that's how they learn they're on his black list."

Methusal couldn't imagine Mrn. M being on anyone's black list. "He changes his mind so quickly about people?"

Mrn. M laughed softly. "He's mercurial, is the Presidente. But he's always done well by my husband and me."

"What sort of people does he invite, then? Just high ranking officers?"

"Oh, goodness, no. Prominent business men, or people who grant him special favors. Sometimes he invites a whole family, if someone has done something especially wonderful for Zindedi. On occasion, he invites people from the street—a direct slap in the face to those who aren't invited, but should be."

"How wonderful," Methusal murmured. "When do the invitations usually go out?"

"Soon," she predicted. "He'll send them to the mail distribution center. All except for a select few, of course. Those are hand delivered. I imagine those have already been delivered."

Methusal glanced at Mentàll. His glittering, sharp gaze said he was thinking the same thing she was; their opportunities for securing official invitations had just widened considerably.

△ △ △ △ △

It would be their first night to sleep together on the big bed.

After helping to wash the dinner dishes, Methusal reluctantly entered the room she shared with Mentàll. Slowly, she changed in the relief room, and then, even more slowly, exited.

Methusal eyed the bed, and then her fake husband sitting on the far side. She was certain he would keep his promise not to touch her. All the same, she nervously smoothed her high-necked nightgown. It would feel weird to crawl into bed with him sitting right there.

Behran would not be pleased with this arrangement. At all.

Without looking up, he said, "I will go to the relief chamber. You may go to bed first, if it will make you feel more comfortable."

"Yes. Thank you."

He did so, and she slipped under the covers and scooted to the far edge of her side of the bed. If she stayed here all night, a half-length would separate them. A safe distance. Even a respectable distance.

Well, maybe not. She closed her eyes.

His footsteps soon reentered the room and the bed moved beneath her. Quilts rustled as his long body slid beneath the sheets. She lay on her side, teetering on the edge. After a few more small movements, the light snuffed out.

He said, "Good night."

"Good night," she mumbled.

Silence ensued. Then, "I promised I will not touch you."

"I know."

"You are about to fall off the bed."

"I won't. I have good balance."

A tiny sigh escaped. "Good night, Methusal."

"Mmhm."

Again, her behavior made it clear that she feared him. It chagrined her. Once more, she'd acknowledged that he held all the power in the relationship. Hadn't she decided to change all of that? Wasn't she supposed to be figuring out how to manipulate his base desires so she would come out the victor?

Huddling on her side of the bed was accomplishing none of her goals. Methusal wondered what a more experienced, crafty woman might do.

She had no idea. A few half-baked, risky plans came to mind as she drifted toward sleep. One might actually work. She yawned. If only she could remember it in the morning...

"No, Methusal." The deep voice thundered behind her.
She whirled.

"Love one another." The Prophet's eyes blazed like fire. "Live at peace with your enemies."

"I can't."

"Why not?"

"When I do, he gets too close to me."

"And?"

"I can't let that happen. I can't."

"You fear, Methusal. Perfect love casts out fear."

"I don't have perfect love. I don't know what that is."

"Come to The One. Ask him to fill you with his love. Ask him to help you fulfill your destiny."

The memory of sheeting rain, and war, and fleeing for her life from her enemy filled her heart with fear.

"I'm sorry," she gasped.

A terrible silence ensued.

Sudden, gusting winds buffeted her. Gray clouds roiled overhead, and the flat landscape grew darker.

She felt very alone.

A still, quiet voice told her, "Your actions will affect others' destinies. You must listen, Methusal."

She whispered, "And if I don't?"

"It is your choice. Choose to love, or accept the consequences."

"You will punish me?"

"No."

She felt relieved.

"But many others will suffer."

Dark images filled her mind. She was locked in a dark jail cell. Rain poured down all around her. She was trapped, and Mentàll... Mentàll's eyes blazed with hatred and rage. And hurt. His lips curled back in a snarl, and he lifted his blade high and struck the lock.

"No!" she gasped with terror.

He hated her. He had not looked at her that way in almost a year.

And she couldn't stand it.

It was clear his hatred was destroying him. And just as clearly, she knew that he would not harm her. But he would destroy himself.

"No," she whispered.

"Love, Methusal," the quiet voice said. Then stronger, so that it reverberated through her soul. "Love."

She awoke with a gasp. It was dark. And she was alone. Mentàll was not in the bed.

Her heart still thundered from the dream. It seemed so real—just like the first dream she'd ever had of Mentàll.

At least she hadn't slept-walked this time.

If the nightmare had been one of her prophetic dreams—if it had been from The One—then he wasn't pleased with her plan to manipulate the Dehrien Chief. Or her plan to pounce when he was weak in order to achieve her own goals.

She hadn't felt right about the plan from the beginning. So she wouldn't pursue it.

But that wasn't enough. The One demanded more from her concerning the Dehrien—and possibly regarding her other enemies, too.

Why? Mentàll was a strong, indomitable man. He needed nothing from anyone. Certainly not from her. He was happy alone. He was impervious to hurt or insult—well, mostly. Humanness did live in him. She'd seen it more than a few times.

But how was she supposed to love him? What did The One mean? She had forgiven him—at least as much as she was able to do. Was she supposed to treat him kindly, like during the war, when she'd cared for his wounds?

Again, she wondered why her actions would matter to the Dehrien at all.

Methusal stared at the ceiling, feeling tense and confused. *Why* did her life have to be entwined with his? From the beginning, it felt as if fate had bound them together.

Would she ever be free of him?

Her prophetic dream three years ago had warned that if she tried to escape, she'd be caught by him forever, bound in a dark prison of her own making. But if she listened to The One's decrees to love...then maybe she could free herself from Mentàll. A paradox. Logically, it made no sense. But if a little kindness could separate her from him forever, wouldn't it be worth the effort?

Small acts of kindness couldn't kill her. Could they?

Methusal closed her eyes. Her head ached. Why did everything have to be so complicated?

The door opened. A dark figure entered, blanketed in shadows.

"Where were you?"

He sat on the bed. A quiet sound indicated that he'd shucked off his tunic. He lay back with a sigh. "I went to the base."

"Alone? Why?"

"I have Zindedi documentation that proves I am a Commander. But I realized tonight that I am not registered in their files at the base."

"You think Mrn. M gave the General your name? Do you think he'll check on you?"

"Even if he does not, someone might in the future."

"So you filed false papers."

He grunted softly. "Yes."

"It's almost morning."

"I do not need much sleep, Methusal. If you will be quiet now..."

Methusal fell silent, and soon his even, quiet breaths indicated he'd fallen asleep.

Methusal closed her eyes. She felt disturbed. He'd gone off without telling her where he was going again. What if something had happened to him? How would she have known where he was, or how to help him?

He must believe he was invulnerable. And he still did not trust her with his plans.

The arrogant man. She had a good mind to wake him up and give him a piece of her mind.

She went up on one elbow and stared at him.

Interrupting his sleep would be cruel.

She flopped back down. The man infuriated her. If she did anything foolish, he was on her in a flash. Did he think he could operate under a different set of rules?

She went up on one elbow again, itching to shake him awake. She did not. Instead, she flopped back down and childishly gripped the covers and yanked them as she rolled over to the edge of the bed.

An equally hard yank sent her sprawling backwards. Mentàll loomed over her, outlined in black against the pale light glowing through the window. Softly, he said, "Speak what is on your mind, Methusal. I am too tired to play games."

"You should have told me where you were going," she told him. "What if something had happened to you?"

"You would care?"

"You're the commander of this team. Of course I care! Don't do it again. It's foolish. And reckless."

"Now I answer to you?" Humor laced the low words.

"Of course you do. Aren't we married in the eyes of the Zindedis?"

He chuckled softly. "So now you choose to exercise your rights to wifely benefits."

"I doubt that would work, even if we were married," she returned tartly.

"Do not be so sure," he murmured. "If you were my wife, I would happily provide you with every benefit you could desire."

Heat flushed through her. "Well, I'm not. So settle for giving me basic courtesy. If you go somewhere alone, I need to know where."

He lay back with a tired grunt.

She went up on one elbow and looked down at him. "Well?"

"Since it concerns you so deeply, I will tell you next time. Unless it compromises your safety."

She flopped onto her back again. "Fine."

"And Methusal," his words slurred a little now, "next time, a wifely kiss would be more welcome than stealing my blankets."

"That'll be a cold day," she informed him. But his quiet, deep breaths told her he'd fallen asleep again.

Methusal closed her eyes, but it was a long time before she fell asleep again.

Chapter Twenty-Eight

Day 12

Had she awoken early enough?

Moving clumsily on her still unfamiliar crutches, Aali made her way into the courtyard of the Chief's compound. Early morning sunlight shone through the arched doorway, spreading golden sparkles of light over the lush, potted flowering plants and trees.

Despite the beauty around her, melancholy threatened, feeling like a dead weight on her spirit. It was her birthday. And she'd have to spend the next eight weeks alone in a strange town with strange people, and as a guest in a very strange household. Dastn was her only friend, and he'd leave soon.

If he hadn't already.

"Aali." The familiar, deep voice made her turn so fast she bumped her injured leg.

She winced, but the pain melted into a burst of sunshine when she saw Dastn smiling at her. His pack was already on his back, and a large, clumsily wrapped package in his hand.

He offered it to her. "Happy birthday."

"You knew?" she said, amazed.

"Of course." He nudged the light, airy package into her hand. "Go ahead. Open it."

She couldn't help but grin. "I love presents!" She ripped open the parchment and stared. Then she giggled uncontrollably.

It was a grass hat dyed a cool shade of green. A huge, pink straw flower perched jauntily on one side. It looked silly. Outlandish. And she loved it.

"For the trip home. So you won't get sunburned."

"Thanks, Dastn. You can be sweet when you want to be." She slapped the hat on top of her head.

He eyed her for a moment, his dark eyes intent and thoughtful. "Sixteen?"

"Yes." How did he know? Again, she wondered.

"Sweet sixteen. Never been kissed." It sounded like both a question and a statement.

She gave him a bold, impudent grin. "You could."

Had she just said that? Her stomach felt fluttery.

His right brow slanted up, matching the wicked tilt of his spiky hair. "But I won't."

Aali pulled off the hat to cover the warm feeling that suddenly grew in her. "Thank you."

"I knew I had to get something just right for you. Not too sweet, and not too ordinary. Fresh. And sassy."

The smile in her heart grew bigger. But she played it cool on the outside. "You did okay. For a boring old man."

Dastn laughed softly. "See ya, Aali." He strode away, and disappeared through the courtyard gates.

Tears burned her eyes then. She didn't like being a crybaby, but every once in a while was okay, she reasoned.

"Aali." A small hand tugged at her own. She looked down at the dark-haired little girl with the strange, pale eyes. "It's time for breakfast. And Great-Grandma wants to meet you."

△ △ △ △ △

Light streamed in the window when Methusal finally woke up the next morning. It was late. Maybe halfway to noon. She sat up fast. Mentàll's side of the bed was empty again. Before she could take a guess about where he was, the relief room door opened, and he entered the room wearing only light tan breeches.

His chest gleamed bronze in the golden morning sunlight. Silver flashed from the medallion he always wore around his neck. The medallion with the two peaks. It had been his father's—the father he'd never met, and he didn't know his name, but hated all the same.

She realized that she was staring. Amusement flashed in his eyes. Before he could make an inappropriate remark, she said, "I was looking at your medallion. So don't get a swollen head."

His smile deepened anyway, annoying her.

"Why do you wear it? I thought you hated your father."

He pulled on his tunic. "It is a clue to my past."

"Have you found any answers?"

"Why do you want to know?"

"I'm curious."

"That is all?"

"Of course that's all. It's not like I want to know everything about you."

He moved closer, buttoning his tunic. "And yet you do, don't you?"

She eyed him. "What do you mean?"

"You know many intimate things about me, Methusal. Things you will never forget."

Her cheeks warmed. It was just like him to turn a completely innocuous conversation into something else. "Stop it."

His smile lingered. "And I know many things about you. Like in the middle of the night, when you are deeply asleep, you snore. Softly."

"I do not!"

He sat down and pulled on his boot. "You do. It is...enchanting."

"Please." She snorted.

"Do I snore? No one has ever told me before."

Those pale eyes held hers, as compelling as clear crystal. She couldn't look away. He was deliberately trying to deepen the connection between them by asking these questions. She knew his purpose, and yet she couldn't escape the snare of his gaze.

"Do I, Methusal?" he asked softly.

"You don't snore," she said shortly. "In fact, I never hear you at all."

He finished tying his boots. "Good. I would dislike being an annoyance."

"You're much worse than an annoyance," she said grumpily. "But I'm sure you know that. What are we doing today?"

"We will find the mail distribution center."

"And then?"

"I will follow the mail carriers and see if invitations are being delivered today. However, it is possible they have not been delivered to the distribution center yet. You will watch the palace, and follow any couriers who head for the center."

"I'll be free of you all day?" She grinned.

He eyed her with no amusement. "I will also visit the Merry Spirits for the midday meal. Perhaps I will learn information from the sailors there."

"They're more likely to speak freely at night, when they're drunk," she pointed out. "Maybe I could go then. Men are more likely to loosen their tongues with a woman."

Mentàll stared at her, his face almost comically blank with shock. "No."

"Why not? I can take care of myself."

"They would think you were a.... *No.*" His cheekbones tinged red.

She'd unwittingly gotten under his skin—so easily, and it was so unexpectedly satisfying, too. "We could go together," she suggested. "Then..."

"*No!*" The word thundered, making her jump. Tension tightened his frame, but she unwisely pushed on.

"Why not?"

"I will not allow those men to touch you..."

"If they do, they will quickly regret it."

"...or *look* at you with..."

"Looking won't hurt me, Mentàll. Let me do my job."

"If you were there, I would not be able to do mine." An implacable, unyielding expression stared back.

"So I'm supposed to watch the palace all day. That's it."

"You may watch the docks, too. But stay safe. Do nothing foolish," he said harshly.

Her jaw dropped. "I don't believe this. How can you have two sets of standards? You can do anything you want, but I can't? If you let me scout alone, it's only for easy, safe jobs. The only time I get to do something interesting is when I'm with you!"

He turned his back on her, putting items in his pockets. "I am glad you find our time together so compelling."

She growled between her teeth. "It's not *fair*. Treat me as an equal, Mentàll."

"I do. But I will not allow you to take unnecessary risks."

"But *you* can take unnecessary risks?"

"I am more advanced in kaavl than you are."

How could this man rile her up so easily? "I can do anything you can do. Don't talk down to me."

He faced her again. Frustration hardened his features. "Do not argue with me. I am the Commander of this mission."

Without thinking, she closed the distance between them and set her jaw. "You're a power hungry whip. That's what you are."

He heaved a harsh breath. Unexpectedly, his hand went to her hair and gently slid down the soft strands. Her breath caught in surprise.

"I will allow no man to harm..." His low voice grated to a halt. "I will not allow it. Other jobs are fit for you, Methusal. I will not allow you in a spirit house with drunken men. Accept that, and do not argue about it again."

His hand in her hair felt remarkably like a caress. It melted her defenses, because it actually felt like he cared about her. That this was why he was denying her wishes. His fingers grazed her healing wound. It didn't hurt.

"How is your head?"

"Fine." A small pause elapsed. "And your arm?"

The faintest smile glimmered. "Fine."

Uncomfortably, she stared back at him. A tiny part of her waited, irrationally wondering if he'd stroke her hair again. Those discerning eyes watched her, as if gauging her thoughts. Then his big hand cupped her head and slid, slow and sure, down the strands again. A nameless, soothing peace relaxed her.

She drew a trembling breath. "All right. But I'm worthy of a more dangerous assignment. Next time, please give me one."

In a low voice, he said, "I respect your kaavl abilities, Methusal. But I will do as I see fit."

She moved away from him. "You infuriate me."

"You do not want a man who will bow to your wishes."

"I want a man who will treat me with respect."

"I want to protect you, Methusal. That is the highest respect I can pay to anyone."

Was it true? And yet he never lied. "I still don't like it," she mumbled.

"But you will accept it. Get ready. We will leave soon."

Then Methusal realized that she was still wearing her nightgown. She had stood here arguing with him in nothing but her night clothes! If that wasn't testament to the unthinking intimacy they had achieved, what could be? It bothered her. It also bothered her that she had stood as still as a pet apte while he had stroked her hair. What was wrong with her?

She firmly closed the relief room door behind her. It didn't help much.

△ △ △ △ △

"Do you have your papers?" Deccia asked anxiously.

Timaeus gave her a teasing grin. "They're in my pocket." He pulled on his pack.

"Good. Did you look at them?"

"Do I need to?"

"Umm. It might be a good idea."

With a puzzled frown, her husband pulled the false military papers from his pocket and unfolded them. His frown deepened when he read the first line.

"Please don't question it," Deccia whispered. "I just want to keep you safe."

His expression cleared, and he kissed her. "It's a good idea. I'll carry them with me all the time. Are you working on the other papers today?"

She nodded. "I hope to have them finished by the time you get home tomorrow."

His hands settled on her hips and he pulled her in for a thorough kiss. "I'll be home before you know it. Don't worry, Decc."

Deccia didn't answer, but she offered a brave smile when he pulled away. "Have a good trip. I love you."

"I love you, too." He gave her another lingering kiss. Then, with a decisive, quick turn of his shoulders, he left her. Deccia watched him stride down the hill. *Please don't let the Zindedis capture him, The One. Please!*

△ △ △ △ △

A little while later, Deccia and Hendra headed to town for supplies. Sozla and Behran remained behind, working on the detonator. A quiet, excited energy emanated from them, and Deccia wondered if they were close to making it work.

When Deccia entered the market, the pungent scent of spices teased her nose. Funny. She'd never noticed them before. A closer inspection revealed that tied bundles of dried plants hung upside down over the front counter, where Ceri loaded a woman's purchases into her basket. She did a double take. *Ceri!*

Relief filled her heart. The General hadn't captured her! Before Deccia could greet her friend, the woman at the counter turned toward the door. Olita.

"Well!" The Dakarran woman offered the Koblanis a wide smile. "Our visitors have returned to town." Her small eyes darted left and right. "Where are your men? Have they reported for duty yet?" Her teeth gleamed, looking as sharp and pointy as wild beast fangs.

"They haven't received their orders yet," she said coolly.

Olita's dark eyes narrowed. "Seems awfully suspicious to me. Why would they order my man to the base, but not yours?"

Deccia glanced at Hendra, trying to formulate an answer.

Hendra said, "Our men have trained for months." True, if one counted fighting in the Quasr War. "They're ready to fight now. If I'm not mistaken, the men ordered into training are either completely inexperienced, or have been out of the service for a long time."

Olita's round face flushed. "Are you suggesting my man needs training? He's a *Commander!*"

Hendra flinched. "As a Commander, I'm sure he is needed to train the recruits."

"Yes." Olita's feathers did not settle, however. With a glare, she limped toward the door. "Insolent apte brains," she muttered. Snorting to herself, she left the shop.

Good riddance. Deccia hurried for the counter. "Ceri! Where have you been? I've been so worried about you!"

Ceri's pale green eyes sparkled. "I hid out for a while, just to make sure the General was gone." She whispered, "Thanks for knocking him silly with that can. If you hadn't, I don't know where I'd be right now."

"I know what it's like to have a horrible man chase you. And how..." Deccia bit her lip, "...unspeakably awful it is when they catch you."

"I'm so sorry."

Deccia shrugged, wanting to forget about it. "Can I ask something?"

"Sure."

"Why did the General say you were his?"

"I'm *not!*" Ceri scowled. After a sharp, assessing glance, she leaned forward. "If I say why, will you tell anyone?"

"Of course not."

"I haven't been home to Carachki in months. I can't. And it's all his fault." Anger tightened her voice "He won't leave me alone."

"Why not?"

"General Fitrn thinks I belong to him, but the truth is, I was pledged to his brother."

"His brother?"

"The Presidente has another son?" Hendra said.

"Yes."

"What happened?"

"My father was a Commander. He knew the Presidente well, and they were friends. Anyway, when I was a baby, they agreed I would marry the Presidente's youngest son." Ceri fingered the writing stick on the counter. "I didn't mind," she said softly. "I fell in love with him when I was sixteen. Anyway, I thought I was in love."

"And then?"

"And then he left." Ceri shrugged. But it was clear she hadn't dismissed it so easily at the time.

"Where did he go?"

"I don't know. He disappeared without saying goodbye." A flush touched her cheeks. "It's clear he didn't love me."

"Have you seen him since? Did he explain what happened?"

Ceri's eyes darted away. A small silence elapsed. "Not...not really."

She was lying. Deccia wondered why, because she'd taken a risk by telling them this much.

"Anyway, Fitrn decided I belong to him, since his brother rejected me. He says the agreement is still valid."

Hendra said, "Why don't you tell your father that you don't like General Fitrn?"

"My father is dead. And I'll never be free from Fitrn. He's like a whip with an apte. He enjoys stalking. He relishes cornering his prey. He feeds off of fear, like...like an eater of souls. So you see, he cannot know I'm still here."

"We won't tell anyone," Deccia promised. "But what if he comes back?"

"Then I'll hide in the forest again."

Had the Zindedi girl been hiding in the forest for the last five days? How had she survived in the cold and damp, all alone? Concerned, Deccia said, "If you ever need help, please come to us. We'd be glad to help you."

Ceri accepted the pledge of friendship with a smile, but her eyes sparkled, looking suspiciously bright. She drew a breath. "Now. What can I help you find today?"

△ △ △ △ △

Deccia pondered Ceri's story as she and Hendra left the market. Heavy, bulging bags weighed down her arms.

So, the awful Presidente had spawned yet another son. Interesting. But if Ceri had fallen in love with him, he must not be too bad. Then again, he'd left without telling her why or goodbye. Ceri had probably gotten off lucky. In that family, there was probably a high chance he was just like his father, his Uncle Greisn, and his brother Fitrn. Crazy, and evil incarnate, in other words.

Anger and a disgusted revulsion twisted inside her, thinking about Fitrn and his hateful family. Her nails stabbed painfully into her palms until she willfully relaxed her clenched fists.

General Fitrn's brother had returned, and Ceri had seen him. This Deccia knew for a fact; inner intuition never led her astray when she felt a truth this certainly.

Then why had Ceri pretended that she hadn't seen him? The lie seemed strange, and a little suspicious.

With a frown, Deccia hurried by Olita's store, imagining the woman's malicious eyes watching them. The Dakarran woman hated them. Deccia had sensed her deepened malevolence at the market. While Olita had never been exactly pleasant, her attitude toward Deccia and the others had undertaken a drastic change for the worse.

Maybe Olita felt resentful because the Koblani men were still at home with their "wives," while she had lost both of her men to the military. Regardless, Olita could prove to be dangerous. Deccia would warn the others.

Few of the Dakarrans seemed to like the Koblani team, and it seemed strange. She wondered why. At home, everyone liked them all.

An unsettling possibility came to mind.

Perhaps Olita and the other Dakarrans had sensed from the beginning how much the Koblanis disliked them. Maybe they had sensed Deccia's hatred, too. Hatred fed on hatred. She should know.

Distressed, she walked faster down the narrow, grassy country lane. It couldn't be true. Surely Olita and Vitnia weren't sensitive to anyone's feelings besides their own.

There she went, being judgmental again. The Prophet had admonished her to forgive her enemies and to live at peace with them. But how? How was that possible when war lived in her heart? She despaired over her struggle yet again. From the moment she'd stepped onto Zindedi soil, she had battled her hatred and fear of the Zindedis. Praying to The One with Methusal had helped a little, but not nearly enough.

Again, it all came down to that depraved General Greisn, and the horrible, wicked things he had done to her. She wanted to weep and scream to the heavens that it wasn't *fair*. Why was she the one who was still suffering? Why was she the one who had to forgive, when *she* was the one who had been abused?

Silent, hot tears filled her eyes and dripped down her cheeks. She didn't want to be weak. She didn't want to be a failure. Deccia averted her face, looking out at the weeds.

"What's wrong?" Concern was plain in Hendra's voice.

She wiped the tears with the sleeve of her coat. "How can I forgive someone who never regretted what he did to me? It wasn't *right,* what he did."

Compassion softened Hendra's features. "It will never be right," she said quietly. "If you want the truth, I think forgiveness is a gift for ourselves. To help us let go of the pain and let go of the tormenter, too. The One will deal with them. It still hurts, though. Even though Jascr is dead, it still hurts."

"I know," Deccia whispered.

Softly, Hendra said, "What did the Prophet say? 'It is mine to avenge; I will repay,' says the Lord.'"

"I know. But I still feel *hatred* inside me. And what's worse, my anger at him spills over onto all of the Zindedis here. I feel this overwhelming revulsion, and...and *dislike* and even hatred for them. But it's not because of anything they've done. It's because of this horrible ugliness inside of me. I hate it. I don't want to be that person."

"We both need help. And healing, too." Hendra caught her arm. "Let's stop for a minute and pray."

Deccia closed her eyes. Hurt, despair, and anger still twisted painfully within her. She certainly had no answers. She could not do this on her own anymore.

Soft and soothingly, Hendra said, "Dear The One, you know how we feel about the men who hurt us. You hate what they did to us. I know it wasn't your will for us to suffer like that. Deccia is hurting. Please heal her and deliver her from the fear and pain and hatred. I ask that for myself, too. It's like a dark pit, The One. We need help to get out. Please deliver us both. Amen."

Hendra smiled. "I memorized a verse when I was little. Maybe it can help us both. It says, 'Do not be overcome by evil, but overcome evil with good.'"

Deccia wiped away her tears. Her soul did feel lighter now. It was a relief to share her pain with someone who understood, and who cared. "Thank you, Hendra. I'm so glad to have a friend like you."

Hendra smiled, clearly pleased. As they headed toward the cabins again, the Dehrien girl's steps quickened eagerly. She clearly hoped Doc was home. Although Hendra had disguised her worry well with constant work, Deccia had often caught her stealing glances out the window, waiting and watching. She'd become progressively quieter, too, as the days passed by and Doc did not return. Deccia understood the fear Hendra felt.

Timaeus. Had he reached Carachki yet?

△ △ △ △ △

Doc still hadn't returned. It was late afternoon now, and Hendra had just finished placing the tubers in the oven to bake for dinner.

He had been gone for three days. How hard could it be to find the powder mine? How far had he and Goric gone?

Had he been captured?

She felt sick to her stomach with anxiety.

"Behran, look," Sozla cried. "Do you see?" Her head was very close to his. They both stared at a small, circular contraption on the table. "See? It made a spark."

Hendra moved closer, intrigued. "How?" she said. "What happened?"

Sozla smiled up at her. "If we pull the spring down with the thread this far, and then cut it, the spring hits the flint hard enough to make a spark."

"Let's try it out for real." Behran jumped up. "I'll get one of the powder balls."

Behran had made more wax balls with powder on the inside, with a wick trailing out of each one. Hendra had noticed that he'd encased different amounts of powder inside of each ball of wax.

Right now, he grabbed one of these, and she followed the two outside to a flat stone near the well. The sun had lowered to the tree tops and it was chilly. Sozla carefully placed the small detonator on the rock, attached it to the wick, and then tied a short piece of thread around the spring, cinching it down almost flat. Behran eyed it, adjusted a few things, and then stepped back, apparently satisfied. He pulled a knife from his pocket.

"Stand back," he advised. "I don't think there is much powder in this one, but..."

Hendra backed up a few paces, but Sozla only one.

Behran cut the thin thread, the spring shot up, the flint sparked, and the wick lit. A tiny flame licked toward the ball of wax. He grabbed Sozla's hand, pulling her further away.

The flame licked at the wax, melting it, and then
BOOM!

The detonator exploded and pieces flew through the air, but luckily fell short of them all. A puff of black smoke and a singed, faintly putrid smell wafted through the air.

"Yes!" Behran pumped his fist. "Good job, Sozla!" He lifted the slight girl high in the air in a brief, whirling hug, and then deposited her on her feet again.

Red flushed Sozla's cheeks, and her eyes sparkled.

The door burst open and Deccia ran out. "What happened?"

"It works!" Sozla cried. "The detonator works." She rushed forward to gather up the pieces of their mechanical baby.

"Careful," Behran cautioned. "They might be hot."

"The bombs are ready?"

"No," Behran said. "We've figured out the self-triggering detonator. Now we have to duplicate a bunch of them. We still need to figure out the timers. That might be the hardest part. We want to be able to set up the bombs hours in advance. The longer, the better."

"You've done a wonderful job. Congratulations," Hendra said. "Mentàll is going to be so pleased."

Behran grinned, and the two inventors hurried back inside the cabin.

Still shivering, Hendra followed more slowly. She wondered if the Dakarrans had heard the explosion. The plume of smoke hadn't gone up very high, so they wouldn't see that, at least. Maybe they'd think the explosion came from the military base. She hoped so.

The kitchen felt toasty warm after the cold outside. Hendra checked a pan of raising biscuits under a towel, and then the meat stewing in a pan. Dinner would be ready soon. Already the sun dipped toward the horizon.

The kitchen was warm and quiet. Behran and Sozla talked quietly at the table, and Deccia sat at the other end with parchments spread around her. Carefully, she applied ink to paper, copying more military documents for the men.

Dusk thickened outside. Hendra lit the lamps in the kitchen, and then retreated to the colder living room and lit one near the window. It would shine as a welcoming beacon, showing the way home, if Doc or the others were close enough to see it.

The sharp scent of smoke curled into her nostrils when she blew out the firestick. It was lonely in this dim, quiet room.

Deep purple enshrouded the landscape outside. The black forest looked cold and lonely.

She rested her forehead on the cool pane. No sign of Ryon. The high, thick clouds blocked every ray of light.

Movement caught her eye. A thick, bundled shape headed for the porch steps. It was a man, wearing black, with a thick scarf wound around his neck. As if sensing her stare, he turned to look.

Doc.

Fierce joy shot through her. She ran and flung the door open. His dark eyes focused only upon her.

"Doc," she said softly, and reached for him. His cold, gloved hand curled tight around hers. He moved to the side to let in Goric, who was behind him, and at the same time ripped off his other glove with his teeth. He tossed it to the couch. His bared hand took her free one, holding it firm and strong.

She gasped. "You're freezing!"

Goric muttered, "Me, too," and headed for the kitchen.

Hendra realized then that she was holding both of Doc's hands, and blushed furiously. She tried to disentangle herself, but he only released one hand. He removed his other glove, tossing it onto a nearby chair. Meanwhile, he still held her anchored close to him in the quiet, secluded living room.

"Sorry my hands are so cold," he said huskily, and offered his other hand again. Hendra closed her warmer fingers around his. It was the least she could do. He'd just suffered through three days and nights in the cold.

"They feel like ice," she said softly. "What happened? I...we've been worried about you."

"We followed a bunch of roads that led us nowhere."

"You didn't find the big mine?"

"The only military carts we saw went to the small one. We searched down every path, but found nothing."

"I'm so sorry." Hendra felt his frustration as keenly as if it were her own. "I'm glad you're back," she said softly. "Behran and Sozla just got the detonator to work."

He offered his first smile. "So that was the explosion I heard."

"I hope the Dakarrans don't get suspicious."

"It sounded like a gun. I wouldn't worry about it." Quietly, he said, "I'm glad to be home." His gaze held hers, as warm and intense as an embrace. He'd missed her. A blush warmed her cheeks again. Finally, and with apparent reluctance, he released her.

"Come into the kitchen," she urged. "It's warmer."

In the other room, Goric hunched in a chair, scowling. Behran must have just asked him a question, because he was looking at the Aestoff man expectantly.

"We looked everywhere," Goric muttered. "What more do you want? Should we stay out and freeze for another three nights?"

"I asked which way you went on the beach road. West or east?"

"East," Doc said, taking a chair and straddling it. "We traveled two days east, and investigated every side road we found."

"Why did you not go west?" Sozla inquired.

Sounding sullen, Goric said, "Riln said all the carts came from the east. We've never seen a cart go west."

"We need to search the base and find a map," Doc said. "We could waste another three or four days following dead ends."

"Good plan," Behran agreed. "Should we wait for Riln and Tabor before going on the base again?"

Hendra would rather not wait for Riln. The man created trouble everywhere he went. "We could slip in and out faster with fewer people," she suggested.

"But security is doubled at the base," Doc said. "We may need people to distract the guards, and other people to search the base."

"I agree. We need more kaavl players," Behran said. "So we'll wait until they get back. Until then, we'll keep watching. Hopefully their security will soften up over the next few days. It may be our last chance to get on base before Day Zero."

Day Zero was the day they'd set off the explosions. It coincided with the night of the Presidente's ball, and was only seven days from now. Hendra would be in charge of setting the detonators inside the base. Once again, she hoped she was up to it. She didn't want to disappoint Mentàll or fail her team, either.

She glanced at Doc and found strength in his steady gaze. He believed in her. Perhaps she should, too.

△ △ △ △ △

Methusal dutifully watched the palace and docks all day long. Tedious and boring couldn't quite describe the experience. By five o'clock, she was ready to scream with frustration.

No palace messenger delivered mail to the distribution center. And the docks were quiet.

Her mind wandered during those crawling hours. She wondered if Deccia had finished forging the fake invitations. They may need to use them. In addition, they needed to return the invitation before the Commander's wife discovered it missing. Something told her the woman would raise a shrill alarm if the theft was uncovered.

Earlier that day, at noon, she had watched the Dehrien Chief enter the Merry Spirits for the noonday meal. She wondered what exciting things he was learning while she ate lunch on a quiet bench in the park, watching mothers play with their children.

In the afternoon, things quieted down even more. Bored beyond words, Methusal repeatedly paced between the palace and the Merry Spirits. Military soldiers streamed in and out of the latter all day. Mentàll left at two. At about five o'clock, two Commanders went inside, deep in serious conversation.

She couldn't help but wonder what they were discussing. Had the Presidente given them new instructions? Methusal itched to know what they were talking about.

Unfortunately, she'd noticed that no women went into the spirit house.

If only she could find a place to hide out of sight, so she could listen to the conversations inside. Maybe in the back. She'd seen a large trash bin...

But when she reached the back, a woman wearing a short red skirt and an elaborate, scoop necked, puffy white tunic stood there, inhaling from a smokestick. Her long brown hair straggled in curls down her back. She spotted Methusal before she could hide.

"Hey." She ground the smokestick beneath her heel and rasped, "You the new girl? Your shift's about to start."

A multitude of thoughts shot through her head. "I'm not exactly dressed..."

"Change inside." She jerked her head toward the door. "Come on in. I'll train you. I'm Tineia. Who are you?"

Upon closer inspection, the woman looked to be on the beaten side of forty. "I'm Midi."

"The last waitress left behind her uniform." She eyed Methusal. "Should fit you."

She followed Tineia into the dark interior of the spirit house. Warm air, thick with the sting of smoke, enveloped her. Clinking glasses and men's hearty laughter colored the close atmosphere.

"This way." Tineia skirted a long counter where a man poured drinks, and headed for a side door.

"Hey," yelled a man. "You the new one? Come over here, sweetie. I'll show you *everything* you need to know."

Revulsion swept through her. Was she doing the right thing? And yet think of all the conversations she could listen to if she worked here.

Mentàll would not be pleased. And yet it was clear no invitations would be delivered today. And the docks were quiet. Wouldn't this be the best use of her time?

Mind made up, she followed Tineia into a small room and quickly changed. The skirt showed her knees, and the bosom of the white tunic drooped alarmingly. "The top is too big. Can I pin it up somehow?"

Tineia gave the neckline a cursory appraisal. "It's fine." Her eyes lingered on Methusal's necklace. "You're married?"

Her fingers flew to it. "Um... Yes."

Pity flashed on the other woman's face. "Did your husband send you?"

"No! In fact..." Methusal bit her lip. "We need extra money. What he doesn't know won't hurt him."

Tineia nodded, but her gaze softened. "All right. I'll give you a few pointers. Stay away from the fat one at the counter. And the two skinny ones in the corner. I'll take care of them. Take your tips as soon as they give them. Move fast, and watch out for their hands."

Methusal took a deep breath. "Okay. How long do I work?"

"How long can you stay? You say your husband doesn't know."

"I need to be home in two hours."

"Good. Let's see how you do tonight."

Methusal followed Tineia into the dimly lit, smoky room. The tavern appeared to have no windows. Oil lamps hung above the bar counter, and candles flickered on each table. All of the men watched her entry with obvious, unconcealed interest.

At the counter, a stout man with small eyes and full lips waved his empty mug. "Come here, sweetie. Fill me up." He leered. "Then I'll return the favor."

Methusal suppressed a shudder. She was relieved when Tineia headed for the disgusting man.

A mug slammed down near the door. "Here!"

Her first customer. If only she knew what she was doing. As she hurried over, something pinched her bottom, hard.

She gasped. Instinct made her whirl, and her foot connected with the man's arm. Too bad it wasn't his face. His drink capsized. "Hey!"

At least the smirk left his expression. Red flushed up to his receding black hairline. Spirits pooled on the floor.

Fear gripped her, and she wondered if she'd just blown her cover.

Then the men sharing his table laughed. "Caught you a feisty one, Sergeant."

"Come're, sweet thing," said another. "I'll teach you how to fight."

Tineia murmured, "Keep moving." To the men, "I'm sorry about the accident. A free round of drinks?"

The dark-haired one spluttered, but eventually accepted the peace offering. Methusal, meanwhile, picked up an empty mug in the back of the room and hurried to refill it. As she did, she noted that the two Commanders were sitting in the far corner of the room. Their expressions looked tense, and they spoke in low voices. She concentrated into kaavl to listen.

"You sure they're coming? What about the Presidente?"

"Naw. The General's his mouthpiece."

The front door banged open. "Commander!" cried a young solder. "Fijorn fell from the upper mast!"

One of the Commanders jumped up.

"I'll pay," said his companion. "Lunch tomorrow? I want to prepare for the meeting. If we can."

"Tomorrow." The Commander barreled out the door, listening to the sailor's high-pitched, urgent voice.

She hadn't learned much. But the Commanders would meet again tomorrow for lunch. Apparently, they wanted to prepare for some sort of big meeting with the General.

She wondered where the meeting would take place, and when. And who exactly would be there.

"New girl!" called a man, banging his mug on the table. "Another drink."

Any thought of quitting the job tonight died a quick death. The Commanders would meet here tomorrow. So she'd need to keep the job until then. That meant she would need to work hard today. And not kick any other customers.

Methusal spent the next two hours ignoring indecent proposals and dodging quick, sly hands. A few men managed to pinch her thigh, and one brushed her breast. That contact made her flesh creep, and the unpleasant memory lingered throughout her shift. Even though it had been fleeting, she felt defiled, and longed for a bath to cleanse the contact from her mind.

"You did a good job," Tineia said, when Methusal changed clothes at the end of her shift. "Here are a few tips you missed."

Methusal had left some money untouched, just to avoid the long arms and grasping fingers of the men at the table.

"Thank you."

"You're quick." Tineia's tired dark eyes glimmered. "Will you be back tomorrow?"

"Yes. For the lunch shift, if that's okay."

"Of course. Can you work until seven again?"

It was the last thing she wanted to do. But the other woman obviously needed help. Tineia was the only waitress working tonight.

"Yes, thank you. That would be fine."

Methusal made her way through the dark to Mrn. M's house. She was exhausted, and craved the cheery warmth of Mrn. M's home. The filth of the spirits house seemed to cling to her. She wanted to be somewhere decent and good again.

Unfortunately, Mentàll would be wondering where she'd been. She'd need to think up a reasonably truthful cover story.

Even as she climbed the porch steps, the stink of smoke from the Merry Spirits clung to her. She sniffed the ends of her hair, and then her clothes. The unmistakable, stale smell of smoke filled her nostrils.

She needed to get a bath and change before Mentàll noticed. She burst into the warm house. Mrn. M called from the kitchen, "Hello, dear! Did you have fun shopping?"

So that was the cover Mentàll had given for her noticeable absence. A lie. And most unlike him to give it. She glanced over at him sitting on the couch. Hard eyes glittered back. He wasn't happy. Well, that couldn't be helped.

"I had a great day, thank you. I'm going to take a quick bath. Do I have time before dinner?"

"If you hurry."

Mentàll made a small movement, as if about to rise to his feet, but Methusal fled into their room, grabbed up her backpack of clothes on the way, and slammed the relief room door just as he opened their bedroom door. Her heart hammered.

She twisted both bath tub knobs and quickly stripped off her rank clothes. Then she rolled them into a ball, hoping the small package would emit little odor. Hastily, she stepped into the tub.

Ice cold water bit into her toes. She gasped aloud. That's right. Gorj only heated water in the mornings. She'd have to endure an ice cold bath. Unfortunately, she needed to wash her hair, too.

Taking a fortifying breath, Methusal plunged under the icy water streaming from the tap, and scrubbed her skin and her hair until her whole body tingled. Teeth chattering, she quickly climbed back out and rubbed her cold body with the large, soft towel. Shuddering, she hastily pulled on new, dry clothes. Then she ran a careful comb through her hair. The bullet wound had shrunk to a scab that was half a finger width wide by two long. No sign of infection. Good.

Trying to quiet her shudders, she opened the door and exited with her balled, smoky clothes.

Mentàll wasn't in the room. Thank goodness for small favors. She deposited her clothes in the basket and pulled an old towel over them to further mute the smell. Good. All was well. She pulled on an extra pair of socks for warmth, and then entered the blessed heat of the living room.

"Just in time," Mrn. M bustled to the table, carrying hot rolls. She took in her wet hair. "Oh, my dear. I'm sorry! You must be freezing."

Mentàll eyed her hair with a faint frown.

"I...a flying beast dropped something in my hair. I...I wanted to get it out right away," she lied. And then she felt guilty. "I'm fine." She offered them both a bright smile. "Dinner smells delicious, Mrn. M."

That lady had just delivered gravy and roast meat to the table. She beamed at the compliment, appearing to take Methusal's explanations at face value. On the other hand, hard suspicion glittered in Mentàll's eyes.

When Mrn. M sat, they all served themselves. Methusal kept up a stream of vivacious chatter, trying to appear completely normal. Mrn. M said little, but sent a twinkling glance at Mentàll from time to time. Apparently she found her behavior unusual. Methusal fell silent then, eyes lowered, and focused on the tender, delicious food.

On her right, Mentàll spoke up, his low voice as smooth as butter, "More gravy, Midi?"

She glanced at him, trying to gauge his mood. It proved to be impossible. She offered a syrupy smile. "Why, thank you. You know I love gravy."

"I know you quite well. Little escapes me."

Mrn. M said, "How lucky you are, to have such a devoted husband."

"Yes, lucky," she mumbled, taking another bite.

"Butter for your roll," Mentàll suggested a moment later, all helpful solicitation.

She sent him a narrow-eyed look. "Perhaps later, thank you."

His teeth flashed white, but it wasn't a smile. Rather, a predatory threat. "Later," he agreed mildly.

From then on, her fake husband appeared to relax. Methusal, however, felt more tense by the minute. What story could she tell him? It couldn't be the complete truth, or else he'd forbid her to go back to the Merry Spirits tomorrow. At the same time, she didn't want to lie to him, either.

After dinner, Mentàll surprisingly helped dry dishes in the kitchen while Methusal put them away. Then they followed Mrn. M to the living room. Mentàll caught Methusal's hand and urged her to sit down on the sofa beside him. He leaned back, arm around her shoulders, holding her close to his warm body. Her wet hair still chilled her, so the contact was unexpectedly pleasant.

"What are your plans for tomorrow?" Mrn. M asked, sipping tea.

Mentàll's fingers stroked Methusal's damp hair. It felt soothing. "Whatever Midi would like. I am sure she has many plans that she cannot wait to tell me."

Methusal tensed a little, knowing he was baiting her.

His hand cupped the back of her head and his breath fanned her cheek, followed by his warm lips. "Do you need more dascals, Midi? I am happy to give them to you."

The caress felt warm, even genuine. She felt flustered. What would he think if he knew she'd earned forty dascals today?

"I don't want to empty your pockets, Lozar. What would you have left?"

He murmured, "You may take everything I have. I would gladly give it."

Yet again, she sensed that he spoke on two different levels. Frankly, it disturbed her that she listened for those double meanings.

An inner imp prompted her next words. "What if there aren't enough dascals in the world to satisfy me?"

"Then I would find other ways to satisfy you."

Methusal flushed, for his meaning was unmistakable. Across the room, Mrn. M smiled and looked away. Their hostess didn't appear to be embarrassed, but Methusal was. "Enough," she hissed.

"Tell me. What would you like to do tomorrow, Midi?"

She looked up at the large man sprawled on the Zindedi couch beside her. He appeared to be completely relaxed, but at the same time he played this complex game on multiple levels with apparent ease. He watched her, his pale gaze glittering, but softer than before.

She decided to offer a half truth. "I've found a place I'd love to have lunch."

He nodded. "Done."

"Actually, I made a friend today. Would you mind if we have lunch, and shop together for part of the afternoon?"

His gaze narrowed. "A friend."

"Yes. I'll be back in time for dinner."

Another moment elapsed as he digested this. "If that is what you wish. The next day, however, you are all mine." The words sounded possessive, and just like a husband might sound if he wanted to jealously guard his time with his wife on his honeymoon.

She laid her head on his chest—a brilliant, wifely move, she congratulated herself. "Oh, Lozar. How did I find such a wonderful man as you?"

"I am the lucky one." He stroked her hair. His chest felt warm and comforting, and beneath her ear, his heart thumped, slow and steady. It soothed her. Until this moment, she hadn't realized how tired she was. She had the insane urge to close her eyes and lap up his caresses like an apte flourishing under the loving attention of its master.

Her eyes flew open.

She was not an apte. And Mentàll most certainly was *not* her master! She jerked back.

Amusement glimmered, and she felt even more disturbed. How could she enjoy his caresses, for even one moment? They meant nothing. They were a lie. All if it was a lie. Everything was a calculated pretense to fool Mrn. M. Why did she keep forgetting this simple fact?

Shortly, she said, "I'm tired. I'm going to bed."

He stood with her.

"Don't come," she muttered, and offered their landlady a weak smile. "Goodnight, Mrn. M. Thank you for the delicious dinner."

"It was my pleasure."

Methusal hurried for their room.

Mrn. M murmured, "She's tired, poor thing. Let her sleep. All will be right as rain in the morning."

Mentàll did not follow her. She was glad. Very glad, she told herself.

CHAPTER TWENTY-NINE

THE NEXT MORNING, when Methusal exited from the relief chamber, Mentàll was waiting for her. Slowly, she put her night clothes away and eyed him.

He was deliberately blocking the path to the door. She couldn't leave the room without going through him first. Unfortunately, she'd known this confrontation was coming. It had been brewing since last night.

Even so, she tried to divert his attention to another topic. "You were gone again this morning." She'd awoken early to find his side of the bed empty again.

"I met with Timaeus. He gave me the invitations Deccia copied, and the original. They're in my pack. I told him to follow the coastline and find our ship. He'll give Captain Hilrae his orders to pick us up near Carachki on the evening of Day Zero."

"What else did he say?"

"The Dakarrans are training soldiers. And Doc and Goric are still looking for the biggest powder mine."

"Hopefully they'll find it soon."

"Yes." Mentàll's stance had relaxed. Good. She headed for the door, planning to sidestep him. "Let's..."

Hard fingers clamped onto her arm, drawing her to a stop beside him. He released her. "Tell me where you were yesterday."

Methusal licked her lips and thought about the partial truth she'd concocted to satisfy her suspicious Commander. She already knew she couldn't tell him the whole truth, or else he'd scrap her mission. Important information could be lost. What was more, she'd earned this mission, and so she'd see it through to the finish.

Taking a breath, she launched into her rehearsed tale, which was thinly pinned together with bits of truth. "When I was spying, I spotted two Commanders having lunch in a...a restaurant. I went inside. The waitress was friendly, and I learned the men go in there often. So I thought I'd go back again today and spy."

A long silence elapsed. "Is this the friend you will be shopping with this afternoon?"

Methusal hedged, "She's agreed to spend the afternoon with me. I'm hoping to learn more then, too."

"Very enterprising, Methusal."

Her glance skittered from his gaze to the door. Quickly, she said, "So you see, I won't be able to watch the palace..." When his eyes narrowed, she faltered. "Well, at least part of the time."

"You will have lunch alone, and then shop?"

"Um...yes." Inwardly, Methusal winced at the lies.

That discerning gaze watched her. "You will be done by four o'clock? Then you will watch the palace."

"I can watch all morning, too," she offered quickly, partially sidestepping his question. But the lies weighed on her soul, and she looked away, feeling more and more guilt, because she wouldn't watch the palace at all in the afternoon. *I'm sorry, The One. Please forgive me. I'll tell him the truth tonight, I promise.* And she would. That helped a little. Enough so that she could look him in the eye again. That blue gaze looked very dark now, and entirely unreadable.

Discomfort twisted tighter within her. He hated liars. She didn't want to earn his disrespect. Although why that mattered so much to her, she couldn't say. She swallowed again and looked away. Quickly, she said, "I'll tell you everything tonight."

She made to move past him, but there wasn't enough room to escape through the door. In a low voice, he said, "You know how I feel about liars, Methusal."

"I'll tell you everything later, I promise. You have to trust me."

After a long moment, he moved away from the door. She looked up at him. Still, she could not read his dark gaze, but she sensed his disappointment in her. No. Disillusionment. She bit her lip. "Don't *look* at me like that."

"Then do not *lie* to me."

Unable to stand it another moment, she whirled and escaped from the room. She took refuge at the table, where muffins awaited under a cloth. Mentàll exited the room behind her. She didn't look at him, but waited for him to take his place.

He did not. Instead, he strode for the front door. Its slam shook the entire house.

Mrn. M hurried in from the kitchen, frowning. "Whatever happened?"

Lips trembling, Methusal pleated her napkin with her fingers. It seemed pointless to tell anything but the truth. "We had a fight." A tear slid down her cheek. It took her by surprise.

With a soft, sympathetic sound, Mrn. M rushed to sit beside her. "Now, dear." She patted Methusal's face with a dry napkin. "Don't worry. Spats happen. Believe you me, Charlie and I had plenty of problems when we first got married. Almost as fiery as you two." She gently squeezed Methusal's hand. "Can I give you a piece of advice?"

"Of course." Methusal sniffed, and wondered why it mattered so much what he thought of her. And yet it did. And her conscience accused her, too. She never lied. Why had she started now?

Softly, Mrn. M said, "If you're wrong, admit it. Say you're sorry. And then make up."

"What if he won't forgive me?"

Mrn. M squeezed her hand. "Of *course* he'll forgive you. He loves you, doesn't he?"

Methusal didn't answer.

"Of course he does. I see it plain as day, every time he looks at you." Mrn. M squeezed her hand one more time, and then let it go. "I have one last piece of advice. After that, I promise I won't stick my nose in again."

Methusal smiled a little. It seemed bizarre to receive marital advice for a fake marriage from a Zindedi enemy. Although Mrn. Machblin didn't seem like an enemy. She'd been nothing but a friend since they had first arrived on her doorstep. "I'd love to hear your advice."

"Well, then." Mrn. M. looked pleased. "I know you're a new bride, and I can tell you're still a little tentative..." She offered a kind, encouraging smile. "But, well, men like it when their wives initiate a little... You know. Loving." She flushed a little. "It helps smooth out the rough times. I can see you're a perfect couple. Maybe just a few bumps to get through." She leaned closer. "But it *helps*. Adds a little unexpected zip to a relationship."

Methusal's cheeks warmed. "I...I'll have to think about that." Of course, she'd do nothing of the sort! On the other hand, it would certainly surprise Mentàll if she tried it. A role reversal. A tiny smile tugged at her lips at the thought of his reaction.

"See?" Mrn. M smiled. "It'll all work out for the best. Now, have some breakfast."

Δ Δ Δ Δ Δ

"A report, Presidente." Yalin took a nervous step backward.

The Presidente flicked his fingers at his secretary. The young man fled from the room, closing the door with a quiet thump.

With pleasure, he turned the envelope over in his thick fingers. Had Ostl, his Commander, delivered what was required? Or would it be necessary to make him into an example? Pain tightened in his chest, and then subsided.

Either way suited the Presidente, but he'd prefer to find answers in the letter. With one wrist flick, his knife sliced open the parchment. Impatiently, he unfolded the paper. A smile flickered. And then a chuckle trembled through his jowls.

Finally, one of his men had proven himself worthy. Commander Ostl had compiled a list of all the houses in Carachki which harbored new, out of town boarders. The list was short. The Presidente grunted with satisfaction, scanning it.

Easy enough to investigate. He would send men immediately to track down the Koblani vermin.

A name at the bottom caught his attention, and a surprised chuckle escaped from his throat. He folded the parchment again, creasing the folds with hard strokes of his thumb nail.

Tomorrow he would pay one of those visits. He would be sure to first cut some fresh nasrias. A pleasant encounter it would be. Very pleasant.

△ △ △ △ △

Methusal spent the morning spying on the palace and docks. She did not see Mentàll at all, and wondered what he was doing. Spying on the base, perhaps? She hadn't seen him since he'd stormed out of the house that morning.

He was furious with her. She'd never seen him completely lose his cool before. Not during the thick of battle, not when men had mutinied against him—never. His anger deeply upset her.

Her own lies continued to plague her, too. She wouldn't be able to watch the palace this afternoon or this evening. Mentàll didn't know that. She felt guilty about neglecting her duty, but felt her own mission was much more important. The meeting between the Commanders at the Merry Spirits would only happen once. She believed and hoped the information she learned would be worth all of the misery her lies were causing.

When it neared the time for her shift at the Merry Spirits to begin, she wandered to the north side of town, and then ducked into alleys, carefully doubling back, making sure the Dehrien Chief wasn't following her. She saw no one.

Right on time, she slipped into the Merry Spirits. A quick, suspicious glance inside the establishment calmed her nerves. The Dehrien wasn't inside.

Noisy greetings roared when the men saw her. "Midi! Come 'ere. I'm thirsty," bellowed a red-faced sailor.

"She's servin' me, first," bawled another.

"She's serving neither of you," Tineia asserted, slopping down a drink. "Pay up with me."

Methusal slipped into the side room to change. The Zindedi Commanders hadn't arrived yet. She hoped she hadn't missed them.

The lunch crowd kept her running, and she served not only drinks, but sliced, crisped tubers and thick meat sandwiches. Her stomach rumbled, but she didn't get a chance to eat a snack until most of the lunch crowd had left. By then, her pockets bulged with coins. Better yet, the hungry men had made few efforts to grab her. Well, at least that was the case until they sat back, replete and belching, and their minds turned to matters other than food.

The afternoon wore on. New sailors replaced the old. The new crowd was young, brash, and wanted their drinks now. Their hands were quick, too.

One squeezed a handful of her while she served him a tall glass of spirits. Anger and mortification lit her temper. She whirled and "accidentally" knocked his drink into his lap. He yelped and leaped up, swiping at the cold drink spreading down his pants.

"Maybe that'll cool you down," she muttered. Legs shaking, she retreated to the far side of the room to collect drinks from the drink server.

From then on, she'd moved faster and managed to escape most of the sly, quick gropes.

In the late afternoon, the Zindedi Commanders finally arrived. Tineia was on her break, so Methusal served them. Both men were sunburned, and one had grizzled black and gray hair, and the other was blond and balding. Both looked to be in their fifties, and thankfully showed little interest in her.

They spoke of trivial matters until they finished their meal.

"Talkn from Oesten is coming to the base. Mekl, too, from Paraski."

"Any from Dakarra?"

"No."

"Any guesses for the purpose of the meeting? Last time the General stripped Ankr of his rank. He's still a private."

"I don't know. I'm wearing my cleanest uniform and bringing all my logbooks."

"Good idea. I'll bring one of my men, too, in case I forget something. He can run back to the ship and get it."

The grizzled one grunted. "Think there'll be food there? It'll be at noon."

"Wouldn't count on it. I'm eating lunch before I go."

"Yeah. Don't think that General eats more than a flying beast."

"It's people's fear he likes to eat. Like a whip, devouring his own."

An uncomfortable laugh followed. "Best watch your tongue. He's got spies everywhere."

"What'll he do? Take my ship? He needs Commanders. With all those green recruits..." He snorted. "We'll be lucky to make it to Koblan without losing a few in the sea."

"How's Fijorn?"

"He landed in the drink, the lucky fool. I strapped him to the mast top myself last night. He whimpered and bellyached the whole way up. He's still there," he finished with satisfaction. "An example to the others. He won't cry at heights anymore."

Methusal inwardly cringed at the casually mentioned cruelty. Fijorn had had an accident, and then was further traumatized by being made into a public spectacle. The Zindedis reminded her of the Koblani wild beasts, which devoured weak members of their own pack.

The Commanders' conversation digressed to the incompetent young men they'd soon be receiving from Dakarra and other bases. They grumbled at the training they'd be forced to perform. Apparently, they felt the Presidente should have enforced the draft long ago. He'd refused, apparently. "Likely to keep the General dangling at the end of his whip," snickered one. "The Presidente likes to show who still wears the pants in the family."

"But for how long?" muttered the other. "I've heard tell of chest pains."

"The Presidente will never die. The devil's too scared to have him. He'd probably take over hell."

More quiet laughter.

The men finally left, and before the door closed behind them, she saw it was dark outside now. Maybe another hour until her shift ended. Her feet ached. But at least she'd discovered important information. Everything—the sore feet, the lies—had been worth it.

"How do you do it?" she asked Tineia. At the moment, Methusal was taking a bit longer than necessary to wipe down an empty table. She was trying to ignore a particularly rowdy group of men who had just entered. Two were loudly trying to get her attention, but her thighs felt black and blue from pinches. She felt defiled and filthy, and couldn't wait to leave. She never wanted to return, either. All the same, she'd feel bad about leaving Tineia alone to deal with the horrible beasts.

Tineia offered a small, tired smile. "You get used to it. It pays well. Keeps food on the table for me and my daughter. And sometimes the job has benefits." She flushed. "Sometimes a man will seek you out. It's usually pleasant enough."

Methusal nodded, and gave the table a last swipe. Tineia went very still, her attention apparently caught by something over Methusal's shoulder. "Hmm," she said. An odd inflection lilted her voice.

"What?"

"The one at the bar has taken a liking to you."

Methusal didn't turn around. "Which one?" Another man to avoid.

"The big, good looking one. The Commander."

A sudden chill slid down her spine. She glanced over her shoulder. The man, clad in military black, watched her from beneath his dark cap. Ice blue heat seared into her.

She gulped. Mentàll! *He was here.*

In a panic, she wondered what to do.

Tineia's voice interrupted her muddled thoughts. "I know you're married. But if you go with him, he'll pay well. The officers always do."

It was on the tip of her tongue to admit that he was her "husband," but she didn't. It would be difficult to explain why a Commander's wife would need to make money at a spirits house.

"Go on," Tineia encouraged. "At least talk to him. He might leave you a big tip."

It did seem pointless to avoid him. Their confrontation would either come now or later. Might as well face it head on. She walked toward him.

Immediately, men hooted. "Yeah! Fresh girl is yours, Commander."

Sitting at the bar, as he was, their gazes were nearly level. Silently, she looked into his dangerous, glittering eyes. No words needed to be said—or could be said, because most of the men had fallen silent, clearly straining to hear their interchange.

His hand closed around hers. "You are a pretty one."

"Yeah!" shouted a lout. "Close the deal, Commander."

His thumb stroked the back of her hand. "Come with me. I will make it well worth your while." His words said one thing. His hard eyes said something else entirely.

"My husband would not be pleased," she said faintly.

"You want to please your husband?"

"Yes. Of course."

"In all things?" The ice blue gaze cut into her, as searing as a brand.

She managed a faintly impertinent smile. "His wish is my command."

"I could only wish for a wife as obedient as you."

"How dull that would be. No one to challenge you. Or take your ego down a needed notch or two."

The nearest man flashed her a black look. "You going to take that, Commander?"

Mentàll did not respond. Instead, his gaze still held hers. "Will you come with me? Now." The last sounded like a command.

"I have a shift to finish."

Tineia brushed by. "Go," she murmured.

Methusal drew a slow breath. Much as she'd prefer to postpone the confrontation, it was time to face the Dehrien Chief's displeasure. "I need to change my clothes."

The Dehrien's gaze slid from her face to her neck, to the low scooped line of her top. "You are pleasing just as you are."

Heat flashed, burning her skin where his gaze touched. When his eyes met hers again, hot promise simmered, deep within. Her breaths came quicker. She remained unmoving, even after he released her hand.

"She's ready for you, Commander," called a man down the counter.

It broke whatever spell entangled her. Quickly, she turned and headed for the changing room. It didn't take long to change, but it took longer to prod her feet toward the door. Tineia met her just as she was leaving, and pressed money into her hands. "Your tips. Will you be back?"

Methusal shook her head. "I...I don't think so."

Tineia looked from Methusal to Mentàll, who leaned against the counter watching her, his stare brooding and intense. In a low voice, she said, "He's your husband. Isn't he?"

She considered denying it, but Tineia was no fool. "He's...he's not happy with me."

"Surely he makes enough money?"

"Yes." Methusal searched for another explanation for taking the job. "I didn't want to stay at home alone anymore. I wanted some excitement."

Mentàll strode toward them now, his long strides purposeful and decisive.

"Looks like you found it," Tineia murmured, and left her alone.

The frigid night air felt like an arctic blast after the close, stifling warmth of the Merry Spirits. She shivered, and drew the lapels of her jacket together at her neck.

Silence stretched as they followed the waterfront toward the heart of Carachki. A few lamps lit the path, but shadowed areas lived between them. Mentàll stopped in one of these dimly lit areas and stared out at the bay, which was filled with Zindedi warships.

"You lied to me," he said harshly.

"I know. And I'm sorry. But..." She stopped.

"You would do it again."

She struggled to find an answer.

"Wouldn't you?"

"I wouldn't want to!" she snapped back. "But you make things impossible. I knew you'd forbid me..." She blinked, hating the guilt she felt. She'd broken her own code of honor by lying. It truly sickened her. "I'm *sorry*. I didn't want to lie. I hated it. I've felt awful about it all day, but..." She drew a breath. "Okay. There is no excuse. But I had a lead. I wanted to follow it through, but I knew you wouldn't let me."

Silence elapsed as he took this in. In a low voice, he said, "This incident goes beyond lies and insubordination, Maahr. It is about trust."

"I said I'm sorry."

"You are asking my forgiveness?"

"Yes."

"You will never lie to me again?"

His gaze searched hers in the dim light. He wanted to believe her. That surprised her. Unexpectedly cut to the quick, she touched his powerful wrist. Softly, she said, "I won't. I promise."

The moment of connection ended when his gaze hardened. Tension again stiffened his shoulders. "As I said, this goes beyond lies. Do you like to displease me?"

"What do you mean? I had the perfect, safe cover. I learned important information. Why would that upset you?"

"I told you I did not want you in that place."

"You underestimated me, as usual."

His tone hardened. "As usual, you are insubordinate, Maahr. You did not spy on the palace this afternoon. We do not know if the invitations were brought to the distribution center. Now I will have to break in tonight to see."

"No."

"Yes, Methusal."

"It was worth it," she told him. "I found out that General Fitrn and all the top commanders from Carachki, Oesten, and Paraski are meeting tomorrow at the base."

"When?"

"For a lunch meeting."

"So you did accomplish something of value."

"Of course! I'm not incompetent, like you seem to think. And you don't know everything. You need to trust me."

"You, Methusal, need to trust me."

Annoyed, she glared back. "In this instance, I was right. Admit it. Show *me* some respect."

He looked away, and then back. Finally, in a low voice, he said, "I am glad you discovered the information. However, I am not pleased that you went behind my back to do it."

"How else could I have done it? You'd have forbidden me to go. It wouldn't have mattered that I heard the commanders talking yesterday about the meeting. They said they'd meet again today..."

"You worked there *yesterday?*"

She drew in a quick breath.

"Why didn't you report this yesterday?"

"I knew you'd want to do the mission yourself."

"You are right. I would have." Anger tightened his tone.

"See? You're unreasonable. You don't trust me to do a good job. You want all of the exciting jobs for yourself. That's why I didn't tell you the truth. Because you're a selfish, domineering man!"

"Tell me," he said in a low, harsh voice, "how many men propositioned you, yesterday and today?"

"I don't know. I tried to ignore..."

"How many touched you?" Now his voice was a gravel rasp. "How many put their hands on you?" In the moonlight, darkness edged his cheekbones.

Methusal felt it might be wise not to answer that one.

"*Tell* me!"

"Only a few. Just a pinch here and there. Or...or...nothing much." But her skin still crawled from the contact. She couldn't erase it from her mind.

He swore, loud and viciously.

"Stop it," she whispered.

He uttered another Dehrien curse, then, "Methusal!"

"I told you, it doesn't matter."

"It matters to *me*."

"Why?"

He heaved a harsh breath, obviously trying to control himself. He gritted through his teeth, "You are under my protection. You are my responsibility. I will not let anyone hurt you."

"Anyone except for you, you mean." Shaking a little, she turned on her heel and strode for Mrn. M's house.

She was done with this conversation, and with the emotion shivering between them. She didn't understand him. A soft moment had passed between them when he'd forgiven her. And now he was angry again.

She walked even faster, but he easily kept pace with her.

"Methusal! We cannot go inside the house like this. After this morning, Mrn. M will become suspicious."

"Why didn't you think of that before you started yelling at me?"

He drove his fingers through his hair. "*Methusal. Methusal, stop.*"

She stopped at Mrn. M's garden gate. "What? This situation is impossible. I can't talk to you anymore."

He heaved another harsh breath. "We need to fix our relationship."

Fiercely, she said, "We have no relationship."

"We do."

"The only *relationship*," she waggled her fingers in the air to suggest quotes, "is what Mrn. Machblin sees. She only sees your *acting*. I can't pretend anymore."

"Methusal. You are not..."

"I'm sick of the lies. I'm sick of them *all*."

"What do you mean?"

"Our whole relationship is a lie!"

"It is not," he said through his teeth. "I think you realize that."

"We're not married!"

"Our kisses are not lies."

"They are!" She felt aghast.

Softly, he said, "Is that why you kiss me back?"

"It's an act. Everything's an act! And you're doing an A plus job. You have Mrn. M convinced you're the best thing since running water." She turned, reaching for the garden gate, but he caught her hand.

Low and fierce, he said, "This argument must end. We will look like two happy honeymooners when we go inside."

"More lies."

"I have told you no lies, Methusal. Not one."

She cried out, "You pretending you *care* for me is a lie!" Pain wrenched deep within her. She couldn't explain it, but it hurt badly.

He went silent for a moment. With quiet discernment he said, "Do you want me to care for you?"

"No!"

Mentàll leaned close and kissed her with barely contained, searing heat. "That is what I feel for you. It is not a lie."

She stared up at him. He was so close that she felt his deep, heaving breaths. He had meant the kiss. Mrn. M could not see them.

"Hold my hand, Methusal. You look freshly kissed, and that is what Mrn. Machblin needs to see right now."

Her heart beat faster. Was this another act, or not? A sick feeling gripped her. She felt so confused. What was the truth, and what was fiction? Lies ripped at the fabric of her soul. She could not take another one.

Chapter Thirty

Day 14

AALI'S FIRST MEETING with Great-Grandma had ended up being postponed. Lylitha had suffered several dizzy spells, and she'd needed Aali to constantly watch Trori and Rartn.

But the day of reckoning finally arrived. She hadn't heard the old woman throw a fit during the last few days, but that didn't make her feel any less apprehensive about the upcoming meeting. Maybe she was saving up a whopper for Aali's visit.

She knocked on the older woman's door. A querulous voice demanded that she enter.

"You wanted to speak to me?"

"Sit down, girl! I'll break my neck, looking up at you." Trori's great-grandmother's sharp eyes scanned Aali as she obeyed.

She returned the courtesy. The old lady, wearing all black, sat hunched in a chair. Her hair was gray, and her eyes were the same disconcerting light blue as Trori's.

"Hmmph," the old woman said. "Tall. And too skinny. Don't you eat?"

"Nice to meet you, too. I'm Aali, by the way."

"I know who you are, Aalicaa Storst. You think I'm stupid?"

What a rude old lady!

"Why did you want to speak to me?

"You're new, aren't you? Not boring like all the others around here. Or are you?"

"No one's ever called me boring before. Maybe sassy. Or a troublemaker. But never boring."

The old eyes brightened. "Good. Good." She muttered, "This should be interesting."

"Are you always so rude?"

"Huh?" The old woman cackled. "Of course. An old lady's prerogative. There's no one left to impress."

"What do I call you?"

"GG." The old lady eyed her for several more long minutes, and then said abruptly. "I'm tired. Leave me."

She frowned at this rude dismissal. "I just got here."

"Go!" The old lady flicked a claw-like hand and muttered, "I must plan better for next time."

"What?"

"You will return soon. Now off with you," she ordered in a majestic tone.

Mentally rolling her eyes, Aali did as she was told.

GG was crotchety, but also sharp. Next time they met, she would be more prepared, too. That canny old lady probably knew everything that happened in this house. Maybe even what Mentàll and her grandson Calbn were plotting together.

Aali smiled as she swung on her crutches to fetch the children for lunch.

△ △ △ △ △

Methusal felt rested when she awoke that morning, but emotionally drained from last night's confrontation with Mentàll. Of course, their "discussion" had stopped once they'd entered Mrn. M's house, but she wasn't sure if anything had been resolved.

She was tired of their fights. All she wanted peace—if that could ever be found with him.

When she exited from the relief chamber, ready for the day, Mentàll still hadn't left the room. In fact, he hadn't put on his shirt on because he was inspecting his bullet wound.

She put her nightclothes away. "How does it look?" Not that he needed her help. He was a grown man. And yet, as with every injured beast she'd treated at home, something prodded her to take a look. She had to know if it was healing properly.

"It is fine," he muttered.

Methusal pulled out a coltac leaf. "Let me see."

Humor glinted, which lifted her spirits a little. "Once again, you are like a wolmite with her cub."

"Everyone needs someone to look after them. Move your hand." She brushed it aside, and gasped. Blood trickled from beneath the scab. And at the far end...was that pus? Alarm gripped her. Had blood poisoning set in? The skin around it looked red.

"That doesn't look good. What happened?"

He shrugged. "I bumped my arm this morning. It is nothing."

"You're wrong. It *is* something." She collected a clean, damp cloth from the relief room.

Softly, he said, "You want to take care of me?"

She dabbed at the wound. He watched her intently. Methusal felt very aware of how close he was, but tried to ignore how unsettled she felt.

Again, it was like during the war, when she had tended his wound. And just like then, she'd come to his aid without being asked. Surely this constituted a kind act. At last, she'd followed The One's directive to love her enemy.

An unexpected feeling of peace quieted the discomfort of being so close to him. In answer to his question, she said, "I want to do the best I can."

He stood very still as she carefully wiped away the blood. It occurred to her, in that quiet moment, that the whole weight of this mission rested on his shoulders. He stood alone. She was his only support here in Carachki. He had chosen her to support him.

To her relief, the white patch wasn't pus. She smeared coltac juice onto the suspicious area, and then stuck on a tacky leaf. With a deep breath, she stepped back. Flippantly, she said, "You'll live to see another day. Long enough to spy on those Commanders."

"With you by my side, I can do anything."

She looked up. His gaze held hers. He seemed to mean it. That amazed her. "I'm not so sure about that. I think you could have chosen a better partner for this mission. Maybe someone you don't need to fight all the time."

He smiled. "I still would choose you, Methusal."

"Why?" She actually wanted to know.

"You are a strong woman. And you sharpen me like ore does a blade."

"That doesn't sound very comfortable."

"And I sharpen you. You will not be the same when this mission is over."

"My mother said something similar when I left Rolban."

"Your mother is a wise woman. She sees to the heart of things."

Methusal took a risk. "And what about your mother? What was she like?"

He looked away. She sensed his subtle withdrawal into that dark, remote place inside himself.

Softly, she said, "You still don't want to talk about her?"

"I loved her," he said abruptly. "With all of my heart. I don't remember her very well."

"She loved you with her whole heart, too. I know that is true."

Vulnerability flashed. He turned away. "Yes."

Methusal pressed on, even though she knew she was flirting with the danger of upsetting him. Something told her this was what he needed. So she'd do the right thing. Even if it meant he attacked her, snarling, teeth bared, like the wild beast she'd always believed him to be.

"Why don't you like to speak about her? Or is it me? You don't like to talk about her with me."

Pain flashed, darkening those silver blue eyes to the color of a thunderstorm.

"Why do you want to know?"

"Is it true I remind you of her?"

"No," he said, low and vehemently.

Curiously hurt, she said, "You were touchy whenever I brought her up during the war."

At last, he pulled on his tunic. "Your kindness to me reminded me of her," he said roughly. "But that is all. In truth, my mother was more like Deccia. Sweet and gentle."

"And I'm not." His words stung, although she knew he had not meant to hurt her.

"Are you?" Could that be a trace of humor?

"I'm about as sweet and kind as you are."

"So you see," he said softly, "we are a good match."

"I *want* to change. I want to be a kind, loving person."

"Sweetness does live inside you, Methusal." More humor flashed. "Deep inside. I see it from time to time."

She glared, and then remembered that this conversation was supposed to be about him. "Why don't you like to talk about her?"

"Why do you like to get under my skin?"

She drew an exasperated breath. "During the war I got to you somehow," she guessed. "And the only other person who's gotten under your thick skin was your mother. And Hendra, of course."

He turned his full attention upon her. The faintest smile curved his lips. "Do you want to see into my deepest heart? Is that true, Methusal?"

"I'm curious. I want to understand what motivates a man like you."

"A man like me. Do you still think I am a lost cause? Or do you think a warm heart beats, deep inside of me?"

Her throat closed for a moment. She swallowed with difficulty. "That's the question, now isn't it?"

"What do the good scriptures say? Seek and you shall find, if you seek with your whole heart."

"That's about seeking *The One*. Don't talk blasphemy."

"It is the same if you want to know the truth about any person. You must seek to know who they really are. You must look below the surface. If you dare."

"I *dare*. I think there must be something good in you. Something your mother used to love."

His smile turned faintly mocking. "Can you find it, Methusal? Or perhaps it is an impossible task. Perhaps that part of me died long ago."

"No. If that was true, your love for her would be dead, too."

"Perhaps we are both works in progress, Methusal. What we are to be is not yet seen."

And that's what confounded her. Who was this man, really? Was he the man who still harbored a tender, child's love for his mother, or the ruthless man with ice running through his blood? How could the two coexist? The man was a paradox. Methusal could not figure him out. And that disturbed her most of all.

"For now," he said softly, "I am your Commander. Are you ready to follow my instructions?"

"I'm ready to spy on the General's meeting. I'll follow every instruction that helps us accomplish that goal."

"The correct answer is, 'Yes, Kaavl Commander, sir.'" An echo from the war, when he'd coerced her to submit to his authority. Some of that same tone reflected now. Yesterday's insubordination was not forgotten. He would allow no more.

"I will follow your instructions," she agreed softly. "Kaavl Master. Spokesman elect for *all* of Koblan."

The corners of his mouth jerked up. His teeth flashed in a grin. He'd never directed his full smile at her before. It disarmed her. She blinked, mesmerized. And then she smiled back. Her spirits lifted. It just might be a good day after all.

And maybe they would discover what the top Zindedi officers were up to.

△ △ △ △ △

In the late morning, Methusal and the Dehrien Chief slipped onto the base through the back fence, ready to spy on the top Zindedi meeting. They'd first changed into Zindedi military uniforms in the shack on the edge of the city. Now they headed for the main part of the complex, blending in easily with the hundreds of milling Zindedi soldiers. Privates, most of them, and young. Many wore wide-eyed, scared looks.

As they strode for the Commander's office, she said, "Will you break into the distribution center again tonight?" He had reported that no invitations had been delivered last night.

"I hired a boy to watch. He will report his findings in a note."

"What if he takes your money and lies about watching?"

"I will check the distribution center tonight. If he tells the truth, I'll pay him the other half of his wages tomorrow. It will prove if he is trustworthy for future missions."

"Good idea. Now we can focus on more important things." She sharpened her hearing as they neared the Commander's office. It seemed like the logical place for the meeting to take place.

"I don't hear anything. Are they here yet?"

"It is almost noon." His gaze focused upon a black painted cart. Ornate, swirling gold and red designs adorned it. He murmured, "Looks like General Fitrn is here."

"We could split up," she suggested. "I'll take the north half of the base..."

"No."

She frowned. "Why won't you ever trust me? We're wasting time. They could have started the meeting already."

He said nothing for a moment, but his features looked austere beneath the black cap. Then, harshly, he said, "We will meet back here in ten minutes."

"Unless we find them," Methusal interposed. "That person would have to stay and listen. We can't miss any information."

Slowly, he nodded, although his faint frown said he wasn't pleased with the idea. "Ten minutes," he repeated harshly, and cut south.

It seemed unlikely that the top military men would meet in the outbuildings which housed powder and ammunition, she decided. They'd want a place with chairs, and perhaps access to drinks from the dining hall. So that meant somewhere within the barracks area.

From prior excursions, she knew the barracks stretched in military rows between the dining hall and recreation hall, and more rows extended west, beyond the recreation hall, toward the base's main entrance. She and Mentàll had only given the area a cursory investigation, because it clearly contained only military housing. What if they'd missed something?

She skulked toward the dining hall, mingling with the pimple-faced young men. Carefully focusing her kaavl hearing to filter out the noise around her, she carried, planting her source of hearing inside each barrack she passed.

"...ing General."

A coarse laugh.

"Why can't we go home first?" A whiny snivel.

On and on it went. She strode quickly, listening to and then dismissing each building in turn. Nothing important happening in the dining hall. She itched to find the top Zindedis without Mentàll. That would prove she was a competent, useful kaavl soldier, and did not need his constant supervision. Better yet, she could start spying without him.

△ △ △ △ △

"Presidente! Welcome."

"Nasrias for you." He offered them to the woman at the door. Pleasurable anticipation tingled within him. He knew she would love them. They were her favorite flowers.

"Thank you!" she gasped, and sniffed deeply of the succulent yellow blossoms.

The Zindedi leader motioned for his bodyguard to stay outside, and he followed his hostess indoors. "Your garden is as lovely as ever, Mari."

Mrn. M turned and dimpled at him, revealing a strong resemblance to the enchanting girl he had been enamored with years ago. At that time, she had been his cousin's wife, so he had made no overtures toward her. Now, nothing stood in his way.

"Sit down," she urged, ushering him to the most comfortable chair. She settled the nasrias in the center of the small table in the living room, and took a chair adjacent to his. "It is good to see you again," she smiled. "To what do I owe the honor of your visit?"

The Presidente relaxed his stocky frame. The chair was a little stiff for his taste, but it was the best this poor woman could offer. Perhaps someday he could offer her more—if she passed his test today.

He chuckled pleasantly. "I fear I have been ignoring you. It has been two weeks since I saw you last."

Mari flushed. "I feel spoiled, that's what I feel. You take time out of your busy schedule to visit me. And you bring such lovely flowers each time."

"I am happy to do it." He smiled genially.

"Charlie would so appreciate how good you are to me."

His smile became stiff. *Charlie.* Must she bring him up every time he visited? The man was dead. Couldn't she see that he was ten times the man Charlie had been? She was blind, and a fool.

Soon his patience would wear out. But one of the purposes for his visit today was to see how much of a fool she really was. Or perhaps she was a traitor. Discomfort tightened his chest, and he tried to relax. He did not want pains to attack him here.

His perceptions of Mari could not be so erroneous. He had not misjudged her.

Quickly, she arose. "Would you like tea? Perhaps your favorite cakes?"

"No, no. I don't wish to be a bother. Regrettably, I can only stay for a few moments."

"Oh." She sat back down.

"I have been worried about you, Mari. Your home looks well kept, but Charlie's death pay surely is not enough to meet all of your expenses."

"Thank you, Presidente." *Presidente.* Another source of irritation. She would not use his given name, even though he'd instructed her to do so. "...But I'm managing just fine. I take in boarders, you know."

He affixed a pleasant smile upon his face and folded his hands across his thick midriff. "Good, good, I am relieved to hear that," he murmured. "But still, if you need anything, I insist you come to me. It would be my pleasure to help."

"Thank you." Her eyes looked bright. She was pleased, he deduced.

"Good. Tell me, then. Do you have boarders now?" Anticipation sharpened within him.

"Oh, yes." For the first time, Mari relaxed back in her chair with a soft, wry smile. "Indeed I do. They are a pair, to be sure."

The Zindedi leader smiled and leaned forward a little. He did not have to pretend interest. "Oh? Tell me about them."

"Well, Midi is as sweet as she can be. And Lozar is charm itself." Her cheeks pinkened a little.

Jealousy stiffened the Presidente's spine, but he kept his expression bland. "Oh?"

Mari shook her head. "But the two of them together... Sparks fly. More than at a bonfire."

"They fight?" he asked pleasantly. So. If these were the Koblanis, as he suspected, their fights proved they were still enemies. Their marriage was a sham. Good. He felt well satisfied, and strangely relieved

She snorted. "Yes. Often. But they always make up. They're honeymooners, and just have a few problems to work through, is all. But I have confidence they will be fine."

"Where are they from?"

"Dakarra. Lozar is a Commander. He fought in the south of Koblan. Perhaps with General Fitrn. He's never said."

"Indeed. I will have to ask my son." The Presidente frowned. "Lozar. The name is familiar, but I cannot place his face..."

"He's a big man. Very tall, with blond hair. It's an unusual color—almost white. And has distinctive, pale blue eyes."

Fierce elation gripped him. Only one man on the planet fit that description. *Mentàll Solboshn.* His number one enemy.

However, the Zindedi leader kept his features carefully expressionless. "Yes. I remember him now."

"And Midi is about Ceri's age, with beautiful, long brown hair."

"I am pleased that you have such excellent boarders. How long are they staying?"

"A few more days, and then Lozar will have to report for duty."

They would leave in a few days' time. For where? Koblan? Had they believed his words of peace?

The Presidente did not believe this. He must squeeze more information from Mari's willing lips. It was clear she was beguiled by the Koblanis. A fault of her soft, generous heart, the Presidente deduced. It was a weakness, but not a traitorous defect. However, he did wish that Mari had more discernment.

With deliberation, he said, "Are they coming to the ball?" Mari's invitation had not yet been sent. No doubt she felt anxious about that, and was wondering if she would be invited. He had intended to deliver the invitation himself, but now...now he would need to modify his plans.

Mari's eyes brightened. "They haven't been invited. But they are curious about the ball. They've asked me a number of questions about it." She looked at him expectantly. When he did not respond, she looked away, swallowing quickly.

Good. She felt uncomfortable. A just punishment for stupidly harboring spies. Spies who were interested in the grand ball.

Pleasurable plans whirled in his mind, each more satisfying than the last. He would send orders to his son at once. And he'd also order that all of the invitations be delivered tomorrow. Except for Mari's.

Retribution on his enemies would begin immediately.

△ △ △ △ △

Methusal could not find the meeting place for General Fitrn and the commanders. It was nearly time to meet Mentàll, and she had exhausted every option.

She had overheard a lot of gossip between the soldiers, however. The privates would practice shooting skills this afternoon, and a few men mentioned seeing the General earlier. Awe and fear tinged their voices. But no one mentioned the location of the top level meeting.

It was time to meet Mentàll. Disappointed, Methusal headed past the recreation hall again. A man with a gun over his shoulder stood outside the double doors. She listened intently, but heard nothing at all inside.

Nothing.

Her steps slowed.

Wasn't that strange? With all of these men on base, wouldn't a few be inside? She glanced at the gray double doors. The soldier stationed outside looked bored. She sharpened her hearing to listen to a location just inside the doors. Quiet breaths from two men.

Excitement prickled. *Guards.*

The General and his top commanders must be inside. But why couldn't she hear them?

A mystery. And that meant she needed to get into the building.

Unfortunately, it looked like the double doors were the only way in. All of the windows were shut, and there were no shrubs that would conceal her attempt to break into one. She had to go in the front door. Somehow.

An idea flashed to mind, and she walked quickly for the dining hall. She fingered the edges of her beret, making sure all of her hair was safely tucked inside, and then strode into the kitchen as if she belonged there.

Twenty or more men worked quickly, making sandwiches, flipping meat in a pan, and arranging platters. Warm, spicy smells filled her nostrils, and her stomach growled.

Methusal looked for the drinks area, or for anyone carrying a tray. She spotted a man with spiky blond hair who was pouring hot water into a silver pot. Delicate cups, placed upside down on plates, rested on a tray beside him. On the nearby counter were six more trays. Each appeared to hold three plates of varying sizes, all covered by black pottery lids with red handles. Methusal positioned herself next to a tray near the end.

The man filling the tea pots glanced at her. "Good. You're ready. Ngev! Histl!" He shouted three more names. "Come help." He whipped off his apron, crammed on his cap and jacket, and picked up the first tray. He hoisted it over his head. "Follow me."

Methusal followed the Zindedi men out of the dining hall, carefully holding her heavy tray. It was awkward to balance overhead, and it seemed silly, too. But perhaps it was a Zindedi custom reserved for serving the highest officers.

Outside, she walked close behind the Zindedi soldiers, but kept a sharp eye out for Mentàll. She saw him a moment later, lurking near the corner of a building. She felt it when he spotted her, too. That pale gaze pinned her as sharply as a knife could skewer an apte.

Guards opened the doors to the recreation hall. Taking a deep breath, she stepped inside.

Just as she'd heard with kaavl, a guard was positioned on either side of the exit doors inside. Directly ahead of her, the serving men's boots clicked across the wooden floor of a massive hall. At the far end, they entered a door and filed left down a hall, and then up a narrow flight of stairs. Then they marched down another narrow hall.

Methusal still heard nothing, and stopped with the others when the leader halted outside of a smooth white door. He rapped twice with a metal mallet. The sound clanged.

The door swung open, and Methusal saw that the thick door was made of metal.

As she silently filed inside the room after the others, she saw that all of the walls looked unnaturally smooth. She guessed the entire room was encased in ore. It appeared to block out sound.

So they had soundproofed the room to prevent anyone from overhearing their sensitive plans. The Zindedis must indeed be paranoid.

A long wooden table occupied the sparsely furnished gray room. Six commanders were seated around it, and General Fitrn sat at the head of the table.

General Fitrn.

For the first time, the folly of her actions hit her. He might recognize her and think she was Deccia.

Methusal looked down at the floor, averting her face from the Zindedi.

The kitchen steward led the way to a long side table positioned against the left wall. He motioned for the other food bearers to come near. Then he picked up a cup and saucer, along with the teapot, and headed for the table. The other servers and Methusal did likewise.

The head steward served the General, and Methusal sidled to the far end of the table, endeavoring to avoid the commanders she'd served at the spirit house, for fear they'd recognize her. She placed the saucer and cup before a thin, scowling man and retreated to the side table while the main steward poured the drinks.

"Enough!" The General waved the steward off before Methusal's man could be served. In silence, he obeyed. The thin man scowled more deeply, his thick black brows bristling.

"Mekl. Give a report on the ships in Paraski," the General ordered.

The thin man said, "They are all ready. We await only powder from eastern Zindedi."

"And you, Talkn?"

"We have powder. We are waiting for fresh recruits to man our ships," said a florid, heavy-set man.

"Men and powder will arrive tomorrow at Paraski and Oesten. The final shipment in Carachki will arrive soon enough." The General flicked a slim finger at the head steward.

With alacrity, the man lifted the largest plate from a tray and approached General Fitrn. Methusal and the others quickly followed suit and served the other men. The seventh soldier speedily poured tea into Mekl's cup.

Methusal was glad now that she'd learned a little about serving at the Merry Spirits. At least she knew how to move quickly and unobtrusively. She placed the plate before Mekl and whisked the lid away, revealing red, creamy soup.

"Leave us!" the General snapped, motioning to the servers. "Mergev, you stay. Choose one man to help you. The others are dismissed. *Now!*"

She needed to stay too, so that she could listen to their conversation. *Please, The One.*

Methusal risked turning her face toward the main steward. He hovered behind the General, who fastidiously blew on a spoonful of steaming soup. The steward scanned the row of men. Methusal's heart sank when his gaze rested on the man beside her. He opened his mouth. Inexplicably, however, he then glanced at Methusal. Curtly, he nodded.

She'd stay!

The others filed from the room and the door clanged shut.

An uneasy silence fell as the General and commanders ate their soup. Methusal got the distinct impression that the commanders were afraid to speak unless spoken to.

The General slowly tasted each spoonful of soup. He dabbed a napkin to his thin lips after each bite.

She wondered if he liked the uncomfortable silence. Did he feed off of the subtle fear emanating from his lower officers?

When the General finished his soup, the steward whisked away the bowl. With a silent hand motion, he ordered Methusal to clear the other bowls. It didn't seem to matter if the commanders had finished their soup or not.

Plates with slices of urchet meat, tubers, and gravy were served next.

Methusal's stomach gurgled alarmingly.

Talkn chuckled. When displeasure sharpened the Zindedi General's features, Talkn fell abruptly silent.

The meal continued in silence. The General ate rapidly now. Would they discuss the mission at all? Or would they wait until she and the steward had left?

Frustrated, Methusal leaned against the wooden side table, trying to appear inconspicuous. If only the General would start talking!

All too soon, General Fitrn sat back. He'd only finished half of his meal. The commanders, even less.

General Fitrn's delicate burp seemed to be the steward's cue to clear the table. Methusal silently helped him, and then served the last dish; a spice-scented cake filled with cream, and drizzled with red sauce. It looked delicious. Methusal tensed her stomach muscles, hoping to avert another growl. It worked. For the moment.

The men greedily eyed their cake, but the General did not touch his, so they didn't touch theirs, either.

"So." General Fitrn rapped his fork on the table. "Have you no questions? Your lack of curiosity is disturbing."

The grizzled commander from the Merry Spirits said, "We await your orders, General. I think I speak for everyone when I say we are eager to defeat the Koblanis."

"Good." Fitrn's smile looked false. "It is time to discuss our enemies. And our plans."

The commanders leaned forward, as if eager to hear every word that fell from the General's lips. Those lips thinned in a curl of disgust. "Talkn. Explain our goal for Koblan."

"To get the ore, General, sir. And to kill as many Koblanis as we can."

His narrowed, flat gaze pinned another commander. "Mekl?"

"We will kill all of their leaders. We will capture their kaavl players and torture them into revealing their secrets."

A fine chill swept down Methusal's spine.

Another commander spoke up, perhaps emboldened by Mekl's statements. "We will capture the kaavl leaders of the resistance. The Dehrien, Mentàll Solboshn, and Methusal Maahr."

A smile curled the General's lips. "My father says they are on Zindedi soil."

The commanders' dismay was evidenced by the quick babble of voices. General Fitrn's curt hand motion silenced them.

"They are in Carachki, pretending to be one of us. Pretending to be married. Soon, each will be tortured into revealing Koblan's kaavl secrets. Once we understand how to use this ...*kaavl*..." disdain twisted the word, "...Koblan will be helpless before us. They have few weapons. No central government. No Presidente. They are weak. Exploiting their lush treasures will be a pleasure."

"But how will we take their ore?" asked Talkn. "Kaavl soldiers roam all over Koblan. How do we fight against them? They appear out of nowhere, and then disappear!"

"He's right. We have no weapon against kaavl. It's like magic."

"*It's not magic!*" the General shouted. His vocal cords stood out in violent ridges. His face, however, looked calm. Disconcerting. "Our *spies* have learned kaavl. They have written home about it. There is nothing magical about it."

"Then why hasn't anyone in Zindedi learned it?" asked Mekl. "Haven't the spies' letters described how to learn this kaavl?"

The General waved a hand. "They claim it takes years of practice. I don't believe it. As I said, we will extract their kaavl secrets, and then we will kill every kaavl man, woman, and child we meet on Koblan."

"We will attack the whole continent, then?"

"No. Our target remains the same. But once that stronghold falls, the rest will soon collapse."

The General took a tiny bite of the cake, and his face twisted into a moue of disgust. "Take it!" His fist hit the dish and sent it flying off the table. Pottery shattered, and cake and cream spattered onto the wall.

Red flushed the General's face. "*It is unfit to eat!*" he screamed. "Throw it on the floor," he ordered the commanders.

Talkn doubtfully eyed his dessert. He licked his lips. With a small sigh, he pushed the plate over the table's edge. Crockery smashed, one dish at a time, around the room. The sound echoed, magnifying to a ringing cacophony in the metal encased room.

The head steward's face went unnaturally pale. Hastily, he knelt and began to clean up the mess. The General stared at him, his lips curled back in a maniacal snarl. The steward looked down, quickly tending to his task. Either he was not aware of the General's continuing glare, or he was wishing he was invisible.

Fitrn flicked off the man's cap and grabbed him by his hair. He forced his head backward. "The rings for you, soldier."

The steward's throat bobbed. "Yes sir."

The General shoved him backwards, hard, knocking him off balance. He fell onto the floor.

Legs shaking a little, Methusal quickly knelt to gather up dessert fragments. Her hands trembled.

An unearthly silence reigned from the General's end of the table. Swallowing, she moved more quickly.

Boots clicked across the floor. The General. Heart pounding, she grabbed a spoon which fallen on the floor and shoved it up her sleeve. Too bad it wasn't a knife. If only she had *her* knife! Yet again, she had forgotten to bring it.

Foolish. *Foolish.* If she survived this, she'd carry it all the time.

Black, polished boots appeared in her line of vision, spaced apart to avoid the spattered dessert. The fastidious General didn't want to step in the gooey mess. A weakness, and one she could use to her advantage.

"Look up, soldier."

Methusal tensed, and did her best to focus into kaavl.

Sensory input rushed in. The door, two lengths away. One commander was between her and freedom. Of course, even if she made it out of the room, there were no guarantees she'd make it outside alive. There could be untold numbers of soldiers in the hallway right now.

"I *said* look up!" the General snarled.

Methusal looked up into his dead, flat eyes. Pleasure lurked in his faintly curled lips.

"Are you responsible for this mess, soldier?"

How should she answer that loaded question?

Carefully, she said in a low voice, "I'm cleaning it up."

Swifter than thought, a black boot kicked her wrist, scattering the pieces she had gathered. Pain flashed, followed by a numb, tingling sensation. Methusal remained where she was, squatted and hunched over. Now what? What game did the insane General want to play?

"You're useless!" General Fitrn stated.

She remained silent.

"Aren't you?"

Agree? Say nothing? ...Probably not. "Of course," she murmured.

"Of course?" The General laughed. It sounded disbelieving. "Of *course?* You beg to be taught a lesson, soldier."

Methusal slowly picked up the pieces again. The General's boot connected with her side. Sharp pain, followed by nausea, shot through her. Bile rose in her throat, and she was glad she hadn't eaten anything recently.

She allowed the spoon she'd hidden up her sleeve to slide to her palm. She gripped it tightly.

A violent hand swept the cap from her hair, and Methusal sprang to her feet. The General gaped at her clipped up hair, and then his gaze went to her face. Shock gave way to a vicious snarl. "You!" He lunged for her throat.

Methusal was ready. She arced up the spoon handle, wanting to hit his groin, but missed. The spoon dug into the soft flesh of his stomach. He gasped, and she stomped on his instep and rammed the spoon deep into the tender area of his neck. He gasped again, hands flying for his throat.

Methusal spun and ran for the door. A twist, and it was open.

"Not so fast," snarled a voice. Bony hands gripped her wrist, and an arm choked around her neck. Methusal stabbed blindly at her attacker, and then grabbed at his sleeve and shoulder cloth and twisted forward and down, pulling him awkwardly over her shoulder. Mekl's long body collided with the metal door, slamming it shut.

The others were almost upon her. In a frenzied panic, Methusal wrenched the door open, fighting against Mekl's weight sprawled against it, and squeezed out. A frowning soldier approached from the end of the hall. Methusal whipped out her trusty spoon and flung it, straight and true, at his eye. He screamed.

Heart pounding and feeling sick, she ran down the stairs and down the short hall. She stopped just before the door leading to the massive main hall, and wondered how she could possibly escape past the two guards stationed at the front doors.

Boots clattered on the wooden floors upstairs.

Should she pull her hair pins out? Maybe seeing a woman would shock the guards long enough for her to devise a plan of escape.

Or maybe not. Feet pounded down the stairs now. No time to lose. She strode out the door, head held high, narrowed eyes focused on the door. Her goal—escape.

Only one guard stood there now. But a tall one. A big one.

He looked her way, and ice blue froze straight into her soul.

Mentàll. She felt such intense relief that she wanted to weep. She ran to him. Kaavl input continued to flood in—the men behind her, about to come through the door, and the bodies of the two guards lying to the right, in the shadows.

The Dehrien's fingers bit into her arm and he yanked her out the front door. The outside guard had disappeared, as well.

They walked fast, around the corner of the building. Mentàll headed toward the front gate with quick, decisive steps.

Sounds tickled into Methusal's ears. "They're following us," she gasped.

He didn't answer. A few steps later he cut right, following a wall, and then right again. Now they were heading for the eastern, back portion of the base. But they still had to pass through the barracks area. Not to mention pass by the recreation hall and the dining hall area again. But from the sounds she heard, the commanders and soldiers seemed to be focusing their attention on following their cold path to the front gate.

General Fitrn's sharp voice cut into her ears. "They haven't gone this way, fools! Search the entire base!"

But Methusal and Mentàll were making good time. They ran behind the barracks, and when they came to an open place, they casually strolled in order to avoid attracting attention. Whenever they came within eyesight of other soldiers, Methusal modified her steps so Mentàll would block their view of her. Her beret was missing, and her pinned up hair made it obvious she was a woman.

Swiftly, they reached the back fence and slipped through into their friendly gully. Mentàll wasted no time in heading for Carachki. But before they left the gully at the edge of town, he stopped.

Cold eyes surveyed her. "Take down your hair and remove your jacket. You must look like a Zindedi woman when we go into town. You no longer pass as a soldier."

Methusal tugged off the jacket and plucked the pins from her hair, so it tumbled down around her shoulders. The Dehrien watched, his expression remote. The coldness, however, gave her a clue about his true feelings. He was angry.

A small, unexpected smile tugged at her lips. How well she knew him. His displeasure didn't disturb her, however. Instead, after escaping from that awful General, she felt oddly euphoric. She'd spied on their meeting. She knew their deepest goals for Koblan. And she'd stuck a spoon in the General's neck. She wouldn't think about the soldier whose eye she had probably damaged.

"Why are you smiling? This is not a humorous situation, *Maahr*."

She looked back at him, battling that ice blue gaze. "I know you are unhappy with me, and I know you were worried about me. I'm sorry about that."

A silent moment passed. "Tell me what you learned," he said in a muted, controlled voice.

Methusal climbed out of the gully, and on the way to the shack where they would change clothes, she told him everything. Her spirits lifted when he fell silent, digesting it all. She had discovered critical intelligence, and they both knew it.

After changing, they strolled for the docks, and then took a turn around the Presidente's palace. All seemed to be quiet today. The sun sank toward the horizon. Mentàll said little during this time. Methusal took this as another sign of her success. Once again, she had discovered vital information completely on her own.

As they closed Mrn. M's gate behind them, she said, "Will you finally admit that I'm a competent kaavl soldier? I discovered every scrap of information yesterday and today without your help."

He remained silent. Encouraged, she pressed on, "We know they plan to attack one stronghold..."

"We do not know *where,*" he interrupted, his voice like slick ice.

"We know they want to kill the kaavl players..."

"They want to kill *us.* They want to torture you. If you had not escaped..."

"But I did," she said cheerfully.

"*Methusal.* The General knows you are in Carachki. He has memorized your face. Deccia hurt him in Dakarra. *You* injured him here." Vehemently, he said, "You can be sure he wants your blood."

"He can't have it."

He gripped her arm, stopping her from opening Mrn. M's door. "You do not understand how his mind works."

"And you do? Is that because you remember how you felt when you wanted to kill me? So now you understand his bloodlust? Is that it?"

"Yes, I understand him," he said harshly. "I am not proud of it. I understand that he will do anything...*anything* to make you pay."

"Because I hurt his pride?"

"Yes. You embarrassed him in front of his commanders. He will search this town from top to bottom until he finds you. He will torture you." His voice was rough. "And then he will kill you."

Fear prickled into her heart. "He won't find me. I'll wear disguises. I'm smarter than you give me credit for. After all, *you* never killed me, did you?"

An eerie silence elapsed. "I could have, Methusal. Many times. But I did not. Because I am not insane."

She looked up at her old enemy, standing in the glow of the porch light. Tall and forbidding. At times, he still frightened her, but not like he had before. Never like before. "You want to protect me now?"

"Yes. But you must follow my every instruction. Do you understand?"

"I will follow your orders. But sometimes a risk will need to be taken, Mentàll. I'll take those risks, for the good of the mission. You need to accept that."

"You will do what I tell you."

"Risks will..."

"You will do what I *tell you* to do."

She frowned. "Why can't you admit that I did something of value today? Is it because you can't stand to be proven wrong? Can't you admit I could be right about something?"

He uttered a short, Dehrien curse. "You are blind, Methusal."

"I am blind to none of your faults," she snapped. "But just once, I'd like for you to say I've done a good job!"

"You have done an excellent job. But you are impulsive. You do not think through your actions. How did you plan to escape today?"

"I don't know. Honestly, I don't think I could have planned an escape. I think I trusted you to be there for me."

"What if I am not there for you, Methusal? What then?" That rough rasp actually sounded like he cared for her—as if that might be why he was being so hardheaded right now. That thought lifted her spirits. She endeavored to ignore his dark frown.

"Hopefully that day never comes. For now, my mission was a success." She smiled and impulsively grabbed his hand. "Come on. Let's go inside."

△ △ △ △ △

Hendra hid in the thick forest and peered around a tree, her heart pounding. Thick bark pressed into her gloves and cold mist seeped through her clothes. The thick fog, which had lingered all day, could not conceal the two powder carts and scores of men streaming from the Dakarran base. All wore packs on their backs. All were heading toward Carachki.

A touch on her shoulder made her jump.

"My shift," Goric said, his murky eyes reflecting the color of the fog.

"Are Tabor and Riln back yet?"

"No." And from the curt word, he didn't appear to care.

Goric had never been a friendly man, but he'd become even more withdrawn over the last several days. Hendra wondered why.

"Two powder carts left the base," she reported. "I'll tell the others."

"Good thing Riln's not here, or he'd want to blow them up." A bald statement, and yet caustic humor bit through it, too.

Hendra hesitated. She'd never taken the time to get to know Goric. Mostly because she suspected he didn't want to be known. She wondered if he liked to be alone, or if he'd just lived as an outsider all of his life, and so that was the role he'd become accustomed to playing.

Hendra understood the feeling. She had spent most of her childhood trying to be a shadow, too—trying to avoid her father's mean-spirited attention, and wishing those who wanted to hurt her would leave her in peace.

"You're right," she said. "If we didn't need his help to get on the base, I'd wish he wouldn't come back." Hastily, she added, "At least not for a long time." She didn't want him dead, of course.

"What do you know about Riln?"

"Not much. He's from Tarst. He mutinied against Mentàll during the Quasr War. But you know that."

"What else do you know?" Goric watched the base.

The question seemed strange. "Why do you ask?"

"I observe people. Riln acts suspiciously. No one seems to ask why."

"He's a hot head. I'm not sure if that's suspicious."

Goric shrugged. "Think what you want." His tone was dismissive. Clearly, he was used to people ignoring his opinions.

"I don't like Riln, either. But he hates the Zindedis. He'll fight to the death to defeat them."

"He'll fight to the death. But who will he take to hell with him?"

"Do you think he's dangerous to our team?"

Goric's eyes flashed, looking as bleak as a winter day. "Of course. Zindedis won't be the only ones who die with him."

"I hope you're wrong."

"Everyone believes I'm wrong about everything." Resentment twisted through the words. "I've never measured up to anyone's standards. I probably never will." He watched the base, his posture rigid, and slightly hunched.

Hendra remained silent for a moment. "Maybe you should be the man *you* want to be," she suggested. "Who cares what others think? It's your life. You're the one who'll have to answer for your actions in the end."

Goric really looked at her then, his gray eyes sharper than their normal dull color. "It's not so easy."

"When is it ever easy to do the right thing? Follow your conscience, and The One's ways, and you'll be a man that you can be proud of."

Goric looked away again.

Hendra got the feeling that he'd just shut her out. "I'll talk to Behran about Riln."

"Good luck," he said curtly.

Silently, Hendra made her way back to the cabins. And she thought about what Goric had said about Riln.

△ △ △ △ △

Mentàll ate swiftly and methodically at dinner. He was courteous when Mrn. M spoke to him, but his answers were short, bordering on curt. On occasion, Methusal felt his gaze on her. When she looked up, his eyes glittered with unknown, tightly leashed emotions. Disturbed, she looked away. He was still upset. But why?

Mrn. M watched them with a faint frown. Great. Now the Kaavl Master was compromising their cover. Methusal wanted no part of it. And she wouldn't be sucked under by his bad temper, either.

She smiled at Mrn. M. "I love the flowers on the table. Aren't they nasrias?" She'd noticed the yellow flowers the minute they'd returned home this evening. Their sweet, heavy fragrance filled the room. They had not been on the table this morning.

Mrn. M dimpled, pleased. "A friend brought them today."

Methusal wondered if it was the male "friend" who had visited Mrn. M last week. She smiled. "Very thoughtful."

"Perhaps I should plant nasrias in my garden. I have just the spot, and I love them so..." Mrn. M rhapsodized on about her garden, and which flowers would bloom next, for quite some while. It was fine with Methusal. All the better to ignore her frowning, fake husband.

After a while, Mrn. M departed to bring in dessert. For a moment, Methusal was left alone with the Dehrien Chief.

"What's wrong?" she hissed. "Mrn. M is getting suspicious."

"What is wrong, Methusal, is that you are uncontrollable."

Mrn. M returned. He said nothing, but a deep, severe frown remained as he ate dessert. Methusal honestly couldn't figure him out. Why was he so angry?

The last time he'd been like this was after the Zindedi soldier had whipped her. He'd been angry then, like now...but it was more than that. Both times her life had been in danger. Maybe, as she'd thought earlier, he wasn't so much angry as he was upset at the thought of something bad happening to her.

She glanced at him as he silently ate his dessert. His expression looked stern, and his lips straight and unsmiling.

A bemused smile tugged at her lips. Could it be? Had he actually been that worried about her?

Mrn. M sent Methusal another worried look, but it softened when she saw Methusal's smile. Their hostess stood. "Tea for you two?"

Mentàll demurred, and so did Methusal. Mrn. M carted the dirty dishes to the kitchen. When Methusal rose to help, their landlady said, "Relax tonight, dear," She winked at Methusal, and then glanced meaningfully at Mentàll. The older lady's marital advice returned to mind.

Methusal took in the Dehrien Chief's severe expression. Should she? Dared she? It certainly would alleviate Mrn. M's worries about their marriage. And it just might jolt her "husband" out of his foul mood.

Some reckless part of her wanted to do just that. What would it be like to startle him?

Alarmingly, she wanted to know. She could not explain why the thought of turning the tables on him made her heart beat faster with anticipation.

When Mentàll headed for their room, she slipped between him and the door, forcing him to a stop. Surprise flickered across his features.

He was so close that she could smell the clean scent of his shaving soap. He'd shaved just after their mission. His crisp white shirt emphasized the breadth of his shoulders, and he seemed very large, so close like this.

She swallowed, determined not to lose her nerve. "You've had a hard day, I know." With a smile, she put a gentle hand on his shoulder. He stiffened. "It's all right, love," she whispered. "I'll soothe away your tensions." Boldly, she reached up and pulled down his head.

The action took him by surprise. His eyes dilated black, but he gave only the slightest resistance before allowing her to tug his head down further. She kissed him.

It felt strange, having all the power, to be the aggressor. He didn't move, or respond. She took it as a challenge—after all, Mrn. Machblin was watching. It needed to be a good performance. She drew on all of her limited knowledge and pressed her lips against his, persuasively sliding and softly nipping at his until an unexpected tremor ran through him. He opened his mouth to hers and fiercely deepened the kiss.

Methusal trembled when the fake caress abruptly exploded out of control. She clung to him as molten heat poured through her body. "Ment...," she choked out.

With one swift movement, he swung her up in his arms and carried her into their room. A kick, and the door slammed shut, and he carried her to the bed. He looked down at her, his breaths deep and harsh. "Shall we continue?"

She felt vulnerable, lying there, but a perverse, irrational part of her insanely wanted to reach for him.

"No." She shook her head for emphasis.

"Why?"

"I was only pretending."

"No."

"Yes," she whispered.

He clenched his fists, visibly trying to restrain himself.

"Explain yourself," he ordered in a guttural voice.

"Mrn. Machblin was getting suspicious. And...and she told me the other day that she thought...she thinks we need help. Our relationship is bumpy, she said, just like her and her husband's was. She told me I should...that we needed some unexpected zip. I thought she was getting worried about us again, so I...I took her advice. I couldn't warn you. It had to be a surprise."

His harsh breaths slowly quieted, but his dilated eyes still burned. "You planned this?"

"I decided it at the last minute." She sat up, feeling vulnerable lying on the big bed. "I hope you understand."

"I understand perfectly," he said harshly.

Methusal sensed that he still teetered on the edge, battling for control. He could so easily continue what she had started. Heart beating rapidly, she watched him. Long moments slid by. She saw when at last control slipped over his features, masking his expression.

"You did well." He turned away, and began rifling through his pack, his shoulders stiff.

She gathered up her night things. "Are you going in the relief room now?"

"No." He didn't stop digging through his pack.

Inside, she took her time getting ready, hoping that by the time she came out, all of the tension would have blown over.

He lay on his side of the bed, reading a parchment, when she entered the room again. She put away her clothes and crawled in on the other side. She lay with her back to him. "Good night," she offered.

For a moment she thought he wouldn't respond, and then he said roughly, "Good night."

After a moment, she said in a small voice, "What's wrong?"

A silent moment passed. "I did not expect you to do that. You fooled me."

Uncomfortable heat prickled. "You mean you thought I meant it?"

Another silence. "For a moment." He hadn't wanted to admit it.

An apology hovered on her lips, but remained unspoken. After all, didn't he continually play games with her? Instead, she turned over, so she could see him. "Was my decision so bad?"

"No. You secured our cover with Mrn. Machblin."

"Then what's wrong?"

The cool, pale gaze held hers for a long moment. "Do you truly want to know?"

Danger whispered a warning through her mind. "Maybe not," she said softly.

"Next time give me a warning."

"Like you warn me?"

"You like to play with fire, Methusal. Know that the next time you will be burned." He blew out the lamp.

Of all the gall! She flopped back onto her other side and muttered, "You can serve it, but you can't take it."

A hard hand pulled her shoulder, forcing her flat onto her back again. He loomed over her.

She said, "You promised not to touch me."

"You promised not to provoke me."

She pulled free and turned back onto her side. "Good night." She pulled the quilt up to her chin in a cocooning, protective gesture and tried to ignore him.

After a moment, she felt his weight shift as he lay back down. Her pounding heart slowed. What was wrong with her? Did she want a confrontation with him, here in bed? After what had just taken place?

Long, silent moments passed, and she gradually relaxed. He would stay true to his word.

Methusal stayed awake for a long time, questioning and second guessing her actions after dinner. Why had she kissed him? Had it truly been to protect their cover, or had something else motivated her actions?

No easy or palatable answers came. But she finally admitted one thing to herself. She had wanted to disturb him tonight. That's why she'd so eagerly taken Mrn. Machblin's advice. She'd been feeling full of herself and had wanted to provoke him, true enough. She'd wanted power over him, and she'd wanted to shake him up. And she'd succeeded a little too well. Just thinking about her instant, heated response to his caresses made shame burn her cheeks. What about Behran? Why did she keep forgetting about her fiancé when she was with Mentàll?

Guilt consumed her. Could she be any more self-destructive? She marveled at her own foolishness.

Chapter Thirty-One

DAY 15

THE PRESIDENTE STARED AT THE MESSAGE in disbelief. Great snorts escaped from his flaring nostrils. Impossible! It was not *possible*. Surely his military was not so incompetent.

Pain, like white lightning, shot from his chest to his groin. He had no time to breathe before agonizing spasms seized his chest. He gasped, his mouth gaping soundlessly; wanting to scream, but refusing to succumb to the temptation. He must remain strong. Others could suspect no weakness in him. Once the takeover of Koblan was complete... Once the ore was his, then he could relax and begin to transfer the reins of power to his son. His *deserving* son.

Apoplectic rage again seized him, squeezing the air from his lungs. His heart pounded like a hammer, shooting painful bolts through his chest and down his arm. He slumped forward, feeling dizzy, and rested his forehead on his desk, touching the paper that had started the attack.

Calm, he told himself. *Calm.*

He gasped for air, heart thundering. The air felt heavy and thick in his lungs. His ears rang as loud as the squeal of the first man he'd ever killed. The Zindedi leader lay still, closing his mind to all thoughts until the pain at last began to subside.

Then he pushed himself upright. He felt as if he'd been run over by ten carts. His vision was blurry, and he squeezed his eyes shut, ordering his body to obey him. He opened them again. Clear. Good. Again, he saw the message before him. He read it once more while taking calming breaths.

Yes. Lozar is listed as a Commander from Oesten in the files on base.

The Koblani had made it onto the base. *Into Ostl's office.* The incompetence of his staff blazed through him yet again. The Koblanis could have been on the base a countless number of times. Every piece of equipment, every piece of intelligence was compromised.

Rage flushed his face, and with a violent arm, he swept everything off his desk. Writing instruments, books, a vase and his tea cup...everything smashed.

A very long silence elapsed. And then the office door cautiously opened. Yalin peered around the corner. "Sir?"

"*Leave me!*"

"But General Fitrn is here..." He yelped, and abruptly disappeared.

The Presidente's prized son strolled into the office, twirling his whip. Glittering eyes surveyed the mess on the floor.

"Father. Unfortunately, your morning is about to become more unpleasant."

With low force, the Presidente stated, "The Koblanis have been on the base."

Disappointment registered on the General's features, which lifted the Presidente's spirits. His son said, "I almost killed the woman yesterday. She spied on our meeting."

He should not feel so surprised. His enemies would pay dearly, and soon. "What happened to your neck? It looks like someone stabbed you with the wrong end of a knife."

The General flushed. "It is not important. I intend to find the Koblani girl and kill her."

"You will listen to my orders and follow them exactly. Now, listen closely." The Presidente gave his son specific instructions. He even magnanimously authorized the General to inflict retribution upon the Koblani of his choice. "But allow her to live," he thundered. "I have plans to torture them both soon. Let them taste fear. Let it crawl in their bellies. But *I* will be the one to snap their necks. Is that clear?"

"Yes, Father." The General smiled and licked his thin lips. Unholy light brightened his flat, light brown eyes.

"Double the guards on the base," the Presidente ordered, deliberately breaking into his son's pleasurable ruminations. "The meeting was compromised."

"The girl learned nothing of importance. We did not discuss battle plans until after she left."

"All plans must be changed, you fool. The commanders have loose lips. We must assume the Koblani spies know everything we know."

His son stiffened. "The last of the troops should arrive tomorrow."

"Good. Order them to transfer weapons to the ships soon. We will sail for Koblan in six days. All preparations must be complete."

"Dakarra has a large shipment of powder to send to us."

"You will retrieve it and return with it the night of the ball. Deliver it directly to the ships." The Presidente chuckled. "The Koblanis will be occupied at that time."

The General tightened his shoulders and sat very still. Finally, his thin lips barely moved. "I am not to go to the ball?"

The Presidente smiled and leaned back, his satisfaction complete. "I trust you to supervise the powder, arms, and men. What more could you desire?"

His son said nothing. His rigid features masked his disappointment. But clearly he was not happy.

The Presidente smiled with pleasure. "Good. You are dismissed. We will meet again in two days."

The General stood, heels clicking sharply on the floor.

"Send in Yalin. Report your success with the Koblani girl tomorrow."

"Yes, *sir*." It was a barely disguised snarl.

The Zindedi leader's lips twitched, drinking in the small taste of victory over his prideful and overly confident son. The sharp cuts of humiliation would continue to hone him, much like the small slices the Presidente had carved into his young psyche from a tender age. This is one son who would do him proud. His other... Rage again formed a knot in his stomach. The lack of correspondence from that son had eaten away at him for days. He should have reported reams of information by now.

"*Yalin!*"

His secretary burst into the room, clutching parchment and ink. "Yes sir!"

"Send a message. Write, 'I *want* the name of my brother's assassin. Answer by tomorrow, or be marked a traitor.' Send the message to Oortn at once."

"Yes sir!" Yalin disappeared.

The Presidente drew a deep, calming breath. His youngest son was worthless. It was just as he had feared, ever since the moment that weak, sickly baby was born. He should have died at his mother's breast. Instead, he'd been pampered and spoiled for eight years until his mother died. Now he was utterly useless! A complete disappointment in the simplest of tasks. Pain threatened in his chest. Either his son would deliver the information tomorrow, or he'd order his death. After all, it was twenty-five years overdue.

△ △ △ △ △

"The invitations are at the distribution center. We need to get an early start." Mentàll finished lacing his boots and stood. "Are you ready?"

Methusal fingered her wet hair. It was clean, thanks to another hasty bath. How she longed for a long, leisurely soak. But experiencing that small pleasure—or any other small, normal pleasure—was unlikely. Five more days until the ball. Five more days until they could go home. And then she'd finally leave this man behind and get on with her life with Behran.

"You are silent. Why?"

She flushed. "I was thinking about Behran."

With predatory grace, he closed the distance between them. "Would Behran approve of our passionate embrace last night?"

"It was an act," she said in a dampening tone. "Like all of the others."

He smiled, his teeth showing sharp and white. They reminded her of wild beast fangs. Softly, he said, "So, the lies continue."

Yesterday he had been the one who had appeared disturbed. Today he was flying in full form, as arrogant and full of himself as ever.

She changed the subject. "What's the plan for today?"

"We will split up. You have wanted your own assignment. Today you will have one. I will follow a mail carrier out of town and steal an invitation from him. You will watch where the invitations are delivered in Carachki. Pay attention to the ones sent to ordinary homes. It is unlikely the Presidente knows everyone by sight. Especially average Carachki citizens."

Methusal smiled. "A day on my own. What could be better?"

"But the night remains ours," he murmured. "I look forward to that."

Methusal rolled her eyes and escaped from the room. Mentàll at his most unpredictable was not someone she wanted to spar with this morning.

"Good morning!" Mrn. M called cheerily. Breakfast steamed on the table. Meat, fresh bread, and straw-colored, fluffy eggs.

"Yum!" Methusal settled down to tuck in.

Mrn. M sent a glance from Methusal to Mentàll, and a small smile curved her lips. Evidently their acting last night had convinced the Zindedi woman that nothing was amiss in their relationship. Warmth flooded Methusal's cheeks, remembering the kiss she had initiated. Even more disturbingly, when the Dehrien Chief had kissed her back. It had not felt fake. It had not felt fake at all.

She didn't want to think about it. At least they would spend today apart. A needed break.

Her gaze fell on the vase of nasrias Mrn. M had put on a side table near the kitchen door this morning. "So," she said with a smile to their landlady, "do you have a secret admirer?"

Mrn. M blushed. Her giggle sounded like a young girl's. "Oh, my, no. The Presidente is not..." She gasped, and her hand went to her mouth.

"Presidente?" Methusal stared. "The Presidente was *here* yesterday?"

To her right, Mentàll forked up eggs with one controlled, fluid movement.

"Well," Mrn. M said. "It's not common knowledge, you see. For security reasons, of course. I shouldn't have told you."

Smoothly, Mentàll said, "We will tell no one."

"Well, good." Mrn. M seemed to relax. "He does it out of the kindness of his heart, of course. He and my Charlie were cousins, and great friends, as I've said before. He's concerned about me. Yesterday he asked if I have enough money. I said I do, because I take in boarders."

Methusal's throat tightened. "You told him about us?"

"A little. It was kind of him to be concerned."

"You are friends with the Presidente, then," Mentàll said.

"We have been friends for many years." Mrn. M stood. "I really shouldn't speak about it anymore."

"Of course," Mentàll murmured.

Methusal wondered how much Mrn. M had told the Presidente. Did he suspect that she and Mentàll were Mrn. M's boarders? If so, wouldn't he have arrested them already? She glanced at the Dehrien Chief. Nothing could be read in his blank, carefully frozen expression. But no doubt plans whirled, made and discarded in that brilliant, strategic mind right now.

After breakfast they left the house and walked toward the distribution center.

"Should we move?" Methusal asked. "Find a new house to live in?"

"We will stay where we are. Leaving would draw suspicion to us."

"But if he *knows*..."

"He has not arrested us. I think we are safe for now. If he does suspect us, he has chosen not to act upon it. Yet. That means he wants to play a game of whip and apte."

"He could attack at any time."

"Yes. We will need to scan the house each night before we go inside. We must be ready to escape at any moment. Until he shows his hand we will wait, and we will watch."

Methusal shivered against the cold, and drew her jacket more tightly about her. "I don't feel safe anymore."

"I knew this day would come. If necessary, we will go into hiding. But I think for now the Presidente wants us alive."

"Why?"

His smile curled back like the fangs of a wild beast. "Because he is planning our torture and death. Right now he is trying to devise the most evil, depraved ways to make us die."

"*Mentàll*," she gasped.

"He is a man who likes grandiose posturing. He will orchestrate our deaths to celebrate the launch of the new war against Koblan."

"You mean..."

"We have a few more days to live. Soon the Presidente will show his hand. I will formulate the best plan to defeat him."

"Aren't you afraid? Even a little?"

He smiled again; a sharp baring of his teeth. "I look forward to the challenge. The Zindedi Presidente will cower in fear to me, Methusal. I will be victorious in the battle between our lands."

Fear slithered through her. She hoped he was right. The Presidente could strike at any time, and anywhere. That meant they needed to stay focused into kaavl every minute of the day. Mentàll could do that. Of this, she had no doubt. But she wasn't sure if she could. Small things still distracted her. She hoped the Presidente's men did not strike during one of those small lapses.

△ △ △ △ △

Hendra left Goric watching the base as she headed back to the cabin for lunch. At least it was clear today. All the same, it was cold, and she was glad to reach the cabin. Shivering a little, Hendra entered the warm kitchen, where she hoped Doc would be. Sure enough, he was straddling a chair at the kitchen table, talking to Behran and Sozla. The dark-haired girl grinned at him, her eyes sparkling with fun.

"No, Doc. We cannot use long strips of rope as a timer. First of all, the Zindedis might see or smell the smoke. Second, they are dangerous. We plan to blow up powder. A small spark could blow everything up...boom!"

Doc grinned back. The twinkle in his eyes made it clear that he had been teasing. "We can't have that."

"No. Mentàll wants us to orchestrate all of the bombs to explode at midnight."

"What kind of timers will you make, then?"

"Look." Sozla pushed a round, metal object across the table. "The last time we went to Dakarra I found this in the market. It is a time keeper. It accurately measures hours and minutes. If Behran and I can somehow use the hour hand as a trigger for the bomb, we will successful."

"Sounds complicated," Hendra offered.

Sozla glanced at Behran. The fun in her gaze darkened to quiet admiration. "Behran has a few ideas. We will experiment until we find something that works."

"We have three days," Behran said grimly. "If we have to, we'll work at it all night, too."

Sozla nodded.

"We only have three days to find that huge powder mine, too, before we have to go to Carachki," Doc said. "We need to get on that base soon."

Behran looked out the window. "Tabor and Riln should be back by now."

"Riln makes me nervous," Hendra said. "Goric feels the same way. What if Riln does something to jeopardize the whole mission?"

"I'll talk to him," Behran said. "But we need both him and Tabor to get on the base."

She bit her lip and glanced at Doc, who was quietly watching her. He said, "What aren't you saying?"

Hendra lowered her voice, not wanting to make a big issue out of her uncomfortable feelings. "How long have you known Riln?"

His brows rose. "A few years. Why?"

"It's just something Goric said." She frowned and looked away, not sure if she should say more. Much as she disliked Riln, she didn't want to slander him, or put malicious suspicions in others' minds about him.

"What did he say?"

"Goric seems to find his behavior suspicious. And, well...so do I. A little."

Behran had been listening. "You're questioning his loyalty?"

Hendra flushed. "I don't want to. And I feel bad to say this. But we know Zindedi has sent spies to Koblan. No one suspected Verdnt. Who's to say a Zindedi hasn't infiltrated our kaavl team?"

Everyone at the table fell silent, and stared at Hendra.

Now she felt even worse. "I don't want to slander anyone, but isn't it a possibility?"

"Is what a possibility?" Timaeus and Deccia had just entered the kitchen by the back door, their noses red with cold.

Feeling even more put on the spot, Hendra admitted her suspicious thoughts.

Timaeus shoved his hands into his pockets. "It's possible. We'd be fools to think it's not."

"A traitor?" Deccia looked appalled. "Living here among us?"

"We don't know if it's true," Behran said.

"I know," Hendra agreed. "I feel bad. Maybe I shouldn't have said anything."

"We should be careful," Doc said. "You and Timaeus are right."

Sozla sent Doc a long look. "So. Was Riln born in Tarst? Or is he an immigrant?"

"He moved from Wyen about five years ago."

More silence elapsed.

"That doesn't mean he's a traitor," Behran said.

"Of course not," Deccia agreed. "I mean, how many other people on this team grew up in a different town than the one they live in now on Koblan?"

"I emigrated from Dehre to Rolban," Behran admitted.

"Goric is from Aestoff," Deccia said.

"Tabor is originally from Aestoff, too," Hendra said. "But I know you were born in Dehre, Behran. We grew up together, remember?"

Behran grinned. After a moment, he rose to get a glass of water from the sink.

"So now what?" Deccia asked. "Are we supposed to be suspicious of people who emigrated from other towns, just because we don't know where they're truly from?"

"We should definitely be careful," Doc said. "But suspicion can fracture the team. We can't have that, either."

"On the other hand," Behran said, "Riln makes no effort to hide his behavior. Maybe that proves his innocence."

"If threatening to shred our cover just so he can kill Zindedis is *innocent*," Hendra muttered.

"You may have a point."

"He makes me feel uncomfortable. I'm not saying he's a traitor, because logically I realize that is unlikely. But I just don't trust him. At all. He likes to stir up trouble. Have you forgotten all the arguments he's started with you?"

Behran fell silent, and then his hand went to her shoulder. A comforting gesture. "I'm not dismissing your worries, Hendra."

"I know." But she still felt conflicted about bringing up the whole subject. She wasn't sure if she'd done the right thing.

"Hey." Behran's arm went around her shoulders in a comforting squeeze. Dark blue eyes met hers. "I'll watch Riln. You can be sure of it. But for the time being, I think it will be best to treat everyone the same. If, by some chance we do have a traitor among us, we don't want to tip our hand."

She felt a little better. "You're right. Thank you, Behran."

His arm tightened, and then let her go. When he stepped away, Doc glanced at Behran, and then sent Hendra a long, considering look.

Then she realized she hadn't shrunk away from Behran's casual embrace. Even though it had felt a little strange to be so close to him, it hadn't frightened her. The gesture had been friendly. Nothing more, and she'd accepted it as such. She had just trusted him.

But Doc's touch made her feel so jumpy.

Maybe it was because he wanted more from her than simple friendship. He reached deep down into her soul and pulled out thoughts and feelings she was frightened to face. Even though she trusted him completely, she wasn't ready to expose those deep, dark, hurt places to him. She was afraid of what might happen if she did.

She offered Doc a ghost of a smile. "For now we'll have to trust each other. As much as we're able."

His gaze held hers. "That's all anyone can ask."

△ △ △ △ △

In the late afternoon, Deccia traveled to town with Goric. The military facility was quiet, now that most of the new recruits had left, and Timaeus was watching it right now. A few higher ranking officers still remained, of course—and of course all the powder barrels the base had been collecting remained behind, too, waiting for General Fitrn's arrival.

Goric walked silently beside her. Over the last few days he'd become more moody and withdrawn than ever. Deccia wondered why, and glanced at him now, trying to read his state of mind. She sensed that he was unhappy and a little angry. Back at the cabin, he had responded in curt phrases whenever anyone spoke to him.

Now he stopped abruptly. "I'll wait here."

They'd reached the edge of Dakarra, and Deccia hadn't even noticed.

"I won't be long," she promised.

He shrugged and turned away to find a hiding place. The Dakarrans still hadn't see him, or Riln, or Tabor. When the military had rounded up fresh recruits for the war with Koblan, it had seemed like a good idea to continue to keep their presence and identities a secret. It still seemed prudent.

Deccia headed for the market. Although she enjoyed chatting with Ceri, she hated going into Dakarra. Invariably, she met up with one of the three busybodies.

Fortunately, she did not see Vitnia, Olita, or Tisnia on the street, so it was with a feeling of relief she slipped into the market. Ceri was helping an elderly woman package up her purchases.

Deccia quickly gathered supplies for dinner tonight and tomorrow. Cloth shopping bag overflowing, she unloaded her purchases on the counter and waited while Ceri added up the total.

The Zindedi girl grinned at her. "According to Tisnia's swollen big toe, it's supposed to rain tomorrow."

With a laugh, Deccia rolled her eyes. "I feel lucky that I haven't seen her—or Vitnia—today."

"Lucky you. I get that treat every day."

"I'll be glad to go home." Deccia shut her mouth. How had that slipped out? Who would want to return home from a "vacation"?

Ceri didn't seem to find her statement unusual. Sympathy edged her smile. "Dakarra's not everything you hoped it would be?"

"It's quieter at home. People are friendlier."

A perplexed line appeared between Ceri's brows. "I thought you were from Carachki."

"Oh. Uh..." Deccia floundered. For a second, she'd let down her guard with Ceri, like she have would have with a real friend. "I live in Carachki now. But I...I grew up in the country. My grandparents still live there, in fact."

Ceri nodded, but her slight frown remained.

Deccia paid the bill and changed the subject. "I hope Tisnia is wrong. I'm sick of the fog and the rain."

"Tisnia is wrong about what?" The market door slammed shut and heavy feet slapped across the wooden floor. The faint, huffing breaths behind Deccia told her the newcomer's identity. Olita.

"We were talking about the weather," Ceri said shortly.

Olita stopped beside Deccia and thumped a basket onto the counter. "I need meat. My man likes it thick and juicy, so none of that bony gristle like last time. Tell Hasr."

Ceri disappeared through the back door.

"So." Olita faced Deccia with narrowed eyes. Her lips twisted into an unpleasant line. "You're still here. And your husband too, I assume."

"For a few more days."

"A few more days." She snorted. "Your husband's a slacker. I told my man about him last night."

Alarm prickled. "What do you mean?"

"I told him a bunch of military men are vacationing up in the hills. Asked him if that's normal." She smiled. "Apparently it's unusual. Very unusual, in fact."

"Their papers are in order."

"So you say. Maybe my man will stop by and take a look."

The horrid woman!

Deccia offered a false smile. "How wonderful. I'll have to bake a cake. What kind does he like?"

Olita's lips curled back into a snarl. She snatched the packaged meat from Ceri and unrolled it. "Too fatty," she pronounced. "Cut it off." Ceri disappeared again. To Deccia, she snapped, "You have a smart mouth."

She smiled. "What kind of cake, did you say?"

Olita huffed. "Anything sweet. But it won't help, if your man's papers aren't in order."

"Don't worry, Olita. They are in order. I look forward to meeting your husband. What is his name?"

"Radl." Olita turned her scowl upon Ceri.

With a sympathetic wave to her friend, Deccia escaped from the market. But she was trembling. That awful woman! Threatening to send her husband to attack them. She had to warn the others.

Deccia practically ran down the road toward the cabins. Goric appeared by her side.

"What's the rush?"

"I'll tell you at the cabin. It's awful. Just *awful!*"

Deccia ran up the hill to the big cabin. Panting, and arms shaking, she set the food on the counter. Everyone but Timaeus had congregated in the warm kitchen. She'd give anything to have Timaeus here right now, and to feel his support. Somehow, when he was with her, she knew everything would be all right.

"We have a problem," she told the others. "Olita is going to send her husband soon to check the military papers."

Shocked faces stared back at her. Behran's tightened into grim lines. Goric faded into the far corner and hunched there with his arms crossed.

"Why?" Hendra asked.

Sozla said, "Because she hates."

And Deccia hated Olita. The fury of that emotion shivered through her. The horrible woman wanted to hurt them. She was despicable. *Evil.* Just like that vile General...

Doc took her elbow and urged her to the nearest chair. "It'll be all right. Don't worry. We'll think of a plan."

"Tell us everything," Behran said.

Deccia did. Even the ridiculous bit about baking a cake. Behran laughed at that.

Sozla, however, scowled. "Do not make a cake. He doesn't deserve one."

Goric spoke from his corner. "What is the saying? 'Feed the beast'?"

Feed the beast before it eats you.

"He probably won't come today," Hendra said. "It's late. Tomorrow is soon enough to bake it. I'll help you."

Deccia didn't think a cake would smooth things over with Olita's husband, who was a Commander in the Presidente's military. The only comfort she felt was that she'd finished copying military papers for each of the men. They'd be protected. Only Riln and Tabor still needed to receive theirs.

Doc and Behran exchanged a silent look. Doc stretched. "All this talk of cake is making me hungry."

Deccia turned to the stove, glad to think about something besides Olita and her husband. "I'll start dinner."

Chopping vegetables and sautéing meat soothed her jittery feelings, and when Timaeus returned at dusk, her nerves settled a little more. Behran and Hendra left to spy until lights out at the base.

Preparations for dinner finished all too quickly. While the meat cooked, Deccia itched to keep her hands—and mind—busy. Seeing Goric sitting alone, reading a book in the living room gave her an idea. She smiled to herself and whipped up a special treat at the stove.

When everyone lined up to help themselves to dinner, Deccia had the pleasure of watching Goric's mouth gape open when he stared into the giant pan of whipped pudding. His favorite, she remembered, from the ship. He swallowed hard, and then sent her a faint, glimmering smile. He scooped three ladlefuls onto his plate. And Riln wasn't even there to tease him about it.

△ △ △ △ △

At the mail distribution center, Mentàll bid Methusal goodbye. "Be careful," he warned in a low voice. His hand curled around her shoulder and lingered for a moment, as if unwilling to release her.

"I'll be fine," she encouraged. "I'll see you back at Mrn. M's tonight."

He stepped away, but his gaze was unusually dark. He seemed troubled.

Methusal wiggled her fingers. "Goodbye."

With a faint frown and a quick twist to his shoulders, he was gone.

Four mail carriers had already left the distribution center, she quickly discovered. One wore a pack, complete with water bottle. No doubt he planned to hike to Oesten and Paraski. Mentàll was following him. Methusal would follow the carrier who would head into the heart of Carachki—and away from the high priced homes and Feldon Street.

The short, chubby fellow with a ring of thinning orange hair headed southeast into the city. Methusal followed at a discreet distance. The morning was crisp and cold, but gloriously clear. She wondered if it ever warmed up in Zindedi. Back home the hot season would be beginning soon, and the rains about to taper to nothing.

She focused into kaavl, staying aware of her environment, although with her hair up in a cap like a boy's and wearing plain black clothing, few would think she was a girl. A good disguise, should she happen to cross paths with the General. Not that that was likely in this area of town. The houses here were run down, with dingy yards full of weeds.

Methusal kept a close eye on her mail carrier. At the moment, she carried with vision to watch him around the corner. The streets were so flat and open that her presence could quickly become suspicious, especially if she followed him all day long.

He pulled a large, tan colored envelope from his bag and knocked on the front door. *An invitation.* Methusal watched, every sense on alert. A woman with a baby on her hip opened the door. She took the envelope, turned it over with an apparent lack of interest, and then shut the door in the mail carrier's face.

A good lead. Surely the Presidente didn't personally know that woman or her husband. If Mentàll failed to steal an invitation from the mail carrier, they could steal this one later, nearer the night of the ball.

Feeling ebullient, she continued to follow the mail carrier. He delivered no more invitations, however. For lunch, he stopped and ate beneath a tree in the park near the Presidente's palace. Methusal's stomach growled. After a while, the man headed back for the mail distribution center and disappeared inside.

An hour dragged by. Other mail distributors returned, and it became clear that they had finished delivering mail for the day. At least she'd found one lead.

Now what? She had all afternoon to kill. Spying on the base might be a good idea. Maybe something new was going on.

It seemed as good an idea as any. She'd spy from a distance, which would please Mentàll.

She headed for the northern edge of town and found the empty shack where they often changed clothes. It provided a good view of the base from its perch on the small bluff.

But when she peeked out the empty window, she gasped. A mass of dark clad men marched toward the base. Easily a hundred men. Maybe more. And two powder carts.

Clearly, the ships would be overflowing with soldiers soon. Was Zindedi planning to double the number of soldiers sent during the Quasr War? Triple? How would Koblan ever defeat them all?

"So." The sibilant hiss came from behind her. "The spy is spied upon."

Methusal whirled.

General Fitrn stood in the doorway, fondling the whip in his hand. His stance looked casual, as if he was merely passing the time of day. But tension stiffened the muscles beneath his well-tailored uniform, and she got the distinct impression that he wanted to spring upon her and cut her throat.

"General," Methusal said in a low, masculine voice.

"Do you take me for a fool?" The man's thin lips stretched into a cruel smile. "I have come for you, Methusal Maahr. You have made a fool of me twice too often. Dakarra. Now here. It is time for you to suffer the humiliation that you so richly deserve."

Methusal kept her expression blank, and relaxed utterly into kaavl. She berated herself for the lapse in concentration that had allowed the General to sneak up behind her. And his men...she counted six men's breaths outside the door. Her only hope was to escape through the window.

She estimated the distance behind her, to the window. Three handbreadths. And of course the short, sheer bluff below it. A risk she would have to take.

"Come with me now," Fitrn said. "And I will go easy on you."

He was lying, of course. The flat brown eyes gleamed like dull gems.

"Come!" His whip unexpectedly licked out, spitting pain above her ear.

"I'll come. No need to be so unpleasant."

He watched her, his gaze as hard as a whip beast's.

In one smooth motion, Methusal lunged backward. Her hands shot up and out the window, and she grasped the upper ledge. A swift hoist, and she was through the window, sitting on the ledge. The next instant she brought her knees up. With her feet on the lower sill, launched herself up and backward...into nothingness.

Methusal didn't hit the ground for one long, heart-stopping moment. The bluff blurred as she fell straight down, and then suddenly her hip hit something sharp. A branch. She grabbed it, breaking her fall. Here, the bluff sloped at a graveled angle. Releasing the branch, she slipped down the rest of the slope.

She glanced back up. The General looked down, his expression smooth and undisturbed, and she wondered why.

When she leaped up, a wave of black clad soldiers closed around her. Before she could gasp, they'd grabbed her arms and swiftly wrestled her to the ground.

"So you see, Methusal Maahr." The General's voice came from the top of the bluff. "You are no match for me. Soldiers! Carry the spy to my house. I intend to have a nice long chat with her."

△ △ △ △ △

Aali was getting anxious. She'd discovered nothing about the Dehrien Chief's nefarious plans yet. GG had not summoned her again, and she didn't know who else to question.

Calbn was a closed, forbidding man. And Lylitha lay in bed most of the time. Although it looked like Calbn's wife could give birth at any minute, apparently she still had two months left to serve in her pregnancy. So Aali waited.

"All of my family lives here." Trori told her one afternoon while Rartn napped. She toed herself back and forth on a swing which hung from a tree near the center of the courtyard.

"You mean in this compound?"

"Yes. Me, Rartn, Mama, Daddy, and Great-Grandma. We're the last of the M'ntoyans. The invaders killed Grandpa," the little girl said matter-of-factly. "Now he lives in heaven."

"What about your grandmother?"

"She died a long time ago, like Great-Grandpa. Mama says Great-Grandpa died because he couldn't take dealing with Great-Grandma one more day."

Aali giggled. "She *is* a little strange. But you have her beautiful eyes."

"Great-Grandma says I take after her. But I don't want to be like her. She's mean."

The little girl fell silent, heels kicking through the air beneath the swing. After a moment, Trori clutched Aali's arm. "I want to show you something. Come on."

Aali allowed herself to be tugged to Rartn's door. There she stopped. "He's taking a nap, Trori. I don't think we should wake him."

"We won't. Shh." The little girl put a finger to her lips and tiptoed in. Aali clumped on her crutches as quietly as she could. Worried, she eyed Rartn, but the small boy didn't move. He lay on his back, mouth open and snoring.

Trori pointed at her brother and giggled. Then she carefully pulled open a drawer in the table next to Rartn's bed. She opened a box inside and pulled out a silver medallion on a long, silver chain. "Look," she breathed. "It'll be Rartn's someday, when he grows up."

"Why are you showing it to me?"

"Because it's special. And Rartn won't let me touch it when he's awake. He throws a screaming fit." After a moment of silence, Trori continued reverently, "Daddy has one, too. Rartn's and Daddy's are the only medallions left. There used to be three, but one got lost. Great-Grandma says they've been in the M'ntoyan family for hundreds of years."

Trori's little hand kept bobbing about, so Aali couldn't get a good look at the silver disk. She said, "Why does Rartn get it, and not you? You're the oldest."

"Only boys can have it." Trori sounded a little jealous.

"Can I hold it?"

"Sure." Trori generously transferred the prize to Aali's hand.

She scrutinized the round, flat piece of metal. It fit inside the palm of her hand, and smooth markings were engraved upon it. "Are those the Quasr twin peaks?"

Trori shook her head, and then nodded. "Well, sort of. It's mostly an 'M,' for M'ntoyan, but it's supposed to look like the peaks, too."

No words were engraved into it. Just the twin peaks, and a finely worked edging. She flipped it over. It looked the same on the back. She handed it back to Trori. "It certainly is heavy."

"It's made of a rare metal," she said, and carefully laid it back in its box.

Rartn began to stir.

"Quick! Let's go!" Trori squealed, and dashed for the door.

Rartn's eyes popped open, and then his mouth circled open, too. A mighty roar bellowed from his tiny person. "Maa..maaaa!"

"Drat!" Trori cried out.

"Bother," Aali muttered, and tried to sooth the boy. "Shh, Rartn. It's time to wake up. Come on, we're going to play a game."

But the boy did not stop screaming. A second later, Calbn flung open the door. "What is going on in here?" he demanded with a thunderous frown.

Trori hastily championed Aali's feeble story. "We're waking up Rartn. It's time to play."

The gray eyes narrowed at Aali, and then at his daughter. "Trori. Tell me the truth. Were you showing Aali the medallion?"

Trori looked guilty. "Only for a second, Daddy."

Rartn screamed louder at this. "*Mine!* It's mine!"

Aali wanted to clap her hands over her ears and run away. "I'm sorry, Chief Calbn. I never should have let Trori bring me in here."

The little girl stamped her foot. "Daddy, it's so boring! Why can't I show Aali the medallion?"

Calbn's mouth looked grim, and his features harsh. "The medallion belongs to the M'ntoyans only. Outsiders may not look at it. It is not meant for their eyes."

Aali gasped at the ridiculousness of this statement. "Don't worry. I won't steal it, Chief!"

He glared at her, "You'll let *me* decide what you may and may not see in my own home. These are my children, my medallion, and you have no place here!"

She took a step backward, feeling attacked and a bit frightened, but she called on her kaavl training to try to conceal it. "Fine, Chief Calbn. Then I will leave Trori and Rartn in your capable care. Please excuse me."

Pressing her trembling lips together, she swung for the door. She brushed by Calbn, who did not move. Anger seethed inside of her. The ungrateful man! She was doing her best to care for his children, and this was the thanks she got? Yes, she was grateful for a room to stay in until her leg healed. But she would not put up with verbal assaults.

Aali stumbled into her room and slammed the door shut. She burst into tears.

△ △ △ △ △

Methusal sat in darkness on cold, packed dirt. Metal manacles held her wrists together in front of her. An hour ago—maybe more—the General had thrown her downstairs into his basement. She'd managed to briefly grab the stair railing to slow her fall, but her hips and thighs hurt, and she knew she'd have huge bruises later. Then Fitrn had left, locking the door at the top of the narrow staircase behind him. She'd checked the lock. It worked from the outside only. The thin stream of light under the door was the only light in the chilly basement.

She had no idea why he'd left her, or when he'd be back.

Her stomach gurgled, reminding her of how hungry she was. But hunger was the least of her concerns.

She had to get out.

She'd already stumbled around in the pitch black cellar, searching for a weapon, or for any high, blacked out windows she could break. She found neither. Nothing except for a chair, high walls, and a locked cupboard.

Did he torture people here?

Sick fear knotted her stomach. She was alone. Mentàll was out of town, and wouldn't return for hours. When he did return, he'd have no idea where to find her.

What was she going to do? Tears threatened, but she blinked them back. *No crying.* The General would try to break her. Of this, she had no doubt.

The man was sick, just like his uncle. Like the Presidente. How had such a deranged family gained control of the Zindedi continent?

The lock clicked at the top of the stairs. Heart pounding, she sprang to her feet. Blazing light appeared in the doorway, and then polished boots clicked on the stairs. Two hulking men followed General Fitrn inside and stationed themselves at the bottom of the stairs.

"You have not made yourself comfortable," the General remarked. He circled the room, lighting several lamps that were located high overhead. "Sit!"

She ignored his command. "What do you want with me?"

He approached. The skin of his face tautened as he screamed, "Bow to me, as your superior! Rous! Chirdl! Seize her."

The two large guards strode toward her. This couldn't be good. Methusal stumbled backward and sat down hard on the chair.

The General waved the men back. "How easily Koblani scum are broken." Hard, bony fingers gripped her chin and forced it up. "Tell me. How many of your people are in Zindedi?"

The Zindedi Presidente knew Mentàll was here. After all, he'd sent the preliminary peace agreement to the Presidente. "None," she said sullenly. She could not give up information too quickly, or the General might think she was hiding more information than just Mentàll's presence.

The slap of the baton hit her lip and blood spurted, dribbling down her chin.

"The truth, Methusal Maahr."

She licked her lip and glared. "You know there are two of us. Why even ask the question?"

A nasty smile curled his mouth. "Your lover."

"No!" Methusal recoiled in shock. And then she realized that she was perilously close to blowing their cover. "He is my husband."

"*You lie*. Tell me you *lie*," he screamed.

Fear shivered through her as she eyed his contorted face. His eyes bulged like ripe fruit.

His reaction seemed over the top—insane, even—but at the same time she sensed the calculation behind it. "Why would I lie?"

"You are enemies," the General snapped. "My father is not a fool. Neither am I." He strutted back and forth, slapping the baton against his leg.

"We got married a few weeks ago. He'll kill you if you hurt me." She wasn't sure why she continued to cling to the fiction of their marriage. After all, the Presidente knew they had been in Carachki for some time. He probably knew where they lived, too. But he didn't know the truth about their relationship. It appeared that the idea of her marriage to Mentàll irrationally enraged the General. Instinct made her stick to the story.

He gave a sharp, mocking laugh. "Profess your love for him. If you expect me to believe you, tell me how much you worship this Dehrien Chief. The man who held you at knife point. The man who almost raped you. The man who attacked Rolban, lusting after its ore."

How did he know all of this? "He didn't want the ore."

The whip, which had been dangling from his belt, suddenly flicked out and connected sharply with her shoulder. It curled through the hair at her nape. Methusal swallowed hard, but didn't cry out. Fear made her feel sick to her stomach.

The General said, "Get down on your knees. Tell me all about your tender feelings for your enemy."

He retracted the whip. It tightened momentarily around her neck, and then sprang free, pulling some hair out with it. Tears seared her eyes. She wouldn't obey him. The man wanted to dehumanize her. Humiliate her.

"Rous."

Her chair jerked sideways and she fell to the floor. She struggled to her knees, but a heavy boot in her back prevented her from rising. Now she indeed knelt at the General's feet. She wanted to scream with rage, and wished, with everything within her, that she still had her knife. The General's men had disarmed her.

"Speak," the General commanded calmly.

Methusal stared at his polished black boots. She licked her lips, tasting the metallic bite of blood in the lower left corner. "I love him," she said stonily.

"Why do you love him? Do you enjoy men who hurt you? Perhaps you would like my attentions."

Revulsion slithered through her. "Mentàll is not like that. He protects me. He won't let anyone hurt me." For the first time, she realized that this had been true ever since he'd saved her life on that cliff during the Quasr War. "And he's a brilliant strategist."

"All qualities of an excellent commander. But you are not really married. Admit this truth."

"We *are* married."

A long silence ensued, and then Rous removed his boot from her back. Methusal attempted to straighten up from her hunched position, but the whip hissed and stung deep into her back. She cried out in pain.

"Tell the truth," he said coolly.

"I *am*. We're mar..." Another jolt of pain slashed into her flesh.

"The truth," he said patiently.

"I am..." Another shock of pain. Tears dripped down her cheeks "Why do you *care?*" she snarled. "What does it matter to you?"

"It does not matter to *me*. I am only interested in the truth."

Fitrn didn't care. So why was he torturing her about this insane topic? Who else would want to know?

The Presidente. But why?

"We're married," she said stubbornly. "I love him with all of my heart."

"Lift her up." The General sounded bored. "Attach the rings."

Rous dragged her to her feet. Chirdl removed her manacles, and then forced her hands overhead. Two chains dangled from the ceiling. Attached to the end of each was a metal ring that looked like a manacle. Chirdl snapped each open, and then forced her arms overhead. A ring snapped shut around each of her wrists. Rous released her and she dangled from the rings. She scrabbled for the floor. Only her toes touched.

The General smiled. "I will return."

He and his henchmen left, leaving all of the lights blazing. The door clicked shut.

Methusal was alone. Her arms felt like they were being pulled out of their sockets. And it was hard to breathe. Trial and error quickly taught her that if she balanced on her toes she could release the tension in her arms and breathe more easily. Tears trickled down her cheeks. How long would they leave her like this? What did the General plan to do next?

△ △ △ △ △

Hendra and Behran hurried toward the warm lights of their cabin. Home. They'd spied on the base until lights out. It was cold and clear tonight, and Ryon had shone down on the grassy landscape surrounding the military base. While that had prevented them from getting close enough to overhear conversations, she had noticed that a few powder carts had been moved from the back of the base to the main entrance.

Shivering, and coat pulled tightly around her, Hendra opened the door to the cabin and stepped into the blessed warmth...and noise.

Across the room, Riln guffawed. Tabor stood quietly near the couch, his bulky shoulders still encased in his black military jacket.

So, they'd finally returned.

Riln roared a greeting, and shook Behran's hand as if they were the best of friends, and had been separated for months. Hendra headed for the kitchen for a warm cup of tea. Doc took the chair next to her at the table.

"Tell us what you learned," Behran encouraged Tabor. "Where were you?"

"Mentàll sent us to eastern Zindedi."

"Eastern Zindedi?" Hendra sat forward, surprised. "Why?"

"Powder mines. We found one. A big one."

"Will we blow it up?"

"Mentàll never tells us anything," Riln complained, sprawling back in his chair. He smiled. "But it was a great adventure."

He liked the great outdoors. Mentàll had been smart to order him out of the cabin for a few days.

"What happened while we were gone?" Tabor asked.

Behran relayed the pertinent facts, and ended with the bit about Olita's husband.

"We might need to abandon the cabins," Timaeus said. "We should prepare for that."

"I think all of the men should stay out of the cabins tomorrow," Deccia said. "And take your papers with you."

"He'll come back if we're not here the first time."

"But it'll buy us another day," she countered. "One day closer to Day Zero. Another day for Behran and Sozla to figure out the timers."

To Hendra's surprise, Riln didn't suggest killing the Commander when he arrived at the cabin. Instead, he demanded, "What else has been going on at the base?"

Goric said, "Troops marched for Carachki a few days ago. Powder carts, too."

"Powder carts?" Riln sat bolt upright. "You let *powder* carts leave the base? *Fool!*"

Goric flushed.

Hendra spoke before a fight could break out. "I'm the one who saw the carts leave."

"Of course." Riln's lips curled back in disgust. "This is what happens when you let an apte do a man's job."

"Riln!" Doc said sharply.

"She's useless. Maybe she's good at baking." He flicked a finger toward the stove, "Or cooking pudding for soft men." He raised an eyebrow at Goric, whose flush darkened. "But let the real men do the hard, dirty work of war."

An alarming ringing sounded in Hendra's ears. She bolted to her feet. "You wouldn't know a real man if you saw one! You're a rash, irresponsible hothead. We can't trust you with one simple mission. If it was up to me, I'd order you back to the ship!"

Now red suffused Riln's face. "Insolence from the apte. Too bad your spine didn't show up when the carts left. When we needed it most."

Hendra was not a violent person, but she wanted to slap his red, mocking face. She hissed, "If we blew up the carts, the Zindedis would know we're here. How smart would that be?"

"What does it matter? It would mean less powder to attack Koblan. Isn't that what we want?"

Voice tight with anger, Doc said, "We're not going to jeopardize the whole mission over two powder carts." His fingers closed around Hendra's. They felt like a warm anchor in the storm. "We'll blow up nothing until Mentàll says so."

Hendra sat back down, trembling. Her face felt hot from her uncharacteristic outburst. What did the others think of her now? But a quick glance proved that everyone else was staring at Riln. Varying degrees of anger and shock registered on their faces. Goric looked as though flames might shoot out of his eyes. Doc still held her hand, and she was glad, because it made her feel like he was there for her, no matter what happened.

Calmly, Behran said, "Doc is right. We'll follow Mentàll's plan to the letter. He's the leader of this mission. Either you agree, or you're gone, Riln."

Riln jerked his chin dismissively. "Just stating my opinion. Not a big surprise no one will listen."

"Our plan, Riln. Do you *agree*?"

"Yeah." A harsh breath exploded. "I'll sit on my hands if I have to."

"Good," Behran said. "Then you should know that Hendra and I saw more powder carts near the main gate today. No telling when they'll leave, but it will probably be when Fitrn returns."

Riln cursed.

"We need to get on that base," Doc said. "We need to find the map to the last powder mine here in western Zindedi."

Tabor's calm voice spoke. "We'll go tomorrow night."

Behran nodded in agreement.

"We can't let those powder carts get to Carachki," Riln scowled. He stared at the others. With a muffled curse, he surged to his feet. "I can't take this!"

The kitchen door slammed.

Silence reigned. Uneasily, Hendra glanced at Doc. He looked troubled, too. "How do we know what's the right thing to do?"

He squeezed her hand. "Mentàll wants to time all of the explosions for midnight on Day Zero. We have to follow orders. We need to trust him."

Trust Mentàll. Would everyone trust her cousin? That was the question. Riln had mutinied against Mentàll during the war. Surely he'd be willing to do so again. And who would mutiny with him? Mentàll had invaded Rolban—the home of three of the people on this team. His only true endorsements for leadership were his victories against the Zindedis during the Quasr War, and orchestrating this entire mission. Would his word be enough to keep this team together? And what if a Zindedi spy did lurk among them, even now?

If the team fractured, it could mean death for them all.

△ △ △ △ △

Methusal didn't know how long the General left her alone, but her arms screamed with pain when the Zindedi at last returned. Minus his henchmen, this time.

"Have you enjoyed the rings?" he said pleasantly.

Methusal wanted to spit some of the Dehrien Chief's colorful curses, but she bit her tongue.

He raised his hand. A key dangled from a ring. "I will happily release you. Are you ready now to admit the truth?"

"I will lie if you want me to," she said. "But nothing will change the truth."

He stared at her, his eyes glittering like dull, dirty brown stones. He had not broken her. She felt a flare of triumph. He would *not* break her.

As if sensing her thoughts, hatred deepened the General's gaze to a malevolent, muddy black. A knife appeared in his hand, and he pressed it against her cheek. No soul lived behind those dead eyes. Just an empty, frightening vacuum. The man was insane. He had no scruples, and no conscience.

Her fear licked into horror, and then into terror.

"Yes." He smiled. "Now you see I would enjoy killing you."

"Then why don't you?"

Surprise, and then rage flashed. "You will answer my questions first."

"Why should I cooperate if you plan to kill me?"

"To avoid pain. I can make your death quick and painless, or I can drag it out for days...perhaps weeks. Until you beg me to end your life."

Methusal believed him.

His eyes gleamed with triumph, and he stepped away. With fastidious care, he wiped the already clean blade on a white, square cloth and resheathed it. "How many Koblanis are on Zindedi?" The question sounded casual; even off-hand.

"Two. I told you."

"How many kaavl players are on your continent?"

"I don't know. We don't keep records."

"Ah, yes. Because Koblan is weak. Not unified. Backwards. It will be a pleasure to rape the lush bounty from your helpless land."

She said nothing.

"How many Koblanis are on Zindedi?" He pulled out his whip.

Methusal swallowed. *The One help me.* "Two."

He hit her. It knocked her off her toes, searing pain through her aching shoulder sockets. But she did not cry out.

"When does your ship return?"

"I don't know."

Another lash.

The questions kept on, repeating over and over again. Methusal's back burned, her arms burned, her calves spasmed.

Time lost meaning. She felt lightheaded and her brain groggy with pain. At last, the General walked away and called up the stairs for his henchmen.

The men appeared, each carrying two pails of liquid that sloshed on the stairs. With despair, she eyed them. Now what?

The General lifted the first bucket and approached her. He came very close. "I will break you," he said softly, and his hand ran suggestively from her neck to breast. She struggled not to respond, although the contact made her want to crawl out of her skin. He stepped back. "And it will be a pleasure."

With an upward thrust, cold water doused her face, shooting up her nose. She coughed and choked. Another bucketful followed. One pail soaked her chest and the other, her legs. Freezing water dripped down her entire body. The General headed for the stairs.

"I...I will die tonight if you leave me like this." Her teeth chattered. Spasms of cold shook her entire body.

The General nodded to his men. "Lower the rings."

Blessed relief, she could stand on her feet again. But her arms were still uncomfortably suspended overhead.

The General smiled. "Sleep well." He blew out each of the lamps in the room. His blazing lantern disappeared upstairs, and he and his henchmen left. The door slammed.

Alone. In the dark, and freezing. Shudders of revulsion and cold convulsed through her body.

Methusal finally allowed herself to cry. She tried not to think about the way the General had touched her, or his implied threats for tomorrow. The man was insane.

She'd freeze to death if she couldn't free herself.

Methusal twisted her hands, and struggled to pull them through the narrow metal rings. When she finally stopped struggling, her wrists felt raw. She could not escape.

Was this it? Would she have to remain here, chained and helpless, and let the General do whatever horrifying things he wanted to do to her?

No!

She struggled yet again, but only succeeded in hurting herself more. Her manacled position reminded her of aptes she had treated; many of whom had escaped from traps. More than a few had gnawed off a limb just to escape.

She wept. Great sobs shook her. "Help me, The One! *Please.*"

She shuddered uncontrollably now. She was so cold. Her wet clothes felt like clinging sheets of ice. If only she could warm up!

Exercise.

The thought came to her out of nowhere. Of course. Whenever she went for a run, she got warm—sometimes even hot.

It was awkward to run in place. And painful, because the jarring movements rubbed her sore wrists on the rings. She settled for marching. Her hunger pains had long since subsided, but as the long minutes and hours passed, she began to feel lightheaded. Lifting her feet became more and more of an effort. She was so tired. So cold. It was hard to tell if she felt any warmer.

Endless time stretched on. Was it dinner time? Midnight?

From time to time, she fell into a light doze, but always the painful bite of the rings jerked her out of that comforting escape.

A faint scratching sound brought her out of her half-conscious stupor.

The General?

Half-baked, vengeful fantasies had slipped through her mind over the last few hours, mixed with longing thoughts of home, and of Mrn. M's warm, welcoming house and a table full of food.

The scratching came again. She tried to quiet her chattering teeth, and listened harder. Only one man's breaths. He was alone. One of her violent fantasies—the most logical of them all—swam through her mind again. She could swing by her wrists and grab the General around his throat with her legs. With the right torque, she could break his neck.

She wasn't sure if her plan would work or not, but it was her only chance. She took a step backward and started swinging. Although she'd managed to grab a bit of the chain above the manacles, excruciating pain still burned her wrists. She ignored it.

Footsteps crept down the stairs. She swung higher and higher. It seemed strange that Fitrn wasn't carrying his lantern.

Something black and big loomed out of the shadows. Rous?

He was close. A foot tap to the floor subtly changed her direction and she flew forward, feet pointed skyward like a spear. At the very least, she could knock him down.

Her feet connected with a solid chest. A guttural "Oomph" escaped from the man. He staggered, but didn't fall. Instead, he grabbed her feet with hands as strong as tempered ore.

Violently, Methusal struggled like a wild thing. She spat the Dehrien's most vile curse. "*Scienth!*"

"I thought we were past name calling, Methusal."

Never had that harsh voice sounded so wonderful.

"*Mentàll!*" She choked on a sob of relief. "Let go. My wrists. They hurt."

Immediately, he released her, and then his big hands skimmed up her body. It almost felt like they trembled a little; but maybe that was her own body shaking. "You are wet," he said harshly.

She shivered convulsively again. Relief and fear mixed together, turning her emotions inside out. "Can...can you free me? They're locked...in...in some kind of rings."

The Dehrien's hands felt deliciously warm on her skin as he gently fingered her wrists. He slid his thumb between her skin and the manacle on her left wrist, searching for the locking mechanism.

He let go, and she felt very alone again. It was so dark that she could barely make out his shape. "Can you free me?" she asked anxiously. "You won't leave me, will you?"

"Of course not." The statement was tightly controlled and forceful. Tiny sounds indicated that he'd pulled something from his pocket. Then he grabbed her leftmost manacle and jammed something again and again into the lock that held her. A *pop*, and it clicked open.

Her shoulder protested, screaming pain as she lowered her arm. Mentàll gripped the other manacle. Another violent, controlled series of jabs into its locking mechanism, and she was free.

Her shoulders hurt unbearably. And the change in position pulled at the skin of her lacerated back. Tears of misery ran down her cheeks. She was so cold. She shook so hard that she could barely stand.

"Come." He touched her back.

With a gasp, she flinched.

Silence followed. "What did he *do* to you?" he hissed.

"I want to go home," she whimpered. "Please take me."

He took her hand in his large, warm one and headed for the stairs. Her legs didn't want to work. They felt stiff with cold, and her feet felt numb. They hit the ground before she expected them to, and she stumbled and fell to her knees several times. Only Mentàll's hand, gripping hers, prevented a face plant into the dirt.

She staggered to her feet again and swayed, gripping his solid arm as an anchor. Shivers ravaged her.

"I'm so c..c..cold, Mentàll." A jagged sob escaped, and finally, tears overwhelmed her.

"Methusal." His low voice was rough, and if she didn't know better, sounded agonized. Stripping off his jacket, he wrapped it around her shaking shoulders. "I am sorry," he whispered into her hair. "This will hurt." He lifted her in his arms and carried her out, moving fast. Hot pain licked into her back, but it was nothing compared to the comfort and safety she felt, cradled in Mentàll's arms.

Before she knew it, they were on the dark streets. It must be the middle of the night. She couldn't stop shaking long enough to ask questions. Such as how he'd found her. Or how he'd broken in and out of the General's house. It didn't matter. She was safe now.

He carried her into Mrn. M's silent, dark house and into their room.

"Don't put me on the bed. I'm all wet."

He ignored her instructions. "Take off your clothes, or I will do it for you."

Shivering convulsively, she struggled to pull his jacket off of her shoulders. A pale thread of moonlight filtering through the drawn curtains provided the only light in the room. She felt a soft whisper of movement. Her nightgown lay beside her now.

"Can you do it?" His voice sounded harsh, and urgent.

Methusal managed to shake off his jacket. It fell to the floor. She felt his fingers on her shirt buttons. She didn't protest. The lighting was so dim that she wasn't afraid he'd see something he shouldn't, and she was too miserable to care. For such big hands, his were agile. He peeled off her shirt, leaving her scrap of a bra. He left her there, shivering and shaking, while he lit the lamp.

"What...what are you doing?" she whispered, shaking in spasms now. She crossed her arms protectively, concealing herself from his view.

"I am looking at your back." His voice was tight.

"Hurry, please. I'm so c..ccold."

Cool gel slid over her skin, dabbed on by his warm fingertips. A press adhered the coltac leaves to her skin as a bandage. It took a little while to treat all of the wounds. Finally, he was done.

Methusal felt cold, exposed, and fragile. She shuddered, teeth clacking. "Please...please turn off the light. I don't want to get dressed in front...in front..."

The light flickered out, followed by a puff of smoke.

Her nightgown settled over her head, and then around her shoulders. Roughly, he said, "Take off your bra."

Covered by the soft, drooping folds of the gown, Methusal obeyed. Then Mentàll helped her put her arms through the sleeves.

"Can you stand?"

Methusal staggered to her numbed feet. Her legs felt like quivering appendages of ice. He unbuttoned her pants. Delayed modesty kicked in, and a prickle of icy heat. "I can do that."

He backed up. She got the breeches partway down her thighs, and then had to sit down, because she was shaking so hard. He went down on one knee and pulled them the rest of the way off. She felt vulnerable as he knelt there looking up at her with dark, shadowed eyes.

He stood, urging her to lie back. Cool covers and the heavy quilt draped over her.

More tears slipped out. She was so cold. At this point, she didn't think her freezing body could ever warm up the sheets.

After some quick movements near the window, Mentàll slipped into bed, too.

He would be warm. Methusal wanted to wriggle closer. She looked at him just as he reached for her. "Come to me, Methusal," he said huskily, and she turned to him. He pulled her flush against his hard, warm body. She felt shocked. He still wore breeches, thankfully, but his shirt was gone. His skin felt deliciously warm—even hot—against her own. Gratitude surged.

"Th..thank you." She pressed her cold nose against his warm chest and shivered. "And...and th..thank you for r..r..rescuing me."

His arms tightened around her. Harshly, he said, "I would never leave you. And I am sorry I could not get you out sooner."

Tears slid down her face. At last, she felt completely safe. But the horror of what she'd been through felt like a crouching wild beast in the dark recesses of her mind. Exhaustion battled it, and so did the peaceful security she felt in Mentàll's arms.

He murmured words that she did not understand. She felt his warm breath in her hair, and he kissed her forehead. "Sleep."

Chapter Thirty-Two

W HEN M ETHUSAL AWOKE late the next morning, he was gone.

She lay in bed for a long time, reluctant to face the day. Reluctant to think about anything. She felt toasty warm cocooned under the bed covers. The air beyond the blankets felt frosty on her nose.

The door opened, and the Dehrien Chief entered. He frowned. "You are well this morning? You are not sick?"

Methusal shook her head. Her mind felt clear and her throat fine. She shivered when she sat up. "It's cold in here."

Her back, shoulders and wrists ached, but only a little blood had oozed from her abraded wrists. They might be painful and unsightly for a while, but would heal quickly. Her back throbbed, and she wondered how bad it was. Thankfully she'd worn a shirt through the entire assault.

He sat on the edge of the bed. A faint smile tugged at his lips. "Would you like me to hold you again?" Much as his embrace last night had been platonic, now his tone held a wicked hint of something else.

Methusal flushed. "No."

He measured the heat in her cheeks and his smile edged higher, looking satisfied. A few heartbeats passed, and his smile faded. "Tell me what happened."

Methusal didn't want to tell him. She didn't want to think about it.

With surprising gentleness, he said, "Where did General Fitrn capture you?"

"At the shack." She drew a breath, reluctantly accepting that she must face the memories. "It was after lunch. I don't know where he came from, or how he found me. No one followed me all morning."

"What did he do to you?" His voice sounded carefully controlled.

In halting fits and starts, she told him. The muscles in his body tensed with the telling, and by the end, his clenched fists were white.

"I will kill the *scienth*." Violence shivered through the low words.

"You can't. We have to follow the plan."

He stood. Raged pulsed in palpable waves from his tense body. "The man does not deserve to live. I will kill him, if I get the opportunity."

"You won't jeopardize the mission for me."

"I *will not* allow him to lay a hand on you again."

"Mentàll..."

"Do not argue with me," he rasped. He paced away. The crisp shirt rippled across the broad planes of his back. It reminded her that beneath the cloth veneer of civility, hundreds of scars marred his skin. A silent testimony to the countless beatings he had endured.

He knew how she had felt yesterday; the feelings of helplessness. The pain. The humiliation. Tears filled her eyes, but she blinked them back. She didn't want him to see them. She didn't want him to act rashly on her behalf, as he had done for Hendra, when he'd beaten his uncle to a bloody pulp.

And he would do the same for her. Methusal knew this now without question. For a man who showed only ice to the world, fire glowed, deep in the belly of the wild beast. ...If indeed he was a wild beast. Already, over the past year he'd saved her life more times than she could count...six times now?

He was no longer her enemy.

It seemed wise to change the subject. "I don't understand something. Why did the General try to make me admit that we're not married? He said *he* didn't care. Does that mean the Presidente does? And why would he?"

"The Presidente is afraid of us. The thought of us working together as one weakens him with fear."

"That seems like a strange thing to fear."

"He is insane. We do not need to understand his fear. But we must capitalize upon it."

"Can really we beat them? They have so many ships and men."

"Trust me, Methusal. My plan will bring them to their knees." The Dehrien's searing, implacable gaze held hers. "They are fools, and their vulnerable underbellies are showing. It will require only a few strategic moves to crush the Presidente's power to dust."

In his gaze she read his absolute certainty and self-confidence. She believed him. The Dehrien Kaavl Commander was a formidable man. If anyone could succeed in this impossible task, he could.

His lips curved up. "Good," he said softly. "Yesterday I procured invitations from a low ranking officer in Oesten. Today I will spy, and you will stay here."

"No," she said at once. "I am perfectly fine..."

"The General will be looking for you."

"I'll be careful. And shouldn't we return..."

"*No.*"

She scowled at his high-handed command. "I won't stay here like a scared apte."

"I will not allow you to put yourself in danger again. You are injured. Take care of your wounds today."

Mutinously, she stared back.

"Spend the day with Mrn. M. I will be back by dinner." That pale gaze held hers, demanding compliance.

"I'll see you later," she agreed.

He sent her another uncompromising look, and then headed for the door. "I expect you to obey me. I am your commanding officer."

"Are wives held to the same requirements as subordinates?" The provocative words tripped off her tongue before she could stop them.

When he glanced back, the ice blue gaze smoldered with sudden, intense heat. He advanced toward her. "Do you want to change your responsibilities to those of my wife?"

Her heart beat a little faster. "No." Thankfully, her voice was even.

Those discerning eyes searched hers. Softly, he said, "Are you sure? Because I am willing to change the game now. You need only say so."

Now she felt decidedly hot. What had possessed her to provoke him? She shoved aside the covers and put her feet on the cold stone floor. Only a handbreadth away from him, she looked him squarely in the eye. "I'd sooner shiver to death in that awful cellar."

He smiled. "I think you would always prefer to come into my arms, Methusal."

She blushed even hotter, and hated herself for it. "Get out."

Those blue eyes cooled again. "I will see you tonight."

"Tonight." She said agreeably.

The door closed with a quiet click behind him. As soon as he left, Methusal scampered to his side of the bed and swiftly untied his pack. At the bottom, she found what she was looking for. She tucked it under the mattress, and then gathered clean clothes and went into the bathroom to deal with her wounds and get dressed.

△ △ △ △ △

The sweet, delicate scent of baked cake filled the warm kitchen.

Deccia pulled the warm dessert from the oven and glanced at Hendra, who sat at the table. They were alone in the cabin. All of the men had gone to scout except for Behran, who had retreated into the woods with Sozla to work on their timers. It was gray outside, and threatened rain.

"Smells delicious," the Dehrien girl offered.

"Thank you." Deccia dropped the potholders onto the counter. Sick nerves wiggled in her stomach.

"Are you going to put tagma jam on top?" Hendra asked.

"No."

Hendra smiled and sipped tea. Her face looked serene, although Deccia knew more went on beneath the surface than the Dehrien girl allowed the world see.

Deccia sat down too, and swallowed lukewarm tea. "Are you ready?"

"What's to get ready for? We have to be the perfect hostesses to Olita's husband." Softly cloaked ore threaded through her words. A reflection of her cousin, Mentàll.

Deccia smiled. "I was proud of you last night. I'm not sure I could have said those things to Riln."

Uncertainty crossed her features. "Do you think I crossed the line? I don't want to be belligerent."

"You could never be belligerent. I think he's intimidated by you."

Hendra laughed. "No."

"Why else do you think he picks on you?"

"He's a bully. He likes to pick on the weak."

"Maybe partly, but..."

A hard knock sounded at the front door. Both girls peeked out the kitchen window. Two Zindedi soldiers stood there. One was Nygev, Vitnia's husband, and the other was a large, stocky man, who wore the medals of a Commander.

Deccia took a deep breath and headed for the front door. Moisture dampened her palms. What would Methusal do in this situation? One thing was for sure—she wouldn't be intimidated by these men. Pasting on a fake smile, she flung open the door.

"Good morning!" she chirped. "Hello, Nygev. And you must be Commander Radl. Pleased to meet you."

Radl was a tall, thickset man with wide, bushy black brows and a pock-marked face. From his stony expression, he didn't want to pass social pleasantries.

"Get your men," he barked.

"They're out." Deccia's smile remained pinned in place. "But they should be back at any time. Would you like to come in for some cake?"

"Get their papers."

Deccia frowned. "I'm sorry, but of course they took their papers with them. Wouldn't you like to come in..."

"*No!*" he bellowed, and shoved by her. "Nygev, search the place."

Nygev didn't meet their eyes as he traveled from the kitchen to the two empty bedrooms. "No one here, sir," he finally reported.

Radl stepped closer to Deccia, bristling menace. "We'll return tomorrow. Your men had better be here. If they're not, we'll drag you both down to the base for questioning." He smiled, showing crooked teeth. One was black. His voice lowered. "I don't think you'll like that."

Coolly, Hendra said, "What time will you come tomorrow?"

Radl sent her a contemptuous glance and turned on his heel. "Nygev." He marched out the door. Boot steps *thunked* down the stairs.

Hendra closed the door. "I guess that means we get to eat the cake."

△ △ △ △ △

"Did you two have a good time last night?" Mrn. M inquired at breakfast. It turned out that Mentàll had not left the house after all. He must have decided to stay in order to shore up the fiction of their marriage. "You must have been out late. I didn't hear you come in."

Methusal glanced at the Dehrien Chief and discretely pulled her shirt cuffs down to cover her red, angry looking wrists. That's all Mrn. M needed to see. She'd think Mentàll was abusing her. And thankfully she couldn't see the lacerations on her back, either. Five had broken through her skin. They were painful, but not too serious. She'd heal soon enough, and was thankful for the coltac leaves that she'd brought to Zindedi.

"I wish we'd come home earlier," she said. "It was hard to get up this morning."

Mrn. M dimpled. "Did Lozar surprise you?"

"Well...yes..." She wasn't sure what fabrication he had cooked up to explain their absence last night.

Mrn. M clasped her hands. "It's so romantic that he decided to go find you. I imagine you were having fun shopping, but to be swept off to dinner like that, and a show. Well. I have to admit I wish Charlie had done that a few times."

Methusal smiled at her "husband." "I never know what to expect from Lozar. He keeps our relationship fresh and exciting."

A knowing light glimmered in his eyes, and the corners of his mouth deepened into a smile. "I have never spent a dull day with Midi. Nor do I intend to."

Methusal looked away. Her heart beat faster. He had just admitted that he liked the friction between them, and he wanted to keep things that way. "What are your plans today, Lozar?" she asked, just to put him on the spot.

"I must spend time at the base." To Mrn. M, he said, "I have experience training troops, and a number of them arrived yesterday."

"I heard that." Mrn. M frowned. "I imagine the war against Koblan will start soon."

Wondering about her frown, Methusal said, "Aren't you for the war?"

"Oh, I suppose the Presidente knows best. But so many men have already died..." Tears shone in her dark eyes. "I just wish more men, especially the young ones, would not have to die. And you, Lozar," she clutched his hand, "you will be careful, won't you?"

"Of course. Thank you."

With a pat, Mrn. M released him. "I'm a foolish, sentimental old woman." She began clearing the table.

Methusal helped. When she returned to the dining room for the last load, Mentàll met her at the door, now wearing his black military jacket. With a swift hand on the small of her back, he drew her in for a kiss. It shocked her to feel his warm lips on hers in such an intimate, possessive caress.

"Be a good girl, Midi," he murmured. "I will see you tonight."

"Bye." She watched him leave, pulling the black cap down securely over his blond hair. Where was he going, really? To kill the General, like he'd threatened? Or to spy—and if so, where?

Troubled, Methusal finished clearing the table. Mrn. M sent her a sympathetic glance. "You miss him already, I see. That's good. It means a solid foundation has been built for when he leaves for war."

Methusal looked down. "I don't want to think about that."

"I know, dear. But it's a fact. And I think we are both practical women, are we not?"

Methusal met her eyes. "Yes."

While washing dishes in the kitchen, Methusal said, "When the Presidente was here the other day, did he bring your invitation to the ball?"

Mrn. M frowned. "No." She shook hot, soapy water from a glass and handed it to Methusal to dry. "It surprised me, I'll admit. I wonder if I've offended him. But I can't think how."

"Of course you haven't. Isn't he rather...unpredictable?" Or insane, like his brother and son.

"He's mercurial. But he has always been kind to me. I just can't imagine..." Perplexed lines wrinkled her brows. "Perhaps I should let it go. If I'm meant to go, I will. If not..." She shrugged. "I won't worry about it."

"Good idea." But it did seem strange that the Presidente hadn't given Mrn. M an invitation yet. After all, he'd sent out all of the remaining invitations yesterday. Why would he exclude her, the wife of his cousin and best friend? And the woman he visited every two weeks? It made no sense. The oversight—if it was one—made her feel uneasy.

And as far as invitations went, she had one under the mattress that needed returning. Mentàll would not be pleased with her plan for today, but that could not be helped. If he had an extra knife, she would take it. He would be pleased with that, at least.

△ △ △ △ △

A full day passed before Calbn issued a stiff, written apology to Aali. She suspected Trori and Rartn had been driving him crazy.

With no further comment, Aali returned to work, caring for her two small charges. But she took her meals with the children, and whenever she saw Calbn, she hobbled the other way. She did not like the man, which made him even more suspicious in her eyes. Not only was he unpleasant, but he was also friends with Mentàll. Not a good combination. She felt more convinced than ever that the two were plotting something evil. If only she could discover what it was!

Finally, GG demanded that Aali come visit again.

"Sit down. Have tea."

When Aali complied, the old lady pushed a plate toward her. "Have a slice of cake." With shaking hands, she poured brown, steaming liquid into a cup, and held it out to Aali. She accepted it before the liquid could slosh onto her leg.

"Thank you." Aali noticed the double peaks stamped into the cup's fine pottery. She'd never seen it on the dishes in the dining hall before. She said as much to GG.

"Of course they don't have the stamp." GG looked smug. "They're common. Mine are family heirlooms. Passed down only to those who appreciate them most. Certainly not to that Lylitha!" She snorted.

The engraving reminded Aali of Rartn's medallion. "Are those the Quasr twin peaks?"

"Of course. It is the Quasr symbol. Also the M'ntoyan symbol. One and the same." The old lady took a sip, and so did Aali. The bitter liquid burned her tongue. She put down the cup.

"I had a husband—dead," GG announced suddenly. "And two sons—dead. A daughter-in-law—dead. Life is cruel, young Aalicaa. Don't forget it!"

She didn't know what to make of those strange comments. Maybe go with it? Spy, and learn all the information she could? That had been her plan for some time now. If anyone knew the Chief's plans with Mentàll, it would be GG. She seemed to know everything that went on in her little world of the compound

"Trori said invaders killed her grandfather. Why?" she asked.

"Power, of course. Why else?" GG frowned. "He was Chief of Quasr, just like his father before him, and like my father before that."

"Chiefs aren't elected here?"

"Of course they are. But everyone knows the M'ntoyans are the best rulers. We've ruled for two centuries."

My goodness, Aali thought. Time for a shake up! "You said you had two sons. What happened to the other one?"

"Nosy, aren't you?" GG stared at her for a moment, as if considering whether to answer or not. "Wild beast attack thirty-one years ago. He was a wanderer, just like his father."

"I thought your husband was Chief." Aali felt confused.

GG's eyes snapped. "You are an impertinent, nosy girl!" She lapsed into silence and nibbled on a cake.

"Are you mad?" Aali asked. "Should I leave?"

"I'll tell you when to leave, girl!" GG frowned harder. She sipped tea. "Tell me about your family. Don't leave anything out. I'll know if you do."

"My father is Petr Storst. He used to be Chief of Rolban. My mother died a long time ago. Deccia is my sister, and my cousin, too. My parents adopted her from my aunt and uncle when she and Methusal were born. They're twins."

"A double blessing." The old woman nodded. "Tell me the names of your aunt and uncle. And your cousin's name."

"Hanuh and Erl Maahr. And my cousin is Methusal Maahr."

"I've heard the name. Mahre's descendent?"

Aali nodded.

GG muttered to herself, "A fine catch."

Aali wondered what she meant by that.

"Tell me about that young man of yours. Dastn?"

Her heart fluttered. "He's not mine. He thinks I'm a kid."

"Mmmhuh," GG snorted. She sipped more tea.

Aali decided to ask another of her prepared questions. "What was M..."

"Quiet!" GG snapped. "I'm thinking."

Time passed slowly, and Aali fidgeted. Her leg itched, and she wished she could scratch it. Maybe walking on the crutches would help.

GG said imperiously, "Don't let Lylitha run you ragged. She's a slug monster. Lazy!"

"She's pregnant!" Aali said indignantly. And Lylitha looked ready to give birth any minute. Not that she was an expert, mind you. But big was big.

"No excuse. Don't you have a broken leg? That's not stopping you, is it?"

"You *are* mean!"

GG cackled. "Always mean what you say, and say what you mean. I like you."

She wasn't sure if that was a compliment.

"I'm probably the oldest person you've ever met," GG said slyly. Those pale, keen old eyes focused on Aali, like a flying beast about to attack its prey.

She found that she wanted to upset GG's complacent pride. Clearly, she thought she was unique and special. Rude old lady. Wouldn't it humble her to realize she wasn't the only old person still living on Koblan?

"Nope. I have a grandfather. Methusal adopted him into our family."

"Grandfather!" GG snorted. "I'm a *great*-grandmother."

"He doesn't have any family. But Sims is old enough to be a great-grandfather."

The old woman's tea cup smashed to the floor. White bits bounced, and a dark brown puddle slid long tentacles across the stone floor. Aali quickly moved her cast out of the way, and shot a concerned look at GG.

"Are you okay? Are you burned?" From that quick glance, the old woman seemed fine. Except that her face had turned crimson.

"Get out...Get *out!*" GG screamed. Her whole body visibly quaked. "Get out, I tell you!"

Horrified, she wondered what was wrong. The old woman looked to be in the throes of a fit. She grabbed her crutches.

"What is it?" Lylitha appeared in the doorway.

"I don't know. We were talking. She asked me questions, and then she suddenly...flipped out."

"Please go watch Rartn and Trori. I'll deal with GG." Lylitha slipped into the room.

∆ ∆ ∆ ∆ ∆

Invitation securely tucked into her waistband, Methusal headed for the expensive houses on the hill. She'd bought a stylish hat and clipped up part of her hair so it looked shorter than it actually was. She focused intensely into kaavl. No one followed her. Of this, she felt certain. If the Presidente knew where she and Mentàll lived, his spies were keeping a discrete distance. Why? Why would he allow his enemies to wander his city at will?

Taking a circuitous route, and sticking to alleys, she hurried to Commander Ostl's house. She had no desire to meet up with General Fitrn today. It had always been difficult for her to remain in a kaavl state of mind, but yesterday proved that she needed to try harder. A lot harder.

She wondered what the General had done when he'd found his cellar empty this morning. Had he hung someone else up in the rings as punishment?

Chills prickled down her skin. Again, she wanted to block out yesterday's horrifying ordeal from her mind, but she couldn't. Especially not when she saw General Fitrn's gray rooftop in the distance. Her back burned from the lashes he'd given her, and her arms still ached, too. The man was a monster. If Mentàll hadn't come...

Stop it. Concentrate.

She recognized the high hedge surrounding the Commander's house. Good. Now she'd scout out the lay of the land, and then slip inside and return the invitation. No one could know it had been stolen. Otherwise, the Presidente might figure out that they wanted to attend the ball.

Methusal crept closer and knelt in a shadowed section between two hedges. Intensely concentrating into kaavl, she projected her hearing inside the house.

"I'm telling you, I had it in my drawer!" said a shrill voice. "Cidla, where did you put it?"

"Ma'am, I have not touched it. I did not know it was there."

"You're *lying!* Who else could have taken it?"

"Drumela." Commander Ostl's voice. "Mine is here. Are you sure you didn't misplace it?"

"*Misplace it?* For months, I've been dreaming of going to that ball! I did not *misplace* it. I've bought the perfect dress. I *have* to go! Get me another invitation, Ostl. Get it now!"

"The Presidente cannot be ordered about like..."

"Like what? Like a faint-hearted Commander who pees in his boots every time the Presidente speaks? Be a *man,* Ostl. Get me that invitation!"

"I'll try, but I cannot promise..."

"Then *I* will speak to him. He's coming for lunch tomorrow, isn't he? With that dreadful General. If need be, I'll do your speaking for you."

"You will be *silent,* woman!" Ostl thundered.

A short silence elapsed. "Don't you care about me, Ostl?" Drumela asked in a smaller voice. A sniffle reached Methusal's ears. "I have longed to go to a ball since I was a little girl. It is my *dream!*" Delicate sobs punctuated the quiet. "Don't you see why I'm so distraught? My dream is shattered. All those years... Oh, Ostl, have *mercy.* Help me, please!"

"I'll write a note, explaining the situation. However, I will not ask for another invitation. If he gives one, so be it. If not, you must accept it."

"I can *never* accept it!" Hysteria edged her tone. "To have it so close, and then ripped away...it's unfair!"

"Quiet! I've heard enough of your nonsense. I have to go."

"But the note. You'll write it now, won't you?"

"Get me parchment and ink."

Still crouching in the bushes, Methusal wondered what to do next. The Presidente couldn't suspect that Methusal and Mentàll wanted invitations to his ball. But when Ostl sent the message, it would be too late.

Maybe she could still put the invitation back where she'd found it. The Presidente would learn the truth tomorrow, when he had lunch with the Commander.

While Methusal waited for the Commander and the errand boy to leave, she pondered why the Presidente and General would meet at Commander Ostl's house tomorrow. Probably a secret meeting concerning the war. Definitely a meeting she needed to listen to.

Drumela said, "I need to lie down, Cidla. I have a headache. Search the house again, from top to bottom. If it's here, I want it returned immediately."

"Yes, ma'am."

The house fell silent. Methusal waited until the housekeeper's footsteps faded before she crept to the back door. Thankfully, it was unlocked again.

She slipped inside. Drumela was in the bedroom, so she couldn't risk putting the invitation back there. One thing was for certain—wherever she put the invitation, the housekeeper was sure to take the blame. First, for stealing it, and then for fortuitously "finding" it again. Methusal felt bad about that. But it could not be helped.

Pots banged in the kitchen. Methusal sidled past the couch to the desk. Carefully, she slid the top drawer open a crack. A quick poke and the invitation disappeared inside. Gently, Methusal closed it just as a knock sounded at the front door. The housekeeper's flat, slapping footsteps hastened to answer.

Methusal froze, although everything within her urged her to flee. If she made a run for the back door, though, the housekeeper and anyone at the front door would have a clear view to see her. Maybe she should stay crouched beside the desk for a minute longer. Hopefully the person would leave soon.

The door swished open. "General Fitrn," the woman squeaked. "Sir! How may I help you? Commander Ostl has just left."

A short gasp sounded, and boot steps clicked into the entry hall. "You stupid woman. I am not here to see the Commander."

"Then, wh...who, sir?"

Methusal carried with vision. The General had stopped near the short, squat housekeeper. He stroked her hair with disturbing familiarity. "Tell me, Cidla. How often does the Commander hide a fugitive in his house?"

"F...fugitive?" The woman's eyes rounded. "I am sure I don't know what you mean, sir."

"At this very moment, a fugitive roams your house. A prisoner." General Fitrn unsheathed his whip, and a tremble slid through Methusal. "I must question her at length."

How had he known she was in this house? She had been so sure no one had followed her! Panic made her palms sweat.

"Let...let me call the lady of the house."

The General's thin lips parted in a smile. "Of course. You won't mind if I search in your absence."

The woman's hands fluttered, and then her plump person hastened for the stairs.

The General's clicking steps entered the Commander's study. The desk, supported only by spindly legs, was not a good hiding place. Methusal wildly searched for a concealing spot. A half-length to her left was a tall, potted plant in a dark corner. Swiftly, she scrunched into the corner, partially hidden by the tree. She slipped the knife from her ankle strap and gripped it tightly.

The General paced, nonchalantly twirling the whip in his fingers. Her heart pounded in terror, and she remained very still. The torture he had inflicted upon her last night fast forwarded through her mind, making her feel sick to her stomach. What if he found her? What horrible tortures would he do now? She couldn't endure it. Never again.

She held her blade in a death grip.

General Fitrn continued to pace, idly flicking the whip at various items in the room. A vase trembled, but didn't totter. A snap made a paper on the desk jerk skywards, and then float downward in soft, undulating waves.

It occurred to her that he didn't appear to be looking for her very hard. In fact, a few moments later he coiled the whip up and lay it on a chair. He also disarmed himself of his favorite baton and other weapons, and then took off his cap and placed it on top of it all. Very strange.

Scuffling sounds reached her ears. A quick carry spotted Drumela descending the stairs wearing a robe and slippers. She stopped short in the doorway. "Oh. It's you." Her lower lip pouched out into a pout, "You gave Cidla a conniption, and woke me up from a nap."

She crossed over to a table, lifted an ornate, blue glass bottle, and poured liquid into a crystal glass. After an appreciative sip, she flipped her blond hair over her shoulder. "What do you want?"

The General advanced upon her with a pleased, rather frightening smile. "As I told your housekeeper, a fugitive has escaped. I have reason to believe she is here. I have already searched the downstairs."

"Oh." Drumela arched a brow. "Would you like me to aid in your search?"

"It is not a question of want. I need your help in my quest. If I cannot search this house to my complete satisfaction, I will be back with soldiers. Your husband's career will be over. On the other hand, if I find the fugitive now, with your help, Ostl will have nothing to fear."

Slowly, Drumela said, "I must, then. For the sake of my husband's career."

"Good." He smiled.

"Under one condition."

A flush suffused his face. "You are not the one to make demands."

"But how happily I'll help you if I receive one small favor in return."

"What's that?" he asked through tight lips.

"Another invitation to the ball. Mine was stolen. Perhaps by that useless Cidla."

Unknown thoughts flickered behind those cold, dead eyes. "All right. If my mission here is completely satisfied, then yes."

"Good. Cidla!" she shouted.

The housekeeper appeared, wringing her hands. "Yes, ma'am?"

"General Fitrn will be arriving tomorrow for lunch, and so will the Presidente. The General would like for you to serve his favorite cream torte and roast meat with poached tubers. Do you have all of the ingredients you require?"

"No, ma'am. The torte requires fresh spices. Would...would you like me to get them now?"

"Yes. I will show the General out when he finishes his search."

Cidla bobbed her head. "Of course, ma'am." Moving on remarkably swift feet, she headed for the back of the house. Moments later, a door slammed.

"Now." Drumela cast a languid gaze over the General. "In which room would you like to begin?"

The Commander's wife led the General upstairs. Methusal stared after them, puzzled. And then she choked back a horrified gasp. They couldn't be about to... *No.*

She couldn't escape from the house fast enough. She closed her ears to the sounds already coming from upstairs and ran for the noise of downtown Carachki.

Her skin crept, and she tried to block from her mind what was happening in Commander Ostl's home. She actually felt sorry for Ostl. From the little she'd seen and heard, Drumela and Fitrn seemed like a perfect match for each other.

She wandered the area around the Presidente's palace. It was quiet today. She slipped down to the docks. Recruits and powder carts choked the area. Stockpiling weapons on the ships had begun.

Methusal bought lunch, and then found a quiet bench where she could unobtrusively watch the activities. A Commander let loose a string of invectives at the slow moving soldiers. A few minutes later, an officer struck a new recruit. She flinched. He struck the young man again. It made her feel sick, seeing the soldier's weakness, and his inability to protect himself; to see him being forced to endure whatever cruelties his superiors decided to lash upon him. Helpless. Just like she had felt yesterday evening.

Last night's events again flooded her mind in agonizing detail. The pain. The humiliation. The absolute terror she'd felt.

Hot tears filled her eyes and slid down her cheeks. Face down, hidden by the wrapper of her sandwich, she wept. The horrible Zindedis. The horrible, *horrible Zindedis.* When could she finally go home? When could they *all* go home? She missed the goodness and simplicity of Rolban.

△ △ △ △ △

Hendra surveyed the small bedroom she shared with Sozla. All of her belongings were tucked into her pack. Tomorrow morning she'd be ready to evacuate the cabin. She toed the pack under the bed and glanced out the rain streaked window. They'd have to camp in the cold, damp woods for almost three days. At least the rain had stopped for the moment.

Tonight they would infiltrate the base for the last time before Day Zero.

Sozla entered the room. "Dinner will be ready soon. We'll have the meeting after."

"Is Goric back? Or Riln and Tabor?"

"No." Sozla pulled open her bag and scooped items off the shelf.

"How is the timer coming?"

Sozla smiled. "Behran is working on a brainstorm. He said it'll be ready to test after dinner."

"I'll see if Deccia needs help."

But Deccia was snuggling with Timaeus on the couch and insisted that the stew needed no work. "It'll be done in thirty minutes."

Hendra left them alone and entered the savory smelling, quiet kitchen. Behran labored over time pieces on the table. Doc stood at the window, looking outside. He wore his coat.

"Are you going out?"

He offered her a quick smile. "I was thinking about it."

She approached. "Why?"

With a gentle hand on her elbow, he urged her closer to the cold pane. His hand fell away. "Look," he said quietly. "A mama wolmite and her cubs."

The silver pointed wolmite sat on the opposite hill near the tree line. The fading light shimmered off of the iridescent flecks in her coat. Her black nose sniffed the air while white balls of fluff gamboled near her haunches.

"She's beautiful," she breathed. "But if we went out, she'd run away." Wolmites were fiercely protective of their cubs.

"That's why I'm still here."

Hendra took in his quiet absorption in the scene. Doc would never frighten an animal. He went to such lengths to never frighten her.

"Are you ready to go to the base later?" she asked.

"I could ask you the same question."

"I'm nervous. The guards are doubled. I hope we don't get caught."

"Tabor stole wire cutters today. We'll go in through the back fence."

That sounded like a good idea. Better than trying to get through the multiple guards watching the main gates. "Are

you still going? I mean, if you don't need to pick the lock..."
She'd rather Doc didn't go, and that he'd stay safe here.

"I'm going, Hendra. We have dozens of buildings to search."

The cold seeping through the glass made her shiver. "I hope we find the map to the powder mine quickly."

"You're cold. Take my jacket." He shrugged it off.

"I'm not cold," she protested. "The window is just a bit chilly."

His smile deepened. "Isn't that what cold means?" His jacket's warm weight enveloped her. It smelled just like him. Spicy, warm, and secure. His arm around her shoulders slipped down, so his fingers curved around her waist. The pressure was light, and she knew he'd withdraw at her slightest twitch of discomfort. Instead, she stood very still, enjoying being so close to him, and better yet, feeling no fear at all. She didn't know why, but decided not to question it.

She soaked up the moment, savoring his presence, his scent, and the tingle she felt, deep in her belly, being so close to him. In this one perfect moment, she felt like she belonged with him—that she belonged *to* him. Joy unfurled. She'd never thought...

The front door slammed.

"Leave me alone, Riln." Goric sounded irritated.

"Why weren't you at your station?"

"Why weren't you at yours?"

"Stop it." Deccia's voice. "You sound like children. Dinner's ready."

Doc's arm slowly fell away and they turned as the others entered the kitchen.

Sozla had joined Behran at the table. They sat close together, elbows touching, examining Behran's masterpiece. "See?" Behran murmured. "I think that will work." The two shared a smile. "Now to test it."

"After dinner," Sozla touched his wrist. "We need to eat."

"Is the timer ready?"

Behran grinned. "We'll see. If it is, we'll need to get more supplies from the store tomorrow."

Riln sloshed his bowl onto the table. "I'm ready for action."

"We'll go at lights out," Behran reminded him.

Riln shoveled large spoonfuls into his mouth. "I'm ready. Those Zins better stay out of my way."

△ △ △ △ △

Good. Very good. The Presidente patted his mouth with the pure white napkin, hiding his smile from the General, who sat across from him. He took a sip of spirits. "It is a shame Ostl's wife misplaced her invitation," he murmured. As of yet, Ostl had said nothing about it yet, fool that he was. "Was she distraught?"

His son's thin lips curved. "I smoothed her feathers."

"Ah." The Presidente chuckled and replaced his cup. Neither his son nor Ostl realized the importance of the missing invitation—not that that surprised him, of course. He was Presidente, after all. "Good. And you promised her a certain something in return?"

"Yes."

"Good. Yalin will provide it." And Yalin would deliver another of the coveted invitation packages tomorrow, too. Yes. His plan was falling neatly into place. How simple it would be to gather his enemies in hand and crush them with his fist. Violent satisfaction gripped him, and a warning pain shot down his arm.

"Father? Are you all right? Your face is flushed."

Not for one moment did the Presidente believe his son's concerned, solicitous words. The pup would pounce on power at his slightest slip. He ignored the question. "Did you find the Koblani girl? Did you interrogate her?"

"Yes." Fitrn sprawled back in his chair. A cruel smile pulled at his lips. "I tortured her, but let her go, as you requested."

"What secrets bleated from her lips?"

"She insists that she and the Dehrien are truly married." Speculatively, the General watched the Presidente. "She pledged her undying devotion to him."

Fury flashed, followed by a burning, agonizing pain. "It is a lie."

"I don't think so."

The fool! What did he know? And yet the thought of his enemies giving joy to one another, working as one... *Love.* Abhorrence crawled through his gut. He wanted to vomit. He wanted to scream. He would defeat it. He would *kill* it.

...If it was true.

He relaxed a little. His son was young, and ignorant to the wiles of women, unlike himself. Women held few mysteries for him. It was conceivable the Koblani slut had tricked his son. Yes. She had lied. Never could his instincts be so wrong about people. Methusal Maahr and Mentàll Solboshn were enemies, and he would divide and destroy them. Soon they would die.

Temper spurted. *Very* soon. And he'd enjoy watching every tear drop, and each blood droplet paint fear across their bodies. Every scream would help balm the itching hatred, deep in his soul.

△ △ △ △ △

After dinner, Behran cleared the table of everything except for his timepiece and a flat frying pan. Hendra and the others gathered to watch.

He lay the timepiece in the pan. A short length of twine extended from it.

"It's complex," he explained, "but I tied a thread to the mechanism inside that moves the hour hand. We can set the timers twelve hours in advance. Every time the hour hand goes around, it tightens the tension on the timing string inside. When it hits twelve hours, the tension on the string is so tight it pops the thread, which releases the firestick chip, which sparks flame to the twine. Of course the timing can't be perfect, but I've tested the thread and it's pretty uniform. It should work fine."

Sozla said, "I see you are turning the hour hand twelve times. That means twelve hours have passed on the timer?"

"Yes." Behran carefully set the timer down. "This may take a few minutes."

The detonator and powder weren't part of the experiment, so Hendra guessed that nothing would blow up.

Long minutes passed. Riln crossed his arms, shuffled impatiently, and then shoved his chin right and left with the heel of his hand, making cracking sounds.

"It's close!" Behran sounded excited.

Hendra craned closer.

A moment later, flame flared from the back of the timepiece. Fire swiftly licked down the short length of twine.

"Yes!" Behran hit the table with his fist and leaped up. "We did it, Sozla!" He grabbed the slight girl in an exuberant hug.

Sozla blushed bright red. Behran grinned down at her, but when he saw her reaction, quickly let her go. Flushing a little, he bent to examine the singed time piece.

"Still works," he said. And we have four more. Plus three detonators made."

"Won't we need a lot more?" Hendra spoke up. "Mentàll and Methusal need quite a few for Carachki, too."

"Yes. But to make them, we'll need more time pieces. That will determine how many timers we can make. Detonators aren't a problem. I have plenty of springs and flints. If we run out of time pieces, we'll have to use long, slow burning rope timers."

Not the most ideal solution. Zindedi guards might see them, or smell them.

Deccia said, "I'll go into town early tomorrow with Sozla and get the supplies you need."

"Don't forget. I'm supposed to meet with Mentàll tomorrow night," Timaeus said. "The timers and detonators will need to be ready by midmorning. And it might be a good idea if you show me how to set them up. Then I can show him."

"I'll show everyone now. We can have a refresher on Day Zero. And I think we'll only be able to send a few timers with you now, Timaeus. Doc and I will bring the rest to Carachki on Day Zero."

For the next hour, Behran coached each person through the process of setting up the timer and detonator, and even attached it to a ball of the wax that encased a pinch of powder. However, he didn't allow the timer to go off. So no explosion.

At last, he said, "We'll need to make more of the wax balls tomorrow. They'll need large amounts of powder inside, so they'll make big explosions."

"Do we have enough powder?" Hendra asked.

"No. We'll need to get more on the base tonight."

∆ ∆ ∆ ∆ ∆

Hendra crouched on the far edge of the dark field. Rain drizzled down, soaking into her hair and slicking down her face. Everyone was there except for Deccia. They'd search the base in teams of two.

Ten lengths away, Riln and Tabor squatted at the fence, looking like dark shadows. They were cutting the wire. Few guards patrolled this back portion of the base tonight. Most were congregated at the entrance gates. Hopefully it would be a simple matter to get in, find the map, get the powder, and get out.

Timaeus' whistle warbled like a flying beast settling in for the night. Riln and Tabor collapsed flat into the mud. A guard approached, and then squelched by.

The men resumed work. Minutes later, they slipped through the small opening and their black shapes disappeared behind a nearby building.

Hendra and the others waited. The guard meandered back and lingered near the cut fence, staring into the black night.

Precious minutes ticked by. No doubt Riln and Tabor had begun their search for the maps and extra powder. Hendra hoped Riln's bloodthirst wouldn't sabotage the mission. Knowing him, he'd kill anyone who crossed his path. It wouldn't occur to him that his actions could jeopardize the entire mission. Or would it?

Behran nudged her arm. "Come on."

Cut wire snagged on Hendra's clothing and sliced the back of her hand as she struggled through. She sprinted across the open compound to the building where Riln and Tabor had vanished. Of course, they were gone.

When everyone finally joined her, they split up. Hendra and Doc were to search the weapons making facility again. Behran, Sozla, Goric, and Timaeus would search the officers' buildings for information on the large powder mine.

Hendra wanted to take no chances. Before darting across an open space to the next building, she peered around the corner and focused hard. For long moments, nothing happened. It had been over a week since she'd practiced seeing the future.

Finally her vision shifted, warping into that odd, half-here, half-there feeling. Soldiers crossed the pathway. None looked this way.

"Come on." She touched Doc's arm.

Carefully, they crossed to the east side of the base. Few people were out in the rain, which made things much easier. They bypassed a group of soldiers who were congregated near a building, laughing and telling coarse jokes. At last they came within sight of the weapons building.

"Guards," Doc breathed.

"Remember the big doors at the back, near the ore mine? Maybe they're not guarded."

"Let's try."

After more stealthy maneuvering, they hid behind a piece of abandoned equipment and surveyed the back of the structure. Two guards and a large lock secured the doors.

"Now what?"

"We'll knock out the guards and pick the lock," Doc said calmly.

She gasped softly. "Are you crazy?"

"We have to find that powder mine. It's huge, from what I've heard. It could fuel the war against Koblan for years. We have to destroy it. So we need to get in that building and see if we can find a map. And there's extra powder in there for the detonators, too."

"How, then?"

Doc hesitated. As a doctor, harming people could not come naturally to him. It didn't come naturally to Hendra, either. She'd run from violence for her entire life.

A pale green moonbeam broke through the clouds and touched Doc's hair, turning it a dark, coppery green color. It also reflected off of pieces of metal on the ground. Several long rods. Hendra lifted one. It was heavy.

"It's the right length for a kaavl stick," she whispered. "If we get close enough, I could knock them out."

Doc's lips thinned into a grim line. "You take one, and I'll take the other."

Swiftly, they approached the eastern fence. No soldiers guarded this side of the weapons facility, because it had no entrances into the building. Hendra and Doc crept to the corner and peered around at the two guards. One paced stiffly, and the other lounged against the wall. Hendra looked into the future, waiting and watching for a time when both soldiers faced away from them.

"Now," she whispered.

Silently, they rushed the guards. Too late, Hendra saw why they'd turned away. Two new guards appeared. But they couldn't stop now. She and Doc bashed their rods on the first guards' backs, just as the new ones let out a startled cry for help. Hendra rushed them. Her twirling rod hit one in the arm, and another on the side of the head. One man bellowed and went down. A piercing whistle rent the air

"Hendra! Come on." Doc grabbed her arm and sprinted for the nearest building. Breaths heaving, they stood close together. Shouts erupted all over the base. Hendra didn't need to see into the future to know that they needed to escape right now.

Doc grabbed her hand and she ran with him to the back fence. The patrolling guard raised his gun. "Stop!"

Without thinking, Hendra flung her rod like a spear. It hit the man's chest and he went down with guttural moan, clutching his chest. Hendra slipped through the fence and waited anxiously until Doc joined her.

Where were the others? Had anyone found a map? And what about the powder?

They hadn't had enough time on the base. And it was all her fault. If she had looked into the future just a little longer, she would have seen the new guards approaching.

Riln and Tabor sprinted into view. They grabbed the groaning guard under the armpits and dragged him away from the cut opening. Riln punched him repeatedly in the face until the man slumped, unconscious, to the ground. He followed Tabor out.

"Got some powder," Tabor muttered, patting a bulge in his jacket.

"Good job," Doc said.

At least that was one piece of good news.

Lights blazed all over the base now. Muffled shouts came from the barracks.

Anxiously, Hendra waited for Behran and the others.

Long minutes ticked by. Zindedi soldiers ran to the weapons facility. Others marched in pairs, brandishing torches, and searching between buildings. They were getting closer. Soon it would be too late. The Koblanis would not be able to escape.

"Oh The One, please," Hendra whispered.

And then a slight figure appeared. Sozla! She slipped through the fence, and Goric was close behind. Then Timaeus. Long, nail biting moments later, Behran appeared. He carefully pulled the cut wires together, and then sprinted with the rest of them into the safety of the damp, dripping woods.

Riln said, "What idiot alerted the Zins?"

Hendra didn't want to say anything. But she wasn't a coward. "It's my fault. We were attacking two guards when two more appeared. I didn't see them coming. They shouted the alarm."

Riln spit vile curses.

"I got it," Behran said quietly.

"Got what?"

"The map." He grinned. "When the alarm went up, the Commander left his office. I had plenty of time to look, and I found the map."

No wonder he'd come running out last. "You have it?"

"In my pocket." He patted it.

Hendra felt a hundred times better. "Thank goodness."

Goric spoke up. "I'll look for the powder mine tomorrow."

"I will go with you," Sozla said.

Goric's brows shot up in clear surprise. "Why?"

"It will be our job to blow up the powder mines, no? I would like to see them before Day Zero."

"Don't you need to make the timers with Behran?"

"I have been confined to one place for too long. I need a fresh perspective."

It seemed like a strange statement to make. Behran shot Sozla a quick glance, but said nothing.

Goric shrugged. "Fine. But I'm going fast. You'd better keep up."

"Perhaps you could teach me a little kaavl. I want to be prepared for Day Zero." Sozla sent him a quizzical look.

"I can't teach you much in one day. You'll have to trust me on Day Zero."

"Of course," she murmured.

"Changing the subject," Tabor said in his quiet, deep voice. "Twenty carts are lined up at the front gate."

Riln muttered, "We should have blown them up."

"They won't leave for Carachki until the General arrives," Hendra said. "I heard the soldiers say that a week ago."

"Plans change, apte girl. You can't trust those Zins."

"I wonder if they've moved the powder from their storage buildings to the carts," Sozla said.

"I guess we'll find out on Day Zero," Hendra replied. But Sozla had a good point, and so did Riln. What if all of those carts were filled with powder? How could Mentàll and

Methusal blow up all of those powder carts, in addition to all of the powder already in Carachki?

"We need to blow them up *now*," Riln said loudly.

"Tomorrow Timaeus will ask Mentàll what to do with the powder carts," Behran said.

"Sitting on our hands will lose us Koblan," Riln said. "War's messy. It's time to get our hands dirty. Now."

No one answered.

△ △ △ △ △

Mentàll did not show up for dinner. An hour slipped by, and then two. Fear lodged deeper in Methusal's heart as the minutes slowly passed by. What was wrong? Where was he?

"Don't fret," Mrn. M said. "They've a lot to prepare for. More than once Charlie kept late nights."

Abruptly, Methusal reached for her jacket. "I'm going for a walk."

"No. I'm sorry, but I can't let you. It's not safe for a girl to wander the streets alone. Not at this time of the night. He'll come home safe enough. You'll see."

Methusal didn't like sitting still and worrying. Maybe later, after Mrn. M was asleep—and if he still hadn't returned yet—she'd go out and look for him.

She wondered how Deccia could handle it when Timaeus walked to Carachki alone. Not to mention when he was gone overnight. How did she handle the worry? Not that her feelings for Mentàll were anything like Deccia's for her husband, of course, but worry was worry. And the Dehrien Chief was the head of this mission. What would she do if something happened to him?

For the first time since arriving in Carachki, Methusal felt alone. She wished Deccia was here, or Behran. Yes, Behran. It disturbed her that she hadn't thought about him much lately, except to wonder what he was doing, and if he was all right.

She longed to talk to someone who would understand.

More time crept by. Finally, with her stomach firmly tied in knots, she bid goodnight to Mrn. M. "I'll see you in the morning."

"'Night, dear. I'll leave the door unlocked for him."

"Thank you."

In the room she shared with Mentàll, Methusal lay down in the dark, not bothering to undress. In a little while, when Mrn. M went to sleep, she'd go out and find him. Until then, she'd take a short nap.

She fell into a restless sleep.

"Deccia!" Methusal spotted her sister sitting on the porch in Dakarra. She was glad, because she'd been wanting to speak to her.

Deccia smiled and nodded ahead, toward the woods. "He's over there."

Who? Behran?

She would love to see Behran, of course. But he was not whom she was looking for.

Or was he?

She headed for the woods. But no matter how fast she walked, the forest remained the same distance away. Frustration and fear grew. She had to reach the woods.

And yet now a tremendous force, like a giant, invisible hand, pressed against her chest, preventing her from moving forward.

Was she going in the wrong direction?

Wildly, she looked around. Where was he?

Who was she looking for?

Maybe if she made it back to Mrn. M's, she would remember why she was here. Even if that meant leaving Deccia, that was what she must do. She turned around.

With a gasp, Methusal sat straight up in bed. She was home, in Mrn. M's house.

It was late.

She slipped across the room to the door. It creaked when she opened it, and she peered into the living room. The fire had burned down low, and the pale glow from Ryon streamed through the front windows.

He wasn't there. Could he be outside?

She drifted across the stone floor. A turn to the knob, and she looked out.

Nothing. No one.

Ryon's pale green light washed the leaves in the garden a pale, silvery color. It looked so quiet and peaceful. She needed the peace. She craved it. Something was terribly wrong. She needed to make it right. If only she knew what to do.

Dew splashed cold, wet prickles against the soles of her bare feet.

"Methusal?" The voice seemed to come from far away. Behran?

She stooped to pluck a flower from the carpet of grass and sniffed it.

"Methusal, what are you doing?"

"Behran?"

A strong pair of arms scooped her up, her knees dangling over one steely forearm, and the other arm supported her back. Pain stung, and then vanished.

"I am not Behran," the harsh voice said, carrying her back inside the house. He toed the door shut.

Deep peace relaxed her. Finally, she had found him. Methusal snuggled closer and mumbled, "I know. Kiss me?"

Her rescuer stopped in midstride. "What?"

"Kiss me."

He drew a deep breath. "Who am I?" His voice sounded thick.

Methusal reached up and tried to tug his head down, but he resisted.

"Who am I?" he insisted in a harsh whisper.

Methusal sighed. "Mentàll."

"Yes." The word, deep and low, sounded satisfied.

He laid her on their bed, but she wrapped her arms around his neck, refusing to let him go. She did not know why she longed so for his closeness, for his touch, but whispered again, "Kiss me."

He muttered a soft word, but complied. His mouth seared hers, and she gripped him tighter, her whole body quivering in response to his caress. With unknown strength, she pulled him down closer, so his hard shoulder grazed hers. His muscled arms vibrated with tension against her. Their mouths moved and tangled with wild, fierce heat. Hot lightning shot through her, igniting a molten fire deep within her. And still she wanted him closer.

She didn't want him to stop, not ever.

But even as she thought it, he lifted up, pushing away from her.

"No," she protested.

He dipped his head to kiss her again, fiercely, hungrily. With a soft curse, he pulled back.

"Mentàll..."

Harshly, he whispered, "You are asleep, Methusal."

"No."

"Yes." He pulled free, and she felt bereft and alone.

"Mentàll," she mumbled. "*Mentàll.*" She sat up with a soft gasp. For a moment the dream mingled with reality, and she stared blankly into the dark room. A dream. She'd been having a dream. About Mentàll.

"No... *No!*" She flopped back, covering her face with her hands. "What is *wrong* with me?" she whispered.

A faint noise *clicked.*

And why did her mouth feel cool and minty, like freshly chewed tagma leaves? She shot a panicked glance at Mentàll's side of the bed. He still hadn't come back. Legs trembling, she got up and searched the room. He wasn't there.

She lay back down. He was still out. It had only been a dream.

On the heels of this relief, worry returned. Where was he? Was he safe? Was he captured? Should she go out and look for him?

It would displease him if she did.

Methusal curled up into a tiny ball and decided to wait a little longer. Her eyelids grew heavy.

When she opened them again, dawn's pink light glowed through the window. The Dehrien Chief still hadn't returned.

CHAPTER THIRTY-THREE

METHUSAL SAT UP FAST. She'd slept the entire night away. And Mentàll still hadn't returned.

Worry overwhelmed her. And then last night's insane dream returned, like a fist punch to her solar plexus.

What in the *world*…

No. It made no sense at all.

She shook her head in confusion, and folded her arms tightly against herself. She'd been looking for someone. Behran? Mentàll? Maybe she had been longing for Behran, but then Mentàll, with whom she spent every waking moment, had intruded into her subconscious mind.

Yes. She clung to this thin explanation. Of course. Dreams were crazy. An apte could turn into a wild beast, and dry land into the sea. Dreams made no sense at all.

Feeling a little better, her mind returned to the present dilemma. Where in the world was Mentàll?

She threw on her clothes, brushed her long, tangled hair until it was smooth, and slipped into the living room. She glanced anxiously down the hall. No sign of Mrn. Machblin yet. Good.

She crept toward the front door, skirting the back of the couch, from which emitted a gentle snore.

Snore?

A quick glance located the missing Dehrien Chief. He lay sprawled on the far too short couch, his cheek resting on the rough fabric of the couch arm. One leg was bent, and the other long leg dangled off onto the floor.

Methusal had never seen him asleep before. He always woke up before she did. Her gaze traveled back to his face, and she smiled a little. The harsh, angular planes were gentler in sleep.

But what was he doing out here? What if Mrn. M saw him?

Much as she hated to do it, since he looked so peaceful, she had to wake him.

"Mentàll," she whispered, touching his shoulder.

He immediately sat straight up, which startled her, and sucked in a deep breath. "What?

"What are you doing out here?"

He did not reply for a moment. "I didn't want to wake you."

"What if Mrn. Machblin saw you? She'd get suspicious."

Mentàll glanced at Methusal, his eyes sleepy and slightly unfocussed, as if still trying to regain his faculties. The rough, red pattern of the couch fabric had imprinted into his cheek.

"That looks painful." Without thinking, she gently touched it. "Does it hurt?" The rectangular groves felt deep and bumpy in his skin.

He went very still.

She froze. What was she doing?

And then, ever so slightly, he pressed his cheek into her hand. His eyes found hers, dark now with some fierce emotion. Longing? It couldn't be. Not Mentàll Solboshn, Dehrien Chief. He couldn't be longing for the gentle touch of another person...*her* touch.

Her heart beat faster and she didn't know what to do. And then she did.

Softly, her thumb stroked the bumpy indentations on his cheek, and then she slowly withdrew. "Those couch marks look uncomfortable."

He seemed to come fully to his senses. His shoulders straightened and his angular face stiffened back into its usual implacable lines. "No," he said, and stood. He disappeared into their room.

"Good morning, dear!" Mrn. Machblin bustled into the living room. "Did you have a good night? Ready for breakfast?"

"Let me help you." Methusal felt unsettled by her encounter with the Dehrien Chief. It helped her equilibrium to set the table and do other small jobs, such as slicing bread for toast.

Why had she touched him so gently like that? And she'd wanted to do it.

Last night's dream again filled her mind. And so did the truth.

She almost cut herself, slicing the bread. She'd been worried about Mentàll when she'd fallen asleep. She'd been searching for *him* in her dream.

Had she longed for him last night, instead of Behran?
No.

Methusal placed the bread on the table, and set out cups and plates. No, of course she hadn't.

She'd wanted to treat him with kindness, she told herself, just like the Prophet had directed. Just like she had nursed his cut cheek during the war. He was a human being, after all. She even cared if whip beasts were injured. And that couch burn had looked painful.

Of course. That's all it had been.

The problem was, she wasn't sure if she believed what she was telling herself right now.

Delicious smells of fried meat and baking biscuits drifted from the oven.

Mrn. Machblin carried two mugs of tea into the dining room and set one before Methusal. Her bright eyes rested on Methusal, but then a frown drew her brows together. "Did you and Lozar have a fight last night? I know it's none of my business, but... Well, I came out around midnight and saw him asleep on the couch."

Midnight? Methusal thought he'd been out for most of the night. She swiftly improvised, "He didn't want to wake me."

"I see. Let me check the biscuits."

Hopefully, their hostess didn't think they'd had another fight.

Her mind involuntarily returned to waking Mentàll on the couch. This time, she set aside her own disturbing reactions, and for just a second relived his.

A bit of wonder took root in her soul. That large, intimidating man had responded to her touch. He had seemed to *like* it. At one time that thought would have frightened her, but now it didn't. Instead, it filled her with an inexplicable joy. On its heels another, softer emotion slid through her.

"The biscuits are done. Why don't you see if Lozar is ready?" Mrn. Machblin suggested.

Methusal slipped into their room and found Mentàll securing his pack shut. He didn't look up.

"Breakfast is ready. I'm afraid Mrn. M thinks we've had another fight. She saw you sleeping on the couch last night."

The Dehrien Chief stiffened, but finished buckling the last strap into place.

"You weren't out late. Why didn't you come in here to sleep?"

"I do not need to tell you everything, Methusal."

She ignored a stab of hurt. "Were you spying?"

"Yes. I traveled to Paraski to count the number of their ships."

That still didn't explain why he hadn't come into their room last night. Evidently, he didn't intend to tell her why, either. Fine. He could be distant and cold if he wanted to be.

And then, as he came toward her, she saw the red marks on his cheek again. And she remembered the moment on the couch when he had revealed his vulnerable side. Her annoyance evaporated.

He reached for the door, but she didn't move from in front of it. His eyes narrowed. "Are you ready?"

"Yes." Boldly, she slipped her hand into his.

He paused, his other hand frozen on the knob. He stared down at their interlinked hands, as if trying to understand the reason behind it. Then his fingers folded around hers. "Mrn. Machblin."

"Yes."

He sounded so harsh, and so matter-of-fact. Then why did the fingers wrapped around hers feel gentle, as if holding a priceless, valuable thing?

Surely, she must be imagining things.

He ushered her into the living room. Mrn. Machblin stopped bustling about and smiled when she saw them. "Good. All is well. Care for juice?"

Methusal said, "Yes, thank you," as Mentàll pulled out her chair for her. His hand lingered, holding hers, until she was seated, and then the warm pressure fell away. He helped Mrn. Machblin bring the last items to the table.

Methusal smiled, looking at all of the delicious food piled on the table. Before sitting, Mrn. Machblin leaned close to her and whispered, "You look radiant, dear."

Did she? She felt happy, Methusal realized in surprise. In fact, joy bubbled up inside her and spilled out in her grin to the other two at the table. Mrn. M smiled to herself and slathered jam on toast, but when Mentàll glanced at Methusal, he stilled, as if transfixed. The tiniest smile crept into his glacier blue eyes and thawed them. Just for that second, Methusal glimpsed a completely unexpected side of him. Gentle and relaxed. And happy?

Soft emotions tugged at her heart. She wanted him to be happy. She wanted that very much.

∆ ∆ ∆ ∆ ∆

Early in the morning, while fog still enshrouded the landscape, Deccia, Sozla, and Goric headed for Dakarra. Deccia had a bad feeling about today.

At dawn, she'd clung to Timaeus before he'd left with the men to find a camp spot in the forest. She wouldn't see him again until tomorrow. Behran planned to finish four timers and detonators in the woods, and then he'd send them with Timaeus to Carachki later this morning

Again, Deccia relived Timaeus' kiss and the feel of his strong arms around her. "I'll be back before you know it," he'd whispered into her hair. He felt so solid and strong.

Fear coiled through her heart and she clung to him, unable to let go. Fear told her that if she did, the world would snatch him away from her forever.

She buried her face into his neck. "I wish I could go with you, Timaeus." If she was with him, surely he'd stay safe.

"I'll be back tomorrow morning."

At last, she released him. "Please be careful."

"I'm always careful. I want to live to see you again." Gently, he kissed her. "I'll see you tomorrow."

"'Bye, Timaeus." It made her feel sick to her stomach to watch him go. With every step he took, it felt like she lost a little more of him. "Come back to me soon," she whispered, and tears slipped down her face.

Now Deccia blinked back more moisture. It felt like he was lost to her forever. That she'd never see or touch him again.

It had to be a lie. It had to be only fear talking. And yet when they'd sailed to Zindedi she'd had that premonition of darkness. Of losing someone she loved. Today that feeling was so strong it tasted bitter in her mouth.

Sozla touched her arm. "Are you all right?"

Goric glanced over and then away, hands shoved deep into his pockets.

"It's Timaeus. I have a horrible feeling something bad is going to happen. I'm afraid I'll never see him again."

"I will pray with you."

"Will you?" Deccia gratefully clutched her sleeve.

The two girls stood close together, hands clasped, and eyes closed. Goric stood a good distance off, staring into the fog. "The One," Sozla said. "Please keep Timaeus safe. Protect him from the Zindedis, and protect his life until Deccia can see him again. Amen."

"Amen," Deccia sniffed, wiping her eyes. "Thank you."

"Of course. So much of life is out of our control. I have found the only way to find peace is to pray."

When they slipped into the outskirts of Dakarra, Goric disappeared. Sozla would meet him again on the north side of town for their walk to the beach road.

At least Deccia had seen no sign of Commander Radl yet, or Nygev. Not that it mattered. The Koblani men were safely hidden in the woods. Only Hendra had remained in the cabin, packing up the last of the supplies. When the men returned for the last load, they'd leave the cabin forever.

Warm lights glowed from the market, and Deccia was glad to see it was open this early. She'd been worried it might not be.

It felt chilly inside the building. In the back, Ceri shoved wood into the round stove. "Good morning!" she called out. "You got an early start."

"We want to go on a picnic if it clears up. I thought I'd get some supplies."

Deccia placed bread, dried meat and other nonperishables in her bag, along with fruit and vegetables. It would be their last visit to the store, and the last time she'd see her friend, Ceri. A pang of sadness slipped through her.

Sozla finished quickly with Behran's list and dropped the supplies into Deccia's bag. "I only found five time pieces," she said in an undertone. "We need more."

Ceri's sharp ears caught the statement. "Do you need something?"

Sozla smiled. "Our husbands like the time pieces. We thought we'd give them as gifts to our relatives. They are so ornate and beautiful."

"Tisnia might have more in her shop. She'll open up soon."

"Thank you. We will check."

Deccia placed the items on the counter for Ceri to tally up. The Zindedi girl made no comment on the wire and other metal odds and ends mixed in with the "picnic" foods. "I hope it clears up soon," Ceri remarked. "I'm sick of the fog and rain."

"Me, too." Impulsively, Deccia said, "We'll be going home soon. I hope it's nicer there."

"When are you leaving?"

"In a few days."

"Oh." Ceri's face fell. "Be sure to stop by before you go."

Deccia's smile wobbled and she nodded, not trusting herself to speak. "'Bye." Gathering up the bag, she quickly left the shop. She hadn't expected to make a friend in Dakarra. Maybe hatred didn't completely darken her heart for all things Zindedi. That was a smidge of comfort for the state of her soul.

Across the street, shadows moved in Tisnia's shop. Deccia pulled her coat more tightly around her against the chill and urged Sozla to go find Goric. "You have a long trip. I can find the time pieces."

A frown wrinkled Sozla's brow. "If you are sure. Timaeus would not like me to leave you alone."

Unexpected temper spurted. "Timaeus isn't here. I'll be fine."

Sozla left with a frowning, backward glance, and Deccia huddled beside the shop door, her arms crossed. She hoped Tisnia would open the shop soon.

The gray sky lightened as she waited, and pale strips of blue flirted with the clouds. A large figure appeared on the street, wrapped in a long brown cloak. Her limping waddle identified her. Olita.

The Dakarran woman scowled at Deccia, and swerved to rap on Tisnia's door. When it opened, Deccia followed her inside. She needed to get those time pieces and go. Radl could show up at the cabin at any time, and she needed to get back before the men returned for the last load. She had no idea how to find the new camp on her own.

Warm light glowed in the back of the store. Vitnia was there too, her spare frame garbed in black, and her arms crossed. Her black eyes narrowed when she spied Deccia.

The three cronies huddled together as Deccia perused the shop. She strained her ears, struggling to pick up on any information about Radl's trip to the cabins today.

Olita stamped her feet and rubbed her hands. "Soldiers dragged my man out of bed at one in the morning," she said querulously.

"Mine, too," Vitnia muttered. "What do you think it's about?"

"Spies broke into the base."

The other women gasped. "Eastern Zins?"

"Most likely. They don't know for sure. Guards are tripled now." Olita sent Deccia a baleful look. "They need every man."

Deccia fought the urge to move quickly. Slowly, thoroughly, she scanned the shelves. *Oh, please let her have some time pieces.* It would be poetic justice if the bomb timers came from one of the women who had been so nasty to them during their stay in Dakarra. Too bad it wasn't Olita's shop.

Maybe it was wrong to think such vengeful thoughts.

Her eyes lit upon a round, ornately engraved time piece. Seven others lay right beside it. They were marked twelve dascals apiece. She had enough to pay for them. Gleefully, she scooped up all eight of them and headed for the counter, eager to leave the mean-spirited women as soon as she could.

"Is that it?" Tisnia said in her high, breathy voice.

"Yes." Deccia pulled dascal notes from her small purse.

"Two hundred dascals."

"But the sign said twelve dascals apiece."

A small smile split Tisnia's long, full face. "Two hundred dascals."

"Nine hundred dascals." Vitnia's features looked sharper than ever. Her black eyes glittered at Deccia.

Deccia said nothing for a moment. What game was Vitnia playing? She barely had two hundred dascals. And securing the time pieces was her first priority. Quickly, she counted the notes into Tisnia's hand and scooped the time pieces into her bag.

Vitnia's claw-like hand grabbed her arm. "You owe me seven hundred dascals."

Deccia shook off the other woman. "What are you talking about?"

"Rent was due two days ago. You owe me six hundred for the week, plus one hundred in late fees."

"Oh." Deccia had completely forgotten. "I'm sorry. I have more money at the cabin."

"I want my money now."

"I don't have it. I can get..."

"I want it *now*. Maybe you should give those time pieces back to Tisnia, and she'll give me the first two hundred you owe me."

Tisnia opened her mouth, but said nothing.

Deccia tightened her grip on the bag. "I have the money at the cabin," she said firmly. "I can bring it to you later."

Vitnia jutted her chin closer. "I don't trust you. You're a spoiled, pampered rich girl. You need to learn to pay what's owed. Nothing comes for free. Now, give me that bag. You'll get it back when I get my money." She seized the shopping bag and gave a mighty yank.

Deccia gasped, and yanked right back. "Let go! I said I'd get you the money."

"Radl will get the money," Olita interposed. "Him and his men are going to drag their worthless men off to war today. He'll get everything that's owed you, and more."

With a final glare at Deccia, Vitnia released her grip on the bag. "I want eight hundred dascals now. No. Make it a thousand!"

Deccia wrapped her arms tightly around the shopping bag. Her heart pounded, but she forced herself to speak calmly. "You'll get your money, Vitnia. Good day."

On shaking legs, she swiftly exited the shop.

Thank goodness Timaeus was gone. And thank goodness they were leaving the cabins this morning. She had to warn the others about Radl's true intentions.

∆ ∆ ∆ ∆ ∆

It felt strange to be alone in the cabin. Hendra hoped Doc and the others would find a good camping spot soon. And she hoped that Commander Radl would arrive after they'd carted the last load of supplies into the woods.

She rubbed soap on a cloth and scrubbed the crusty egg pan.

Footsteps creaked on the floorboards. She spun around, hands dripping soapy water on the wooden floor. Riln stood behind her, looking large with his black coat, black hair, and black eyes.

The two of them were alone in the house. Instant panic surged.

He shouldn't be here. *This wasn't right.* Memories of her stepbrother flooded her head—black-haired, black-eyed Jascr cornering her alone in an outbuilding. Touching her. Forcing himself upon her.

Hard won instinct managed to hide her fear. "I thought you went with the others," she said pleasantly.

"Tabor thought someone should guard you."

And he'd chosen Riln? "How comforting." She turned back to the dishes.

He joined her at the counter.

Hendra fought the urge to cringe from him. Why was he standing there? Didn't he see that she didn't want to speak to him? Was he so insensitive?

Yes. Yes, he was. Or maybe he intended something altogether different. Maybe he intended to take advantage of his time alone with her, after all. Panic fluttered again. She drew slow, calming breaths. *Please protect me, The One.*

"Why don't you go outside and keep watch?" A quick glance took in his unpleasant, hostile smile.

"I just checked. I think I'll stay right here."

Nerves felt like rochers crawling over her skin. She scrubbed the dishes, trying to ignore him.

When his arm brushed hers on the way to grab a cup from the sink, she staggered backward, fast.

She'd just revealed her fear. Warily, she stared into his eyes.

Amused, opaque black stared back. "You think I would hurt you?"

Hendra didn't say anything for a long moment. If he hadn't thought of attacking her, she didn't want to plant ideas in his mind. Evenly, she said, "You do. Every day."

"You're an apte." His eyes glittered.

Gathering up her threads of courage, she asserted, "I don't like you. You're rude and arrogant and mean. And not just to me. To Goric, too."

Disgust curled his lip. "Goric's a mama's boy."

"And you're a real man because you trample other people's feelings?"

He shook his head. "I have you figured out, apte girl. Doc needs to cut you loose. You'll lead him a pretty song and dance. But in the end you'll bleed every drop of self-respect from him. He'll never have you. Because no one's good enough for you." He grinned, and it wasn't a nice one. "I have your number, apte. You can't handle a real man. If you could, I'd show you one."

She shuddered in revulsion, but still held her ground.

"Doc knows where I stand," she said tightly.

"Yeah. Right." His lip curled.

"Step off!"

"I'll step off." He leaned closer. "But first, tell me something."

His largeness frightened her. His *closeness* terrified her. Hendra fought it. "I said, step *off*."

His finger chucked under her chin. "Don't you like men to touch you?"

Panic scorched her. Instinct screamed to run. Pride and pure grit fought it. "*No*. I don't. A man hurt me. Over and over again." She stared at him, her face feeling like a block of wood. "And do you know what? You're just like him."

He jerked back when comprehension flashed. Disgust, incredulity, and then bewilderment crossed his face. He took another step backward, and his gaze flicked down her body. "No."

Hendra trembled. She hadn't wanted to expose her darkest secret to this man, but it appeared to have shocked him. And finally, he'd backed off. "Leave me alone, Riln." She turned to the sink and rinsed the breakfast dishes.

Riln left.

△ △ △ △ △

When Deccia reached the hill to the cabins, she'd seen no sign of Radl or his men. The landscape looked peaceful. Tall grasses quietly rustled in the breeze.

She burst into the cabin, where she found Riln and Doc piling supplies on the living room floor. Hendra plopped a big pot and spoon next to her backpack.

"Deccia," she said. "Did you find time pieces?"

"Thirteen. We have to get out now. Where are Behran and Tabor?"

"Behran's at the new camp. Tabor's our look out."

Deccia hadn't seen him when she'd approached the cabin. He must be well hidden. She fought a curl of unease. "We have to go. Now." Quickly, she explained what had happened in Dakarra. And Radl's threats.

"Everything's ready."

"I'll do a last run through," Doc said. "Is everything out of your cabin, Deccia?"

"Yes. Timaeus already carried my pack out into the woods."

Doc checked the bedrooms, and then disappeared into the kitchen.

"Could you carry these blankets, too, Deccia?" Hendra asked. They intended to borrow Vitnia's blankets for a few days, and then return them.

"Sure." Deccia gathered the blankets in her arms just as a sharp rap came at the door.

With a sick feeling, she dumped the blankets on the couch. After a quick glance at the others, she went to the door and opened it a crack. Commander Radl stood outside, flanked by a thick-set man. Two additional soldiers, guns cocked, stood behind them. Where had they come from? She'd seen no one a minute ago.

"Good morning." She tried to affix a pleasant smile upon her face. Her gaze went from Radl to the stocky man, and then paused. For a moment, she couldn't breathe.

The second man closely resembled the dead General Greisn. Stocky. Black hair. Jowly face. Medals pinned in precise rows across his chest.

A slow tremor seized her. It couldn't be him. And yet hatred overwhelmed her. Her fingernails dug into the doorframe, even as her mind registered that the man's eyes were brown, not amber. And the medals indicated he was a Commander, not a General. Still, hatred festered, like a pustulant wound about to spew poison.

"Why have you come with soldiers, Commander Radl? They are not necessary."

Radl planted a massive hand on her chest and shoved, hard. She staggered backward, and he and his companion stepped into the room.

"What's this?" His gaze flicked over the pitiful piles on the ground. "Planning an escape?"

A ruckus sounded from the kitchen.

Doc staggered through the doorway, his arm wrenched up behind him. A black clad soldier shoved him another step forward.

A grimace contorted the doctor's face. The soldier held a gun to his head.

△ △ △ △ △

After breakfast, Methusal took her courage in hand and reported to Mentàll the conversation that she'd overheard yesterday between Drumela and Ostl. A top level meeting would take place between the Presidente and General Fitrn at noon, and she suggested they might want to spy on it.

She'd skated on the specifics. After the peaceful truce they'd forged this morning, she didn't want another fight. She'd neglected to mention where she'd overheard Drumela's conversation.

Shrugging into his black jacket, he'd followed her outside, asking few questions, for which she was grateful, and also a little suspicious.

As they headed for Commander's Ostl's house, she deliberately changed the subject. "How many ships are in Oesten and Paraski?"

"Fifteen in total."

"Will we blow them up, too?"

"No. We will blow up Carachki's powder buildings and ships."

"The ships?" Methusal blanched. "But what about the men on them?" She thought of the green recruits she'd watched suffering yesterday under the officers' harsh treatment.

"They will die. This is war."

She gasped. "Half of those soldiers are young. I'll bet they've never hurt anyone in their lives."

"Compassion for your enemy, Methusal?" Those pale eyes glittered. "Perhaps that is your weakness."

"Compassion is a strength, not a weakness."

"Do you feel so tenderly for all of your enemies?"

She smiled, refusing to let his subtle topic change ruffle her. "Does tenderness frighten you?"

"Nothing frightens me. You should understand that well." They entered Commander Ostl's neighborhood from the north side.

"So you say. But I think tenderness is foreign to you. Hatred and hostility, though, are familiar friends. You're much better at dealing with those, aren't you?"

"How little you know me, Methusal."

"You keep saying that. But I think I know you a lot better than you think."

His gaze caught hers for a moment. "You may be correct, Methusal."

That surprised her.

The Dehrien Chief ducked behind a hedge. Five houses down the street, a black coach rolled into the parking space behind Commander Ostl's house. A military cart followed. Soldiers spilled from it and took up positions all around the house.

"The Presidente has arrived," he said grimly. "The building three doors down is vacant. You will listen to their conversation from there."

A bit of relief relaxed the tension she'd been feeling. As they slid from shadow to shadow toward their destination, Mentàll murmured, "You did not think I would allow you to be in the same house as that predator, did you?"

"I'm a soldier," she reminded him. "You don't need to baby coddle me."

He did not reply.

"Come." He slipped between two large trees, heading for the back door of a large house. The lock was broken.

The wooden floors inside looked dusty, and the large room was vacant, except for a flowered couch.

"They'll see our footprints," she warned.

"The Zindedis will not check this house. They are fools," he muttered, stalking into the adjacent room, and then upstairs. Apparently satisfied that they were alone, he took her elbow and urged her to the couch.

His touch and his nearness unexpectedly made her heart flutter, and when she sat down, she made sure a full cushion length separated them. Behind them, the sun streamed through the window, warming her hair.

Those ice blue eyes glimmered. "Now who is frightened?"

She ignored him, and closed her eyes.

"Relax," he murmured.

She frowned.

"You are safe here," he said softly. "I will protect you."

Annoyed, Methusal opened her eyes again. As usual, his deliberate, provocative statements made her want to respond like a contrary urchet. "I'm supposed to trust you?"

"You *do* trust me." He smiled. "Don't you?"

She closed her eyes again and flipped out words she didn't really mean. "Just because I've aligned with a wild beast to fight a whip doesn't mean I trust the wild beast."

Softly, he said, "You promised to tell me no more lies, Methusal."

She glared again. "Will you please be quiet? I need to concentrate."

He sprawled back, his arm resting along the back of the couch. His fingertips nearly touched her shoulder. Methusal fought her instinct to scoot further away. Why was he behaving like this? He was deliberately trying to get under her skin again. After their closeness this morning, she'd thought...

And then she wondered if he was trying to push her away and create distance between them. Maybe physical intimacy was fine with him, but emotional intimacy was a different matter.

Well, she wanted distance too, didn't she? She should be grateful for his efforts to create space between them again. She tried to ignore the small twinge of hurt she felt in her heart.

"I'm concentrating," she said, more to redirect her own thoughts than to speak to him.

The sun felt nice and warm on her hair. She slipped utterly into kaavl.

△ △ △ △ △

Hendra couldn't tear her eyes away from Doc. Pain spasmed across his face. The soldier had shoved the doctor's elbow nearly up to his shoulder blade. It looked close to snapping.

A quick glance took in the Commanders in the middle of the room. The two Privates stood just inside the doorway, their guns cocked and ready.

Beside her, hatred blazed from Deccia's eyes. Riln stood near the men's bedroom door. Aggression oozed from his tense, slightly hunched posture.

Commander Radl's black gaze drilled into Deccia and Hendra, and then flicked to Riln and Doc. "Where are the other two?"

No one spoke.

He focused upon Hendra. With a step, he closed the distance and roared, "*Where?*"

She jerked back. "I...I don't know."

Radl punched her. Pain shattered her thoughts. Blood squirted from her nose and gushed down her lips.

"Hendra!" Doc lunged forward, and then choked back a moan of pain.

The others stared at her. Deccia gasped. With a mighty roar, Riln charged Commander Radl. A knife flashed in his fist, and the Zindedi crumpled to the ground.

△ △ △ △ △

The Presidente shoved aside the plate filled with food. Nearby, the plump housekeeper visibly twitched, and then tightly clasped her hands together. Clearly, the ignorant woman did not know how to properly treat a person of his importance.

"Clear the table, woman!" The Presidente frowned at Ostl. The balding man gulped, and a bead of sweat appeared on his shiny forehead.

The housekeeper hastily cleared the table and disappeared.

"Shut the doors," the Presidente ordered.

With a speed belying his stocky build, Ostl closed the double doors leading into the hall, and then resumed his seat beside General Fitrn.

The Presidente pulled a leather valise from its resting place beside his chair. He extracted a dirty, wrinkled parchment and shoved it with one finger across the table. "Your next assignment, Fitrn."

Distaste curled the General's lips. Quickly, he perused the short document. Unknown thoughts flickered behind his stony expression.

Helpfully, the Presidente said, "Your brother has spoken. He names my brother's killer and describes him."

"What am I to do with this?"

"He is in Dakarra. Or close by. You will travel to Dakarra today and capture him. You will bring him back to Carachki, along with the powder, on the day of the ball."

The General flicked the paper onto the table, clearly dismissing its importance. "Many men meet his description. Dark hair. Dark eyes. Taller than average. His true name means nothing. Names can be falsified."

Temper erupted. "Then you will arrest every suspicious man you see!" The fool. "Are you incompetent? Should I assign another man in your place?"

General Fitrn's narrow shoulders stiffened. "It is done." With clipped, precise strokes, he folded the misused parchment and aligned it next to his water cup.

"While you are at it," the Presidente said mildly, "seize every foreigner in Dakarra, including your brother, of course. It is time to wipe the continent clean of the filthy Koblanis." Hatred spurted through him, as raw as a meat cleaver. Pain seized his heart, but he struggled to ignore it. Soon all of the Koblanis would pay with their lives. He needed only to be patient, because soon all of his plans would come to fruition.

He cleared his throat and took deep, even breaths. He hoped the pain would diminish, and not worsen, as it often did these days. He spread a map of the Koblan continent on the table. "Take no notes," he instructed. "And speak no words. We must assume ears live in the walls."

Ostl and the General leaned forward to look at the map, which was positioned to the Presidente's best advantage. He wondered if the fools could make sense of it upside down, and smiled to himself. "Here," he pointed, "is where we will make our attack."

"But..."

"Silence," he thundered. His thick finger moved down the page. "General, your troops will march this way, along the coast. When you reach this landmark, you will head into the mountains. And here," he jammed his thumb onto the map, "is the prize."

The General said nothing for a long moment. Then, through pinched lips, he said, "All of our ships will attack from this one direction?"

"Yes. They will secure the supply line to the coast. We will gain the prize before anyone on the continent knows what has happened."

Ostl's gaze flicked from the Zindedi leader to the General, but he remained silent, revealing none of his thoughts.

Long moments slid by.

Finally, the General's dull, light brown eyes met the Presidente's. Contempt lived there. But also a tight, resentful obedience. "As you wish." But a blink revealed his lust for power, and a cold, determined desire to gain it, no matter the cost.

For the first time, apprehension unfurled in the Presidente's heart. When Fitrn returned from the war, he would try to kill him. Pride followed on the heels of his fear. Here was a son of whom he could be proud. He would rule Zindedi and Koblan with a hand of ore, just as he, himself, had done for years.

A small smile crossed his lips. "You, my son, are destined for great power. And I will make certain you achieve it."

His son's thin lips curved, but soulless ice stared back. "I am awaiting that day." He rose. "Are we finished? I must head for Dakarra."

Temper bubbled in him at the impertinence. Already the pup was trying to usurp his power. He barked, "Succeed in your mission, or do not bother to return."

An irritated muscle clenched in the General's cheek. He turned on his heel and exited through the double wooden doors.

Well pleased, the Zindedi leader turned to the Commander. "You, Ostl, will send a runner to each ship's captain, telling him our destination. It may not be written down. The Commanders cannot tell another soul. Do you understand?"

"Yes. Yes, of course," he stammered.

"Choose a trustworthy man. Lives depend upon secrecy."

"I understand, sir. Your instructions will be carried out to the letter."

"Good. Has your wife received her new invitation yet?"

Ostl blinked. "I did not... How did you know she misplaced it?"

The Presidente smiled to himself and lit a smokestick. After a deep, pleasurable inhale, he said, "An informant told me." He eyed Ostl over the red, flaring tip. "One who is intimately acquainted with the needs of your wife."

Red suffused Ostl's face. His meaty hands fisted, and then relaxed, and then fisted again. The Presidente watched, enjoying the sport of seeing Ostl squirm with uncertainty, not knowing if he had been insulted, or if his relationship with his wife had been maligned. Afraid to call the Presidente out on his true meaning.

The Presidente puffed rings toward the ceiling, enjoying the other man's torment. It was gratifying to watch the visible thoughts flickering across Ostl's face. Confusion gave way to anger, and then to blind vengefulness.

"Yes." The Presidente chuckled. After another deep inhale, he stubbed out the expensive smokestick. "I see you know what to do." He gathered up his valise. "Order my coach to the door."

Ostl strode out, his strides long and angry.

The Presidente chuckled again to himself, and joined his host on the front porch. "Tell Drumela I look forward to seeing her at the ball. She is a ravishing woman. All must enjoy her beauty."

"Yes, sir." The words gurgled in Ostl's throat.

The Presidente's black cart arrived. A man alighted to help him up the steps. Before entering the dark interior, the Presidente pointed at Ostl. "Remember. Secrecy at all costs."

Ostl nodded, and with a sigh, the Presidente settled back into the plush cushions of his coach. It was so easy to torment a simple man. His mind turned to more complex enemies, and the tortures he wanted to inflict upon them.

His blood thrummed faster. Soon all would fall into place. It was hard, however, to be patient.

Sharp pain squeezed in his heart, and then vanished.

Soon the Koblanis would fall into his trap. If he had procured any insight into the prideful Dehrien at all, the bait would be irresistible.

Glee unfolded, and pain exploded in his chest.

He panted slowly, closing his mind to his pleasurable visions. He would see Mentàll and Methusal dead before he passed through hell's gates.

△ △ △ △ △

Hendra could barely think because of the pain throbbing in her nose. But Doc's abrupt scream jolted her from that fog.

He sagged forward onto his knees. In one unconscious movement, Hendra grabbed a metal spoon from a nearby pot and lunged at the soldier.

"Stop!" The soldier jammed the gun into Doc's head. But already the spear-like handle of the spoon drove straight for his jugular. Doc's good arm elbowed into the Zindedi.

The gun exploded, and Doc and the soldier collapsed in a heap.

Doc! Hendra fell to her knees beside him.

He groaned, and his eyes slitted open. "Doc," she whispered with relief.

A glance proved the soldier was dead. Violent scuffles struggled behind her.

Tabor had entered the fray. The soldiers at the door lay in a crumpled heap, and Riln fought the remaining, stocky Commander—she recognized him as the commander of the Dakarran base. Knives flashed in the dim light. They circled each other in a slow, deadly dance.

Riln lunged, and then the Commander lunged. Each drew blood.

Hendra turned back to see if Doc needed help moving away from the fight.

A metal clang sounded, and a body thumped to the floor. Hendra cast a quick glance over her shoulder. The base Commander had fallen. Deccia stood over him with a metal pot.

"Good work," Tabor said. "Help me tie him up."

While Deccia assisted Tabor, Hendra helped Doc to his feet. His face was white, and his right arm hung limply at his side. She whispered, "He dislocated it, didn't he?"

He nodded, his lips white. "Tabor." It came out in a whisper. Louder, he said, "Tabor."

Tabor looked up from lashing together the Commander's wrists.

Doc said, "When you've got a minute."

Hendra looked at the bodies on the floor and felt a numb, sick sort of shock. She wasn't sure how many were dead.

Deccia helped Tabor tie up one of the men at the door, her face expressionless.

The two tied up men must still be alive. That meant three were dead, including Radl, Olita's husband.

"I can't believe this," she whispered.

Riln heard her. His face was ruddy—likely invigorated by the violent combat. "Get used to it, apte girl. It's war." He'd finally killed a Zin, which he'd been itching to do for weeks. Exultant satisfaction glowed in his eyes.

Hendra wanted to be sick.

Sitting back on her heels, Deccia said, "What should we do with them?"

"Kill 'em," came Riln's prompt reply.

"Too messy," Tabor said. "We can't leave clues that they've been here, or else the whole Zindedi military will come after us."

Riln rolled his eyes. "What do you suggest, then?"

"Buy time. Cover our tracks. We'll drag them into the woods and bury the bodies. We'll tie the others to trees."

"To trees?" Riln snorted. "They'll get free in five minutes."

"They'll stay unconscious."

"How?"

Hendra turned to Doc. "Do you have more pain powder? It put me out for over twelve hours."

"We need them to be unconscious for two days."

Through white lips, Doc said, "We can give a double dose. Any more might kill them."

Tabor nodded. "Give me instructions. Where's the powder?"

Under Doc's directions, Deccia and Tabor dosed the unconscious men by letting the liquid run down their throats. Tabor stood. "Riln, help me." He hoisted an unconscious soldier over his shoulder and headed for the forest. With a muttered curse, Riln followed with the base Commander.

Tabor had forgotten that Doc needed help with his arm. "Let me help you," Hendra told him. "Tell me what to do."

He gave his head a tiny shake, as if even that movement pained him. He'd refused any pain powder a little earlier, because he said he wanted to keep his mind clear. "Riln's stronger. It'll go quick and easy. I'll be fine."

He didn't look fine, but she didn't argue with him. She urged him to sit down on the couch. To Deccia, she said, "Let's clean up the blood." First, though, she washed the blood from her own face as best she could. Afterward, Doc insisted on feeling her nose with his good hand. "It doesn't feel broken. You should be okay, Hendra."

It throbbed like a stubbed toe. But she knew it couldn't compare to the pain Doc was enduring right now.

She'd avoided the distasteful clean up task long enough. Already Deccia was scrubbing up the blood of the soldier Hendra had inadvertently killed, but she'd first turned him over and stuffed a cloth into the wound to stop more blood from flowing out. Horrible guilt pressed into Hendra. That man was dead because of her actions.

She turned to Radl, who lay unnaturally sprawled on the floor. Blood oozed from the wound in his chest. She had to roll him over in order to clean up the blood. He still felt warm, and his muscles flaccid as she pushed him. Nausea rose in her throat.

With a gulp, she ran for the door and vomited into the bushes. This was a nightmare. Men lying were dead in their cabin. And yet outdoors, for the first time in days, the sky had cleared to a sunny, deep blue.

Taking a deep, cleansing breath of cool air, she returned inside and scrubbed the floor until the rag was in shreds. And then she buried it. Afterward, she retreated outside to watch for more soldiers.

△ △ △ △ △

"He's insane," Methusal said, opening her eyes. She felt surprisingly relaxed after the long kaavl session of listening in on the Presidente's meeting with Commander Ostl.

"What are his plans?"

"Hunt down General Greisn's killer."

Mentàll's brows flew together. "They know Timaeus killed him?"

"No names were mentioned. But the description matched Timaeus."

"How do they know?"

"The General's brother is in Dakarra. Somehow he found out the truth. Today Fitrn will travel to Dakarra and seize all of the strangers in town."

But it seemed strange that anyone in Zindedi could have discovered that Timaeus had killed General Greisn. No one knew, except...

A horrible thought occurred to her. "What if Fitrn's brother is on the Dakarran kaavl team? If he is, that means he's been a spy on Koblan for years."

The Dehrien Chief paced across the room to look out the window. "It is possible. I was to meet Timaeus tonight. I will find him early and warn him." He looked at Methusal. "Anything else?"

"He's sending all of their ships to one location on Koblan. They intend to take some prize by force. He didn't say much, except that 'ears live in the walls.' I'm sure he pointed to locations a map. He didn't say anything else." But the other, unspoken things... Methusal felt disgusted.

Mentàll frowned, lost in thoughts of his own.

"He's sick," she said, pushing herself up from the couch.

"How so?"

"He taunts his son. He praises him, and cuts him down at the same time. He tormented Ostl for the fun of it." She headed for the front door. "He wanted to upset him. He knew what Fitrn had done..." She cut short the sentence.

"What did he do?" Mentàll was right behind her.

She jumped. With a quick turn, she stepped away from him. "I'd rather not say."

Those light blue eyes watched her intently. "Tell me. What did Fitrn do to Ostl?"

"It wasn't to Ostl. It was to his wife." Methusal shut her mouth. "We should go. You need to warn Timaeus."

They headed for the street, and then cut north, taking the long route back to Mrn. M's house. Methusal thought the subject had been dropped until Mentàll said, "How do you know about the General and Drumela? Is it another of the things you overheard yesterday?"

She didn't look at him. "Yes. I overheard it." It was the truth. And she'd heard a lot more, too. She tried to block out the memories.

Silence ensued. She chanced a glance up at him, but could not read his expression. It made her feel uncomfortable.

"Where did you hear this conversation, Methusal?" His voice was even.

She bit her lip. Here was the confrontation she'd been trying to avoid. But she would not lie to him. "At Ostl's house yesterday. General Fitrn was there. And Drumela."

A moment elapsed while he digested this. Methusal did not look at him, because she didn't want to see his displeasure.

He said, "He defiled her. In Ostl's house."

"She was a willing..." Methusal stopped. She would not go into details with Mentàll.

"So, you returned the invitation." His voice was deceptively calm. "Tell me what happened."

After taking a fortifying breath, she outlined yesterday's illicit mission.

His stride lengthened, but he said nothing.

"The invitation needed to be returned. I did what had to be done," she said, in the face of his silence. "Don't ask me to stay home and lick my wounds, because I won't. I can't."

When he still did not reply, she turned in front of him, forcing him to stop. A faint flush tinged his cheekbones, and cold ice stared down at her.

She said, "Say something."

"I cannot trust you."

That hurt to the quick. "Of course you can. I completed a necessary mission. You know that's true. If Tabor was here, you would have ordered him to return the invitation yesterday. Why didn't you give that assignment to me? I'm not a child, Mentàll. I'm a soldier. Treat me like one."

Before he could speak, she rushed on, "Do you want to know the truth? I feel like you don't trust *me*. Why else would you tell me to stay at Mrn. M's all day? We needed to return the invitation. So I did. And I found valuable information, too. How else would we know to warn Timaeus? How else would we know their plans?"

"I am glad you learned about the meeting. But your safety is my primary concern. You disobeyed orders. You deliberately put yourself in danger."

"I disagree."

"You were in the same room as the General. What if he had seen you?" His cheekbones darkened to maroon, and his breaths deepened and harshened.

"He didn't."

"He would have dragged you back to that cellar." His voice rose. "He would have defiled you, and killed you, and I would not have been able to stop him!"

Again, fire glowed, deep in the belly of the wild beast. "Give me important assignments, Mentàll. Then you'll know where I am every minute of the day."

"You are insubordinate."

"Yes." Recklessly, she snapped, "Maybe you should have left me at the ship."

"*Methusal.*" He shoved a hard hand through his hair.

She drew a trembling breath. "I don't like making you angry. I don't want you to be frustrated or disappointed in me. But the truth is, I have a mind of my own. Isn't that the reason why you asked me to come with you?"

"Do not disappear again without telling me where you are going."

"If something comes up, I'll leave you a note."

"*No.* You will tell me, face to face. You will not sneak off behind my back again."

"I wasn't sneaking…"

"You have been lying and sneaking. *I cannot trust you!* I need a soldier I can trust, Maahr."

"Then be reasonable! Let me do my job. You can't protect me from everything." And that was the crux of the matter, she realized. He didn't want to let her out of his sight because he wanted to protect her.

"I am the Kaavl Commander. I decide what is best for you."

"If you won't give me important assignments, I'll make up my own."

A short silence elapsed. "Then you will go back to the ship."

"No."

"If I cannot trust you, Maahr, you will not stay here." The hard edge to his voice said he meant it. He had had enough.

"You need me."

"I can succeed without you."

"No."

His implacable stare said he could.

She drew a deep breath. "I won't go."

"You will go, if I have to carry you over my shoulder. If necessary, I'll tell Captain Hilrae to lock you in your cabin."

"You don't mean it."

"Don't I?" he said silkily.

Angry frustration churned in her. "Fine. What's the difference between being locked up on the ship or in Mrn. M's house? I'm useless to the mission either way."

He resumed walking. "Then we are agreed. After I warn Timaeus, I will escort you to the ship."

"*No!*"

"It is settled." His long strides ate up the ground

She jogged to catch up with him. "No, it is not settled."

He stopped abruptly. "Do you want to plead your case?"

To beg him, in other words. She crossed her arms and glared. "Give me an assignment, and I'll follow it."

"You will follow my directions to the letter." He watched her, his gaze hard.

"Yes. All right." She expelled a breath.

"You will attempt no mission without first discussing it with me."

"Yes. Fine!"

"Pledge by all that is holy."

That cut to her heart. He did not ask her to pledge on her honor. "I pledge by all that is holy."

"Good." He started walking again.

"I just wanted to help the mission," she said in a quieter voice.

"I understand. But your safety is my responsibility. I will not go home and tell your father that you are dead because I could not control you." His voice still sounded very harsh.

"I'm sorry." She did appreciate that he wanted to protect her. But she also wanted to be given important assignments. "What is my assignment today, while you're gone?"

"Doc and Behran need to be hired on to work at the ball. Find them jobs, if you can. If not, we will need to detain two workers so they can take their places."

An important job, but the task probably would not be dangerous. "Thank you."

"Be safe. Take no unnecessary risks."

"I could say the same to you."

They'd reached Mrn. M's house. Soon he'd leave to intercept Timaeus. "Will you be gone overnight?" Last night's worry returned. This time she would be prepared.

"No. I will return this evening."

When they entered the house, Mrn. M rushed from the kitchen, her cheeks pink and eyes sparkling.

"They came!" she exclaimed, clutching an envelope to her bosom. "The Presidente sent them this morning!"

"Your invitation to the ball?" Methusal grinned.

"And not just mine!" Trembling fingers plucked three crisply folded parchments from the envelope. "He sent along two extras. One for a special man in my life," she giggled like a schoolgirl, "and one for my daughter. He even apologized for sending it late. He said my Charlie's heroic deeds will be honored at the ball, and...and...it's just *overwhelming!*" Fanning herself, she collapsed into a chair.

"I'm so happy for you." Methusal sat on the nearby couch, ready to listen to more of Mrn. M's rhapsodies. Mentàll disappeared into their bedroom, and then reemerged moments later, pack on his back. "Will your daughter come, do you think?"

Mrn. M's joyful spirits visibly deflated. "No. Of course not. He included that invitation to please his son. Ceri would never go to that ball."

Ceri. The name tickled in Methusal's memory.

"I must go," Mentàll said, and dropped a kiss on Methusal's head. "I will be back tonight. Perhaps late."

"'Bye." Methusal looked up at him. His warm palm unexpectedly stroked her hair, and something inside of her relaxed. All was forgiven. She read that in his eyes.

"Sweet dreams, Methusal. Do not walk outside alone tonight." His eyes gleamed.

She blinked, because a horrifying thought suddenly occurred to her. Had she *slept-walked* last night? Had he carried her inside, and...and had she *kissed* him? A hot blush suffused her cheeks.

A small smile tugged at his lips, and he headed for the door.

If that was true, then he'd slept on the couch because...why? Because she'd basically thrown herself at him last night? Methusal gulped back a gasp of horror. It couldn't be! Surely, it had all been a dream.

"Lozar," Mrn. M said. "Before you go. It seems a shame to let these extra invitations go to waste. Would you two like to come with me to the ball?"

Surprised, Methusal stared at their landlady, and then at Mentàll. It was too much to process. After all of the time and effort they'd spent trying to procure invitations, now Mrn. M wanted to *give* them two?

His eyes had narrowed, but he said smoothly, "Thank you, Mrn. M. We would be pleased to accept."

Her face lit up. "Good. I'll send your names to the palace for approval."

Approval? Brows raised, Methusal glanced at Mentàll. His slight head jerk told her to follow him outside.

As she rose, she remembered to smile at Mrn. M. "Thank you so much! I would love to talk about dresses, if you don't mind. But first I'll see Lozar out."

She joined him on the porch. "You think it's a trap."

"Yes."

"But how would the Presidente know Mrn. M would invite us?"

"He knew."

"How?" And then realization dawned. "Mrn. M would never betray us like that."

"We cannot trust her."

"Mentàll!"

"We can trust no one. Her innocence or guilt is irrelevant. It is clear the Presidente wants us at that ball."

"Why?"

His smile looked chilling. "To kill us, of course."

"Then maybe we shouldn't go."

"We will go." His teeth looked like the fangs of a wild beast. "The Presidente is the one who will suffer complete defeat. He is the one who will beg us for mercy."

"I hope you're right." As he headed down the steps, she added, "Be careful. The General is heading for Dakarra, too."

When he grinned at her, her heart unexpectedly fluttered. "It almost sounds like you care."

"I don't want you to die. Who would take me to the ball, then?"

His chuckle sounded rusty. And then he was gone.

Her mind turned to her own assignment, and she wondered how to go about finding jobs for Behran and Doc.

And then she thought of two people who might be able to help. As she went inside, another name finally clicked into place in her memory. Ceri. Deccia had a friend in Dakarra named Ceri.

△ △ △ △ △

By the time Riln and Tabor returned for two of the dead bodies, Hendra felt nervous to still be at the cabin. It was already late afternoon. The longer they stayed, the more likely it was the military would arrive, looking for their missing comrades.

A scream erupted from the cabin. Doc! Heart pounding, she ran inside.

He lay on the sofa, sweat beaded on his white brow. Tabor stood over him, frowning. "Did that do it?"

"I think so," he gasped. With a grimace, he lifted his arm from the couch. "Good thing I'm left-handed."

Deccia wrapped a sling around his arm and helped him sit up.

"We found a gorge," Tabor said. "We'll hide the bodies there. Then we'll come back for you and the last soldier."

"Hurry," Deccia urged. "I have a bad feeling. At least bring that last soldier into the woods now. If someone comes, they'll know what happened."

Tabor obliged, and then he and Riln each hoisted a dead man over his shoulders. "We'll be back in forty minutes," he promised, and headed for the woods.

Hendra hovered near Doc. "Are you all right?"

He smiled, and she was glad to see that the white lines of pain had eased from his mouth. "I'm fine, thank you."

Deccia said, "I think we should move everything out into the woods now. I don't want to stay here any longer."

Hendra agreed. She felt more like a sunning, silly apte each extra minute they stayed in the cabin.

As they quickly moved the blankets, packs, and assorted odds and ends a good distance into the protective forest, Hendra kept a sharp eye on the road. So far, no one was in sight.

Finally, the cabin was empty. And the floor had dried, leaving only the faintest stains where the blood had pooled.

"Goodbye, cabins." A grim smile edged Deccia's lips. "And goodbye, Vitnia. I guess you won't get your money, after all."

Hendra wondered about the cold look in her eyes. "Are you all right?" she asked her friend.

"I'll be fine once we leave for home." Deccia headed for the woods, not waiting to see if Hendra followed.

Hendra decided to go check the road one last time.

Taking no chances, she slipped into the future before peering over the crest of the hill. Two dark heads popped up, and then a skinny body and an overweight, limping woman came into view. Both held their skirts bunched up, clear of the grasses.

Hendra gasped, dropped to her knees, and crawled quickly backward. Then she darted for the cabin. There wasn't time to escape into the forest without being seen. A hand touched her shoulder, and she almost cried out.

"Shh." Doc pulled her between the two cabins. He took in her expression. "Who is it?"

"Vitnia and Olita."

"They'll need to think we're gone. And that we left a long time ago."

"I know. Where can we hide?"

Doc took her hand and circled to the back of the main cabin. He pulled her down to sit beside him, with their backs against the cabin wall's rough wood. Tall grasses waved above their heads. "They probably won't come back here," he whispered.

She hoped not.

Thumping footsteps climbed the stairs to Deccia and Timaeus' cabin. Mutters reached Hendra's ears, and then the footsteps entered the bigger cabin.

"They're gone!" Vitnia snapped. "They cleaned me out! I knew I couldn't trust that girl."

"I wonder where Radl is."

"Probably went to the base. Or maybe he's hunting them down." A vicious chuckle punctuated that thought.

Olita giggled.

"They took my best pot!" Crockery smashed on the floor. "I'd love to get my fingers around that girl's neck, and squeeze..."

"I'll tell my man to give special attention to their husbands when he finds them."

Vitnia cackled. More footsteps click clacked. "And they took all the blankets!" Curses spewed.

"We might as well go. It'll be dark soon."

"I want to see if they left anything behind. Maybe a clue so we can follow them. I'm checking outside."

"It's a waste of time."

"I don't care. I'm scouring this hill until I find one clue. *What I'd do to kill them!*" The kitchen door slammed.

Now Vitnia was around the corner, and only two short lengths away.

Hendra pressed closer to Doc, trying to breathe evenly.

His comforting hand gently squeezed hers. "See the future, Hendra. Tell me when we need to run."

△ △ △ △ △

Methusal guessed the ball would need waiters, dishwashers, and all sorts of serving personnel. But who made those hiring decisions?

Mrn. M seemed the logical person to ask first. That lady had pulled out her ball gown from last year by the time Methusal reentered the house. After exclaiming over the beautiful gown, and talking to about dresses and hairstyles for a while, Methusal casually said, "How many people normally come to a ball?"

Mrn. M put away her ornate, purple and blue dress with puffed sleeves and a long, full skirt. "Two hundred, easily."

"Wow. Think of all the food they'll need to prepare."

"They've already begun. Of course, most will be made fresh the morning of the ball."

"The Presidente must have a huge dining room."

"Yes." Mrn. M headed for the kitchen. "Tea?"

"No, but thank you. I think I'll go and look for a dress in the shops soon."

Mrn. M set the kettle on the stove, and then turned to Methusal with a smile. "To answer your question, the Presidente uses his ballroom as the dining room, also." She sighed. "Oh, the cakes and confections piled high on gold trays! And the delicious foods on the buffet table. Three kinds of meats, and breads and fruits..." She clasped hands to her bosom and sighed. "And the dancing, before and after. It's such a treat."

"Think of all the people it must take to make it run smoothly."

"Oh, yes. The Presidente spares no expense. He hires at least a hundred people to take care of the guests."

"My goodness!" Methusal said nothing more, hoping Mrn. M would divulge more information.

"The kitchens train their own staff, of course, but the servers and trash keepers and valets come from the community."

"It must be a coveted position, to work at the Presidente's ball."

"Oh, likely. I wouldn't know about that side of it."

Methusal talked to Mrn. M for a little while longer, and then headed for the docks. While Mrn. M may not know much about the serving side of the ball, someone else she knew might.

△ △ △ △ △

"We can't run," Hendra whispered. "They'll see us."

"Then we'll have to lie down."

Bewildered, Hendra looked at him. "You mean in the grass?"

"It's our best bet." He went down on his left elbow, his back to the cabin wall, and then slid on his side into the tall grasses growing close to the house. He was almost totally concealed. "Come here, Hendra."

Anxiety tightened in her chest at the thought. But the grass where they'd been sitting was flattened. If she could slide between the stalks, up next to Doc, hopefully Vitnia wouldn't spot them through the thick, wild weeds. And being close to the wall was best, so Vitnia wouldn't accidentally step on them.

It was a good plan. Still. With trepidation, she went down on one elbow and crept up beside him. He was very close, and he smelled nice, of clothes baked dry in the sun. His bound up, injured arm touched her lower ribs, and the heat of his muscled thighs touched hers.

They fit together. Hendra closed her eyes as unreasoning panic fought the pleasure of being so close to him.

"Hendra." His breath touched her lips.

"What?" His smoky blue eyes were so near that she noticed the little silver flecks in them. Fear made each breath a laborious effort.

"I won't hurt you. I would *never* hurt you."

"I know." She drew in a ragged breath. "I know you won't." Hendra tried to relax. She tried to think about something else. But Doc's beloved features were all she could see. His straight nose, straight brows with the slight hook on the ends...and his lips, outlined by his closely trimmed red beard. She drew a quick breath, remembering how she'd kissed him when her mind was loopy with drugs. It had felt nice. Very nice.

Desire for another kiss warred with an irrational fear that urged her to escape from the closeness between them.

Doc glanced upward. "She's coming."

Hendra looked through the grasses to the pale, gray-tinged sky. Dusk was coming fast.

Vitnia's shoes crunched over the pebbled earth near the well, and then shuffled for the back corner of the house, where they lay hidden. Hendra focused on the tall, waving grasses, and into the future.

Heavy footsteps lumbered onto the kitchen porch. "It's getting dark, Vitnia. I need to start dinner for my man."

Her man, who would never come home again.

"Give me a minute," Vitnia snapped. Quick footsteps rounded the corner. Hendra didn't breathe. She saw Vitnia clearly. Slowly, the future warped into the present.

An endless moment passed. Had Vitnia seen them?

"Vitnia," Olita whined.

"All right. All right!" Vitnia retreated. "But I have a feeling they're not far off."

Their footsteps receded. Hendra and Doc lay very still, not daring to move; not sure if it was a trap, designed to lure them out into the open.

Long, slow minutes dragged by.

Hendra whispered, "Do you think it's safe?"

"Not yet." His chest rose and fell against hers. The movement felt sure and steady.

On the other hand, quick, shallow breaths pumped air through her lungs. At least Doc's arm was bound to his chest. Knowing he couldn't reach for her helped to calm the irrational flutters of panic that kept clawing at her.

She hated the fear. It made her want to scream with frustration. Because a part of her wanted to be close to him, more than anything else in the world.

"How is your nose?"

Hendra's gaze went to his. Her heart thumped harder and her mouth felt dry. "It aches. But it's not too bad."

"Good." His eyes were more a smoke than blue color right now. She saw the wanting in them. He wanted to kiss her.

"Doc." She drew a panicked breath.

"Hendra," he said softly.

For a long moment he didn't move, but his gaze remained locked with hers. When her breaths quieted, he slowly closed the distance until his lips touched hers.

Hendra didn't move. The magic of his mouth felt heavenly. But when her eyes fluttered closed, an edge of panic fought the pleasure.

She wanted to retreat into that safe cocoon deep inside her. Panic told her that she couldn't let him in, because then she'd be exposed to him. Vulnerable. She couldn't have that.

When his warm mouth left hers, her eyes fluttered open again. Her heart felt like a fist, driving in painful, agonizing beats.

His breaths were uneven. He wanted more. She saw that clearly. But tenderness and patience tempered the smoky fire.

Softly, he said, "I'm sorry. I didn't mean to frighten you."

Hendra shook her head. "I liked it," she whispered. "But it scared me, too."

Loud rustles in the grass made her gasp. She rolled away from Doc, her body tense, ready to fight.

Riln stared down at them. "Done fooling around?"

△ △ △ △ △

Methusal eyed the Merry Spirits across the street. It looked quiet; maybe because the ships were humming with activity. Scores of men scurried on the docks, carrying boxes and barrels. They were finishing preparations for their attack on Koblan. Twenty ships at the docks, and five at anchor, all bristled with men and arms. How could she and Mentàll ever stop them all?

Her gaze returned to the Merry Spirits. Dared she go in the front door?

Why not? General Fitrn was gone. And if the Presidente had wanted to capture her before the ball, he'd had plenty of opportunities at Mrn. M's house.

She crossed the street and opened the door to the dark, smoky interior of the Merry Spirits. Taking a deep breath, and squaring her shoulders, she went inside. Loud shouts and coarse jokes greeted her arrival.

"Midi!" shouted the corpulent officer at the bar. "I've missed your sweet form. C'mere and give me a drink."

Tineia swatted his backside with a wash towel as she passed by. "Keep your pants on."

The officer made a rank suggestion, and gulped spirits while Tineia smiled at Methusal. "What brings you here? Do you want your man to chase you to the docks again?"

Methusal blushed. "No. Things are going well. I came down because I have a problem I'm trying to solve. I hoped you might be able to help me."

"Of course." Tineia folded her arms, and her smile indicated pleasure at the thought.

"I have a brother and friend coming to town and they need work. They want to work at the ball, because they heard it pays well. I'm not sure how to get them a job, though, or if it's even possible." The lies came a little too easily.

Tineia's gaze narrowed a bit. "You thought I would know?"

"It seems like you know everything that goes on in this city."

Tineia smiled again. "Yes. Pretty much."

"Do you think they have any hope of getting a job like that? What steps should they take?"

"When will they get here?"

"Tomorrow."

Tineia nodded. "I have a friend who might help. Do you need to be home early tonight?"

"My husband will be out late."

"Good. My shift is over at eight. Can you come back then?"

"Of course. Thank you, Tineia."

"Just a word of warning. When we visit my friend, don't let him know you're a Commander's wife. He has a problem with the military."

∆ ∆ ∆ ∆ ∆

Doc quickly led Hendra deep into the forest while Riln remained behind to wait for Goric and Sozla, because neither of them knew the way to camp. Hendra carried her pack and an armload of blankets.

Dusk rode swiftly into the forest, blanketing the earth in deep shadows. It smelled tangy and fragrant, and grew colder by the moment. She didn't look forward to sleeping out in the open.

It took a half an hour to reach the campsite, which consisted of a fire with two logs pulled up alongside it.

Deccia was stirring something in a pot hanging over the fire, and Behran sat cross-legged in the dirt, assembling the timers and detonators.

He looked up when they arrived. "Goric and Sozla aren't back yet?"

"Riln's waiting for them."

Hendra helped cut up vegetables to toast over the fire. Behran finished the bombs and placed them in his backpack. Later, when complete darkness closed around them, voices rang in the forest. Sozla's laugh identified them before they broke into the small clearing.

"Yes, Goric. You know it is good I went with you. Otherwise, we'd still be going in circles."

The flickering fire revealed Goric's scowl.

Riln snorted in derision. "Useless."

"Did you find the powder mine?" Doc asked.

"Yes," Sozla said. "It was difficult. A few small roads are not marked on the map."

"Good work."

Goric retreated to the far end of a log, where he sat alone.

"Dinner's ready," Deccia announced. "Stewed meat with bread. Hendra has cut up vegetables to roast over the fire."

The hot meat tasted good, and better yet, the bowl warmed her cold hands. Doc had already placed his steaming bowl onto the ground beside her, and now returned with a roasting stick full of skewered vegetables. Using his good arm, he held the stick over the crackling fire. "I'll share with you," he offered with a smile.

"Thank you."

Others settled down with their steaming bowls, too. The fire's white smoke wafted in a cloud over Goric, where he still sat alone, wolfing down meat from his bowl. Deccia took a seat nearby, and made an effort to talk to him.

Behran was the last to serve meat into his bowl. A spot still remained at the end of Hendra and Doc's log, next to Sozla. He seemed to hesitate, but took it.

"How was the mission?" he asked, just as Sozla took a big bite.

She looked up, surprised, and then her eyes sparkled. She chewed rapidly. "Good."

Hendra listened to Behran and Sozla while she watched Doc slowly turn the vegetables over the fire. They were already a delicate, golden brown, and her mouth watered.

"Done." He offered her the skewered end. "You first."

"Thank you." With a small smile, Hendra used her spoon to slide half of the vegetables into her bowl. Then she pushed the rest into Doc's bowl. "It must be hard to eat with one hand."

"I'll manage." He held the bowl steady with his knees and ate neatly with his left hand. A comfortable silence ensued. Sozla laughed at something Behran had said. Across the fire, Deccia, Goric, Riln, and Tabor sat silently. Deccia stared into the flames, as if lost in her own thoughts.

At last, the Tarst doctor pushed his bowl to the side. "Are you ready for tomorrow night?"

"I hope so." Thinking about infiltrating the base—of being in *charge*—twisted her stomach into knots. Why had Mentàll chosen her, instead of Tabor? "I hope there will still be powder left on the base to blow up."

"You'll do a great job. But be careful."

Doc would leave for Carachki tomorrow. She didn't want him to go. She shivered, because it felt as if an icy wind just blew over her soul. "You, too."

Doc fished a blanket from the ground behind them and, with amazing one-handed dexterity, draped it around both of them. He hesitated. "Can I put my arm around you?" He wanted to. That much was plain.

She smiled softly. "Yes. That would be nice."

His arm secured the blanket around her shoulders, and his body heat warmed her as they sat close together, hip to hip.

"Better?"

Hendra nodded, not trusting herself to speak. She felt quiet joy, being so close to him.

Her feelings for him continued to grow. She couldn't stop them. And yet what did that mean for their relationship? She could handle sitting close beside him like this. But he held her as a friend. No pressure. No expectations. On the other hand, when he'd kissed her at the cabin she'd been ready to jump out of her skin.

Had anything truly changed, then? Even though she cared about him more and more every day, maybe this friendship was all she could handle. Doc definitely deserved more. Riln was right. She should let him go. She couldn't give him false hope. She shouldn't. But for now she would sit close beside him and pretend everything was all right. That they could possibly have more.

After the mission was over—that would be soon enough to face the harsh truth.

△ △ △ △ △

Methusal got a bite to eat, and then wandered the lamp-lit Carachki streets, looking at dresses in windows, and mingling with other shoppers as dusk deepened into night. Mentàll had warned her not to go out alone tonight—not that she was truly alone, with all of these people around. And it was safe in the heart of the city at this hour.

Again, last night's dream slipped through her mind. She wished she would stop thinking about it. It had been a dream. Nothing more. And as for curfew—she'd better keep focused into kaavl and watch for soldiers, just to stay on the safe side.

She hoped Tineia's mysterious friend would be able to find work for Behran and Doc.

Behran. She'd see him tomorrow, at last. She'd missed him, but in some ways it seemed strange that he would actually arrive in Carachki tomorrow—that he would enter the world that she and Mentàll had created for themselves here.

But the mission would end soon. *Everything* would end soon. And then they would head home. An odd, empty space opened up inside her at the thought.

Just before eight o'clock, she left the comfortably crowded streets of downtown Carachki and headed for the spirit house. The further south she went, the darker the streets became. Street lamps were sparse, and she intensified into kaavl, avoiding the faint breaths of a man in an alley, and the footsteps of two patrolling military men. Although she'd learned the military didn't enforce curfew in the heart of the city at night, the outer areas appeared to be fair game. She spotted and avoided several pairs of soldiers before reaching the Merry Spirits.

Tineia waited for her behind the spirit house, her arms crossed, and shivering in her mid-length, fur trimmed coat. "Come on," she said, and headed quickly for the southwestern part of town. No streetlamps brightened this area. Only Ryon lit the landscape—that, and the feeble light spilling through curtains in the squat houses. Bracken, broken pots, and hand carts littered the front yards of most houses. The aromatic scent of stew wafted from one building, and a baby squalled in another.

Despite the dark and the lateness of the hour, Tineia did not seem afraid. Instead, she strode through the neighborhoods as if they were her own.

Methusal kept her ears alert for soldiers. "Do you live around here?"

"A bit further north. But my family lives a few blocks away from my cousin."

"We'll visit your cousin?"

"Yes. As I said, don't mention you're with the military."

"I won't." Methusal couldn't help but ask, "Do you have a big family?"

"Seven brothers and sisters." Tineia grinned. "How about you? Besides your brother, of course."

"A twin sister."

"A twin! I always wished I had a twin. Did you trick people? Or aren't you identical?"

"We're identical." Methusal offered this last bit reluctantly. The truth couldn't hurt, could it? Who would Tineia tell? Besides, the Presidente and General already knew she was in Carachki.

"Here we are." Tineia stopped before a small house that looked much like the others. Dim orange light filtered through the window. "His name is Esim." She rapped on the door.

No one answered.

She knocked again, louder.

The door wrenched open, revealing a huge man with wild hair and a bushy beard. "Whatd'ya want?" he snarled.

"Play nice, Esim," Tineia said, brushing by him to walk into the house. "I've brought a friend."

Esim glared at Methusal, but moved back the barest fraction, indicating she might—just *might*—be welcome in his home.

The first thing Methusal noticed was the smell. Rotten food, unwashed clothes. Sweat. Dishes cluttered the counter and table, and debris covered the couch and floors.

Tineia frowned at her hulking cousin. "This is a rocher's nest! What happened to your cleaning woman?"

Esim scowled. "She gave up. Whatd'ya want?" The dim light revealed his broad face and squashed nose. Dark, unkempt hair stuck out in every conceivable direction and his tunic strained across his round belly. His bare feet revealed broken, yellowed toenails. Methusal wondered how this man could possibly help Behran and Doc get jobs at the ball. He seemed incapable of caring for himself.

Tineia got right down to business. "Midi's brother and friend need jobs at the ball. I want you to help her."

"Why?" He lumbered with a noticeable limp for the kitchen, where he rummaged through a brown sack and pulled out a bread roll. He popped the whole thing in his mouth and chewed. The bun protruded from his lips while he masticated the food. It made Methusal feel a bit sick to watch.

"Because Midi is my friend. Help me, Esim."

Spittle, mixed with white bread, dribbled down his chin. A thick finger suddenly pointed at Methusal. "You with the military?"

"No." True enough.

"What about your brother. Or friend?" Suspicious, crafty green eyes watched her.

Methusal knew she had to be careful. Every able man was supposed to be in the military. "They were enlisted. But both got injured in the war with Koblan. And my mother needs help with the farm, since my father died. Money is tight. If you want the truth, my brother is glad to be out of the military. They treated him horribly." She stopped embellishing the tale. Too much detail might raise Esim's suspicions.

"Unhuh." He still eyed her with suspicion.

"Are you going to help, or not?" Tineia demanded. "I can't wait for your answer all night."

He fished a writing stick from a clump of curled up, stale bread ends and scribbled something on a scrap of parchment. Tineia took it, and with a nod, gave it to Methusal.

She quickly scanned it.

Give these two jobs as trash keepers at the ball. Esim.

He chuckled, and shoved more bread into his mouth. "No one knows trash like I do. Give that to Pruvin on Bay Street, near the square. He owes me."

"Thank you."

Tineia headed for the door. "Goodbye, Esim. Thank you."

They left the giant man chewing bread alone in his foul kitchen.

Methusal gulped in a breath of fresh air. "Thank you so much, Tineia."

Tineia smiled and headed north, toward downtown, which was where Methusal needed to go, too. "I'm happy to help. And if you want to add more excitement to your life, stop by the Merry Spirits again. I always need help."

"Thank you. I'll remember that." Street lamps began to dot the corners as the neighborhoods improved in appearance. "If you don't mind me asking, why does Pruvin owe Esim?"

"I don't know the whole story. Esim's past is pretty gray. Rumors are he gets rid of unwanted trash—at a price."

"Like..."

"Like dead people."

"Oh!"

"You won't say anything, right?"

"Never."

"Good. I have to go." They were still a few blocks south of downtown Carachki. Tineia smiled, and patted her arm. "Take care."

"You too." With regret, Methusal watched her only Zindedi friend disappear into a dark alley. Chances were, she'd never see her again.

∆ ∆ ∆ ∆ ∆

Head resting on her pack as a pillow, Deccia wrapped a blanket tightly around herself and stared into the dying embers of the fire. The violence and the horror of the day replayed through her mind.

Three Zindedis were dead. Radl, Olita's husband, was dead. A small part of her felt sorry for Olita. The Zindedi woman had loved her husband, and would never see him again. Deccia understood that kind of love. If she lost Timaeus...

The empty, haunted feeling again gripped her.

She turned her mind away from the fear, thinking instead about the remaining threats of the tied up Private and Commander. They were unconscious for now. But what about when they woke up, and what if they managed to free themselves? They knew their friends had been murdered. They would send the army to track down the Koblanis.

The base Commander's features loomed behind her eyelids and she felt a rush of hatred so vicious it choked her. He had reminded her so much of Greisn. She hated Greisn. *Hated him.* She wanted to block out the memories, but the filthy sense of defilement continued to ooze over her soul.

He'd never leave her. Neither would the dreams, in which he continued to stalk her.

Deccia wept. She hated it all. She hated Zindedi. If only she could go home with Timaeus.

Timaeus. An animal cry worked up high into her throat. She pressed the blanket into her mouth.

Something was terribly wrong. Somewhere, Timaeus fought alone.

Curled up into a tight ball, she prayed for him until she lost the battle for consciousness. She slipped into the familiar nightmare world where the General stalked her. But now evil imprisoned Timaeus in her dream, too. Forever, they would be lost to each other. The General would make it so.

△ △ △ △ △

Lamp light pooled on the stones of Feldon Street, pushing the shadows into the manicured yards of the cottages. Methusal walked swiftly, listening intently for danger, but heard nothing suspicious.

At Mrn. M's gate she relaxed, slipped inside the yard, and hurried up the dim porch steps. The lights were on inside. That meant Mrn. M was up. She'd have to explain why she hadn't found a dress yet, although she'd spotted several that she had liked.

As she reached for the doorknob, a movement to her left made her gasp and whirl.

"Methusal." A gravel rasp.

"Mentàll! You scared me to death. You're back so soon?"

"I found Timaeus earlier this afternoon. He gave me the detonators." He rose from the porch bench.

She scanned his features in the dim light. She could not read his expression. "How many detonators?"

"Four."

"Four! That's not enough."

"We will improvise. And hopefully Behran will bring more tomorrow."

There was a note in his voice that she could not decipher. "Why are you out here?"

"I was waiting for you."

"I finished my mission." She gave him the note, and briefly told him about her evening.

Mentàll pocketed it. "You did well. I will give it to Behran and Doc tomorrow." The tension in his tone, however, belied his approving words.

"What's wrong?" After a moment, she said, "I did my mission like you asked."

"I said you did well." His voice sounded tight.

"Then why are you upset?"

"I did not expect to return before you. I did not expect you to stay out so late."

"It's hardly *late*."

"Soldiers are out. It is dangerous."

"For you, too."

He stared at her silently.

"What?" she said.

He drew a harsh breath. "Mrn. M said you had been out all day. She thought you'd lost track of time shopping. I knew better. I looked for you in the shops and restaurants."

Needless to say, he hadn't found her.

He grated, "I came back here, thinking you had returned."

"I was fine. I did my mission like you asked."

"I asked you not to walk alone at night, Maahr."

"Which order should I follow?" she said softly. "Which is more important to you?"

"Your *safety* is most important to me. Didn't I make that clear today?"

"I did what I thought was best. You need to trust me."

"The Presidente wants you dead. And the day Fitrn captured you—I *knew*. I could not eat, I could not rest. I ran all the way back from Oesten. I could not stop until I found you."

"You knew? How?"

He heaved another harsh breath. "You *swore* you'd follow my instructions. I told you not to go out after dark. What was I to think when I came back and you weren't here?"

"I didn't think you'd be home yet."

"So that excuses insubordination?"

"It was hardly insubordination," she said with frustration. "You're being ridiculous! I did my mission. What more do you want?"

He closed the distance between them. "I want you to be safe. I do not want to imagine soldiers defiling...." He fell silent.

Now she understood why he was upset. More softly, she "Mentàll. I'm sorry that I worried you."

"Thank you." He turned toward the door.

"You're still upset."

That pale gaze pinned hers. Finally, and with the faintest of smiles, he said, "How will you quiet the beast?"

He was daring her, and suddenly she felt reckless. She curled her fingers around his wide, strong wrists. Going on her tiptoes, she kissed his bristly cheek and quietly said again, "I'm sorry. I didn't mean to worry you."

Tension relaxed out of his shoulders, but before she could withdraw, his broad palm cupped the back of her head. He kissed her deeply. The thorough suddenness of it shocked her. His tongue plunged into her mouth, stroking, and demanding her full response. She felt his frustration in the kiss, and then his hunger, mixed with a restless longing. Heat inflamed her senses, and she swayed into him.

She enjoyed his warm, velvet touch too much. She didn't want him to stop.

With trembling arms, she pushed at his chest. "Enough," she whispered.

His blue eyes looked disoriented, but even when they cleared, he did not loosen his possessive grip. His uneven breaths matched her own. "It is not enough. It is never enough, Methusal."

After another long moment, he released her. "Remember this."

Faintly, she said, "What? Your kiss?"

"Yes. I like how you feel in my arms." Harshly, he finished, "And the taste of you. I cannot get enough."

Her heart hammered harder. "We should go in. Mrn. M will be wondering where we are."

Mentàll caught her hand. "I want more, Methusal."

Panic prickled now. "I won't *give* you more." She tugged free and hurried inside. But the tiny trembles didn't quiet. They continued shimmering through her, like a ringing glass.

Mrn. M smiled when she saw them. "Such the gentleman. I see he found you, Midi. No dress yet?"

"No."

"Do you have room for dessert? I've made Lozar's favorite tart."

"Of course." Methusal took a seat, and to her surprise, Mentàll helped their hostess carry dessert dishes to the table.

"Thank you." Mrn. M dimpled at him, and retreated to the kitchen for a forgotten item.

Methusal eyed him. "You've certainly won her over."

"Now I need only to win you."

Methusal averted her eyes and pulled a tart onto her plate. "That, Mentàll, is the impossible mission."

CHAPTER THIRTY-FOUR

DAY 18

IT WAS ALMOST TIME TO GO. Deccia surveyed camp. Her pack rested against a nearby log, and Doc still wore his sling, although he'd take it off later, in Carachki. He didn't want to appear injured when he petitioned for a job in the palace.

Across the clearing, Behran again demonstrated how the timers worked to Hendra and Sozla. A frown of concentration knit Hendra's brows together, and she paid close attention. Tabor and Riln had gone to check on the Zindedi prisoners.

Timaeus wasn't back yet.

She wasn't surprised. It was too soon. And yet she knew he wouldn't be back. Her numbed brain accepted this, but her heart could not. Tears filled her eyes. Yet again, as she had done since waking up in the black pre-dawn, she fervently prayed for his life.

She wanted to get going. Perhaps foolishly, she hoped to find Timaeus on the trip to Carachki.

The others weren't ready yet.

Drawing an uneven breath, she glanced over at the one other person who also appeared to be feeling alone in camp. Goric. He sat on a rough log, scowling. Talking to him might help her to think about something besides worrying about Timaeus. She approached him. "Are you ready for your mission tomorrow?"

"As ready as I'll ever be," he said shortly.

He did not want to talk, and she wondered what might be wrong. She focused her empathic heart upon him. He seemed unhappy—but more than that, troubled, as if he was conflicted about something.

"What's wrong?"

He scowled again. "Like you need to know."

Prickly as a rotarhudge. But that didn't bother her. She sat on the log, too. "You're a valuable member of this team, Goric. Sozla didn't mean to hurt you with what she said last night. And you know you have to ignore Riln."

His murky eyes narrowed. "Why are you so nice to me?"

It felt like an accusation, which made Deccia feel defensive—probably as he had intended, she swiftly understood. Another of his mechanisms to push people away. He was a difficult man to understand.

"Do I need a reason, besides basic human decency? I'm an empath, Goric. I like to understand people." She searched for the right words to explain it, but couldn't find them. "I know you feel like an outcast. I know you've never fit in anywhere. But I think underneath all of your scowling and pretending to accept others' low opinion of you... I think you have a lot to offer."

He shrugged and looked away, still scowling. "Yeah. Right."

"Stop feeling sorry for yourself," she advised. "Stand up and be who you are. Ignore people like Riln. He puts people down so he'll feel better about himself. It's pathetic. If you believe in yourself, others will, too."

His scowl knotted tighter, and then gradually relaxed. Sharp, intelligent eyes stared at her. A hint of the true Goric within. It actually unnerved her, because this was the first time she'd sensed how deeply he'd buried his true self. "You really think so?"

"I know so."

He nodded, and after a moment offered a very small smile. "All right."

"You'll do a great..."

"They're gone!" Tabor boomed, dashing into camp. "We have to move."

△ △ △ △ △

Pale sunlight streamed in the window when Methusal awoke. The bed felt soft and warm. And empty. She always knew when Mentàll was there, and when he wasn't. His body, a short half-length from hers, always felt like a safe, anchoring weight. When he was there, she slept deeply. When he got up, she always swam toward consciousness, struggling to become alert to danger.

Water ran in the relief room.

She yawned and stretched. Tomorrow was the big day. They'd plant the detonators and go to the ball. But what would they do today?

She decided to remain in bed until Mentàll came out. No sense shivering in the cold room, waiting to get dressed in the warm relief chamber. It would probably be moist and steamy from his bath. Methusal shut her mind to the image of him rising from the tub, water sluicing from his tanned, broad shoulders, like it had done by the stream at the end of the Quasr War. Of course, he'd worn breeches then. Now... She would think no further.

How she longed for a long, hot bath. To relax and feel weightless, and to feel all of her troubles drift away like soap bubbles. It sounded like heaven.

Methusal closed her eyes, imagining the warm water lapping under her chin.

"Methusal."

Her eyes flew open. Mentàll stood over her, wearing his black jacket. She sat up on an elbow. "Where are you going?"

"To set up a place for Doc and the others to stay. I'll be back in an hour."

"No mission for me this morning?"

His gaze traced her features, and a faint smile tugged at his lips. "None that you would accept."

The moment he left, she gathered up clean clothes and scampered into the relief room. A twist to the hot water tap, and steaming water thrummed into the tub. Humming happily to herself, she dribbled in a generous portion of Mrn. M's purple bath soap. She sniffed with appreciation. It smelled sweet, like flowers. Delicious.

As soon as the tub had filled, she slipped into the delicate bubbles and sighed. Smooth and creamy bubbles. Hot water. And plenty of time to take a leisurely bath. She washed herself and her hair, and then stretched out in the long tub.

Soap bubbles puffed in mountains over her. Their delicate flower fragrance teased her nostrils. The water felt warm and soothing.

She leaned back against the smooth, slippery tub until her ears were submerged and her head gently touched the back of the tub. It was a warm, silent, peaceful world. She smiled in bliss. Lethargy stole through her limbs. It felt so comfortable that she could doze off again...

A vague noise teased at her subconscious. The water felt cool now, and she had the odd sensation that someone was watching her. Her eyes slitted open.

Mentàll looked down at her.

"Mentàll!" With a gasp, she sat up, crossing her arms to cover herself. A quick glance proved that clumps of soap bubbles still mostly covered her. She glared up at him. "What are you doing in here? Get out!"

He didn't move. The eyes that held hers were dilated black, and burned with fierce longing and intense need. Last night's kiss seared her mind. Warm agitation stirred.

His gaze drifted down over her arms, and then returned to her face. Her skin burned where his gaze had touched. "I called you three times. You did not answer."

"How long have you been staring at me?" Why did her voice sound choked and breathless?

"A moment. I thought you had drowned until I saw you were smiling."

"I was enjoying some peace and...and *privacy*. Please go. Now."

Mentàll offered her the towel, but with a glare, she refused it. It would have meant exposing herself to him.

A hint of a smile tugged at his lips. He draped the towel over the tub's edge. "Ten minutes. I have a mission for you this morning." Then he left, quietly closing the door behind him.

Heart pounding, Methusal remained where she was, half afraid he'd open the door again and come back in. But he did not.

She quickly stepped out of the tub, dried herself off, and dressed. She combed her long hair, jerking at the tangles in an effort to prevent her mind from reliving when he'd watched her lying naked in the tub. And the intense heat she'd seen in his eyes. It should have deeply offended her—his coming into the relief room and looking at her that way.

But it hadn't. He hadn't meant to invade her privacy. He had been worried about her. And while desire had been in his eyes, she'd sensed a deeper emotion than lust. Her heart beat faster, remembering it. As if he yearned for *her*, and for her alone. It made her feel beautiful, and desirable. Something she'd never felt before.

Methusal yanked at another tangle. Was she insane? She did not want him to desire her. She did *not*.

△ △ △ △ △

After the monstrous fit GG threw several days ago, she had not called for Aali again. In fact, the few times GG ventured out of her room, she had glared at Aali as if she were the devil.

What was wrong with that old woman? Aali didn't understand her, and didn't want to, either. Maybe she was unbalanced.

Since GG wasn't available for questioning, she tried to find other ways to achieve her spying goals. True, Trori and Rartn accompanied her every minute of the day. But that could prove to be a good cover, she quickly realized. People ignored the children. Therefore, since she was always with them, people ignored her, too.

She really wanted to investigate Calbn's office.

But how? And when? Certainly not while the Quasrian Chief was around. He disliked her and distrusted her. Ever since the medallion incident, his gray eyes felt like cold ore every time they touched her.

She shivered, feeling those cold eyes on her now. She tucked her crutches more securely under her arms and watched Calbn hug Trori and Rartn.

"I'll be back for lunch," he promised. "Be good."

"We will, Daddy!" they chorused.

With a frown for Aali, Calbn slammed the door leading into the courtyard. And then he was gone.

"What do you want to do today?" Aali asked.

"Let's play Hide and Find!" Trori said.

"Where? Outside?"

"No. Let's hide in our rooms, the kitchen, and Daddy's office!" Trori said.

Aali's heart leaped at the very idea. Could it be so easy? "Does your father let you play in his office?"

"Oh, sure. All the time," Trori said airily.

"Really?" She felt doubtful, but didn't try to discourage the idea, either.

Trori re-explained the hiding rooms to little Rartn, and the game began.

It didn't take long for Aali to find Rartn the first time, but Trori was nowhere to be found. Calbn's office was the last resort. Knowing Trori, it should have been the first place she looked. That little girl liked to live on the edge. Much like herself, she had to admit.

She pushed open the heavy wooden door to Calbn's office. "Trori," she called out. Rartn dogged at her heels. "Are you in here?" She heard a distinct giggle. "Uh oh, Rartn, I think I heard a squeak! What could it be?"

"A monsta?" Rartn suggested with a grin. He grabbed Aali's hand and held it tight.

"Help me look," she whispered. The two shuffled inside. Aali closed the door behind her so Trori wouldn't dart outside and hide somewhere else.

Suddenly, Rartn broke free. "I'll look! I'll look!" he squealed.

Good. Aali saw her chance and hobbled across the room to Calbn's desk, which was situated in front of a large window. Papers were strewn all over it. Heart jumping with excitement, she lifted one page and scanned it.

It detailed plans to expand the docks downtown. Nothing interesting. She picked up a different one. Notes from a Council meeting about cleaning up garbage. Frustrated, she reached for another.

"I found her!" Rartn cried out. The two children ran across the room at the same moment the office door flew open. She froze, paper in her hand. Calbn strode in, his face as dark as a thundercloud. The paper fluttered from her fingers and onto the desk.

"Trori. Rartn. Out!" he hissed. "See Cook."

With a frightened look, Trori glanced at Aali and then the two scampered out. Calbn didn't bother to close the door before he advanced on her.

"Explain why you are in *my office!*" The sentence ended with the force of a gale.

"We... We were playing Hide and Find."

"Did you find Trori under the papers on my desk?" he asked caustically.

"Of course not! But she could have been under..."

"I saw you through the window." His voice made her skin crawl. "Do not lie to me, Aalicaa."

She licked her lips. "I was curious," she admitted. "I saw the papers, and wondered what they said."

"You have no business being in my private office!" he shouted. In fascination, she watched the cords in his neck bunch up in fury.

She sidled out from behind the desk. "Of course. We won't come in here again. Trori didn't think you'd mind…"

"Do not use my daughter as an excuse! You came here to spy."

Aali opened her eyes wide, hoping she'd look innocent. "Spy? Why would I spy, Chief Calbn? Do you have something to hide?" The last was a daring question, and she flinched when he made a sudden movement toward her. He stopped, though, before reaching her.

Relief, sharpened by fear, pumped through her. The man was close to losing his temper. Maybe even close to throwing a fit, like his grandmother. Frightened, she swung quickly on her crutches for the door.

"Stop," the Quasr Chief ordered, his deadly voice shaking. "You will remain here until I have finished speaking to you."

She cast a longing look at her avenue of escape, but obeyed his order and stopped moving. She mentally tried to harden up her emotions so she could endure whatever tongue lashing Calbn planned for her.

He said, "You are a guest here, but twice you have invaded our private quarters."

"It is my job to go into Rartn's room."

"And what right do you have to be in my office? None!" His voice cut like a sharp knife.

"You think I broke my leg so I could stay here and spy?" Aali injected a note of incredulity in her voice. It sounded authentic, too, she was pleased to note.

Calbn cut his eyes to the ceiling. "Of course not."

"I would be home, Chief, if I hadn't broken my leg." No need for him to know that she would have spied before she'd left.

He took a step toward her. "I don't trust you, Aalicaa Storst. I know you're up to something."

She lifted her empty hands. "I'm not hiding anything. But you have made me curious, Chief. Why are you attacking me? Unless, of course, you have some dastardly secret that *you* are hiding." Aali knew she was pushing matters, but she wanted to know how Calbn would respond. She wanted to know if he and Mentàll were plotting evil together.

"You are a nosy girl!" The ugly force of his rage shuddered through her spirit. The Quasr Chief frightened her. He jabbed a finger at her. "Get out. If I find you in here again I will throw you out in the street!"

She trembled. The Quasrian Chief was not a man she wanted to cross again.

All the same, she struggled to keep up her façade of innocence. "I won't allow Trori and Rartn to play in here again. You have my word on that." She hobbled out as quickly as she could.

The door slammed behind her, and the impact sent a shockwave through her nervous system. She wanted to burst into tears, but didn't, because Trori had run up.

She put a gentle hand on Aali's arm. "Did Daddy scare you? Mama says sometimes he has a nasty temper."

"I'm okay." Aali forced a smile. "But we can't play in his office anymore."

Trori clung to her hand. "I'm sorry. It's all my fault you got in trouble."

"No. It wasn't." She wouldn't let the little girl take the blame. After all, Aali had wanted to go into the office. She certainly hadn't discouraged it. And Calbn had exploded in temper because he'd caught her rifling through his private papers. What was even more frustrating was that she'd found nothing. No proof of evil doing. No proof of any nefarious deeds. Although he had certainly *acted* like he was hiding something suspicious.

She'd need to be a lot more careful next time. And there would be a next time, because it seemed glaringly obvious to her that Cabln was hiding something.

Unfortunately, she still felt shaken and upset by his outburst. Calbn was suspicious of her. GG appeared to hate her. Only the children seemed to like her.

The weeks ahead suddenly seemed unbearably long and lonely. Would Dastn ever return?

∆ ∆ ∆ ∆ ∆

Methusal and Mentàll stood outside Mrn. M's house. A cold, damp breeze blew this morning, and clouds scudded in from the north. Methusal pulled her warm leather jacket more closely about her and said, "What are our plans for today?"

"We need more detonators and timers. Even if Behran brings more, we'll need as many additional ones as he can make. If we find the parts, I can give them to Behran and he can make more tonight."

"What do we need?"

"You can find the time pieces. I will find the rest."

It seemed a simple enough task. "How many do you want?"

"Twenty. We'll meet here in an hour."

"How about on Bay Street? I want to find Pruvin."

"Do not make contact with him. Doc and Behran will speak to him."

She rolled her eyes. "I won't jeopardize our cover."

"One hour." The cool blue gaze lingered on her face. An echo of the earlier intensity burned. After a hesitation, he turned and strode up the street.

Methusal watched him go. His black jacket hugged the breadth of his powerful shoulders and cut in at his waist, accenting the long, lithe lines of his body. The black cap mostly covered his hair, but a bit of the white blond gleamed in the fitful rays of the sun.

She couldn't explain why she watched him. Or the warmth—and was that pride?—she felt in him. He'd done a great job leading this mission.

A cold gust swirled through her hair and snuck down her collar. With a shudder, she clutched it closed at her throat and hurried for downtown.

The time pieces were simple enough to find. She spread her purchases out among several shops in order to avoid suspicion, and then spent a few minutes admiring a green, beautifully cut gown in an expensive looking shop.

Afterward, she headed further south for Bay Street. The narrow lane was situated a few blocks north of the dock, and the scent of fish permeated the air. Vendors hawked their wares and women prodded the fish, testing its freshness before nodding for it to be wrapped up.

Methusal pretended to be interested in the fish, too. When she found a stall temporarily free of customers, she slipped in and poked the slimy, pink flesh. The stall owner, a short man with curly gray hair and a smokestick parked between his teeth, said, "What you lookin' for?"

"I'll know it when I see it. Is Pruvin around today?"

"Yeah." He tipped his head left. "Down there, supervising a clean-up."

"Thank you."

Methusal wandered in that direction. It wasn't hard to pick out Pruvin. He was yelling at a pimple-faced youth with blond hair. The hapless lad had spilled a barrel of fish guts, and the stink made her stomach roil.

Bald-headed Pruvin wore a blood spattered white shirt, and his large belly drooped over his belt. "Do you have a brain?" He swore. "I'm left with imbeciles!"

"I'll clean it up!" promised the teen.

Pruvin chewed him out at length, punctuating his comments with colorful curses, and then stormed into a shop. "Trash Collection" was inscribed in brown on the window.

Easy enough to tell Behran and Doc how to find the shop later. Methusal sidled further down the street, keeping a watch out for Mentàll.

"Did you find him?" The Dehrien Chief appeared at her elbow.

She jumped. "Stop doing that!"

"Are you practicing kaavl?"

Chagrined, she admitted, "Not at the moment. I found Pruvin, though. He's at the shop that says 'Trash Collection.'"

"Good. And I see you found the time pieces. Give them to me, please."

"Why?"

"I will meet the Dakarran team on their way into town. I'll give them their orders then."

She blinked in surprise. "But I'm coming, too. I want to see Deccia. And Behran," she quickly added.

His eyes gleamed at her inadvertent oversight. "It will be safer if I go alone. The Zindedis cannot know they are teamed up with us. I will not let the Presidente's men follow me."

Methusal looked around. "Are they following us now?"

"See that soldier on the corner? He has been watching you. Two blocks east, two more have been following me."

She'd had no idea. Why hadn't she been practicing kaavl? Was she so foolish to feel safe, even for a moment, in the Zindedi capitol? "So they *do* know who we are."

"I suspected no less. Go back to Mrn. M's. You will be safe there. I will lose my spies easily enough."

"Could you tell Deccia that I found a gown I like at 'Dress One?'"

"Good. Tomorrow you can tell her in person before you trade places."

"We'll trade places?"

"Deccia will pretend to be you. The soldiers will think you're shopping, when really you will be setting detonators on base."

Just like Mentàll, to think of every contingency plan. "How will it work?"

"She will go into the bake shop early, when it is crowded. At seven, she will slip into the relief room. Shortly after, we will arrive. You'll take her place in the relief room, and she and I will leave together. Both of you will wear black tomorrow. Then I will leave her alone to shop.

"After she's bought everything you need, she'll go to Mrn. M's house, where she will pretend to have a headache and lie down. She'll slip out and head over to the ship. When you get back to Mrn. M's you'll slip in the back way, and she will not know the difference."

"Good plan."

His teeth flashed in a surprising grin. "I am glad you approve of one of my plans."

Methusal felt a catch in her heart when she looked up at him. When he was relaxed like this, with that razor fine tease to his tone, he was at his most dangerous. Because right now, for one wild, insane moment, he was utterly irresistible to her heart.

Drawing a quick breath, she looked away, trying to break finely spun connection between them. "I want to go to the Presidente's gardens next. I have a hunch." She was ready to battle for this idea. After all, if the soldiers hadn't arrested her yet today, they weren't likely to do so later, either.

To her surprise, he didn't argue. "Do you have enough money?" He reached into his pocket.

His chivalry disturbed her, although she wasn't sure why. "I think I have enough."

"More is always better," he murmured. He took her hand and pressed dascals into her palm. The notes felt warm from his body heat. Unthinkingly, her fingers curled around the money.

"Be safe, Methusal. Remain in kaavl." He leaned in close, and his warm lips brushed her cheek. "I will see you later. I want to take you out tonight, so be back by six."

She stared up at him. "You want to take me out? To dinner?" Her voice squeaked. "Why?"

"It is our last night together before the ball. I want to make it special."

"I don't... I mean, that's not necessary." It sounded like a dangerous idea. Definitely not a good idea at all.

He only smiled. "Six o'clock." And then he was gone.

△ △ △ △ △

After Deccia, Doc, and Behran disappeared south through the woods, heading for Carachki, Hendra and the others broke camp. They needed to move to a safer place in case the Commander and his men came looking for them. As they undoubtedly would. And soon.

"We'll head west," Tabor decided. "According to the powder map, the forest runs west for quite a while. It ends in the mountains."

Sozla pulled on her pack. "How far will we go?" Her dark eyes looked sober. Hendra had noticed that her gaze had lingered on Behran before the trio had left a little while ago.

"I don't know. But we're not safe here. Take only what you need. No pots. Only one blanket apiece."

"I'll spy on the base," Riln announced, shouldering on his pack. "As soon as I know what's going on, I'll find you."

"We'll stay together," Tabor said tightly. "Let's go."

Riln's face flushed with temper. "I won't run blind. Head straight west. I'll catch up with you soon." He strode east, out of camp.

"Fool," Tabor muttered.

Hendra, Sozla, and Goric followed Tabor through the crunchy underbrush. The day was crisp, clear, and cold. The lack of fog could be a good thing or a bad one, depending upon if they'd need to hide later.

Hours passed, but Riln didn't catch up with them. No one appeared to be following them, either, so Tabor decided to stop for lunch.

Hendra was glad for a rest. Her legs ached. And she was worried about getting back to the base in time for tomorrow night. They'd have to backtrack a long way.

"Maybe we should wait here for a while," she suggested. "Maybe Riln will catch up soon and tell us what's going on."

"I agree," Goric said, gulping water.

A frown flickered between Tabor's dark brows. "Okay. We'll wait for a while."

They sat in silence, munching on jerked meat. Other soft, crunching noises stirred the silence.

Tabor's neck and shoulder muscles tensed. Hendra slipped on her pack, and so did the others. "I'll find out who it is," she offered. "I'll catch up with you."

Tabor hesitated, clearly not liking the idea.

"I can see into the future. It'll give me extra time to escape."

He nodded, and the threesome disappeared into the forest. Heart in her throat, Hendra crept east, concentrating hard on the bushes and trees in front of her.

A man's voice muttered. Then an ugly, feral snarl rent the air.

Bent double, Hendra crept closer and peered into the distance. Black uniforms. The ones in the lead clutched ropes and seemed to struggle with whatever was attached to the other end.

Another snarl rent the air. Men swore and yanked on the leads. A gray animal, its ears silver-pointed, leaped forward, fighting against the tether.

Wolmites!

Hendra spun and ran back.

"They've caught a scent!" shouted a man.

Boot steps crunched and claws scrabbled across the earth. Heart racing with fear, Hendra sprinted after her teammates. Luckily, they hadn't gone far.

"Wolmites," she gasped to Tabor. "They're tracking us. One got a whiff of me."

Tabor abruptly cut north. "The stream. It'll cover our tracks. And rub yourselves with dirt and leaves. It'll help cover our scent."

Hendra grabbed up handfuls of fallen leaves and scrubbed her clothes and hair with them as she ran with the others. The snapping snarls of the wolmites grew closer, although the men were still out of sight.

Apparently Tabor had purposefully paralleled the stream the whole time they'd been hiking, because they reached it within moments. He splashed down into the middle and headed west. Hendra followed as quickly as she could. The sound of the wolmites grew louder.

Tabor had just rounded a corner. She cast a fearful glance backward. A hard stare, and the Zindedis appeared, peering down the stream. Had they just seen her?

Or had she seen into the future?

Moments later, Hendra rounded the last corner.

Tabor kept up the grueling, jogging pace, sloshing and sliding over the wet rocks in the stream. Hendra's ankle turned. It hurt as she ran on, but that couldn't be helped. She couldn't stop.

They kept going, even as dusk fell. Hendra was glad wild beasts did not appear to live on Zindedi. One less predator to worry about.

She hadn't heard the men or the wolmites for some time now, but that meant nothing. Her ankle ached, but not too badly. The icy water was good for it.

Tirelessly, Tabor slogged on, and the night grew cold and dark around them. Only Ryon's green, silvery light reflected off of the ripples of the stream. Hendra's stomach rumbled.

"Please. Can we stop?" Sozla said. "I do not think I can go much further."

A hill rose to the north. "We'll climb up," Tabor decided. "It'll give us a good view."

Hendra's legs felt heavy when she left the icy stream, and her feet felt like chunks of ice. The rest of her body was warm from exercise, but already the night air felt cold against her face. When they stopped, she would feel even colder.

The hill top offered no trees for concealment or shelter. An icy wind whipped, flattening the tangled, grassy weeds. While Tabor scanned the countryside, Hendra pulled off her wet boots and socks, and then she and Sozla shielded each other with flapping blankets and peeled off their wet clothes and pulled on dry ones.

It made little difference. Hendra shuddered uncontrollably now, even with her blanket wrapped tightly around her shoulders. She struggled to chew some meat and bread with chattering teeth, and fantasized about the hot meat from last night. And Doc's warm arm around her, too.

"We'll take turns keeping watch," Tabor said. "Hendra, you go first. Then Sozla."

Nothing stirred during Hendra's watch, and afterward she rolled up in her blanket and pulled the ends over her head. It was freezing. She wondered if Doc and the others had made it to Carachki, and if they were staying in a warm inn tonight.

Her teeth clacked. Where was Riln? And she wondered if the Zindedis given up the chase. It seemed unlikely. One thing was for sure—the guards would be on full alert at the base tomorrow night.

△ △ △ △ △

Methusal hoped her hunch was about to pay off. She studied the map posted outside the towering, dark green maze in the Presidente's garden. Gray clouds now completely obscured the sky, and a cold rain spit on her cheek. Few people were wandering in the gardens. She'd easily lost the soldier following her a few minutes earlier. He was a distraction she could do without right now.

Using the writing stick she'd brought, Methusal traced the intricate maze on a scrap of parchment. As she did so, the wind strengthened and flecks of rain hit harder. She shivered, and eyed the inky entrance. It had looked ominous the first time she'd seen it with Mentàll and Mrn. M. Now, alone, it looked even more sinister.

Mentàll had found the secret fountain in the center of the small maze. Wouldn't the Presidente hide an even greater treasure in the center of this huge one? What could it be?

A prize for the intrepid?

Or perhaps evil lurked in the heart of the garden.

Methusal dismissed this chilling notion and plunged into the maze.

At once, darkness enshrouded her. The hedges grew three lengths high, and only a little gray light filtered down to the stone path. But it was protected from the wind, and a little warmer. Light, infrequent raindrops touched her skin.

She slipped utterly into kaavl, absorbing multiple sources of input at the same time. The soughing trees outside, the rustle of leaves in the strengthening breeze, the drip, drip of water eleven lengths to her left...it all streamed into her brain. Next, she carried with vision, peering around corners before she arrived, and following paths she knew were dead ends according to the map. It was the perfect place to practice kaavl, because the sensory inputs were so few. She was alone in the maze. That was good news.

Methusal practiced jumping from one sensory carry to another, faster and faster. It gave her a headache.

She wondered if the Primary level came effortlessly to Mentàll. Although she knew the Dehrien Chief could handle multiple input simultaneously, she didn't think he could carry with vision or hearing. With fewer sensory inputs to track, wouldn't it be easier to surrender utterly to kaavl? Of course she had no idea what his kaavl gifts were, because he'd never told her. Perhaps he dealt with more input that she could imagine.

She wondered which kaavl gift had told him that she was captured, when he was all the way over in eastern Zindedi. Certainly, it was one she'd never heard of before. And she remembered that during the Quasr War he had seemed to sense the safest path to take faster than she could carry with vision or hearing.

The Dehrien Kaavl Master definitely had skills he hadn't shared with her.

Methusal zigzagged deeper and deeper into the maze. The walls narrowed, and the stones of the path became smoother.

One final twist, and brighter light and a mist greeted her. The heart of the maze was a two length square in size, and carpeted in grass. In the center sat a giant, stone square.

She moved closer to read the large metal plaque on top.

Herein lies the defeated presidente of Zindedi. May all who enter take heed, lest you suffer the same fate.

Only tombstone. She looked up at the gray sky. *Why did I want to come here, The One?*

Mist sprinkled on her skin. She looked back at the squat, ugly tombstone. It was repulsive. A testament to the current Presidente's violent past.

The mist slowly thickened to fat raindrops. Time to go home. She'd found nothing.

And yet... Her fingers traced the engraved lettering on the plaque. "May all who enter take heed," she whispered. What did that mean? All who enter the heart of this maze? Or those who *enter* somewhere else?

Her fingers slipped over the metal surface. On a hunch, she pressed lightly on every raised letter.

The round part of the letter "e" in "fate" moved. Her breath caught, and she pressed harder. It popped beneath the metal plaque. She pushed at the plate. With a grating sound it slid in a semi-circle left, revealing a black, gaping hole. And a ladder.

"What is *this?*" she whispered. She glanced around, but kaavl confirmed that she was alone.

Dared she?

Of course. She had to see where it led. Wishing she had a torch, Methusal swung her legs into the hole and carefully descended. The two length ladder ended at the beginning of a stone path. She looked up at the reassuring gray square of light, and then at the black, narrow passage ahead. Mentàll would not be pleased.

After four small steps, the passage became pitch dark. Her hands slid along the damp, gritty wall, and she carefully made her way forward.

It felt like she walked blindly for an eternity. Everything was completely silent.

When she estimated that she'd gone at least two hundred lengths, the path sloped upward. Sounds finally reached her ears. Clinking dishes.

Now she crept forward with even more care. Her hand hit a wall straight ahead. Her other hand flew out and confirmed it; the end of the passage. And the noises were louder now.

She patted the wall. It was wood now, instead of dirt and stone. A metal hook scratched her finger. A latch? After feeling for the catch mechanism, she carefully released it from its loop. The door rolled sideways, but no light entered the passage. Another touch encountered more wood. Carefully, she patted the rough surface until she found another latch. This time, the door opened outward.

The damp smell of old leather and wet cloth met her nostrils. It smelled like a coat closet. Straight ahead, light shone under a door.

Methusal crept forward, focused upon the crack of light. She carried with vision into the room. It was a gigantic kitchen, paved in smooth white stone. Cabinets were made of a light-colored, polished wood, and the counters were made of more white stone. Shiny metal pots hung from hooks, and ten cooks rushed about, assembling trays.

"If the Presidente does not desire urchet, deliver the slug next," ordered a portly, red-faced man.

"What if he doesn't want that, either?" fretted a narrow-faced woman.

"Be ready to make whatever he wants on the spot!"

To the right of the door stood a soldier with a hand on his gun. He was young and stood stiffly, on full alert. No doubt he was guarding the secret door. Or did he even know of its existence?

Methusal sat back on her heels, unable to believe what she had just found. She was *inside* the Presidente's palace. Mentàll would not believe it.

She'd seen enough. Time to go. Crawling backward, she crept back into the passage and drew the first door closed, but did not lock it. She left the rolling one open. Who knew if they'd need to escape tomorrow night? Having the doors open might make all the difference.

△ △ △ △ △

The Presidente folded the parchment with a pleased smile. So. His foolish enemies had gobbled up the bait. A deep chuckle rippled in his belly and rumbled out, growing in volume until he shook with mirth. It sounded spine-chilling, even to his own ears, and yet he felt nothing but pure joy. No spasms pained his heart.

It was a sign. All would go as he planned.

"Yalin!" he shouted.

His skinny secretary burst into the room. Already, apte-like fear had scored permanent worry lines into his young face.

"Take down my orders, and send them to my personal guard." With succinct words, the Presidente laid down the law.

When Yalin scuttled out, the Presidente chuckled again and stuck a succulent smokestick between his teeth. Yes. At last, the torture of his enemies would begin.

△ △ △ △ △

Methusal arrived back at Mrn. M's just before six, so she didn't have a chance to tell Mentàll about the secret passage before they headed off to the restaurant. He insisted on holding her hand, which disturbed her. His hand felt big and warm, and very secure. She shouldn't feel like she belonged with him, and yet she did.

Behran was already in Carachki, after all. She'd see him tomorrow night at the ball.

But thoughts of Behran left her mind when Mentàll ushered her into a warm restaurant lit by a crackling fire at one end, smoldering torches on the walls, and flickering candles on the tables. It was a soft, intimate setting. A romantic setting. Her nerves tangled into knots. What had he planned for tonight?

The waiter took their jackets before seating them at a table draped with snow-white cloth, and with a thick, sweet smelling candle in the center. They faced each other over the steadily burning flame.

"Menu?" The waiter extended one to Methusal.

"Oh. Thank you."

After the man took their drink orders, she glanced around the restaurant—anywhere but at Mentàll. "This is nice. Have you been here before?" Finally, she looked at him. A crazy thought entered her head, and she swallowed. "You haven't, have you? With another woman, I mean."

His teeth flashed in an obviously surprised smile. "Would it bother you if I had?"

"Fine. Don't answer." The waiter delivered bread, and Methusal tore off a hunk. "Anyway, I don't care."

"Then why did you ask?"

She sent him a cool look, mentally chastising herself for bringing up the subject. "Never mind. Let's talk about something else."

His hand covered hers, warming her chilled skin. "I have not brought anyone else here. You are the only woman I desire to be with."

Her cheeks warmed, and she tugged her hand free. "I see."

His gaze ran over her flushed cheeks. Softly, he said, "Does that truth disturb you?"

She didn't answer. Instead, she bit off another piece of bread, and deliberately changed the subject. She told him about investigating the secret passage. Hopefully, that nugget would sever the unnerving intimacy already threading between them.

To her surprise, he said nothing.

"Aren't you going to lecture me for sneaking into the palace?"

"No. Because then I would need to censor myself. I have already been there."

"What?" Her mouth fell open. "Why didn't you tell me? Oh, I know. You're the Commander. You don't need to tell me anything."

"I was going to tell you about it tonight. We will both need to know how to escape tomorrow night."

Why was he always one step ahead of her? "Are you always so perfect? You figure out everything first. It's hard to measure up."

His smile vanished and the blue eyes darkened. "I am far from perfect. You know my darkest sins. Can they ever be forgiven?"

"I already told you that I forgive you, Mentàll. But trust demands a higher price."

"I understand." His gaze held hers as the waiter poured amber liquid into their cups. When he left, Mentàll raised his glass to her. "To new beginnings. May we never forget the lessons of the past, nor be afraid to step with faith into the future."

His glass touched hers, and the quiver of sensation shivered through her fingertips, up her arms, and sped toward her heart. Methusal gulped the spirits, trying to drown the fanciful thoughts. She should think about Behran. *Why did she keep forgetting about Behran?*

In the far corner of the cozy restaurant, a man strummed a melodious instrument.

When the food arrived, the urchet meat was tender and succulent, the logne leaves delicately flavored with a sweet dressing, and the tubers mashed to light perfection. Mentàll persisted in drawing her into conversation about the restaurant, the food, Carachki, and her feelings about the Zindedi people she'd met. He listened intently to her short responses.

Methusal didn't want to be rude, but for self-preservation purposes she thought it might be best to keep their conversation to a minimum. But no matter how hard she struggled to resist, his intense, focused attention made her feel giddy—as if she was special and important to him. She could so easily let the music and his company go to her head.

And he wanted her to take that final step. His small smile wooed her, and so did his low voice, pitched only for her ears. He was charm itself.

After the waiter took their dessert order, Methusal abruptly pushed back from the table. "I'll be back in a minute." Her heart pounded. She needed to get away from him.

In the relief room, she eyed her flushed face and sparkling eyes with a feeling akin to horror. What was wrong with her? He was seducing her, and she was *letting* him. "Oh The One, help me." She splashed cold water on her face.

It helped. A little.

Feeling more sober, she returned to the table. A berry tart glistened on each of their plates now. Hers was a tagma tart, and his was made of a lighter color, unknown berry. "That was fast," she said, arranging her napkin on her lap again.

"You have water drops in your hair." Amusement glinted.

She swiped at her face. "It's warm. I needed to cool off."

They ate in silence.

"How is your tart?" he asked.

"Fine."

"Mine is delicious. Would you like a taste?" He extended his fork to her. A delicate, fruity square was ensnared on the tines.

"Umm. No."

"Why not?"

"It's yours. I'm fine with what I have."

"Until you taste something new, you cannot know what you are missing." He spoke of more than the tart.

"I'm happy the way I am."

"Are you?" he murmured. "Is that why my tart tempts you?"

She gasped. "It doesn't tempt me. *You* don't tempt me!"

Her face burned when every eye in the place turned to stare at her. She stiffened her shoulders and silently ate her sweet, predictable dessert.

Afterward, Mentàll paid for the meal, and then helped her on with her coat. The cold air outside was a shock after the warm restaurant.

His warm hand took hers, and he tugged her between two buildings and turned her to face him. He was too big. Too close. She backed up, but a stone wall stopped her. "What are you doing?"

"This." He cradled the curve of her jaw in his big palm, and just looked at her. Her heart beat faster. Much as she didn't want to admit it to herself, she liked his touch. And she wanted more.

"Should I stop?" he murmured.

For some reason she couldn't find it in herself to say "no."

He didn't move for a very long moment, clearly giving her the opportunity to escape. When she she made no move to do so, he leaned forward.

His kiss was exquisitely tender. The blood rushed to her ears and her heart pounded. She unthinkingly clung to his jacket. And still the gentle assault went on and on. When at last she surrendered to the aching need inside of her and tentatively responded, he delved deep, giving more of himself to her. Her hands slid up around his neck and burrowed into the short, soft hair at his nape while his palms slid to her waist, pulling her closer to him. It felt good. It felt right.

This was wrong.

"Mentàll. Stop," she mumbled. It hurt to say it. But she wanted more, and this wasn't right. It wasn't. "Let me go."

With obvious reluctance, he did as she asked.

Silently, he wrapped her hand securely in his and walked her home. Methusal did not protest this small intimacy, even though she should have. Her traitorous, foolish heart still craved contact with him.

What was wrong with her? What about Behran?

△ △ △ △ △

Lights blazed in Mrn. M's house when they returned.

"She is not alone." Mentàll stopped Methusal from turning the door knob.

She listened intently. "A man is with her."

"Who is he?"

A sliver of light peeked through a curtain, so she carried with vision into Mrn. M's living room. "A soldier. He's a captain with a special insignia."

"He is waiting for us."

"Should we run? We could hide somewhere until tomorrow." A thought occurred to her. "We don't need the invitations now. We could sneak through the passageway into the ball." The more she thought about this, the better the idea sounded. "The Presidente wants us at the ball as his 'guests,' right? If we sneak in instead, we could turn all of his plans upside down. We'd have the upper hand."

"No. He would not be fooled. He would triple the guards, because he'd know we'd try to break in. It is better to let him think he holds all of the power."

"But what if that soldier arrests us?" she hissed. "What if he drags us off to jail?"

"He is alone, and no other soldiers are near. He is here for another purpose. If necessary, I can overpower him." Mentàll twisted the door knob. "Follow my lead."

When they entered, Mrn. M turned a flushed face to them and quickly stood. "Here they are, Captain. I *assure* you, you have nothing to worry about."

The Captain was a slight man with lank, dark hair and close-set eyes.

Mentàll extended his hand and shook the other man's. "What is the problem?" he said cordially.

"The Captain..." Mrn. M drew a short, agitated breath. "He believes you might be *spies*. I have assured him..."

"Sit," the Captain invited, as if the house were his own. He sat in Mrn. M's special chair and crossed his legs. His eyes reminded Methusal of a whip's—alert, shrewd, and shifty. An unpleasant man. Not one to cross, either.

On the couch, Methusal and the others faced him. She felt exactly like she had when she'd been accused of murder—on the spot. And ill-prepared to defend herself.

Mentàll's arm went around her shoulders and a little of her fear eased. His body posture was relaxed and confident. "You have an issue to discuss, Captain?"

"Reports have surfaced that a pair of Eastern Zindedi spies have infiltrated Carachki."

"Oh." Mentàll crossed his ankle over his knee, and his thumb gently stroked Methusal's shoulder. "We are from Oesten, as my military records state."

The Captain's dark eyes gleamed. "Records can be falsified, as you well know...Commander."

"True. Who are these spies?" An authoritative edge bit through his tone, indicating he meant to take control of the conversation. "How can we protect the Presidente from them?"

The man's dark eyes flickered. "Provided you are not the spies, of course."

"Of course."

"Reports state the man and woman hate each other. Only their love for Eastern Zindedi unites them. However, they pose as a married couple. You are new to Carachki. Before allowing you into his ball, the Presidente ordered me to secure proof of your true marriage and affection."

Mrn. M sat forward, hands clasped, visibly trembling with indignation. "Midi and Lozar have lived here for two weeks. I assure you they are married, and very much in love!"

The Captain eyed Mentàll's hand on Methusal's shoulder. "It appears to be so." But he made no effort to rise from his chair.

"This is outrageous," Mrn. M said. "Can you not see? What other proof do you need?"

The Captain's lips stretched into a chilling smile, and he relaxed further into his chair. "Perhaps I will stay the night. I must be fully satisfied of their true marriage union."

What did he mean by that? Methusal glanced at Mentàll. He leaned close, so his lips touched her ear. Hot sensation licked, and she stiffened, breathing faster. She had trouble focusing on his low whisper.

"He requires one final proof."

What proof?

And then a burning blush seized her whole body. She pressed her lips together, afraid her true feelings would blurt out. The pervert! The disgusting slug. How did he plan to secure that knowledge? Did he plan to...to *watch* them? Her chest felt tight, and she could barely breathe because of the horror of it all.

Calmly, Mentàll said, "You may stay as late as you like, Captain. But my wife and I are tired. We want to make an early night of it. If you wish, you can return in the morning and we can talk more then."

The man's eyes flickered from Mentàll to Methusal, and then down her body. An unpleasant smirk curled his lips. "I will stay."

Mentàll shrugged and stood, offering a hand to help Methusal up. "Good night, Mrn. M. By the way, we will not need breakfast. I plan to take Midi out. Captain, we will see you in the morning, no doubt."

"Goodnight." Anxiety tightened Mrn. M's voice, and she looked from them to the Captain. Her frown devolved into a scowl. "Perhaps you would like tea, Captain."

"That would be lovely."

In their room, the Dehrien Chief closed the door behind him. Methusal felt better when he locked it. She shuddered and paced the room with agitation, her arms crossed. "That horrible man."

"We will have to convince him."

She spun back. "What do you mean?"

"We will need to make him think we are making love."

"*No!*" Another hot blush seared her skin. "I won't. I'm engaged to Behran..."

"We will pretend. It will not..."

"*Why?*" she exploded. "This is sick! It's perverted!"

"The Presidente wants to torture us. If we hate each other, as he thinks we do, then forcing us to prove our intimacy would be abhorrent to us. It would sicken us." He came closer. "He wants to make us suffer."

"He's right. It would be awful, and I hate him."

"No."

"No?"

"No, he is not right. It would not be horrible. It will be extraordinary between us, Methusal. I think you know that."

She backed away. "I'm not going to...to have *sex* with you. Forget it! I won't let you twist this situation around to your advantage!"

A smile glimmered. "If we ever make love, Methusal, we will be alone, and it will be very private. Just you and me. All of our attention will be focused only upon each other."

She gasped aloud. "You are..."

"Here, tonight, we will do what is necessary to fool the guard. It will drive home to the Presidente that we are unified, and a force to be feared. For he does fear our unity. Why else would Fitrn try to beat the truth from you? Why would the Presidente send the guard to torture us? He is insecure. And each of his moves only proves his weakness. We can defeat the Presidente, and we will. But first, we will deliver this small blow to his confidence. After tonight, he will believe we are fully married. And then he will fear us even more when we meet him tomorrow night."

"It's insane that such a small thing could scare him."

"He understands only hatred. Not love. He fears what he does not understand."

She looked into his eyes. "We don't love each other."

He said nothing for a moment. "He will think we do, and that is all that matters."

Did it take a wild beast to understand another wild beast? Mentàll seemed completely confident in his insight into the Presidente's bizarre, twisted psyche.

"This is insane," she repeated.

"Are you with me? We will fool the guard together."

"I won't take off my clothes."

He smiled. "You will not need to."

A tremble started, deep inside her. Everything in her screamed to flee, before it was too late. But she said, "You won't take advantage of me."

His smile deepened, like a wild beast anticipating a juicy morsel. "Trust me."

Illogically, she wanted to smile. Was he teasing her? "I don't. But I will."

"Good." He went to his side of the bed and divested his pockets of their contents and lay them on the bedside table. But she stood still, suddenly paralyzed by second thoughts. How could they convince the guard of anything? Was she supposed to moan? Make sounds? Her cheeks flushed hot at the very thought.

His low voice said, "Are you ready? We will have to make it sound as if we're about to become intimate."

Methusal's cheeks burned. "Stop," she hissed. "I don't think I can do this."

A chair squeaked in the living room, and then a thump sounded outside their room. A quick, unconscious carry proved her worst fears.

She whispered, "He's right outside our door!"

Mentàll spoke in a normal voice. "Change, Midi. Come to me when you are ready." The bed squeaked when he sat down.

Methusal still hesitated. Should she? Or was she about to make the most foolish decision of her life?

His unexpected smile disarmed her. He flicked a finger toward the relief room. With a roll to her eyes, she obeyed. It was time to sleep anyway. Nothing different than normal. At least, so far. She put on her long, soft gown, buttoned it to her throat, brushed her hair, and then returned to the room with raised brows and hands on her hips.

He'd taken off his boots, but nothing else, she was glad to see. He stretched out on the bed, hands behind his head.

"You look beautiful." His voice was low, like deep velvet. "Come here."

Her nerve endings, still inflamed from his after dinner kiss, reawakened. If she hadn't seen the tinge of amusement in his icy blue eyes, she would have bolted.

She sat on the bed and bounced on it for good measure, making it squeak. She had no idea how he planned to convince the Captain that their marriage was real, and she felt apprehensive about what was to come, to say the least.

"Relax," he said. "Lie down."

"How about I bounce a few more times?" she said, trying to keep a note of levity.

"It will not be enough."

She felt very aware of his large body, lying close by. Under normal circumstances, he'd honor his agreement with her father to behave himself. Would he tonight? She'd need to make sure he did.

She lay on her back and stared upward. The lamp on his side flickered, casting smoke and odd shapes across the ceiling. That horrible Presidente, and his equally disgusting Captain. This entire situation boded disaster.

Mentàll went up on one elbow and looked down at her. "You'll need to make sounds," he murmured.

Her face burned. "I can't."

"I was afraid of that."

She crossed her arms and glared. "Don't forget our agreement."

"As if I ever could." His low tone vibrated along her nerves. "Kiss me," he said, and relaxed onto his back.

Feeling uneasy, Methusal went up on her elbow and scanned his familiar features. The proud, prominent cheekbones. The pale, glittering eyes. His blond hair, with the bit that kicked up at his hairline. No amount of water or smoothing ever held it down. His mouth, which could unlock turbulent emotions inside of her. Her gaze returned to his eyes, which watched her carefully.

He said, "If you kiss me, I won't be accosting you." He smiled just the tiniest bit.

"And why should I kiss you?"

"Trust me."

Methusal knew she shouldn't. "How will that make any difference? How will the Captain know?"

"Trust me," he said again.

Reason screamed *no* in her mind. This whole thing was crazy. But his wits had saved them in the past, and so had her instincts. If he thought he knew what he was doing...

Trepidation built in her heart, but she slowly lowered her mouth to touch his. His lips felt warm, and she pulled back the tiniest bit. He lifted his head and captured her mouth with a feather soft kiss. He relaxed back against his pillow.

Her heart beat faster. She felt like she was stepping into a fire with her eyes wide open.

She dipped her head to kiss him again, and he returned it with a gentle insistency that stirred a languorous warmth inside her. A dangerous warmth. His hands slid up her back, urging her to rest her torso on his chest.

"What are you doing?" she whispered.

"Trust me. Kiss me one more time."

"Just one more?"

"One more," he agreed in a low voice, which reminded her to speak so the guard could hear.

"One more," she said with a faint sigh.

When she kissed him again, he took command. He explored her lips with a leisurely deliberation, and then coaxed entry. With a shudder, she allowed it. His kiss slowly deepened, becoming intimately, acutely pleasurable. His hands caressed her back and slipped down to her sides, running too close to sensitive spots. "Mentàll," she choked out.

He rolled them over so he was over her, holding himself up with one arm. With a quick movement, he ripped his shirt over his head. He kissed her more thoroughly, and Methusal felt herself spin out of control. Her hands curled around his sleek, hard shoulders, while her body ached for more of his touch. She felt his hand slide, stroking up her abdomen.

"Mentàll," she moaned softly. Tension spiraled in her, waiting for more intimate contact. His thumb brushed the sensitive underside of her breast. She didn't recognize the long, sighing moan that slid from her lips. And still she longed for more. The fever he had lit in her burned to be fed, and only he could deliver the satisfaction she craved.

She arched her neck back when his kisses touched her chin, and then trailed down to the hollow of her throat. "*Saltisienna,*" he muttered thickly. She felt his deep, heavy breaths. He kissed up her neck again to the point under her jaw bone.

"Has any man touched you like this before?" His words sounded dark and possessive.

"No," she breathed, pulling him closer, begging for his touch again. He met her need, and she gasped.

"Good." She heard the deep satisfaction in his voice. He kissed her more, and he gently stroked her until she was mindless and trembling, aching with need for him. Her breaths came in soft gasps, and when she touched his skin, it felt like fire. At her tentative caress, a deep, guttural groan escaped from his throat.

"Mentàll." She didn't recognize the low, aching sound of her own voice.

With an agonized groan, he rolled onto his back, pulling her with him, so she lay on top of him. His eyes were dilated black, and she felt in his hard body that he wanted her. Even worse, she wanted him, too. Badly.

His eyes blazed blue fire. He murmured, "I could take you now, and you would let me."

It was true. He held her, hands possessively around her waist, for long moments, until his harsh breaths slowly quieted. "Behran is a fool," he grated at last.

Cold reality shocked her.

What was she *doing?* What had she *done?* She pushed up, struggling to free herself. "Behran and I are waiting until we get married!"

His grip tightened, so she couldn't pull away. "Is the Captain gone?"

She listened. After all, that's why they were in this compromising situation to begin with. "Yes. He's joking with Mrn. M about us. He seems to have believed it."

"What about you?" he said quietly.

Methusal looked down at him, but didn't know what to say. She felt confused and ashamed. Loyalty to Behran warred with what she felt for this man. And what could explain why she had responded to him the way she had, and how she had let him touch her? It didn't bear thinking about. And yet she couldn't stop. Part of her shamefully wanted to relive it, again and again.

Her fingers strayed up to stroke down his wayward tuft of hair. His face gentled, and he captured her hand and pressed a kiss into her palm. Her nerves melted again. She couldn't look away from his eyes. They looked clear, for the first time ever, as if the ice had melted and she could see into his soul.

"Remember this, Methusal. You can have me—you can have this—any time you like."

His words slammed into her spirit.

"Mentàll." Her eyes traced his proud features, and she swallowed. "Mentàll...you should only give yourself to someone you love. And someone who loves you back."

"I have made my choice." The determined glint in his eyes told her she should take this as a warning. He rolled them over to their sides and looked down at her. "Goodnight, Methusal."

"Good night," she whispered. She didn't understand him. Not at all. He left her, pulling the quilts off of the bed. With soft sounds he rolled up in them on the floor. The man with limitless self-control had deliberately left their bed.

Shouldn't she be grateful for his self-restraint? Another man might have taken advantage of her inexperienced, trembling eagerness, and taken her.

She closed her eyes as remorse finally fell down like cold, driving drops of rain, filling her heart with regret. She pulled the covers over her head. What had she done? What had she *done?* Tears slid down her cheeks.

CHAPTER THIRTY-FIVE

THE NEXT MORNING, when Methusal awoke, guilt pressed hard upon her conscience. Water ran in the relief room, signaling that Mentàll was taking a bath. She didn't want to open her eyes. She didn't want to face the day.

She had betrayed Behran.

Tears filled her eyes. She had shamelessly—no, *eagerly*—responded to Mentàll. If she loved Behran, how could she allow—worse yet, *enjoy*—another man's touch?

Was she a wicked, depraved girl, to enjoy such things? She squeezed her eyes shut. Hot tears leaked out, soaking into her pillow. *Oh The One, please forgive me. Please! I'll never do such a thing again. Never!*

The water turned off in the relief room. Methusal hastily wiped her face and scrambled out of bed. She would not be lying there, feeling vulnerable, when Mentàll came out. Never again would she lie in his bed. Never again would they share a night together. Tonight, after the ball, they would return to the ship.

When Mentàll left the relief room, she took his place and quickly readied for the day. They were supposed to meet Deccia early in the bake shop.

When she exited, Mentàll was pocketing a small roll of money. He tied his pack closed. "Take what you need for the return journey to the ship. Only what fits in your pack. Take seven detonators with you. Mrn. M must think we are going on a day hike, and then shopping. We can't cause suspicion."

Methusal couldn't explain why, but the very thought of contemplating speaking to him hurt, just like tearing a bandage off a wound.

Instead of looking at him, she reached for her pack. "How will we get our backpacks to the ship?" Because after they'd changed for the ball later, they'd leave this small house forever, never to return.

"Leave your pack in the abandoned shack. Deccia has instructions to take them to the ship this afternoon."

Methusal piled money, small necessities, and her favorite clothes into the bag. "The ship is near Carachki?"

"It is a half an hour west, in a protected cove."

She fingered a detonator, still reluctant to make eye contact with him. "How do I set these up?"

His fingers brushed hers to take it, causing a small shock to go through her. To her embarrassment, she jerked back. "Like this." With quiet words, he explained. "Set the timers after noon passes, and then set them to explode at midnight."

"All right. Thank you." She put them in her backpack and tied it securely shut. It looked a little bulky, but she'd left quite a few Zindedi clothes behind, neatly piled in a drawer. And she'd left the nightgown in the laundry basket. She never wanted to wear it again.

"Methusal."

"What?"

"Do you want to talk about last night?"

Finally, she looked at him. "I want to forget it ever happened."

"I will not forget."

"It was a mistake."

He said nothing, but continued to watch her.

"I shouldn't have..." She found it hard to say the words, and tried again. "I shouldn't have responded..."

"To me?"

"Yes."

"But you did. You desired my touch. Just as I desired yours."

She couldn't deny that. But she could make one thing clear. "Lust means nothing."

"Desire is an important part of a relationship between a man and a woman."

She could not believe she was having this conversation with him. "Desire is only a small portion of a relationship," she informed him. "The biggest part is love. I *love* Behran. That is what will last."

Mentàll watched her for a moment. "Do you desire Behran?"

She gasped. "How dare you? That is none of your business!"

"I can give you everything Behran cannot. But you are afraid to take it."

"Except for love. Right?"

He didn't answer.

Feeling inexplicably sick to her stomach, she said, "That's because your heart is made of ice, isn't it? All you care about is war, and power. But power, most of all. Isn't that right?"

"Do you still not know me, Methusal?"

"How can I? You won't let anyone inside!"

He said nothing, but turned away. "Get your jacket. It is time to go." His voice was harsh.

"Now you're the one who's afraid."

He shrugged on his black jacket. "I fear nothing."

"Don't you? You're afraid to trust people." She knew that was because he'd been abused as a child. More insight flashed. "That's why you taught Kitran all those strange principles about channeling emotional energy into kaavl. Because that's what you've done your whole life. You won't let anyone in. You won't let anyone hurt you, so you pump all of your anger and hurt into accomplishing your goals. Kaavl. Power. You've become a cold shell of a man."

Silkily, he said, "Did you feel cold when I kissed you last night?"

"We're talking about you. Not me."

"I assure you, Methusal, I am not dead inside. You know this. You are the one who is afraid to face the truth."

"Base, animal impulses mean nothing. I love Behran! Those are the feelings that will last."

Harshly, he said, "Stop lying to yourself, Methusal."

Suddenly she couldn't stand his presence, or this discussion for one moment longer. She yanked open the door and burst into the living room. His hand gripped her shoulder.

"Do not run out of here. She will think the newlyweds have had a fight."

"So what else is new?" She strode quickly, wanting to be free of him. He easily matched her pace, and put an arm around her shoulders before she reached the outside door.

He said over her head, "We will be out all morning, Mrn. Machblin."

That lady smiled at them, her rosy cheeks dimpling. "You have a good one, now." She turned her approving gaze from Mentàll to Methusal, who forced a smile in return. Somehow Mentàll had won over the older woman's approval and affection.

Mentàll's arm remained around her until they reached Feldon Street. Then Methusal shrugged it off. "That's enough, don't you think?"

"Mrn. Machblin would be dismayed to learn that our honeymoon is over."

"If she had you for a fake husband, she'd understand."

Mentàll's smile disappeared and his manner cooled. "We will need to hurry to reach the bake shop at the crowded time."

"I know I'm supposed to set the timers in the powder buildings on base. But what will you do?"

"I will set the timers on the ships."

"How?" Concern flared. "They'll notice you. You're too big to blend in."

"Worried?"

She didn't answer. "What is your plan?"

"They are still loading supplies onto the ships. I will pack detonators inside the barrels, if I can. Or attach them to other flammable equipment, if necessary."

"But if the detonators aren't in the powder barrels, they won't make a big explosion."

"True. But they will burn."

"So the ships will catch on fire and then explode."

His teeth flashed like a feral beast's. "Yes. If we are fortunate."

They arrived at the bake shop. Before going inside, Mentàll put a hand on Methusal's wrist. "Be careful."

She met those pale blue eyes and saw he meant it. He did not like the idea of her going on the assignment alone. Her irritation with him melted with alarming swiftness. "I'll be careful," she promised. More quietly, she said, "You, too."

"I intend to take you to the ball tonight. You may be certain I will return."

His habitual arrogance made her lips twitch with reluctant humor. "I'll pray all goes well for us, and for the other teams, too."

Because tonight was it. If someone was going to die, like the Prophet predicted, today must be the day it would happen. She hoped it wouldn't be Mentàll, or herself, or Deccia, or Behran... She hoped the Prophet was wrong.

△ △ △ △ △

"Come," the Presidente said, settling back in his chair and trying to relax. An uncomfortable sluggishness had plagued him all morning. It disturbed him. Tonight was the ball. Finally, he would get to execute his enemies. He wanted to feel in prime, vigorous health for it. Perhaps he should take a nap later.

His personal guard, the Captain, slunk into the room. His eyes and hair were as black and lifeless as ever. "I have gathered the information you require."

The Presidente's thick lips stretched into a smile. "Good. Did they succumb to the pressure?"

A lascivious smile pulled at the Captain's mouth. "A better performance I have never heard."

The Presidente frowned. "What happened?"

"Their activities did not sound forced. If fact, they sounded enthusiastic, if their groans and moans of pleasure were any indication."

"They fooled you!"

"No. I have had many women. I can tell when they fake it. The sounds I heard were genuine. They appear fully unified, in body and spirit."

"No!" With a violent arm, the Presidente drove everything off his desk. Vases smashed, books thumped, a glass of water sloshed and shattered. Pain seized his chest, and he gasped.

The Captain stood silently while the Presidente doubled over, his face planted into the desk, helplessly trying to seize control over his traitorous, weak body. Pain pierced the Zindedi leader's sternum. He could barely breathe. For one wild moment, he thought this might be it. Now he'd meet his brother in hell.

He wasn't ready. The ball was tonight.

Using every ounce of strength he possessed, he concentrated on his breathing, calming the rigid tension in his neck.

The pains slowly eased, and with one hand pushing hard on the desk, he forced himself into an upright position.

The Captain regarded him with blank eyes. "Would you like water, sir?"

The Presidente heaved a careful breath and rested his arms on the empty, polished surface of his desk. "I am fine," he growled, in order to hide the wheeze in his voice. "It was a spell, and it has passed. You have done good work. You will watch the spies at the ball tonight. If they leave the room, detain them."

"Kill them?"

"No! I have plans for those two."

"If they threaten me, I will kill them."

"As a last resort, Captain. Do you understand?"

The Captain clicked his heels together and saluted. "Understood, sir!"

"You are dismissed."

The Presidente took more deep, calming breaths, and waved Yalin away when he tentatively stuck his nose in the door. So. His enemies were truly unified.

Hatred rose in him, as vile as corrosive poison. He would *kill them.* He would make them suffer. Yes. Perhaps it was even better that they loved one another. Watching their lover die would increase the torture that each suffered. He chuckled. Tonight he would relish hearing them cry out in horror to each other with their last, dying breaths.

Pain rent his arm. He drew another slow, calming breath.

Tonight. Tonight he would reap his satisfying, bloody harvest.

△ △ △ △ △

In the crowded, noisy bake shop, Methusal left Mentàll in line and headed for the relief room in the far back corner. The door was closed, and she sharply rapped on it. "Deccia?"

The door opened a crack, and then Deccia pulled her inside. They fiercely hugged each other. The room was tiny.

A small window over the relief stool let in a grimy stream of light.

"I'm so glad you're all right," Deccia sniffed, pulling away. "Lock the door, just in case."

Methusal did, but her concerned gaze remained on her sister's watery gaze and puffy eyes. "What's wrong?"

She twisted her hands. "It's Timaeus. I have a horrible feeling about him. Something is wrong."

"He should be fine. Mentàll saw him and warned him two days ago."

"Warned him about what?" Deccia's eyes darkened with anxiety.

"Didn't he tell you? General Fitrn has gone to Dakarra to find his uncle's murderer."

Deccia's hand flew to her mouth. "How does he know? Someone told him it's Timaeus?"

"Yes. Fitrn's brother is in Dakarra. He sent a note to the Presidente, telling him the information."

"General Fitrn's *brother* is in Dakarra? Who is he?"

"I don't know. But it's possible he's on the Dakarran kaavl team."

Deccia gasped. She sat down abruptly on the relief stool. "But everyone on the team is from Koblan!"

"I know. But who else would know that Timaeus killed General Greisn? Only Koblanis were in the room when the General died. All of the Zindedis were dead."

"But maybe word got out somehow. Maybe it leaked to a Zindedi who escaped home."

"It's possible."

Deccia's face was white. "Methusal, this is too much. Fitrn's *brother* might be on the Dakarran team?"

"If he is, it means he's been a deep spy on Koblan for years."

"But *who*? Who would betray Timaeus? Oh, thank goodness I changed his name on his military papers!"

"The Presidente didn't mention a name. But the description matches him. Actually, it could match Tabor and Riln, too."

"But the spy—Hendra and the others are with him right now!"

"Mentàll told Timaeus the facts. He can warn them."

"If he made it back to Dakarra."

"Of course he has. Don't think like that, Deccia."

Tears slipped down her sister's cheeks. "I want to believe he's safe." However, she obviously did not.

"You said you have a bad feeling?" Dread caught at her spirit.

"Yes. A black, hopeless feeling. Like when I was trapped in that pit."

A fist pounded on the door.

"Just a minute," Methusal called.

"How will you escape? No one can see us together."

"I'll go out the window. But we'd better get down to business. I found a green dress I like. It's in the window of a shop named 'Dress One,' on Bay Street."

"I'll get everything you need. Don't worry."

"Mrn. M thinks we're hiking all morning. If you could bring the dress to her house in the early afternoon, that would be best."

"Okay."

"I should go."

"Wait." Deccia stood. "Tell me what's been happening here."

"The Presidente knows who we are, and where we live. But he wants us at the ball. So when you go to the shack, make sure no one follows you."

"All right. And what about Mentàll? What's been going on with him?"

A tide of guilt and confusion swamped her. "Don't ask."

"That bad?" Deccia said sympathetically. "Or that good?"

She flushed. "Deccia! He's a wild beast, and that's it."

"Methusal, I love you. But don't lie to yourself."

"He confuses me," she admitted. "But I'd be a fool to trust him. I still think he's plotting something against Koblan."

"With Zindedi?"

"No, not with Zindedi. Something on his own. And I think somehow he needs me to get what he wants."

"How? Why?"

"I don't *know*!" Anguished, she said, "I'm so confused. Nothing is ever simple with him. He's always plotting ten things at once. I just *can't* trust him." Her voice broke.

Deccia hugged her. "It's okay," she whispered. "If you're falling in love with him, it will be all right."

Methusal stiffened. "I am *not* falling in love with him. I love Behran!"

Wise, discerning eyes looked back at her. "Follow your heart, Thusa. Really listen to it. And pray for wisdom. One day soon, you'll have to choose who makes you happy—who completes you, and who you can't breathe without. And when he's gone, you feel like there's a hole inside you the size of Koblan. If he's hurt, you wish you could suffer for him." Tears filled her eyes.

"Like Timaeus," Methusal whispered, and hugged her sister tightly. "It'll be all right, Decc. He'll be fine."

"I hope you're right." She pulled back and wiped her face. "I need to go. Green dress. Dress One. Right."

Another loud bang punctuated the air. "Open up!"

Methusal clung to her sister's hands. "I'll see you at the ship."

"Yes. Tonight."

"Tonight it will all be over." A wave of foreboding hit her. Yes, it would all be over tonight. But for whom?

"Climb out the window," Deccia urged. "Hurry."

Just before Methusal wiggled out, a thought hit her. "I learned a funny thing the other day. Mrn. M has a daughter named Ceri. And she ran away from Carachki."

"Because of General Fitrn?"

"Yes."

"Really." With surprised thoughtfulness, she said, "It has to be the same Ceri."

"Be careful at Mrn. M's. She has close ties with the Presidente. He visits unexpectedly."

Her sister smiled. "Don't worry. I'll be taking a nap. Go. Quickly."

More loud, impatient banging came at the door. "Open up!"

"I'm coming!" Deccia said. "Be safe, Thusa."

"You, too." Methusal wiggled the rest of the way out the window and dropped into the empty alley. After a quick look both ways, she piled her hair up under her beret and made her way north. It was still early yet, but she wanted to see what extra security might be in place at the base.

△ △ △ △ △

Riln met Hendra and the others in the early afternoon, when they were halfway back to Dakarra. He waited on a boulder by the stream, poking a stick into its gurgling depths.

It had been a miserable night, and Hendra had hiked all morning huddled inside her blanket. Even when the noon sun beat down, she still felt cold, even though she wore full Zindedi military gear in readiness for tonight's mission. Her ankle ached, too, and it grew worse as the day progressed. They'd met no Zindedi soldiers so far. That was the good news. Riln's bristly face, however, conveyed bad news.

"Where were you?" Tabor said curtly. His stance made it clear he intended to resume hiking at any moment.

Riln rose. His large, black clad body reminded Hendra of a wild animal rising from its lair. "Spying on the Zins. You'll thank me I didn't turn tail and run, like the rest of you did."

Abruptly, Tabor headed east again, his shoulders visibly tense. "Report what you know. We have a lot of ground to cover."

Riln's swaggering strides easily kept pace with Tabor's. Hendra lagged behind, feeling no desire to be near the obnoxious Tarst man. Clearly, he felt he'd found extremely valuable information. It appeared his ego had swollen to the near bursting point.

"They found the tied up Commander," Riln said. "And General Fitrn is in Dakarra. He's sent soldiers all over the countryside, looking for us."

"What are their orders?"

Riln's lips curled back. "Does it matter? If they shoot, we're dead. If they capture us, we're dead."

"What are their *orders*?"

"Capture first. Shoot to kill second."

"Are they still trying to track us?"

"Most went back to the base. They're gearing up to move powder. The General wants to leave this afternoon."

"We'll have to track the powder at dark," Tabor decided. "Goric and Sozla will take care of the powder mines. Hendra will still lead a team on base."

Riln barked out a laugh and said over his shoulder, "Good luck, apte girl. I'm not going with you."

"I'd be happy to go alone," she informed him.

"Hah. You'll be a tasty treat for the wolmites."

Tersely, Tabor asked, "What do you mean?"

"Guards with wolmites are patrolling the base. No one will get by them."

A chill prickled down Hendra's skin, remembering the snarling, vicious wolmite from yesterday.

Sozla said, "What other information did you discover?"

"Oh. Someone finally admits I made the right choice to stay behind. That I was *man* enough to face down the whole Zindedi military." This last was directed at Tabor.

Hendra felt the urge to roll her eyes.

Tabor's jaw clenched. Quietly, he said, "Apparently Riln found no more information."

"No. We have to wait until dark to get near the base. I'm going to hide on the road to Carachki. I can't wait to ambush those Zins."

"What about Timaeus. Have you seen him?"

"No."

Hendra wondered what Timaeus had done when he'd returned to the cabin and found it empty. Would he return to Carachki? Or wait for the ship to come pick up their team just south of Dakarra? Maybe they'd meet up with him on the beach tomorrow.

Tabor said nothing for a long while. He dropped back to walk beside Hendra. "We'll check out the base. If it's too dangerous, we'll join Riln on the road to Carachki tonight. We'll concentrate on destroying the powder carts, instead."

"But Mentàll wants me to blow up the powder on base."

"Your safety would be his first concern." Tabor's steady, protective brown gaze held hers. "As Mentàll's next-in-command, I ask that you follow my orders."

"Fine." But disappointment made her eyes sting. Mentàll had trusted her to lead a mission on base. Now she may never have the opportunity to prove she could successfully complete such a tricky, dangerous task.

"Good." Tabor addressed Sozla and Goric. "You two will cut south before we reach the cabins. Blow up both mines. We'll meet you at the beach west of Dakarra tomorrow morning. I'm not sure when the ship will arrive. We'll wait in the woods until we see it."

When they stopped much later for dinner, Hendra soaked her swollen ankle in the ice cold stream, and Tabor distributed one explosive device to each person. Two were left over, so he put an extra one in Hendra's pack, and kept one for himself.

Riln looked on with a disgruntled expression. Clearly, he wanted to have two, also. But Hendra could think of nothing more frightening than Riln carrying two explosive devices. One could prove disaster enough.

"We're almost to our cabin," Tabor said. "Split up, and take your positions."

△ △ △ △ △

Methusal squatted in the protective gully, trying to decide what to do. Soldiers crawled all over the base, and guards had quadrupled at the back fence. She wasn't sure how to get by all of the guards. Worse, soldiers streamed in and out of the powder buildings loading barrels into carts.

Did they plan to empty all of the powder buildings? If so, she'd need to get inside soon and place the detonators in the barrels before they left the base.

First, though, she had to figure out how to get in.

High overhead, the hot sun beat down on her head. It was noon. Five hours remained before she needed to return to Mrn. M's to get ready for the ball.

Should she try to go in the front gate instead, and blend in with the soldiers returning from the ships? She'd already left her pack at the shack for Deccia, and had stuffed the seven detonators into the pockets of her Zindedi uniform.

Getting the timers inside the powder barrels might prove difficult, and setting the timers to explode would also take precious time. Maybe she should set the timers on the detonators *before* she arrived on base.

Though dangerous, it seemed like the best plan.

One by one, Methusal pulled out the seven detonators and carefully set the timing mechanism for twelve hours. She pushed in all the knobs and the clocks quietly started to tick. Now she had seven live bombs, all ready to explode at the same time. With care, she lodged them back into her pockets. Hopefully, Behran's invention wouldn't backfire and explode early.

Methusal concentrated into kaavl. Soldiers' boots crunched on the ground near the fence. An angry officer shouted at a Private.

The hot sun soaked into her black uniform. She stifled a yawn and focused upon the building nearest her. Relaxing utterly into kaavl, she carried with vision. It was if she invisibly stood at the corner of the building. She heard and then saw the guards clomping along the fence. A glance to her right revealed a stocky soldier and a skinny one carting barrels on their shoulders. Sweat glistened on their brows.

"Heavy," grunted one.

"Hurry up. Sergeant Kirkwn is coming."

Methusal followed their gazes. A young, tawny-haired soldier strode toward Methusal, and she stifled a gasp. It was the man who had captured and threatened to whip her.

She mentally followed him to the next building, where she saw and heard everything perfectly. A calm serenity enfolded her. It was so easy, as if...

She drew a quick breath, which broke the carry. Methusal became aware of the sharp stones she sat upon, the prickly bushes growing tall about her, and the blue sky overhead. She felt utterly and completely relaxed. That serenity remained, even though excitement charged through her blood.

She must have just experienced the Primary level.

Kaavl had been effortless. She'd carried with both hearing and vision simultaneously, and moved from location to location on the base with effortless ease.

The Primary level!

Unfortunately, she couldn't dwell on her breakthrough, because her brief reconnaissance had proven one thing—she wasn't getting in through the back fence. Too many people were working there.

It took her quite a while to circle back to the main road, where she joined a group of soldiers heading toward base with an empty cart. She lagged behind them with her head down.

They paid no attention to her at all. At the entrance gate, she moved a little closer and entered the compound with no problem.

Once inside, she slipped away, toward the powder buildings. The industrious barrel moving was still underway. Several powder buildings were empty. Several were half full. She followed soldiers inside one of these and inspected a barrel as she jockeyed it back and forth, pretending to try to get a good grip on it. A wooden peg secured the lids shut. She moved to a barrel in the far back corner and spent precious time trying to loosen one. When the soldiers came back in, she picked up the barrel next to it and carried it out. It was heavy.

On her next trip inside, keeping her back to the others, she managed to work the peg almost free.

Footsteps sounded behind her. "Hurry up, soldier!"

"Yes, sir!"

Swiftly, she gripped another powder barrel and heaved it up in her arms. Head down, she hurried outside. The reprimanding soldier dogged her footsteps, and then continued to watch her. She worked quickly with the others, trying to deflect suspicion away from herself. When finally his attention turned elsewhere, she slipped back into the building.

Hastily, she yanked the plug out of the barrel. The lid stuck. She scraped her fingertips raw, trying to wiggle it open. Finally, just as footsteps entered the building, she popped it open. Swiftly, she stuck a timer inside and snapped it shut again. Footsteps came closer, and in a panic, she slammed the plug in with the heel of her hand. Pulling the barrel into her arms, she swung around and stared into two hard, tawny eyes.

Sergeant Kirkwn.

At once, she lowered her eyes and tried to sidestep him.

A painful grip on her arm stopped her. "Do I know you, soldier?"

"No. I don't think so, sir."

"Look at me."

Panic pulsed through her. Bracing her nerves, Methusal looked up and stared hard into the officer's eyes. "Yes, sir?"

Recognition registered, and his eyes narrowed. He knew she was a spy. And she knew he was a spy for eastern Zindedi. Why else would he have stolen papers from the Commander's desk several weeks ago?

The Sergeant stared at her for a long time, obviously trying to decide what to do. "You have your orders, soldier?"

"Yes, sir." Her gaze didn't waver from his.

He released her arm. "I have a special assignment for you. Follow me."

As she followed him outside, she slipped utterly into kaavl. Her pounding heart felt like a roaring in her ears. She deposited the powder barrel in the cart and followed the Sergeant's crisp, military steps. He headed for the back fence.

He wasn't watching to see if she followed him. She could easily escape. Still, she was curious. So she warily followed him.

He stopped at a maintenance shack. Methusal made no move to follow him inside. A moment later, he returned with a broom and flipped it into a horizontal position. Before she could take a defensive posture, he struck her legs. The sudden, sharp pain made her cry out. She twisted sideways, and he struck her again, hard across the back of her shoulders.

"Worthless, lazy Pit!" His vocal cords stood out, and his face looked purple. He hurled the broom at her, and instinctively, she caught it. "Sweep the empty buildings. Now! Go to it!"

"Yes, sir!" Legs shaky, she quickly walked away from his glaring eyes. Now she understood. He was giving her free reign to roam the base and create whatever havoc she liked. But to the others, it looked like he was punishing her.

Soldiers watched her hurry to an empty powder building. Some looked away. Some sniggered.

But she was alone. For all intents and purposes, she could do whatever she wanted now. She could sweep anywhere, and no one would question her. Quietly, she swept the empty room, and then moved to the next building. This one had been emptied of all but eight barrels. Was that worth a detonator? Yes. Who knew how many more detonators she'd have a chance to set?

Methusal found a stick to pry off a lid, and set a detonator inside the barrel. Five more to go.

The afternoon sped by as she methodically swept every powder building. Three remained full of powder. Two others were half full. She set a detonator in each. It was almost five o'clock when she'd set the last one. Time to head back to Mrn. M's for the ball. She rested the broom against the wall and quickly left the building.

"Finished, soldier?"

Methusal drew in a quick, startled breath and spun.

Sergeant Kirkwn leaned against the wall, chewing on a weed stalk. His eyes looked as hard as ever.

"Yes, sir. Do you have another assignment for me?"

"No."

She turned away.

"Where are you from?" His voice sounded casual, but it prickled like rocher feet down her spine.

She glanced back. "Does it matter? We are all united. With one purpose."

His gritted teeth flashed in a false smile, and he straightened. "Go. And don't come back."

"Yes, sir."

Methusal swiftly left him. Unease hastened her footsteps. Zindedi officers were unpredictable and cruel. She did not want to give him a chance to change his mind.

She followed a powder cart off the base. It was all so unexpectedly easy. Zindedi's defeat was only hours away.

△ △ △ △ △

Hendra and Tabor could not get very close to the base. Every time they drew near, leashed wolmites snarled and lunged.

As the sun dipped toward the horizon, a thick mist rolled in from the ocean. Hendra and Tabor stared down at the quiet military base from a hilltop. The powder carts had left two hours ago. Below them, the restless wolmites paced the fence, staring at the woods, saliva dripping from their muzzles. They looked ferocious. Only the beasts' collars and tethers protected the Zindedi soldiers who walked near them. More than once a wolmite lunged at a soldier. A few young soldiers ran. The handler's whip flicked out, chastising the animal, and the wolmite returned its attention to the woods.

Crouching back on his heels, Tabor pulled a water skin from his pack. "We're not getting on the base tonight." He tilted the skin and drank.

"I know." It didn't ease the frustration she felt.

"Most of the powder is in those carts, anyway."

He was probably right. But she felt as if giving up on the base amounted to failing her mission. It seemed wrong to leave the Dakarran base without inflicting some sort of damage upon it. Mentàll had entrusted her with that specific mission.

"It'll be dark soon. We should go."

Hendra fingered her pack. "How far can you throw a rock?"

Tabor's eyes looked hard and impatient. "Thirty lengths. Maybe more. Why?"

"I have an idea." Hendra pulled an explosive device from her pack. After setting the timer to go off in six hours, she wrapped it up in a neat, tight bundle inside one of her tunics.

"What are you doing?" He frowned.

"The powder buildings are along the western fence, right?"

"Yes."

"The roofs are flat. When it's dark, you could throw this onto one of them. At midnight it would detonate. My shirt would catch on fire, and so would the roof. After that, it's just a short trip to the powder inside."

He raised one dubious brow. "I might miss the roof."

"It's worth a try, don't you think?"

"If you want my opinion, we've wasted enough time here. We need to catch up to the carts and help Riln."

Hurt nipped. "Go, then. It's my mission. It's my responsibility."

"I won't leave you."

"Either help me, or leave." Ore cooled her voice. Not long ago, she would have run from a confrontation with a man. But now, perhaps thanks to Riln, new strength had grown inside her.

His gaze assessed her. "All right. I'll do it, since it means so much to you."

"Thank you." She turned away and strapped on her pack again.

Dusk spread its large, dark palm over the landscape. Soon, its fist enclosed their hilltop.

"Let's go." Tabor hiked down for the western fence.

A wolmite howled. Ryon was half full, but only a faint glow made it through the fog. The beasts were no more than dark, furry blobs.

On the flat land, they went down on their hands and knees and crawled closer to the base. A wolmite snarled, and its handler swore.

"Close enough," Tabor whispered. Shadowy buildings loomed through the fog. Flexing his bicep, he rotated his arm twice.

Hendra handed him the cloth wrapped bomb.

"Hope it doesn't explode when it hits."

Hendra hadn't thought of that.

Tabor stood up in one swift movement. With a violent lunge, he hurled the package skyward. It disappeared into the mist. A wolmite erupted into a snarling, ferocious fit.

He dropped back down beside Hendra. "Let's go."

Bent double, they fled for the protective forest.

Shouts came from the base, but Hendra couldn't tell if they were directed at the wolmite, or if someone had raised the alarm because they'd found the detonator.

At least they had made one attempt to attack the base. She felt pleased about that.

△ △ △ △ △

Methusal felt a surprising sense of relief when she entered Mrn. M's house and spotted Mentàll sitting on the couch, ankle crossed over his knee. He looked up when she entered. "Midi. I thought you were resting."

She drew in a quick, dismayed breath. That's right. She was supposed to have snuck in through the back window. She glanced toward the silent kitchen. Mrn. M was nowhere to be seen. "I went out for a bit."

His pale eyes looked flat, as if lost in thoughts of his own. Quietly, he said, "You had no problems?"

"None." She would have said more, but Mrn. M bustled into the room.

"Midi! I'm glad to see you're up. Are you feeling better?" Concerned dark eyes peered at her.

"I'm fine, thank you."

"Good, good. Your dress is lovely. I found the lip balm I told you about. Here. Just keep it." Mrn. M offered her a tiny purple pot with a lid that looked like a ball. "It's not my shade, but it will go perfectly with your skin tone."

Deccia must have shown Mrn. M the dress. With a smile, she accepted the gift. "Thank you. I'll wear it tonight."

"You need to get ready, dear. The Presidente is sending a carriage to pick us up in an hour."

"He is?"

"Oh, my, yes." The older lady dimpled. "He says I need to arrive in style, seeing as Charlie will be honored tonight."

"How wonderful." Methusal cast a sidelong glance at Mentàll, wondering what he thought about this new development. As usual, his expression was impossible to read.

"I imagine this will be our last night together." Mrn. M clasped her hands together, and her dark eyes glistened.

"Yes," Mentàll agreed. "Tomorrow the war begins. I will need to report for duty." He glanced at Methusal, and unexpectedly extended a hand to her. Wondering what he intended, she went to him and let him wrap his long, warm fingers around hers.

"Oh." Mrn. M pressed her hand to her mouth, blinking rapidly, but a tear escaped. "Young love. You two remind me so *much* of Charlie and me. We started off as a hot, tumultuous affair, but ended so sweet..." She blinked and sniffed and wiped more tears away. "I wouldn't have traded a *day*." Her voice broke. "It makes me happy to see you two so in love. It gives me hope, you see. Love still lives on." She drew a shaky breath. "I'm glad we're all going to the ball together to honor Charlie. It seems right, somehow. I want you two to have a special, special time."

"Thank you, Mrn. M." Methusal smiled softly at her Zindedi friend, and felt a catch of sadness. The older lady had been nothing but kind to them, and yet they intended to betray her trust. They would bomb her country, and they'd never see her again after this evening. Suddenly, it was important to her that Mrn. M understand how much she meant to them. "We're grateful for everything you've done to make our honeymoon special. I will never forget."

"Oh." Mrn. M waved a dismissive hand and dabbed her nose with a small, delicate cloth. "It was the least I could do. You are my guests, after all. But enough of my blathering. I need to get ready. But first, a cup of tea." She bustled into the kitchen.

Mentàll still held Methusal's hand. With a tug, he drew her off balance so she tumbled down beside him onto the couch. What was he up to now? Unfortunately, she couldn't create a scene and try to wrestle free—not with their sharp-eared landlady in the next room.

"She is right, you know," he murmured.

She looked into his intense, ice blue eyes. Warning sizzled. He was much too close. Their thighs practically touched. Her heart beat faster. "About what?"

"About us."

With a faint frown, she whispered, "She believes in an illusion."

"Does she?"

"Don't start this." She became aware of silence in the kitchen. A quick carry revealed that Mrn. M was standing at the counter near the door, quietly stirring her tea. She was probably listening to them.

Mentàll's eyes gleamed. He knew it. His thumb gently caressed her wrist. "You have captured my entire passion," he said quietly.

"Stop," she hissed.

"I will not. I love you, Midi. Do you not know that by now?"

Her heart jerked. Flustered, she whispered, "Don't."

"Don't what?"

"You don't know the meaning of love."

Mentàll lowered his head, and his warm breath caressed her lips. "Teach me." The words sounded husky. It sounded like a plea from his heart.

But wasn't this all an act for Mrn. M?

"I can't," she said, with a hint of panic.

"Then who will save my soul from the dark side?"

"Only The One can forgive you and save you."

He kissed her, and the unexpected sweetness of it made her heart pound. He whispered, "Yours is the forgiveness I want." With helpless capitulation, she kissed him back. Something in her soul reached up, wanting to melt into him—to give him anything he desired.... To make him whole, if she could.

When he withdrew, she felt dizzy.

Mentàll searched her eyes and murmured, "Yes. You know."

Knew what? His heart? She felt completely confused. The kiss was like nothing she'd ever experienced before. It had felt spiritual, like a melding of his heart to hers.

Trembling a little, she stood. She swayed slightly, her equilibrium off. "I'm going to change for the ball."

He watched her, blue eyes still holding hers, delivering the same message as his kiss. Taking a quick, shaky breath, she escaped into their room.

∆ ∆ ∆ ∆ ∆

In the relief room, Methusal tried not to think about what had transpired on the couch. And yet her mind kept returning to the feel of Mentàll's warm lips on hers, and the surge of emotion in her heart that had burgeoned up, wanting to meet and fuse into him. It scared her.

He had said he loved her.

No. He'd said he loved *Midi*. In any event, wasn't it all an act? So why did she keep thinking about it?

"If you're falling in love with him, it will be all right." Deccia's words.

"I am *not*," she whispered to her reflection. "I am *not* falling in love with *Mentàll*." It was insane. Preposterous. Wasn't it? Hadn't he been her enemy for over three years? And what about Behran? Didn't she love *him*?

Besides, she had more important things to worry about right now. The ball, for example. Not to mention meeting the Presidente and presenting the peace agreement tonight.

The uneasy feeling she'd battled all day intensified as she thought about the evening ahead. Something bad would happen. She felt it clearly, like a black mark on her soul. A stab of fear panicked her for a moment. For one crazy moment, she wished they could run away to the ship and not go to the ball at all.

And yet, for Koblan, they must. For Koblan, she had to gird up her courage and meet the enemy, like Mentàll planned.

Methusal took slow, deep breaths, trying to calm her nerves. She brushed her hair until it shone, and then carefully applied the lip balm Mrn. Machblin had given her. It subtly darkened her natural lip color, and added shine. Then she slipped off her clothes and lifted up the green ball gown.

She'd become used to the foreign fabric of the tunic and breeches she wore every day, but this fabric was altogether different. Soft, smooth, shiny, and a deep, beautiful emerald green. The mirror revealed that it exactly matched the color of her eyes. Deccia had tried it on for her, so it should fit perfectly. She slipped it on, with difficulty fastened the clasps in the back, and then looked at herself in the mirror again.

A stranger looked back. She was accustomed to wearing clothes that hung straight, and basically covered her shape. This dress hugged tight to her skin, and showed every curve she possessed. A flush darkened her cheeks. The neckline plunged, in her estimation, showing a hint of her bosom. The shimmering fabric nipped in at her waist, and then hung in a cascade of flowing lines and simple accents of decorative beadwork.

Methusal had never thought of herself as pretty before, but the dress made her so, she decided. She felt exposed, though, showing so much of her skin and figure, and bit her lip as she slipped on the matching slippers. She could do this. Koblan's future and safety were at stake, so she would face whatever gauntlet was thrown before her, and the first step was mustering the courage to wear this dress without embarrassment. Last of all, she placed her knife and the paper she'd drawn of the maze into her bodice. Just in case.

She gave herself one final look. Her green eyes looked luminous, and her cheeks faintly flushed as she pushed open the door to the relief room.

Mentàll stood across the room, at the door. His back was to her, and in a glance she noticed how the tailored black jacket emphasized the broad power of his shoulders, and the black pants accented his lean hips and legs.

Hearing her step, he turned and went very still. His gaze swept down her, taking in every detail.

"Do I pass?" She wanted to inject lightness into the question, but could not.

"You do." He held out his hand, and she slowly crossed the room to accept it. His gaze didn't let her go as he lifted her hand. His warm lips settled on her inner wrist, at the pulse point.

The shock of it went to her toes, and she couldn't hide the surge of emotion that shot through her. His gaze still held hers.

She swallowed. "You wasted that one. No one is here to see."

"I wasted nothing." He tucked her hand under his arm and opened the door.

△ △ △ △ △

It took two hours to catch up to the military caravan heading for Carachki. Five soldiers trailed General Fitrn's cart, which followed at the rear of the procession. Two of those men wrestled with wolmites on tethers.

"The breeze is from the south," Tabor whispered. "They can't smell us yet."

The strengthening breeze rippled through Hendra's hair. The mist had vanished, and the open road looked black and menacing under Ryon's half-light. She wondered how long the soldiers would march before stopping for the night. And she wondered why the General had waited until late afternoon to start the trek back to Carachki. "We'll need to pass the wolmites if we want to get to the front of the caravan and throw the explosives in the carts. They'll smell us then. What will we do?"

"I don't know. Our scent might blend in with the Zindedis'. I think the biggest danger is if the wolmites hear us."

"Maybe we could go out and around them, in a big half circle, and then cut in ahead of them. We could wait for them to come to us."

"Good idea."

Bent double and running fast, Hendra and Tabor sped in an arc away from the road, and then cut back in after they'd passed the caravan. Still no sign of Riln. They squatted, hidden by bushes on the side of the road, waiting for the procession to catch up.

The front cart rolled into sight, pulled by a plodding urchet. A soldier with a wolmite flanked the cart.

Under his breath, Riln muttered, "We'll let them pass. Assess their weaknesses. Then we'll plan our attack."

Hendra nodded. The wolmite drew nearer, and she barely dared to breathe. Would it smell them in the bushes? Would it lunge, snarling, in their direction?

The wolmite's yellow eyes gleamed in the dark, staring in their direction. Its mouth hung open in a strange smile. Saliva gleamed on its tongue. It strained on its tether, leaning for their side of the road.

"Hiy!" The handler yanked the lead. The wolmite whirled back, snarling, and the soldier's whip cracked. The wolmite jumped and skipped ahead several paces. A low growl muttered in its throat. It slunk forward, periodically glaring over its shoulder at the handler.

Cart after cart rolled by. Five. Ten. Hendra spotted the end of the line and finished her mental tally. Fifteen carts. They traveled in a tight, close group, and were guarded by two soldiers per cart. Five wolmites paced with them. Getting close looked impossible.

Silently, Hendra waited for the final carts to approach and pass, wondering how they'd attack the powder caravan with only four bombs. And where was Riln, anyway?

The General's black cart rolled nearer. It looked like a specter of death, and Hendra shivered, imagining the cruel man inside.

Three soldiers, dressed in Zindedi black, trailed the last powder cart, cushioning the space between it and General Fitrn's cart. One walked close behind the cart, head down, shuffling along. He walked so close to the vehicle that it looked like he was holding onto it. Odd.

The soldier behind him whipped up his gun and shoved it into the first man's spine. The man jerked upright, and then slumped down again, plodding forward. A sick feeling gripped her. The man wasn't holding onto the cart. He was *tied* to it.

It was too dark to see him clearly. Who was he? A soldier being punished, or had Riln been captured?

The prisoner tripped, and a different soldier cracked a whip across his shoulders. His face flinched sideways, contorted in pain.

Hendra gasped in horror, and she clutched Tabor's arm.

It wasn't Riln. The prisoner was Timaeus.

△ △ △ △ △

The carriage that brought Methusal and the others to the Presidente's palace was enclosed, and upholstered in soft red and black cushions. It rolled smoothly over the stone streets, as if floating on a rich liquid, or over calm seas. It inspired a false sense of peace, considering their destination and the likely tortures the Presidente had planned for them.

Unease crawled through the pit of her stomach.

She sat beside Mentàll, with Mrn. M across from them. That lady exclaimed about the wonders of the ride every few moments, and peeped outside at the lamp lit streets going by.

Mentàll held Methusal's hand the entire time. She didn't protest. Truthfully, it leant her courage. His grip was firm and confident. He already saw the mission as a success, of course. She needed to do the same. But the black knot of fear would not subside.

Inside the gates of the Presidente's palace, soldiers in full dress uniform helped them down onto the smooth pavement. Lights blazed over the arched entry, illuminating the wide open, huge double doors to the palace. Brilliant light, sparkling chandeliers, and warm laughter, punctuated by a woman's shrill giggle, rushed out to meet them.

A black-suited man with white gloves accepted their invitations, and another took Methusal's coat and ushered them inside. The gigantic ballroom lay straight ahead. On the far right side, black-clad servers streamed from a hallway into the ballroom. It probably led to the kitchen and the secret passage.

Hand still firmly secured in Mentàll's grip, she entered the grand room. Tables draped in white cloth encircled the room. On them were glass vases overflowing with yellow nasria blossoms. In the center of the room clustered groups of conversing people. White, sparkly gowns shimmered. Other women wore slinky black sheaths. A few, like Methusal, had chosen to wear bold colors, and they garnished the room like bright jewels. Most of the men wore black uniform dress jackets, like Mentàll. Everyone in attendance looked perfect, and their hair was impeccably coiffed. Practiced, social smiles hovered on their lips.

Mrn. M moved to the side and chatted with a distinguished woman who had artistic white streaks in her black hair.

Methusal felt out of place. All of the women, to a one—including Mrn. M—looked poised and practiced. Her own smile felt fake, and she wondered if she should have done something to her hair. Couldn't everyone tell she was an imposter? Mentàll, on the other hand, with his arrogant bearing, could fit in anywhere.

Her warm palms felt slippery with sweat. To her relief, Mentàll released her hand, and she swiped it against her dress. Unexpectedly, his arm went around her shoulders, tugging her close to him. "All will be fine," he said in a low voice. "Appear confident. Little else is required with this group of people."

His gesture comforted her. "I'll do my best." She searched the room for Behran or Doc, but saw neither.

Mrn. M returned to them, her eyes sparkling. "Doria told me we're to be at the head table. Let's claim our seats."

They followed her to the long, rectangular table at the far right side of the room, near both the kitchen and the stage. Musicians tuned their instruments, readying for the night of revelry.

Few people had claimed seats at the table yet. Mrn. M chose a spot on the end and draped her shawl over the chair. "Sit if you want," she invited. "They'll bring out drinks shortly." Then she fluttered off.

Mentàll pulled out Methusal's chair, and as she sat down, arranging her skirt, a waiter appeared in her side vision. A white cloth was draped over his black-clad arm. "Your drink of preference?" The amused lilt in the familiar voice made her look up.

"Doc!"

"Shh." The red-haired doctor grinned back. "Punch, madam?"

"Thank you. Where's Behran?"

"He's around. His job is clearing tables. I got promoted to waiter. Must be my charm." As he poured pale pink liquid into their cups, a beak-nosed man at a nearby table snapped his fingers, demanding Doc's attention. With an apologetic smile, he left them.

Methusal craned her neck, scanning the room for a glimpse of Behran.

"Your fiancé just left the kitchen," Mentàll murmured.

Methusal turned quickly, and relaxed when she saw Behran's tall, familiar form. He wore all black too, and carried an empty tray. As if sensing her stare, he glanced over and smiled. A relieved rush of air filled her lungs and she grinned back. He disappeared into a throng of people.

"You feel relieved, now that you have seen your fiancé?" The soft words didn't hide the edge in the Dehrien Chief's voice.

"Yes. I'm glad he's here. I'm glad he's okay." And of course she was glad to see him. She hadn't seen him in over a week, although it seemed much longer. A little of her anxiety eased, knowing he was here.

"You have missed him?" That hard, remote gaze locked with hers.

"Every day." It was the truth. But it was also true that she hadn't thought about him as much as she could have on any of those days. That bothered her. And yet, didn't everything about this assignment disturb her? Tomorrow, on the ship, everything would return to normal.

In silence, Mentàll drank from his cup.

No one was nearby, so she murmured, "When will you present the peace agreement?"

"Just before midnight. With luck, he will be here. If not, we will search for him."

"What if he orders soldiers to arrest us before then?"

"Then I will present it sooner." He scanned the room, seeming to pay little attention to her words.

She hissed, "How can you be so calm? He wants to kill us! He'll probably make an example of us in front of everyone here."

"Are you in kaavl?" Those cool eyes met hers.

"No."

"Focus. Koblan's future and our lives are at stake tonight."

The musicians struck up a jaunty tune. A loud murmur swelled, and then fell abruptly silent. The crowd parted, allowing a thick, stocky man, clad in Zindedi black and red, to enter the room. His coarse hair was dark, liberally sprinkled with gray, and his eyes looked like coal.

The Presidente. A prickle ran down Methusal's skin. The resemblance to his dead brother was uncanny.

"Welcome, friends! Resume the festivities. Drink your fill." A deep, throaty chuckle rolled from his barrel chest. "This will be a night none of you will forget."

Top ranking military men closed in around him, blocking him from view. Methusal focused into kaavl, as she had done earlier at the base. But too many stimuli battered her brain here. She couldn't make sense of it all. So she focused only on the words exchanged between the Presidente and his men. Unfortunately, all she heard were officers trying to outdo each other in lavishing praise upon the Zindedi leader.

She took note of the soldiers guarding every entry into the room. Sergeants threaded through the crowd, nibbling appetizers. They failed to blend in—mostly because their sharp eyes were constantly roaming the ballroom. She wondered if they were the Presidente's personal guards, or if they were looking for her and Mentàll. But surely everyone must know they had arrived by now.

The orchestra segued into a grand, sweeping melody. It seemed to be a signal of some kind, because most of the people meandered toward the tables, but a few couples took to the dance floor. The women swirled by on the arms of their men. They looked very grand and refined and graceful.

Mrn. M bustled up and settled into her chair with a sigh. "Why don't you two go out and dance?"

"I've never danced in my life," Methusal admitted. "I could never look like those people."

"With the right partner, you can do anything." She turned to Mentàll. "Surely you could lead her, Lozar."

He slightly inclined his head. "I know a few steps."

He seemed so remote now, as if locked away in that icy shell of his. So different from the man who had held her hand when they had entered the ballroom. Was it because he was on high kaavl alert now? Or was there another reason why?

In any case, he didn't appear to possess a burning desire to take her onto the dance floor.

Methusal told Mrn. M, "I think I'll just relax."

"Perhaps later, then. It's such fun. You must try at least one dance tonight."

"Maybe," she agreed.

A black uniform appeared at Mrn. M's elbow. "Does someone want to dance?"

It was the Captain who had spied on them last night. It appeared that he'd washed his greasy hair, but apparently not his mind. She didn't like the way his eyes flickered over her bosom.

"I was just telling Midi that it is so much fun to dance. She only needs an experienced partner."

"A novice." The Captain's smile looked lascivious. "As it happens, I am experienced. I would welcome the opportunity to introduce you to the pleasures of dance."

"Thank you, but..." When the Captain's eyes hardened to stony orbs, Mrn. M squeezed her arm and gave her a warning look.

"Just one, dear. It would be fun."

Clearly, in the Presidente's palace, a request was an order. She affixed a gracious smile upon her lips. "Of course. Thank you, Captain."

His lips curled back in a satisfied smile, and he crooked an arm to her. In a soft swish of skirt over the polished floor, Methusal accompanied the Captain to the center of the floor. He clasped her right hand in his cool, clammy one, and pulled her close with a hard, pinching grip at her waist. He was a little taller than she was, and although he was thin, a coiled energy, like in an aggressive whip, radiated from him.

His breath smelled of rotten fish. Methusal wanted to bolt. Instead, she accidentally stepped on his toes, trying to make sense of the steps.

He laughed softly. "Listen to the music, girl. One two three...one two three."

Methusal swiftly caught the hang of it, and he twirled her around the dance floor, his teeth gleaming in a disturbing smile. "You are a quick learner," he murmured. "A quality your husband must appreciate." His hand on her torso moved, as if trying to find a more comfortable position. But as they passed by the head table, his thumb brushed her breast.

She trod hard on his toe. He gave a sharp, surprised chuckle, but his hand retreated. "Was that move for your husband's benefit?"

"No. Slug."

The Dehrien Chief's cold eyes watched them pass.

The Captain chuckled again. "Your husband is a possessive man. He hates allowing other men to touch you."

She said nothing.

"I suppose that is as it should be. He wouldn't be possessive if he didn't have great passion for you." A smirk slithered across his face.

Would this dance ever end? The Captain's hands felt sweaty, and even though his wandering hand had retreated, he held her too close to him.

"I want to dance with my wife." Mentàll's harsh voice felt like a welcome draught of cool water. Without waiting for the Captain to agree, she swiftly extricated herself and turned into Mentàll's waiting arms.

His fingers curled securely around hers, and she stepped close to him, so that the fabric of their clothing almost touched. He would allow no one to hurt her. She felt protected and safe in his arms.

With a disgruntled lip curl, the Captain left them.

"How eagerly you come into my arms," the Dehrien Chief said in a low voice. A hint of a smile warmed the ice.

"He was horrible." A tiny shiver went through her, and his palm gently stroked her back, drawing her nearer.

Moments passed as they danced in smooth, fluid harmony. Now she felt like she was too close to him. She pulled back and looked up. "The Captain thinks you're a possessive husband."

"Does he."

"Your glare was inspired. He thinks you hate letting other men touch me." She smiled, to make light of the comment.

Mentàll did not return it, however. He drew her in for a slow turn and said into her hair, "He is right."

She stiffened. "We're not married," she reminded him.

"I am well aware of that fact. Your fiancé is watching us even now."

"Behran is not jealous. He knows he has nothing to worry about."

"No?" He seemed secretly amused.

"You're my enemy."

"And yet I've saved your life countless times."

"You're untrustworthy." Did she even believe what she was saying? No. But a self-protective part of her still fought to break the intimacy that was growing between them. Especially with Behran here. Especially because of that.

"And yet I did not take advantage of you last night."

"A whip beast," she persisted.

His small smile faded, and anger flared in his pale eyes. "Would you like me to treat you like a whip beast would?"

Fear—something she hadn't felt in his presence in a long time—flared. She pulled back. "No." It was a denial and a plea.

"Stop," he said harshly. He drew her close to him again. "I will not."

Relieved, Methusal cautiously rested her head against his shoulder.

He whispered a Dehrien epithet above her head, and ran his hand down her back. "I am sorry. I did not mean to scare you."

"You haven't treated me like a whip. I'm sorry for saying those things." At last, she quietly admitted, "I don't know what to think about you anymore."

He drew a deep breath, but whatever he'd been about to say was lost in a sharp horn blast.

"Take your seats. Dinner is now served."

Back at the table, Mentàll held out her chair for her, and then Doc and the other waiters served the first course of a sumptuous feast.

On a dais adjacent to the stage, the Presidente sat alone at a small round table. After a murmur to the tall, skinny young man who served him, Mrn. M was soon summoned to join him. She left Methusal and Mentàll with a pink face and sparkling eyes.

Methusal enjoyed every morsel of the delicately seasoned, sliced slug monster, baked tubers, and a frothy sweet dessert baked in a pastry shell. She'd never tasted anything so delicious in her life.

Throughout the dinner, she repeatedly caught the Presidente's hard eyes upon both her and Mentàll. She couldn't help but wonder if he wanted them to enjoy the meal. He probably intended for it to be their last one.

No soldiers had accosted them yet. How long did he plan to continue this charade of peace?

Every now and again she glimpsed Behran and Doc going about their duties. It made her feel better to know they were close by, in case something went wrong. As it undoubtedly would. The black unease in her stomach knotted tighter as the evening progressed. The dinner, interspersed with dancing and speeches, lasted for hours. When dessert was finally cleared away, it was an hour before midnight.

After the meal, the Presidente honored Mrn. M's dead husband, and with flourish presented her with a medal in his honor. Tears slipped down Mrn. M's cheeks as she accepted the award. Her bearing remained regal as she thanked the Presidente, and then she returned to the main table to join Methusal and Mentàll.

"My lands." She pressed her hand to her mouth, eyeing the gold orb nestled in the ornate basket. Complex etchings encircled the outer portion, and the center simply said, "Presidente's Seal of Honor, Charlie Machblin."

"I cannot believe it. Charlie would feel so honored." To Methusal, she said, "The Presidente has only awarded three of these. Doria's husband was one. It's too bad he passed away before he could enjoy the honor."

Maybe the Presidente only awarded this "honor" to dead men, Methusal speculated. Men who had served their country well, but who could never attempt to usurp his power.   Another sign of his insecurity. She glanced at Mentàll.

His eyes glittered at the Zindedi Presidente. "Soon," he murmured.

Soon what? She concentrated into kaavl again, chastising herself for forgetting. She needed to remain alert every second, and not become absorbed in a meaningless award ceremony.

"Relax! Enjoy!" the Presidente boomed. He marched for the back of the stage and disappeared through a door.

"Dance with me." A tense restlessness simmered in the Dehrien Chief.

Without a word, she followed him onto the dance floor and allowed him to pull her close. With smooth precision, they circled the ballroom. Finally, she ventured, "What are we doing?"

"It is almost time. The soldiers have been murmuring together for the last few minutes."

"They mean to take us now?"

"They await only a signal."

"But the Presidente just left." Comprehension dawned. "Oh. He doesn't want to be here when it happens. He'll come back after we're captured and parade us in front of his guests."

"Exactly," he murmured. "His evening's final triumph would be to capture the leaders of the Koblani resistance. It would signal victory to his militia."

"The perfect way to launch the war against Koblan. We can't let them capture us. What will we do?"

A mirthless sound came from his throat. "They are heading for us now."

Fear tensed her muscles.

"Relax. Hear them coming," he whispered. And then, unexpectedly, he twirled them toward the palace entrance and into the midst of a swirling throng of revelers. "The hall to the left has stairs that lead upstairs. Meet me there." And then he was gone, like a mist fleeing before a strong wind.

Methusal felt utterly alone. Her brief panic resolved into intense, deadly concentration. She was certain Mentàll meant to accost the Presidente in his private chambers upstairs.

She glimpsed an approaching sergeant, ducked down out of view, and slipped left, through the twirling bodies. Now she wished she'd worn black, instead of green. Black would blend in better.

The soldiers had not anticipated that their prey would vanish from under their noses. Disjoined murmurs touched Methusal's ears, but by then she'd already reached the hall and slipped up the narrow stairway. Mentàll waited for her at the top.

They now stood in a wide hallway carpeted in plush, geometrically woven rugs. Ornate torches burned above each closed door, lighting the hall as bright as day. White, glossy paint gleamed on the walls and carved doors. Inlaid gold designs gilded the doors.

It was as quiet and still as death.

Methusal carried, projecting her hearing into each room. Most were silent. But then she stiffened. "I hear the Presidente's voice. Two doors down, on the right."

"How many are with him?"

Methusal listened carefully, filtering out sounds from other rooms, and listened for voices and breaths. "One. The Captain."

"And in the other rooms?"

"I hear quiet breaths in a few."

"Take out your knife." Already a long, wicked one rested in his palm. "I will go in first. Come in only if I need help."

Heart in her throat, she pressed her back against the wall beside the Presidente's door. Mentàll tried the knob. It didn't move. He pulled out a short length of wire and delicately probed the lock. A faint click, and the knob silently turned in his hand.

With a final, warning look at her, he opened the door.

"Well." The smile in the Presidente's voice made prickles crawl down Methusal's skin. "A welcome surprise."

Instinctive fear choked her. "Mentàll," she gasped. "It's a tra..."

A horn sounded, and eight men erupted into the hall.

△ △ △ △ △

Horror choked the breath from Hendra's lungs. *Timaeus*. Timaeus was captured!

Beneath her fingers, Tabor's muscles hardened into sinewy cords. He'd seen, too.

General Fitrn's cart rolled past, followed by the five soldiers and two wolmites.

"We have to rescue him!"

"We will." Tabor sounded grim.

"Where is *Riln?*" It figured that the one time they needed him, he was nowhere to be found.

"He can't be far."

"Unless he already did something rash and they've killed him."

"It's not like you to be so pessimistic, Hendra." Tabor stared at the road ahead, his face hard.

Hendra was surprised that her cousin's right-hand man had ever noticed anything about her. In Dehre, she was like a ghost, slipping from her tent to the orphan's shelter and back.

She said, "Riln has been nothing but trouble from the start."

"Miss me, apte girl?" Riln's large, silent appearance made her gasp. He laughed loudly.

"Shh!" Tabor said, still staring at the road up ahead.

"They have Timaeus," Hendra said. "We're thinking of a plan to rescue him."

"Blow up the powder carts. That'll distract them."

Tabor shook his head. "We can't take that chance."

"Why not?"

"If one powder carts blows, the rest will follow. It'll kill Timaeus."

"You don't know that."

"I saw the munitions building blow up in Quasr. It took out an area four times its size. If one powder cart blows, so will the one behind it. It will be a chain reaction, all down the line."

And the urchet and all of the men within range would blow up, too. And Timaeus, tied to a cart—the thought of it made her feel sick.

Riln said, "If we don't, they'll kill him anyway."

Hendra fiercely turned on him. "Riln, you're like a rotarhudge, trampling everything in your path. Timaeus' *life* is at stake! We have to *think*. We have to figure out the best plan possible."

"You won't get near those carts."

"We can..."

"What do you plan to do? Run up and say pretty please?" he mocked.

Hendra felt the violent urge to slap him. "Be quiet! Let me think."

Riln headed down the dark road. "Count me out. I won't sit on my hands and do nothing."

Appalled, Hendra ran after him. "Don't do anything rash. Wait for us to make a plan."

"I'm done taking orders from him," Riln thrust his chin in Tabor's direction. "He ran like a girl when the soldiers chased you in the woods. And I sure as hell won't listen to you, apte girl."

Now she felt even more frightened and horrified. Riln had been itching to confront the Zindedis for weeks. Likely, blowing them all to pieces would give him a bloody thrill.

"Tabor," she said urgently, pausing for him to catch up.

"Riln's right. We can't get close without a big distraction."

"But Timaeus could *die!*" she said in anguish. "We could *all* die if we blow up the carts."

"Hide in the bushes, apte girl," Riln called back, clearly disgusted.

Tabor strode ahead to talk to Riln.

Hendra ran to catch up again. "No, Tabor! His plan is crazy."

"We have to do it, Hendra. We have no other choice."

Feeling a breathless, choking sort of despair, she listened as Tabor told Riln that it would be best to cut the thread between the detonators and the timer, which would immediately ignite the flame. They'd throw them at once into the carts. Thankfully, Behran had had the foresight to build in a delay so it would take a minute or more for the flame to eat through the wax encasing the powder. Hopefully then the explosion would rip into one of the powder barrels and cause a chain reaction.

Hendra had a bad feeling about this. Very bad.

The men pulled detonators from their packs and exposed the trigger thread. Tabor asked Hendra to give Riln her extra explosive device. The men would each throw two bombs into the carts. "Remember—cut, and as soon as you see the spark, throw it," Tabor told Riln. "Let's leave our packs here. We'll get them on the way back."

Hendra reluctantly set her pack down, too.

"This is it." A fierce, anticipatory grin stretched Riln's lips. He lumbered into the dark.

"*No,*" she whispered. Surely, there had to be a better way.

Then why did her brain feel frozen? Why couldn't she figure out how to save Timaeus without putting everyone's lives in jeopardy? Everything was spiraling out of control. Riln had finally wrestled control of the team into his own hands.

Oh The One, please help us save Timaeus.

Δ Δ Δ Δ Δ

The soldiers attacked Methusal and Mentàll like voracious wild beasts. Knives flashed, and one sliced into her arm. She was surprised the Zindedis didn't try to shoot them.

Mentàll fought with his usual cold, brutal efficiency. Two men fell from his blade, and one from hers, before they were forced into the Presidente's room by the five remaining men. A wild slash from Methusal's knife found an enemy's jugular. He collapsed, just as Mentàll killed another.

A movement behind her made her retreat sideways in an attempt to fight the man before her and the one behind her at the same time. Mentàll fought three men all on his own.

A knife blade poked into the base of her skull.

"Drop it," hissed the Captain.

Her hesitation allowed the charging soldier to stick his knife tip into her chest. A warning. Concede, or die.

Methusal dropped her knife.

The Captain yanked her backward by the hair and slammed her against the wall. An unholy light burned in his black eyes. "You sounded nice last night. I'd like a piece of that." Methusal blocked out the horror of his touch by focusing hard into kaavl. His molesting hand left other parts of him vulnerable.

Methusal kneed him as hard as her hampering dress would allow, and then delivered a hand chop to his windpipe and swept his foot out from under him. A hard shove, and he sprawled backward, onto the floor. The paper with the maze directions fluttered down. Like a coiled whip, he lunged for her legs, but she sidestepped and grabbed for her knife. In her side vision, Mentàll felled the last Zindedi.

"Stop. Or I'll shoot." The Captain rose fast, pointing a short, ugly black gun at her.

Swifter than thought, the Dehrien Chief lunged forward and twisted the Captain's wrist. The Zindedi officer screamed, and the gun clattered to the floor.

"Scienth!" Cheekbones tinged red, Mentàll punched the officer with a fury and violence Methusal had never seen from him before. The Captain staggered under the onslaught, and his attempt to stab Mentàll ended with another scream of agony. He fell to his knees, clutching his obviously broken wrist. A river of blood poured from his nose.

Mentàll spit a guttural epithet at him.

The Captain looked up, and his black eyes blazed like a demon's. "Kill her," he hissed.

Both Methusal and Mentàll spun. An officer in the doorway trained his gun on her.

Methusal froze. She was about to die. At close range like this, she could not escape a bullet.

"Shoot!" bellowed the Captain.

Mentàll's shoulder hit her hard, and she toppled over just as the gun blasted. The Dehrien's body jerked. He seemed to fall in slow motion as the boom resonated throughout the room. He landed heavily beside her and lay unnaturally still.

Chapter Thirty-Six

"No!" Methusal screamed. She scrambled up on her knees beside him. Deep crimson flowed from a hole in his chest. Instinctive medical training made her press a hand to the wound to stop the bleeding. "*No,*" she gasped. "No!"

His chest jerked, stuttering under his effort to breathe.

"*Mentàll.* Mentàll, no!"

A harsh gurgle escaped from his throat. No! It couldn't be. *No.* She crumpled onto his chest. "Oh, The One, please *no.* Don't let him die!"

The Zindedi soldier helped the moaning Captain stand up. "Get reinforcements," the Captain choked out.

"They're coming," the soldier said. "I'll get you to medical."

"No. Stay here," the Captain gasped.

The officer helped him out the door. "You need help. You're losing blood, Captain. The woman can't go far."

Their footsteps receded down the hall.

"Thusa...Methusal." A thin whisper touched her ears.

Her head jerked up. He wasn't dead! His breaths were thready now, rather than gurgling, and his face was parchment white.

His hand lifted a fingerbreadth from the floor, and then dropped. "Treaty," he gasped. "Shirt. Take. Presidente. Now."

"No! I won't leave you. You'll bleed to death. And they'll be back, and who knows what they'll do to you."

She yanked and ripped at her dress, and managed to tear off a long piece of material. Then she tore off another piece to stuff into the wound. She worked quickly, knowing time was of the essence. She wadded up the cloth, and then worked the long strip down, beneath his shoulders, and around his chest. She tied it as tightly as she could. His breathing was too shallow and fast. Fear made her hands shake.

"Go," he choked out. "Before...too...late."

"No," she whispered.

"Commanding...officer. Order...y..." He was getting weaker, and she was terrified. She fought a grief that threatened to overwhelm her. She shut her mind to it, trying to focus. Trying to keep her head straight.

He was speaking to her. She should listen.

At the very least, she could honor his last request. She swallowed back a sob that threatened to break her, and slid her hand inside his shirt. His skin felt cold and clammy, and then she felt the crisp parchments. She pulled them out.

"Good." He gave a small grimace. "Go."

"I won't leave you." She fought the tears burning in her eyes. Words couldn't express everything she wanted to say to him; everything she needed to say, but didn't know how. "I...I..."

He closed his eyes, face white. "Go."

"Methusal!" Behran's voice had never sounded so welcome. And Doc was with him.

"Thank goodness," she cried out. "He's been shot." Quickly, she filled them in on the most pertinent information. "How did you get past the soldiers? More will be here any minute."

"We heard the shot," Behran said. "We ran up the servant's stairs. Luckily, I had a steak knife, and killed two in the hall."

Doc took over compression. He looked up. "We have to get him out now."

"There's a secret passage near the kitchen," Methusal said. "It's in a coat closet. It ends in a maze in the Presidente's gardens. I have the map..." She scrambled to find the paper on the floor, and pressed it into Behran's hand. She stared into his deep blue eyes, and then at Mentàll. Fear choked her. "Take him now. Quickly. The coat closet is guarded. Be careful."

"You're coming with us." Behran scooped up two guns near the fallen soldiers.

"No. He asked me to bring the peace agreement to the Presidente. I'll follow you when I can."

"Thusa..."

"Behran," Doc said. "Let's go."

With a final, anguished look at her, Behran lifted Mentàll under the shoulders. Doc gripped his feet. And then they were gone. The whole episode had lasted only a few minutes.

The soldiers would return at any moment.

She had to find the Presidente. But where had he gone? She'd heard his voice in this room, but he'd vanished before they'd entered. At least, she thought he had. He could have slipped out during the fight.

But Methusal didn't think he'd gone far at all.

Boots tramped at the far end of the hall. But no shouts. Hopefully they hadn't spotted Behran, Doc, or Mentàll. *Mentàll.* A fist of pain clenched her heart so hard that she could barely breathe. He'd taken the bullet meant for her. He was dying—*dying* right now, because of her. A sob ached in her throat, but she choked it back.

Stop it. Think. Grieve later.

The soldiers would arrive in less than a minute.

Mentàll wanted her to deliver his final message to the Presidente, and so she would deliver it. It must be vital. She must pull herself together.

The Presidente. If he hadn't left by the main door, then how had he escaped?

A secret passage.

Swiftly, she knocked on the wall, listening for a hollow sound. At the same time, she sharpened her kaavl senses, listening to the soldiers in the hall march closer. Ten lengths, nine...

A hollow echo. Her fingertips ran over the engraved paneling, rapidly pushing at each of the intricate leaves and tiny flowers.

With a soft groan, the wall moved, revealing a narrow, open door. Pitch black waited beyond.

Four...three...

Methusal slipped into the darkness and pushed the wall back into place behind her. She blindly felt her way forward with her hands.

The passage headed left. But as her body traversed that dark, narrow hall, her heart traveled with Mentàll. *Please, The One.* Please *don't let him die.*

△ △ △ △ △

After circling far ahead of the caravan again, Tabor and Hendra crouched behind a bush and waited for the carts to approach. Riln lay in wait across the road, ready to chuck his detonators into the first cart. Tabor would do the same to another cart, further down the line.

A sick feeling of fear churned in her gut. Riln's plan wouldn't turn out well. She felt it, deep in her heart. But what could she do to stop it?

Only her kaavl gift could possibly make a difference in their fate. She concentrated hard on the carts and shifted into the future.

A bright orange flash exploded into the night. She jerked back.

Another ball of fire exploded. Soldiers ran, their mouths wide open in shock. Urchet pieces rained down on the road. Another cart...and then another exploded, in lightning fast procession. The glare lit the night sky, illuminating the General's black carriage at the end. Figures ran as the ball of fire exploded down the line, charging for the black carriage...and for Timaeus, tied to the last powder cart.

Tabor's light touch made her gasp. He said, "We threw them."

She grabbed his arm. "Tabor. They'll blow in two minutes. Once the first cart goes, we have less than a minute to get Timaeus free before his cart blows up."

"You saw it."

"Yes."

"Then let's go." In a crouch, he ran north, for the General's carriage.

Wolmites snapped and snarled.

"Hiy!"

"What's wrong with the stupid beasts?" The men wrestled against the wolmites.

Hendra followed Tabor, pulling her knife from the belt of her Zindedi uniform.

"Spies!" shouted a man. "Release the wolmites!"

Claws scrabbled on the earth. Hendra ran faster, gripping her knife tightly in her cold hand. Three carts to go...two.

A great furry weight hit her shoulder, and she stumbled and dropped to her knees. The wolmite's hot breath snarled in her ear. One bite into her neck could kill her. She plunged the knife backward, into the beast's belly. A high pitched whine rent the air. Teeth snapped against her hair, and barely missed her ear. Frantically, she plunged the knife again and again into the beast. It was awkward, since it was behind her.

The beast's weight abruptly lifted. Rough hands jerked her up. "Come on." Tabor.

The night sky exploded into a ball of fire.

Men shouted in surprise.

Hendra ran with Tabor, trying to keep her footing. The ground shook...the very air exploded with each forceful blast.

Timaeus. Timaeus. They had to reach Timaeus.

Tabor boldly entered the milling mix of Zindedi soldiers, and so did Hendra. No one seemed to notice.

"It's coming this way!"

"Run!"

General Fitrn erupted from his carriage. "Save the powder!" he screamed. "Drive the carts off the road!"

Urchets and carts lumbered suddenly right, nearly knocking Hendra over. She sprinted for the last one, and there was Timaeus, staring straight ahead with an empty, hopeless look on his face. Tabor lunged forward and sawed at the rope binding his hands. Timaeus' face lit up. He spotted Hendra, too, but his half smile vanished as quickly as it came. "Look out!"

A whip snarled around Tabor's neck and knocked him to his knees. "What are you doing, soldier?" hissed the General.

Tabor gasped, pulling at the whip, wiggling it loose. "If the cart blows, the prisoner dies."

General Fitrn stared down at him, his thin lips tilted in a peculiar smile. "That is my concern. Not yours."

Thankfully, Fitrn was paying no attention to Timaeus or Hendra. She frantically sawed at his bonds. Explosions still rocked the earth. The plodding urchets weren't moving fast enough to escape the blasts. Worse, they were bunched together and heading in the same direction off the road. Explosions rolled down the line.

She didn't have to look to know it was almost too late.

Another knife appeared. With one violent silver flash, the last of the cords broke. Timaeus staggered free, and they ran.

The carts continued lumbering off the road, and the ball of fire followed. One after another, they exploded with deafening roars. Urchet pieces and wooden bits of cart flew like deadly spears.

"Get down!" Timaeus cried. Hendra collapsed on her knees just as the final cart exploded.

△ △ △ △ △

Methusal's foot hit an obstruction and she pitched forward into the inky black. Hard stair edges bit into her knees and hands. "*Ow*."

Arms trembling, she pushed herself back up on her feet. She bit her lip, forcing back the irrational urge to scream with the utter frustration and helplessness she felt. Mentàll was *dying* because of these horrible Zindedis. And their evil Presidente wanted to conquer Koblan. Why should the Zindedis hold all of the power? Why could they arbitrarily decide the fate of an entire continent?

They couldn't. They *wouldn't*. It wasn't fair. It was *wrong*.

Anger swallowed up her weak, impotent feelings of grief, and grew stronger with every step she took upward.

Mentàll was certain that the explosions would bring the Presidente to his knees. All she had to do was deliver the demands written into the peace agreement. She could do this for Mentàll, and for Koblan. She *would* help deliver defeat to the Zindedi Presidente.

The passage ended on a small landing which faced a closed door. The catch was easy enough to find. Methusal listened before triggering it. The Presidente could be on the other side. Or more soldiers.

Kaavl revealed one man's heavy, raspy breaths. She was willing to bet it was the Presidente.

∆ ∆ ∆ ∆ ∆

The door latch clicked, but the Presidente did not bother to look up. He scowled. "Go, Yalin. I have no use for you now."

"Perhaps you have use for me." The cool, feminine voice made him freeze. Slowly, he raised his eyes.

A slim young woman wearing a sleek, emerald ball gown stood just outside the open door of his secret passageway. Methusal Maahr.

A faint smile puffed out his cheeks, and he settled back in his chair, thick fingers laced across his belly. Although he despised the Koblani whore, he again noticed, as he had earlier in the evening, what a beauty she was. Dark hair cascaded halfway to her waist, and her skin was the warm color of his favorite sweetener.

Nothing of sweetness softened her face, however. Her jaw was set, shoulders straight, and she wore the ball gown like a military uniform. Her green eyes glittered like cut glass. She held a parchment in her hands.

He allowed a chuckle to escape. "So. You have found me. Where is your husband?"

"As if you don't know. Your men shot him."

"He is dead." While he'd wanted to kill the Dehrien himself, he felt gratified that he would now witness Methusal's heartbreak over her lover's death.

However, her expression remained like a stone. "He lives. And he has escaped the palace with help from our friends."

Rage flared, and pain seized his chest. Willfully, he tamped down his anger. The woman could be lying, although it was true he read no sorrow in her eyes. Only a black, cold kind of rage.

With deliberation, he said, "Perhaps you should run home as well. Like the apte you are."

She stepped forward and placed the parchment on his desk. "I have brought our demands for peace."

Now a true laugh gusted from his chest. "Demands?" His fist hit the paper. It fluttered wildly into the air, and then curled down to the floor. He longed to grab the insolent girl and drag her across his desk, but she remained just out of reach. And the lingering pain in his chest cautioned against such action. Instead, he bared his teeth. "You possess no power to make demands, little girl. A finger snap and you are dead."

"I wouldn't be so hasty, Presidente. Even now, at my signal, we are prepared to unleash destruction upon your land." Her dead-set expression made it clear that she meant her words.

For that reason alone, the Presidente laughed at her. "You are nothing." Contempt dripped from his words. "You and Koblan are weak and helpless. Your husband is dead." Methusal flinched. With satisfaction, he concluded, "Tomorrow my ships will set sail to rape and conquer your land. You are powerless to stop me."

"You are wrong." The Koblani woman gracefully stooped to retrieve the parchment. "If you want to avoid utter destruction, you will read this peace agreement."

The Zindedi leader leaned back in his chair and looked down his nose at her. "You read it," he suggested. "But I warn you, when it is finished, your illusion of freedom ends. I will order my guards in here, and I will personally torture you in every way I see fit."

No emotion flickered in her cold eyes. He felt disappointed. But soon she would beg him for mercy. Soon the ice princess would become his delectable plaything. He smiled. "Read," he commanded, and licked his lips.

The paper trembled a bit her in her hands, and fierce elation charged through him. Yes. This would be even more satisfying than he had thought. Perhaps he would not wait until she'd finished reading before ordering his guards in. He smiled and listened, his eyes locked onto Methusal's down-turned face. She began to read.

∆ ∆ ∆ ∆ ∆

Mentàll's list of demands staggered Methusal. He'd obviously felt utter confidence as he'd written them. Of course, he hadn't known he'd be dying while she stood here, trembling, reading his ultimatums to the Zindedi Presidente.

Stiffen your spine, she ordered herself. *Be strong.*

A creeping sensation told her the Presidente was undressing her with his mind. Cruelty carved unpleasant lines into his thick, jowly face.

Fear crawled through her belly like a slithery whip. Keeping her voice steady, she slowly finished reading the document. Surely, it must be almost midnight. She had to stall for time. The Presidente couldn't order his guards into the room. Yet.

"In sum," she stated, looking the Presidente straight in the eye, "We will refrain from destroying your entire continent under three conditions. First..."

"I will *not* call off my attack," Contempt rolled like low thunder from the Zindedi Presidente. "I will not travel to Koblan in three weeks, begging for peace. And I will *never*," he learned forward, the cords bulging in his neck, "take orders from a *woman*. Or a weak continent with no ruler." He raised his hand, fingers prepared to snap.

"*Mentàll* is our ruler." The words blurted out.

His fingers remained still.

"You see?" She shoved the paper across the desk. "His name is first. He is First Chief of Koblan. He is our ruler."

Shrewd brown eyes stared back at her. "He is dead."

"He is not." She stared at him, willing it to be true. Willing him to believe her cold, emotionless words.

"Regardless. You are an impertinent, insolent girl. Worse, you are stupid. You cannot harm my land. We both know that. Both Koblan and you are helpless beneath my power. Now you will taste exactly how helpless you are. Guards," he said calmly. His thick fingers snapped.

The door slammed open.

Inspiration struck—perhaps insane, perhaps fruitless. As she heard the heavy military boots rush in, Methusal flew across the room to the window. She threw the drapes open and swiftly raised her arms overhead, and then swept them down to her sides. To the Presidente, it would look like a signal. Of course, her theatrics were meaningless. No one was watching.

Rough hands grabbed her arms, wrenching them behind her.

"Bring her here," the Presidente said.

She struggled like a wild beast, fighting the two men who held her captive. They dragged her across the floor to the Presidente's desk. His stocky body rose from the plush chair. Cruel, hot eyes rested upon intimate parts of her person. His hand twitched on his belt buckle. An unholy smile pulled at the corners of his mouth.

"No!" Methusal struggled, and viciously kicked every man within range. One blow hit a man's knee. Another, an instep and ankle. More boots ran into the room. Two men dragged her backward, onto the floor. Concentrating wholly into kaavl, Methusal kicked and kneed and struggled, refusing to give up. Refusing to face the terror clawing at her mind.

It took six men to subdue her. The Presidente walked toward her. She would not be afraid. She would *not*. She wouldn't give him the satisfaction. But when the Presidente loomed over her, she wanted to vomit. She wanted to scream by all that was holy, for The One to strike the man dead on the spot.

"Now we will see," chuckled the Presidente.

An earsplitting, tremendous *BOOM* rocked the entire room. The Presidente thunked heavily down on all fours, trying to keep his balance. Orange fire burst outside the window, lighting up the entire nighttime sky.

"What the..."

Another explosion shook the palace.

One of the soldiers who was holding her cried out in fear and ran to the window. Another bomb exploded. The Zindedi leader collapsed into a seated position beside her, looking dazed. The other men had loosened their grips on her. Methusal seized her chance and wrenched free.

Another boom shook the palace floor as she staggered to her feet.

"*What is that?*" screamed the Presidente.

Methusal whirled. "A promise of things to come," she spat. "One ship. Three weeks. Quasr. Come prepared for peace. Or we will finish your destruction."

"Don't let her escape!"

But three bombs exploded then, one after another, knocking everyone off of their feet. Methusal crawled as fast as she could for the door, and then scrambled up the instant the shaking lessened. She charged out, clipping the Presidente's skinny, frightened secretary on the way. She flew down the stairs, past soldiers, taking full advantage of the fact that everyone was dazed, bewildered, and frightened.

The ballroom was a scene of mass hysteria. Women screamed. Men shouted. A black sea of impeccably clad people rushed outside into the courtyard. Methusal was one of the mob. Already men rattled the Presidente's palace gates, shouting to be let out. A guard hastily unlatched them, and Methusal streamed out with the others.

It was bitterly cold, and she longed for her warm leather jacket. She'd never wear it again. And if there was any justice, she'd never see the Presidente's palace again, either. If only she'd brought a detonator to the ball.

△ △ △ △ △

The deafening blasts roared like judgment day in Hendra's ears. Pain stabbed into her arm that she'd protectively clamped over her head.

"Get up. Let's go!" Riln shouted.

Men screamed. Hendra scrambled up. Sharp bits of debris dug into her hands, and an awful, putrid smell permeated the air. Timaeus stumbled to his feet, too, and Hendra looked wildly around for Tabor. He was upright, but so was the General. He was pointing a gun at Tabor's heart.

He shouted, "Tell your friends to surrender. Or you die."

Horrified, Hendra glanced from Tabor to Riln, Timaeus, the General and back to Tabor again. Tabor's hard eyes told her to go.

But Fitrn would shoot him. Hendra stared at the General and deliberately warped into the future.

Fitrn shot Tabor, and then turned the gun on Timaeus. Deccia's husband fell, and then Riln toppled. Last of all, Fitrn stalked for Hendra, his eyes like molten ore. He pressed the gun to her head. "Now, my pretty," he hissed. "You will come with me."

A shudder of absolute horror jerked her into the present. Spots swam before her eyes. *No.* It would not happen. She would not let it happen.

She still held her knife. With one swift motion, she hurled it at the General's jugular. As it flew through the air, fury contorted the General's face into a maniacal grimace, and smoke erupted from the muzzle of his gun. Tabor crumpled to the ground. The General spun for Timaeus just as her knife hit his shoulder. The shot flew wide.

"Run!" Riln shouted.

The three dashed for the underbrush. Hendra was in the lead. Another shot exploded, and a body fell heavily to the dirt. She spun in horror. Riln bent over Timaeus.

"He's shot in the leg." By sheer brute force, he hauled Timaeus to his feet.

Timaeus' teeth were gritted in pain. "Can't...make it. Run! Save yourselves."

"No!"

General Fitrn shouted orders, clutching his shoulder. Soldiers ran after them.

"Go," Timaeus gasped, struggling free of Riln, and crumpled onto the ground. "Tell Deccia...I love her."

"No!" Hendra cried out again. "Timaeus!"

Riln grabbed her by the tunic and yanked her into a dead sprint.

"No," she sobbed out. "*No!*"

"Quiet, you little fool. Do you want to die, too?" His grip painfully twisted the tunic into her neck, half-choking her.

"Let me *go.*"

He did not listen, but charged through the underbrush, dragging her along with him.

After long moments, the sound of the soldiers faded. They'd given up pursuit.

What were they going to do to Timaeus? Shoot him in cold blood? Drag him back to that horrible General? Hendra couldn't see through her tears. She sobbed helplessly, struggling against Riln every step of the way. "We have to save him!" she cried. "We can't leave him there to die."

Riln didn't answer. Long minutes passed as he forced her to march on. No more shots were fired. Behind them, fire and smoke still roiled into the sky.

Finally, Riln slowed down and released his brutal grip. Winded, Hendra breathed in harsh gasps. "We have to go back and save him! They're still running around, confused. We could slip in..."

"No."

"No?" Everything within her suddenly exploded into a bright kaleidoscope of fury. "You're a horrible man, *and I hate you!*" she screamed. "I'll save him, even if you won't, you apte!" Turning on her heel, she ran back the way they had come.

"You want me to kill every Zin? I'm happy to do it," he shouted after her. "But we'd both die."

"You're a slithering, spineless slug."

"I'm no coward!" he exploded.

She stopped. "Then prove it," she said coldly. "Help me rescue Timaeus."

"He can't walk. How will we get him to Dakarra?"

"We'll kill the General and take his cart." Uncharacteristic, vengeful bloodlust seethed in her heart.

"We accomplished our mission. The powder is gone. Tens of Zins are dead. It's time to go home."

"You...you *apte!* You talk big, but you're *gutless*."

He lunged for her.

She jerked sideways, heart pounding. "Stop it!"

"Don't call me an *apte,* girl," he snarled.

Fear calmed a bit of her fury. Hendra drew great, shaky breaths. "We can't leave Timaeus there with that horrible General. Don't you see that?"

"If we die, then who will tell Deccia what happened to Timaeus?"

Yes. Deccia would want to know.

Hendra didn't want to give up and leave Timaeus alone. But if Riln wouldn't help her, she knew she'd never be able rescue Timaeus on her own.

Long, sickening moments passed by. At last, she conceded bitterly, "We'll tell her. Then Mentàll will send a rescue mission for him."

"Maybe."

Hendra was done talking to this callous man. "Apte," she muttered, heading for the road to Dakarra.

It seemed strange to her that Riln—who had wanted to kill Zindedis from the moment he'd arrived—suddenly wanted to retreat and go home.

Hendra nearly stumbled over their packs. Riln took Tabor's as well as his own, and they marched in silence for the woods that flanked the Dakarran beach.

△ △ △ △ △

Methusal didn't see Behran, Doc, or Mentàll anywhere near the harbor. Twelve ships blazed like infernos at the dock. Their masts were thin black stripes against the orange, leaping flames. As she watched, another ship, adjacent to a blazing vessel, exploded with a deafening *BOOM*.

Lifting her skirts high, she ran west, following the road that hugged the Zindedi bay. She saw no one. Surely they hadn't come this far already. Worry and despair choked her.

Had they escaped from the maze? Had Doc needed to stop and administer more medical care to Mentàll?

If he was still alive.

She wouldn't think about that.

Methusal ran until the road ended. A cart was parked at the end, and an urchet quietly chewed leaves nearby. Had they already transported Mentàll here by cart?

A bit of hope returned. She cut left, toward the rocky shoreline, and walked as fast as she could. Ryon lit her path.

Her transient hope quickly bled to blackness as time passed. Fear gripped her heart more tightly with every step. Even if they'd managed to get Mentàll to the ship, was he still alive?

At last, excruciatingly long minutes later, she spotted the masts of the *Sea Mistress* gleaming in the distance. She cut across a field of windswept grass, heading for the small, protected cove. Small waves licked ashore on the deserted beach. The moonlight illuminated the small rowboat bobbing next to the ship.

She cupped her hands to her mouth. "*Hello!* It's Methusal."

Movement flashed on deck, and then the small boat slid through the waves toward her. It ground ashore, and moonlight glinted off of Behran's blond hair.

"Behran!" She went into his arms and stood there, trembling, holding onto him. "*Behran.*" Her voice broke. Her heart began to break, too, but she couldn't let it. Not yet. She had to get to the ship. "Mentàll." Her voice caught. "Is he dead?"

"Not yet. Doc's working on him."

She nodded. "Let's go." Quickly, she climbed into the boat. Behran rowed for the ship, the long oars glistening with water in the moonlight.

At the ship, rough hands helped her aboard, and then the sailors pulled up the small boat while others hauled in the chain and anchor, readying to sail north for Dakarra. Apparently, she had been last person they had been waiting for.

Methusal descended the ladder into the lamp lit cabin. Deccia sat at the dining table, looking worried. When she saw Methusal, she leaped up. "You're safe." She hugged her, but Methusal pulled back after only a moment of comfort.

Only one thing mattered. "How is Mentàll? Where's Doc?"

"In Mentàll's cabin." Deccia's hand stopped her. "A crewman is helping him. We need to wait."

"I *can't*. Finally, the torrent of emotions overwhelmed her. Hot tears gushed from her eyes. "I can't wait."

Behran watched her, his gaze dark.

Deccia urged her to sit down on the couch. "Pray for him, Thusa. That's all we can do right now."

Methusal wept. Mentàll couldn't die. *He couldn't.* Feeling overwhelmed by helpless fear, she prayed for him. Over the long minutes that passed, she prayed without ceasing, her knees drawn up to her chin, sitting curled in on herself on the couch.

Δ

To be continued...

*Final book of the Kaavl Chronicles series
Kaavl Conqueror, coming Spring 2017.*

Author's Note

I sincerely hope you enjoyed *Kaavl Calamity*. *Kaavl Conqueror* will finish the series, and it will be published in Spring 2017.

I originally wrote Kaavl Calamity and Kaavl Conqueror as one (very long!) volume. Although it is one continuous story, the length made it necessary to separate it into two books. The cliff hanger ending seemed the best place to divide the two. I know a few readers don't like cliff hanger endings, but I hope the publication of the final book in Spring 2017 will be able to answer all of your questions without a lengthy delay.

One final note. As a small press author, getting my books before readers is a real challenge. You can help! If you liked this book, please consider writing a short review on Amazon, B & N, or the retailer's website where you purchased the book. Each review encourages Amazon and other online retailers to promote the book to more readers. Each and every review counts, and means so much!

I love to hear from my readers. Please drop me a note at jennettegreen@jennettegreen.com.

Best wishes always,
Jennette